Chronicles of Arax

Book 2

The

Siege

of

Corell

Benjamin Sanford

STENOX PUBLISHING
Clarksburg, MD

First originally published by Page Publishing 2021

Artist: Karl Moline

ISBN 979-8-9886249-2-9 (pbk)
ISBN 979-8-9886249-3-6 (digital)

Printed in the United States of America

CHAPTER 1

"*Help me, Cronus!*" *she cried piteously, her beseeching cries greeted with red eyes and curved fangs as the creatures made sport of her. Her raiment was torn away, and blood squeezed from her bound limbs as they held her down, defiling her virtue. Smoke, black as a midnight sky, drifted above Central City in thickening billows, choking what life remained. Cronus's noiseless shouts were trapped in muted rage as he stared helpless upon his beloved Leanna as if he was only a ghost, impotent to aid her.*

"Cronus, wake up!" Raven's voice echoed from above, drawing Cronus from his nightmare. His eyes opened, gazing up at the thick branches overhead, blue sky peeking through the breaks in their emerald boughs. *Where am I?* he thought before collecting himself. Sweat poured off his fevered brow, shaking the tortured dream from his mind. "You all right?" Raven asked, standing over him, shaking his head as if Cronus was a victim of a terrible accident.

Was he well? His terrible vision was so richly vivid. He feared it was premonition. While in captivity, his dreams were often pleasant, always a haven from Kriton's torturous ministrations, which plagued his waking hours. Now that he was free, his dreams cruelly transformed into nightmares. Would his waking hours now be his reprieve and sleep his torment? "I am well thanks to you, *my* friend." He smiled easily, gaining his feet as Raven slapped him upon the back.

"That's what friends do, Cronus. Besides, I owed you a couple—one for saving my neck when we first met, and the other for—"

"Cordi's death was not of your doing, Raven. Let it not plague you." His smile eased as he placed a hand on Raven's shoulder.

"It was my fault. I allowed Nels Draken aboard, which led to such folly."

"Yes, and instead of slaying the pirates, he took them captive in order to sell them into slavery. They escaped and killed Cordi in their flight. The blame lies at Draken's feet or the pirates who actually slew my brother. As for you, Raven, only omnipotence would grant you vision to see how any decision could bring about such consequences. You were a warrior before coming to my world. As such, you should know that commanders can only plan and order their men forth. They can never guarantee their safety or outcome."

"Thanks, pal." Raven smiled. "Now let's get moving. It'll be dark soon, and we have to get you back to Leanna." Lorken and Alen were tending to their mounts, fastening their saddle packs and gear. "Here. Eat this." Raven offered him another strip of dried douri. "As soon as we reach the ship, we'll get you some real food."

Cronus bit into the meat, savoring its flavor. Compared to the fetid gruel he had been fed in the dungeon, the dried douri was the sweetest delicacy he could remember. His weary eyes drifted skyward as he descried a faint shadow pass overhead. "Raven." He pointed.

Raven craned his neck, catching sight of the winged form passing to the north. "Psst, Lorken," he whispered harshly, drawing his friend's attention. Lorken looked up as he finished strapping the saddle pack to his magantor, giving Raven a curious look. Raven pointed skyward, and understanding washed over him. They froze in place as the Benotrist scout circled back, sweeping low over the trees. The rider saw movement on his first pass and returned southward, paralleling the border of the tree line that separated the forest from the open grasslands to the west. He spied the movement amid a small clearing just within the forest's edge.

Drifting lower, just above the bristled peaks of the serried torbins, he flinched as intense blue light burst from the trees ahead. He jerked his reins to no avail as the giant eagle's head tilted unnaturally to its flank while its wings slackened. Panic gripped his heart, realizing the bird was dead. He followed its clumsy descent, half gliding and half falling, tumbling through the treetops. Freeing his feet from the stirrups, he prepared to jump free in case the magantor's body flipped, trapping him below its cumbersome bulk.

They tumbled through the upper boughs of the trees, the force of their needled branches knocking him from his saddle before he was ready. The world spun in dizzying horror as he struck one branch after another. The snapping of bones intermixed with breaking branches as he gasped for air throughout his descent before smashing into the forest floor.

When the poor fellow opened his eyes, he found himself upon his back, staring skyward with the faces of three strangers standing over him. One was a gaunt, black-haired Araxan, but the others were terrifying to behold, their builds, clothing, and weapons matching the description of the men he was sent to find. He cringed at the sight of them, struggling to rise and flee, but only his arms obeyed him, feeling nothing below his waist.

"Who are you?" Raven asked. The fellow did not answer. He merely lay there, staring at Raven with disordered vision.

"Where are you from?" Lorken asked with similar result.

"He's dressed differently from the magantor riders we left at Fera," Raven observed, noting the man's gold tunic with its pleated kilt and his polished steel breastplate and greaves.

"Where are you from?" Lorken asked again.

"I fear not death, only dishonor," he answered, collecting himself.

"We don't have to kill you. Your back is broken. If you don't start talking, we'll do the same to your arms and leave you here for the bugs, birds, and wildlife to finish you at their leisure." Raven smiled evilly. The broken man grew fearful of such a prospect.

"If you answer our questions, we'll give you a quick death. If not, you will still die, and Tyro will never know of your courage," Cronus said. The man considered their words, torn between duty and a horrible end.

"He is from the imperial magantor stables at Plateres," Alen said, recognizing the uniform as he came within the fellow's field of vision.

"My name is Quanten Tul, magantor ranger of Plateres," the man conceded.

"Plateres?" Raven asked.

"Plateres is an imperial holdfast many leagues north and east of Fera. It houses nearly a third of the empire's magantors," Alen said.

"Were you searching for us?" Raven growled, balling his fist under the broken man's chin, twisting the collar of his tunic around his neck.

"Argh." The man coughed. "Yes. All...of our host...seek your wh-whereabouts."

"Packaww! Packaww!" The distinctive cry of magantors screeched through the crisp late-day air, drawing closer. They gazed skyward; their view obscured by the thick-needled boughs branching overhead.

"What were you to do if you found us?" Cronus asked, returning his gaze to their captive.

"Relay your position to our comrades with haste."

"Where's Thorton?" Raven growled, knowing Ben was their greater threat. The man scrunched his face, not understanding the question. "He's the Earther who serves your emperor. Where is he?" Raven shook him forcefully.

"I know not!" he weakly replied as Raven's shaking painfully bobbled his head.

"They must have seen him go down," Cronus said, explaining the magantors coursing overhead.

"He doesn't know where Ben is, Rav. He could be anywhere." Lorken sighed.

"Yeah, and with a hundred magantors sweeping the skies north of us, it won't take long for Ben to fix our position and shoot us out of the sky!" Raven grunted, releasing his hold on the man.

"What if we head due south to Rego?" Cronus asked, regarding the obvious avenue of escape.

"What about the south?" Raven asked, grabbing hold of the captive's tunic collar again.

"There are fifty magantors guarding the approaches to Tuft's Mountain," he hurriedly answered.

Tyro was forcing them east, into the wilderness, denying them the quickest routes to Rego and the sea. If they continued east, however, they could spread out the Benotrist scouts and break north to the coast or south over the Plate Mountains to Torry North. The problem was in moving east without Thorton seeing them. The night would not mask their presence from his scope. Of course, if they saw him first, they could take him out before he returned the favor. In this deadly game, the first shot would likely win. "Packaww! Packaww!" The shrill screams again echoed above as their riders drew near.

"Rav, wait one hour and head due east. Head east for three days before breaking north," Lorken advised, drawing his pistol and blasting a hole through their captive's brain as Raven released his grip on the fellow's collar.

"Where you going?" Raven asked as Lorken started making his way to their campsite.

Lorken stopped midstride, craning his neck over his shoulder. "I'm leaving."

"We stay together, Lorken. Splitting up is—"

"Rav, they are looking for a group of five magantors. We lost Terin and the Yatin to who knows where. That leaves us. Thorton wounded your mounts purposely to slow us down, not to separate us. I will head northwest to draw them away. Wait an hour, head east, and hope Thorton isn't looking when you do."

"I'll lead them astray. You stay with Cronus," Raven insisted. He would be damned if he let Lorken risk himself for their sakes.

"You won't make it, Rav," Lorken said, turning around to face him. "You can barely maneuver. Magantors aren't star ships, and though you are a better pilot than me, this is different. My skills are far superior, and if any of us can break through to the coast without getting shot down, it's me."

"This is insane." Raven snorted.

"Trust me," Lorken added while tossing his good comm to Raven. "You'll need that when you get close. Try not to break it."

*****

He burst through the treetops, the magantor's dark wings pounding emphatically neath the waning sun. The fading daylight played off the magantor's ebony feathers, contrasting the evergreen of the forest roof. There, above the trees, the world came into view, where the western grassland met the forest's edge. The forest stretched beyond the eastern horizon, disappearing into the approaching night.

"Packaww!" The sound of Benotrist magantors screeched through the crisp evening air. He pivoted in his saddle, finding two magantors closing fast from the east. Lorken could see the beasts' bellies as they coursed through the firmament high above. A cursory search found three more approaching from the northwest, closer than the two closing from the east. He cleared the treetops, turning northwest and driving headlong to meet the three. The cool air pressed upon his face, framing his countenance with a terrible resolve.

"Packaww!" his magantor screamed, coursing the northern sky. Lorken's stomach rose to his throat as they rode the wind. The three magantors before him held two riders per mount, a rider and an archer. Lorken knew they had to draw very close for their arrows to strike true through the strong wind. Blue laser streamed across the heavens, striking the lead avian where the breast and neck joined. The bird's body slackened, listing leftward before tumbling in rapid descent. Its riders were thrown clear, their screams waning as they fell.

A second blast took the next magantor in its right wing, spewing feathers and blood as it screeched its displeasure, nearly throwing its riders as it bucked. Its left wing flapped emphatically, compensating for its right. It circled sharply right, struggling to ease its descent.

The third magantor veered left, fleeing Lorken's deadly aim. Lorken opened the scope on his pistol, fixing the riders in his sights, his laser catching the archer in the back. He could see the body go limp in the saddle, seated aft of the driver, who continued east, forsaking the chase for a chance to live. Lorken shifted aim over his shoulder, spewing hurried, errant blasts toward the two closing from the east. The hurried volley missed its mark but drew close enough to frighten the magantors, sending them astray. Lorken ignored the disordered foes and sped north and west as fast as his mount could press.

*****

They stole away like ghostly shadows, passing to the east, hugging the treetops to avoid casting their silhouettes in the night sky. They kept close, one to the other, lest they lose each other in the dark like Terin and Yeltor. Lacking the technology that he had grown accustomed to, to guide them, Raven relied on Cronus's sense of direction, trailing his magantor as they sped through the night air.

Pale moonlight played off the evergreen of the forest roof, lighting their path. He was thankful the moon was not in its new phase, for it would've multiplied the difficulties and dangers of their journey. They would continue east for three days before breaking north for the coastline and pray the *Stenox* would be there.

CHAPTER 2

He soared through the firmament, the crisp morning air contorting his face as he pressed northward. Miles of open farmland stretched to the horizon. From this height, Lorken could not discern the faces of the peasants below, staring up as he passed overhead. He contemplated their miserable lot, toiling dawn to dusk in unforgiving elements. Some were Benotrist farmers, managing their freeholds and working to their own pace. Most, however, were Menotrist slaves, toiling under the lash of overseers on large rural estates.

Lorken took great pleasure whenever he spotted a Benotrist overseer brandishing a whip. He would sweep down from above, fixing the cruel offender in his sights, and fire. He despised slavery, and though he couldn't free those in bondage below, he could gain a measure of justice by slaying some of their oppressors.

Crack! The sound of the whip whistled in the morning air. The Menotrist field slave cried out, the overseer taking wicked delight in motivating his charges. The blow struck the wretch's back, raising a vicious welt neath his unbroken tunic. Some of the farmlands of the Benotrist Empire were small freeholds worked by landowners and their kin. Most, however, were worked by gangs of field slaves on vast estates. The miserable wretches worked dawn to dusk, their ankles shackled with two-foot chains as they labored.

Those slaves unfortunate enough to dwell in the western half of the empire were gelded, branded, and collared, wearing a tunic that barely reached their knees and no shoes. With planting season near its end, they were aligned shoulder to shoulder above the furrows with satchels of seed flung over their shoulders.

*****

"Stop dawdling, Vella!" Snargos barked. Vella stumbled, the blow of the whip knocking him from his feet. He quickly corrected himself without spilling any seed lest he receive another blow for that offense as well. Those to either side of him went about their tasks, ignoring their comrade, or risk being punished in kind. Snargos was liberal with the whip, and Vella hurried to keep pace with the others.

Snargos rewound his whip, trailing several paces behind the row of Menotrist slaves. He snatched a water pouch from the slave girl at his side. She stood submissively beside him with downcast eyes and dozens of water pouches flung over her narrow shoulders. Snargos regarded the shapely wench as he guzzled, taking lecherous pleasure in her charms, knowing her fellow Menotrists were no longer equipped to do so. The male slaves were given female names to further humiliate them, and Snargos took pleasure in calling them by said names.

"Shall I give them water, master?" the slave girl asked.

"Nay! Let them finish these last furrows," Snargos snarled, pushing the pouch into her chest.

"Yes, master." She bowed, stepping away as he whipped another.

"Don't dawdle, Gretas. You are a full step behind the others!" Snargos growled.

Zip! Blue laser streamed from above, striking Snargos between his shoulder blades. He cried out before stumbling to the dirt, his cruel face planting in the soil. The field slaves gazed skyward as the magantor passed overhead with a strangely dressed, black-skinned man riding the great bird, brandishing a small object in one hand while the other was outstretched with only the middle finger extended.

*****

11

Lorken holstered his pistol, soaring through the sky, continuing north toward the coast. He could easily discern the upturned faces of the field workers below, just as he easily spotted the overseer among them before he took his shot. He took great pleasure in blasting such wretches. He despised slavery, and though he couldn't free those in bondage below, he could grant them some measure of justice by slaying a few of their overseers. This was the third one he killed this morning. It provided him something to do to pass the time as well as leave a good trail for the Benotrists to follow, hoping to draw their pursuit from Raven's and Cronus's wounded magantors.

By midday, he spotted three small specks to the northwest, their dark silhouettes bold against the clear sky. Lorken drew his pistol, depressing the Scope Up button of the weapon. Gazing through the scope, he spied the three magantors, each bearing a single rider. He released a relieved sigh, for Thorton was not among them. "Well, in that case," he said, taking aim.

The Benotrist scouts' eyes drew wide as blue laser streamed through the air, piercing the breast of the lead magantor. Blood and feathers spewed from the gaping wound, the large avian releasing its death scream. "Packaww!" the great bird shrieked, its life measured in seconds, blood streaming from its wound. Its outstretched wings drew in, preceding its tumble, its rider thrown clear with its violent descent. The Benotrist scout's screams were drowned in the wind as he sped to his death a thousand feet below. The others sped off, breaking away from the dangerous Earther as laser blasts pierced their magantors' wings at the tips, displacing feathers as their birds continued apace, escaping south and west. Lorken continued north, unchallenged and unopposed.

*****

She dismissed the servants attending her magantor, cinching the saddle straps herself. Tosha prepared her mount, her countenance a veil of indifference, masking the turmoil of her heart. The others counseled her to be cautious, to let others search for the fugitives, but she would have none of it, insisting to lead a sizable party herself.

Scouts had returned throughout the night and early morn, detailing any anomaly they had seen. When scouts returned at midday with reports of missing comrades over the forests to the east, she knew what direction to begin her search.

The north wind swept over the upper battlements, swirling around the magantor platforms that jutted from the ramparts atop the palace. Gargoyle encampments surrounded the castle, their cook-fires stretching endlessly, the Emperor's gaze following them to the horizon. He stood upon the precipice, his arms folded over thick robes, surveying his domain, standing at the outer lip of Tosha's magantor platform. Any steps to his left, right, or front and he would fall to certain death since the naked edge of the platform having no rail or wall along its exposed sides. Standing at the edge, upon the highest platforms of Fera, most men would feel a tingling course their legs, begging caution as they neared the precipice. Tyro felt no such apprehension standing upon the dark stone platform, his hardened eyes and even breath betraying none of the storm within.

"Father," Tosha said, greeting him, stepping to his side.

"Child," he answered, regarding her briefly before returning his gaze to the horizon. She stood upon the platform dressed in dark leather trousers and shirt with knee-high boots and a shortsword upon her left hip. A gray fur cloak draped her shoulders, and black hair trailed her silver helm bound in braids.

"I am ready," Tosha said, pulling thin gloves over her slender fingers.

"I have men more suited to this task. What profits you this quest? The risk outweighs the gain."

"I'll see Raven returned in chains. He will be punished for his insolence."

"He is dangerous," he warned.

"Not to me."

"And how would you cow him? Only death will stay his hand, but you desire him alive."

"The lives of his friends are the currency with which I shall purchase his chains. The choice shall be his, and I know what it shall be."

"You bargain with that which is mine. I will have them, all of them, for their affronts to me and my realm." Tyro's icy voice was but a whisper upon the wind, a quiet malice that brokered no compromise. He would have them eventually, each begging for death before his throne, a death he would not grant, but there were other uses for them if his suspicions proved true.

"The others mean nothing. If I must grant them safe passage to collar Raven, then I shall do so," Tosha said firmly.

"Commander Naruv shall oversee the pursuit and apprehension of the fugitives, child. You are to only observe and remain with his command post. Am I understood?"

"Yes, Father."

"Thorton wounded two of their magantors. I doubt the beasts are strong enough to bear them for long. That shall leave them with a difficult choice: whether to remain together at a slower pace or to separate. The Earthers are far too heavy to share a mount. I suspect they'll dispose of your slave and the Yatin they freed, using their magantors to escape," Tyro said, for he would be so inclined to do so in their place.

"Nay, Father. Raven, Terin, and Lorken will not forsake a friend, even one recently embraced."

"Then they are foolish as they are brave, though it is difficult to know where one ends and the other begins," he said as Commander Naruv stepped onto the platform through the magantor stall behind them, passing under the roof that covered the stall but not the outcropping from which the magantors took flight.

"My emperor," Naruv greeted, taking a knee upon the dark stone.

"Rise, Commander!" Tyro said.

The Benotrist magantor commander gained his feet, his countenance indicating the confidence natural to a man of such rank. He was of a stature to Tosha with wisps of silver encroaching his dark mane. He was long in service to his emperor, fighting at his side throughout the Benotrist-gargoyle revolution. He wore polished steel greaves, helm, and breastplate over a golden tunic with four braided azure cords circling his shoulders, indicating his rank as commander of telnics.

"We have established our forward observation sites, concentrating east and south. All of our commands from Fera to Nisin shall be warned of the fugitives over the proceeding days. Several scouts reported sighting the darkest-skinned Earther heading north after he slew two of our magantors and wounded another, but we have found no sign of his comrades," Naruv reported.

"Very well. My daughter shall accompany you, along with Kriton, third among my Elite. He shall serve as her guardian until she returns."

"As you command." Naruv bowed and withdrew.

Tosha stepped back under the roofed section of the platform, loosening the tether that bound her magantor's leg to the floor. She climbed into the saddle, guiding the great war bird onto the outer lip of the platform, its powerful talons strutting along the black stone. Tyro stepped aside as the princess urged her magantor off the end of the platform, its wings spreading as it caught the wind, sailing through the firmament, circling the high citadels of Fera.

With a wave of her hand, she sped off to the east. Scores of magantors soon joined her, their riders launching from the half-circle platforms that jutted from the battlements surrounding the upper palace, their numbers filling the skies with their winged forms.

Kriton launched his own magantor amid the others, the bird especially trained to bond to one of his kind, for magantors held a natural animosity toward gargoyles. Third among Tyro's High Elite, he was the finest gargoyle sword in the empire, second only to Morac's fell hand. He rode the foulest breed of magantor, a gray-and-black-speckled avian with piercing black eyes and misshapen, lethal talons. Beast and rider lazily circled the upper battlements before passing to the east.

Tyro watched as Tosha disappeared along the horizon before returning his gaze to the necklace in his hand, his fingers tracing the shape of the carved faces over and again.

CHAPTER 3

Leanna stood nervously gazing through the viewport of the bridge, her heart pounding, hope and doubt weighing upon it in equal measure. The Benotrist coastline was but a sliver upon the horizon, a thin line of gray and green against the clear morning sky. The hem of her dress swayed below her knees with the rocking of the ship. Her tired eyes and sleepless nights could not dim her outer beauty or spoil her gentle spirit.

They had lost all contact with Raven and Lorken at Fera, the signal on Raven's comm cutting off completely and Lorken's but a faint whisper somewhere to the east of Fera. Strangely, Lorken's comm appeared to be near Raven's signal while Lorken's signal drew near the coast. Unfortunately, only Raven's original comm had long-range capability, rendering Lorken's able to only communicate over short distances. This dilemma prevented them to know if they had found Cronus or not.

The anguish of not knowing pained her heart, robbing her of every pleasure. Sleep was fitful, her food was bland, and the others' good humor went for naught to lighten her spirit. Arsenc repeatedly embraced her, offering his shoulder for her to cry upon. Brokov took her under his wing, teaching her the operation of the ship, giving her tasks to occupy her mind. It was his pragmatic way of being kind. Zem was less helpful, simply stating Cronus's odds of returning to her, his cold logic not intending to dampen her spirits, but what other result could she reach when Cronus's odds were so poor?

Argos's gruff manner was little better, as he snorted his approval of Cronus's bravery at Tuft's Mountain and simply declared that whatever befell him, his fell deeds were now immortalized in the annals of warfare. It was Kato whose passion and optimism went furthest to mend her heart. Of all the Earthers, he seemed the most amenable to her Araxan culture. Kato spoke passionately about the righteousness of the Torry cause, pushing the others to take greater action against Tyro's realm for the sake of all mankind. He spoke with optimism on Cronus's fate and told her to never surrender hope to despair. The fates brought them this far, and she should trust them until they proved false, he said.

Brokov sat in the captain's chair beside her, his fingers interlaced under his chin as he surveyed the coastline ahead, his eyes fixed to the point along the shore where Lorken's beacon indicated. "We'll know soon enough, Leanna," he said, trying to reassure her.

"You have no means to see if he is alone?" she asked again, though the answer was always the same.

"Without their comms and the structural analyzer, we only have the transponders that we placed under Raven's and Lorken's skin. We only know their location. Whether they are alone or with others, we can only guess," he patiently explained. "That's why we have to resort to primitive means of establishing contact," he added before pushing his comm switch. "Light it up, Zem," he commanded.

From his position in the weapons room belowdecks, Zem depressed the forward laser switch. A series of thin lasers erupted from the bow of the *Stenox*, angling skyward above the coastline. Within moments, a single stream of blue light passed overhead from the rugged coastline ahead.

Before Brokov could deploy a submersible to retrieve their friend, Lorken took to the air, soaring over the white-capped waves as he flew toward the *Stenox*. Lorken circled the *Stenox*, his magantor's wings full with the wind as he descended, landing upon the stern as the others emptied out onto the deck to greet their friend.

Leanna rushed to the stern of the second deck and was hurrying down the ladder before he had dismounted. "Cronus?" she asked, running into Lorken's arms as his feet met the deck.

"He's alive," Lorken said, his words sweeping over her with relief. "He was half starved, weak, and badly bruised but alive and intact when I last saw him," he reassured her as she remained in his embrace, feeling as though she could hold Cronus through Lorken's touch.

*****

"They are still moving east," Brokov said, running his finger over the map of Northern Arax from the eastern approaches of Fera to the northern steppes of the Plate Mountains. They were gathered around the small table in the dining cabin with the digital map alit upon its glossy surface.

"They should break north by tomorrow, but they are making poor time by the looks of it," Lorken said while scratching his ear.

"Yes. Their wounded magantors must be slowing their pace," Kato surmised. Lorken had relayed their tale, telling the others of everything that had transpired at Fera and thereafter. Brokov mentally admonished himself for not planting a tracker on Terin as well. Now their young friend was lost to them. They could do little but shadow Raven's beacon and hope he reached the coast.

Leanna stared at the map with renewed intensity. Her elation with the news of Cronus was now tempered by the grim odds before them. He was still hundreds of leagues from his freedom, surrounded by foes and his body weak from abuse. She sighed, taking Kato's words truly to heart. The fates had brought them this far, and she trusted them to bring him through.

*****

He stood upon the precipice overlooking the surrounding lands from the highest ramparts of Fera. His mouth twisted cruelly, reflecting his dark countenance. He stared out at the austere assemblage, lost in thought. Fanciful visions danced genially before him, visions of victories past and conquests yet to come. The world was but a game board, and he the master player, moving his pieces across its face with strategic brilliance.

He fondly recalled the fall of the Menotrist kingdom and the glorious rise of his new empire from the scattered holdfasts of that decrepit realm. He savored his vengeance extracted for their many affronts, for all that they had taken from him. He refused to rest upon his victories, extending his empire to nearly the breadth of Northern Arax, toppling kingdom after kingdom, only pausing to consolidate his gains. His complete victory was all but inevitable. Soon, the lands of the south would topple like top-heavy stones before his advancing legions.

He could see his banners flying above Corell, relegating the mighty Torry fortress to a mere vassal state of his growing empire. Let the Torries celebrate their modest victory at Tuft's Mountain. He would see their kingdom laid waste. Once Corell was taken and King Lore slain, he would place a new lord upon its ancient throne, a lord loyal to him and him alone.

The legions gathered below would be the instrument of the Torries' destruction. Even from these airy heights, he could see their banners blowing proudly in the wind. The bloody red-and-gray ax on a field of black, which represented the 4th Gargoyle Legion, assembled nearest the castle. Farther afield, he could see the black-mailed fist on a field of white of the 5th Gargoyle Legion. The fractured white skull of the 6th Gargoyle Legion and the black whip and gray chain upon a field of green of the 7th Gargoyle Legion rested farther beyond.

"Kai-Shorum!" Gargoyle chants echoed through the howling wind, their hissing voices joined in a ghastly chorus beneath the stormy sky. Tortured clouds gathered overhead, casting an ominous pale over those below. Morac galloped forth from the massive north gate of the castle astride a blood-red ocran with black breastplate, greaves, and helm over his gray tunic. A scarlet cape billowed in his wake, and his eyes shone through the empty eye sockets of an ape skull affixed to his steel helm. Scores of his fellow Elite preceded him in columns of two, parading forth with determined purpose.

He stopped at a fair distance, circling his mount to face his emperor, who stood upon the ramparts above, presiding over the grand procession. Morac drew his golden sword, holding it aloft, the shrouded sun illuminating its ancient blade, alighting it a fiery red. The gargoyles' chants faded to an eerie quiet, their crimson eyes drawn to the magic of the sword. They stared with mouths agape and eyes wide with wonder, captive to its mystical power.

Morac lifted the sword toward Tyro, saluting his emperor before shouting their war cry: "KAI-SHORUM!" The gargoyle ranks echoed his war cry, their guttural, hissing chants spreading to the horizon in a thunderous chorus. "Nordhenz!" they shouted, glorifying their emperor with the title to which he was known to their foul race.

Nordhenz—the human foretold in gargoyle prophetic lore to lead them into a golden age, an age where the gargoyle race would assume its rightful place as the apex species of Arax. Without human allies, however, they could never achieve such lofty aims, allies who would forever be joined to their cause and them to theirs. Nordhenz was the human who would bring their race to this time, the time when their legions would finally be unleashed upon the kingdoms of the south with their full fury.

Morac waved his sword in the air as he galloped forth between the gathered legions, riding along the east road. The legions followed in kind as he led them eastward. Tyro overlooked the legions' procession as they began the long, arduous march. "VICTORY! CONQUEST! MUTILATION! DEATH!" he commanded, his chief lieutenant echoing his command. Soon, Tyro's words rang through the air on the lips of the gargoyles, their chants echoing over the Feran Plain like a harbinger of doom.

CHAPTER 4

They soared through the heavens, passing between the towering snowcaps that straddled the Vorun Gap. Terin drew his cloak tightly about his shoulders, the chill air cutting through its thin material. Yeltor assured him of the brevity of his shortcut over the Cress Mountains. They had never pressed their magantors to such heights, attaining the airy reaches of those towering peaks. Wisps of smoky air escaped his lips as they swept over the gap, passing between the jagged gray slopes that rose to either side, melding with the glaciers covering their summits. The view was one few men would ever know, and he would remember it to his dying day.

They had traveled many days since losing their comrades east of Fera. Terin followed Yeltor's advice, doubling back westward, skirting the southern approaches of the Black Castle. They traveled by night for two days, using the dark to mask their movement before daring to chance the skies in the full light of day. They spotted fewer Benotrist magantors the farther south and west they traveled. The last one they saw was the morning prior, a single bird passing far to their north. They set camp each day along riverbanks, catching fish from the streams for their dinner. They were far enough from Fera to chance a fire to cook their game.

Strangely enough, they encountered little trouble during their trek across the Benotrist lands, as Tyro's eyes were drawn elsewhere. Terin could well guess where since they originally intended to head straight east and north for the coast to meet the *Stenox*, most likely holding to that course and drawing most of their pursuers with them. That was, of course, if his friends had not already been slain or captured.

"Packaww!" their magantors screamed, sweeping over the Vorun Gap and the foothills beyond. Yeltor smiled as the lush green of the Voltaran Forest stretched to the horizon. He was home at last. They would next set down in Yatin land, far beyond Tyro's reach.

The Siege of Telfer
A week ago
Day 2

Telfer Castle rose from the Voltaran Plain like a fist of an amethyst giant punching through the surface from its subterranean keep. The Purple Castle, as it was more commonly referred, was built with five walls connected by massive turrets spanning one hundred feet in diameter. Each wall stretched four hundred feet in length and rose one hundred feet high with an eighty-degree slope. Each turret was higher still by a fair measure, nearly the height of three men, over-looking the walls to either side. A wide walkway, five meters abreast, ran inside the perimeter of each wall, connecting each turret and allowing the defenders to shift men from one place to another with relative ease.

Heavy trebuchets and catapults were placed upon each turret with lifts affixed to each to bring stone missiles from the base of the fortress. A large portcullis and gate were centered on the south-fac-ing wall, providing the only entry point to the castle. Behind each turret ran wooden walkways that connected to a massive inner keep that overlooked the outer walls by another fifty feet. Each walkway ended at a separate gate to the inner keep. Further battlements lined the roof of the inner keep with five sides, mirroring the outer walls.

Two raised platforms rose farther above the inner keep by the height of two men each. The first platform, called Jovan Crest, rested behind the north turret. The second platform, Farin Crest, was wider than its contemporary and rose behind the southeast turret. From these platforms, the garrison commander could oversee Telfer's defense. Several towers rose higher still, protruding from the inner keep's center, the most prominent of which was Yangar's Finger. It was a strongly built citadel protruding straight into the air in dark-purple stone, complementing the lighter hue of the castle proper. Telfer bore the namesake of the king who ordered the construction of the massive fortress fifteen centuries ago, during the reign of the old Western Kingdom.

General Morue stood upon Farin Crest, overlooking the surrounding lands with guarded apprehension. The Cress foothills lined the horizon to his northeast, peaking above the Voltaran Forest, which skirted the western edge of the Cress Mountains. The forest arced south and west, stretching to the southwestern horizon, skirting the castle at a fair distance. The rolling hills that shadowed the length of the Salamin River ran northwest beyond his line of view. The open Voltaran Plain stretched from the edge of the forest that ran south and east to the Salamin foothills to the north before disappearing along the western horizon.

Morue sighed as his weary eyes beheld the gargoyles of Yonig's legion positioned around the castle, forming a perimeter a league from the castle walls. They had chased them since Salamin Valley, harrying the Yatins' retreat throughout. Morue bitterly recalled the horrors of that arduous trek. It took days to reach the safety of Telfer after the gargoyles turned their flank, Prince Yanku's ill-advised offensive and subsequent cavalry charge dooming the Yatin Army.

With a full muster of forty telnics, Morue could have held Telfer against 200,000 gargoyles, let alone the 50,000 that Yonig brought to bear. Of the 30,000 men that Morue commanded at the outset of the battle of Salamin, he returned to Telfer with less than 12,000. Many had fallen in battle while countless wounded were left behind along the bitter trail, and untold others were simply missing, cut off, or captured. A few stragglers broke through the loose gargoyle perimeter, chancing death for the safety of the castle walls. As the days passed, however, the gargoyles arriving to join the siege bolstered their ranks, sealing their perimeter.

Further damaging was Yanku's decision to leave only a token force of two telnics to hold the palace, sending three telnics far south and east to gather reinforcements and fill the muster. The palace was woefully unprepared for a quick siege, which they were now presented. Adding to their woes, hundreds of people from the surrounding villages had poured into the castle since word spread of the disaster at Salamin Valley. They had little food stored to feed those who could not wield a sword. With summer now upon them, the food stores were running low.

Morue counted several gargoyle telnics surrounding the palace, yet there was no sign of Yonig or the main body of his legion. Where were they? Obviously busy cleaning up the remnants of Morue's army, which he lost during the retreat. His subordinates urged Morue to send out forays to assail the weak gargoyle detachments encircling them before their reinforcements arrived, but Morue dismissed such suggestions as madness. The gargoyles would like nothing more than to bleed their ranks outside the castle walls. Yonig would gladly trade two gargoyles for each Yatin, as an attack on the palace itself would cost far more. Morue planned to hold the palace at all cost and would bleed Yonig's legions if they dared to take it. For that, he needed every man he could find to defend these ancient walls.

Day 4

The red claw on a field of black, the banner of the First Gargoyle Legion, paraded before the north wall of Telfer, heralding the arrival of General Yonig, the gargoyle commander. Yonig's main body of twenty telnics skirted the castle in disciplined ranks, unnatural for their kind. They broke off northwest of the castle, circling Telfer in two equal columns before posting south and east of the fortress, guarding the likeliest avenues of approach of any relief force.

Unlike their lesser-armored brethren, these twenty thousand wore breastplates, greaves, and helms. The heavy armor hindered their ability to fly, but they were better suited for straight up engagement against Yatin infantry. Traditional gargoyle tactics favored maneuvering and flanking their opponents but were ill-suited for frontal engagements, where their exposed flesh fared poorly against well-armored humans in disciplined ranks.

Tyro had led the Benotrist revolution by blending the two tactics, using human Benotrist infantry to engage the Menotrists in classic lines of battle while his gargoyles were set loose to wreak havoc in the Menotrists' flanks and lines of communication. Yonig simply applied the same tactics within his all-gargoyle legion. His twenty armored telnics played the role that their human allies performed while the remaining thirty telnics retained their favored tactic of wreaking havoc wherever they were sent. Once released in battle, gargoyles succumbed to a mindless bloodlust, forsaking all discipline for the frenzied passions of the moment. Yonig had beaten such base instincts out of his chosen twenty thousand, his brutal discipline a testament to his iron will.

A long baggage train followed the legion, an endless column of wagons laden with weapons, tools, provisions, and shackles. The Benotrist wagon drivers and slavers were the only friendly humans in Yonig's camp. Accompanying this column were thousands of Yatin prisoners joined by the neck in a coffle, their arms pinioned behind them.

Day 5

General Morue stood upon Farin Crest, staring intently out over the Voltaran Plain as Yonig tightened his encirclement. The Yatin prisoners were put to work, digging earthworks and trenches about the castle. Whether their purpose was to keep the defenders in or a relief force out, he could not discern. The captive Yatin soldiers toiled under the lash, the whistle of the gargoyle whips echoing over the wind, their ghastly sounds reaching the highest battlements.

Benotrist magantors circled overhead, spying the castle's disposition and scouting the eastern and southern approaches. Others ferried messages north and west, informing General Yonig of happenings with the other legions. Yonig ran his clawed digit over the map unrolled across the face of the table in his pavilion. A Benotrist messenger stood rigidly before him, pointing out the places on the map. Commanders Vorztez and Tolessk stood to either shoulder of the lone human, their wings tucked to their sides as their crimson eyes followed his explanation. Vorztez commanded the heavy-armed portion of Yonig's legion while Tolessk commanded the rest.

"Admiral Mulsen has engaged the Yatin 1st and 2nd fleets here," the messenger said, his finger stopping at Cull's Arc, the coastal region north of Tenin Harbor. "He dispatched both fleets and has moved south to cut the sea lanes to Tenin. Commander Torab has completed the land side encirclement of Tenin," he added, sweeping his finger along the land side approaches of Tenin Harbor.

"What of the Yatin 3rd fleet?" Yonig asked.

"Still anchored at Faust," the messenger answered, running his finger along the Muva, stopping where the river met the coast.

"I see." Yonig's crimson eyes alit, savoring the harvest of victories their forces had attained.

"And the 3rd Legion? What progress have they made?" Commander Tolessk inquired intently.

"They are sweeping rapidly south, even with the twenty telnics they have dispatched to join the siege here," the messenger stated firmly. "It seems they are marching unopposed, save for pockets of local resistance. The road to Mosar appears open."

Yonig's original plan was to use two legions to contain the Yatin forces at Telfer and Tenin, freeing the 3rd legion to march upon the Yatin capital. The Yatins' decision to engage him at Salamin Valley was most fortuitous. He had reduced the Telfer garrison by two-thirds and now shifted strategy, dispatching twenty telnics of the 3rd Legion to join him there to take Telfer rather than contain it. They were a mere day away from adding their might to his forty telnics.

The foolish Yatin prince's blunder would gift him Telfer far sooner than he planned. Once the castle had fallen, he would join with the third legion in their advance upon Mosar. By the time the Yatins could muster their armies along the eastern and southern borders, the Yatin Campaign would have already been won.

"Return to the reinforcements from the 3rd Legion. Tell them to hold position here." Yonig's claw stopped at the western approaches of Telfer, where the rolling hillside met the Voltaran Plain. "There they shall rest until dusk on the morrow. At that time, they shall force a night's march to join us before dawn."

"Yes, General Yonig." The messenger bowed.

"Tell them to be ready for battle upon their arrival!" Yonig added as the messenger bowed again and withdrew.

*****

As the late-day sun dipped toward the west, the gargoyles had erected over a hundred large Xs made of crossed timbers, setting them around the palace beyond archer range. The defenders atop the walls stared with grave misgivings, wondering their purpose. Not long after, Yatin captives were brought forth and affixed to each, their limbs bound to each point of the X. Yonig had ordered those prisoners whose labors were most lacking throughout the day to be among the unlucky chosen. Two gargoyles stood before each X, brandishing whips.

Many of the captives knew what was to transpire and resisted being bound to the boards but to little avail. Most were subdued by a dozen gargoyles, their dark-clawed hands digging painfully in their flesh as they bound them in place, stretching their limbs to their upmost. A great horn sounded, signaling to commence. The sound of two hundred whips cracked the air, followed by the horrid screams of their victims.

Men atop Telfer's battlements cringed at the sight of their fellows suffering at the hands of these red-eyed demons. Some cried, some emptied their stomachs, but most seethed in quiet rage. General Morue pounded his fist into his hand, losing count of the lashes that had fallen. Eventually, their screams died out, their tortured flesh succumbing to their captors' brutality. Some still lingered, but most hung dead upon the boards, the flesh of their chests, stomachs, and faces torn away.

Once the lashes had fallen one hundred times, the gargoyles lowered their whips. Thousands of gargoyles rushed forth, swarming each X, feasting on the humans' flesh. The waning sun shone dully over the plain, casting their blood-soaked fangs in a ghastly light, their chants echoing hauntingly over the battlements above.

Day 6

The next morn found the Yatin captives attending to their labors with great vigor, each hoping to avoid being chosen that night. General Morue faced growing dissent among his telnic commanders, many arguing to attack the gargoyles and free the prisoners, believing they might strike quickly and withdraw to the palace before the gargoyle host could fully respond.

"No!" Morue growled. "Any man I lose outside these walls is worth five times that number within," he said, berating Telnic commander Baryak for offering such foolish counsel.

"The men grow restless. It's unbearable witnessing our brothers' treatment by these foul creatures!" Baryak countered.

"That is Yonig's intent!" Morue strode across the stone floor of Farin Crest, his nose a breath away from Baryak's. "He tortures our men to draw us out. Tell your men that the prisoners are already dead. If they desire revenge, then stand to post and bleed Yonig's legion upon these walls!"

Day 7

"Kai-Shorum!" Gargoyle war cries broke the stillness of the predawn air, signaling their advance. They ran apace along the weathered soil, slowly gaining lift to carry them aloft. The walls of Telfer rose imperiously to their fore as they taxed their wings to attain them.

"To arms!" The command swept the Yatin defenders throughout the palace as the lookouts spied the advancing foe. Men stumbled wearily from their slumber, struggling to gain their bearing as they stepped to post along the walls and ramparts. Their bleary vision quickly corrected as they beheld the breaking dawn, revealing the winged forms dotting the heavens.

"Kai-Shorum!" the gargoyles screamed, breaking upon the walls like high tide upon the shore. Arrows spewed from the battlements, striking naked flesh wherever they struck, as the gargoyles forsook armor that hindered their flight. Hundreds fell, feathered shafts striking their face or breast. They tumbled from their serried ranks, dropping to the ground below with terrible force. The first wave wavered under the withering archer fire but pressed on, swarming the battlements upon each wall. Yatin shields and swords met the enemy at the battlements, denying them a toehold upon the wall. The gargoyles reached the airy heights haggard and spent. The first wave was thrown back, and the second followed, pressing on toward the walls as arrows flew to greet them.

Gargoyles passed over the battlements, their bellies exposed to spear thrusts and archers at close range. Many tumbled onto the defenders below, their innards spilling upon the stone walkways. Yatin discipline and position doomed the second wave as it had the first, but no sooner had they stemmed the tide than the third was upon them. The gargoyles attacked all five walls simultaneously, two hundred upon each wall with every wave, hoping to break the Yatins' weak points wherever they might be.

Trebuchets atop the turrets roared to life, loaded with shards of iron half a finger's length with jagged points protruding from their center. Hundreds were loaded upon their slings and flung over the ramparts, tearing large holes in the gargoyle formations. The pointed barbs rarely killed but painfully impaired their targets, leaving them easy prey for the Yatin swords greeting them upon the battlements.

Yatin archers took careful aim, spending their arrows judiciously, as much of their stores were depleted at Salamin Valley and the retreat that followed. General Morue lamented the loss of so many archers at Salamin. With nary five hundred left to man the walls, he could only wonder what his once full complement might have done. With three hundred archers to each wall, he doubted a single gargoyle would have attained the battlements without a shaft embedding their flesh. Alas, it was not to be, and he had to make do with what little he now had.

The third wave reached the walls, their numbers thinned by the withering archer fire and the trebuchets, the survivors faring poorly against the defenders' thick shields and fresh blades. The shrieking screams of dying gargoyles echoed over the din, many tumbling from the ramparts, their bloodied bodies pounding against the slanted walls as they fell. Yatin swordsmen held the front while men armed with spears stood behind them, reaching over their comrades to strike at the enemy.

The gargoyles continued their assault despite their losses, sending wave after wave. With the sixth wave, the gargoyles assailing either wall adjoining the north turret shifted upon the turret proper, forsaking the walls to overwhelm the turret from both sides. Yatin archers manning the turret loosed their volleys with little regard to target, unable to miss in the crowded sky. Trebuchets managed one last volley, cutting large swaths among the gargoyles' serried host.

The withering fire could not stem the tide as the gargoyles swarmed over the battlements, setting down upon the turret among the defenders. The defenders thrust madly into gargoyle flesh, their blades imbued with blood. Those to the rear turned about-face, leveling their swords upon the gargoyles setting down behind them. Those who could interlocked their shields, protecting their fellows to either side while stabbing furiously between their shields.

Most, however, stood among a broken line with gargoyles setting down all around them. Spears impaled gargoyles only to be discarded, as their wielders were unable to dislodge them amid the close ranks. Gargoyles swarmed over the catapults and trebuchet crews, their blood spilling upon the slick stone.

More waves followed, converging upon the north turret. General Morue ordered reserves forward from the inner keep. The north portcullis of the inner keep raised as Yatin infantry marched forth, four abreast along the walkway that connected the north turret to the inner keep. To either side of the narrow walkway was a perilous drop into the bowels of the fortress. With shields guarding their fore, flanks, and overhead, they marched in force.

Gargoyles poured over the north turret, their bloodlust overcoming fatigue and fear. The Yatin relief column drove swiftly onto the turret, stemming the tide. They were hindered by the corpses littering the turret floor, the bodies of gargoyles and men twisted in unnatural angles or ripped open with jagged wounds, their innards spilled beneath them. One pile was nearly the height of a man, corpse after corpse piled one upon the other.

One gargoyle crawled atop the macabre mound, his eyes glowing a fiery crimson and his bloodstained fangs salivating as the Yatin reserves flooded the turret. The creature sprang from the pile, its terrible scream piercing the ears of the Yatins below. Spear tips met the creature at its chest, protruding out of its back as it thrashed in its death throes. The Yatins swept around the corpse piles, driving upon the gargoyles wherever they stood. Many of the original defenders at the battlements' edge still lingered, slashing frantically with weakening sword arms. Desperation drove their exhausted limbs to fight on with gargoyles swarming all around them.

The Yatin reserves eventually secured the north turret, only to be pushed back as more waves converged. The gargoyles surrendered five of their number for every defender but pressed on. General Morue withdrew his men from the turret, ordering all his archers upon the battlements of the inner palace to concentrate their fire there. Trebuchets and catapults atop the inner keep added their fire in kind, riddling the gargoyles serried there.

Morue again ordered his infantry forth, driving the gargoyles from the north turret. Elsewhere, the gargoyles converged upon the southeast and southwest turrets. The Yatins raised the portcullis on the southeast and southwest walkways that joined the inner keep at their respective turrets, sending infantry forth to quell any footholds the gargoyles might gain.

No sooner were the walkways serried with Yatin infantry than Benotrist magantors passed overhead, their riders bearing torches. The Benotrists touched the flames to ropes protruding from large leather pouches before dropping them on the walkways below. The sacks exploded in flames upon impact, spreading a gelatinous material over the walkways amid the Yatins' crowded ranks. Men thrashed violently, their limbs covered in flames as they stumbled into their comrades, knocking men from the walkways to their deaths below.

Morue shifted his archers to the inner battlements overlooking the turrets in contention along the south wall.

The defenders upon the outer walls fought bravely, bleeding the gargoyles for every inch gained. Smoke drifted above the battlements, choking men and gargoyles alike. Some gargoyles broke from the outer walls, springing forth toward the inner battlements but faring poorly for the effort.

The morning hours lingered painfully, every moment an eternal struggle. The cries of dying and wounded men rent the air as the battle raged atop the palace. Yonig ordered more waves forth, pressing his attack. The twenty telnics of the 3rd Legion had forced march throughout the night to join the battle, arriving just before dawn. Minus the ten telnics he had lost at Salamin Valley, he now commanded sixty, with which to take Telfer. He ordered what few magantors he had to again assail the palace. Three of the great birds soon took flight, driving for the inner keep.

The Yatins atop Jovan Crest shouted the alarm as the magantors drew nigh, passing high above and beyond the range of their projectiles and archers. Men stared helplessly, frozen in place, not knowing where the flames might strike yet prepared to run where they weren't. The eyes of the defenders drew wide with wonder as another magantor swept beneath the lead avian from the side, its rider brandishing a silver blade that shone with a luminous azure glow. The mysterious rider swept beneath the Benotrist magantor, his blade running the width of the bird's belly before passing to the opposite side.

The afflicted magantor released a bloodcurdling scream, its innards spilling below as it thrashed violently, throwing its rider. The Benotrist fell, his limbs flailing helplessly, impacting the surface shy of the palace walls. His magantor fared little better, landing roughly at the battlements' edge before slipping off the wall, its blood smearing the purple stone as it slid along the wall through its descent.

General Morue stared in disbelief as their mysterious benefactor circled through the firmament, driving straight for the trailing Benotrist magantors, who seemed out of sorts as their frightened eyes beheld the glowing sword drawing near.

Terin drove headlong into the Benotrist magantors, his foes helplessly transfixed by the raw power his sword invoked. He soared over top of them, his magantor plucking the first rider from his saddle, its powerful talons piercing his chest and back before depositing him in open air.

The last magantor rider started to turn away but was caught unawares as Yeltor drove his mount under his wing, thrusting his blade along its left wing. The bird screeched painfully, its master leading it away. "The fool!" Yeltor growled in dismay, catching sight of Terin setting down upon the southeastern turret, jumping from his saddle, his sword dancing in his hands. Upon their approach to the palace, his young friend was overtaken by a strange urge and sped off to join the fray, leaving Yeltor struggling to keep pace.

Terin jumped from his mount, slashing madly as he moved amid his foes. The turret was overrun with gargoyles, their winged forms crawling over the battlements, swarming the ramparts and pouring into the palace. Yatin soldiers held them at the adjoining walkways but gave ground as the foul creatures pressed their advance. They crawled over the dead and wounded, feasting on the flesh of the fallen. Smoke choked the fetid air, the stone floor slick with blood, while mangled corpses littered the turret.

Terin moved nimbly among the gargoyle host, following the will of the sword. He took one creature across the neck, its head spinning above as its body fell away. Another turned to flee as he caught it across its back, its squeals paining his ears as chest slipped from torso, the blow halving the creature in two. Others looked up unexpectedly from their feasting, only to be met with a slash across their outstretched arms. They retracted their bloody stumps before Terin felled one with a thrust to the chest and halving the other from shoulder to opposite hip.

Yeltor set down upon the turret atop the piling corpses his young friend left in his wake before rushing to Terin's side. He struggled to find a foe to face, as the gargoyles peeled away from Terin's advance. The creatures' feral eyes dulled with timidity, drawing away from Terin like a parting sea. He caught sight of Terin cleaving swords in half with every swing of his blade, the metal shards flying in every direction as he moved through their melting ranks. Yeltor followed in his wake, slaying witless gargoyles that had forsaken their sword skills with their courage. It was almost too easy.

Great cheers rang over the din, the joyous sounds of men pouring onto the turret to aid their mysterious benefactor. The gargoyle attack broke upon the ramparts, their survivors fleeing whence they came. Terin stood upon the turret, blood splattered upon his face and raiment and dripping from his sword, surrounded by cheering Yatins. Overcome with the fatigue of battle that his sword had mysteriously masked, he was bereft of breath and nearly toppled in exhaustion. Yeltor announced his rank, and the two were ushered to Farin Crest to present themselves to General Morue.

*****

"After we crossed the Cress Mountains, we continued on before seeing the palace beset by the enemy. Terin sped off to engage the Benotrist magantors, and I hurried apace to join his endeavor," Yeltor explained to General Morue. Morue's nondescript countenance betrayed little of the thoughts running through his tired brain. The fate of their fallen prince sickened him but only strengthened his resolve to fight to the bitter end. The rest of Yeltor's tale seemed fanciful in its improbability, yet he needed to look no further than the fair-haired Torry who stood humbly in his presence to validate the truth of Yeltor's tale.

"What say you, Terin Caleph?" Morue asked as they stood upon Farin Crest, surrounded by Yatin defenders clearing the battlements of the dead.

"He speaks true, General Morue, though he omits his courage in his quest to free your prince. He faced certain death in that endeavor and only stands before you now by the will of providence," Terin said, his eyes drifting to Yeltor's impassive face, who spoke not a word in his own defense.

"Providence?" Morue questioned. "More likely your timely intervention. It seems we are indebted to you twice over, young Torry."

34

"You are fighting the enemy of my kingdom, General. Saving Yatin lives that are spent to kill gargoyles saves our lives as well," Terin explained, his skin blushing with the general's praise.

"Our people have been enemies for hundreds of years, young Caleph. Perhaps the friendship of our greatest warriors, men such as Yeltor and yourself, can overcome the hatred and history our peoples share."

"We haven't the luxury of our petty squabbles any longer, General. The enemy is at our gates, and we must unite against them. But I am no warrior, General," Terin said, correcting the misperception.

Morue gave him a look. "You slew scores of gargoyles upon the turret below, Terin. If you are not a warrior, then what are you?"

"I...I am a scribe and apprentice to Minister Antillius," Terin sheepishly explained.

"A scribe." Morue laughed like a madman, overcome with fatigue and suffering, his mind beset with worry since their bitter defeat at Salamin Valley. The gargoyles slew thousands, tortured hundreds of his men, and nearly conquered Telfer, only to be thrown back by a Torry scribe.

*****

Yonig stood before his pavilion along the southern perimeter of his siege lines, staring north toward the castle, his eyes dull with calm as he surveyed the Yatin fortress. The late-day sun played upon the left side of his face. The reports of the attack were a mixed lot. His plan nearly worked. The sudden assault took the Yatins by surprise, and the tactic of converging upon the turrets worked better than expected. Telfer might have even now been his had the boy not interfered, a boy wielding a bewitched sword.

His sudden appearance magically stripped his gargoyles of their wits and courage, thus breaking the attack. The casualties exceeded five thousand dead, missing or severely wounded. The Yatin losses were likely far less, perhaps under a thousand if reports proved accurate. His next attack would have to be very well-planned.

"Commander Tolessk!" Yonig called out, summoning the nervous-eyed commander forth.

"My general," Tolessk said, bowing low, as if expecting Yonig to hew head from body for his failure.

"See to your troops. Have them ready for battle come dawn. Bring forth two hundred prisoners for torture and death. Have your troops feast upon their flesh in full view of the castle, lest our Yatin friends grow boastful of their small victory."

"As you command," Tolessk acknowledged and withdrew.

"Commander Vorztez!" Yonig summoned the commander of his heavily armed contingent. Vorztez had sat out the morning's assault, his armor-laden troops unfit to attain the palace walls.

"Yes, my general." Vorztez bowed his head, stepping forth. The formal greeting acknowledged the hierarchy within the gargoyle ranks, the subordinate always bowing his head to his superior, offering his neck to his superior's sword if he chose to take it. Such fealty was most effective in maintaining discipline and loyalty within the legions.

"Prepare your troops for battle. We renew our attack at dawn."

Day 8

The sound of horns rang through the palace in the predawn air, jarring Terin from his slumber. He donned his sandals, struggling with the laces in his dark chamber. Drawing his sword, he stepped without. Men rushed past in the outer corridor, shouting excitedly as they made their way to the palace roof. Yeltor joined him in the corridor, showing him the way to the battlements.

Stepping onto the roof of the inner keep, Terin quickly regarded their magantors housed safely in the stalls of their stables before taking position overlooking the north turret. The shrieks of gargoyles echoed over the din, drawing near in the darkness somewhere to their north. The Yatin archers loosed their volleys, firing blindly in the dim light. The sounds of steel meeting steel rang out where the attackers assailed the battlements.

The soldiers upon the battlements exerted full effort in blocking the gargoyles' advance with their shields as the men armed with spears behind them struck at the enemy. Hundreds of gargoyle bodies fell from the battlements where they were struck down. The first wave broke just as the second drew near, but that fared little better, placing no claim upon any part of Telfer's walls.

Glowing flames dotted the sky, drawing ever closer amid the third wave. Yatin archers fixed their aim upon them as gargoyles bearing torches and sacks of gelatinous material drew near, touching flame to sack and casting them over the battlements. Most were struck down before delivering their cargos, Yatin archers feathering them with arrows, their stricken bodies tumbling with their torches through their descent. A few struck true, spilling flames upon the battlements to either wall adjoining the north turret. Men drew away from the festering flames, and others stepped forth to douse the fires igniting their tunics, though the fires burned through their skin regardless.

The Yatins were soon pressed upon the west and east turrets as the sounds of battle rang out in either direction. Terin stood uncertainly upon the battlements of the inner palace, unsure of the path to take, as his sword provided no direction but to keep him in place. The sound of battle soon echoed behind him upon the southeast and southwest turrets as well as the wall connecting them. The gargoyles were pressing their attack on all sides, or so it seemed.

The walls of the great fortresses of Arax were highly built to tax any gargoyle attack. The winged creatures exerted much effort to gain enough lift to attain the walls and could not hold in flight for long. The walls of Telfer, though lower than the airy heights of Fera or Corell, were still high enough to cause the gargoyles great duress. They reached the walls tired and spent and were easily dispatched by the rested men awaiting them upon the battlements. Few gargoyles had the strength to fly above the walls, and those that did fared poorly all alone, as their brethren lingered upon the ramparts below them.

Terin soon noticed an eerie silence upon the north turret and the flame-kissed walls adjoining it. As the light of daybreak illuminated the eastern sky, heralding the coming dawn, panicked shouts rang out along the southern battlements. "THE MAIN GATE!"

*****

They approached afoot under the cover of night, avoiding detection as the lookouts fixed their gaze ever skyward, not believing the gargoyles to approach by land. The coming dawn revealed the Yatins' folly as 12,000 armor-clad gargoyles closed upon the main gate over the flat ground that stretched south of the palace for some leagues. The morning sun reflected off their polished helms, breastplates, and greaves like flickering starlight upon a dark sea.

There amid their foul host, teams of ocran pulled forth a great battering pike. It was well-constructed with a massive iron head in the visage of a magantor. It was suspended by great cables and support towers to each corner of its wagon and could be thrust forward with terrible force. The ballistae intended to counter this threat were otherwise engaged with the countless waves of gargoyles assailing the battlements above.

The armored gargoyle ranks afoot interlocked their shields overhead, warding off any projectiles cast down from above while the great ram was brought forth. Arrows spewed from the archer slits aligned to either side of the main gate as the ram drew nigh. The gargoyle driving the ocran team tumbled from his seat, arrows piercing his chest. His replacement fared little better, struck down as quickly as he took his place. The loss of neither seemed to slow the weapon's advance, and the archers shifted aim to the ocran pulling the great pike into place. Scores of arrows struck the lead animals but were too late to stay the advance. Within minutes, the gargoyle crew positioned the great pike before the main gate.

*****

The gargoyles assailing the wall connecting the southern turrets slowly drove the defenders back in places, their tenuous holds ever strengthening with their repeated attacks. Yatin reinforcements

38

rushed forth from the inner palace and the adjoining walls, but not as quickly as the next gargoyle waves setting down upon the battlements, protecting their brothers below from Yatin fire from above.

Thud! The sound of the great pike striking the main gate echoed hauntingly over the din. The significance was not lost on the weary defenders as General Morue ordered a thousand men to the gate tunnel below. The tunnel ran from the main gate to the central courtyard, nearly two hundred yards in length. It was widely built to accommodate three full wagons abreast. If the main gate gave way, which rested where the tunnel met the outer edge of the south wall, the gargoyles flooding the palace would be funneled through that corridor.

A thousand men could hold that narrow point for hours while men atop the battlements withered the enemy congested without. The twelve gargoyle telnics afoot at the base of the palace would be easy prey if only the Yatins still held the wall above, but the lightly laden gargoyles assailing those airy heights flooded over the ramparts like a dark wave cresting the shore.

Terin lifted his sword, splitting the curved blade of the gargoyle before him, disarming the helpless creature, a swift follow-through lopping its wretched head, sending it flying over the edge of the serried walkway as he rushed forth from the inner palace. Yeltor's shield blocked a hasty strike intended for Terin's back before thrusting his blade into the gargoyle's chest, struggling to guard his young friend's brash charge into the fray. Before retracting the bloodied steel, he found Terin well ahead of him, his fell blade striking down gargoyles in his path like a child swatting down straw soldiers. The gargoyles crowding the serried causeways melted away like ice in the summer sun.

Terin ran forth, charging onto the southeast turret, his silver blade bathed in azure light. He came swiftly upon a dozen Yatin defenders with their backs pressed against the inner edge of the battlement. Scores of gargoyles pressed upon them, hacking wildly with their curved swords and their teeth snapping like frenzied beasts. Terin swept into the gargoyle mass, his sword slicing several with each swing, their proximity to one another playing to his advantage.

The creatures broke their attack with his advent, taking to flight, the mystical blade robbing them of their courage. The Yatin defenders were equally stunned, frozen in place as Terin swept the enemy from their path before passing on.

"Forward!" Yeltor shouted, following close on Terin's heel, ordering his countrymen onward.

"Ahhh!" they shouted, rushing forth to press the attack and retake the turret.

Yatin reinforcements flooded the turret where Terin had passed, swarming the battlements as the young Torry swept onto the south wall that connected to the southwest turret, the Yatins following close behind. He dodged a high-arching blow, drawing his blade across the offender's thighs. The gargoyle tumbled forward, his legs falling away as Terin passed on. Another hasty strike met his blade, breaking asunder as it met his silver blade.

The gargoyle wave approaching the battlements reeled in panic, causing those that followed to crash into them midflight. Some were stunned, falling to their deaths. Others recovered during descent, spreading their wings and soaring just above the armored gargoyles below. Some of the fallen struck their comrades on the ground, the weight of their descent smashing the unfortunates below that failed to dodge their fall.

General Morue stared awestruck as Terin raced along the south wall, sweeping the gargoyles from the ramparts. He watched in disbelief as Terin raced onto the southwest turret, dispatching the gargoyles there with apparent ease.

Crack! The sound of the main gate giving way sparked the defenders' urgency as armor-clad gargoyles poured through the tunnel. The Yatins retaking the battlements above cleared the few gargoyles that remained, allowing the trebuchets on either turret to fix their aim upon the gargoyles' ground assault. Stone missiles and balls of flame arced over the battlements, striking the gargoyle ranks congregated before the main gate. Archers took position along the length of the south wall, pouring their fire into the enemy below. The gargoyles assailing the battlements above broke off, scattering to the four winds.

Yonig stood before his pavilion, staring bitterly as the azure glow of Terin's blade danced along the wall above the main gate, sending his assault force in disordered retreat. His ground assault fared little better, struggling to push through the tunnel, where their numbers counted for naught in those deadly narrows. Archer slits lined the length of the tunnel, striking his troops from either flank, the enemy slowing their pace to a crawl, bleeding them for every step gained.

The true devastation came from above, as the Yatins took easy aim upon his serried ranks gathered without. The foul Yatins cast not only stone and flames upon his helpless troops, but his own dead as well, their falling corpses forming deadly weighted projectiles. He had seen enough and ordered retreat. As his troops slowly withdrew from Telfer's south wall, he could hear the Yatins shouting a name, a name he would never forget: "CALEPH! CALEPH! CALEPH!"

They heralded his name as he stood upon the battlements bereft of breath and drenched in blood. Yeltor stood at his side, his own blade caked in the blood and flesh of the countless gargoyles he had slain. "Well done." Yeltor smiled, placing his heavy hand upon Terin's shoulder.

Day 11

They skirted the castle, soaring over the gargoyle encampments that circled the beleaguered citadel before setting down near the large pavilion erected along the southern perimeter. Gargoyles stared skyward as the twelve magantors circled overhead, their dark-ebony wings fully outstretched, gliding through their descent. Their riders were an odd collection of Benotrist warriors, former free swords, two gargoyles, and a strangely attired human whose build and carriage were well-known, even to the most ignorant of their kind: Thorton. Draping to either side of the magantors' necks were lengths of cloth with a golden sword with a whip woven along its length dividing a moon and stars upon a field of black. It was the sigil of Tyro's High Elite.

"Leave us!" Ben Thorton ordered, dismissing General Yonig's aides from the pavilion, leaving Nels Draken, Zelo, Neon, and himself alone with the commanding general of the Yatin Campaign.

Yonig appraised the Earther with guarded contempt, wary of the power the Earther wielded. "To what purpose have you ventured here, Thorton?" Yonig asked.

"Your orders, General. We have need to see them." Nels spoke with calm diplomacy, hoping to assuage the general's ire.

"My orders?"

"The orders you received to commence the invasion of Yatin," Thorton said, weary of needless delay. Yonig's eyes slightly flared a fiery crimson before abating, obviously incensed by Thorton's tone. He retrieved a scrolled parchment from a satchel resting against the leg of his map table. It had a broken royal seal. He presented it to Draken, who quickly read its content. "Well, what is it?" Ben growled.

"As we suspected, his orders were altered," Nels confirmed.

"Altered?" Yonig hissed.

"Aye, General. It appears Admiral Mulsen took it upon himself to commence the Yatin Campaign sooner than the emperor had planned," Nels affirmed.

"Mulsen!" Yonig snarled, growling the admiral's name like swallowed nails. "Why?"

"He likely feared your legions gathering at the border may be discovered by the Yatins if you were to wait any longer. Admiral Mulsen has planned the Yatin Campaign for many years and did not wish it ruined by mere happenstance when the fruit of his ambition danced so temptingly near." Nels shrugged.

"And does our emperor place blame upon me?" Yonig's nostrils flared.

"That was for us to determine, General," Nels explained.

"And?" the general asked warily.

Thorton took a menacing step forward, staring down at Yonig with unsettling calm. "If we thought you guilty, you'd already be dead."

"Then what orders does the emperor have for my command? I have conducted this campaign as—"

"Continue with your conquest of Yatin, General. We shall deal with Admiral Mulsen as befits his treachery. You originally intended to envelop Telfer and contain the Yatin troops therein. We see your victory at Salamin Valley has afforded you an opportunity to seize the castle outright," Nels affirmed.

"And I would have already done so had it not been for that foul wretch wielding that glowing sword of his!" Yonig hissed.

"Glowing sword?" Thorton asked.

"Yes. He arrived some days ago riding a magantor with another human. They came from the northeast," Yonig explained. He continued expounding the events in detail, and Thorton knew he might need to linger longer than he planned.

*****

Terin stood upon the battlement, his hands resting on a rampart, staring off to the west, the setting sun slipping beneath the horizon. He had lingered at Telfer far longer than he intended. Come the morn, he would continue his journey, hoping to reach Torry North and report all that he had seen. The Yatins looked upon him with awe. He found their reverence unnerving and undeserved. He merely followed the will of the sword and was as much its servant as it was his.

"I thought I would find you here," Yeltor said, stepping to his side.

"Just breathing a little fresh air before bed." Terin smiled easily.

"Fresh air?" Yeltor questioned, lifting a dark brow, regarding their surroundings. The fetid air was thick with the smell of burning corpses. The palace furnaces had been working for days to dispose of the dead. Most of the great palaces of Arax were equipped with shafts that ran from their upper levels to vast furnaces below. The dead were simply thrown down the shafts from the battlements, where the furnaces could dispose of them before disease took hold. While under siege, the defenders could ill afford to venture outside the walls to attend the dead but could safely dispose of those piled upon the battlements.

"I've grown accustomed to it," Terin answered.

"You're too young to grow accustomed to such things." Yeltor sighed.

"No one should, but such is war," Terin reflected. The dead were so many that the defenders could not burn them all before they began to rot. They had bled Yonig's legions in both assaults, perhaps spoiling his taste for another such attack.

"We part ways on the morrow, Terin. You have done my people a great service, and I as well."

"It was you who led us away from Fera. Without you, I would be lost somewhere in the northern wilderness."

"Humble as always." Yeltor grinned. "Remember what I told you."

"Follow the mountains south for one hundred and twenty leagues to the gap of Rulon. Pass through the gap and follow the Rulon River southeast to its mergence with the upper Nila," Terin said.

"Very good. And I'll follow you most of the way before breaking southwest for Mosar," Yeltor said.

It was paramount that Emperor Yangu be apprised of all the happenings at Salamin Valley, Fera, and Telfer. General Morue was loathe seeing them go but understood the importance that they spread news of the gargoyle invasion to their respective capitals. He had sent riders at the outset of the invasion to Mosar and the Yatins' 2nd and 3rd armies along the southern and southeastern border, advising them to fill their musters and ready for battle, but received no word of their progress. If they tarried too long, then his garrison was doomed.

Day 12

The breaking dawn found Terin and Yeltor upon a magantor platform. They were readying their mounts when the cries rang out. "Gargoyles!" Rushing to the battlements of the inner palace, their eyes swept the heavens, stopping north of the palace, where a dark mass filled the sky, dotting the horizon like a vermin swarm feasting on ripened crop. Yeltor was stunned that Yonig would press his attack after such heavy losses, but there they came once again.

*****

The Yatins on the north wall held firm as the enemy drew near. The archers held their fire until the gargoyles closed within range, releasing their first volley upon the serried mass. As the first arrows flew, twelve magantors broke free of the gargoyle formation, soaring high above the battlements with balls of flame hanging from their saddles.

"Fire!" men shouted as the deadly volleys spewed upon the battlements, flames splashing upon the stone walkways that adjoined the north turret. The gelatinous material ignited upon impact, spreading upon the purple stone and sticking wherever it touched. Men doused in flames flung themselves over the walls, preferring a quick death to the burning pain.

Archers loosed their volleys upon the magantors above but to no avail, as the cursed beasts remained above their range, circling the skies above like carka waiting to feast upon carrion. Soldiers rushed to douse the flames while others held the battlements as the first gargoyles attained the walls. Spears and swords greeted the gargoyles at the walls' edge, driving the fore ranks from the battlements.

The gargoyle second wave followed close behind, snapping their jowls, slather oozing from their expectant fangs. Yatin soldiers held firm, driving their blades into whatever flesh they were offered. Flashes of azure light spewed from above, sweeping along the ramparts of the north wall and turret, striking down Yatin defenders with mindless ease.

The Yatins farther back gazed helplessly as Ben Thorton sat astride his magantor, decimating their defenses with his terrible weapon. He fired methodically without cease, raining laser fire upon the Yatins' foremost ranks. The gargoyle third wave met far less resistance. They swarmed over the ramparts along the north turret and its adjoining walls, sweeping away the defenders like windblown leaves.

Men cried out, fleeing toward the safety of the inner palace or the adjoining turrets.

Fires to either flank trapped many along the causeways, forcing them to stand their ground. Many held their position, stopping the gargoyle stream like rocks protruding from a riverbed, but Thorton targeted them group by group, his laser spewing into their midst, breaking their defense as gargoyles exploited their misfortune, tearing into their shattered formations. The Yatins remaining upon the north turret were slain to a man, gargoyles slaughtering them before passing on.

Thorton signaled his comrades to set down upon the turret to establish a command position from which to direct the following waves. Their descent was cut short as one of their magantors released a terrible cry. He turned in his saddle, catching sight as the bird tumbled, blood pouring from its breast, its rider thrown clear, a terrible gash running the length of its sternum. His eyes found the source of their misfortune as the young Torry whom Raven had befriended circled above, brandishing his silver blade, which emitted a luminous azure glow along its length.

Terin swept beneath the Benotrist magantor, his blade outstretched above him, cutting through the giant bird's chest like brittle parchment, passing on before his stricken foe could drop upon him. He circled about in the serried sky amid the enemy magantors. His eyes found Thorton passing below, preparing to set down on the north turret. The Earther pulled up, cutting his descent, his eyes fixed upon Terin circling above. Terin swept beneath another magantor, passing under its left wing and cutting the outstretched appendage in half, sending the stricken avian thrashing helplessly as it fell.

Great cheers rang out throughout the palace as the defender's laden hearts lifted. Terin followed his second kill by diving below, passing over the gargoyle ranks serried along the causeway linking the north turret to the inner palace. His bird lowered its head, smashing scores of gargoyles from the walkway, breaking their charge and lifting the spirits of the Yatins who held tenuously to the causeway's far end.

Thorton's magantor soared through the firmament, circling the palace, keeping Terin in view. Leveling his pistol, he squeezed the trigger, training his sight on the brash Torry. If Tyro wanted Terin captured, he couldn't do so without maiming him to some degree. Blue laser sliced the air, lighting the sky in a deadly stream above the citadels of the fortress. Yatins gazed skyward, forlorn of hope, many turning away, as their young benefactor was certain to meet his end. Gargoyles stopped in place, their expectant eyes awaiting Terin's demise.

Terin's blue eyes drew wide as the azure light rushed to meet him. His arm gave way to the will of the blade, bringing the flat of the blade before his face. The laser met the ancient metal above the hilt, reflecting off its bright surface.

Thorton stared in disbelief as the laser returned to him, striking his magantor's right wing. The bird screamed its war cry, its wing fixed painfully stretched as it veered sharply right, passing over the east wall. The remaining Benotrist Elite broke, following their stricken captain in his retreat. Nels Draken observed Terin curiously as he sped from the palace roof, wondering the significance of what he had witnessed.

Terin wasted little time setting down upon the inner palace, dismounting in a flourish to join the battle afoot. He was startled to find Yeltor setting down beside him, suddenly cognizant that his friend had followed him into the sky and back again. They ran apace, moving across the battlements of the inner palace amid the flurry of battle. Arrows arced overhead beneath the gray sky, the clash of steel ringing in the air. A few gargoyles assailed the upper battlements of the inner palace, springing through the air from the outer walls, throwing their lives futilely into Yatin spears.

Terin and Yeltor swiftly descended the stairwell to the lower platform, passing through the crowded corridors that led without before stepping onto the causeway that connected the inner keep to the north turret. Making their way through the Yatins holding tenuously to the vital walkway, Terin and Yeltor weaved carefully between the serried troops until reaching the fore.

Terin broke free of the Yatin fore ranks, driving headlong into the gargoyles pressing their front with Yeltor trailing close behind. They swept the gargoyles from the causeway like water from a broken dam, driving them back whence they came. Terin split swords raised desperately to block him, slashing gargoyle flesh that failed to flee his blade. The Yatins followed Terin onto the north turret, sending the gargoyles gathered there to the four winds.

*****

Ben Thorton trained the barrel of his pistol on his magantor's head and fired, putting the animal out of its misery. His fellow Elite gathered about, standing upon the Voltaran Plain with the shadow of the Purple Castle to their west. Two of their brethren were slain, and four magantors were dead or beyond saving.

"What now?" Zelo hissed, raking his clawed digits over his ebony skull.

"Two of us will double up. We'll return to Yonig's pavilion and think on how to proceed," Thorton snarled.

*****

The waning sun lingered in the western sky, hanging above the horizon like a lover's kiss. Yatin soldiers in battle-stained tunics and armor stood in ordered ranks upon the roof of the inner palace to see them off. General Morue regarded them fondly, grateful for their timely intervention and for sparing the garrison twice over. The third assault failed, and another four thousand gargoyles were slain. Of his own men, Morue lost eight hundred, a costly amount but a fair exchange for the enemy dead.

Terin swallowed past the lump in his throat as these brave soldiers saluted him with fists to hearts, honoring him with their respect and affection. He loathed leaving them to a precarious fate, but he needed to return to Torry North and warn his king of all he had seen, just as Yeltor had to return to Mosar and relay the news of Prince Yanku to his emperor.

Terin touched his fist to his heart, saluting his Yatin friends before climbing into his saddle. His large war bird strutted along the roof before springing into the air. Yeltor followed, and they circled the inner keep in full view of the defenders manning the outer walls before passing on.

Day 29

"Kai-Shorum!" The gargoyle battle cry greeted the breaking dawn. Yatin archers spewed their deadly volleys upon the gargoyle host drawing upon each wall. Benotrist magantors again attained the firmament above, dropping deadly fire munitions upon the battlements below. General Morue oversaw the palace defense from atop Farin Crest, resigned to his probable end this day. His men held back the encroaching tide, but cracks were slowly taking hold. Hundreds of gargoyles fell from the sky, struck down by arrows or stones. Hundreds more were driven back at the rampart's edge by Yatin spears.

Blue laser streamed from above, taking Morue full in the chest. Thorton fired upon Farin Crest, slaying dozens of aides-de-camp and commanders of rank. He swept over the east wall where the defenders were most distressed, shifting his fire along their line. Soon, large fissures opened along the Yatin wall, their voids filled by gargoyles swarming the battlements.

By nightfall, the gargoyles swarmed the palace roof, sweeping away the last vestiges of Yatin resistance. Gargoyle hordes swept through the palace like an ill wind, slaying nearly everyone in their path. Blood soaked every corridor and holdfast of the palace as the Yatins fought to their deaths. By the next morning, Telfer had fallen, its garrison killed to a man save for 215 captives, most of whom were women and children. They were given over to Benotrist slavers for disposition. Yonig did not savor this victory, for it bled his legions of thirty-two telnics. He would garrison the fortress with ten thousand troops before continuing his march south. With the loss of three more magantors, Thorton's party was forced to journey to Tenin by ocran, limiting their mobility for much of the campaign.

CHAPTER 5

Staring off to the west from the windswept ridge, he watched the sun settle in the western sky, casting long shadows over the narrow vale below. They set camp just within a tree line that ran north and south along the top of the ridge with forests covering its far slopes, stretching endlessly eastward. Recently sown fields covered the western slopes of the ridge, their long furrows running the length of the ridgeline and the width of the vale to the opposing ridge, which mirrored the one on which he stood. A small stream meandered the vale with modest homesteads dotting its embankment to either side. Whether the homes were of Benotrist farmers or Menotrist serfs, he could only guess. They had set down upon the hillside at the break of dawn, staying within the shelter of the trees to conceal their presence from the locals' prying eyes.

Cronus drew his cloak tightly about his naked shoulders, staying the night chill as he scanned the valley floor. He descried men in the distance working the fields of the opposing bank, beyond the narrow strip of trees that straddled either bank of the stream. As soon as the last field hands retired for their homes, they would again take to the sky, hoping to take flight unseen.

For five days, they flew east, traveling at night while resting by day, using the light of the moon to illuminate their path. They had planned to turn north two days past, but their slow pace forced them to push farther east before attempting the northward shift, hoping to avoid the more populous regions of the northern coast. Their magantors were tethered far enough within the tree line to not be seen.

Two days—the thought ran continuously in his mind—two days north to the coast, to the *Stenox*, to Leanna, two agonizingly long days before he could see her beautiful face and hold her in his arms. Her image danced genially before him, conjured by memories of their last parting. He could still see her perfect face and sparkling blue eyes, losing himself to her enchantment. Would she still look upon him with the same affection?

He felt a pitiful wreck, a beaten-down soldier whose glory had dimmed since last she beheld him. He felt the ache in every joint, the lingered pains of his harsh confinement. He was malnourished, yet five days of a rough but steady diet went far in restoring his frame. After two days of hard tack, Raven started shooting any critter they came upon, cooking them over stones he heated with his pistol. They dared not use a fire, fearing the smoke by day or light by night might betray their position. They remained ever vigilant, as Benotrist magantors swept the skies above with annoying regularity. He wondered how many birds Tyro sent to hunt them. Far too many it seemed.

"Supper's ready," Raven said, approaching through the trees, trampling foliage like a lumbering moglo. Cronus craned his neck, catching sight of his large friend pushing low branches out of his way, cursing as his jacket caught on the thistle limbs of a low-hanging bough. "Argh!" Raven grunted, venting his ire on the offending branch, snapping it from its trunk before stomping it underfoot.

Cronus looked on curiously at his friend's antics, ever thankful that the local peasantry was not near enough to hear the disorder. "What have you cooked this time?" Cronus smiled, stepping away from the edge of the tree line.

"I don't know what it is. It had four legs, a long snout, and about wee big," he said, stretching his hands about shoulder width apart to indicate the creature's size.

"Probably a Terlak," Cronus surmised.

The underbrush and foliage quickly thinned several yards within the tree line, easing their brief trek to their campsite. Cronus stepped gingerly over the raised roots and fallen branches, his feet bound with the animal hides of Raven's kills. The sandals he took from a dead Benotrist during their escape had proven unfit for their forest environ.

"Packaww! Packaww!" The terrible screams rent the air, piercing their ears like dagger tips twisting in their skulls. They wasted no time running to their campsite toward the sound of their magantors' cries. Cronus spied movement amid the trees ahead, a large shape thrashing violently as if possessed. Several steps closer and they could see the large shape to be one of their magantors, thrashing violently, beset with smaller creatures clinging to its back and wings, biting into its flesh. The bird screamed again, smashing emphatically into tree trunks, trying desperately to dislodge the wretched things tearing into its body.

The chaotic scene unfolded before them in a horrific panorama. Their first magantor was beset, thrashing about, its legs jerking its tether to its utmost. Their second magantor was upon its side, its throat ripped open, its blood pooling the ground in rivers of bright red. Alen staggered, his back to them, sword in hand, swinging madly, fending off another of the creatures, which drove him from their prey. The creatures stood upon their hind legs with vicious, knife-sharp claws upon their fore limbs and two rows of dagger-shaped teeth. They were covered in thick fur in hues of gray and brown and could reach the height of a man's thigh when standing erect. One reared up before them, its jaws snapping and black eyes glaring, blocking their path.

Raven drew and fired, blasting a hole clean through its center. "What the hell was that?" he grunted.

"Gragglogg!" Cronus answered, rushing past his friend with sword drawn to aid Alen, who was now upon his back with a gragglogg biting into his thigh.

"Argh!" Alen cried out as the creature's fangs cut through the meaty part of his leg, just north of his right knee, before Cronus's blade took the creature's head, just above the nose. The gragglogg's teeth eased from Alen's sundered flesh, its still corpse falling away as Alen's hands went to his leg, holding it in anguish.

Raven and Cronus stopped short of the magantor that still lived, avoiding the giant bird's massive bulk from crashing into them as it thrashed about. They needed to dislodge the graggloggs from their magantor's back but couldn't step near the avian. Raven took careful aim, training his sites on the gragglogg attached to the back of the magantor's neck, its vicious fangs closed emphatically into the bird's flesh. He struggled to keep his sight on the target as the magantor bucked and thrashed, his aim shifting with the struggle.

Zip! The laser struck nearly true, piercing the gragglogg's hind quarter. It squealed, though refused to retract its fangs. Before he could fire a second time, the magantor's tether snapped, freeing the giant eagle from its hindrance. The magantor burst through the tree line, toward the open fields to the west.

"Kill it!" Cronus shouted in vain, Raven's laser striking empty air, the magantor passing from sight. Along his periphery, Cronus caught sight of the graggloggs biting into the other magantor, taking their fill of its dead flesh. Several moved off the carcass, closing quickly upon Alen's prone form. "Raven!" he called out, alerting his friend.

Zip! Zip! Two of the creatures tumbled over, laser skewering their innards. Cronus moved to protect their fallen comrade. Raven shifted his aim, laser spewing from his barrel, striking the creatures feasting on their dead mount. His hurried blasts fell all along the magantor's carcass, some blasting graggloggs and some striking the trunks of the trees beyond while others struck the magantor, splashing guts, blood, and feathers into the air.

The creatures sprang from the dead magantor, charging Raven with blood-maddened eyes. His hurried shots focused as they drew near, striking the lead animals, hoping their fall would deter those that followed. *Zip!* A third tumbled in the dirt. *Zip!* A fourth. *Zip! Zip! Zip!* Three more dropped in succession, two dead, the third squealing with its spine severed, flopping upon the ground with its jaws snapping.

A gragglogg lunged at Cronus, and his sword tip met its mouth, impaling its throat. He kicked the creature free of his blade, retracting the sword as another followed. He cut that one across its snout, blood spraying his face as it fell back, squealing in pain before pressing its attack, its feral eyes fixed with a hatred no mere animal should have possessed. Cronus spun his blade, taking the creature's front claws, then its life with a thrust through its center.

"ARGH!" Cronus turned at the sound of Raven's shout, finding his friend with a gragglogg biting his right arm and his pistol falling from his grip. Raven snatched the weapon with his left, pointing the barrel to the creature's head and firing several times. Blue laser poured into the shattered skull as Raven pried the creature from his arm. He spied a dozen graggloggs dead at Raven's feet as he rushed to guard him. "Little bastard got me!" Raven cursed, throwing the gragglogg off him before kicking its carcass.

Cronus's eyes swept their surroundings, finding no signs of living graggloggs. Alen lay upon the ground, favoring his right leg, which had begun to swell. He moaned in agony as the creature's poison took effect. Raven winced in pain, his right forearm aflame.

"Take off your jacket, Raven."

"What? I'm all right," he said, trying to wave off Cronus's concern.

"Take it off, Rav, NOW!" The panic in Cronus's voice forced Raven to reconsider his bravado. He holstered his pistol, stretching awkwardly across his body with his left hand.

Cronus helped him pull off his jacket before the swelling of his arm fully expanded. Raven snarled as he turned his forearm, examining the needled bite marks that barely broke the skin. His Space Fleet jacket saved his arm, but he didn't know what poison that damnable creature possessed or how much the creature was able to inject. Alen was now unconscious, his leg twice its normal size. Cronus looked to Raven for any sign that he might succumb, but his Earther blood resisted the sleepiness that the gragglogg poison induced, but not the swelling, as his forearm was nearly doubled in size, rendering his right hand useless.

"What does the poison do?" Raven asked.

"It puts you to sleep and swells wherever the fangs touch, rendering the flesh numb for days. You are still awake. That's good, for I can't carry you both," Cronus said, rummaging through their dead magantor's saddle pack, stripping anything of use while Raven checked on Alen's wound. The fang marks were vicious and deep but had missed the vital arteries in Alen's leg. Cronus bound Alen's wound with strips of the magantor's saddle skirt, which had protected the bird from the leather of the saddle. He fixed a sling for Raven's arm while Raven hoisted Alen over his good shoulder while Cronus carried Raven's pack.

They followed the path of broken tree limbs and tramped underbrush where the other magantor fled, the trail leading to the edge of the tree line, overlooking the valley to the west. "As if this journey couldn't get any worse," Raven growled.

There at the base of the hill upon which they stood, their magantor lay upon the tilled rows near the homestead below. The local peasants had emptied out of their homes, surrounding the dead beast while brandishing their tools as weapons, hacking away at the graggloggs feeding off the dead magantor. A trail of blood and feathers littered the fields, forming an unmistakable path to their campsite. "We best move before they trace the blood up here," Cronus said.

*****

They traveled south, staying within the tree line as it paralleled the small stream in the valley below. Moonlight shone across the open fields off their right, filtering through the porian and lupec trees, lighting their path, even the ambient light could not reveal every root that ran aboveground.

"Umph!" Cronus turned about as Raven went tumbling in the dirt, tossing Alen aside lest he crush the Menotrist under his bulk. Raven growled and cursed as he gained his feet, then kicked the offending root and the trunk of the lupec to which it belonged.

"Feel better?" Cronus grinned.

"I swear Tyro planted these trees on purpose!"

"Yes, that was obviously his plan all along. He knew there would be a day that a motley band of renegades would raid his castle, slaughter hundreds of guards, desecrate his beloved statue, and escape to the wilderness where his tree roots could torment them for his amusement," Cronus whispered so as not to wake the local peas-

55

antry in the event Raven's shouts, moans, and cursing hadn't already done so.

"I wouldn't put it past him." Raven snorted, grabbing Alen with his good arm and tossing him over his shoulder as if he was a sack of feathers.

They continued south for several leagues, hoping the peasants who had found their magantor hadn't discovered their footprints and trail, though they were unlikely to do so in the dark. Even if they had such skills, it wouldn't be long before their overlords did. Cronus had to find a home they could hold up in while Alen recovered or find some ocran and ride swiftly as they could before Tyro's pursuit caught up with them.

Just before dawn, they came upon a dry creek bed that ran from the ridge southwest to the valley floor. The clear moonlight illuminated the open valley, where the dry creek joined the flowing stream below. At their conjoint rested a small cottage made of rough-cut logs and a makeshift stone chimney. The cottage was surrounded by tilled fields with no other dwellings in sight save for a small stable. They followed the dry creek bed, walking upon its dry stones to mask their sign.

Raven stepped carefully, not wishing to trip upon the unforgiving rocks. Of course, a good tracker could easily guess their route of travel once he lost their footprints along the ridge. Thankfully, they passed over a large stretch of hardened soil; but once word spread of a dead magantor with a saddle rig matching those in service at Fera, Tyro's patrols would flock to their campsite and scour the countryside to smoke them out.

They approached the dwelling below from the windowless side where the chimney rested to mask their approach. Their feet imprinted in the moist soil that surrounded the homestead, especially Raven's large boots. "Harrumph!" a moglo beast snorted from its pen beside the barn, loud enough to wake half the valley. Raven felt like plugging the dumb animal where it stood, but the damage was done.

He set Alen's still form on the ground beside the chimney wall of the house while reaching his left hand across his body to draw his pistol. He followed Cronus to the front door, skirting the side of the dwelling. Cronus kept a hand on the hilt of his sheathed sword, hoping not to alarm the residents with a drawn blade. A knock on the door preceded a long wait until it finally opened. They were met by a pair of green eyes peering through the crack of the door. "Who—" A man's voice echoed behind the door before Cronus interrupted.

"I am Cronus Kenti, Torry born and Torry loyal, commander of unit, and I vow upon my sacred honor that if you allow us to enter your home, no harm shall befall you by our hand."

The man's frightened green eyes shifted nervously from Cronus's imposing figure to Raven's hulking form. He closed his eyes and reluctantly opened the door. What choice had he, a mere chattel peasant, against the likes of such men? As Cronus and Raven stepped within, they were met by a dim candlelight upon a small table in the room's center. The chimney was off to their left, centered on the wall. A woman who appeared in her fifth decade, though was likely much younger, stood beside the hearth with two younger girls, neither having attained their seventeenth year.

The man standing before them looked far older than his thirty-five years would have indicated. He was stick thin with silver hair overtaking his yellow mane. He wore a knee-length brown sackcloth tunic. An iron collar was affixed to his neck, indicating his chattel status. The three women wore similar garments and collars. Two thin mattresses of sackcloth stuffed with feathers rested upon wooden platforms on the dirt floor to their right.

The womenfolk were startled by Cronus's intrusion but shrank in abject terror at the sight of Raven, and Cronus noted their apprehension. "Be not fearful, ladies. My friend shall not harm you in any way. We were waylaid by a pack of graggloggs last evening. My friend's arm was bitten, and another friend rests without with a terrible wound to his leg. We ask only to lodge briefly here before moving on," Cronus explained.

"I am Gervis," the man answered, stepping toward the women. "My wife, Naira, and my daughters, Lena and Misa," he said, indicating the women and their relation to himself.

"Your collars. Are you slaves?" Cronus asked curiously.

"We serve the land, land which is owned by our proctor Flagen Tines, to whom our peonage is owed," Gervis answered ashamedly.

"You are not Menotrist?" Cronus asked.

"Nay. We are Venotrist."

Cronus nodded in understanding. The Venotrist tribes were age-old enemies of both the long-ruling Menotrists and the downtrodden Benotrists. With the Benotrist subjugation of the Menotrists, the Venotrists were put upon soon after, their lands quickly conquered by the Benotrist-gargoyle alliance. The Menotrist culture was being systematically exterminated through mass gelding of the majority of their male population, using only the most diminutive to copulate with their females. Such biological engineering would result in a permanent servile ethnicity bred far smaller and weaker than other men and easily enslaved. The Venotrists, however, were treated far more gently. They were bound to the land and allowed to retain their base family structure.

"I'll fetch Alen," Raven said, stepping without. He quickly returned with the former Menotrist slave flung over his shoulder, depositing him upon one of the beds. The Venotrist family looked away, ever fearful of the large Earther. Gervis was of a size with Alen, and the women were smaller still, none exceeding fifty-five inches, and despite Cronus's assurances, they could not circumscribe the fear that governed their hearts. Raven had seen that look countless times during his time on Arax. "I'll be outside," Raven said, not wishing to cause these peasants any more grief than necessary. *Best I leave before they piss themselves,* he thought sourly before stepping out.

"My lady, would you see to my friend?" Cronus bowed his head, backing a step toward the door and waving an open hand to Alen, who lay upon his back, his eyes fluttering in delirium and fever. Naira blushed at his reference of her as *my lady*. They were little more than slaves, yet this Torry commander treated her with great deference. She curtsied as she stepped past him to see to Alen.

She found him shivering, his flesh aflame and his leg swollen painfully. His upper body was swallowed by Raven's jacket. There was little she could do other than seeing that he rested comfortably until the poison ran its course. If the wound was fresh, she could have attempted to draw the poison out with heat, but it was too late for that now.

"My wife will see to your friend. It will take a few days for him to recover. Do you wish me to send word to our proctor that you require assistance, Commander?" the man, Gervis, asked.

Cronus's eyes hardened suspiciously at that suggestion. "That would be ill-advised, good sir. We are fugitives of the Benotrist emperor."

"Fugitives?" Gervis shifted nervously. "I...I do not understand."

"I am Torry, and we are at war," Cronus said as if that was obvious.

"War?"

"You do not know?" Understanding eased Cronus's expression. *Of course, these people wouldn't know. Their masters would never share such news that might embolden them to flee to Torry North.*

"No. We are told little, and nothing that would be of use." Gervis sighed.

"I am sorry that we must impose upon you until my friends are well enough to travel. I would pay you in coin, but I have nothing of worth to gift you."

"Coin would do us little good, for we are forbidden to own wealth of any kind. This land, the moglo beast in our stable, this home, and even the clothes upon our backs are the property of Proctor Tines."

"And where dwells this proctor of yours?" Cronus asked, sickened by the treatment these people suffered.

"Two leagues upstream rests a hamlet. Clustered therein are two dozen cottages of Benotrist tradesmen of varying guilds. Resting high upon the east bank of the stream is a well-built home of stone, log, and mortar, spacious and richly adorned. Therein dwells our proctor. His dwelling is surrounded by fifty acres of arable land, worked by gangs of Menotrist slaves."

"That close." Cronus scrubbed his hand over his face, wondering if their overseer's proximity was to their detriment or benefit.

"Very close, and..." Gervis paused nervously.

"And what?" Cronus didn't like the tone the man was using. It was often used in relaying ill news.

"My eldest daughter, Lena, she must go to our proctor's home tomorrow."

"Why?" Cronus asked darkly.

"Every Venotrist household is pledged to serve our local proctor, rendering shared service. Each household must provide a full day's labor every fourth day. Our share begins on the morrow. Lena serves as a maid to our proctor's wife for four consecutive days, then returns to our home for twelve days before serving again."

Cronus pondered their dilemma. If they kept the girl there, they risked the proctor investigating why she had not shown for service, which would draw attention to them. If they let her go, she might tell the proctor of their presence.

Cronus stepped without, finding Raven sitting upon the ground beside the stable, his back resting against the wall. His holster was untied from his right thigh and shifted further across his waist to be drawn by his left hand. His right arm was still severely swollen and numb.

"How are you feeling?"

"Like crap." Raven snorted.

Cronus nodded grimly, regarding Raven's swollen right arm. It would be useless for a few days longer. "How well can you shoot with your left hand?"

"Not as good as my right," he said, which answered nothing. "I'll manage well enough as long as Thorton doesn't show up unexpectedly."

"These people will tend to Alen. I'm going to scout ahead. Maybe you should wait atop the ridge. From there, you should have a clear view of the valley floor."

"Where are you planning to scout?"

"Their master's holdfast is two leagues south of here. I need to get a closer look. He should have ocran stabled there somewhere. I'd prefer magantors, but that is overly optimistic."

"You plan on riding all the way to the coast? We'll never make it."

"The northern coast? No. The way is far too populated. The mountains block our southern route, and the enemy is to our west."

"That leaves east, and it's hundreds of miles," Raven pointed out.

"What choice have we?"

"None," Raven conceded.

*****

Cronus spent the better part of the day following the ridge-line south, keeping to the trees as he spied the valley floor through the foliage. Venotrist farmers had conveniently cleared the western slope of the ridge over the years, providing Cronus a clear view of the stream that coursed the vale. Gervis's information proved correct as Cronus came upon the small hamlet resting at the conjoint of a stream merging from the east. The eastern stream cut through the ridgeline that he followed.

He found the holdfast that Gervis described resting just north of the conjoint, resting high off the bank. It sat midway up the ridgeline with a commanding view of the hamlet to its southwest and the river flowing north along the vale and the adjoining stream flowing from the east. A gang of Menotrist slaves hobbled along the gentle-rising slope, chained in a coffle while bearing buckets of water from the stream. They seemed to be heading for a water trough between their master's home and the stables just east of the master's abode.

Cronus wondered why they carried water from the stream when he could see a solidly built well amid the estate but surmised that the Benotrist overseers wished not to tax the well to provide water for their charges. It was just as easy to assign their slaves the laborious task of moving such amounts of water. Cronus counted at least thirty slaves in the coffle, joined by their necks with a chain linking their collars.

The forest pushed below the ridgeline, closer to the holdfast, providing cover if he chose to get closer. It would be of use when he planned to steal the ocran they would need. He was torn between chancing it soon in order to flee before their pursuers received word of their magantors' fate and by the need to wait for Alen's and Raven's restored health. He chose the latter and would wait a few days more.

*****

By late the next morn, Alen emerged from his delirium, greeted by the sight of the young girl swabbing his warm brow with a cool cloth. She possessed a comely face dimmed only by her sackcloth dress and sweat-stained flesh. Her light-auburn hair was neatly combed, and her green eyes sparkled with curiosity as she regarded him.

"Where…" His attempt to rise was met by her small hand to his chest.

"You must rest, Alen. You are in no condition to move about," she admonished.

"How…"

"I am Misa. Your friends brought you here yester morn. You were bitten by a gragglogg and have been asleep ever since," she explained.

"Where are my friends?" he asked nervously.

"They wait without. The one called Cronus has visited you much since they brought you here. The large, strange one keeps much to himself."

"Raven," he said.

"Yes, that is his name. He seems a strange companion to a Torry commander and a royal slave," she said.

"How did you know that?" he asked ashamedly.

"The mark upon your left thigh, a feminine crown, is the sigil of the Benotrist crown princess, or so Commander Kenti claims. It marks you a royal slave. How come you of your freedom? For I see no collar upon your throat," she asked curiously.

Her remark was not judgmental, but he blushed in embarrassment of his former status. "I was freed before we fled Fera, though now it matters not. We are all fugitives of the throne, and our lives will surely end terribly if we are caught."

"Your friends seem determined for that not to happen," she said, dabbing her cloth in a bowl of water before touching it again to his brow.

Alen knew she thought Raven and Cronus to be fearless warriors who could overcome great odds to secure their freedom, but she did not know the men and gargoyles that pursued them. Thorton was as deadly as Raven, and Morac wielded an unbeatable weapon. Their only hope was to stay ahead of the pursuit, which was now unlikely.

"Your collar?" Alen asked, noticing the foul adornment around her neck. "Are you—"

"We are Venotrists, bound to this land by our proctor," she explained.

"A slave to the land or a slave to men is still a slave," he said bitterly.

"Yes," she conceded. "Such is our fate."

"Fate can change," he said. "Look at me. I am sore, wounded, and so very tired, but I am free. My friends saved me, then taught me how to save myself."

"You are very brave."

"No, I am a coward, as I was raised to be. Only mercy and dumb luck have spared me a worse fate. But no matter how fearful we are, we must all stand against the Benotrists and their gargoyle allies."

"They are too strong, Alen. What hope have we against them?"

"We can kill them!" he said bitterly. "And if not, we can flee. We can go to Torry North and join them in battle, helping them in any way we can."

"We are not warriors."

"You can fetch water. You can serve meals and mend tents. You can forage for food. You can be taught to feather arrows or sharpen blades. We can fight by helping those who wield the swords and notch the arrows. And as insufferable as your lot now is, it shan't be long before our Benotrist overseers apply the tactics that they have honed on the Menotrists to your people. They will emasculate the strongest of your men, breeding a race of weaklings to serve forever under their dominion. Then you can never revolt or flee, for it shall be too late."

*****

Cronus found Raven at his post inside the tree line, overlooking the valley below. He kept a vigilant watch on the northern and southern approaches while staying within the foliage for concealment. "How fares your arm?" Cronus asked, stepping under the low-hanging boughs of a lupec. He could see that the swelling had subsided. Raven's arm was freakishly large without the swelling but appeared to have returned to its natural state.

"Better, but my hand is still numb." Raven shook his hand, trying to shake off the last vestiges of the poison.

"Thank the fates for small favors." Cronus sighed in relief. The gragglogg attack could've gone much worse. Of course, it could've gone much better as well, he reminded himself. Either way, they needed Raven's gun hand restored to full health if they harbored any hope of escaping this land.

"I killed these critters earlier. You think Gervis's wife minds cooking them for me?" Raven asked, pointing out the two malisks lying at his feet. They were twice the length of a man's foot with brown fur, short snouts, and floppy large ears. Their claws were used more for climbing trees than means of defense. Raven had slain a tersk the day before, beseeching Gervis's wife, Naira, to clean and cook the animal for all of them to share.

"I'll ask her, Rav, but we must destroy the evidence thereafter, lest their proctor finds the bones."

"Why? What difference does—"

"Hunting game of the forest is punishable by death. If their master finds any evidence of our kills, he will punish Gervis and his family," Cronus explained.

"Hunting game is outlawed?" Raven made a face at the idiocy of such a law.

"Hunting rights are consigned to the Benotrist ruling class. The Venotrist peasants are forbidden to partake. They are limited to fishing one day out of five in the river to supplement their meager portions of their bounty that they are allowed to keep."

"No wonder they're all the size of my kid sister," Raven remarked, regarding their diminutive stature. "Tell Gervis's wife that if she cooks these up, I'll dispose of the bones with my pistol."

"I shall. We'll all need the nourishment if we plan to leave by sunup on the morrow."

"Tomorrow? Is Alen well enough?"

"He's awake, so we have to chance it. It won't take Tyro's scouts long to discover our magantors. The rain last night helped mask our tracks, but it's only a matter of time before they search house to…"

"Packaww! Packaww!" The distinct sound of a magantor broke the stillness of the late-morning air. Raven and Cronus slowly crouched so as not to draw attention to any sudden movement that scouts were trained to spot. Gazing through the foliage that gathered at the forest edge, they spied a single magantor flying southward, parallel to the stream below.

They withdrew ever slightly as the great avian drew close. It appeared to soar several hundred feet above the valley floor. They spied a single rider upon its back, most likely a messenger or scout. Whether it was a routine patrol or he was sent to find them, they could not know. They waited for him to pass before creeping close to the forest edge to gain a better view.

"That's not good," Raven commented as the magantor appeared to descend as it continued south, most likely to set down at the hamlet upstream.

"Perhaps, or it might be routine. Either way, we should gather…" Cronus drew back as a dozen ocran with men donning gray helms and breastplates over black tunics approached Gervis's small home from the south, along the east side of the stream. From afar, he could easily discern their sense of purpose, as several broke from their formation, circling further east around the home before cutting back north of the cottage, cutting any avenue of escape. The others rode up to the homestead.

Cronus and Raven could hear the shouting of commands but little of their meaning from their position along the ridge. They could see Gervis emerging from the home and kneeling as the soldiers dismounted, pushing him to the ground as several entered the dwelling with swords drawn.

Raven drew his pistol, taking a step forward before Cronus put a hand to his shoulder. "Not now," he warned. "It will only reveal our location, and they will certainly reciprocate by killing our friends." They could only sit and helplessly watch as the soldiers dragged Alen from the cottage along with Gervis's wife and younger daughter. They were all bound and flung over their mounts before returning whence they came. Two of the soldiers lingered briefly, scanning the surrounding vale before following their comrades south.

*****

Alen winced painfully as his hands were bound behind him as he was tied across the saddle in front of a Benotrist soldier. His body bounced painfully, tied across the saddle, with every twist, bend, and bump magnified exponentially. The brief ride to the proctor's holdfast seemed far longer than its true distance.

The holdfast was a well-built house of stone, log, and mortar, resting upon the east bank of the river with a commanding view of the hamlet below and the northern and eastern approaches. He could see several magantors tethered to posts driven deep into the ground just south of the holdfast. A large stable rested northeast, and various holding sheds and shanties surrounded the estate.

The holdfast was abuzz with activity. Dozens of riders were constantly coming and going. Alen spotted several Benotrists wearing the sigil of Tyro's Elite, a golden sword with a whip woven along its length dividing the moon and stars. He did not recognize their faces before he was dumped upon the ground before the door of the main house. He felt two guards gripping his bound arms, jerking him to his feet before dragging him within.

His eyes slowly adjusted to the dim light of the spacious front room as they transitioned from the bright sunlight without. The outline of the room came into focus. A massive hearth was built in the far wall, which was the center of the structure. A number of men in dark mail were gathered around a table in the room's center, each pointing out positions on a map that was unfurled across its surface. He was forced to his knees as Gervis, Naira, and Misa were similarly handled and knelt beside him.

"We fetched them, Commander!" the leader of the men who captured them declared as he stood rigidly beside his prisoners. A well-built man with silver tinting his dark mane stepped away from the table, his dull-brown eyes fixed studiously on Alen. His sandaled feet stepped briskly across the stone floor, stopping before him as Alen attempted to lower his eyes. The man gripped his chin, jerking his head upward to again meet his icy glare.

"You are the personal slave of Princess Tosha?" the commander sternly asked.

"Yes," Alen answered warily, wishing to add *former slave*, as he was freed, but such distinction now seemed moot.

"Where are your friends?"

"I…know not. I was waylaid by a gragglogg. They brought me to these people's home. When I awoke, they were gone," Alen explained, regarding Gervis and his family.

"Hmm." The Benotrist commander snorted derisively.

"We found this in their home," the man who brought them added, holding forth Raven's thick jacket.

The commander took it in hand, examining its strange texture and large size. "Explain this." He directed his command to Gervis, who knelt beside Alen, his pallid lips quivering.

"It belongs to one of his comrades, master," Gervis answered quickly.

"Which comrade?" the commander asked. Gervis hesitated, struggling to recollect Raven's name, as the stress of the moment was robbing him of his senses.

"Answer him, Gervis, or it shall go much harder for you and your kin," another man warned as he stepped forth. He was a slender-built fellow with long dark hair and soft features and wearing a voluminous green robe.

"Yes, Proctor Tines." Gervis bowed his head before the man who owned the land he was bound to. "He is called Raven. He came to us several days past with another man named Cronus. I know not where they fled."

"What about the others?" the commander inquired, his eyes narrowing menacingly.

"There were no others, master. I swear by—"

"You swear? What worth is the word of landed slaves? None. Tell it true, Venotrist, or I'll cut the answer from your wife's breast," the commander warned, though his voice barely raised.

"I...I swear upon my life that—"

"He is telling true," Alen said, not wishing to cause Gervis any more grief on their behalf. "We were separated upon our flight from Fera. The others are lost to us."

"The word of a Menotrist slave means less than this wretch's." The commander kicked Gervis in the chest, knocking him to the floor.

"I am a slave no more. I earned my freedom!" Alen dared utter.

"Freedom?" the commander sneered. "A Menotrist slave at least has worth. What value are you now? None, it seems. Your life rests upon the mercy of the emperor. I see by your slight stature that you are a bred slave. Perhaps he shall allow you to return to that station." Alen went numb. He would rather die than return to that mean existence.

"Shall we torture him to further loosen his tongue?" one soldier asked of the commander, regarding Alen with malicious intent.

"Nay. The princess demands that no prisoners are to be touched without her consent. We wait."

And so they waited, kneeling painfully upon the stone floor of the proctor's home as the hours dragged slowly along. Alen wondered how they were discovered until it was revealed that Gervis's eldest daughter confessed to their proctor of the strange visitors to their home and begged of him to spare her family any punishment. She had kept quiet until a large party of Benotrist warriors arrived at the holdfast the night before claiming to have discovered the slain magantors some distance north and were looking for dangerous fugitives from Fera who might be nearby.

No sooner had she confessed than a dozen riders sped off to search her father's home. Any hopes Lena harbored of having her family spared repercussions were soon laid bare by their ill treatment. Lena soon joined them on her knees with her hands bound behind her and head bowed in shame of her betrayal.

Alen could not discern how much time had passed. He had fallen over several times in exhaustion, the weakness of his wound still lingering. His captors cared little for his excuse and beat him back to his knees. He learned that their commander's name was Kaul Retave, a magantor commander and chief lieutenant to general Naruv, commander of Tyro's magantor contingent.

He also learned that the local proctor was named Flagen Tines, a quiet-spoken master whose prose matched his cruel nature. He spoke of stripping Gervis of his landed status and selling his wife and daughters to a brothel and sending him to the mines or galleys. He put forth the possibility of keeping his daughters as his personal slaves, allowing Gervis to contemplate the unspoken implications of such an arrangement.

Alen's heart pounded with trepidation as two familiar faces entered the dwelling. The first was a gargoyle of considerable size wearing a gold half tunic that fell to his knees and a blood-red cuirass with the symbol of Tyro's Elite emblazoned upon his chest. His curving fangs and blood-red eyes were the conjuring of any mortal's nightmare. It was Kriton, third among Tyro's Elite and keeper of the dungeon of Fera.

Kriton stepped off to the side, posting near the door while surveying the room. If Kriton evoked the darkest imaginings of Alen's fearful heart, the one who followed him was no less terrifying. Tosha strode into the room, her black boots echoing off the stone floor, taking measure of her surroundings.

"Your princess stands in your midst!" Kriton shouted, drawing the attention of those gathered therein. The men quickly took note, kneeling in unison as she stopped at the center of the floor.

"Rise and report!" she commanded.

Commander Retave gained his feet, beckoning her to the map upon the table, where he reported their discoveries. She regarded

Alen briefly before stepping forth, following the commander's explanation as he pointed to different locations on the map.

"You found Alen here?" she asked, jabbing her finger to the point on the map representing Gervis's home.

"Yes, Your Highness, along with the article I earlier mentioned," the commander explained.

"Raven's jacket," she affirmed. "The others couldn't have gotten far. I want this entire region cordoned off." She swept her hand in a sweeping arc around the vale. "How many trackers have you here?"

"Three, Your Highness. They spotted fresh sign running from the slaves' home to the east ridgeline. The fugitives masked their prints well, but the larger man's boots are difficult to miss."

"Yes, he is difficult to overlook," she said dryly. "Without their magantors, they should still be close by. I want every tracker within two hundred leagues sent here. Did your trackers find sign for only two, or were there others?"

"Just the two, Highness," Retave answered.

Where are the others? she mused. Earlier sightings claimed one Earther heading north for the coast, a dark-skinned man traveling alone. It was likely Lorken. If Raven and Cronus were there, where were Terin and the Yatin? It mattered not, she reminded herself. She came to fetch Raven, and he was now within her grasp. But why did he leave his jacket? This piqued her curiosity, and she called for Lena to be brought forward. The young maid was roughly handled and brought before her.

"Let her stand!" Tosha commanded as the soldiers started forcing her to her knees. She lifted the girl's chin, bringing her timid brown eyes to Tosha's golden orbs. "Why did Raven leave his jacket?"

"He…" Lena hesitated.

"Answer, slave!" Commander Retave growled.

"He was bitten, and his arm was too swollen to wear it," she blurted fearfully.

"Bitten?" Tosha's heart went to her throat. She wanted Raven captured but not harmed.

"That was when I last saw him. I know not his condition now," Lena added.

"Is this so?" Tosha asked Gervis, who was kneeling beside Alen some paces away.

"His right arm is much restored, though his hand is yet numb, mistress," Gervis answered quickly.

"Numb," Tosha whispered. Perhaps this might be easier than she thought. If Raven was hurt, then where would they be hiding? It was not in their nature to leave a comrade behind, but if Raven was hurt, she doubted they would chance a rescue, and that was if they even knew where Alen was. She struggled to quell her anxious heart. She needed to find Raven before her father's more brutal minions did. She might yet coax his surrender if she safeguarded his friends' lives, offering them sanctuary in her mother's realm.

She could see Alen favoring his right leg, the vicious gragglogg wound visible beneath the hem of his tunic. He looked pallid and well-used, and she doubted he would last more than a few days in the wild even if Raven was able to rescue him. She would see to his wounds and remove him to Bansoch, where he would be safe from her father's reprisal but continue in her service as her slave. It seemed a kinder fate, for males such as Alen could not survive on their own, she reminded herself. He was bred for servitude and would continue as such in her mother's realm.

Raven was another matter. Her mother would surely question her wisdom in attempting to tame such a male, but he would sire strong heirs for both her mother's queendom and her father's empire. Was that not the purpose of a royal consort? By offering to safeguard his comrades, he would surely acquiesce to her demands.

The sounds of shouting echoed without, drawing her attention from her thoughts of fancy. Commander Retave stormed across the floor, closing upon the front door to investigate. Opening the door, his eyes drew wide as a burst of blue light took him full in the chest. He tumbled backward, dropping dead in their midst. Hands went to sword hilts as Tosha and the others stirred to action.

One soldier attempted to open a shuttered window. No sooner had he lifted the blocking beam and pulled the window within than laser took him between the eyes. Tosha crouch-walked toward the doorway, stealing a glance around the edge. Men were running in all directions, but many more littered the ground. Some were slumped over the ocran trough, their blood spoiling the water therein. One fellow crawled over the ground between the main house and the stables, his legs trailing useless behind him.

The screech of magantors taking flight was met by laser fire striking them in their throats before they could take to the air. From her position, she could only hear their painful death cries as laser swept from her front, passing to her right, where her magantor was tethered. She traced the source of the laser to the corner of the stables where Raven stood, decimating her men to great effect. He fired without cease, his right hand seeming no worse for its wear as he went from target to target, killing her men with methodical precision. A few stray arrows filled the air, each a poor attempt to stay his fury, the archers who loosed them paying dearly for the effort.

He paused ever briefly as their eyes met across that deadly space. She thought his eyes might reveal anger, disappointment, or regret, but he only shook his head as if he wasn't surprised and shifted his aim, striking a fellow he spotted through the window to her left. She didn't know if she should be honored or insulted that he all but ignored her.

"Is there a backdoor?" Kriton hissed at the proctor.

"Yes, through the hallway to the back," the man franticly answered, his shaking finger pointing in the direction indicated.

"You five, come with me!" Kriton counted out those nearest him. "We'll try to flank these scums. The rest of you, STAND YOUR GROUND!"

*****

Cronus cleared the stable as Raven decimated the grounds surrounding the holdfast, catching one soldier by surprise, thrusting his blade into his gut before he drew his sword. He found two Menotrist stable boys, their necks bound in collars, denoting their status. He sent them scurrying off. A wiser man might have slain them to silence their tongues, but he wasn't keen on spilling the blood of innocents, at least not yet.

Raven waited without, sweeping the grounds with discriminate fire. He had lost count of how many he had slain, but a fair guess put the number over thirty, their corpses littering the fields and grounds like festering carrion. His targets were now more careful and in full retreat, abandoning the holdfast in whichever direction took them from his deadly fire. He spotted two retreating forms at the base of the ridge, running apace toward the hamlet below. It was a fair distance, but Raven took steady aim, fixing the nearer of the two in his sight. The laser took the fellow between the shoulder blades, his face planting on the rough soil. The next shot struck the second soldier in the hip, sending him limping into the village, slipping from sight.

Raven spotted another attempting to flee southeast, angling toward the adjoining stream before joining the river that ran through the vale. His first shot missed its mark, passing over the soldier's left shoulder. The second struck the Benotrist somewhere in the back as Raven watched him tumble in the high grass.

Cronus saddled three ocran before stepping without once Raven's laser fire ceased. Stepping into the clear, he was greeted by an awesome sight. Dozens of bodies lay strewn across the grounds, their still forms resting in whichever angle they fell, smoke drifting above their open wounds. Raven stepped into the open off his left, waving him on with his pistol toward the main house in the holdfast center. Cronus moved swiftly afoot toward the front-left corner of the dwelling as Raven stepped toward the front.

"I saw you in there, Tosha. Come on out! Tell your men to throw their weapons on the ground and to exit slow, real slow!" Raven commanded. His command was met by a brief silence, and then he caught sight of Alen passing through the front door, staggering with his hands bound behind him and a knife to his throat. He could spy Tosha behind him with her left hand wrapped around Alen's forehead and her right holding the knife.

"Stay your weapon, or I'll slice his throat, Raven!" she warned, forcing Alen forward several paces.

"Let him go and surrender, Tosh, and I'll let your men live. What's left of them anyway."

"It is you that should drop your weapon and surrender. You cannot escape this land, Raven. Surrender to me and I will provide your friends sanctuary in my mother's realm," she countered, gripping Alen ever tighter.

"Sanctuary? More like slavery. Save your generous offer for the next moron that'd believe you."

"It's a better fate than my father intends. At least my way keeps each of you safe. Such was my intent before your savagery at Fera. You ruined everything—killed hundreds of my father's men and nearly lost your own life along the way—and for what? Is the life I offer you so wretched that death is preferable?" she asked bitterly.

"To trust you ever again would require a whole lot of assumption on your end and a lot more stupidity on mine, wife."

Cronus sprinted from the corner of the dwelling, running up behind her before driving the pommel of his sword down upon her right elbow. Her grip weakened as he tore her away, throwing her to the ground before her comrades rushed from the open doorway to protect their princess. Several stepped through but were met with laser fire. Two dropped dead while the others withdrew.

Raven marched up to Tosha, grasping her left arm with his free hand and pulling her to her feet, ignoring the knife in her other hand. She brandished it in front of his face. Raven holstered his pistol and stripped the knife from her hand, tossing it away.

"You know, I used to live a nice, quiet life before I met you, Tosha." He glared.

"Quiet? There's nothing quiet about, Raven. Even the sound of your breath carries for miles!"

"I was quiet enough to sneak up on your little establishment here."

"Raven, we don't have time for you to argue with your wife. We need to move out," Cronus said, freeing Alen's hands.

Before Raven could command the others to step outside, a large shadow descended. He looked up to see Kriton springing from the rooftop, his wings stretched to their utmost, easing his descent. His ears arced back as if pressed by the wind, and his fangs curved menacingly over blood-red lips. With no time to draw his gun, Raven caught him full in the chest, collapsing under his weight.

They tumbled in the dirt, rolling on the ground, as Kriton's five companions rushed around the side of the dwelling with blades drawn. Several others emerged from the doorway, reacting slow to their turn of fortune. Cronus moved quickly to the side of the doorway, catching the first to step through at the knee. The fellow screamed, his face planting in the ground, his body an obstacle to those who followed.

"Alen, help Raven!" Cronus bellowed, backing away as the men rushing around the corner of the dwelling closed upon him. Alen barely took a step before Tosha was upon him, grabbing his arm and twisting him to the ground. She was warrior bred and raised and far stronger than a weak slave could hope to challenge her.

Raven and Kriton wrestled in the dirt, each grunting, twisting, and biting. Raven's pistol slipped free of his holster, lying upon the ground as they unwittingly rolled away. Cronus noticed it as he backed away from the onrushing Benotrists, hopelessly outnumbered. He broke in a full sprint toward the weapon as Tosha, too, took note as she stood over Alen, holding his arm behind his back. She pushed his arm aside as she lunged forth, hoping to beat Cronus to the treasure.

Raven gained his knees, flipping Kriton over his shoulder, slamming him into the ground before pummeling him with his fist. He cut the knuckles of his right hand on Kriton's fang as he punched him in the face. He shifted his attention to Kriton's chest, pounding the wretch.

Cronus dove into the dirt, his outstretched hand grasping the pistol as Tosha fell atop him. He turned to his side, drawing the weapon close with her clinging desperately to his back before spraying laser upon his pursuers. Raven gained his feet, kicking Kriton's ribs for good measure before helping Cronus. He reached down, peeling Tosha from Cronus's back as his friend blasted away. Raven pinned Tosha to the ground, binding her hands behind her with a strip of binding leather she had tucked into her sword belt. He removed her sword and similarly bound her ankles.

Cronus was familiar with Raven's pistol and could strike targets close by where his poor mechanics were not visible. His hurried shots dropped the three Benotrists nearest him, sending those who followed scurrying away. Raven came to his side, retrieving his weapon and striking several who were beyond Cronus's aim. Raven walked among the fallen, shooting each in the head to make sure of them.

"Where's Kriton?" Cronus asked.

Raven turned sharply to where he had left the gargoyle bloodied in the dirt. He was gone. "That overgrown bat has more lives than a cat!" he growled.

"What's a bat?" Cronus smiled, knowing full well that his friend would struggle to describe the alien creature before eventually giving up and growling.

"Never mind." Raven snorted, skipping the attempted explanation altogether.

Cronus laughed, feeling much restored to his former self. "Alen, you'll find three ocran saddled in the stable. Fetch them!" he commanded before entering the main dwelling to free Gervis and his family. Within minutes, Gervis and his wife and daughters emerged from their proctor's home, rubbing their wrists where they were bound. Cronus followed after, dragging a disheveled Flagen Tines in tow. The cruel proctor had a bruised face where Cronus dealt him a blow. Cronus threw him to the dirt between Raven and himself.

"Who's he?" Raven asked.

"Our proctor," Gervis answered warily, staying a fair distance from their master. Raven and Cronus shared a look. They knew well the tales of Benotrist cruelty to the Menotrist slaves and Venotrist serfs. Men like Tines took wicked pleasure in castrating, blinding, raping, and torturing their slaves.

"You deserve a far meaner fate than I can give you," Cronus said, stepping forth and slashing his blade across Flagen Tines's stomach, spilling his innards as the village master crumpled to his knees, his screams echoing through the vale. Had Cronus had the luxury of sparing his life, he would've dealt the man the mercy he offered his slaves—gelding and blinding and binding him to a grain wheel to live out his days in all the misery his kind deserved.

But that was the way of the Benotrists, gargoyles, and the Menotrists before them, each committing greater atrocities upon their foes for lesser slights committed upon them. Each revenge built upon the last, bringing no limit to their mutual cruelty. He needn't repeat their barbarity—just kill them and be done with it.

But that didn't mean men like Flagen Tines couldn't suffer an agonizing death. There had to be some measure of justice, after all. He would leave him where he knelt, dying slowly with his guts spilled upon the ground. If only Kriton could meet such a fate, but alas, the foul creature had escaped them.

Raven fished his comm from his trouser pocket after remembering a crunching sound during his struggle with Kriton. There it was in his hand, broken in three parts. "Crap!"

*****

They found the Menotrist slaves whom Cronus had first observed days ago shackled in their holding pen just north of the main dwelling. They freed them and sent them on their way, armed with whatever weapons they took from the dead. Most were too frightened to dare an escape until Cronus simply asked them what use the life they lived was. Their days were measured by the lash and suffering. No pleasures were left to them, and only death could free them from their miserable lot. Besides, the Benotrists would kill every slave in the holdfast once they found their master and their soldiers slain.

Their tentative first step to freedom soon cascaded into a full sprint to the hamlet below with blades raised and revenge in their hearts. Gervis, on the other hand, thought it better to return to his homestead and hope none of the surviving Benotrists knew of him. Nearly all his master's men were among the dead, and he could never hope to flee without being caught. Benotrist fiefdoms ran endlessly in each direction, and he could never circumvent their endless patrols. Cronus and Alen bade them farewell while Raven killed every ocran that remained.

Tosha said not a word as Raven freed her legs and lifted her into the saddle before climbing up behind her as Cronus and Alen mounted their own ocran. "Lead the way," Raven said, regarding Cronus, wrapping his arms around Tosha to grasp the reins.

"You will pay dearly for this!" Tosha snarled as Raven kicked his heels into the animal's flanks, following the others east along the north bank of the adjoining stream.

"I'm sure I will, sweetheart," Raven said, kissing her neck before she reached back and bit his nose.

CHAPTER 6

The morning sun broke upon her face through the foliage above, stirring her awake. Tosha turned her face from the hurtful glare, cursing the dawn, as she wished nothing more than to sleep, though how well she could sleep with her hands bound behind her, one could only guess. She struggled to sit up, shifting on an unforgiving tree root that afflicted her legs throughout the night. Raven had again covered her with his thick jacket, which fell to her side as she arose, her midnight hair dropping below her face and obscuring her vision.

She shook her head, attempting to throw her dark tresses behind her, to no avail. She blew her hair, pushing it clear of her eyes to take stock of her surroundings. Alen rested the farthest away, sleeping beneath a large porian, his back to her, curled up beside its thick trunk. Cronus was nowhere to be seen, most likely attending to the necessary bodily functions that she also needed to address.

Their ocran were tied off to a tree beyond Alen's sleeping form. In the opposite direction, she found Raven, his head propped up on the trunk of the tree he slept beneath with his arms folded over his chest and sleeping with blissful content. Oh, how she wanted nothing more than to kick him. How dared he lay there comfortably as if he hadn't a care in the world whilst she suffered her bonds!

Why not? she thought gleefully and stormed toward him to render the blow. The attempted strike failed as she tumbled to the ground, her left ankle caught upon the chain that bound her to the tree where she slept. "Ow!" she cried, her face planting into the damp soil.

"Well, that's not very ladylike." Raven smirked, appraising her with one eye open as if he couldn't be bothered to exert any more motion than that.

"Enjoying yourself?" she asked coolly as she sat up, dead leaves and foliage clinging to her face and hair.

"Immensely." He smiled.

Oh, how she found his smugness irritating. He had taken wicked delight in tormenting her these past days. She told him repeatedly how she had planned to remove him and Cronus from Fera and provide Terin and Lorken safe passage to the *Stenox*. So many lives would have been spared, and they would have been safe from her father's current pursuit. Raven disregarded her plea, saying how little faith he placed in her lying tongue.

After all she had had offered him, he treated her thusly? Did her maidenhood count for naught? By the binding laws of Benotrist tradition and her mother's native isle, they were wed. Was a life with her so terrible?

"You look a little jumpy, Tosha. Do you have to piss?" he asked curiously.

"Must you be so crass?" she reproached. "Yes, I do."

"All right." He slowly gained his feet, taking the key to her shackles from his trouser pocket. He spun her around, unlocking the manacles binding her hands.

"What of my leg?" She lifted her left foot, displaying the thick shackle wrapped around her bare ankle where her trouser leg was pushed north of.

"Fat chance, my darling wife. You have enough slack in your chain to do your business on the other side of your tree."

She glared daggers at him as she retreated, kicking his jacket aside as she circled the tree where her shackle was tethered. Her not-so-subtle curses rang through the forest, waking Alen from his slumber. He gained his feet as she reemerged, regarding Raven most discourteously. Alen stood uncomfortably as Tosha reached the end of her tether, berating Raven for every offense he had ever rendered and many more that he hadn't. He simply stared down at her as if she was a yipping tiny dog.

Raven found her foul tongue amusing but was far enough away to avoid her reach. She had already slapped him a dozen times, bit him twice, and kicked him in the shin, knee, stomach, and groin since taking her captive. He had taken her over his knee for each offense and spanked her, declaring that her father was remiss to not have done so during her upbringing. Their continuous banter was giving Alen a headache.

"I fetched us some breakfast," Cronus happily declared, entering their midst with four fish in his left hand. His initial smile quickly eased into a startled frown as Tosha and Raven continued their argument, oblivious to his arrival.

"You're a hopeless, dull wit with the manners of a gragglogg. To think I believed you suitable to serve as my consort!" she snapped.

"Where I come from, we actually ask someone to marry us before doing so without their consent. You might've let me in on your little scheme before bedding me and drugging me in that order!" Raven growled, though she held her ground, refusing to back down.

"We drank of the same cup offered by my father. Were you ignorant of its significance? You entered my bedchamber at my behest. Would any other than my consort be so honored? Perhaps I have misjudged your intellect," she answered coolly, her chest rising, her words coming quicker than her breath allowed.

"The cup again, huh!" Raven snorted derisively. "You might excuse my ignorance, being from a different world and all. How the hell was I to know that taking a sip from a cup meant marriage in your backward kingdom? You might want to back off on who you call a dimwit, *girl*, and take a look in the mirror."

"Oh, how you will suffer for your insolence!" she said, shrieking as if he had thrown hot water on her. "If you think to insult me without rep…" Raven pinched her lips shut with the fingers and thumb of his right hand, hoping to silence her shrieking banter. After a few mumbled words, she jerked her head away, freeing her lips before biting down on his fingers.

"Why, you little—" Raven growled, shaking his wounded fingers as she cut him off.

"Don't touch me without my leave, peasant. I could have your hand removed for such an affront!" she reproached.

"Why you…" He grunted, stepping forth to seize her and administer her another spanking, as he had done repeatedly these past days.

"Rav, wait," Cronus said, stepping between them, placing a hand to his friend's chest. "There's a nice lake just down this hill. Go wash while Alen and I cook these up." He lifted the fish tied to the string in his left hand. Raven glared at Tosha over Cronus's shoulder, snorted, and stepped away, her eyes following him through the trees as he passed from sight. "If you desire affection from him, you'll find kindness a more effective strategy, Princess," Cronus offered before stepping away.

"It is too late for such sentiments. Raven hates me." She sighed, her shoulders sagging with defeat.

"Hates you?" Cronus turned back, regarding her curiously.

"Yes. He hates me. We are far too different to ever agree. I was a fool to believe otherwise."

"Different?" Cronus smiled, shaking his head. "You are far more alike than either of you care to admit."

"If we were kindred souls, he would have understood the difficulty of my position. He would—"

"He loves you," Cronus said, the words freezing her in place.

"Loves me?" she repeated to herself, failing to believe it. "If that were so, then why has he treated me thusly? Why chain me like an animal or slave?" she countered.

"Could he trust you not to run or slice his throat whilst he slept? You have given him little reason to trust you, Princess."

"I granted him my hand and maidenhood. Any man would accept such gifts with gratitude and reverence. He loves me you claim. What proof have you to back such a boast?"

Cronus regarded her kindly, stepping near, placing a hand upon her shoulder. "No one has treated him so harshly as you have and lived. What else but love could restrain him?" She was taken aback, her scowl softening with Cronus's reassurance. The Torry commander possessed an uncanny ability to calm the stormiest of hearts. He was a true friend to Raven but did not harbor resentment for her father's ill treatment toward her. He thought only of his friend's interest. She had feared Cronus would be a wedge between them, urging Raven to cast her aside or slay her outright, but such was not his nature.

"I now see why he went to such lengths to save you, Commander Kenti. You are a true friend." She regarded him in a new light.

"So is Raven, Princess."

"Let me speak with him," she asked, raising her left ankle where the chain dangled from the manacle.

*****

She made her way down the hill, her ankle free of the manacle but her hands bound before her. Cronus did not trust her completely and compromised on her restraints to allow her limited movement. She paused before stepping from the tree line, spying Raven's naked torso in the water, his broad, muscled back facing her as he washed the stink from his flesh. The lake water must be cold, but he seemed to tolerate it in order to clean himself. The mere sight of him stirred the strangest feelings within, clouding her judgment whenever she thought of him.

Her furtive glance drifted to the shoreline, where his clothes were strewn in his usual disordered fashion. Her plan to speak with him was quickly forsaken for a different opportunity. She crept from the foliage that concealed her, her eyes searching desperately for his holster, which she could not find.

"Looking for this?" He startled her, his hand on his holstered pistol. Raven stood from the water in all his natural glory save for the holster strapped around his waist.

She stifled a laugh, appraising his assets with a bemused smile. "I see everything that I was looking for." He shook his head, knowing full well she was just as apt to kill him or kiss him with equal consideration. She stripped off her trousers, fur boots, and loin garment before trudging through the shallows to join him. Her bound wrists prevented her from stripping her shirt, but she didn't plan on getting that wet.

The cold lake water felt like ice, and she saw Raven's pimpled skin, proving he wasn't immune to its effect. "Do you ever part with your weapon?" she asked lasciviously, stepping near. She lifted her bound wrists over his head, settling them behind his neck, looking into his deep black eyes, which seemed to stare right through her.

"Considering the company I'm keeping these days, I doubt it."

"You don't trust me." She pouted playfully, her eyes trailing the length of his lips.

"Did you hit your head or something?" he asked, taken aback by her sudden mood swing. One moment, she wanted to kill him; the next, she flirted shamelessly. He had never understood women, and who could blame him? They were strange, exotic creatures who tempted him and drove him crazy at the same time. It seemed Cronus somehow found the one sane woman on the entire planet. *Lucky bastard,* he thought wryly.

He was entirely convinced that Tosha had a few screws loose in that pretty head of hers and wondered how he had stumbled into this mess in the first place. It all went back to Molten Isle, when he first laid eyes upon her. He was instantly smitten at that fateful moment, and she had consumed his thoughts ever sense.

"You always speak so strangely." She smiled, ignoring his jibe. No man other than her father ever spoke so openly to her. She found it intolerable and thrilling in equal measure, often evoking different responses from her. His lack of deference to her high station was insulting. It often led to her harsh rebuke toward him but also evoked something else. She felt a strange quiver within whenever he looked into her eyes or spoke to her as if she was his equal.

Perhaps the strangest feeling was how safe she felt whenever he was near. She was born and bred to be fearless and to lead, to have others bow and look to her for direction. Men on her mother's isle were little more than consorts at best and chattel at worst. They were nothing like the men on the continent and certainly not akin to Raven in any way.

She was never taught to favor strength in a mate or needed to be protected, but she was hopelessly drawn to him for those very reasons. She fancied sitting on her mother's throne one day with him beside her, her consort, her guardian, her lover.

He spoke fondly of his kin who dwelled on his home world. Would his affection for their own children be any less? Alas, he was too proud to come with her willingly. If she desired him beside her, she would have to drag him to Bansoch in chains. Such measures would surely sour him to the role she intended for him to assume, and if her father captured him first, she shuddered to think of what he might do. Raven's offenses to the Benotrist Empire were only growing in severity. Now that he had captured her, she could only imagine the punishment her sire intended upon him.

He stared down into her golden eyes for what seemed an eternity, wondering what was going on in that head of hers. She closed her eyes, rising upon her toes to reach his lips. And then it happened. Her expectant kiss was suddenly forsaken as her stomach quickly soured, depositing its contents on his chest. He unhooked her arms from around his neck as she bent over, emptying her stomach into the water. "Are you sick?" he asked, ignoring the vomit coating his chest, touching a hand to her back. She looked up to him with bloodshot eyes and pallid lips, wondering how she could feel so awful.

*****

Raven cleaned her up, donned his clothes, and scooped her into his arms, carrying her back up the hill. She nestled her face in the crook of his elbow, her head spinning. The smell of Cronus's cookfire in their campsite sickened her. The thought of eating fish nauseated her further.

"What's wrong with her?" Cronus asked as Raven set her down beside their packs.

"She's sick. Hand me the key to her manacles," Raven said. Cronus fished the key from his pack, and Raven freed her hands and stripped away her foul, stained shirt. Alen found a spare tunic in their saddle pack, and Raven slid it over her head as the others turned away, sparing her dignity. "Wash that in the lake," Raven said, tossing her shirt to Alen. "Her other clothing as well. I left them beside the shore." Alen gathered it up and hurried off to attend to the task as Raven wrapped his jacket around her.

*****

By midday, Tosha felt much improved, and they continued eastward, skirting the north side of the lake, keeping within the shadow of the forest. Tosha held tight to Raven's back, her bare legs exposed by the brevity of the tunic she wore as she wrapped them over his thighs. Whatever had afflicted her seemed to have passed.

Far off to the south, the sound of a Benotrist magantor screeched through the air, its presence an ominous reminder of the peril surrounding them.

CHAPTER 7

"I like this not, my prince," Jentra again advised as they stood beside the cookfire. They stood upon a half-barren hilltop overlooking the thick forest that stretched endlessly north and west. They were well beyond the Torry border, setting camp in the hostile wilds that skirted the northwestern frontier of their native realm. They were many leagues out of Central City, visiting the holdfasts and settlements along their route of travel.

The prince disregarded the king's summons, insisting they would journey to Corell once this more pressing matter was attended to. Jentra rightly questioned what pressing matter drove them to venture far beyond their border and into these dangerous lands. He had learned over the years that Prince Lorn's mind was impossible to change once one of his *premonitions* took root. Now here he was, the prime of King Lore's High Elite, following his crown prince on a journey that was surely a waste of time at best and dangerous at worst.

"What troubles you most, my friend, that I have failed to heed my father's summons or that we have ventured far into the wilds with nary a dozen men or that we have lit a fire, proclaiming our presence to anyone for leagues around?" Lorn asked, his sea-blue eyes twinkling with amusement, reading the apprehension in his friend's countenance.

Well into his fifth decade, Jentra was a seasoned warrior whose loyalty to the crown was above reproach. He was fair of hair with chiseled jaw and a stout stature, standing sixty-six inches. He always questioned Prince Lorn's odd decisions but followed them nonetheless. His prince's strange premonitions were always proven true for some strange reason, and Jentra should have known better than to doubt him now, but he rightly wondered what purpose would drive him to venture there. Lorn simply regarded him with his deep blue eyes as if privy to some revelation that would soon be answered.

The Torry crown prince was a tall, well-built man, who stood near sixty-nine inches with flowing black hair and a handsome face. His mature countenance belied his true age of twenty-four years, Jentra often forgetting how young Lorn truly was. When Lorn told the elder warrior of his plan to venture into the wilds for a purpose only the prince knew, Jentra growled his misgivings but followed him faithfully into the unknown with twelve fellow members of the Torry Elite. Each was similarly attired in sky-blue tunics and silver breast-plates, greaves, and helms, marking them as Torry Elite.

"I would be lying if I claimed to hold no doubt on the wisdom of this journey, my prince, but I should know better to trust your premonitions," Jentra conceded, though he hadn't a clue as to how this expedition could end fruitfully. At best, it would be a complete waste of time. At worst, well, at worst, it could end very poorly.

"You are right to question decisions that sharply contrast your own good sense, my friend. If I am to be king one day, I would be best served by honest counsel rather than false pleasantries, for no man is all-knowing, not even kings." Lorn smiled, placing a hand upon his friend's shoulder.

"Whether a king is all-knowing or not is less import than his people believing it so. Your wisdom and right to rule must be beyond reproach." Jentra regarded him with his steel-gray eyes.

"My right to rule is based upon nothing more than the fortunes of birth. For the trials ahead, the realm requires more of its future king than such happenstance. Our people must believe in what I advise even if I am not present to light the path. Yah has awakened me from my slumbering ignorance, opening my eyes to his greater vision. It is his path that I now follow. He has illuminated the path so clearly that even blind, I could follow its course."

Yah, Jentra thought sourly. The ancient deity worshipped in the days of King Kal thousands of years ago had resurfaced of late, gathering a scant following of believers. His prince was one of the precious few who worshipped the long-forsaken god. *If Yah were truly omnipotent, why had men forsaken him for nearly two thousand years?* Jentra rightly questioned.

Lorn faithfully adhered to the deity's principle that all men were flawed and prone toward their darkest inclinations. Men needed to acknowledge such weakness and turn to Yah to purify their wickedness. Lorn claimed that his was a god of love and forgiveness, but Jentra could not look past Yah's judgment and rebuke of man's nature. It seemed a strange paradox that his simple soldier's mind could not comprehend.

What could not be dismissed were the visions this so-called god had gifted his prince. Whenever Lorn was visited with such imaginings, they always proved true. Such was their recent venture to Torry South. Lorn ignored his father's summons to attend his war council in Central City before the hostilities with Tyro erupted in the Wid River Valley and Tuft's Mountain. Jentra adamantly urged him to join the campaign and to lead the army in his father's name. Lorn ignored the call, assuring Jentra that General Bode would win a great victory and that Yah had another pressing task that he should attend.

And so as war loomed at Rego, they had traveled to Torry South and ordered the muster of the 4th Torry Army and the partial muster of the 1st Torry Army. Lorn ordered the 4th Torry Army to assemble north of Cagan Harbor and the First to assemble southeast of Cagan, positioning them to respond in any direction as needed. The citizen soldiers of both armies seemed ill-prepared at the outset, and his intervention went far in organizing them into combat readiness.

With the threat of a Yatin invasion ever threatening the northern border of Torry South, the opportunistic Macon Empire to their south, and the war raging in Torry North, they certainly did not lack in potential adversaries. Lorn's timely intervention might have preserved the Torries' southern realm from disaster. The soldiers were sent back home, however, ready to be called again once the need arose.

Now they reversed course, coming north after meeting with Squid Antillius and Lorn's sister, the princess Corry. They traveled by magantor to Central City, where Corry and her escort continued to Corell. Lorn accompanied Minister Antillius to his home in the countryside outside Central City. From there, they continued by magantor to their present locale, there in the thick, wild forest that stretched to the Cress Mountains, which divided the Yatin Empire from Torry North.

"Packaww!" The cry of a magantor broke the stillness of the night as the great bird circled overhead, passing beneath the shadow of the waning moon. The Torry Elite drew swords, circling their prince, watching warily as the magantor descended, setting down upon the far side of their fire, amid the dew-soaked grass that covered much of the hillside.

"Hold!" Jentra commanded, stepping toward the lone stranger, who climbed down from his mount. The figure's visage emerged from the night's shadow, taking Jentra aback by the young face staring back at him.

"I mean no harm," the young man said, spreading his hands apart to dim his threat.

"State your purpose, or go whence you came!" Jentra commanded.

"I am Terin Caleph, apprentice to—"

"Minister Antillius," Lorn interjected, stepping past Jentra to receive Terin.

*****

He spent the better part of two days in the saddle since passing the gap of Rulon, ever watchful for enemy scouts in the surrounding heavens. Terin found few settlements dotting the lands east of the Cress foothills and doubted their loyalties. He pressed on, setting down at night in any clearing far afield of any settlement. When he spied Lorn's cookfire from afar, he was strangely drawn toward the distant flame, obedient to the will of his sword. Whoever had lit that fire in this barren land was a friend, at least his sword believed it so, and what choice had he but to follow its will?

"Come, Terin. Join us by the fire. I am eager to hear your tale," the strangely familiar dark-haired man said, greeting him, drawing him into their midst. The elder man, dressed in the sky-blue tunic and silver armor that matched the uniform of the others, seemed ready to speak out but simply closed his mouth and followed them. Terin recognized the tunics and armor as those worn by the Torry Elite. What a dozen of the king's chosen were doing in these far reaches he could only guess.

Terin should have been taken aback by the stranger's odd familiarity, but it seemed they were of a kindred spirit, as if joined by unseen, ethereal bonds. "Are you hungry, Terin?" the man asked, waving an open hand to their fair offering—strips of meat well-cooked on a spit.

"Thank you." Terin thanked the man and quickly partook. He was famished and was far from his last warm meal.

"You are most welcome, son of Jonas." The stranger smiled, catching him off guard with the remark.

"How do you know that? How do you know who I am?" Terin asked warily.

"Oh, I have heard much of Terin Caleph—first from our mutual mentor, one Squid Antillius, and of course, my sister, who shares a certain fondness of you."

"Your sister?" Terin was as confused as before, his thoughts thrown off-kilter by the man's words, which were laced with hidden meanings that he was too tired to discern. "Who...who are you?"

"He is Prince Lorn II, son of King Lore and your future king!" Jentra interjected.

Terin paled at his familiarity and quickly knelt. "My prince, forgive my lack of protocol. I did not—"

"Rise, Terin. Do not trouble yourself, for you did not know." Lorn took his hand, pulling him to his feet. "There, that is better. It's always good to look a man in the eye."

"Your sister is the princess Corry?" Terin asked.

"Yes, though she often curses her misfortune of having one such as I as her brother, but one mustn't question the will of Yah with the placement of our birth." He smiled, hoping his pun would ease Terin's guarded mood.

"Is she well, Highness?"

"She is with great thanks to you, or so I have been told. I bade her farewell at Central City not five days ago. We traveled there together from Cagan Harbor after your hasty departure in the company of Captain Raven. I missed you at Cagan by mere hours, whereupon I was well-schooled in your exploits by our mutual friend Antillius and my sister. Now are you going to keep your prince waiting, or are you going to tell what transpired since you ventured north?"

And so he told his tale, recounting the journey to Fera and their escape. When he explained that he had lost sight of Cronus and Raven during their flight, the prince seemed unconcerned, as if he was privy to knowledge that ensured his friends' safety. It was the telling of events in Yatin that drew Prince Lorn's greatest interest, his mood growing somber with its full telling. At the conclusion of his tale, an awkward silence passed between them as Lorn stared into the fire, deep in thought.

"You should rest, Terin. You have journeyed far and must be weary after such travels. Jentra will see you to where the others are bedded down."

"My gratitude, Highness." Terin bowed before stepping away.

"It is I who is grateful, son of Jonas," Lorn answered quietly after he departed, his eyes fixed to the dancing flames.

Jentra drew Terin aside, escorting him back to his magantor to fetch his bedroll. The old soldier spoke little, and Terin thought he must have offended him in some way. Terin had many questions but doubted Jentra would answer them, so he simply fetched his things, following him to where he was to sleep, the two not sharing more than a few words.

*****

Terin awoke the next morn to the sound of birds singing in the distance. The Torry Elite were already awake as he sat up, breaking camp in good order. He caught sight of Jentra and Prince Lorn in a heated discussion some distance away along the hillside, out of earshot.

"Your father would not approve!" Jentra warned, hoping to cull Lorn's madness.

"The danger is imminent, my friend. We must do this now. Any delay will mean certain defeat."

"We move on the word of a *boy*, a boy who has no knowledge of warfare? What he speaks of is highly suspicious. Gargoyles assailing a fortress as well-built as Telfer is one thing, but to believe it shall fall is quite another. The sight of the enemy has clearly overwhelmed his senses. It is a common affliction for young eyes to see the enemy in greater numbers than they are."

"His numbers of the gargoyles surrounding Telfer were given him by General Morue. I saw no naivety in Terin's eyes. He knows of what he speaks. Our mission is done here. We return to Central City and, from there, back to Cagan."

"Your father's summons—"

"Can wait. We must see to our southern realm. My father has General Bode, Minister Monsh, and Squid to advise him," Lorn said, stepping away to see to his magantor.

"How did you know that boy would find us here?" Jentra asked, his question stopping Lorn in place.

"Does doubt still cloud your heart, old friend? How many miracles must Yah render before you accept his omnipotence?"

*****

He soared through the firmament, his golden hair trailing in the wind, an easterly gale pressing his face. The early summer air refreshed his tired lungs as he closed his eyes, bathing in the midday sun. The sound of the wind and the movement of his magantor's feathers offered the only break to the eerie silence of his flight. The lands below passed with casual indifference—from the endless plateaus of the northern steppes, to the rugged peaks of the Cress Mountains, and to the thick forests of the wild expanse that separated Torry North from the Yatin Empire.

From his airy view, Terin merely regarded their diverse beauty, not the details that a closer look might have revealed. Only when he set down did he realize the stark difference from one environ to the next. They were well within the Torry heartland, the thick forest long giving way to the open pastures and villages that dotted the landscape. He could see farmers working their fields, greeting them with a wave of their hands. Terin waved back, comforted by the familiar lands of his native realm.

Lorn regarded Terin over his left shoulder. The young Torry was keeping pace, his magantor's wingtip drawing even to his own. The others followed just behind, fanning out to either flank in a V formation with Jentra guarding his right. They continued south and east, finding the Stlen River and following it eastward.

By late day, the citadels of Central City graced the horizon. Terin's blue eyes drew wide with elation as he spied the familiar structures of their capital city coming into focus. The glorious beauty of those ancient edifices seemed less grand from these airy heights, as if they were mere models placed upon a map. Though diminished from this view, they were still grand and only grew in magnificence as they drew nigh. The marble columns of Leltic Hall stood prominently in the city's center, boldly reminding him that his view might have changed, but he was still just a boy after all.

Lorn signaled them to follow as he sped downward, sweeping over the rushing waters of the lower Stlen before veering north, forsaking the city for the countryside. Their wingtips graced the treetops that lined either side of the roadways that ran to and from the city. The farmlands north of the city gave way to the gentle-rolling hillsides skirting the length of the central valley. They circled over a small clearing that rested upon the west bank of a meandering small stream.

There amid surrounding porians and the gentle-flowing tributary rested a modest dwelling made of log and brick with a slate rooftop. An equally small stable was off to the side, and Terin wondered who dwelled in this secluded home far from the beaten path. They set down one by one upon the matted grass that carpeted the clearing amid the towering porians that circled them. Sunlight broke through the trees, alighting the front of the dwelling.

"Who lives here?" Terin asked, dismounting and stepping to Lorn's side as the prince approached the closed door centered on the front of the small dwelling. He was struck by the tranquil beauty of the secluded setting. The sound of birds and the quiet feet of small animals of varying sorts melded with the gentle lapping water of the stream that ran behind the cottage. Terin wondered who dwelled in such a place to warrant a visit from the prince of the realm. Certainly, no great regent, lord, or potentate would claim such modesty for their residence.

"This is the home of Squid Antillius," Lorn answered as the door opened, a familiar bearded face greeting them.

"Terin!" Squid gasped, stepping forth to embrace the boy he doubted to ever see again. "Beyond all hope, my boy." He stepped back, regarding Terin. The boy looked tired, famished, and well-used but alive.

"I said I would return, Minister Antillius." Terin smiled, fishing Tyro's sealed scroll from his satchel, giving it to Squid.

"And you heeded my counsel on following the will of your sword?" Squid asked, examining the rolled parchment before tucking it away.

"I did."

"Of course. How else could you have otherwise returned? Come. Come inside and share your tale. I am eager to hear its full telling." Squid ushered them within.

*****

They sat before the glowing hearth, some seated upon cushioned chairs while others sat upon the stone floor or stood along the great room's periphery as Terin relayed his tale. The Torry Elite had yet to hear of Terin's adventures at Fera, and Prince Lorn desired that they hear it. Terin stood before them, recounting the lengthy tale from the rescue at Molten Isle to his departure from Telfer.

The late afternoon had turned into night before he finished. The eyes of the Torry Elite were a mix of disbelief and awe with a little in between. For the few who took his words for simple truth, his fell deeds were worthy of their regard. For those who doubted the likelihood of the tale, their disbelief was quashed as Squid asked Terin to draw forth his father's sword.

A metallic ring echoed in the still air as he drew the silver blade, holding it before his face as its ancient metal emitted a luminous azure glow, lighting his countenance in a pale light. The men gathered around gasped in unison, bewitched by its mysterious power. It was the first time Lorn beheld its alluring beauty, though he had foreseen it in his dreams. "May I hold it?" Lorn asked.

Terin did not hesitate to obey his prince, offering him the hilt in his outstretched hand. Lorn lifted it aloft, the power of the blade coursing up his arm before filtering throughout. He stood transfixed by its ancient power. He marveled at its weight, wondering how a blade so powerful felt weightless in his grip. It was a sword built for kings, and a lesser man might have claimed it for his own, but Lorn knew the sword was meant for Terin and returned the blade to its master.

"It is a wondrous weapon," Squid said, stroking the silver strands that coursed his beard, sitting in the high-backed chair before the hearth.

"Do you know the blade's origin?" one fellow asked.

Squid regarded Lorn momentarily, and the prince nodded for him to proceed. "I believe it to be one of the nine Swords of Light." The others shifted in awe, their ears perking at Squid's utterance. The Swords of Light were thought to be mere legend, stories told to young boys to ignite their imagination. The thought that such a legend was, in fact, real and before their very eyes was difficult to comprehend.

The Swords of Light were forged by the smiths of ancient Tarelia and gifted to their generals, who ventured forth from their ancient holdfast to establish colonies across Arax. The Council of Tarelia was the last bastion of King Kal's realm, sworn to preserve the laws, values, and knowledge that King Kal's realm once held to and enforced throughout all the land before falling to ruin.

The remnants of that ancient kingdom dwelled along the northern shore of Lake Monata, building the great Citadel of Tarelia and preserving the knowledge and history of their parent civilization while the rest of Arax descended into ignorance and darkness. After a time, the ancient Tarelians husbanded their strength and sent forth small armies to colonize much of Arax and establish new kingdoms throughout the land, forged in the memory of King Kal's realm. The greatest of these new holdfasts was the Northern Kingdom, whose king set about the construction of Fera.

To him was given the greatest of the Swords of Light, the fabled Sword of the Sun. Such was its power that men were driven to madness when faced with its brilliance. Two lesser blades were the Swords of the Moon, whose power far exceeded the six Swords of the Stars. One of the Swords of the Moon was sent east to one unbeknownst to all save the Tarelians. The other was gifted to the Tarelian general Zar Zaronan, who founded the Middle Kingdom and ordered the construction of Corell.

The Swords of the Stars were gifted to lesser generals, who established smaller kingdoms throughout Arax. Through the ages, the swords were lost and their kingdoms with them until only the Middle Kingdom remained. Eventually, even the Sword of the Moon, wielded by the kings of the Middle Kingdom, was lost as well, though the kingdom endured. The Middle Kingdom was eventually renamed after its greatest monarch, King Torry, who expanded its borders to the coastal kingdom of old Cagia.

If Terin's blade was the fabled Sword of the Moon, then it belonged by right to the House of Lore and the royal heir, Prince Lorn II. Such was not lost on Terin as the young Torry knelt before the crown prince, again offering him the sword.

"Prince Lorn, the Sword of the Moon belongs to—"

"To you, Terin. It belongs to you," Lorn said, refusing him, helping him to his feet before taking the blade, returning it to Terin's scabbard.

"My prince, the sword is yours by rights!" Jentra could not still his tongue, his eyes pleading for Lorn to take possession of the ancient weapon.

"The blade has a master, one chosen by an authority far greater than I. It did not fall into Terin's hands by mere happenstance, Jentra, but by the will of Yah."

"But you shall have need of it where you intend to go," Jentra pleaded.

"No." Lorn smiled, placing a hand upon Terin's shoulder. "Terin has the greater need. Terin, you shall answer the summons my father has ordered of me. You shall stand in my stead. The king has called for me, but I shall send him a far greater servant in my place. I trust you to see Minister Antillius safely to Corell. The king will desire to hear of your adventures and will have need of your sword arm."

*****

The next morn saw them off, Lorn and his Elite traveling to Cagan Harbor while Terin and Squid took the heavens, setting their course eastward for Corell.

CHAPTER 8

They coursed through the air, surveying the Torry heartland in all its majesty, the lush valleys and rolling hills dotted with homesteads, stretching as far as the eye could see. Squid Antillius sat behind his apprentice, sharing the magantor saddle as his young charge guided the avian ever eastward, using the road that ran from Central City to Corell to navigate.

It was almost too easy, Terin thought. He and Yeltor struggled mightily to navigate the hundreds of miles of northern expanse upon their flight from Fera, flying toward the setting sun until the Cress Mountains broke the horizon. This was far easier, keeping constant watch on the road below to navigate.

He often stared off to the south of the road, knowing his home was somewhere in the vast expanse beyond the horizon and wondering what his parents were doing at this time. Were they well? What were they doing at this moment? He wondered if they were gazing skyward, able to see his magantor in the heavens and not realizing their son rode upon its back.

They set camp for the night just south of the main road, far from the nearest dwelling. Squid thought it wise to avoid the good citizens of the Torry realm. They held good intentions, but their good manners and proper protocols would needlessly delay them, so they chose the privation of the open road. They cooked salted meat that they packed for their short journey as well as a few vegetables picked from Squid's garden. Squid regarded Terin fondly as they sat across from each other with the small fire between them, each resting on their packs. Terin spoke very little, often staring into the dancing flames, lost in thought, transfixed by the flame's beguiling allure.

"What troubles you, my boy?" Squid asked, running his fingers through his silver beard.

Terin lifted his weary blue eyes, regarding Squid pensively, his somber thoughts betraying his laden heart. "My friends," he answered quietly. "I know not their fate."

"Whatever Cronus's fate may be, Terin, it is far preferable to where he stood had you not ventured to Fera. He, Raven, and Lorken are far from helpless, and you would be wise to remember that rather than plaguing yourself with dark possibilities."

"Even if they have slipped Tyro's grasp, Cronus might die anyway. He looked so weak when I last saw him. What hope—"

"You did your best. Whatever the fates intend for Cronus, it is beyond you now. You must make peace with it."

"How can I make peace when they are under the shadow of that dark land and that evil tyrant?" He sighed bitterly, recalling Tyro's dark countenance.

"Take heart in their strength to endure, my boy. Cronus and your Earth friends are made of hearty stock."

"You did not see how poorly Cronus looked, Squid. He looked starved and beaten, but his eyes betrayed his full suffering. Why are men like Tyro so cruel?"

"It is difficult to say, Terin. Some men are cruel by nature while others become so. It is said that Tyro was driven to madness by the loss of his woman, a woman many believe was his wife. He blamed her loss upon his half brother and his Menotrist kin, exacting vengeance upon them," Squid explained.

Terin had never heard this tale before, wondering what of it was actually true. "I thought he wed Queen Letha of the Sisterhood?"

"That was much later, long after he toppled the Menotrist kingdom and forged his empire. It was said he spent many years searching for his lost love, but she was either dead or so far removed to be never found. It is said that his heart waxed cold from that day on, and he vented his hatred upon the Menotrists for their cruelties inflicted upon his mother's kin through the ages."

"I thought he joined the Benotrist rebellion, and it was they who led the toppling of the Menotrists," Terin said.

"Yes, Morca led the Benotrist revolt long before Tyro joined their fledging ranks, but they were little more than a nuisance. It was Tyro that transformed them into the lethal force they became. It was his sword and his alliance with the gargoyles that carried the day, all because of a woman, or so the legend goes."

*****

They set out at daybreak, rapidly passing over the Torry countryside. Much of the western provinces of Torry North were an equal blend of forests and farmlands. Rich vineyards and orchards ran the length of the upper Stlen. Terin could make out people below, their narrow silhouettes waving back as they flew overhead.

The road ahead disappeared into the thick Zaronan forest. From the sky, the trees' thick branches and leaves seemed little more than the trimmed palace grounds of a giant. The forest stretched for countless leagues before sharply transitioning into open farmland. Beyond the forest edge, rising above the plain like ghostly slivers against the azure sky, arose the citadels of Corell. They drew Terin's eyes once they broke the horizon like spear tips striving to pierce the heavens, their magnificence dimmed only by distance until they drew near.

There, rising above the open plain, stood Corell, the White Castle. The massive fortress, built ages ago by the men of the Middle Kingdom, had stood undimmed since its founding. Its white walls overlooked the surrounding farmlands like a mountain of stone on an emerald sea.

Corell's outer walls rose 160 feet, their outer slopes grading eighty degrees and joined by twelve massive turrets that spanned sixty feet apiece. Two turrets faced each primary direction with the other four resting at an inverted angle at each corner of the fortress. The inner battlements rose thirty feet above the outer walls, mirroring their shape and location along the palace's periphery. A wide stone walkway spanning forty feet abreast ran between the inner and outer battlements, wide enough to move large contingents of troops from one part of Corell to another. Large archways were centered on the inner turrets with grated portcullis barring entry during siege.

A massive inner keep overlooked the inner battlements with tall windows and observation platforms upon its roof, the most prominent of which was Zar Crest, where the garrison commander stood post. Several towers spiraled into the firmament above, their citadels jutting like spear tips into the heavens. The most eminent of the palace citadels was the Tower of Celenia, its ivory-hued walls resplendent in the midday sun, presiding over its lesser peers.

The Golden Tower stood out among the spiraled peaks, its auspicious hue a stark contrast to the alabaster of its sisters. Third highest of Corell's watchtowers, its vigilant lookouts were the first to spy the lone magantor closing from the west. "Magantor!" They signaled below, their right hands extended to the western sky. The swoosh of the magantor's wings echoed dully in the crisp air as the great avian swept over the palace, circling the highest citadels, providing the lookouts a full view before descending to the platforms below.

Terin regarded Corell with awe, wondering how such a structure was built by mortal men. The outer walls rose sharply from the grassy plain, stretching to unimagined heights and joined by the massive turrets that circled the structure. The inner battlements mirrored the course and shape of the outer walls with jutting bulwarks and rugged ramparts cast in white stone. The castle interior was a multilayered structure that rose to a height above the outer walls.

The roof of the inner palace was a collage of observation platforms, an inner keep, magantor stables, and towers spiraling into the firmament. The center of the roof was open, providing a sizable courtyard resting at the ground level below. The courtyard was connected to the main gate centered upon the north wall via a wide tunnel, which ran some distance through the bowels of the palace. Any visitors to Corell approaching the palace from the ground would have to pass this way, but Terin and Squid's arrival had no such hindrance.

Their magantor outstretched its long, muscular legs, setting down on an outcropping of the east magantor stable. They were met by an armed flax with polished steel shields and breastplates over white tunics. Each was adorned with red feathers along the center of their helms.

"Who bids entrance to Corell?" the commander of flax declared, standing before his men, who stood statue still with spears leveled.

"Squid Antillius, minister to the king," Squid said with practiced authority, "and my apprentice, Terin Caleph." He waved an open hand toward Terin, who stood at his side.

"Welcome, Minister Antillius." The commander bowed his head. "Please follow."

The commander passed them along to his commander of unit, who passed them along to his commander of telnic, who verified Squid's identity and led them into the main keep. Terin was struck by the stark contrast between the foreboding black stone bulwarks of Fera and the white walls of Corell, bathed in light. Where the former laden his heart with fear and despair, the later renewed his spirit with joy and hope.

They passed through the raised portcullis of the inner keep. Guards in silver armor with golden tunics stood post on either side with silver wings adorning their helms, outstretched above their ears as if in flight. They followed the commander of rank through the lit wide passageways, whose sheen again contrasted the caliginous corridors of the Black Castle. They passed scores of sentries posted throughout the vast keep, taking numerous turns and stairwells to further disorient Terin's disordered state. He felt as if in a dream, straddling that narrow plane between sleep and consciousness.

They stopped short of a wide wooden door centered in a stone archway. The commander lifted the latch, escorting them therein. They stepped within, entering a well-lit chamber some twelve paces square with a solid porian table at its center. Torches were bracketed into the walls, similar to the ones affixed along the lengths of the outer corridor. The austere chamber was sparsely furnished with wooden benches along the table with hundreds of scrolls stacked upon shelves, lining the walls. Three men of an age to Squid stood beside five young men sitting the table, writing on unrolled parchment.

Upon their entrance, the eyes of the men therein drew instantly to them. Upon recognizing Squid, the young men seated at the table came abruptly to their feet and bowed their heads, the older men stepping forth to greet him. The elder men were dressed in deep-burgundy robes with gold stitching at their sleeves and hems. The younger men wore long-sleeved, ankle-length sun-colored tunics with azure stitching along their sleeves and hems.

"Antillius!" the first elder man to greet him said, stepping before his fellows with outstretched arms.

"Chief Minister," Squid greeted in kind, clasping hands with Eli Monsh, the king's chief minister. Eli stood of a height with Squid with piercing green eyes and a smile that put others at ease.

"Antillius," the other gentlemen greeted in kind. The first was Lutius Veda, minister of trade. He stood slightly taller than his fellows with studious pale eyes and a taut expression that brokered little warmth. He had a sharp mind that was wholly concerned with improving commerce throughout the realm. The next to greet him was Torlan Thunn, minister of agriculture. He stood nearly a head shy of Squid with discerning gray eyes, narrow nose, and high cheekbones.

Terin felt their eyes upon him as if measuring his worth and finding him lacking. There he stood before these men of high station and astute intellect dressed in his coarse tan tunic and sandals, threadbare with ill use from his travels. He looked little better than a peasant save for the wondrous sword that rode his hip. He certainly didn't belong with these learned men. All his knowledge accounted for naught in their eyes, or so he believed.

"We are pleased that your plan to rescue the princess proved fruitful. She arrived days ago, alive and untouched. You are to be commended, and the king would insist on seeing you posthaste," Eli Monsh declared.

"It was merely a suggestion. It fell to others to see it through." Squid shrugged humbly. He wondered how much his fellow ministers knew of Molten Isle or of the names that deserved the full weight of their praise. He turned, placing a fatherly hand to Terin's shoulder. "My apprentice, Terin Caleph," he said, introducing his protégé to his fellows.

"Ministers." Terin dipped his head reverently.

"Young Caleph." Eli regarded him. "I have need of your master for a time. I shall leave you in the hands of my eldest apprentice, Aldo!" He called one of the young men forth.

"Yes, Chief Minister," the boy answered, stepping forth to present himself. He stood sixty inches with a lean, proportionate build and shoulder-length black hair. He spoke with practiced reverence and a cultured voice, reflecting his patrician upbringing. The other scribes standing at the table were likely the second or third sons of landed gentry or patricians. They were apprenticed to their ministers by their fifth year and were well-schooled in all matters of the realm.

"See that he is bathed and clothed in proper attire, if you would be so kind, Aldo," Squid added.

"Of course, Minister Antillius," Aldo bowed. Squid stepped without, accompanying the other ministers to treat with the king, leaving Terin in the hands of the chief minister's apprentice. No sooner had the door closed than a second scribe stepped forth.

"Caleph?" the scribe inquired, lifting a curious brow over his left eye. "I am unfamiliar with that surname. Of course, your family must be patrician for you to be so highly placed in the king's service. Minister Antillius is regarded as the king's favorite, and an apprenticeship in his service is *highly* prized." The scribe failed to mask the contempt in his false smile, which was not lost on Aldo.

"My apologies, Terin. I am remiss for not introducing our fellow scribes," Aldo interjected, touching a hand to Terin's shoulder, guiding him hither. "This is Merith, first scribe to Minister Veda." He indicated the scribe who questioned Terin. Merith was slightly taller than Aldo with his shoulder-length blond hair bound behind him in long braids. His long, narrow nose held a superior air, and Terin disliked him immediately.

Aldo introduced a young boy, not older than ten years, named Portius, the second apprentice of Minister Monsh. Another young boy, no older than seven years, named Fabia was the second apprentice of Minister Veda. The last scribe was of an age with Terin named Servas, apprentice to Minister Thunn. The others regarded Terin politely, nodding their heads in a friendly gesture, while Merith continued to appraise him with a critical eye.

"A sword?" Merith questioned, his eyes fixed on the blade at Terin's hip. "Weapons have no place here. To wield weapons is an affront to those we treat with. You will have to discard it or store it in the armory."

"My sword stays with me," Terin said, holding Merith's stare.

"You speak boldly for one so recently placed. You'll do well to know your place, *scribe*, and acknowledge those of us who have served the crown far longer than your brief appointment."

"My brief appointment?" Terin questioned.

"Yes, your *brief* appointment!" Merith declared with a condescending air. "We have practiced our craft since childhood, schooled deeply in the art of state craft and the protocols of the royal court. You, it seems, are little more than a jumped-up peasant who lacks the barest of decorum to ever treat with the lowest of dignitaries. To be a king's minister requires a knowledge you could never obtain. How could you ever hope to treat with the Royal House of Lore? A lifetime would be insufficient to prepare you."

Terin regarded the pompous scribe with veiled contempt, guarding his emotions as well as he could. Part of his anger was that Merith was right, he was unprepared to serve as a minister's apprentice. He could read and write and knew basic math and geography but greatly lacked the knowledge that apprentices such as Merith acquired. He also lacked their high birth. He was the son of a simple landowner who worked his farm without servants or help of any kind. In fact, he knew little of his parents' families. Whether they were bonded farmers, free men, or patrician, he could only surmise since his mother and father never spoke of them.

What Terin did know was that his father was a free landowner and former soldier who fought in the Sadden Wars. His father was a good man, and he could ask for no better. Terin never asked for his appointment but served Squid as best he could and knew that a scribe was never his true purpose. But to have his place questioned by the likes of Merith kindled a rare anger in him. He might have lacked Merith's mastery of statesmanship, but he had many skills that Merith lacked. His father had taught him all arts of combat, and he so desperately wished to unleash them upon this unwitting prude. Terin released a measured breath, losing his anger as he exhaled.

"You are right, Merith." Terin shrugged. "I am the only son of a simple farmer who is an old friend to Minister Antillius. I shall never be a scribe of your knowledge or breeding. I simply do as Minister Antillius asks of me. If you disagree with my place in his service, then feel free to speak with him on the matter. If you lack such courage to do so, then spare me your discourtesy."

Merith opened his mouth to refute Terin before Aldo intervened. "Come, Terin. We should have you cleaned and suitably attired," Aldo said, guiding him without. Once in the outer corridor, Aldo's practiced indifference eased into a devilish grin. "Well-spoken, Terin. Well-spoken indeed. Merith is often pretentious, but you handled him with ease."

"It didn't feel easy." Terin sighed. He was suddenly very tired and desired nothing more than a bed.

"Perhaps, but you made it appear so. And in our chosen vocation, appearance often exceeds truth, especially when refuting the harsh asperity of men like Merith. Of course, the more arduous task is taming the tongue when rebuked by royals and men of higher station. It is at such times that skilled deftness is required to traverse such troubled waters."

"The royal family does not seem so difficult to speak with, at least not when I spoke with them." Terin shrugged as they walked.

Aldo suddenly stopped, taken aback by Terin's statement. "You...you spoke with members of the royal house?"

"Yes," Terin answered, finding Aldo's question rather odd.

"Who?"

"Princess Corry and Prince Lorn."

"When?" Aldo asked incredulously.

"I first encountered the princess during the rescue at Molten Isle."

"Molten Isle? Were you there?"

"Yes. Lorken, Miles Standarn, and I stormed the pirate village and freed Princess Corry and Princess Felicia, but Miles was slain at the village. Lorken and I led the princesses to the shore, where the Earthers' ship transported us to safety."

"You participated in the rescue?" Aldo hadn't realized that Terin actually partook, believing his involvement was strictly aiding Minister Antillius in the endeavor. Instead, he had a direct hand in rescuing the princess.

"Yes. The princesses were held in two different locations, and we needed to seize them simultaneously. The Earthers needed every sword to aid in the rescue."

"But a scribe? Why would they believe you capable of facing pirates?"

"They are far easier to deal with than gargoyles, I can assure you," Terin explained.

"Gargoyles?"

"Yes."

"You have fought gargoyles?"

"Yes, at the Wid River and Tuft's Mountain."

"Were you able to kill any?"

"Yes," Terin answered warily, thinking the question odd.

"Incredible! You must tell me, all of it," Aldo asked excitedly.

"All of it? You mean the battle or Molten Isle or the Black Castle?"

"The Black Castle?" Aldo's voice raised several octaves. "What of the Black Castle?"

And so Aldo asked Terin to start at the beginning, retelling his adventures from meeting Cronus and Arsenc on the road to Central City to his escape from Fera and the siege of Telfer, ending with him meeting Prince Lorn in the wilds. At the conclusion, they reached the base of the castle, several levels below the surface, where a cavernous chamber was dug out around an underground spring. Each of the great castles of Arax was constructed upon solid bedrock with a fresh water source at their center. Torches bracketed into the uneven, rocky walls illuminated the vast chamber, their dim light reflecting off the watery surface. Aldo provided Terin with a tose powder to clean his skin before hurrying off.

Terin stripped off his clothes and set his sword atop them before stepping in the cool spring water. The underground stream sprang from a rocky wall to his left before passing through the opposite wall. It was a strange geological feature that allowed the palace inhabitants a fresh source of flowing water that remained beneath the bedrock for countless leagues before breaking the surface. He felt gripping cold before plunging into the water. "It's best to go full in than dally about," his father always said.

He wasted little time washing away the stench of the trail before climbing out. Aldo soon returned with fresh undergarments, sandals, and a sun-colored tunic that matched his own. Donning the new clothes felt strange, as Terin had never worn a tunic with long sleeves or one that dropped below his knees. He affixed his sword belt about his waist as Aldo handed him a comb to straighten his hair. "Much improved, Terin." Aldo smiled. "We shall make a courtesan of you yet. Come. Minister Antillius awaits us."

*****

They passed through countless corridors and stairwells ascending the palace until traversing a wide-set passageway that ran the center of the main inner keep. Tall windows brightly illuminated the white stone corridor with the light of the waning sun shining upon their ancient walls. Royal guards in gold tunics and silver breastplates stood post along the lit wide corridor with the silver wings protruding from their helms, following them with their eyes as they passed.

Mid distance along the passageway, upon their right, stood a dozen guards posted before an open tall archway. The doors were the height of two and a half times a man and were opened therein. They were made of thick porian timbers. The light therein bathed the outer corridor through the archway as if the chamber was alit by the sun. He found Squid standing amid the guards, still wearing his traveling clothes. It seemed he had been in counsel since they arrived.

"Well done, Aldo." Squid greeted them as they drew near, appraising Terin's attire and comportment.

"As you commanded, Minister Antillius." Aldo bowed his head.

Terin was taken aback by the reverence his fellow scribes afforded Squid. Had he been remiss with his familiarity toward the elder statesman? He suddenly felt even more out of place and wished he were back at Rego. If Squid could read the apprehension in his young friend's face, he revealed it not.

"Come, Terin. We have an audience with the king," Squid said, his open hand directing Terin through the open archway.

"The king?" Terin asked, tentative to step forth.

"Yes, the king. He wishes to hear of your journey. Come along. We mustn't keep him waiting."

They stepped within, walking across the mirrored white stone floor, their reflection playing off its smooth surface. The throne room was a massive, elongated chamber with a series of stone arches along its length, like the ribs of a giant beast. The arches were built from white granite while stones between them were stained in azure with basin torches resting where they met the floor, illuminating their bright surface.

Between each series of arches stood statues twice the height of a man cast in marble with ivory faces and sapphires set in their eyes. Each statue was crafted in the visage of the Torry kings who once sat the throne. They stood in full armor with swords drawn and their crowns upon their weathered brows. Terin regarded them warily as if they might spring to life. The light of the basin torches playing off the azure stone behind the statues looked akin to an artificial sky, further illuminating their presence.

A dais some three meters high rested at the far end of the chamber with a large black throne centered upon it. It was wrought in iron with silver inlays upon its back and arms and wide enough to sit a giant. The dais curved from one corner of the throne room to the other in a half circle with wide steps upon its front rising to the throne. A lesser throne rested to the right of the black throne half the size of the latter and wrought in ivory with gold inlays upon its arms. A dozen royal guards stood post along the periphery of the vast chamber, which stretched twenty-five meters abreast and thirty in length.

Four massive columns rose imperiously upon the dais, their white pillars melding with the ceiling above. They rose from the back of the dais to either side of the thrones. Terin could see numerous men standing upon the dais behind the throne—courtesans and officials, most likely. There upon the throne sat a man of a size to Prince Lorn with similar black hair, which was slightly silver with age, framing his handsome face. He wore a long azure robe with silver edged along its seams over a long white tunic that draped below his knees. An austere steel crown sat on his head with jagged edges along its surface, symbolic of the burden of the king's rule.

Though Terin and Aldo walked on either side of Squid, it was Terin on whom the king's steel-gray eyes were affixed, appraising him as he approached. Terin struggled to suppress the trepidation of his beating heart, sensing the eyes of the entire court upon him. As they neared the dais, Terin noticed the familiar figure of Princes Corry sitting on the lesser throne, her discerning blue eyes regarding him with terrible intensity. She wore a shimmering sky-blue gown that clung invitingly to her achingly feminine curves. He recalled their previous familiarity and found her present coolness unnerving but not unexpected in the cold formality of the throne room.

A dozen soldiers in sea-blue tunics and black capes with silver breastplates and greaves stood guard along the base of the dais, their uniform marking them members of the King's Elite. Upon the dais, at the king's left, stood a grim-faced man dressed in studded gauntlets and dark leather trousers and boiled leather armor. He was well-built, standing sixty-eight inches, with a stern jaw that appeared to be chiseled granite. His hair was sheared, masking his age, which was likely in its sixth decade. Terin felt the man's scrutiny more intensely than the others, wondering what he had done to incur his judgment. They stopped short of the dais and knelt.

"Rise," King Lore said, lifting his finger ever slightly, mimicking the command.

"Your Majesty," Squid greeted in kind. "My apprentice, Terin Caleph," he said, formally introducing Terin.

"Young Caleph, step closer, son of Jonas." King Lore motioned him hither. Terin stepped forth, stopping just shy of the dais, and started to kneel.

"You've already knelt, Terin. Stand," Lore commanded.

"My king." He bowed his head before meeting the steely gaze of his sovereign.

"I am told that you fought bravely at the Wid River and again at Tuft's Mountain," Lore stated.

"I fought, Your Majesty, but I was far too frightened to describe my actions as brave."

"Daring and selfless acts in the face of death while frightened are the true measure of courage. A lack of fright in the face of such odds is merely the empty thoughts of fools."

Terin smiled slightly. "That sounds like something my father would say." At the mention of his father, the old warrior who stood at the king's left scowled more fiercely. Did the man know his father? Terin wondered. If so, then what offense could his father have committed to earn such ire?

"Your father is a wise man, Terin, and as fine a soldier who ever served the Torry throne," King Lore said. Terin was taken aback by such a revelation. His father spoke little of his years as a warrior. Only Squid revealed an inkling of his father's former life, purposely concealing Jonas's great renown at the behest of the king and Jonas, leaving Terin unaware of his significance. "I am told that you rescued my daughter at Molten Isle, killing her captors while affecting her escape."

"I…I helped, sire, but I merely followed my comrades' lead. It is they on whom the praise should fall."

"He *lies*," Princess Corry interjected, her accusatory tone freezing Terin in place. He regarded her warily, her blue eyes fixed to his.

"My daughter claims otherwise, young Caleph, and I know you dare not refute the word of royal blood," Lore admonished. "Tell us what transpired, my dear," he asked.

"Terin entered the hut wherein I was detained with King's Elite Miles Standarn, slaying the pirates who held us as Miles was struck down. His Earther friend followed after, and Terin bravely led us to

CHRONICLES OF ARAX BOOK 2

the shore, risking his life for my own. Without Terin, I would not have been freed without significant risk. His humility is misplaced," the princess said, her eyes softening with her defense of his character.

"I see." Lore scowled disingenuously. "Can I trust you to speak truly with what transpired at Fera, Terin? Humility is a poor virtue when it clouds truth. We have established that you are humble and honest. I would expect no less considering who sired you. You must understand that I have not summoned you before the throne for you to speak half-truths so as not to boast your fell deeds. Speak plainly, Terin, and tell me what transpired after you departed Cagan."

And so he did so, telling his king of their journey north, the road from Tinsay to Fera. He explained all that transpired in that foul place, including Raven's fight in the arena and apparent marriage to Tosha. How Raven managed to free Cronus before their escape, he could only guess. Unfortunately, Terin never had the time to ask, as they were separated upon their escape.

When telling of their escape through the corridors of Fera, Terin could see the attentive eyes of the court hanging upon his every word. He fondly told of Lorken emasculating Tyro's prized statue, which drew the mirth of everyone save for the scowling, leather-clad warrior at the king's side. He could sense the awe of those gathered when he spoke of the destruction wrought by the Earthers' weapons and the concern when he told of the legions gathered at the Black Castle. The king did not ask Terin to speculate on Tyro's intentions in the full view of the court, preferring to speak of such things in private council.

Squid had instructed Terin to not speak of his sword or of Morac's at this time. But how could he explain his actions without the aid of his father's sword? Who would believe him capable of slaying so many at Costelin, Tuft's Mountain, Molten Isle, Fera, and Telfer without nary a scratch upon his flesh? To speak the truth without mentioning the sword would seem the prideful exaggerations of a youth. His telling of the siege of Telfer drew great interest from the ministers and commanders gathered upon the dais. If Telfer fell, the entire Yatin Empire could easily follow.

The king's calm demeanor grew suddenly taut when Terin finally spoke of Prince Lorn. "Did my son say anything pertinent for me?" the king asked. Squid had already told the king of Prince Lorn's intentions to rally the southern armies in the wake of the Benotrist invasion of Yatin. What else could Terin say save for the very words Lorn had instructed him to speak?

"He…he asked for your forgiveness for not heeding your summons, Your Majesty, but hoped you understood his reasons for doing so," Terin explained.

"What else?" the king asked, sensing there was more that Terin meant to say.

"He…he sent me in his place to serve wherever you have need of me, sire. My sword is yours," he declared with as firm a voice that he could muster. Terin could sense the derision on several members of the court with his presumption but surmised the king likely knew the deeper meaning of his words.

"Yes, your sword." The king sighed. "You were never meant to be a minister's apprentice, young Caleph. I am certain you are aware of that by now. You have sworn to me your leal service and your sword. Such oaths I shall hold you to. There is a place at my table this evening for you, Terin. I expect to see you there sans the vestment of a minister's apprentice and attired in accordance to your proper station."

Terin was again taken aback. What had the king truly meant? Was he stripped of his apprenticeship because he was found lacking, or was he to be honored by the invitation to sit at the royal table? Terin again bowed and withdrew at Squid's behest, taking his leave of the throne room. Princess Corry's eyes followed him as he withdrew before summoning a handmaid from the shadows.

The leather-clad warrior standing at the king's left crossed his arms, his scowl easing with Terin's departure. "Your thoughts, Master Vantel?" King Lore asked, regarding the grizzled warrior bemusedly.

Torg Vantel, master of arms of the realm and commander of the King's Elite, snorted derisively. "I see a *boy*."

"A very *brave* boy and certainly one that has proven his mettle," Lore countered.

"That is yet to be proven. The boy has much to learn."

"We all have much to learn, old friend. The boy has learned much under his father's tutelage." At the mention of Terin's father, Torg Vantel's scowl tightened. "You mustn't let your feelings about the boy's father cloud your judgment, Torg. Jonas kept his word as he promised so long ago. He trained his son and sent him to us. Now it falls to you to complete his training."

"Aye," Torg relented. "Come the morn, I shall see what sort of warrior the son of Jonas Caleph can make."

"Considering the boy's bloodlines, I am certain of your success."

"Success or not, the boy is a far better man than his fool of a father or his even more foolish grandfather." Torg snorted.

*****

Terin waited nervously outside the chamber, the glow of torch-light filtering through the open archway, bathing the corridor in light. He was met in his chamber by a palace steward, who presented him with his current attire, a snow-white calnesian tunic that fell about his knees. The ultrafine material shimmered in the torch-lit corridor. He was gifted a new pair of corded leather sandals with straps that crisscrossed his lower calves. His simple sword belt and black leather scabbard completed his outfit. His apprentice robes were confiscated and replaced with this rich attire.

The steward had ordered him to don the clothing and escorted him hither, instructing him to wait without whilst the steward passed within the lit chamber. He returned moments later, beckoning him to enter. "The princess waits therein. Enter and remember your courtesies," the steward advised. Terin regarded him politely and stepped within.

He was greeted by three women seated in a semicircle before a glowing hearth. The glow of the hearth and the torches bracketed along the circular-shaped chamber illuminated the azure-hued walls. A young man stood beside the hearth, his slender arms resting to either side of a large harp. He was dressed in a long scarlet tunic and gold robes. The three women wore long calnesian gowns in varying hues of sky blue, emerald, and silver.

"Come hither, Terin," Princess Corry's familiar voice called out. She awaited him before the hearth, seated between her companions, her silver gown draping over the legs of her high stool. Terin stepped nigh, regarding her bright sea-blue eyes, which stared back at him bemusedly. Her lush golden locks framed her achingly feminine face. Her pursed lips betrayed little, projecting a cool indifference, which confused him further.

The woman to her right observed him with similar regard, her long auburn hair draping over her left shoulder in a single braid. Her forest-green eyes matched the hue of her dress, her lips easing into a slight smile. The woman to Corry's left wore a sea-blue gown, her midnight-black hair wound above her head in a tight coil. Her deep-olive skin contrasted her light-gray eyes.

Terin stopped before them, taking a knee. "Princess," he greeted, bowing his head. Terin felt the intensity of her gaze upon him, wondering how she could manifest greater trepidation in his heart than all the gargoyles he had faced.

"Lift your eyes, Terin," the princess commanded softly, taking far too much pleasure in his discomfort. She almost laughed with his unease, knowing the brave and honest nature of his character and the effect her presence manifested in him. She never kept a subject upon their knees after a formal greeting but lingered in commanding him to rise.

"It is fortunate to see that you've returned safely from your dangerous travels, Terin. When last we spoke, I told you if the choice were mine, I would've forbidden you to undertake such a risk. You have honored your promise to rescue your friend, and I hope you are now free of all vows save for those to the Torry throne," Corry said.

"I am, Highness. I have promised Prince Lorn to serve your father wherever he sees fit to place me."

The mention of her brother dimmed her mirth. She was not surprised he failed to heed their father's summons. He was oft remiss in his duty to the crown, often choosing his own path over the mundane tasks his station demanded. Perhaps her disfavor with Terin's journey to Fera was rooted in her continued disappointment with her brother's adventurism.

"We gladly accept your service, Terin. And I see you no longer wear the vestment of a minister's apprentice. It is well, for you are unsuited for such. I am glad to see you appropriately attired for treating with the king. You look very fetching." She smiled, regarding the tunic she gifted him.

"And where does the king have need of me, Highness?" Terin mustered the courage to ask.

"Very bold to ask such a question of your princess," the woman in the green gown said.

"Terin asks out of naivety, not boldness. He is only bold and brave when facing the swords of our foes," Corry teased. "Rise, Terin." He gained his feet, smoothing his tunic as the princess introduced her companions. "I am remiss in my duty as your host to not have introduced Lady Enora Fonis"—she indicated the woman sitting to her right—"and Illana Ornovis," she finished, regarding the woman sitting to her left.

"My ladies Fonis and Ornovis." Terin bowed.

"You fought alongside my father at Tuft's Mountain," Enora said.

"Your father?" Terin asked before cognizant of her surname. "General Fonis, commander of the 2nd Torry Army." Her father held joint command of the Torry armies at Rego alongside General Bode.

"Yes." Enora gifted him a smile for answering correctly.

"And, Lady Illana, you are the daughter of Vintor Ornovis, regent of Cagan and cousin to the king," he said, recalling Squid's lessons, recounting the names of the great houses of the realm.

"Yes. And I am told you were his guest in the palace during your visit to Cagan, if ever so briefly," the lady Illana said.

"I was." Terin recalled his time at Cagan, serving as Princess Corry's escort before departing with Raven.

"You served well as my escort that day, just as you shall this evening at my father's table," Corry interjected.

"I am honored to do so, Highness," Terin answered, his heart beating emphatically as if traversing thin ice.

"You must tell of your adventure at Fera," Lady Illana urged, her gray eyes sparkling excitedly. "Surely there is more to your trials there than the brevity of your first telling in the throne room."

So Terin told again of his adventures for the ladies' benefit. The princess demanded he start from his time at home. She asked repeatedly of his youth and what his father and mother had taught him. He believed his parents were simple farmers, but Princess Corry knew otherwise. No farm boy was taught the sword in the manner Terin wielded it or taught letters and mathematics the way his mother instructed him. Was Terin truly so ignorant of the nature of his upbringing? She found his naivety endearing.

"Please sit, Terin. We are to be entertained by Ballan," Corry said, waving him to an empty stool between herself and the lady Enora. Ballan was a famed harpist and singer well-known through the higher echelons of the noble class. He bowed his head with deep reverence toward the ladies and began, his slender fingers moving nimbly along the strings of his harp as he sang. Terin had never heard such a stirring melody, the music kindling his imagination as the bard sang. The ballad was a story of the eternal bonds of love and devotion amid the turmoil of heartbreak and loss. He thought of Cronus and Leanna, wondering if their tale would be one of sweet reunion or tragic end.

The bard played one epic after another, a gamut of mournful ballads to joyous melodies. The ladies were moved by his rich voice, his words creating wonderful worlds in their imaginings. Terin steeled his heart, daring not to let his mind drift lest he come undone. The horrific sights his young eyes had beheld came flooding to the surface, testing his resolve not to weep. His heart pounded emphatically, feeling as if it might leap from his chest. Thankfully, Ballan concluded his performance, allowing Terin to return his mind to the present.

"Shall we?" the princess asked, gaining her feet and holding out her arm for him to take.

*****

Terin escorted the princess through the well-lit passageways, a dozen guards shadowing their course. The waning sunlight gave way to night as they ascended the great keep. Terin noticed that the ladies Illana and Enora were not with them.

"Are your companions not joining us at the king's table, Highness?" he asked.

"They are, but we have another matter to attend first. My father wishes to speak with you and Minister Antillius in his private sanctum," she said as they continued on.

"Oh," he said, taking a deep breath.

"Are you frightened, Terin?" She bit her smile lest she burst in laughter.

"I—NO, I am fine, Princess," he lied.

"Such a poor liar you are, just another example of why you would have made an inadequate minister's apprentice." She smiled.

"I am sorry, Highness. I am just not very good at this. I don't belong here. I can see that now." He sighed dejectedly.

She stopped suddenly, turning to face him in the middle of the corridor, fixing her blue eyes to his. "Cease such foolish banter, Terin. You belong here now. Your true place is here, as it always should have been. You were never meant to be a scribe or a minister or a counselor to the king. No, your true place is *far* more important than that. You saved my life, Terin. Do you understand what that means to me? I was chained, starved, and threatened with such ill abuse that..." The words caught in her throat as she recalled that terrible ordeal.

"I am sorry, Princess." Terin regarded her with empathy.

"No." She shook her head. "You saved me. When you broke through the wall of that vile hut, you ended my nightmare. It was like waking to a beautiful sunrise."

"It was my father's sword that delivered you, not I," he conceded.

"The sword obeys the heart of its master. It may lead you and guide you, but never does it supplant your true will. It merely emboldens what is already there. You and your sword are one," she reminded him.

"How do you know so much about—"

"Your sword?"

"Well, yes."
"Come."

*****

The king awaited them in his private sanctum, an oval-shaped chamber some ten paces abreast and twelve in length. The light of the glowing hearth illuminated its white walls, reflecting off the mirrored gray stone floor, where rested a richly woven burgundy carpet matching the shape of the austere chamber. The only furnishings were several high-backed chairs that circled the carpet and a small set of shelves that held various rolled maps, scrolls, and keepsakes of the king. A lone window rested on the near wall, the light of the moon filtering through its open shutters.

King Lore wore a long gray tunic that bore no adornments, the simple garment poorly reflecting his true eminence. He reflected on something his father had oft told him long ago, that though the realm required a certain pomp and ceremony to demonstrate the authority of the kingdom, in private, a king should bathe in humility. A king was still just a man and must be ever mindful of the delusion of self-import that such power instilled. Lore's ancestors had long established a system of checks upon the power of the king, including limitations of taxes upon the populace and due process before the throne for *all* citizens of the realm.

Lore stood before the hearth with his arms folded, staring into the flames, his mind reflecting on matters of the realm. Not in a thousand years had the fate of the Middle Kingdom rested upon so perilous ground. Every decision weighed upon him like burdensome stones. His own son had refused his summons. Should he chastise the boy or trust in his good instincts? He debated at length with Squid on the matter. His old friend counseled leniency with the headstrong prince.

Squid sat to his left, observing Lore with his contemplative gray eyes. "The boy was wise to follow his chosen course, my friend." Squid's gentle voice attempted to calm the disquiet of Lore's mind.

"That is what troubles me most, that he was right to do so but lacks the maturity to accomplish so bold a plan." Lore sighed, his gaze remaining upon the flames.

"Lorn will surprise you with what he is capable lest you forget who his father is."

"Your faith in my son is well-intentioned, Squid, but I hope not misplaced."

"Lorn's judgment is sound. The southern kingdom must be made ready. Tyro's legions are sweeping through the Yatin Empire, and time is fleeting."

"But he intends to lead an army into Yatin to aid our age-old enemy. Such a move requires a seasoned hand rather than a zealous youth. This could all end very badly."

"Perhaps, but to do nothing at this juncture would be far worse. We must trust in Yah to see us through."

"Yah?" Lore turned, regarding his friend curiously. "I am new to this faith you and Lorn have converted me to. Forgive me if my faith in the deity lacks the omnipotent bonds you both have forged to his divine will."

"Your faith is stronger than you confess, my king. You have entrusted Terin to the will of the sword even though in doing so, he ventured into the enemy's lair and returned."

"That was your faith, Squid, not mine. Had I known he might follow the Earthers to Fera, I would have forbidden it. We are fortunate that he wasn't slain. Tyro might well have had Terin's blade to add to the one he now holds."

"Yes, the one he now holds." Squid ran his fingers through his beard, gaining his feet to stand beside his friend.

"Morac's blade, the one gifted him by Tyro, the very blade Tyro used to forge his empire, it is clearly one of the Swords of Light, but which one? If it be one of the lesser swords, one of the six Swords of the Stars, we may endure, but"—Lore sighed—"if it is the Sword of the Sun..." His voice trailed off with that dark implication.

"Terin claims he crossed swords with Morac upon the battlements of Fera and that Morac's blade was stronger and alit a flaming crimson as if kissed by fire. There can be little doubt that Tyro has the Sword of the Sun," Squid said somberly.

"The Sword of the Sun, the greatest of the Swords of Light," King Lore concluded, hoping it were not so but could no longer deny such a hard truth.

"I fear it is so," Squid said.

"Then Terin may hold the fate of our kingdom in his hands."

"Only if he wields the blade. He offered it to Lorn, and your son refused him. Lorn said the blade was intended for him and sent him to you to act as your shield against Morac."

"That is a heavy burden for one so young," Lore reflected.

"He has been prepared for this since birth. Jonas has taught him well."

"He is still a boy, and Morac has been reared by the finest sword masters in Tyro's empire, and he holds the better sword."

"A boy who has accounted well for himself. Few men have weathered the dark lord's fury," Squid said, handing Lore the imperial scroll with Tyro's seal.

"The boy?" Lore asked, breaking the seal, reading the parchment.

"Yes. He delivered our missive and was given this by Tyro's own hand just before their escape from Fera."

"He is no coward," Lore said, handing Tyro's reply to Squid after finishing with it.

"Tyro has many faults, but wasting words is not among them," Squid said dryly, handing it back to his king, who tore it up, tossing it into the fire. They had asked for peace, and Tyro offered it in exchange for their surrender and the heads of King Lore and Prince Lorn II.

"Father."

Corry's voice drew Lore to the doorway. She entered therein with Terin beside her. Terin stepped forth and knelt before him. The king placed a hand upon his head, regarding the boy carefully. "Rise, Terin," he commanded. Terin gained his feet, met by Lore's gray eyes, which studied his with terrible intensity. "Many questions you must have, I surmise," Lore asked.

Questions? Terin thought. He had more questions than the king could answer in a lifetime, but he might as well start with the most pressing: "If I am not to serve as Minister Antillius's apprentice, then where shall I serve you, sire?"

"By now, you well know that you were *never* meant to serve as a scribe or minister. It was merely a false road we had you follow."

"We?"

"Your father, Squid, your grandfather, and I." Lore smiled wryly, knowing his answer would likely lead to even more questions.

"My grandfather? I know nothing of him, not even his name or if he still lives." Terin was taken aback.

"Oh, he is still quite alive, and you shall know his name when he deigns to grant it. You need only know his pride in the man you have become. As for our collective wisdom in your false placement as Squid's apprentice, it was a test."

"Test?" Terin asked, overwhelmed by the totality of the king's revelations.

"A test, a test of you *and* the blade you wield, a test to see if you are worthy of this blade," Lore said, stretching his hand to the hilt of Terin's sword, lifting it from its scabbard. The king held it aloft. Moonlight filtered through the open window, bathing the silver blade in lunar light. The ancient metal burst in a luminous azure glow as if ordained by the heavens. The light was lucent yet bright and denoted an ancient power undimmed since its forging.

Squid and Corry stared in awe as Lore's eyes ran the length of the blade, examining it with the studious indifference expected of a king. He spun the blade, his hand moving with the ease of a master swordsman, before returning it to Terin's sheath. "You pass the test, young Caleph," Lore assured him, touching a hand to his shoulder. "Now sit, and we shall attempt to answer your many questions." They sat upon the king's direction, Terin waiting expectantly as King Lore sat across from him. Corry sat to his right, and Squid beside the king.

"Before I tell you where you shall serve, I should first explain the origin of the sword you wield. Its forging precedes the founding of the Middle Kingdom, in the bellows of the ancient smiths of old Tarelia. Legend says that a star fell from the heavens, and from its remains, the Jenaii found mysterious metals whose properties were unlike any found in all of Arax. The Jenaii brought the materials across the great sea to Arax, gifting them to the Smiths of Tarelia. From these strange materials were forged the Swords of Light, each a wondrous masterpiece unrivaled by smithcraft before or since.

"Such was the strength of those metals that the Smiths of Tarelia built kilns of unimaginable size and power to achieve temperatures so great as to bend and fold the metals to their desired forms. Even now, our ministers of science and alchemy know not how such foundries were built. The knowledge and skills of the Smiths of Tarelia are but memories, as their ancient holdfast has since crumbled to ruin. Tarelia is no more, but the swords forged in the height of their glory endure.

"The smiths presented their wondrous works to the ruling Council of Tarelia, who gifted them to their largest colonies. The Tarelians established colonies across the face of Arax, each in the image of King Kal's ancient realm in order to restore the peace and order of the golden age of Arax. With the power of the swords, the colonies grew into ever-strengthening holdfasts and kingdoms to counter the gargoyles that threatened to overrun all of Arax.

"Each of the Swords of Light was bound with magic, binding the will of each sword to its master. There were nine swords in all. The lesser of the nine were the six Swords of the Stars. Each of the six was bronze in hue and glowed a luminous gold when held beneath the starry sky.

"Greater than the six were the two Swords of the Moon. Silver in hue, they shone azure and emerald beneath the light of the moon. Yours is the azure blade, Terin. The greatest of the swords and stronger than its lesser brethren is the Sword of the Sun. Its golden-hued blade alights a fiery crimson beneath the sunlit sky."

"Morac!" Terin uttered, horrified that Tyro's minion held the greater sword.

"Yes, Morac wields that mighty weapon." Lore sighed. "When Tyro led the Benotrist revolt against their Menotrist overlords, he was rumored to have found a magical sword that split the blades of his foes and rallied his men to unforeseen victories. We hoped he had found one of the lesser swords and that your father's sword could best him if war were to eventually come between us. Alas, it is not so, as your visit to Fera revealed the true nature of the sword Tyro gifted Morac.

"Squid told me much of your tale before you were called before the throne. That was the reason Squid instructed you to speak not of your sword or Morac's in the full view of the court. If the realm were to know the full threat that Tyro presents, it might instill panic when our attention should be solely focused on the war at hand. Many wars are lost in such a way before a single arrow is loosed or blade drawn.

"I know it was difficult for you to detail your journey to Fera before the court without mention of the blade you wield, but I commend your skill in doing so. Perhaps you might have made a good king's minister in another life, for it matters not, for another path lies before you," Lore explained.

"Your words are kind, sire, but how did my father come to wield this sword?" Terin wondered.

"A wise question." Lore sighed as if haunted by the ghosts of history. "The warriors gifted the Swords of Light by the Council of Tarelia used the weapons to great effect, greatly expanding their colonies and driving the gargoyles from their lands, ever guided by the power of the mysterious blades. The greatest of them was Clorvis Cal, who founded the Northern Kingdom and wielded the Sword of the Sun. His realm expanded across the Feran Plain to the vale of Nisa.

"In those days, the gargoyles had broken from their ancient holdfasts in the Plate Mountains and spread across Arax. Clorvis drove them back into the recesses of the Plate, earning the loyalty and gratitude of the northern peoples. They named him king, and he ordered the construction of Fera and Nisin castles to guard his realm against the gargoyles.

"The Sword of the Moon that you wield was first gifted to General Zar, and he expanded the Tarelian colony that rested at the convergence of the Stlen and Pelen Rivers, which you now know as Central City. He rallied the people who dwelled south of the Plate

Mountains and drove the gargoyles who invaded their lands back into the mountains. The peoples that dwelled in those lands that bordered the southern foothills of the Plate Mountains named him king.

"He ordered the construction of Corell to safeguard his realm from the gargoyles to his north, thus containing them from the opposite side of the mountains from the Northern Kingdom. His realm was commonly called the Middle Kingdom until King Torry expanded the realm to old Cagia. From his reign onward, our realm has borne his name," Lore explained. Terin nodded, for he knew that tale well.

"The warriors gifted the lesser swords expanded the holdfasts that circled the Plate and Cress Mountains to confine the gargoyles to their mountain nests. Others established realms to the south to check gargoyle expansion into those regions. It seemed for a time that the golden age of King Kal might revisit Arax, but alas, it was not to be."

"What happened, sire?" Terin asked.

"The swords were eventually lost one by one, and without them, their kingdoms were overthrown, all save the Middle Kingdom. My ancestor King Vanlar was ambushed at Pharna. He was slain, and the Sword of the Moon was lost. Our kingdom endured and, later, even flourished under the reigns of King Torry and King Toria but without the guidance of the sword. The other kingdoms were not as fortunate.

"The Northern Kingdom had to contend with the gargoyle menace just as we but also the vast hordes of warring tribes that dwelled across the Feran Plain. Eventually, they were conquered by the vicious Menotrist tribes, who, in turn, have been conquered by the Benotrists. Just after the ascension of the Benotrists, your father found the lost sword of the Middle Kingdom in the ruins of ancient Pharna. In his hand, the sword turned certain defeats into victories, which drove the gargoyles from the Plate Mountains and secured Torry North from their threat for a generation."

"But if the sword is the rightful prize of the Torry throne, then it belongs to you, sire," Terin said.

"You are as honorable as your father, Terin, which validates my faith in you. The Swords of Light were gifts from the Smiths of Tarelia, but even more so were gifts of the omnipotence that bestowed their material to the Jenaii, an omnipotence which favored the Tarelians and the Old Kingdom, which they served. That omnipotence could be none other than Yah himself, the ancient deity worshipped by King Kal and forsaken by men thereafter.

"Only the Tarelians kept faith in Kal's god, as did the kingdoms that sprang from their endeavors. Even those kingdoms eventually forsook Yah and forgot the blessings he bestowed upon them. Such was the seed of their ruin, and the swords forsook them as they forsook Yah.

"Only the king of the Middle Kingdom realized his folly after the Sword of the Moon was lost with his father. He ordered his armies to scour the lands that claimed his sire to search for the lost sword. When their efforts were spent for naught, he realized that the blade would only be found by one worthy to wield it. Only then would the sword reveal itself and choose a worthy master. The king ordained that if any subject found the sword, they would be highly placed in his counsel and stand at his right hand. The sword would thereafter belong to the king's new champion.

"The story was passed on from king to prince through the ages, but in its telling, much was forgotten, including the ancient faith of King Kal. Thus, Yah was forgotten," Lore explained. He failed to say that the ancient faith had reawakened, ignited by the smallest of sparks in the heart of his son. The prince claimed to have visions of Yah and had gathered a small host of fellow believers to rebuild the faith, including his father.

"So the sword is mine?" Terin asked uneasily.

"Yes, as ordained by the word of my forebear. The Sword of the Moon was found by your father, as it was intended, and therefore falls rightfully to you, Terin. It is your destiny."

"If the sword is mine, then I am yours to command," Terin vowed.

"Kneel, Terin," Lore commanded. Terin rose from his chair and knelt before the king as Lore gained his feet, staring down at the boy with admiration. "I name you Champion of the Realm and member of the King's High Elite. Rise, Terin!" he declared.

Terin was taken aback. To be named to the King's High Elite was an honor bestowed upon very few, and he felt wholly unworthy to be so named. To be named Champion of the Realm was beyond imagining. It was a post unfilled since its inception, a title created as a boon for the one to find the lost sword of the Middle Kingdom. Who was he to claim such a title? He was no noble, general, or lord. He was only the son of a small land owner.

"You shall earn your place after training under the tutelage of Torg Vantel, the commander of the Elite and master of arms of Corell. He is my strong right hand, and his word is second only to mine. I warn you, Terin, that he is a stern taskmaster and shall drill you without mercy. He will decide when your training is complete. You will report to him at sunrise to begin your training. Let us now partake of our meal. Our guests await us. Enjoy this evening, Terin, for the morrow shall begin your rigorous trials."

*****

The king's table was oval shaped and constructed of sturdy porian with a gray clay surface that ran the length of three men. It matched the shape of the chamber where it was centered. The princess and the king sat at opposing ends, presiding over the austere assemblage of five king's ministers, the ladies Illana and Enora, Terin, and Commander Nevias, the garrison general of Corell. The cupola ceiling arced above, its apex the height of two men, rising above the table's center. The ceiling and walls were stained in hues of silver and gray with basin torches circling the periphery of the chamber. Between each basin stood life-size statues forged in the likeness of the kings of old, most notably King Zar and King Torry, whose stern countenances presided over the chamber from opposing ends.

Once again, Terin was overcome by the prestige of the company that surrounded him. He wondered why they deemed him worthy to sit at the king's table but dared not ask. The other ministers save for Squid and Eli Monsh regarded him with an air of disdain or indifference, perhaps wondering, as he did, why he was present. The princess and her lady companions gifted him reassuring smiles and gestures, setting his mind at ease.

"Ministers, Ladies Enora and Illana, Terin, and my father, allow me to extend the hospitality of the royal table," Corry said, standing at her seat. As the lady of the realm, it was her place to address the king's table and commence the feast. It was a duty she had performed since her twelfth year after the passing of her mother. Corry lifted her goblet from the table, raising it into the air, and those seated at the table followed in kind. Terin waited to see what the others did before mimicking their actions, which meant he was the last to do so. When Corry partook of the wine, touching the goblet to her lips, the others did likewise.

"Well-spoken," King Lore said as Corry curtsied before her sire and sat. Serving girls circled the table, bringing steaming platters of roast moglo and vegetables. The king was offered the first course, as protocol dictated, but he deferred to his guests, as most regents were wont to do. As his father taught him, Lore knew a king should always see to the needs of his guests before his own. He held similar expectations of his generals and commanders of rank. Torry commanders ate after their men.

The serving maids were impeccably attired in long calnesian gowns with tight bodices and flowing skirts that bustled as they moved. The girl who waited upon Terin was a comely maiden no more than twenty years with braided dark hair and a winsome smile. Terin regarded her with polite gratitude as she curtsied and moved on. The king noted Terin's good manners, which merely reinforced his opinion of the son of Jonas.

Terin sat opposite the wall, where large open windows over-looked the surrounding lands. The glow of home fires dotted the Torry countryside, stretching north to the horizon. The view was breathtaking from these airy heights atop the inner keep, starlight painting the clear sky with timeless majesty. Terin reflected on how the beauty of Corell contrasted the harshness of Fera. Did they not share similar construct and countryside? Did they not share a similar place below the starry sky? Were they not both built at the behest of Tarelian warlords?

The difference rested only in the people who dwelled therein. Fera belonged to the Benotrists now, not the Northern Kingdom established by Clorvis Cal. The hearts of the Benotrists had waxed cold, consumed by the hatred instilled by their former Menotrist masters. The hearts of the men of Corell reflected the honor of their king and the traditions established by the Tarelians of old.

"Eat," Minister Veda said, breaking Terin from his thoughts. The elder minister suspected Terin of mimicking their actions, correctly guessing his lack of proper etiquette. The boy was clearly never suited for his apprenticeship and agreed with being stripped of his post. He still wondered why the boy was asked to attend the king's table. No minister's apprentice had ever been granted such privilege for as far back as he remembered. Perhaps his invite was a reward for the part he played in the princess's rescue. Or was there more to the boy than he could visually ascertain?

He recalled the name the king uttered referencing his father: Jonas Caleph. Why did that name ring familiar? Lutius Veda regarded his fellow ministers at the table. Chief Minister Monsh and Minister Antillius sat to his left, and Ministers Thunn and Coran Tevia opposite him. Minister Tevia arrived just after Antillius with troubling news from the city states of Notsu and Bacel. Lutius decided to test the trust the king placed in Terin by bringing Tevia's news to the fore.

"Sire, what of the ill tidings shared by Minister Tevia?" Lutius inquired. Minister Tevia had served as the king's envoy to the city states of Notsu and Bacel for the previous three years. The two cities straddled the vital crossroads that ran from Corell to Tro Harbor and from Pagan to the Lone Hills and points south. Their strategic position rested where the eastern trade routes converged.

Minister Tevia revealed that all trade routes north of the cities were cut, blocking not only access to the eastern Benotrist Empire but also the vital trade routes along the northeast coast to Terse, Filo, Corpii, and Bedo. Caravans traveling south from Notsu were coming under increased attacks, and several had vanished altogether. It was no doubt a prelude to a Benotrist incursion, an incursion that Lore could not allow uncontested.

"Tyro means to set our sights to all fronts. This is but a foray to test our eastern neighbors," Lore said, obviously unconcerned speaking freely on such matters in front of Terin.

"The ruling councils of Bacel and Notsu are most unnerved, sire. I have returned to Corell to share their concerns with Your Majesty," Minister Tevia explained.

"I shall hear their misgivings and act accordingly. General Morton is attending his troops east of Corell. Their muster was called at the outbreak of hostilities and has been filled in good order. I shall hear his counsel before proceeding," King Lore said, regarding each minister in kind.

"As you command, sire." Tevia bowed his head.

"Enough of dark tidings for one night. Let us celebrate the return of young Caleph from his perilous journey." Lore lifted his goblet.

"Terin"—the princess smiled, lifting her goblet toward the young Torry, seconding her father's gesture—"your safe return is most fortuitous. The realm has great need of your leal service in these troubling times."

"In what manner shall he serve, sire?" Lutius asked curiously since the king had stripped him of his apprenticeship.

"As a member of my High Elite *and* Champion of the Realm!" *Champion of the Realm?* Lutius Veda mused, wondering how the boy could fill a post left vacant since its inception. "Terin shall partake of my table this night before submitting to the tutelage of Master Vantel on the morrow," Lore further explained. The mention of the stern commander of the King's Elite gave even the most seasoned ministers reason to pity Terin, for Torg Vantel suffered no fools or slackers. Terin would need all his strength come the morn.

Torg Vantel, Jonas Caleph, VALERA? Lutius gasped, suddenly cognizant of the origin of the boy who sat beside him, and wondered how he would be received by the craggy and ill-humored master of arms. There was more to the boy's lineage than Lutius first surmised, and he wondered if Terin even knew.

CHAPTER 9

Tosha stared into the crackling flames of their campfire, her thoughts a maelstrom of conflicting emotions. It had been seven days since the incident at the lake. Her sickness continued to assail her intermittently, especially in the morning. She had never felt so miserable in all her life. Even broken bones seemed easier to suffer than the illness consuming her. She knew full well the likely source of her affliction with the lateness of her cycle, though no woman she knew suffered thusly. The only grace with her misery was Raven treating her more gently. He left her unchained throughout the day and acted more her protector than captor.

They followed the beaten path, chancing discovery in exchange for speed. They quickly dispersed whenever strangers appeared in the road ahead, taking refuge in the forest that lined the southern edge of their path. Tosha attempted no escape during such encounters, knowing such a move would result in the people's death and her likely recapture. Besides, what could one or two laymen do against Raven? If they managed to stumble upon a large patrol of Benotrist soldiers, she might chance an escape, but part of her desired to stay in Raven's company.

She sat upon one of their saddles with Raven's jacket over her shoulders. She no longer begrudged his offering of it, finding his chivalry oddly appealing. He sat beside her, warming his hands by the fire. Cronus sat across from them, pretending not to notice them as he sharpened his sword with a whet stone, while Alen stood watch along the road that ran east to west at the base of the hill.

Tosha regarded Raven, studying the side of his face as he stared ahead into the fire, lost in his own thoughts. She wondered what his home world was like. What of his family? Were they like him? What was he like as a child? Did he ever love a woman before her? That last thought troubled her, kindling a rage within her heart that constantly clouded her judgment.

He noticed her staring, wondering if something was amiss. "You hungry?" he asked. There was plenty of meat left from their dinner. He wasn't sure what critter it was that he shot, but it sure tasted good, and there was plenty left to eat. Of course, he ate his full share thrice over while the others ate portions no larger than his ten-year-old sister would have chosen.

"I've eaten enough. Have you?" She lifted a dark brow over her golden eye, her tone difficult to gauge, making him question if she was suggesting that he eat more or that he had eaten enough.

"It's not a bad idea to get your fill, kid. You never know when your next meal will be."

It annoyed her how he addressed her so informally, referring to her as kid, Tosh, or wife. Oh, how she loathed that last pet name he called her by. She never expected him to address her by her proper title whilst under his dominion, but he could at least call her by name.

"Did I piss you off again somehow?" he asked, noticing the familiar indignation on her face, but not that he cared.

She couldn't bite the smile that broke upon her face. She would never get used to his bluntness. For such a large man, he was almost like a child, and he had a way of tearing through her carefully constructed facade, rendering her stern appearance useless. "What am I going to tell my mother?" She shook her head.

"About what?"

"About *you*."

"What about me?"

"Need you ask?" She rolled her eyes.

"You think I won't fit in with your mom's side of the family, huh?" He gave her that false hurt look that he employed just to goad her. She again shook her head as he mentioned fitting in with her mother's family, as if the royal court at Bansoch was a cozy family cottage. She chewed the side of her lip to stifle a laugh. *What have I done?* she thought, imagining how he would be received at court. "Doesn't matter, Tosh, since we're never going to your mom's realm anyway."

"Then where shall you take me?" Her mood suddenly darkened.

"With me, back to the *Stenox*. I could use a cabin girl to clean my bunk room and prepare my dinner," he said in all seriousness.

"Cabin *girl?*" She lifted a brow at that suggestion, assuming it was a jest.

"Why not? It's only fair that I captured you that you should be my servant since you had similar plans for me when you drugged me back at dear old dad's house of horrors," he explained, jerking a thumb over his shoulder in the general direction of Fera.

"A royal consort is hardly a palace slave, you dimwit, but perhaps I shall make an exception for you."

"Good luck with that." He shrugged.

"You are still angry with me I see."

"Yep," he grunted as he drew his pistol, pressing the Scope Up switch on the weapon, revealing a thumb-sized square screen that glowed a luminous gray. He peered through the lens, looking passed their cookfire and toward the east. He had done so at various times since sundown, piquing her curiosity at its purpose.

"Why do you keep doing that?" she asked.

"Nightscope, Tosh. I'm just checking on our friends," he answered as he continued to scan the forest-lined ridge that stretched eastward, south of the road below.

"*Friends?* What friends?" she asked in alarm.

"The three fellas that have been making their way toward us since we set camp," he said as if it was of little concern.

"Who are they?" she asked.

"Probably brigands of some sort knowing our location," Cronus answered, keeping still across from them. He was waiting for Raven to signal when they were close. Any movement before then might alert the approaching men that they were detected.

"Brigands!" Tosha said darkly. Such men would slice their throats whilst they slept and steal what they could, willing to kill men for as little as a pair of shoes. They wouldn't hesitate to rape and enslave any whom they did not kill. She would claw their eyes out before allowing them to take such liberties with her. "Why do you tarry? Kill them!"

"Settle down, *wife*. Let them get a little closer," Raven said.

"Why not kill them now?"

"Because I don't feel like walking any farther than I have to when I inspect their corpses. Let 'em get closer, and then I'll shoot 'em."

"And if you hadn't seen them with your little toy, then what? We would likely have had our throats slit in our sleep?" she snarled. "What hope have we of ever reaching your friends? The Plate Mountains block your way south, Tuft's Gap lies hopelessly to our west, and the roads north pass through lands heavily populated by my father's people. That leaves only our present course eastward. You cannot possibly hope to reach the shores of Lake Veneba? Your only sane course is to surrender yourselves to me, and I can remove you to Bansoch and beyond my father's reach."

"I would choose death over your father's mercy, Tosha," Cronus said in a cold voice.

"We'll take our chances with the open road, Tosh. I wouldn't trust you any more than your crazy dad," Raven seconded, peering through the lens with greater focus. Flashes of blue laser spewed from his pistol in quick succession, passing through the still air, striking true some meters away, the cry of wounded voices echoing in the dark.

Cronus sprang to his feet, spinning about, sword at the ready. Raven fired two more times, the blasts taking one of the wounded men full in the chest as he attempted to raise his blade. He fell back between his comrades, a gaping wound in his left breast, dead. The other two lingered, beset with laser blasts to their torsos, writhing in anguish at the forest edge, meters shy of the cookfire. Cronus closed quickly upon them, his eyes finding them by following Raven's second volley to target. He found them strewn upon the matted grass that bordered the tree line, one dead and the others soon to join him. Their weapons rested in their desperate grips, their eyes wide with fright as Cronus stood over them.

"Who are you? Answer true and I shall end you mercifully," Cronus warned, knocking their swords from their weakened grips, leveling the tip of his blade to one of the men's throats.

"B-bounty," the one with the sword tickling his neck squeaked.

"Bounty?" he asked. By now, Raven and Tosha were at his side, and Alen was not far behind, running up the hill at the sight of Raven's laser. "What bounty?" Cronus asked again, running the edge of his blade along the man's throat, drawing a thin trail of blood.

"Him." The man weakly lifted a finger to Raven. "Five hundred thousand certras for h-his capture. Two hundred fifty thousand dead."

"Who set such a sum?" Cronus snarled, pressing his blade tighter against his throat.

"Emperor Tyro."

"How did you find us?" Tosha asked curiously.

"We saw you many days ago at the lake and tracked you here."

"Did you tell anyone else about us?" Cronus asked.

"No, but there are thousands of man hunters scouring these lands, searching for you."

With that, Cronus finished them with swift thrusts to their hearts. Raven scanned 360 degrees, spying a few homesteads in the distance and little else. They set out the next morn, pushing eastward, sacrificing stealth for speed and hoping to avoid large troop contingents blocking their path.

"Bounty, huh?" Raven questioned Tosha as she shared his saddle.

"Did you expect anything less?" she countered.

"Five hundred thousand is a little cheap. I thought I would bring more." She rolled her eyes. "I told you that your father's crazy. It's like my dad used to tell me. 'If you shake any family tree, a few nuts will fall out.'"

CHAPTER 10

"Umph!" Terin moaned painfully, his body striking the sand.

"Up! Again!" the unforgiving voice of Torg Vantel ordered.

Terin sprang to his feet, ignoring the pain in his back and joints lest he incur the wrath of the king's master of arms. Torg's harsh demeanor was well-noted, but Terin didn't sense any malice in the old man, only concern that his pupils master the lesson. When he first set eyes upon Torg Vantel standing beside the king in the throne room, he felt a sudden trepidation rivaling any he had suffered. At that time, he knew the name Torg Vantel, but not the face that it belonged to until he presented himself to the craggy commander of the Elite the following morn.

Torg regarded him with a critical eye, finding Terin to his liking and distaste in equal measure. Terin wondered if he had offended Master Vantel in some way to manifest such interest but did not know how that could be since they had never met before his arrival at Corell.

Terin spent those first days under Torg's tutelage conditioning his body. Torg exercised the poor youth to exhaustion. His rest periods were consumed with mind-numbing repetitions of blocks and thrusts, whether it be with blade or fist. After seven days of such duress, Torg advanced Terin to hand-to-hand training, manipulating joints and instructing him on killing a man with his bare hands. He focused the afternoons on training with his father's sword, which Torg said was unlike the skills used with a common blade. His training encompassed both, as any King's Elite needed the skills handling a common blade, and Terin would be no different.

"There may come a day when you do not wield your father's sword. You must prepare for all contingencies," Torg warned. Terin thought to remind Torg that he had trained with a common blade all his life but wisely decided not to bring it up.

Terin held the silver blade at the ready, gripping the hilt with both hands, eyeing the stake protruding from the sand. He swung wide before striking the target, the stake splitting where it met his blade, the upper half resting upon the lower as if untouched. The upper half stood briefly before toppling from its perch.

"No!" Torg admonished, standing with his arms crossed over his chest. "You must minimize your strike. Your wide swing wastes motion, and speed is essential. An enemy's weakness will only be briefly exposed. You must strike with speed and decisiveness."

"Do I not need strength in my attack?" Terin asked.

"With a common blade, yes. But with the Sword of the Moon, you will either face a common blade or Morac. A common blade will break with your slightest blow, and Morac's blade will not bow to your strongest. To defeat him, you must defend his attack and strike his weakness." Terin nodded in comprehension. "Again, but with a shorter swing," Torg commanded.

Terin obeyed, striking slightly below the first strike, making full use of the stake before it was to be replaced. Terin repeated the process a dozen times before moving to the next stake. Torg had Terin repeat the process until his arms ached before practicing a different skill.

Corry stood behind the parapet overlooking the training arena below, where Torg was putting Terin through his paces. The training arena was a circular chamber in the bowels of the palace with a sand floor and high arches angling to the center of its ceiling. The observation platform allowed her to view the activities below without being seen. Torchlights along the periphery of the arena dimmed the view of those below of those above.

Most mornings found the arena filled with soldiers practicing their swordplay and honing their skills. These past mornings, Torg barred all from the arena save himself and his *new* pupil. Soldiers trained in clothing ranging from a simple loincloth for bare hand training to full tunics and armor for swordplay. Terin had yet to don anything more than a loin garment, as Master Vantel worked him without mercy. Time was of the essence, and the king had tasked Torg with preparing Terin for the trials to come.

Corry observed the sweat glistening over Terin's flesh, the dim light playing off the muscles that ran the breadth of his torso. He obeyed every command Torg issued without pause or complaint, but even from this distance, she could see the exhaustion in his young eyes. She knew he must be weary from his arduous journey and new place and position.

Torg worked him relentlessly from dawn to dusk, taxing both his body and mind. She never heard him utter a single complaint, simply doing everything asked of him. He so desperately wished to please Corry's father for the faith he placed in him. She came to watch his training every morn, reporting his progress to her father. She thought how her first observation of Terin on that memorable day on Molten Isle had changed from a heroic youth to the young man upon whom so much depended.

Five days hence

Terin waited outside the chamber, his tunic soaked with sweat, as he was summoned from his training to Torg's displeasure. He was told that his presence was requested by the king. He was ushered forth despite his disheveled appearance. The guards announced his presence, escorting him within.

"Terin," King Lore greeted him, standing before the glowing hearth with three other men standing to either side. One was Chief Minister Monsh, the second an unfamiliar man in a scarlet robe and piercing green eyes, and the third was that of an old friend who regarded him with familiar dark-brown eyes.

"Yeltor!" Terin greeted excitedly.

"Yes, it is I." Yeltor smiled slightly, which was out of character to his usual rigid demeanor, but the Yatin had grown quite fond of the young Torry. Terin stepped forth, embracing his friend.

King Lore shook his head with mirth. He had called Terin forth to verify the identity of the Yatin who accompanied the minister sent by the Yatin emperor. He didn't expect such an outpouring of affection by the boy. He should have expected no less from what Squid had told him of his character, as Terin seemed to make friends easily and was fiercely loyal. But the boy didn't just make any friends but friends with men of character, strength, and fortitude who apparently reciprocated his loyalty. Even his daughter regarded the boy fondly. He wondered, if Terin had been raised at Corell, as his grandfather insisted, would his easy nature and pure heart have been the same?

"Terin, see to Yeltor's accommodation. You may speak with your friend briefly and hasten back to your training. Torg Vantel is an impatient taskmaster. Now be off, young Caleph, for we have matters of state to attend with Minister Yotora."

"Yes, sire." Terin bowed, guiding Yeltor without. Yeltor walked beside him, his easy smile poorly masking a heavy heart. Terin could see his friend's stiff posture and dour mood. He was unnaturally guarded, even for Yeltor. "Something troubles you?"

"These are troubling times, Terin." Yeltor sighed as they traversed the white stone corridors.

"How fares Telfer? Does it yet stand?" Terin asked, anxious to know of their fate.

"No word," Yeltor said forlornly. "We can only assume the worst."

"How did the emperor receive your ill tidings of his son?"

"Poorly."

"I...I am sorry, Yeltor. You performed your duty beyond the greatest of measures. Your emperor should be proud."

"The Yatin emperor does not share your generous opinion of my...service." He sighed.

Then he is a fool, Terin wanted to say but thought better of it. "If he is displeased, why did he send you here to guard his envoy?" It made little sense.

"I am not here on behalf of the emperor or his envoy. I am banished from my native realm for my failure," Yeltor said dryly as if his words were those of a cadaver.

"Failure!" Terin stopped midstride, forcing Yeltor to halt as well. "You risked all to rescue your prince. You ventured to the Black Castle, where even the bravest dare not tread. How can he hold fault with such effort?"

"A Yatin Elite is judged by success and failure, Terin. There are no consolations for *maybes* and *almosts*. I should feel blessed for the emperor sparing my life, but banishment may be a crueler fate. I shall never see my family again or friends or the land I know as home."

"Make my land your home, Yeltor," Terin blurted.

"You are kind to offer, my friend, but that choice is not yours to gift." Yeltor placed a hand upon his shoulder.

"Then I shall ask the king. He knows your worth and—"

"He has already granted me an audience on the morrow. He spoke at length about a wondrous tale told by you that described me in a most positive light. I was forced to correct your many omissions concerning your exploits upon the roof of Fera and upon the ramparts of Telfer. He was keenly interested to learn the full extent of your fell deeds, especially turning back Yonig's attacks repeatedly at Telfer."

"I spoke truthfully of our battles there," Terin said indignantly.

"You spoke truthfully of battles through your clouded eyes, Terin, not as others saw you. What we others witnessed upon those ramparts was far different from what you claim. Your blade danced in your hands, emitting an ethereal light that vanquished the darkness wherever you went. It was breathtaking to behold, and until you see it from afar, you can never understand the power you command."

"I am training to be a warrior now," Terin said, uncertain about how to respond to Yeltor's praise.

"No longer a scribe?" Yeltor smiled.

"No. I was a poor scribe." Terin shrugged.

"No, you are merely a better warrior."

Terin escorted Yeltor to his chamber, where he was met by a servant to attend his needs. The king invited the Yatin to dine at his table that night, where he would further pick his brain, uncovering the full extent of Terin's exploits. Terin, on the other hand, would return to the training arena, eat a hearty yet bland meal, and retire to his barracks exhausted and spent.

*****

The following morn found Yeltor in the great hall, staring up at King Lore, who sat his throne, taking measure of the former Yatin Elite. "Take a knee, Yeltor!" Lore commanded. Yeltor slowly withdrew his long sword from its scabbard and placed it upon the floor in front of him as he knelt, releasing a measured breath. He earlier asked to pledge his sword and life to the Torry throne, forsaking his native realm. Lore abided his request, and here he knelt to avow such before the Torry king.

"Do you forsake all loyalties to your native Yatin?" Lore's voice echoed boldly off the stone walls of the great hall.

"I forswear all loyalties to Emperor Yangu, the Yatin Empire, and all vassals therein, King Lore!"

"Do you vow loyalty to the Torry throne and realm?"

"I pledge my sword, my arm, and my life to the service of the Torry realm and the House of Lore. I am yours to command, *my king*!" Yeltor vowed.

"Then take up your sword and rise, Yeltor, warrior and guardian of the king."

Yeltor gained his feet, sliding his sword into its scabbard as he fondly regarded the Torry king. If only his emperor were an inkling of the leader that King Lore was, then his native realm would fare better in the troubling days to come.

Eight days hence

Terin found himself standing among a score of the King's Elite in disciplined ranks aligned to either side of the throne at the edge of the dais. He was ordered to bathe and present himself in a formal white tunic and armored silver breastplate and greaves. His fellow Elite were similarly attired, save for the azure tunics that denoted their fully trained status. His tunic was tighter than he was accustomed, and he felt as if he was on display for the full view of the court, though he was but one of hundreds gathered in the throne room.

The king's ministers were aligned behind the throne with their apprentices beside them. He felt Merith's cautious glare out of his periphery, where the young scribe stood beside Minister Veda. He was, no doubt, surprised by Terin's new place in the king's service. He could ill discern if Terin's reassignment was a promotion or a demotion. All that Merith was certain of was that his position within the ministers' apprentice ranks was no longer threatened by the peasant upstart, though he was slightly unnerved by the favor Terin held with the royal house.

Hundreds of courtesans and commanders of rank aligned to either wall of the vast chamber, each dressed in their finery to formally receive the visiting head of state. King Lore presided over the grand assembly, sitting on his throne dressed in flowing black robes over a silver tunic. His coal-black mane fell beneath his austere crown. Princess Corry sat on the lesser throne to his right, wearing an emerald gown with silver folds interwoven in its pleated skirt. Terin's breath caught in the narrows of his throat as he stole a glance, admiring her enchanting beauty. Her eyes shifted suddenly to his, her piercing gaze unsettling his confidence. He quickly averted his eyes, wondering if he had offended her.

Torg Vantel stood to the king's left, surveying the assemblage with the discerning eyes of a seasoned Elite. Little escaped him, not even his young charge's wandering eyes. He would be sure to offer Terin more intense lessons on patience, a virtue Jonas had apparently failed to instill. The boy was not without his merits, however, and Torg took quiet pride in him, lamenting the years lost in watching him grow to manhood. Perhaps Jonas and Valera were right to raise him so far from court. His thoughts drifted to the choices he had made, often in anger, which had caused so many regrets. He should have visited the boy through the years, but his anger at Jonas clouded reason. He quickly shook such sentiments from his mind, returning to the task at hand.

The palace was abuzz recently with dignitaries arriving every day. Representatives of the city states of Notsu, Bacel, Rego, and Sawyer had arrived in recent days, along with the Yatin envoy and numerous Torry ministers, including those recalled from Macon and Nayboria. All had gathered at Corell at the behest of King Lore. The last to arrive was now within the palace, waiting without to be formally received as befitting his regal station.

Haroom! The great horns blared, heralding the royal party's entrance into the throne room. All eyes were drawn to the tall open doors, where two columns of winged soldiers marched forth. Terin's eyes were fixed on the strange creatures. No, they were men who entered the chamber. They were slightly smaller than normal men with gray-white wings protruding from their backs, wrapped about their shoulders. They were black or silver of hair or varying blends of each, draping neath their blue steel helms. They wore thin steel mail over black tunics. Their ears pointed sharply back as if contorted by a pressing gale. Four sharp talons protruded from their slender toes, and the soles of their feet were hard as knotted iron.

The Jenaii! Terin realized. Most referred to them as birdmen or sky travelers. They were an ancient race whose realm's founding preceded the Middle Kingdom. The soldiers parted ranks, stopping mid distance to the throne, making way for a smaller entourage to pass between them. At the head of the vast procession strode a Jenaii with bright silver hair that rolled to his shoulders. He wore a rich azure robe over a gray tunic. A thin golden crown graced his head. His sharp nose and high cheekbones denoted his regal carriage, but it was his piercing silver eyes that evoked a celestial grandeur that filled Terin with awe.

A younger warrior, black of hair and clad in silver mail over a gold tunic, walked behind and to his right, his personal guard, no doubt. The fellow's silver eyes swept the assemblage for any perceived threat or anomaly. The procession stopped short of the throne as a palace steward addressed the assemblage. "Sire, El Anthar, king of the Jenaii, stands before your most high station!"

King Lore stood from his throne as the entirety of the Torry assemblage, save for Torg Vantel, dropped to their knees. The Jenaii delegation knelt in unison, save for their king. Corry stood from her throne and knelt in kind as all yielded to the authority of the king, except the commander of the King's Elite, who was forever charged with the king's safety. He alone knelt to no man, not even his sovereign, as even deference yielded to his sacred charge: the protection of the king.

King Lore descended the dais, stopping before El Anthar, the two kings regarding each other in kind. "Welcome, old friend!" Lore greeted.

"We are welcomed!" El Anthar's crisp voice echoed through the chamber with terrible authority upon his utterance. The palace steward pounded the floor with his staff twice, signaling all to rise.

"It has been many years since last we spoke," Lore said, at least directly.

"Leagues may separate our kingdoms, King Lore, but you and your people are always foremost in our thoughts." El Anthar would have said *hearts* in place of *thoughts* if the Jenaii were inclined toward such emotions. The Jenaii might not openly display the endearing emotions that humans were prone to exhibit but were stoic, brave in battle, and fiercely loyal to their friends. And no friends were as highly regarded as the Torry Kingdoms.

The Council of Corell

Terin stood rigidly along the wall of the council chamber. He spent the better part of the day standing guard in the great hall as the royal court hosted the visiting dignitaries. An army of servants hurried to and fro, bringing steaming platters of moglo and douri, pitchers of wine, and trays of fruits, vegetables, and bread. He stood among his fellow Elite, watching over the festivities for endless hours until the heads of each delegation retired to the quiet of the council chamber, where he joined four members of the King's High Elite to guard the king therein. Princess Corry remained in the great hall, presiding over the festivities in her sire's place.

Terin stood post as Ministers Antillius, Veda, and Thunn entered, taking their places at the large oval-shaped table. Minister Monsh's apprentice, Aldo, stood at the entrance, directing each minister and dignitary to their places. Aldo regarded Terin across the chamber, nodding a subtle greeting of friendship. Terin smiled slightly, acknowledging his friend in kind. He hadn't seen Aldo in days until this morn. He would always remember Aldo's kindness when he first arrived at the palace. He was a kindred soul, and Terin knew that he would make a great minister one day and a far better one than he could have hoped to be.

He caught sight of Merith stepping within, speaking briefly with Aldo before approaching his master at the table. Merith gave Terin a passing glance. He once falsely believed Terin's removal from his former position a validation of his unfitness as his equal but now regarded him warily. A King's Elite was every bit a minister's equal and, in some ways, their superior. Merith posted behind Minister Veda, attentive to his master's needs should they arise.

Terin was surprised to see Yeltor opposite him, standing post beside the statue of King Cot, one of dozens of such works that circled the chamber. He had seen little of his comrade of late, though they shared the same barrack beneath the inner keep. Terin was often too exhausted at the conclusion of his days to do little more than eat and stagger to his bed. His friend presented a stern countenance, surveying the chamber with guarded vigilance.

Though Squid Antillius appeared in an animated conversation with his fellow ministers, he shared a knowing look with Terin more than once, setting him at ease. Squid had yet to name his replacement, and Terin wondered who would be selected for that prestigious post. He reflected on his ignorance of the high honor of his apprenticeship when he first set out for Rego. His parents obviously knew the significance and failed to speak of it. Or had they done so deliberately? Perhaps they wished not to further burden his laden mind with matters that were beyond him.

The last dignitaries to enter were King El Anthar and King Lore, each taking their respective places on opposite ends of the table. The Jenaii warrior who shadowed El Anthar throughout the day followed his regent, standing post behind his king, his silver eyes exceeding Yeltor's attentive vigilance. His slender left hand rested upon the hilt of his sword, a hilt that seemed strangely familiar. The warrior's piercing silver eyes shifted swiftly to Terin, catching his gaze as he quickly looked away. There was something amiss yet oddly familiar about the Jenaii warrior as well.

"Let us commence!" King Lore declared, calling the esteemed assemblage to order. "We have gathered here, allied of common purpose, to share what we know upon the actions of the enemy and to set what course we should collectively follow. Tyro's legions threaten to overtake all of Arax, and none of our lands are safe. We have checked Tyro's ambitions upon Rego, bleeding his legions at great cost. Tyro has crossed into Yatin, sweeping south through the Yatin heartland. Despite his losses upon each invasion, Tyro retains many legions to unleash upon us anywhere along his endless border. Chairman Pontus!" Lore regarded the ranking member of the Regoan council.

The Regoan oligarch gained his feet, smoothing the folds of his burgundy robes, his eyes sweeping the others seated at the table. "I have come on behalf of the populace of Rego and the Wid River Valley to offer our gratitude to the Torry realms for their intervention in the defense of our city and to reassure them of our commitment in the battles to come. We have met the enemy at Tuft's Mountain, standing beside our Torry brethren in desperate battle. Our forces suffered thousands of casualties, but their sacrifice was not in vain, destroying the better part of four legions.

"Our scouts have found no sign of enemy activity anywhere between the Cot and Tuss Rivers. They have spotted a gargoyle force numbering between ten and fifteen telnics camped upon the north bank of the Tuss." Pontus lifted a stick in his right hand, running it along the length of the Tuss River depicted on the large map of Arax that covered much of the massive table.

"Do the gargoyles there appear to be preparing for battle, or are they holding in place?" Chief Minister Monsh asked.

"They have built a line of palisades along large portions of the north bank of the Tuss," Torg Vantel interjected, standing behind the king with his arms crossed over his muscled chest.

"That proves little of their intent," General Morton countered, sitting to the king's left. He commanded the 5th Torry Army, which was mustering northeast of Corell. "Their palisades could be merely a feint to mask another invasion while appearing to be in a defensive posture." Morton was ever cautious and wary of Tyro's strength and tactics.

"Intent is irrelevant, General Morton. We are here to declare facts. Tyro has a gargoyle contingent numbering ten to fifteen telnics camped along the north bank of the Tuss, erecting palisades along its length," Torg reminded him. "Those are the facts as we know them. You may infer the enemy's intent as you like."

"Master Vantel is thoroughly apprised of every scouting report we receive," King Lore added. "Proceed, Master Vantel," he said, waving an open hand over the map before them.

"Aye, sire." Torg circled the table, taking the wooden pointer from Chairman Pontus as the Regoan delegate took his seat. "With the nearest enemy force to Rego along the Tuss, we have ordered General Bode's 3rd Army to Central City, where its casualties shall be refilled with our reserve citizen soldiers that we have mustered. General Fonis's 2nd Army will remain at Rego should the enemy again cross the Tuss. We are sending reserves north to Rego to refurbish Fonis's thinned ranks as well," Torg said, running the pointer along the map at each point indicated. "General Morton's 5th Army has mustered here." Torg indicated a point north and east of Corell. "We have ordered the musters of the garrisons at Central City and Corell. They should be filled within a fortnight. Such is the disposition of the main armies of Torry North."

After a brief silence, Chief Minister Monsh regarded his Yatin counterpart. "Minister Yotora," he said, offering the floor. Minister Yotora gained his feet, Torg Vantel handing him the pointer before taking his place behind the Torry king. At the mention of the Yatin emissary, Minister Zaran of Zulon stiffened noticeably. Zulon and

Teso were ever wary of Yatin adventurism, their two kingdoms suffering several Yatin invasions over the centuries.

"I have come at the behest of my emperor and our Torry host. The Yatin Empire is beset by multiple gargoyle legions commanded by the gargoyle general Yonig. They swarmed over our northern border at the same time they attacked the Torry and Regoan armies at Rego. One legion has enveloped the harbor of Tenin while a Benotrist armada destroyed our 1st and 2nd fleets off our coast before cutting the port's access to the sea. With no relief force available in the surrounding provinces, we can only surmise how long Tenin can endure.

"Our prince led a large host from the palace of Telfer, engaging a large contingent of Yonig's forces at Salamin Valley." Yotora indicated the northwestern approaches of Telfer upon the map, where the battle took place. "Our counterattack was blunted and our prince captured as General Morue withdrew our forces to Telfer, where they are currently besieged."

"What news have you of Telfer?" General Morton asked. "We have two witnesses of the siege in this very chamber," he added, referring to Yeltor and Terin, who stood post along opposite walls of the chamber.

"Witnesses?" Minister Fugoc, representing the ruling oligarchs of the city state of Bacel, asked curiously. He was stern of face with forceful opinions that matched his pugnacious nature, contrasting his diminutive build.

"Witnesses of the battle or the siege?" inquired Chairman Pontus of Rego.

A chorus of whispers passed through the chamber, for many had not heard Yeltor and Terin's grim tale of the siege of Telfer. Minister Yotora pursed his pallid lips, struggling to allow Yeltor's testimony, as his emperor had cast the former Elite from his realm. Yotora inwardly questioned his emperor's wisdom on the matter, wondering how one could fault the leal service of Yeltor after he only failed the impossible task of correcting Prince Yanku's obvious blunder. But Yeltor was no longer his to command, and his testimony was most valuable on the disposition, tactics, and intent of Yonig's legions.

"Yeltor, formerly of the Yatin Elite, and Terin Caleph of the Torry Elite were both present during the early part of the siege. It is to them to testify as to what they saw," Yotora conceded.

"Yeltor, step forth and relay your tale!" King Lore commanded.

Yeltor did so, standing before the table as he again relayed the tale, beginning before Salamin Valley and ending with his banishment by his emperor's decree at Mosar. Most were dismayed at the disastrous decisions made by the fallen Yatin prince. His monumental failure left all of Yatin in grave peril. Had he only garrisoned Telfer with his full army, the palace would have been unconquerable by Yonig's three legions. Without Telfer attained, the gargoyles could not seriously threaten Mosar. But alas, all was now in doubt.

Yeltor's grim tale of the Yatin's ill treatment at the hands of the gargoyles revealed the darkest truth of that foul race's cruelty. As grim as his telling proved to be, it was his tale of Terin's sword that drew the greatest interest. Terin felt many eyes upon him, from mild curiosity and suspicion to awe and wonder.

"He stood upon the battlements, smiting gargoyles and men with practiced ease, his blade alit with otherworldly light. Their swords broke upon his blade as brittle sticks against steel. The enemy fled from his fell hand as we raced to the highest battlements of Fera. There upon those airy heights overlooking the Feran Plain, he met Morac, prime of Tyro's Elite.

"Morac's blade shone fiery crimson, lighting the starry heavens as if it was day, yet the moon presided above in that midnight sky, bestowing its power to Terin's sword. The azure glow of Terin's blade intensified where it touched Morac's fiery sword, staying the hand of Tyro's champion where none had done so before." Yeltor spoke in a haunted voice as if reliving the tale for the first time, the others hanging upon his every word.

"He met Morac's blade, their swords pulsating like bursting stars clashing in the heavens, each vying for dominion upon the celestial plain. And then"—he paused, his fierce brown eyes sweeping the table with terrible intensity—"Terin's blade drove Morac's sword from his grasp, sending the ancient weapon over the battlements, its fiery blade dimming with its descent."

Not a word or whisper echoed in the quiet chamber, for none had heard this part of the tale, not even the king. Most had not known of their escape from Fera at all. Some looked to Terin with awe, others with curiosity, some with pride, such as Squid Antillius, and some with guarded jealously, such as Merith. King Lore, however, shook his head, regarding his named champion. The boy never spoke of disarming Morac. The fact that he had done so should not have been omitted in his telling. It reassured his faith that Terin was intended to wield the Sword of the Moon. But again, Terin omitted facts out of his desire not to boast.

"I could not have done so if not for Cronus. He distracted Morac, allowing me to land the decisive blow," Terin blurted, taking a step forward, his voice weaker than he intended.

"Yet you did land the blow," King Lore said. "And by doing so, you have proven yourself worthy to carry the sword you bear. Your loyalty and honor are beyond reproach in my discerning eyes, young Caleph, but your honesty is still lacking. Stand your post and speak not until called for!" the king admonished. Terin bowed, backing a step, ashamedly taking his place and feeling Torg Vantel's heated glare upon him.

"You may continue, Yeltor!" King Lore commanded. Yeltor finished telling of their flight to Telfer and of the siege, where Terin turned back Yonig's attacks upon the castle. Once again, they learned how instrumental Terin's sword proved to be in turning a battle.

"I thought such swords were a myth, a fairy tale for children," Minister Niotic whispered audibly. He represented the city state of Notsu, which straddled the vital crossroads that connected Torry North to the eastern port of Tro Harbor and the eastern Benotrist Empire to the various city states and realms that lay south of Notsu. Notsu's sister city, Bacel, straddled the northeast corner of the crossroads with Notsu occupying the southwest.

Niotic had journeyed to Corell in the company of Minister Fugoc of Bacel to reaffirm their common cause with the Torry realms. Where Fugoc was short of stature and strong of will, Minister Niotic was lanky and nervous, his lips twitching as he spoke. He was a poor choice when negotiating with adversaries, but his deep knowledge of Notsu's varied interests was well-served in dealing with friends.

"A myth they are not," El Anthar declared, his voice echoing like distant thunder. The king of the Jenaii regarded Terin with a knowing glance, his silver eyes unnerving the young Torry, glowing with terrible intensity. "Terin's sword was gifted to him by his father, who discovered it during the Sadden Wars. He found it among the ruins of ancient Pharna and wielded it in battle, earning great glory and the hand of the beautiful Lady Valera.

"He left the king's service for the simple life of a free landowner, raising his only son in obscurity, hidden from the world, along with the wondrous sword he had found. But now the son has returned to us with the sword of his father at the time of our gravest need." Terin swallowed past the lump in his throat, wondering how the Jenaii king knew so much of his person. It seemed as if everyone knew of his origin except him.

"Should we trust our deliverance to the sword or the boy?" Minister Fugoc asked skeptically, scrutinizing the faith the others seemed to blindly place in Terin.

"Both!" El Anthar affirmed, his glowing silver eyes trained on Terin.

"Could not any wield the sword? Would its power wane if another carried it in battle?" Fugoc questioned.

"Its ability to destroy what it touches would not wane, but its full power would not be realized. To understand the significance of the sword and master, you must understand the origin of the Swords of Light and why they were lost," El Anthar said.

"Enlighten us, King Anthar," Minister Yotora said, echoing the sentiment that many shared.

El Anthar gained his feet, circling the table with his hands behind him in deep contemplation. He paused beside the open window, where the light of the Araxan moon played upon his face. His azure robe rippled softly in the gentle night air. "Long ago, in the land beyond our southern sea, where my people dwelled since the founding of this world, a star fell from the heavens. It broke upon the temple of Yah in the very heart of our ancient capital. The heart of the temple crumbled to ruin as if a giant's fist had stricken it from above.

"Our people were deathly afraid, as our mystics debated its meaning. Some saw it as punishment for failing to heed the will of Yah. Others claimed it a sign that Yah no longer held sovereignty over the Jenaii. The calamity was debated until El Valtor, the chief alchemist, discovered the mysterious metals deposited where the star had struck in the center of the temple's broken floor. They were of an origin unknown to us.

"Each of the metals reacted differently to the celestial bodies that ruled the heavens—the sun, the moon, and the stars. They were of such construct that our hottest kilns could not bend or shape them. It was then that the high priests received the vision sent by Yah, which foretold of a remnant of the devout dwelling beyond the sea. The remnant established a holdfast along the northern shores of Lake Monata and were guardians of vast knowledge thought lost since the days of King Kal."

"The Smiths of Tarelia," Minister Sounor of the city state of Sawyer said. The men of Sawyer were well-schooled in the legends of ancient Tarelia, for their very city was once a mere seedling planted by the Tarelian council.

"Yes, the Smiths of Tarelia," El Anthar affirmed. "Once our priests' visions were relayed to our emperor, he ordered a great armada to set forth, led by his second son, El Ebiorn, to establish a colony upon Arax and to present the divine gift to Yah's faithful in Tarelia. Our ships dotted the sea, their masts full with the wind, stretching to the horizon in all of our glory. El Ebiorn set foot upon the green shores where the Elaris emptied into the sea, establishing our first holdfast of El Tova.

"We were soon set upon by wild tribes of men and murderous bands of gargoyles upon our landing. Arax was populated by such villainy in those days, a land given to chaos and disorder. Only the holdfast of Tarelia stood against the darkness, a beacon of compassion and enlightenment, illuminating the ignorance that surrounded them. It was to them that El Ebiorn delivered the divine gift, forever forging the bonds of friendship that joined our peoples.

"The Tarelian smiths set about constructing vast kilns of unimagined power to achieve the temperatures needed to bend the materials. For two hundred years, they labored, constructing swords from the luminous metals, each a masterpiece, marking the apex of Tarelian smithcraft. They were presented one by one to their ruling council upon their completion. The lesser Swords of the Stars took anywhere from ten to twenty years to forge. The Swords of the Moon and the powerful Sword of the Sun took far longer." He paused briefly.

"The Sword of the Sun was the first and greatest of the swords to be forged, gifted to Clorvis Cal, who used its power to found the Northern Kingdom far beyond the Mote Mountains. To Zar Zaronan was gifted the Sword of the Moon that Terin holds now. He established the Middle Kingdom, joining the colonies previously established by the Tarelian order in the years before.

"The colonies were nearing extinction, beset by gargoyles, warring tribes and savages of all sorts. Zar Zaronan's advent with the Sword of the Moon swept away the colony's threats like a cleansing wind. Such was the power of the Swords of Light, breaking enemy swords along with their spirit and lifting the hearts of those who followed the swords' masters.

"The warriors gifted the swords swore sacred oaths to serve the will of Yah and to rule with humility and justice, and so they did, establishing great redoubts of enlightenment in those perilous days, driving back the darkness from their seats of power. It seemed, for a time, that our labors bore fruit, as the warriors gifted the Swords of Light established flourishing kingdoms across the face of Arax. Alas, our optimism proved false. One by one, the kingdoms established by the Tarelian council passed to lesser men, men who did not serve the will of Yah or had forgotten him altogether. Without Yah's divine bond, those lesser kings suffered grave misfortune.

"One by one, their swords were lost. And without them, their kingdoms fell to ruin, overcome by the barbarians that waited beyond their tenuous borders. No greater fall was there than that of the Northern Kingdom, whose ancient borders stretched from Fera to Nisin, the twin fortresses built to check the gargoyles' advance north of the Plate Mountains. Their fall was as precipitous as their rise. Of all the realms established by Tarelia upon the continent, only the Middle Kingdom endured."

"Why? What set the Middle Kingdom apart from the others?" Minister Fugoc of Bacel asked.

"Upon the loss of the Sword of the Moon, their king repented, vowing to Yah that he would gift the blade to whomever the divinity chose worthy to find it. Yah revealed his will to the king of the Middle Kingdom that he would spare the realm the fate that befell the others if they held to his vow. And so the Middle Kingdom endured, her boundaries growing and receding like the ebb and flow of the tide but enduring nonetheless.

"In time, the line of kings forgot the vows sworn by their pre-decessors, along with their beliefs in Yah and the Swords of Light. The swords passed into legend, forgotten by all, save for the precious few of us who still remember. Ancient Tarelia, the guardians of much of your history and knowledge, were overcome as the first swords were lost. All that remains of their once great citadels are the broken watchtowers along the northern shore of Lake Monata, a deserted graveyard of a lost age.

"And so men had forgotten this sacred tale until a young Torry prince named Lore discovered its telling in an ancient tome. Years later, when Terin's father found the lost sword of the Middle Kingdom, Lore knew it was divine providence and bestowed his blessing upon him and gifted him the hand of the lady Valera," El Anthar said.

My mother? Terin thought, his mind reeling from the revelation. The Jenaii king was so knowledgeable of his parents, and yet he knew so little. Frustrating him further was the fact that he was not allowed to ask of them in this high council. He could feel Torg Vantel's pos-ture stiffen with the mention of his mother. Had he been a suitor for her hand? Was that the reason of his disdain for his father?

Torg seemed much older than his mother, but it was common for high-born maidens to wed men much older. No, that didn't seem right either. El Anthar mentioned that his mother was gifted by the king. Did that infer that she was of the king's household, a distant

155

cousin or ward of some sort? Terin's questions of his parents' origin distracted him as the conversation at the table drifted toward the nature of the swords and the threat posed by Morac.

"If the swords are divine gifts and were lost due to the weak faith of those who inherited them, then what explains Tyro finding the sword wielded by Morac?" Minister Veda asked skeptically, his view of the world shaped by trade and the physical things he could see and touch. He struggled to place stock in fairy tales of far-off lands, magical swords, and a long-forgotten god.

El Anthar's silver eyes regarded Minister Veda pensively. "The properties of the swords allow them to sever anything they touch, be it rock, iron, wood, or steel. Any man or creature can make use of them, destroying whatever they smite. The hierarchy of the swords makes the Sword of the Sun superior to each of its lessers, though not strong enough to break them. The Swords of the Moon are equally more powerful than the Swords of the Stars. It is apparent that Morac wields the fabled Swords of the Sun, the very blade wielded by the kings of the old Northern Kingdom."

"Then is he ordained by this Yah that you speak of?" Pontus of Rego asked worriedly.

"Nay. Yah places no favor for men of such wicked hearts to wield his gift!" El Anthar said indignantly.

"Then how does he wield it? That fact alone questions the very existence of your god or his loyalty to the faithful, as you claim," Pontus questioned.

El Anthar's back stiffened, his silver eyes glowing like embers. It seemed as if he grew taller with his posture alone. Terin almost drew back from the Jenaii king's terrible gaze. "Do not assume to know the will of Yah, Chairman Pontus. Tyro's finding of the Sword of the Sun is the will of Yah. Why he has allowed it to come to pass I shall not presume. No man, Jenaii, Ape, gargoyle, or Enoructan can question his will.

"I am a king in this world, descendant of the kings of the Jenaii. My royal bloodline flows through the millennia to the founding of our race across the sea. No man stands as my superior, and precious few stand as my equal." He regarded King Lore respectfully. "But in the eyes of Yah, I am but a humble servant. I trust in the prophecies of my people and those of the old Middle Kingdom.

"The swords must be wielded by those Yah has blessed. If Morac wields the Sword of the Sun, it is the will of Yah, perhaps to demonstrate his true purpose, that if we place our faith in the hand of his chosen, he shall deliver us. And how shall he demonstrate his power unless he raises up a lesser sword to defeat its better?"

"And what sets Terin apart besides being Yah's anointed?" Torg asked, his eyes fixed sternly upon his young charge.

"Yah designated his bloodline to this task," El Anthar said, stating what he saw as obvious.

"What power does his blood hold? If all men who wield the blade can destroy whatever they strike and cow their enemies, what more can Terin do?" Torg asked, wondering the boy's capabilities.

"Not everyone who takes up the swords instills terror in their foes. The first masters of the swords possessed this ability because they swore sacred oaths to Yah, but their power was limited in its effect. As the swords fell to lesser men, this power disappeared altogether. Tyro instilled fear in his enemies by their fear of the sword's power, not of the man who held it. Terin is Yah's anointed. The powers he invokes from the sword are great and mysterious."

"You have the luxury of patience in placing faith in this boy," Minister Fugoc retorted, jabbing a thumb toward Terin. "My people are not as fortunate. Even now, the drums of war echo in the distance, drawing closer as we sit here in council. My city is but a breath from the Benotrist border, straddling the vital crossroads that join all of eastern Arax.

"Darkhon has cut all routes north and northeast. We are blind to all happenings beyond Lake Veneba. Heralds from Barbeario, Tro, and points between have come to our city seeking the whereabouts of lost caravans, merchants, and ministers bound for our city.

"Our people have returned with grim tales of slaughtered travelers scattered beyond the approaches of Bacel and Notsu. They have spotted columns of cavalry passing in the distance in the dark of night. A fortnight past, we received a herald of Darkhon demanding tribute and fealty to the Benotrist Empire."

"And how did you respond?" Minister Yotora asked, his voice laced with suspicion.

Fugoc glared daggers at the Yatin minister. "Guard yourself, Minister Yotora. My city has been an ever-vigilant watch post upon the gargoyles since our founding. We know our true friends from our false ones. As for Darkhon's emissary, we sent him back to his master, telling him we would bring his *generous* offer before our council. We said we would give him an answer by the turn of the moon." Fugoc referenced Tyro as Darkhon, as he was known throughout eastern Arax.

"You did not refuse him outright?" Commander Nevias, commander of the Corell garrison, asked.

"No, we did not. To do so would have openly revealed our true alignment with the Torry realms. Such an affront would only hasten the Benotrist invasion that is certain to follow. I have not journeyed to Corell as a beggar prostrating himself for whatever scraps you are inclined to lend. Nay, I am here on behalf of the people of Bacel to relay our intent to defy Darkhon and fight to our last drop of blood. If we face him alone, then we shall perish to the man. We shall not beg for your aid but ask that you stand beside us."

General Morton stirred restless in his chair, wanting to speak against such folly, but a look from King Lore stilled his tongue. He argued at length of the indefensibility of holding the crossroads at Bacel and Notsu against multiple legions. Any force sent there might easily be trapped.

"You shan't stand alone, my friend," King Lore assured the Bacel minister. Minister Fugoc returned the king's assurance with an eased countenance while his counterpart, Niotic of Notsu, seemed guarded. Niotic knew well the blade that hung above their collective necks. The crossroads were too ripe a target for Darkhon to easily dismiss.

"Your cities are not alone in their unfortunate proximity to empires that covet your wealth and strategic position. My city is similarly pressed by the ambitions of the Macon regent. King Mortus has blocked our access to Cagan, imposing crippling tariffs on all vessels traversing the Monata. There is little doubt that he shall eventually move upon my city now that the Torry Kingdoms are otherwise occupied," Ambassador Sounor of the Sawyer council stated. Sawyer straddled the mouth of the Monata River at the southwestern end of Lake Monata. Sounor's stately countenance, silver hair, and amethyst eyes bespoke his patrician upbringing. His people's ancient kindred to the Torry realms formed the strongest of bonds among the congregants gathered at Corell.

"King Mortus has ever leaned toward opportunism," Chief Minister Eli Monsh affirmed. It seemed their collective worries only worsened with each testimony. They were beset by enemies upon all flanks, and the Jenaii king had yet to speak on the happenings along the Nayborian frontier.

"Mortus well knows the taxing effects of Tyro's war upon our collective strength. To expect him not to seize the untended fruit that lies so near is utter folly," El Anthar stated. "I shall order my Monata fleet to Sawyer as a demonstration of friendship with your fair city, if your council acquiesces."

"It would be most welcome, King El Anthar." Ambassador Sounor regarded him respectfully. A show of such force might give the Macon Empire reason to pause, though the Jenaii fleet on Lake Monata numbered less than ten vessels. Unfortunately, ten vessels might be all the Jenaii could gift their friends at Sawyer.

"My king has received overtures from our Macon neighbors, offering alliance. The king of Teso received a similar offer. The intent is an obvious move against Torry intervention on behalf of Sawyer," Minister Zaran stated. He was sent on behalf of the twin kingdoms of Zulon and Teso, the realms that controlled the Nila between Torry North and South.

"You will send your king our deepest regard, Minister," King Lore said.

"Of course, great king." Zaran bowed his head. "King Sargov has called two telnics to guard our northern flank should any hostiles emerge through the Rulon gap." The mention of the Rulon gap, the main avenue of every Yatin invasion of the Nila valley, rankled Minister Yotora, fueling the age-old hatred between their peoples. "King Vesn has likewise ordered the three telnics to guard Teso's southeastern provinces." King Vesen, the Teso regent, was the Macon Empire's next likeliest target and Sawyer's northern neighbor.

"We honor your friendship, Minister Zaran." Minister Sounor of Sawyer regarded him. Of course, if the Macons moved against Sawyer, there was little Teso or Zulon could do without strong Torry backing.

"I bring ill tidings as well," King El Anthar said as he circled the table, torchlight playing off the silver of his wings.

"Ill tidings?" Chairman Pontus of Rego asked, wondering what other grim news could possibly beset them.

"There are troubling signs upon the Nayborian border. King Lichu has closed all trade routes between our realms. Our realms have warred through the centuries, but the peace has held for a time. The Nayborians, however, have formally aligned with Tyro through a pact of mutual defense. They have forged a similar pact with the Macon Empire. We must assume they mean to honor their agreement with Tyro.

"They have expelled our dignitaries and have refused our heralds. The border is disturbingly quiet. Our scouts have tracked sizable Nayborian contingents of cavalry and infantry south and east of the Lone Hills, where we lost contact with them. To what purpose they would venture in those wild lands, we can only surmise. When Tyro renews his attack, we expect the Nayborians to strike in kind. When they do, the Jenaii must meet them."

The Torries at the table received the news with expected resignation. The Naybin alliance with Tyro effectively limited any aid the Jenaii might lend the Torry realms. The discussion continued at length, each foreign minister detailing the specifics of troop readiness and disposition as well as provision placement and logistics. The Torry ministers followed in kind, beginning with Minister Veda.

He spoke at length of the status of Torry trade throughout Arax. If the war expanded to Macon and Naybin, as they expected, then the Torries' trading routes would be severely restricted. Minister Thunn detailed the progress in crop yield and the urgency of the harvest preceding an enemy incursion. The remaining ministers detailed the status of their respective responsibilities. When all had testified to the facts as they knew them, the time of decision had come. Minister Yotora looked expectantly to his Torry host, hoping King Lore would provide his beleaguered realm the aid they desperately needed.

"I have dispatched my son to Torry South to ready the 4th Torry Army for march. They shall proceed to the Yatin border to be formally received by emissaries of your emperor, Minister Yotora." King Lore regarded the Yatin emissary evenly. It was no small matter that the Torry crown prince was leading the Torry army to the Yatins' relief. Lore expected the Yatins to understand the full weight of his support, for he was sending his only son to their relief.

He needn't explain that his son had begun this operation without his expressed permission, but now that the boy had done so, the die was cast. Looking at the map upon the table, he knew his son was right to do so. Lore's eyes drifted to the large isle resting off the northwestern coast of Arax, the Federation of the Sisterhood, wondering what part they might play in the war to come.

He was certain that Queen Letha was ever watchful of the affairs of the continent and wary of Tyro's insatiable ambitions. She never forgave Tyro's attempt upon her isle during their brief marriage, but Letha's only daughter was Tyro's heir as well, which further complicated the political landscape. He was certain of only one thing: Letha would never wage war upon the Torry realms, for their bonds were bound in blood.

"My king?" Chief Minister Monsh drew him from his thoughts.

"Proceed," Lore said.

"As King Lore stated, Prince Lorn shall lead the 4th Torry Army to Mosar to reinforce the Yatin defense of their capital." Eli Monsh indicated the points upon the map, running a line with the pointer from Cagan to Mosar. "We have ordered the full muster of the 1st Torry Army to gather at Cagan in the event the Macon Empire strikes our southern kingdom. General Fonis remains at Rego with the 2nd Torry Army to guard the northern approaches of Tuft's Mountain and the upper Nila.

"General Bode shall reposition the 3rd Torry Army to the lower Stlen, below Central City. From there, he can guard our western border and respond to Rego or Corell as needed. General Morton's

Fifth Torry Army has completed its muster and awaits northeast of Corell," Eli Monsh finished, regarding the cautious Morton, whose studious eyes focused intently on the map.

"From there, I shall be well-positioned to counter any Benotrist or gargoyle incursions south of the Plate Mountains or Naybin adventurism to our east," Morton offered.

"Nay!" Lore's voice drew all eyes to him. "Come the morrow, General Morton shall lead our 5th Army and a contingent of cavalry to the crossroads of Notsu and Bacel. If Tyro thinks to seize their vital position with a mere legion, then we shall deny him."

General Morton opened his mouth to counter such folly as he saw it but closed his lips, unwilling to speak against his king before a foreign council. "I shall prepare the army for march, sire," he conceded instead.

"Your opinion on the matter is not to be restrained by slavish obedience to protocol, General Morton!" the king commanded.

General Morton released a measured breath, struggling to vent his words without casting doubt on his king's wisdom. "The crossroads are indefensible against a legion of gargoyles, let alone men, and Tyro can throw either upon Bacel and Notsu with little regard. The crossroads straddle the water resources that are scarce for many surrounding leagues. We might defend the cities with one army if Tyro sends but a single legion, and the populace is armed and willing to stand beside us, but the task would be difficult considering the leagues that separate the two cities.

"Should we concentrate our forces at one, the enemy might flank us and attack the other. If we divide our army, the enemy can destroy us in detail. Our scouts may have difficulty spotting large movements of troops through the myriad of jagged canyons and lush forests that carpet the lands south of Lake Veneba and east of the Kregmarin Plain. Unfortunately, the Kregmarin Plain holds the most defensible terrain for checking the advance of multiple legions, but it is many leagues from a suitable water supply and would place our army closer to the lands that are difficult to scout," Morton argued.

"Then what do you counsel, General?" Minister Fugoc asked harshly. "Should we abandon our city to Tyro and be done with it?"

"Yes!" Morton said reflexively, betraying his true opinion before his mind could stay his tongue. "At least evacuate as many of your people as you are able. Remove them to our borders or to Tro as well as anything of value that can be moved. Reposition your treasuries to Corell, Barbaerio, or Tro. Those who remain must be able to take flight by their own means in the event you declare Bacel or Notsu open cities. Your armies, though small, must remain mobile, deft, and fleet of foot.

"If Tyro attacks with multiple legions, we should avoid contact until his lines of communication are stretched, harrying his supply trains and attacking his periphery. Poison the water sites in the enemy's path, and destroy everything of use that can't be moved. Gargoyles can march many leagues without food or water, but men cannot. We can winnow Tyro's legions until they are at their weakest, and then"—Morton paused, indicating the eastern approaches of Corell upon the map—"we strike!" He struck the table emphatically.

Morton was not prone to emotional displays or military actions with significant risk but knew he could only sway others to his thinking with an eventual plan to engage the enemy. In truth, Morton would harry the enemy while withdrawing to the safety of Corell, letting the enemy waste themselves upon the white walls of the ancient fortress. Alas, such a suggestion would meet hostile derision from their allies of Notsu and Bacel as well as the Torry nobles east of Corell.

"You ask us to forsake our homes so easily?" Minister Fugoc retorted.

"General Morton's advice is sound, and your cities should prepare for the direst eventualities, Ministers," King Lore sagely advised as he gained his feet, stepping toward the window to stand beside El Anthar. The eyes of the council were fixed on the two great kings standing before the pale lunar light.

"None here stands alone," King Lore said, addressing the council, his proximity to the Jenaii king symbolizing his declaration. "If we stand together, each fulfilling their part, we can sever the hand that strikes us. Chairman Pontus, Ministers Niotic and Fugoc, and Ambassador Sounor, each of you must do as General Morton has wisely counseled. Withdraw your treasures, both of coin and flesh, to the safety of the Torry interior. You shall conscript every able male in your municipalities to meet the enemy.

"In turn, we shall stand with you. General Morton shall lead the 5th Army to Notsu, and I shall march beside him." The Torry king would march east! Such boldness struck the majority of the council dumb. The blood drained from General Morton's face, unnerved by the king's decision.

"My people stand beside you, great king. We shall welcome your son and together smite Yonig's legions, vanquishing them from our land!" Minister Yotora declared.

"We stand with you as our peoples have done since our founding," El Anthar's distinct voice thundered.

A thought echoed in Terin's mind, a subtle urge to circle the table and again pledge his commitment to his king. King Lore's bold decision needed a grander affirmation, but it was not his place to do so. No sooner had he dismissed the thought out of hand than the power of his sword emanated from his side, forcing him to act upon his sudden inclination.

He felt his body move without him, circling the great table to approach the king. Terin knelt as he drew forth his father's sword, the light of the moon shining upon its blade. The sword burst in luminous blue light, drawing the awe of the council as they beheld its mysterious power.

"I stand beside you, my king, with the Sword of the Moon that you have trusted to my keeping. I shall be your shield against Morac's greater blade. Where you lead, I shall follow," Terin avowed, the sword's glow bathing his face with otherworldly light.

Master Vantel released a heavy sigh. He was inclined to admonish Terin's forwardness, addressing the king unbidden, but something about the boy seemed to disarm his wrath. He approached the king humbly, sans arrogance or self-import. Perhaps the sword had driven him to act so, as the king had warned Torg Vantel long before he oversaw Terin's training. He was advised to allow Terin to follow the sword's will even if it appeared counter to his training or good sense.

King Lore regarded young Caleph with quiet pride. He stepped toward Terin and placed a heavy hand upon the boy's head. "Your place is here until called for, Terin. You shall remain at Corell and continue to hone your sword craft under Master Vantel and to wait," he commanded.

"To wait, sire?" Terin asked.

"Until you are ready, child. Your sword shall guide you. My daughter shall command the realm in my place and whilst her brother is south. Guard her well." Lore ruffled Terin's hair.

"When the time comes to face Morac and the Sword of the Sun, you shall not stand alone!" the Jenaii warrior who attended El Anthar declared. He strode forth, stopping beside his liege while drawing his sword as he knelt opposite Terin. The assemblage gasped as the Jenaii warrior's blade burst in emerald light as the moon played upon its length.

"The champion of the Jenaii and keeper of the second Sword of the Moon, I present Elos, son of El Elon," El Anthar said, formally introducing his guardian.

The mystery of the whereabouts of the other Sword of the Moon was at last revealed. It was gifted to the Jenaii upon its forging, the sister blade to the sword gifted to King Zar of the Middle Kingdom. Perhaps their cause was not as forlorn as many believed. Terin and Elos arose as one, their swords touching as the pale moonlight played along their mysterious metal, enhancing their illumination to a near-blinding glow.

CHAPTER 11

She stood upon the outer battlements of the east wall of Corell, her golden hair lifting in the midday air as the king's procession disappeared over the horizon. They bade their farewells that morn in the king's private sanctum, her father touching a hand to her face, wiping a lone tear that escaped her eye.

*****

"I never thought to set eyes on another to surpass your mother's beauty until that day she set you in my arms," he said, his steely countenance softening whenever he saw her.

"You should remain here. Tyro's next foray could strike anywhere along our northern border. Why place yourself to our extreme east? Would it not be wiser to—" she protested before he placed a finger to her lips.

"Shh. A king must act as a king. A king must lead lest his soldiers doubt the worth of their cause. Our soldiers have met the enemy at Rego, and no member of our house stood upon the battlefield that day. I must march to the fore and parade with our men beyond the comforts of the palace."

"Is not Lorn doing so in Yatin? Allow him to take up his duty that he has long shirked." She couldn't mask her animosity for her brother's absence through the years. He was prone to adventurism, forsaking his duty for a personal quest that she understood not.

"Judge your brother gently, Corry. He has been distracted from his duty for reasons that are neither petty nor self-indulgent. In time, you shall know the worth of his efforts."

"Perhaps, but you needn't both be absent from Corell. The throne requires—"

"The realm requires our house to sit the throne. You"—he touched a finger to her nose—"you shall sit the throne in my absence."

"Father, I—" she protested before he again placed a finger to her lips.

"You shall rule in my place until my return. You are far wiser than I, Corry, a trait that marks you your mother's child." Her father was prone to speak of her mother, though Corry wished he would not. She died when Corry was a child, and the stoic princess loathed to rekindle the pain of her passing. It was best to bury such hurt. Her father held no such compunction, never failing to speak of his lost queen. When her mother passed, her father never loved again, refusing to wed and sire more heirs.

Her father told her often that love happened once in a single lifetime. Anything before was false, and anything after, empty. She wondered if she would be afforded the luxury of love when royal marriages were often arranged, placing duty over the longings of the heart.

"I am leaving young Caleph to serve as your guard and servant when he is not suffering Torg's tutelage," Lore said.

"Terin should be by your side, Father. It is his destiny to stand by his king! He—"

"He belongs where I choose to place him, Corry, and that is guarding my greatest treasure—*you*." He kissed her forehead before stepping without.

*****

Corry sighed at the memory of their parting. She felt as alone as she had during her captivity in that pirate camp. "Princess?" Terin's familiar voice echoed behind her. She turned as he stepped forth, his hair blowing freely in the breeze, his sea-blue eyes meeting hers briefly before he bowed his head and knelt. She regarded him for a moment, the contours of his limbs displayed by the sand-colored training tunic he wore. He appeared exhausted from his training, his morning spent under Torg Vantel's harsh regimen, no doubt.

"Arise, Terin," Corry softly commanded.

"You summoned me, Highness?" Terin asked. Torg had reluctantly granted him leave to attend the princess once the poor messenger who relayed her order withered under Torg's intense scowl. Terin dreaded returning to Torg, knowing the commander of the Torry Elite would exact their lost time from Terin's exhausted flesh.

"Yes. My father ordered you to attend me as my personal guard and servant when you are not otherwise training," Corry said, gauging his reaction.

"Yes. The king spoke briefly on the matter with me," Terin conceded.

"Very good. I see Master Vantel hasn't spared you his full effort." She gifted him a slight smile, noting the sweat glistening his flesh and the fatigue in his weary eyes.

"Master Vantel has been most generous in his instruction. I lack not in his attention, Highness." He smiled in turn, which made her happy.

"You are a fine apprentice, I am certain."

"I am a poor one, I am afraid. Of course, I couldn't be any worse a warrior than I was a scribe." He shrugged lightheartedly.

"You judge yourself too harshly, Terin. You were a fine minister's apprentice, though such is beneath your present calling."

"You are kind to speak so, Highness. I hope to prove worthy of your father's trust. I feel I should have traveled with him to Notsu," he lamented, regarding the columns of soldiers, ministers, King's Elite, and courtesans who accompanied the king. Even Yeltor sallied forth, riding with the king's royal guard. He bade his friend farewell that morn, thinking how strange it was to see the Yatin Elite now clad in Torry colors.

In the days following the council of Corell, the king was occupied with preparations and seeing off the visiting dignitaries as they returned to their respective realms. Terin was called to attend the king as they bade farewell to El Anthar and the Jenaii champion, Elos. Elos had taken Terin aside, placing a hand to his shoulder and advising him to follow the will of his sword. "Be mindful of the sword's power, but fight not its inclination," Elos had said. The Jenaii warrior did not tend to human emotion, his counsel given as cold truth. Terin nodded politely, conveying his understanding of Elos's sage advice.

He found the Jenaii's piercing silver eyes equally unsettling and calming. They were the eyes of a fearsome yet honorable people, and he wondered how deadly in battle they truly were. Elos regarded him respectfully before stepping away. Within moments, El Anthar had stepped to the edge of the inner battlements, spread his gray-white wings, and sprung into the air. Elos followed, joining their full contingent into the heavens. It was a sight Terin would never forget.

"The king placed you here to improve your swordsmanship and learn the skills required of a King's Elite." Corry's voice drew him from his thoughts.

"I will strive to prove worthy of his faith in me, Highness."

"You have proven so thus far, but rest not on great deeds that you have done, for a future defeat despoils the glories of the past."

CHAPTER 12

She closed her hands through the shallows of the creek, the fish escaping her grasp, her fingers grazing its scaly flesh. Her nostrils flared, angered by her continued failure to snare their supper. She had spent the better part of an hour in the stream with her trouser legs rolled to her knees, attempting to grab fish for their cookfire.

"You're getting better, wife. Perhaps you'll catch a minnow or two before sundown," Raven taunted her. She glared daggers at him as he sat high on the bank with his back against a thick porian, looking all too comfortable.

"Are you just going to sit there? Why don't you lend a hand, *husband?*" She snarled that last word as if it was the foulest word she could conjure.

"Why? You did question Cronus's and Alen's poor fishing last night. You said you could—"

"I know what I said! Are you going to help or sit there all day?"

"You want my help? All right. Step out of the water." He waved a hand to the side, signaling her to step clear. She regarded him warily as she climbed out of the stream, suspicious of that irritating tone that always portended him doing something to irk or annoy her. He remained where he was, sitting on the grass with his back against the tree as if he hadn't a care in the world. Once she stepped clear, he leveled his pistol at the water and fired several salvos of high-energy bursts, causing dozens of fish to float to the surface. "There. All done." He smiled.

Tosha regarded him with a murderous glare. Oh, how she hated him at times. After all their efforts to catch fish these past weeks and all this buffoon had to do was point his little toy at the water and catch all the fish his heart desired, it made her want to choke him.

"Now why don't you be a good *wife* and collect our supper," he said with that irritating smile on his face, holstering his pistol and placing his hands behind his head as he rested against the tree.

"I *am* a good wife," she said darkly, ambling toward him, making her way up the embankment.

Why Raven didn't move before she kicked him, he didn't know, but the look in her eyes when he killed those fish was worth her ire. His laughter after she kicked his knee only fueled her anger further, and she kicked him again. He caught her foot the second time and swept her other leg.

She fell atop of him, her face stopping inches from his own. "You're pretty when you're angry, Tosh." He grinned, looking up into her golden eyes. She opened her mouth to rebuke him but closed her lips, thinking it would only encourage him. She climbed off him and fetched their fish, not speaking a word to him for days.

*****

Cronus stared intently at the map stitched to the leather hide. They had taken it off a Benotrist patrol they ambushed two days prior. The map was quite detailed, depicting the southern region of the empire that bordered the eastern Plate Mountains. Most field maps were stitched to leather hides to weather the environment. Maps painted on parchment were superior in detail and breadth when used in the dry confines of a palace or pavilion but little good when exposed to the rain and soil of the open road.

The patrol didn't appear to be searching for them, and by their colors, they seemed to be vassals of a local proctor or holdfast. They were a half dozen soldiers clad in mustard-hued tunics and gray armor. Raven made quick work of them, attacking their lead mount and working his way to the rear as Cronus and Alen cut their retreat with a rope strung across the trail. Cronus discovered the map in a satchel of one of the slain.

The map was too rare and valuable to belong to a common soldier or lesser vassal. The man was an aristocrat most likely, and Cronus would make good use of his newfound treasure. They acquired seven days' worth of ocran feed, two bows, and better-forged steel swords than those they presently carried. They added two ocran, replacing two of their own, which were nearly lame.

"Where are we?" Alen asked, kneeling beside him, scanning the map spread upon the ground.

"Somewhere along this line." Cronus ran his finger just northeast of the Plate Mountains. "We passed the north-south road. That puts us here. A few more days of hard riding should place us along the northern shore of Lake Veneba." Cronus tapped the map where his finger finished.

"Then what?" Alen asked, his eyes focused on the Benotrist border that ran north of the lake. He had long resigned himself to never escaping this cursed land, but seeing the boundary so enticingly near clouded his pessimism. Could they actually escape?

"Then we go around the lake or over it," Cronus said, stating the obvious. "There are several ports along the north side of the lake—Far Point, Torela, Axenville, and Stapero," he rattled off the names, reading them west to east.

"Will you risk discovery?" Alen asked warily, fearing they would be recognized if they entered any populace areas so near the Benotrist border.

"We may have to risk it." Cronus scrubbed his chin with his hand. The Benotrist border straddled the northern approaches of Far Point and Torela. That would favor them toward the independent ports of Axenville and Stapero, but even those ports fell under strong Benotrist influence. They would find few friends in any of the ports mentioned. "All we need is a boat suitable enough to ferry us south," Cronus lamented, his eye running the length of the north-south road that connected Nisin in the north to the crossroads of Bacel and Notsu in the south.

It would be far simpler to shadow the road south and cross the border, but they had spotted long columns of troops marching south along the road. The troops were far too many to search just for them, and he feared what their true objective might be. Either way, word of their route of travel had likely spread, and they could expect a poor reception at all points between Lake Veneba and the Plate foothills. Even if they circumvented the Benotrists at the border, they would be exposed along the Kregmarin Plain, where water was scarce and where they could be easily spotted by a magantor patrol from afar.

Cronus lifted his head as Tosha stormed into their campsite, her arms full of fish, a vicious scowl gracing her face. Alen drew away as she drew near, dropping her bounty at their feet before marching to the nearest tree and sitting down. Cronus was about to commend her impressive haul when Raven entered their midst. He was about to ask what ailed Tosha when Raven merely shrugged his shoulders as if he hadn't a clue, which clearly meant he was the cause. Alen stepped forward to gather the fish for their cookfire, avoiding Tosha's admonishing stare.

"Well done, Princess. Your efforts exceeded—" Cronus praised before she curtly interrupted.

"I didn't catch them!"

"You didn't—"

"Raven's quite the fisherman. Perhaps you should ask him the nature of this unique skill he seems to have hidden," she said icily.

And so it went throughout the night, Tosha speaking of Raven but never to him. Raven simply ignored her, pretending not to care, but his irritability proved otherwise. Cronus was too tired to be drawn in the middle of their quarrel. Their constant bickering seemed the only thing either of them ever did since they captured her. Cronus thought wistfully of his sweet Leanna. He never recalled arguing with her in any way. He fondly recalled the times he held her, the warmth of her body against his as they embraced. That was love, true love as he knew it.

What Raven and Tosha shared might be love, but their volatile tempers threatened to kill it in its infancy. Raven couldn't forgive her treachery at Fera, and Tosha couldn't forgive him for spoiling her plans. Oddly, she didn't seem angry about him taking her captive, perhaps seeing it as an opportunity to rekindle what they once had. She truly believed she could convince Raven that returning to her mother's isle was to their collective benefit. As the days dragged into weeks, she began to doubt she could do so.

The late evening found Cronus tending the fire as Alen lay fast asleep while Tosha sat beside him, staring forlornly into the crackling flames. Raven sat opposite her, stealing an occasional glance at his wife but finding only derision in return. "I gotta take a leak," he growled, gaining his feet and stepping away. Cronus shook his head at his friend's coarse language, Raven's blunt utterances never failing to make him laugh.

He wondered if all Earthmen were so base in their speech. No. Kato was well-spoken and respectful in his discourse. Lorken and Brokov lay somewhere in between and were both merciless in their goading of Raven. They were akin to brothers or brothers-in-arms, which they actually were. In a way, they were not much different from his own men. He quickly shook such sentiments from his mind, not willing to relive their fell end. He could see Tosha glaring at Raven's retreating form, her golden eyes ablaze, following him with heated fury.

"Your anger serves little purpose," Cronus said softly, "if regaining his trust is your aim."

"Trust?" She nearly spat. "Any delusions I held to ever have such with that imbecile is beyond us. He lives to torment me, relishing my misery." She sighed, her voice losing its ire before yielding to despair. Her morning illness had worsened these past days, waging war upon anything she ate. The fish Alen cooked for dinner barely passed her palate before she threw it up. She expected Raven to mock her misery, but surprisingly, he touched a hand to her shoulder—a clumsy attempt to win her favor, no doubt. After his antics earlier, she felt no such compunction to grant it.

"A little kindness might bear fruit, Tosha."

"To what end? Am I not his prisoner? My life is now his. What fate awaits me once we reach his ship?" she asked darkly.

"We only wish to escape these lands, Princess. I am certain Raven will set you free once we have done so."

"Your faith in your friend's magnanimity is misplaced, Cronus. He shall exact his vengeance on my flesh. He claims I planned his enslavement, yet tonight, it is I that wears his chains."

"That wouldn't be necessary if we didn't fear you would run away," Cronus said.

"Or slit my throat in my sleep!" Raven snorted as he returned.

She stared at him, her countenance betraying no emotion. She simply lifted her wrists toward him for binding. Raven took hold of her wrists, gripping them with one hand while retrieving her manacles with his free hand. He spun her around, binding her hands behind her before pushing her to her knees and walking away.

"He hates me," she said in a dead voice, her eyes trailing him as he stormed off.

"Hates you?" Cronus lifted a curious brow. "Raven is not difficult to predict, Princess. If you bite him, he'll bite back. Of all the emotions that conflict him in regard to you, hate is certainly not one of them. If he torments you, it is merely his childish attempt at revenge for all the slights you intended for him. I've seen Raven angry but never hateful. The only time he leans toward such is when he sees blatant injustice."

"Injustice?" She raised a brow. "One's injustice is another's righteous act. What qualifies as injustice to one such as him?" She lifted her chin toward the direction where Raven went.

Cronus's lips slightly lifted at the corners, recalling a memory.

"It was nearly a year past when Raven and I met upon the wharves of Plestia, a small port south and east of Cagan, near the Macon coast. I was there in service to the crown, and he was there on other matters. We passed a merchant vessel anchored along the wharves, its colors bearing the crimson swords upon a field of gold, the flag of the Casian port of Teris. There was a lad no older than a dozen years, but by his diminutive stature, he could've been younger. He was unloading casks from the hold of the ship onto the wharf, much too large for one so small. His feet were bare, and he wore a threadbare tunic that was no better than a rag.

"The boy struggled up and down the gangplank, straining under the burdensome weight he bore without complaint. Many of the crew of full-grown men loitered upon the deck and wharf, offering nothing but derision and jeers. One fellow stuck out a foot, tripping the child. The boy tumbled to the wharf, the cask he bore breaking upon its fall, spilling its vintage Bedoan ale upon the dock. The ship's captain, a scar-faced, lengthy fellow with greasy golden hair and narrow-set gray eyes, stormed down the gangplank, shouting obscenities that would make a sailor blush.

"He vented his anger on the hapless child, not the wretch who tripped him. He cuffed the child about the head repeatedly. From our view, we could see the iron band about the boy's throat, marking him a slave. Child slavery is forbidden in Torry South, but the harbor magistrates don't enforce such laws upon foreign-flagged merchants. Raven, however, held no such distinction. He stormed across the wharf, knocking sailors aside as if they were made of straw. The captain's foul eyes drew wide as he beheld Raven's approach. Raven beat that man nearly to death. The crew tried to intervene, but he swatted them aside. I had to step forth, as some were tempted to draw steel, warning them that to do so would cause their death by my blade.

"Raven pounded the ship's captain until he lay upon the wharf a blood-soaked pile of flesh. He then beat the sailor that tripped the boy. Raven's face was terrible to behold that day, his dark eyes ablaze as if he could burn men with his gaze. The ship's crew stood down, each fearful of his terrible fury and that they might be next. It was a side of Raven that I would never forget, an unchecked rage that I wish no good man to suffer. It is a fury reserved for evil men, and what man is more evil than one who would harm a child?"

"What of the boy?" she asked curiously. Cronus smiled fondly, recalling what followed.

"Raven took the boy, broke his collar, and paid for his apprenticeship as a blacksmith in an inland village."

"What of the captain? Did he heal and try to retrieve the boy?"

"Raven took the captain and the fool who tripped the boy aboard the *Stenox* bound hand and foot. He thought to slay them outright but knew that death was not the justice they deserved. He sold them as galley slaves in Varabis to a vicious corsair captain who took great pleasure in beating his slaves."

Tosha reflected on Cronus's tale, her ire subdued. Would she suffer a child abused in her sight without intervening? She suddenly thought of all the Menotrists enslaved by her father. Alen was a child when the slave collar was affixed to his neck. He was oft beaten, and she thought nothing of it. Did he see her as a monster the way Raven saw the ship's captain? And what of Cronus's men? She knew prisoners suffered in her father's dungeon but never thought it more than for the extraction of secrets and knowledge vital to her father's cause. Raven shattered such illusion when he told her what he saw in that foul place. She turned her eyes from Cronus, ashamed for what he suffered.

"I am sorry for what my father did to your men," she said, her voice barely a whisper and laced with shame.

Three days hence

They rode neath the shade of the broad-leafed paccel trees, the wind whispering through their upper boughs, rustling the leaves overhead. They braved the cobblestone road that traversed the forest along the northern shores of Lake Veneba. A mere two leagues separated them from the port village of Axenville, an independent freehold that had yet to be absorbed by the Benotrist Empire.

Tyro could seize the port at his convenience, along with the remaining freeholds along the Veneban shores, but hadn't prior to the war's commencement so as not to alarm his future adversaries of his true intent. But despite the port's independence, Cronus was wary of man hunters and mercenaries who frequented freeholds. Even if Axenville did not stand beneath Tyro's banners, his spies and servants certainly dwelled therein.

It was late morning, and Cronus led their party along the narrow pathway, the broad-leafed paccels crowding the road's edge. They rode south and east, drawing ever closer to Axenville and their route of escape. The road ahead suddenly widened to an acre-sized meadow to either side. A small, rocky ridge ran on the southwestern side of the road before disappearing into the forest beyond. The road did likewise, its cobblestone causeway entering the forest at the base of the small ridge. The forest ran to the edge of the ridgeline along its apex.

Raven rode up alongside Cronus, tossing the reins of Tosha's mount to Alen, who trailed them. Tosha sat on her mount, gripping the pommel with her hands bound before her. Cronus knew Raven's demeanor well enough to know something was amiss.

"There's a party of men in the road ahead," Raven warned.

"Coming toward us or away?"

"Toward us."

"How many?"

"Thirty plus. It's hard to tell through the pistol's scope when they're bunched up like that. They're on foot by the looks of it."

"How far off?" Cronus asked, his eyes narrowed as he stared ahead, as if he could see them through the forest.

"Quarter mile, so we best get set up unless you want to head straight into the forest. I say we smack 'em here."

Smack 'em here. Cronus shook his head. Only Raven could speak so casually of dispatching such a force with little more thought than that. They had conducted countless similar ambushes throughout their trek, taking little chance of leaving witnesses to their presence. They avoided contact when possible, sometimes traveling a fair distance, circumventing patrols and avoiding the slaughter of innocent peasants.

"We're too damn close to Axenville to waste half the day lost in the trees," Raven grunted.

"All right," Cronus conceded. "Let's get in position." He and Alen moved apace, riding to the far end of the clearing and up the ridge off their right. The shallow rise allowed their ocran to traverse the rocky slope more easily.

Raven watched as his comrades slipped within the tree line. He did likewise at the northwestern end of the clearing. Passing within the sheltering trees, he tethered his mount to a sturdy bough and waited at the forest edge, crouched behind a thick truck of a paccel.

The position provided a clear view of the meadow below and enough concealment to mask his presence until the quarry was fully exposed in the clearing.

"Keep her secure and quiet," Cronus whispered, leaving Alen and Tosha well within the tree line at the southeastern end of the ridge. With his mount tethered beside theirs, he crept south and east along the ridge before making his way back down the slope, where the trees masked his approach. He kept well within the foliage that bordered the road, waiting for the men to pass. He could hear them through the trees, the sounds of spears clanging off shields and the mingled discord of a dozen voices. The midday sun filtered through the treetops, reflecting off their polished helms. Cronus backed farther into the tree line, keeping well out of sight until they passed.

Raven held his aim as the column of soldiers entered the clearing, waiting for the last to step into the clear. He counted roughly thirty-five soldiers in nondescript gray mail over brown tunics. They carried spears the length of a man with shortswords upon their hips. Half wore their helms while others carried theirs in their free hand. Their shields were slung over their backs, and they were too large a force to be anything but Benotrist militia patrolling the border lands. He noticed a gangly fellow dressed in a knee-length green tunic with a mandolin strapped over his shoulder and his hands bound before him. The man had a mop of brown hair that fell well below his shoulders and a distinct sharp nose that didn't fit his face.

"They probably arrested him to keep his face from the public. No need to scare small children," Raven mumbled. "Time to get to work, I reckon," he added, taking aim at a soldier with decorative feathers affixed to his helm, a primitive sign of his rank, most likely. The soldier marched at the fore, leading the others in a disorganized gaggle.

Zip! Blue laser struck the leader's left cheek, dropping him as if he was a puppet whose strings were cut. The laser exited the back of his skull, striking a trailing soldier in the gut before striking the road in front of another, kicking up gravel upon impact. *Zip! Zip! Zip!* Three more laser blasts followed before the column broke in panic, each blast cutting through their serried ranks to great effect. Their brief inaction swiftly shifted to panic as they broke in each direction as several of their comrades dropped in the road.

Raven's aim followed a group of seven who fled east across the meadow, hoping to reach the safety of the trees. His first blast took the trailing soldier in the lower back, his face planting in the grass as he fell. Laser fire swept them from behind, dropping them one by one, the men oblivious to their comrades' fate behind them until a laser blast struck them down in detail.

Another group turned and ran whence they came, running south and east along the cobblestone road where the forest encroached close to the path's edge. They fared little better, Raven's laser thinning their ranks. Few died on impact while most lingered with laser bursts burning cavernous holes through their torsos, limbs, or necks.

One broke free from his comrades, clearing the edge of the meadow where the path met the forest. He took no more than a third step before laser struck his left thigh. He dropped his spear, tumbling to the ground, the gravel digging into his bare knees. Before he could attempt to gain his feet, Cronus burst from the foliage, driving his sword into the soldier's back.

Cronus swiftly withdrew the blade and hacked a hasty blow to the man's neck before moving to the edge of the clearing. He surveyed the hellish visage as men lay strewn across the gravel road, their twisted bodies writhing in anguish like fish cast upon the sand. Some limped, only to be cut down by Raven's deadly fire. Blue laser flashed brightly across the open ground, lighting the sky with terrible intensity.

Cronus drew his sword close, ready to step forth and finish those who lingered, when the hairs on his neck tingled. Cronus turned, craning his neck to the road as it meandered south through the forest. Panic took his heart, the rustling of branches disturbing the stillness behind him.

Several moments before

Alen waited nervously within the tree line just as the column of soldiers first emerged from the forest along the cobble road. Cronus waited somewhere below and to his right while Raven was positioned farther north and west along the ridge. Their ocran were tied off to the low-hanging branches farther back, save for Tosha's, whose reins Alen held in his hand as she sat on her mount, her hands manacled before her as she gripped the pommel. She wore a loose tunic sans her favored trousers and no shoes to limit her freedom should she think to flee. Alen could barely discern the soldiers moving below, only able to see the tops of their helms through the foliage of the trees.

"A column of unwitting fools marching blindly to their death." Tosha sighed.

Alen craned his neck, fixing his eyes to hers. "Unwitting fools that serve your father."

"All men serve their own interests," she quipped.

"Even slaves?" he asked bitterly of his former mistress.

"Especially slaves. Is it not in their interest to live?" she whispered darkly as he averted his eyes, taking an ill-advised step toward her. She thrust her left foot to his head, catching him unawares, the reins slipping from his weakened grip. She sprang from her mount, snatching the dagger from his belt and pressing it to his neck as he struggled to gain his wits. "Move even *one* finger, and I'll slit your throat!" she warned.

"Raven and Cronus will…" he tried to say as she pressed the dagger deeper into his neck.

"They can't help you now, slave," she hissed, straddling Alen as he lay still. Even with her hands bound, she had enough slack in her chain to finish him if she chose. Why she hadn't was beyond him. She swiftly slid off him, keeping the dagger to his neck as she moved above his head, quickly shifting her hands, only briefly taking the blade from his throat and reapplying it before he could react. "Remove your sword with your left hand and set it aside!" she commanded. Alen obeyed, pulling the blade free of its scabbard and tossing it aside. "Close your eyes!" He did so, feeling the dagger ease from his throat.

Tosha retrieved the sword, tossing the dagger far afield. She wasted little time gaining her mount and riding off through the trees, the sounds of death echoing below with the flash of Raven's terrible weapon spewing deadly volleys. She skirted the clearing, keeping to the trees as she angled for the road at the base of the ridge. She swerved between trees, ducking branches and cutting through the barbed foliage that cut her naked limbs. She burst onto the road, holding the hilt of the sword in her right hand and the reins in her left.

Cronus turned at the sound of snapping branches, catching sight of her as her mount broke free of the trees. She regarded him briefly, her golden eyes narrowed as she beheld the carnage wrought behind him. Before he could react, she turned sharply, kicking her heels, urging her ocran southeast along the road.

Before Cronus could decide a course of action, Alen burst onto the road near the place Tosha had emerged atop his mount with Cronus's in tow. Cronus gained his mount and chased Tosha, keeping her in sight before she slipped away and warned others of their presence with no time to warn Raven lest she escape.

*****

Zip! Laser fire found another soldier in the back, sending him tumbling in the grass near the east end of the clearing. Raven lowered his pistol, surveying his deadly work. The dead and dying littered the clearing, some writhing painfully on the ground, their hands pressed against the gaping holes in their flesh. Some crawled away, their entrails trailing in the matted grass. Others lay still upon the gravel road, dead where they dropped, their bodies twisted in unnatural angles. Some fared better, suffering wounds to their legs, leaving them to Raven's mercy once he descended the ridge.

Raven caught sight of something stirring in the center of the road, a blur of green amid the bodies piled to either side. Raven mounted up and rode to the base of the ridge. *Zip! Zip!* He brained

182

two soldiers in his path, moving carefully beside the road, blasting each of the fallen in the head to be sure of them. *Zip! Zip! Zip!*

He fired, moving methodically in the grizzly task, staying parallel to the road as the green blur ahead stopped moving, hoping to go unnoticed. The blur was likely the gangly prisoner he had spotted amid the column.

"It's all clear. You can stand up now!" Raven commanded, but the fellow remained in place, not trusting the crazed Earther who had cut down a column of soldiers with such little effort.

Zip! A blast struck a corpse nearest the cowering fellow, caving its head and splattering blood in his hair. "Stand up, or I'll do the same for you!" Raven warned as he looked afield, wondering Cronus's whereabouts.

"Mercy, my large friend," the fellow pleaded, rising from the road, lifting his bound hands with a rope dangling between them.

"Who are you?" Raven questioned, not liking the look of him. He was gangly and had a pompous air about him that Raven despised. He reminded him of the nerds who used to irritate him in his formative school.

"I am Galen, a minstrel and bard of great renown among the more learned and cultured. I have performed in the royal courts of Corell, El-Orva, and Fleace, as well as the city states of—"

"You're a humble little fella, ain't you? Why did this bunch take you prisoner?" Raven cut his winded explanation short.

"Though a wandering minstrel holds to no crown or realm, I am Torry born. These simpletons suspected me of nefarious activities. They falsely claimed that I was a *spy*—a spy of the Torry throne, no less. My valiant attempts to explain my impartiality in such things were poorly met by their woeful ignorance of my vocation. Your fortuitous intervention has spared my person a most uncertain fate, my friend."

"Torry, huh?" Raven snorted. The minstrel certainly didn't look Torry. Of course, he didn't look like anything else either. He was tall for an Araxan at nearly sixty-five inches with a stick-thin build and limbs far too long for his body. His narrow face and pointed, aristocratic nose presented a condescending aura that Raven took an immediate dislike to. Raven thought seriously of blasting a hole through the idiot's skull but knew Cronus would scold him if he did. Besides, if he was an enemy of the Benotrists, he might be of some use. Perhaps they might use him as a diversion to further their own escape.

"You seem oddly attired, and you carry a weapon of some mystical properties of which I am unfamiliar. Your name, good sir?" Galen asked curiously.

"My name is none of your business, minstrel. Now why don't you grab a knife and cut your bonds while I finish this rabble?" Raven grunted as he dismounted, tying off the reins to the leg of the nearest corpse. Looking southeast where the road disappeared into the forest, he wondered where Cronus was. He marched quickly across the road, leaving his mount near the minstrel. *Zip!* He fired a blast, taking another in the head as the fellow attempted to crawl away with a severed spine.

"Cronus!" Raven shouted as he drew nearer the forest, his pistol trained on the road ahead where the shade of the forest obscured his vision while standing in the bright light of the clearing. Stepping within the trees, he found sign of Cronus's handiwork but no sign of Cronus or Alen or Tosha. "Come on!" he growled impatiently. "Where the hell are they?" He wondered if they might be repaying him for his fishing prank.

Galen found a blade among the fallen and set it between his feet, working his bonds along the blade until he was free. Once free, he searched the men around him, finding the soldier who took his belt of daggers when they first seized him. He found the soldier still alive, gasping for air with a hole burned through his right breast. Galen thought him dead until the stricken fellow stirred, lifting a shaking hand to the minstrel. He appeared to be pleading for some boon, his pallid lips moving without words as if a simple utterance was beyond him now.

Galen offered a false smile before running a blade across the man's throat. He wiped the blood from the blade on the soldier's tunic and retrieved his belt of daggers, a quick count confirming that all seven were present and in good order. He quickly lifted his tunic, strapping the belt beneath its long folds before smoothing the skirt of the garment, concealing them beneath.

Galen pondered his next course of action. He needed to place as many leagues between this carnage and himself as possible before more Benotrists arrived. After such a slaughter, they would likely scour this entire region with hundreds of soldiers. He needed to be long gone before that happened, which brought his attention to the stranger's ocran standing unattended.

The large buffoon had stormed off along the road, looking in vain for his comrades. They probably fled at the outset, hoping to leave his boorish presence, no doubt. The oaf kept calling out for Cronus, whoever that was. It was all quite pathetic.

Soon, the ruffian stormed up the far end of the ridgeline, cursing obscenities as he trudged up the slow rise. Galen saw him trip on a rock about halfway through his ascent, stumbling clumsily with his face planting in the rough terrain. He gained his feet, shouting even more obscenities while kicking the offending rock as if that would undo his clumsiness.

"Dolt." Galen snickered, shaking his head at Raven's misfortune. He watched as Raven cursed even more upon his search of the tree line before trudging north along the ridge where he had commenced his ambush. He watched patiently as Raven descended the ridge and continued dispatching the soldiers who still lingered, starting toward the northern edge of the clearing. As soon as Raven's back was turned, Galen loosed and mounted Raven's ocran, galloping south along the road.

"Hey!" Raven shouted as Galen disappeared into the forest with laser fire striking the trees as he slipped from sight. Raven growled and cursed, storming across the clearing to follow the road south. In the span of a few minutes, he had lost his comrades and his mount. Axenville was a few miles southeast, and it seemed the only option left to him. Perhaps he would find the rotten minstrel somewhere along the way. This time, he wouldn't hesitate to snuff out his miserable life, correcting his parents' mistake of conceiving him in the first place.

*****

She pushed her lathered mount to its limit, its powerful hooves kicking stones as they clapped the road. She stole a hasty glance over her shoulder, spying Cronus closing fast. Dense forest encroached upon either side of the narrow road, and she thought of forsaking her ocran and losing her pursuers afoot in the thick foliage. She turned a sharp bend, briefly losing sight of Cronus. The road split up ahead, the left fork jutting due east and the right straight south. With little time to weigh her decision, she angled east, leaning in the saddle as her ocran turned sharp at the bend. Her sudden turn caught the riders ahead by surprise as a dozen soldiers in gray mail over forest-green tunics blocked her path.

"Whoa!" their leader shouted, trying to calm his mount as it reared into the air. To Tosha's credit, she stayed in the saddle and retained her grip on her sword as she pulled back on the reins, her ocran stopping short of colliding with the others. Once the initial surprise eased on the soldiers' faces, they regarded her with keen interest, taking in her fair countenance and bound wrists with curiosity. Armed soldiers in the proximity of the Benotrist border likely explained their loyalty, and considering their lustful stares, she decided to play her hand.

"I am Princess Tosha, crown princess of the Benotrist throne!" she declared, leveling her sword toward them. "I was taken captive hundreds of leagues to our west. I have escaped my captors, and they pursue me even now. I—"

"I am commander of flax Favel Cratus of border garrison Baxtel. Our holdfast rests three leagues north and east, Highness." He regarded her with deep reverence, his countenance shifting dramatically upon her outlandish declaration. Word of her capture must have been relayed to the farthest reaches of the empire. What else could explain these men to so quickly believe her?

"The men who follow me, I want *alive!*" Tosha commanded.

*****

Cronus pushed his mount to its utmost, struggling to keep Tosha in view as sunlight flickered through the trees, playing havoc with his vision as shade and light passed with rapidity. He thought to let her escape, needing to warn Raven of their whereabouts, but he had halved the distance to her and hoped to catch her in short order.

Thoughts of her alerting others to their presence or getting her fool self killed weighed equally on his mind. He wished they could safely leave her with one of her father's garrisons and be on their way but doubted they would look the other way while they escaped. Whether they liked it or not, they were stuck with her.

Alen drifted farther behind, still uncertain in the saddle. As a palace slave, he had never ridden an ocran until they fled the hamlet where their magantors were slain. His riding skills had vastly improved but still lacked Cronus's or Tosha's years in the saddle.

Tosha slipped briefly from sight with the curve of the road. He pushed onward, taxing his mount further lest she slip into the forest while out of his line of sight. Cronus's heart sank as he cleared the bend as he beheld the fork in the road ahead. With little time to choose his path, he sped straight south before noticing the cavalry blocking the east fork in his periphery as he passed in front of them.

"Faster, Alen!" he shouted over his shoulder, knowing they had little choice but to outrun their pursuers southward. Any hope of turning back to Raven was impossible with the enemy upon them and their own ocran running apace in the opposite direction.

Cronus guided his mount through the winding roadway, swerving around low-hanging boughs jutting into their path. He continued apace, dipping his head beneath a jagged branch before leaning sharply into a severe turn. He could hear Alen close behind, the sound of the ocran's hooves dulled by the shouts of their pursuers.

"Ow!" Alen cried out, a low branch catching him full in the chest, knocking him from the saddle. His small body lifted briefly in the air before crashing into the cobblestone road. Cronus spared a quick glance, seeing his friend fall, a number of the enemy breaking off their pursuit to seize him. A few continued on, forcing Cronus to distance himself further form his comrades.

*****

"#@&%" Raven mumbled, the curses escaping his lips without cease as he followed the road south. He trudged along, wondering where Cronus and the others had fled while keeping an eye out for that miserable minstrel. Galen! He remembered the creature's fool name, committing it to memory. It was a name he would never forget. "Who the hell names their son Galen?" he growled. "His parents probably hated him once they saw his miserable head emerge from the birth canal. I hated him when I first saw him fifty yards off."

*****

Galen slowed his mount to an easy trot once he distanced himself from the clumsy oaf, smiling for his sudden turn of fortune. Just moments before, he was a prisoner to a band of Benotrist conscripts, and now his captors were dead, and he was free, riding south with a healthy mount, his mandolin across his back, and an open road to Axenville. The small port was where he was originally headed when he was so rudely apprehended.

He received an extra boon after a cursory search of his ocran's saddle packs revealed numerous silver coins, ocran feed, several days of food, and a large bedroll. He needed only to ride to Axenville, sell his newfound ocran, and pay for passage across Lake Veneba. Perhaps he could partake of a fine meal before continuing his journey across the lake. Axenville had numerous taverns along its scenic waterfront where he could purchase such a feast.

The sound of hooves up ahead kicking up stones interrupted Galen's fanciful musings as several riders rounded the bend. His practiced calm faltered as he recognized the sour faces of the riders as they circled him with spears leveled. "How many times must we arrest you, minstrel?" their leader brashly asked.

Galen stole a furtive glance at the one rider he did not know—a woman, no less. She had a strange air about her with midnight hair framing an achingly beautiful face and piercing golden eyes that glared at him with murderous intent. Had he wronged this woman somehow? Perhaps. He often offended those who crossed his path with relative ease. Why should this woman be any different?

"Ah, Commander Favel, I would be remiss to not bid thee a fair afternoon. It is a pleasure to rekindle our brief acquaintance."

"A pleasure?" Favel Cratus asked. "We seized this minstrel early this morn, Highness. I delivered him over to one of our foot contingents. They are most likely the ones that encountered your captors." Galen listened as Favel directed his statement to the woman mounted beside him.

"Highness?" Galen asked bemusedly.

"Guard your tongue, minstrel, for you stand in the presence of royalty!" Favel warned.

"I am humbled, Commander Cratus. To which royal line is the princess akin?" Galen asked.

"None of your concern, minstrel. Now—" Favel said before Tosha interrupted.

"Where did you find *that* ocran?" Tosha asked darkly.

Galen smiled, finally able to look directly at the princess, bowing with practiced deference. "Your Highness, I am humbled in your esteemed presence."

"Where did you find your ocran, minstrel? Answer before I cut your tongue from your pompous mouth!" Tosha leveled her blade to Galen's throat.

"My pardon, Highness. I apologize for my boorish salutation. I—"

"Answer me *now*!" Tosha lost her patience knowing Galen sat on Raven's mount, fearing what had befallen him.

"I relieved this mount from a most unpleasant fellow. He was grotesquely large, uncouth, and ill-mannered. I hope your royal person never suffers his disagreeable presence."

"Is he *alive*?" she snarled.

"Regrettably so, Highness. I was fortunate to flee his insufferable presence, borrowing his ocran whilst he was otherwise distracted. He is now afoot, and I hoped to distance myself from him before he finds me."

"You stole his mount?" Tosha asked with a surprised look.

"Highness, I am not a thief." Galen touched a hand to his heart with pained indignation. "I merely relieved this poor beast of having to bear his former master's immense bulk. It was an act of mercy, not of theft."

"Commander, what was the minstrel's crime?" Tosha asked curiously.

"He is a suspected subversive, Highness."

"Subversive?" She lifted a dark brow.

"He is Torry born, Highness," Favel explained.

Tosha thought briefly, an idea coming to mind. "Release him. Send him on his way."

*****

They watched from the concealment of the forest as the Earther passed, keeping within the foliage to mask their presence. The princess sagely advised them to *not* engage the Earther. She wanted him alive and unharmed. She said it was far too dangerous to confront him in the open. It was wiser to allow him to reach Axenville, where he might be undone in the narrow streets and confines of the lakeshore village.

*****

Axenville was a small trading port with a transient populace that fluctuated with the seasons. Rich vineyards dotted the rolling hills to the east, overlooking the lake. Wealthy landowners moved their goods through the various coastal ports of Lake Veneba, employing small armies to safeguard their lands and trading routes. Axenville, like many of the ports along the lake, was a freehold, holding no allegiance to the surrounding regencies or city states, though its proximity to the Benotrist Empire swayed its sympathies.

Axenville was the demarcation line where the Tartov Forest met the rolling hillside vineyards that stretched east along the northern shore of the lake. The small port was a well-traveled stopping point for merchants, slavers, fishermen, mercenaries, and man hunters searching for fugitives from the far side of the lake.

Galen couldn't swallow his grin as the forest road gave way to the open fields that circled the small port below. He could not believe his good fortune. He had managed not only to escape his captors and abscond with a fine ocran and a pouch of silver but he was also given free passage by the Benotrists, who seemed more interested in the large oaf he robbed.

The road exited the forest, following the west bank of a small stream that led directly through the village. The village outskirts were poorly guarded, allowing any traveler to pass freely between the simple cottages dotting the approaches to the port. The dwellings were an odd mix ranging from thatched huts to strongly built timber abodes. The only stone structures were the village magistrate in the village center and slaver pens near the waterfront.

Galen passed a wooden bridge that traversed the stream to his left, connecting the two sides of the village. The people he passed were a varied sort of merchants, laborers, and local gentry. The wealthier merchants and landowners wore modest robes in hues of emerald, gray, and crimson. Laborers and slaves wore only simple tunics and sandals, the latter wearing iron collars about their necks, denoting their chattel status.

At the far end of the avenue, where the road met the water's edge, was a tavern with the name Severed Skull emblazoned over its front door. It was a single-level structure constructed with weathered dark timbers and a stone footer lining its front. Galen planned to sell the ocran and purchase passage over the lake, but it was late in the day, and he thought to sate his gnawing hunger and dry palate. A hitching post was conveniently driven into the ground in front of the tavern. He dismounted, tied off his reins, grabbed his mandolin, smoothed his tunic, and stepped inside.

The Severed Skull had a large open floor dotted with dozens of men crowding small tables with serving wenches fetching food and ale. A bar ran the length of the back wall with an open doorway behind it that led to the kitchen. Generously placed lanterns brightly illuminated the tavern floor, matching the preference of its naturally suspicious patrons, who viewed dark places as likely traps to be ambushed. Nothing soured a festive atmosphere like a customer being stabbed in the back.

Galen received few strange looks, blending to the environment as well as could be expected. He approached the bar where a barkeep served drinks to those standing along its length. The fellow wore a coarse apron over his dark tunic. He looked to be well into his fifth decade with wide-set green eyes that looked faded with age. He was of a height to Galen with long hair tied behind his head.

"My dear fellow, are you the proprietor of this revered establishment? I must confess, my fastidious nature is not often moved in these nether regions, but even my discerning taste acknowledges quality when I see it." Galen's false flattery failed to move the barkeep, who simply stared at him with obvious indifference.

"We serve food and drink if you have the coin," the barkeep stated flatly. Though Galen could well afford the price, he loathed parting with a coin if there was another way as long as that way required minimal effort.

"Perhaps I might exchange my illustrious talent for a meal and drink?" Galen smiled, setting his mandolin upon the bar.

A minstrel? the barkeep mused. "Play us a tune, minstrel. If the customers favor your song, then you'll have your food and drink."

*****

"Where the hell are they?" Raven grumbled as he trudged along, his heavy boots kicking stones as he walked. The forest gave way as Axenville came into view, resting below the slopes of three small hills. A few peasants working the fields north of the village paid him curious stares but returned to their labor. Before every engagement, Raven and Cronus established specific primary and alternative rally points in case they were separated. Axenville was their alternate rally point and was as good a place to look as any other.

The streets were oddly quiet as he entered the village. He kept a wary eye for crossbows peeking through windows or archers who might try their luck from around corners and rooftops. He first planned to search the waterfront before fetching an ocran from the stables. He would have to steal one now that that rotten minstrel stole his coins along with his mount. The road transitioned into the village's main thoroughfare with various structures of note along either side of the street, but Raven's attention was drawn to the tavern at the end of the avenue and the familiar ocran tied off to the hitching post in front.

*****

"Pluck another tune, minstrel!" several patrons chorused as Galen finished the last verse of "The Maiden's Flower." He sat atop the bar, overlooking the crowded tavern with his mandolin in hand. He had played a dozen songs and ballads without cease, pleasing the tavern's denizens, who offered coin to bribe another tune from his repertoire. He really needed to be on his way but overheard that all the port's boats were currently away, which was unusual. His only concern was if the Benotrists patrolling north of the village thought to enter therein and arrest him a second time. Nay, they would be more than occupied caging that oafish fool who slaughtered their men.

"As you have been a worthy audience, perhaps I shall sing one last ballad to reward your gracious regards," Galen said with a sing-song voice that was much too high. *Which melody should I play?* he mused briefly before the answer came to him. *Ah!* He smiled as the song came to mind. "Perchance, have you heard 'The Offending Minstrel'?" he asked. The patrons seemed unaware of the ballad and collectively shrugged or nodded in the negative as Galen began.

> There dwelled a minstrel from land afar
> Whose wit was sharp and tact ajar
> His king heard tell of his ballads bold

Of love, hope, and fortune gold
Tales of joy and wedded bliss
Of true love and a maiden's kiss
The king desired a ballad true
To woo a lass with eyes of blue
His bride she'd be his with love so tried
Yet the minstrel's song was gauche and snide
Tales of ancient battles lost
Days of dread and rising cost
He bowed to the future queen and king
His voice cracked as he did sing
He asked if 'twas not plain to see
Her mismatched eyes and teeth but three
Her narrow hips and nose so flat
Pallid lips and ears that flap
Death to him the king did cry
But quickly did the minstrel fly

The patrons roared, some spitting their drinks with laughter while others nearly fell off their chairs. Galen bowed his head, sweeping his arms out to his sides, acknowledging their praise. When he lifted his head, his brown eyes drew wide with abject horror. "You!" Raven growled, barging through the front door, nearly tearing it from its hinges. He stood in the doorframe silhouetted by the sunlight behind him, fixing a murderous glare on Galen.

The patrons between them quickly parted once their surprise gave way to self-preservation as Raven stormed across the tavern floor. One half-drunken fellow was slow to step clear. Raven swatted him aside like a loaf of stale bread. "Calm yourself, my large friend," Galen stammered, easing himself off the bar. Raven was upon him before his feet touched the floor. Galen raised his hands to his face just as Raven's left arm backhanded him, the blow tossing him through the air, his right hip striking the unforgiving stone floor.

"You miserable scum!" Raven growled, storming across the floor and seizing Galen about his tunic collar and lifting him into the air.

"Plea-pleas-please, my friend. There is a misunderstanding." Galen coughed, wondering how he would get out of this one.

"Stealing my ocran ain't a misunderstanding, minstrel!" Raven grunted, throwing Galen against the bar, his back striking the wooden counter painfully before slumping to the floor.

"Seize him!" a familiar woman's voice rang out.

Raven turned just as a dozen soldiers in gray mail rushed him. He spotted Tosha at the doorway, her golden eyes staring impassively back at him. His right hand went to his pistol just as Galen lifted it from its holster and backed away along the bar. Raven pivoted, following the miserable wretch with his eyes. He stepped toward Galen just as the first soldier drew his sword, leveling it at his throat. "On your knees!" the soldier commanded.

Raven snatched a mug from the bar, throwing it at his head. The soldier flinched, catching the wooden cup with his nose. Raven scooped him up and slammed him on the floor. Another came at him with a blade ready to strike. Raven caught his arm before he could swing, twisting it behind his back before tossing him into the gaggle that followed on his heels. The men tumbled backward like top-heavy pins.

"I want him *alive*!" Tosha shouted. She could see her men faring poorly and decided to change tactics. "The man before you is the famed Earther Raven! He is a fugitive of the Benotrist Empire. The reward for his capture is five hundred thousand certras if taken alive. Nothing dead!" Her words were as flame to oil, moving the wary patrons to action. The few man hunters in the tavern immediately stepped forth, hoping to gain their share in the reward. The rest of the crowd followed, motivated by greed once they saw others leading the charge.

Tosha shook her head as Raven tossed another soldier across the floor, taking several others off their feet. He grabbed another by the neck with his left hand and punched him with his right. The poor fellow slipped unmoving from his grasp, his nose broken and blood splattering Raven's face. His elbow caught another upside the head, knocking him from his feet. The stifling air was thick with the moans of the wounded and the breaking of bones.

One brave patron climbed atop the bar, jumping on Raven's back to little effect. Raven continued to fight as if the man was a feather resting on his shoulder. The next fellow went low but took a boot to the face before rolling away, spitting teeth. Two others came upon him from opposite sides. Raven grabbed them by their tunic collars, driving their heads together. They fell to the floor, witless and stunned. The next tried a different tact, wrapping his limbs around Raven's right leg, holding on. Raven failed to dislodge him, as too many others drew near.

Raven swung his elbows to great effect, knocking his attackers aside, giving those behind them pause. He wasted little time during the respite to step forward to grab the one nearest him. Dragging the men clinging to his back and leg, he grabbed the fellow by the arm, throwing him headlong into the bar. The sound of cracking wood echoed where his crown met the unforgiving timber.

The man clinging to Raven's back started pounding his right ear. Raven reached over his shoulder, trying to grab the offender, but the fellow drew away, dodging his hands. Raven thrust backward, smashing the fellow's spine against the edge of the bar. The poor wretch screamed, thinking his back broken as he slipped to the floor. "Just grab a part of him and hold on! Hurry before he kills me!" the fellow clinging to his leg shouted in octaves too high for a man.

Tosha had had enough. She stepped without, where dozens of Benotrist soldiers surrounded the tavern. "Commander Cratus, send in two flax!" *Two more?* he thought in alarm, wondering what was transpiring within. Upon his command, the additional soldiers poured through the front door of the tavern.

"Oh, come on!" Raven moaned as the reinforcements poured in just as the barkeep climbed atop the bar, jumping on his back. A second fellow attached himself to his left leg, and another aided the one on his right. Raven punched a drunken patron in the nose as he came straight on just as two more braved the top of the bar and jumped on his back, adding their weight to the barkeep's.

Seeing Raven hindered by those clinging to him, the tavern patrons, man hunters, and soldiers rushed forth, confident in their numbers. They came on without respite, some tripping on the broken bodies that littered the floor. Raven knocked a couple aside, but the third drove his shoulder into his gut. Raven wrapped his arms around the man's back, lifting him upside down, driving his head into the floor. The sound of the man's neck snapping echoed dully through the din. The maneuver cost Raven dearly, allowing others to close in unison, several grabbing for his arms while others piled on his back, grabbed his legs, or threw themselves upon his chest.

"Ow! He's biting me!" one patron cried out, Raven's teeth tearing into his arm. Three more piled on his back, then four, five, and six until the big Earther stumbled under the weight, crashing to the floor. The men wasted little time piling on, ignoring the protests of those suffering their weight at the bottom.

An eerie silence followed. Tosha could only hear the muffled complaints of those buried under the pile of flesh. She could see one of Raven's hands on the floor, protruding from the pile. Her relief of his capture gave way to alarm as the hand failed to move.

"Get off me!" the barkeep pleaded, unable to bear the weight upon him.

"We're not getting off! He's too dangerous!" one of those atop the pile retorted.

"He is not moving. I think he's dead," said one further below.

"Get off him now!" Tosha ordered, trying to quell her racing heart. *Why must he be so stubborn?* She wanted to scream.

The men slowly eased off the pile, wary of Raven stirring and fighting them all over again. No sooner had the last man cleared than several soldiers rushed forth, brandishing shackles. They drew his arms together behind him, but their manacles failed to close on his thick wrists. They used leg shackles instead, fastening two separate pairs to bind his arms in case he was strong enough to break a single pair.

They rolled him over, finding a couple others trapped beneath him. Neither was moving, one clearly dead, his head bent unnaturally with sightless eyes staring at nothing. Tosha knelt beside Raven, pressing her ear to his chest. Relief washed over her as she heard his heartbeat echoing strongly.

She wiped the blood oozing from his forehead where it struck the floor. The blow would've killed lesser men. She was thankful that he wasn't a lesser man. "Bring him!" she commanded after gaining her feet, but then something caught her eye, his empty holster. She hadn't seen Galen take it and wondered why Raven hadn't used it. "Wait! Where is the Earther's weapon?"

"Weapon?" more than one asked curiously.

"He has it!" one shouted, fingering Galen, who had crept toward the doorway.

"Give me that weapon, minstrel!" a commander of flax ordered, taking a step toward him as Galen backed to the doorway. Galen lifted the pistol to surrender it when he inadvertently pulled the trigger. A flash of blue light sprang from the barrel, striking the commander in the chest. The weapon nearly jumped from his hand, his eyes drawing wide at what he had done. He stole a quick glance across the tavern as every eye was fixed to him.

"I, uh," he sputtered, bereft of words. He turned and fled, bounding through the front door and running between the confused soldiers surrounding the tavern. Two moved to block him, as they were instructed to allow no one to pass. Galen raised the strange weapon, pulling the trigger mechanism. Laser splashed from the barrel, spewing haphazardly with his shaky aim and jerky finger. One of the soldiers stumbled, laser piercing his stomach, while the other dove to his right, dodging Galen's errant fire. The panic-stricken minstrel continued on, racing up the street while firing aimlessly over his shoulder in the direction of his pursuers.

*****

Galen didn't cease firing until long after his pursuers gave up the chase. He crossed nearly the length of the port, fleeing afoot west, paralleling the wharves. He passed a few casual onlookers, who paid him little regard while going about their business. He stopped to catch his breath, his heart pounding, looking back whence he came. He lamented losing his newfound coin and ocran, which he had planned to use to purchase passage over the lake. He did have the

Earther's strange weapon and surmised a southern regent or potentate might pay handsomely for such a boon.

First things first, he needed to hide or flee. The village wharves were the next street south, but the docks were the most likely place they would search for him. The avenue where he now stood was narrow with single-level timber structures lining either side. 'Twas little more than an alley with the majority of its structures comprised of residential dwellings. The modest homes were little more than two-room abodes with communal wells at the end of the street and waist buckets set outside their front doors.

Galen crept carefully so as not to overturn one of the foul-smelling obstacles as he made for the next crossway running north just ahead. "I'll cut your throat if you lift that pistol!" a voice warned as he turned into the adjoining alley, greeting a sword leveled to his throat.

There before him stood a ruggedly dressed fellow with thick fur cloak, a brown leather tunic, and numerous bladed weapons strapped to his person. The man looked as if he had lived in the wilds for some length of time. He was certainly no Benotrist but might be a man hunter, which was often worse.

"Drop the pistol!"

"Pistol?"

"My friend's weapon. Drop it," Cronus said, pressing the blade to Galen's throat.

*****

Tosha twisted the cloth, wringing the extra water into the bowl before dabbing it on Raven's face. He lay upon the cot, unmoving since his capture, a vicious gash and raised bump upon his forehead. His hands were now chained at his sides, one fixed to the bars of his holding cell and the other to the bar of his cot. He was stripped to his waist as she examined him for further injuries. He was covered with bruises, incurring most during the scuffle in the Severed Skull.

"You stubborn fool." Tosha sighed, wiping the blood from his cheek and nose. She paused, searching his face for any sign of awareness. It struck her how fearsome he was in others' eyes, but she never saw him thus. He was quite handsome, though masked it with his childish antics and blunt speech.

She was troubled by his present state, wondering the severity of the blow to his head. She never intended his injury, but what choice did she have? They had nearly traveled the length of the continent before she finally caged him, the journey taxing her beyond measure.

She, too, was bruised and battle worn, suffering the rigors of their arduous trek. Her eye traveled to her chaffed wrists, where the manacles had held her during her escape. They were much abused when she ordered her rescuers to break them off with their swords, the blows bruising her further. "If you die, I'll kill you," she whispered in his ear. A part of her wanted nothing more than to curl up beside him on the cot and go to sleep, lamenting all that had transpired since Fera.

If only he had succumbed to the sleeping nectar, they would now be safely in Bansoch, along with Cronus and Alen. She would have arranged safe passage for Terin and Lorken, and all would have been well. Cronus could be reunited with Leanna and gifted asylum in her mother's realm. Alas, it was not to be. Instead, they had risked all their lives to serve Raven's pride, yet the end result was the same, Raven ending in her chains, as she had intended from the start.

"Highness," the even voice of Commander Cratus echoed in the stifling air of the holding cell.

"Commander," she greeted, gaining her feet as Favel Cratus stepped within the open cell and knelt.

"Highness, I present Commander Corvar, commandant of Baxtel," Favel said as a stern-faced soldier with silver hair and piercing green eyes stepped within and knelt. He was similarly attired as his men save for the three golden cords that circled his shoulders, designating him a commander of telnic.

"Rise, Commanders," she said. "What news have you?"

"I am honored to be of service, Princess. We received word of your capture nearly a half moon ago. My scouts, just as those in our adjoining sectors, have been searching for you night and day. It is fortunate that we crossed paths when we did. When I received word of your rescue, I rode here posthaste. I brought an additional two units of cavalry. One I have dispatched to the eastern and western approaches of Axenville to hunt for the Torry commander of unit that escaped you as well as the minstrel that my men had captured earlier," Commander Corvar explained.

"Belay your search for Commander Kenti. I do not wish him killed or harmed. Allow him free passage."

"Highness?" The commandant lifted a questioning brow.

"His death or capture serves little benefit and would only antagonize my prisoner."

Her prisoner. The commandant sighed internally, his gaze drifting to the still form of the Earther upon the cot behind her. The Earther was far too dangerous. He should be killed or at least maimed to prevent another struggle that incurred during his detainment.

"Have all the ships been removed from port?" Tosha asked.

"It has been done, Highness," the commandant affirmed.

"Excellent. I want all avenues of escape closed should my prisoner again slip his bonds. Assign your patrols, ensuring that *no one* leaves Axenville until I have removed Captain Raven to Nisin."

"It shall be done, Highness, though the local magistrate may object—"

"Then you remind him his small port retains its autonomy by my father's benevolence and restraint. I would advise our good magistrate to not invoke my wrath," Tosha said acidly.

"He waits without, Highness, seeking your audience if you desire to grant it," Commander Cratus informed her.

"Send him in," she said as they bowed and stepped without to carry out their tasks.

A moment later, the graceless form of Strutor Vehalas, magistrate of Axenville, stepped within, his wide-set brown eyes and flat nose belying his boisterous demeanor. He was of a height to Tosha and wore thick robes in hues of tan and gray. "Princess Tosha," he greeted as he knelt, his head bowed with practiced reverence. Though he was the appointed head of the independent municipality, Strutor Vehalas wisely greeted Tosha with the reverence her title demanded.

"Rise, Magistrate Vehalas."

"I have procured the items we spoke of earlier, Highness," he offered happily, gaining his feet, expecting his news to please her.

"Caged wagons?" she asked.

"Yes. Axenville's most prominent slaver, Lutus Rarm, has generously offered his finest slave wagon to move your prisoners. It is well-built with iron floor, roof, and bars lining its sides. Even a magantor could not rend its cage. It should suffice for the purpose you intend. Though it is presently en route from Stapero, it should arrive by midday on the morrow."

"I planned to be off come the morn." She frowned.

"My apologies, Highness. The affairs of the slavers who conduct business in our fair port are outside my purview. Lutus Rarm has sent outriders to meet the caravan en route to hurry it along. It is bearing slaves for auction at midday tomorrow. Dozens of larger-estate owners will be arriving throughout the morn to partake. Perhaps Your Highness would care to attend?" the magistrate asked.

"Attend?" She didn't care to waste her time with such frivolities.

"Your presence would assuage the fears of our good citizens regarding Benotrist encroachment and strengthen the hand of those of us who seek union with your father's realm."

Tosha reconsidered, seeing the influence that a royal visit could have in this backwater port. Any peaceful annexation was preferable to a bloody expansion. Much could be gained for a mere delay. "So be it. I shall depart *after* the auction."

"Splendid!" Magistrate Vehalas happily exclaimed.

"What of your blacksmiths? Have they prepared the better-fitting manacles that I require?" she asked.

"They are nearly finished, Highness. They rarely work past sundown, but this night, they are honored to meet your request."

"I shall need them come sunrise."

"Of course." The magistrate bowed. "Do you require them for both of your prisoners or just the large one?" he asked, his eyes briefly regarding Alen, who sat quietly in the adjoining cell. He sat upon the stone floor with his head in his shackled hands, bemoaning his miserable state.

"Nay." She dismissed the notion. "The other is a palace slave. Common manacles shall suffice for his restraint."

"Very well. I hope my hall meets your needs," he said, reminding her of his generosity in her use of the magistrate's hall. To her, the simple, austere edifice failed to match the grandeur of its name. The magistrate's hall was a simple stone dwelling with a front atrium and three small holding cells in the adjoining chamber divided by a narrow door.

"You are most gracious, Magistrate. Your abode has suited our needs sufficiently. I shall retire for the evening shortly. A flax of guards shall be watching over my prisoners once I leave."

"Yes, your commanders of flax and telnic have informed me. My vice magistrate, Kendra Sarn, shall assist as needed."

"A woman?" she asked curiously. Though women held the reins of power in her mother's queendom, those on the continent were not so inclined.

"Yes. Her father was the famed man hunter Zarix Sarn. His fell deeds are held in great renown among the landed gentry of the shores of Veneba. Her name alone is worth ten swords."

"Very well. I have instructed my men to inform me the moment the prisoner awakes. Other than seeing to their needs, your vice magistrate need only keep your good citizens clear of this structure and our route of departure." With that, Tosha regarded Raven for a long moment before stepping without.

*****

"Ugh!" Raven moaned, stirring slowly before jolting awake, pain shooting through his skull. "Ouch!" he growled, lifting his hands to his skull until they were denied by the length of their chains. "What the..."

"Quiet, Raven. You shall alert the guards," Alen whispered desperately through the bars separating their cells.

"Guards?" he asked, dumbfounded by his unfamiliar surroundings. Dull torchlight poorly illuminated the shape of the chamber. He barely made out the bars of his small cell before recalling the events that led him to this sorry state. Taking stock of the situation, he noted that each wrist was similarly chained, but his ankles were shackled together and not to a fixed point.

His small cell was barely long enough for him to lie down and furnished with a cot and a waste bucket, which he might soon have use of. His boots, shirt, jacket, and empty holster were placed on the floor. His blurry vision found Alen in the adjoining cell, staring back at him with a pitiful frown painting his face. "What happened to you?" Raven asked, wrapping his right hand around the slack in the chain attaching his manacle to the bar of his cell.

"Tosha escaped at the outset of our ambush. Cronus and I pursued her while you were engaged. She came upon a detachment of Benotrist cavalry and set them upon us. We were not aware of their presence until they were directly behind us, forcing us to flee south with no way to circle back to you. I...I was dismounted by an errant tree limb that jutted into the road. I was swiftly captured."

"Where's Cronus?" he asked sourly, expecting the worst.

"I...don't know. I believe they still search for him but hear little of what they say."

"He could be dead for all we know," Raven growled. "I doubt Tosha would tell me if her goons had killed him." He grunted, prying the chain off the manacle connected to the bar, freeing his right hand. The snap of the metal echoed audibly in the still air, drawing the guard from the outer atrium, who poked a curious eye through the doorway.

"He is awake!" the guard relayed excitedly to those further without.

"H-how?" Alen stared at the uncanny display of strength.

Raven didn't have the time to explain the effects of DNA manipulation, enhanced strengthening techniques used in Space Fleet's pilot training program, or the countless years of conditioning to build such power. He just needed to escape before they started cutting pieces off him or killing him outright, though Tosha claimed otherwise.

Before he could break the manacle on his left hand, a guard entered the chamber, standing post outside his cell. Within moments, he could hear voices growing louder in the outer chamber until a familiar figure stepped within. She was spartanly attired in tan leather trousers, wool shirt, and gray mail. Swords rode each hip, and her golden eyes shone resplendent in the dull light.

He's awake, she thought with relief. Perhaps now she could finally prove to him that she intended no harm, that her plans for him were as she claimed. Of course, he would protest at first until the futility of his resentment gave way to acceptance. She could prove herself again by protecting his comrades, allowing Cronus free passage with his homeland so near and removing Alen to her native isle. Perhaps acceptance would eventually lead to contentment, the life of a royal consort not lacking for comfort.

"Look what the cat dragged in," Raven said, his sarcasm freezing Tosha in place, stripping away her positive sentiment. She scolded herself for worrying about him, his injury obviously superficial, as he lay there as if he hadn't a care in the world. Oh, how she hated him at times. She feared he might never wake after that terrible blow to his head.

"Cat?" She lifted a brow, understanding the sarcasm but not the word.

"Small animal about wee big with claws and lots of fur. Acts like you," he said, lifting his hands at his sides to demonstrate the length of the animal.

"Hmm," she snorted. Knowing Raven, it was certainly an insult of some sort. The guards flanked her, their spears leveled as if expecting him to pass through the iron bars. "I see you are well," she said dryly.

"My head hurts like hell, but there's no use crying about it."

"Have you ever cried?" she asked, rolling her eyes.

"Only when the Steelers lost the Super Bowl," he said in all honesty. The words meant nothing to her, but she was certain it was another idiotic reference of his home world.

"Do you ever take anything seriously?" She shook her head.

"Other than football? No." He shrugged, reaching his free hand to his left and snapping the manacle that bound it to his cot. Tosha held firm as the guards backed a step. Raven gained his feet, shuffling across the floor, hindered by his shackled ankles. He staggered briefly, holding his aching head as the cell began to spin.

"Raven?" she asked worriedly.

"I'm all right," he said, dismissing her alarm, reaching out toward the bar of his cell door to steady himself.

"No, you're not," she said. He would topple over if he let go even if his ankles weren't bound. Bruises ran the length of his muscled torso, a reminder of the beating he received in the tavern.

"If you think I look bad, you should see the other guys."

"I did. Five are dead, and a dozen badly injured."

"They started it. Actually, you started it," he corrected himself.

"You are insufferable." She sighed.

"And so are you. Where's Cronus, Tosh?" he asked.

"I don't know," she conceded sadly. "Hopefully, he is safely away."

"He can't be that safe with your goons after him," he growled.

"I've ordered my father's men to stand down. Cronus has an open road if he is wise enough to take it."

"And if he doesn't?"

"I ordered that he be taken *unharmed*. If he is taken, he shall accompany you to Bansoch. It is not the life he might prefer, but he shall be safe."

"Safe? I haven't been safe since I met you."

"Not by my choice have you been endangered!" she countered. "But you needn't worry about that anymore. Come the morrow, you'll be safely in a different cage and taken north. You as well, Alen." She regarded her former slave sitting in the cell beside Raven. Alen turned away, burying his head in his hands. She dismissed Alen's self-pity, knowing it was for his best. She would find him a mistress who favored such delicate features in her slaves. He would certainly fare better as a slave in Bansoch than as a free man with little skill to barter.

"You know, Tosh, where I come from, if you marry someone, it doesn't involve cages, chains, and whips. Unless, of course, you're into that sort of thing." Raven shrugged.

She regarded him darkly. She wanted to finally share her wondrous news with him, but his acid tone ruined that for now. "You've earned your chains, Raven. I shall see that you wear them well, whether it is as my consort or my slave. Fair night and sleep well." She turned and stepped without.

Raven watched glumly as she passed through the doorway. *Women,* he thought sourly. They brought him nothing but trouble. "I thought she'd never leave," he growled, sitting down on his cot, examining his shackles, finding them much sturdier than the manacles affixed to his wrists.

"You mustn't antagonize her. She will make you suffer for such insolence," Alen warned in a weak, despondent voice.

"Antagonize her?" He nearly choked. "She's been a pain in my backside since Molten Isle. The first thing you have to learn about women, Alen, is that no woman respects a man that kisses her ass. And I sure as hell ain't starting today. Now I just have to"—he grunted, tugging at the shackles—"find a way to break these and escape these swell accommodations my wife has arranged for me."

"There is no escape for us. I was a fool to believe otherwise," Alen lamented.

"No escape? This ain't the time to be a Debbie Downer, little fella. I'll have us out of here shortly," Raven said, not lacking in confidence, again testing his shackles with little success.

"They made certain of the shackles on your feet. Their iron is far stronger than those they bound your hands with," Alen explained.

"Argh!" He kicked out his feet in frustration. "That is why men and women should live on separate planets! Damn that woman!"

"You must guard your tongue, Raven, for where we are going, such words are blasphemy."

"So what's this island of hers like?" Raven asked, taking another go at the chain.

"Women rule with absolute authority. They are less barbaric than Tyro's realm, but never doubt their potential for cruelty if you disobey."

"I don't get it. Are you telling me the whole island is run by women, and the men just take it? Why don't they rise up? They're just a bunch of girls."

"Have you ever weighed anchor in Bansoch?"

"Nope."

"When you do, you will not so casually dismiss their power."

"They're pretty tough, huh? Sounds like a wonderful place." He rolled his eyes, pulling on the shackle.

"Yes, it does," a woman's voice agreed as she stood in the doorway.

Raven and Alen regarded the eavesdropper curiously. She stood at sixty-one inches with light auburn hair woven in long braids and bound behind her head. She wore a knee-length gray woolen tunic with sandals that laced to her bare knees. Steel guards graced her forearms with gray mail protecting her torso. A shortsword rode her left hip and a bow was slung across her back. She was fair of countenance, but her mannish demeanor detracted her natural beauty. She appraised them with studious brown eyes.

"Who are you supposed to be, the queen of the jungle?" Raven asked, not able to help himself. He only hoped she wasn't the one to feed them, or she would probably spit in his food.

"I am Kendra Sarn, vice magistrate of Axenville," she said, crossing her arms, leaning a shoulder against the doorway.

"Sarn?" Raven knew that name from somewhere but couldn't place it. She came off the door, closing it as she stepped within.

"My father was Zarix Sarn."

"I know that name. He's a bounty hunter. I have friends in Tro who think highly of him," Raven said.

"He *was* a man hunter before he was murdered by Tavis Cora," she said darkly.

"Tavis Cora. I haven't heard his name in a while," Raven said. Tavis was a pirate captain in Monsoon's armada during the Troan raids, the very raids that cost Cordi Kenti's life and Raven's falling out with Nels Draken.

"He hasn't been heard of since you killed him, if my sources speak true," she said.

"Brokov actually pulled the trigger, but I slew a number of his crew." He recalled the battle on the open waters north of Tro.

"Brokov?" She lifted a curious brow.

"My friend and crewmate."

"You oversaw it, then. I had sought Tavis Cora at length for his crimes, for killing my father. You have my gratitude for doing so." Raven understood her view, having sought Monsoon for killing Cordi.

"Well, Kendra, if you are truly grateful, why don't you find the keys and let us out of here?"

"And where would you go? Every mount in town is corralled near the slave pens. The Benotrists have encircled the port, ensuring none leave, and every ship has been ordered away until the princess departs. It seems she has taken every precaution to prevent your escape. Besides, I am sworn to my duty to this freehold."

"If you are a freehold, then why are you bound to obey a Benotrist princess?" Alen asked.

"I serve the magistrate of Axenville. It is he that chooses to curry favor with the Benotrist throne. If we offend Darkhon, will any other realm stand in our defense?" she countered, referring to Tyro in the name he was known by in the east. Alen hung his head, for he well knew the answer. The Torry realm could barely hold their own lands, let alone ensure the sovereignty of others.

"How much?" Raven cut to the chase.

"How much?" she repeated, not understanding his question.

"How much to free us? I can pay you enough gold to buy a small kingdom and transport to take you far beyond Tyro's reach."

"Beyond Darkhon's reach?" She laughed. "There's no such place. A corpse has little need for gold, Earther."

"Tyro's not all-powerful, Kendra. I'm a lot scarier than that boob, believe me."

"A false boast considering where you stand, bested by his daughter and wearing her chains."

"Tosha didn't best me. It was that mob that jumped me from all sides, if memory serves right, not to mention that damned minstrel that stole my pistol!"

"The ever-elusive minstrel." She sighed.

"Did they find him?" Raven wrapped his fingers around the bars of his cell, squeezing them as if they were Galen's neck.

"Strange as this day was, his continued evasion is stranger still. Whether that is good news or ill for your hopes of escape, who can guess since he still has your weapon."

"Well, if you hear a girlish squeal in the middle of the night, it'll be him shooting himself trying to use it."

"It is fortunate you no longer have your weapon, or I might have been tempted to join you," she whispered before stepping without.

"Thanks for nothing," Raven snarled as the door closed.

"She seems friendly," Alen observed.

"Ah, she's as crazy as the rest of 'em. It's like my father used to tell me. 'Everyone around here is nuts but you and me, and you're a little bit off.'"

*****

The morning sun broke upon a clear sky as wealthy landowners and merchants made their way into port, along with their small armies of hired swords, retainers, and servants. They gathered in the auction square, resting on the east side of Axenville, a stone's throw from the wharves lining the lakeshore. The auction block was a ten-meter stone square a meter in height overlooking the lower assemblage that spanned 180 degrees on the east face of the block. The upper assemblage circled the lower assemblage and raised twice the height of a man with spacious seating for the wealthiest bidders.

Those gathered in the lower assemblage were small-land owners, farmers, tradesmen, traders, and less prominent merchants. Hundreds of commoners gathered as well for the spectacle. Those crowding the lower assemblage were dressed in plain tunics in hues of tan and gray with sandals and simple cloaks. They were dressed little better than the slaves to be auctioned, standing in stark contrast to their wealthy counterparts seated behind them in the upper assembly.

Wealthy vineyard owners, merchants, and landed gentry sat in shaded luxury upon the upper seating, lounging in cushioned seats and fanned by servants, who brought them refreshments and catered to their needs. The men were richly adorned with robes of purple, crimson, and forest green. The women wore calnesian gowns of gold and burgundy with exotic jewels adorning their fingers and necks and with their hair swept up in decorative braids.

Magistrate Strutor Vehalas ascended the auction block to address the assemblage, pleased with the grand attendance. Many came to see their royal visitor, who sat in the place of honor in the center of the upper assembly. "My good citizens of Axenville and neighboring estates, we are honored to host the Benotrist crown princess to our fair port. Today..." the magistrate began, speaking at length as he addressed the crowd, introducing their esteemed visitors.

Tosha sat above the assemblage, her guards standing post around her, ever watchful for dangers that might spring. The ports along the shores of Lake Veneba teemed with mercenaries, bounty hunters, and fugitives of all sorts. Any might be tempted to repeat the adventurism of Monsoon, but she doubted any would dare with so many guards about. Her greatest threat was her errant consort, who was safely confined in the magistrate's holding cell. Upon the auction's conclusion, she would have the newly forged manacles fixed to his wrists before preparing him for transport.

She wished it hadn't come to this, but his stubbornness brokered little compromise. Perhaps if he knew the truth of her condition, he might've come willingly. But alas, it mattered not now that he was finally caged. She surmised that many in the crowd had come to see Raven rather than her. The Earthers were an oddity that drew curious stares wherever they trod. Word quickly spread after their arrival on Arax of their ridiculous claims of traveling between the stars.

She never believed it despite their impressive display of power and technological prowess. They were likely the remnant of a dead civilization from across the sea, much akin to the Jenaii. Perhaps she was mistaken, and they spoke true. But it mattered not, for wherever they hailed, they were unlike anyone she had ever known. Raven was unlike any she had ever known.

She heard the murmurs in the crowd, the derision spewed on Raven after his capture, believing it a mark upon his perceived invulnerability. Where once he instilled fear, he was now the source of mockery and derision. He was bested by a girl, as if they had defeated him themselves. *They aren't worthy to clean his feet, let alone walk with superior airs as his better. They are fools,* she mused disgustedly. The sooner she departed this place the better.

The magistrate completed his bloviation, giving way to the auctioneer, a clear-spoken fellow with long dark hair framing an overly common face. He was ordinary in every way, save for his piercing gaze, which seemed to penetrate your soul if he looked into your eyes. He was richly attired in an ankle-length emerald tunic with gold stitching along its hem and sleeves.

"Let us commence," the auctioneer began, signaling two strongly built sentries hither, each clad in leather mail and gray tunics. They approached from the west-facing side of the block, where two long slave pens ran west from the assemblage areas. The pens were set sixty inches in the ground with stone walls and sides with iron bars lining their front.

The slaves held therein were divided by age, gender, and docility. They were earlier displayed on the stone avenue between the pens, naked with their hands bound behind them and their left ankles shackled to the ground. There they stood for inspection by potential buyers, suffering the humiliation of lecherous eyes and probing hands. The time afforded potential buyers to see the human stock up close before auction, where they would be clothed and further afield. The slaves were a miserable lot, staring forlornly at their counterparts in the opposing pens, each awaiting their turn upon the block.

The sentries escorted the first slave to the block, a boy no more than sixteen years with long brown hair framing even-set dark eyes. He wore a brief tan tunic, common for those of his caste, with his hands bound before him and feet shackled. The brutish guards flanked the petrified youth, prodding him up the wide, flat steps on the west face of the auction block. The auctioneer directed him to the center of the block, ordering him to turn, kneel, and stand, running him through his paces.

"Our first offering is a debtor slave, new to the collar." The auctioneer rattled off the youth's attributes, history, and potential, enticing bids from vineyard owners and large estates. The lad was the son of a small farmer who passed owing a sizable debt to a local merchant. The merchant took his family as collateral against the debt, keeping the boy's sister for his own household and selling the rest.

Tosha observed the proceedings with disinterest, wishing it over and to be on her way. Commandant Corvar urged her to attend, wishing to gain favor with the independent freeholds that dotted the shores of the lake. Her father's legions would soon require immense logistical support from these lands. The Benotrist and gargoyle legions needed to husband their strength, requiring softer diplomacy with these freeholds rather than the forceful tactics they usually employed.

"Sold!" the auctioneer declared, pointing to a richly attired fellow sitting off Tosha's left, one Evor Xun, who owned multiple vineyards stretching from Axenville to Far Point. His vast estates required a multitude of slaves, especially with the coming harvest. The slave was removed from the block as the next was brought forth. Several slaves waited in line as the guards removed another from the holding pens, replacing the one who stood on the block.

The first slaves to the block were debtor slaves. They were sold to cover debts incurred by themselves or direct kin. They were often trainable but unbroken, and their price varied greatly, often based on aesthetic qualities and labor needs of the buyers. More expensive stock were bred slaves, those raised under the yoke of slavery. They were bred for specific purposes and were fearfully obedient and docile. Others were victims of slave raids, stolen from their homes at swords' point, most of whom were women and children. The cheapest stock were criminals, spared the sword for a life of servitude. Most were petty thieves, those of low character, or indigents gathered off the streets of far-off ports.

Several slaves followed, all purchased by Evor Xun, who exerted his extravagance hoping to impress upon their royal visitor his esteemed station. Tosha cared not, thinking the local gentry little better than peasants. She thought of the wane looks of the poor wretches sold upon the block. She had never paid heed to the plight of slaves or peasants, accepting their station as the natural order, but staring in their eyes this day filled her with a bitter taste. She heard the boastful ramblings in the crowd, urging her to bring Raven forth to prostrate him before her, as if they had bested him themselves. Why was she panged with guilt?

Thoughts of him captive by her hand consumed her. He was rude, brash, and irreverent to extremes, but he was loyal to those he loved and kind to those who were weak. If he were here beside her, he would have certainly vented his fury upon the slavers who profited in human flesh and misery. She could see him now, snapping the auctioneer's neck and challenging the crowd of buyers with a colorful declaration, like, "What are you going to do about it?" She smiled at the thought.

She wondered how her mother would receive him. She had long counseled Tosha to choose a mate from their native isle, a docile companion who understood his role in the royal court. Her mother feared Tosha repeating her own mistake when she fell under Tyro's spell. Only Tosha kept her parents from waging war upon each other, though her mother's mysterious fondness for the Torry realms might still lead to conflagration. Having come to know Cronus, Tosha could understand her mother's opinion on the honor of Torries. He was a good man, and she now knew why Raven risked so much to see him set free. Perhaps she could counsel her father to end his war upon the Torry realms.

Her attention was again drawn to the auction block where a young maid no more than fifteen years was brought forth. Her shackles dwarfed her small frame. She stood no more than fifty-six inches with richly combed auburn hair framing a comely face. Her brief garment displayed her shapely form, drawing the lecherous stares of the men in the crowd. Her sea-blue eyes were wide with fright with undammed tears squeezing from their corners.

"A comely maiden who has recently flowered," the auctioneer declared, detailing her attributes. "A debtor slave whose maidenhood is intact, a perfect choice for a maid to warm your bed or to breed comely slaves." The girl's panicked eyes darted furtively through the crowd, wondering which of the buyers would claim her. Her hopes now lay in a kind master, for freedom was beyond her, forsaken with her broken spirit.

Her eyes found those of Tosha across the sea of cruel faces. Tosha gasped, remembering her desperation on Molten Isle, chained and helpless, vulnerable to the salacious leers of her captors. For the first time, she saw herself in the place of another and felt sorely ashamed for her previous apathy. She could not help the others, but this girl would not share their fate. She would bring her to Bansoch, allowing her a place as a free woman of the Federation.

"Sold!" the auctioneer proclaimed, pointing to Tosha, who placed the highest bid.

"Fire!" A chorus of shouts rang out as smoke filtered above the granaries along the shore front.

"Calm!" the auctioneer pleaded, his hands raised to the crowd. "Let us..." His words stopped in his throat as blue laser struck his chest.

Sometime before

"Haven't you given up yet?" Kendra Sarn asked, standing before his cell with her arms crossed. Raven looked up, dropping the shackles from his grip as he sat on his cot. He spent the better part of the night and morning trying to pry the heavy links apart. He had managed to bend the link closest to his left ankle cuff, but it refused to completely yield. Another few hours might do, but that was time he didn't have. "Those shackles were forged to hobble ocran. You have no hope to break them." Kendra shook her head at his stubbornness.

"Hopeless causes are my specialty." He grunted, grabbing hold of the chain, again yanking futilely.

"Still not giving up?"

"Does it look like I'm giving up? I just spent these past weeks crossing half the continent trying to get the hell out of this craphole of a country. I ain't planning to go all the way back in a cage."

"It is a lovely cage I am told," she said dryly.

"If you're here to cheer me up, you're doing a lousy job."

"You talk very strange. You certainly don't lack for confidence."

He released the chain again, giving her a look. "What is it you want, Kendra? I'm a little busy here."

She gave him a look in return. *Did he just say he was busy? Busy trying to escape? And saying such to the vice magistrate?* He was incorrigible. "The Benotrists shall be here shortly with new chains for your wrists, chains you shan't break no matter your impressive strength."

"Thanks for the happy update. Anything else you want to share?"

"I wanted to thank you for killing Tavis Cora. I owe you for that."

"How you gonna pay me back if I spend the rest of my life—"

"As the pampered lover of the crown princess of the Sisterhood? A life as Tosha's consort hardly seems so burdensome. You need no favors from me."

"Favors. Don't bother. The last woman who owed me a favor for saving her hide tricked me into marriage, drugged my wine, sent thousands of soldiers to hunt me down, bit me countless times, kicked me, and managed to get me beat up by every drunk in your wretched town. So you can keep your favor!"

"The princess did all that?" Kendra struggled not to burst in laughter.

"Yeah. She's a barrel of laughs!" He snorted.

"But she seems quite taken with you." She smiled.

"Oh, we're best buddies. I can't wait to see her this afternoon and see what she has planned for me next."

"I pay my debts, Earther. You killed my father's murderer. For that, I am grateful. But what I owe you on that regard is a debt of honor. I don't owe you my life. You killed a man I wanted dead. I owe you a death, not your liberty. Besides…" She paused, realizing she had gone too far. She had reliable contacts who told her the local gentry planned to depose the magistrate and submit Axenville to the Benotrist Empire for annexation. She advised Magistrate Vehalas of such, and he dismissed her claims as mere fears.

Benotrist annexations were highly unpredictable and could easily mean her head. The Benotrists often disposed of the previous authority in lands they annexed. She was tempted to help the Earther, but what hope had he without his weapon?

"It's time, Earther!" a soldier sneered, leading three others into the chamber, carrying a pair of heavy manacles with massive links connecting them. "The princess commands we clad you in your new jewelry." He smiled, hoisting the manacles aloft with great effort.

"Well, come on in and put them on me, junior," Raven said, deciding the giggling boy's neck would be the first one he would break.

"No." The soldier shook his head. "We shall not repeat that mistake. You will slip your hands through the bars, and we shall attach them thusly."

"Make me."

"If we have to, we shall, but two things will happen if we do, Earther. One is that your little friend here"—he tapped Alen's cell—"shall be whipped for your insolence. The second is that when we do subdue you, your hands will be bound behind you rather than in front. Since you'll be wearing these"—he again lifted the manacles—"for some time, your arms will be quite sore."

He knew that if they put those on him, he would never escape. He would be at their mercy, and only Tosha could shield him from her father's wrath. Tyro agreed to their nuptials to gain him an heir, and knowing his vindictive nature, he would likely cut off parts of him that wouldn't hinder his marital duties.

"If you behave yourself, Earther, we have a gift for you. Bring him in, bounty hunter!" the soldier shouted to someone in the outer atrium. Three more soldiers entered therein, followed by a bounty hunter pushing a chained captive, Galen. Raven's back straightened as his eyes fell on the wretched vermin.

"You do as we ask and I shall place this one in your cell to do with as you please."

If Galen was here, then where was his pistol? And why wasn't Galen in fear of his life? He wasn't even nervous by the stupid look on his face. It made no sense until Raven's eyes found the bounty hunter who stepped from behind the minstrel. Cronus!

Cronus released a breath upon seeing Raven alive and whole. His eyes swept the room. Five guards were spread out between Raven's cell and him, and another stood post behind him. He again locked eyes with Raven and nodded before all hell broke loose. Cronus threw off his cloak, pistol in hand with laser spewing from the barrel. His first shot took the guard to his front right in the small of the back. Two more blasts ran up the guard's spine. Before the stricken fellow tumbled to his knees, Galen's hands were free, slipping up the opposite sleeves of his long tunic, drawing forth knives strapped to either arm.

Cronus spun about, shooting the guard behind him as Galen jabbed his daggers into the neck of the guard nearest him, driving the blades downward inside the collarbone. The guard stumbled to his knees, his voice trapped within the ruined narrows of his throat. Cronus spun again as the others recovered with swords drawn. Cronus squeezed the trigger, the laser taking another guard in the stomach, the second blast missing his shoulder, striking the wall above Kendra, splashing stone fragments upon her head.

Kendra drew her sword the moment Cronus's first blast struck true. She held at the corner of the chamber, observing the battle at hand. With stone fragments raining upon her and three guards down, she made her move. The guard nearest her took one step toward Cronus before she cut him down from behind, her blade slicing his left knee. The guard face-planted on the unforgiving floor, his sword slipping from his grasp. The soldier to her left stopped midstride, torn between Cronus's laser and Kendra's betrayal. He backed a step to gain his bearing, straying too close to the cell.

Raven snatched the fellow by the collar of his tunic, pulling him back forcefully into the bars of his cell. Raven reached his other hand around the guard's neck, twisting his head until the sound of his snapping spine echoed dully through the din. The last soldier afoot drove his blade toward Galen as the minstrel backed a step, brandishing his daggers in either hand.

Cronus fired several blasts, riddling the guard's torso before his blade neared Galen. The guard slumped to the floor, his skin paling with his pooling blood. Kendra knelt over the guard she had crippled, driving her sword into his neck, finishing him. She lifted her eyes as Cronus leveled the pistol at her head.

"Hold on, Cronus. She's with us now," Raven said, giving him pause.

"The door!" Kendra said as another guard stepped within to investigate. Galen threw a dagger, but the guard knocked it away as Cronus shifted aim. The flash of blue laser illuminated the dark chamber, piercing the guard's heavy mail. Cronus fired repeatedly until the guard's dead body toppled over. Kendra gained her feet, moving to the side of the door, taking the next guard to enter at the neck. His hands went to his stricken throat as he stumbled forth, flopping on the floor, blood issuing freely.

Cronus stepped into the doorway, laser blasts issuing from the pistol in the outer chamber, striking targets standing across the atrium. Kendra followed after him, clearing the few who escaped him. Raven could only see flashes of blue illuminating the doorway as Cronus and Kendra secured the outer chamber. The sounds of battle quickly waned to eerie silence until their familiar faces passed through the doorway. Raven's relief at seeing Cronus gave way to rage at seeing the minstrel.

"Shoot him, Cronus! He can't be trusted!" Raven growled.

"He's with us now, Rav, at least until we reach the far side of the lake."

"He stole my ocran! He stole my pistol! He left me to the mercies of a drunken mob!"

"We don't have time for this!" Kendra shouted. "We have to—"

"He is Torry, Raven. He is hunted now, the same as us, and we need all the help we can get," Cronus said.

"Give me my pistol!" Raven held out his open hand through the bars of his cell.

"Rav"—Cronus caught his breath, his heart still pounding from battle—"calm yourself."

"Calm myself?" Raven said in a deadly whisper. "I'll calm myself after I tear off his head and kick it down the street."

"Rav, we don't have time. I trust your faith in your new friend here"—Cronus regarded Kendra—"though I don't know her. I have no time to waylay my fears. I trust your word on the matter and expect the same in return. Give me your word that you shall not harm him and I'll open your cell."

"Raven, please!" Alen pleaded as Kendra opened his cell.

"All right. I won't kill him." Raven snorted, fixing Galen with a murderous look. "Now open this cage." Kendra quickly unlocked the cell, and Raven hobbled forth with his jacket in hand.

"It is good to see you well," Cronus said, handing him his pistol.

"Not as good as seeing you." Raven slapped Cronus's shoulder, nearly knocking the large Torry over. Raven took his pistol, carefully blasting the hinges of his shackles before blasting the broken manacles dangling from his hands. He slid the pistol into his holster as the metal links hit the floor.

"Now what?" Kendra asked, stepping between them.

"We get out of Dodge," Raven growled, "as fast as we can."

"Dodge?" She made a face.

"Don't ask." Cronus rolled his eyes. "We need mounts, and every mount in port is in the ocran pens near the auction block."

"How inconvenient," Galen quipped.

"But you have a plan," Raven said. Cronus always had a plan.

Cronus nodded, releasing a breath. "I have a plan. We shall see how good it is."

"Oh, it's good," Raven said, punching Galen in the chest, the blow sending the minstrel flying across the room. They all gave him a look. "I said I wouldn't kill him. Didn't say I wouldn't hit him."

*****

"Calm," the auctioneer pleaded, his hands raised to the crowd. "Let us…" His words stopped in his throat as blue laser struck his chest. He faltered, then fell, dropping at the slave girl's feet. The next blast took the guard behind her in the neck, passing through his spine. He dropped like a puppet whose strings were cut, tumbling down the steps behind the block.

Tosha followed the source of the laser to her right. Her eyes drew wide before narrowing as she spied Raven standing on a nearby rooftop, pistol in hand. He paused, his eyes finding hers across that deadly space. "You stubborn fool," she whispered.

Soldiers armed with crossbows took up position along the palisade that separated the assemblage from the adjoining street. Raven took aim, striking them in detail, his laser sweeping the palisade before a single bolt was loosed. The crowd gathered in the lower assemblage broke in panic, fleeing to every exit point as Benotrist soldiers struggled to circumvent the mob to engage Raven and take stock of their situation.

Tosha's guards closed around her with shields interlocked and swords at the ready. "Your shields are useless against his weapon. Follow me!" Tosha commanded, moving to the back of the upper assemblage where the stairs led below.

Raven shifted aim to the slaver guards running east between the slave pens. He picked two out of the herd, taking one in the hip and the other in the shoulder with hurried shots before passing on. The first dropped, hitting the ground painfully before gaining his feet and falling again, his hip shattered. The second stumbled, kept his feet, and continued on. The slaves in the pens huddled to the back of their cells, frightened by the strange light raining destruction from above.

"Raven, over here!" Alen shouted, pointing out a score of soldiers rushing down the street behind them. The roof Raven and Alen stood upon graded ten degrees with its high point facing the auction grounds to the south. Such an angle provided some cover and concealment from the soldiers to his front but fully exposed them to those advancing from the north. Alen squatted near the roof's north edge, watching Raven's back as he fired south.

Raven took a knee, reducing his exposure to the Benotrists along the auction grounds, taking quick measure of the soldiers approaching their back side, flooding the street below. He fired into the serried ranks, unable to miss. Several dropped in quick order, laser burning cavernous holes through their chests, exiting through their backs and striking at the feet of those trailing. The fortunate ones died quickly, falling where stricken. Some staggered with injured shoulders, hips, and limbs. Some limped away, and others crawled, desperate to flee the carnage. Those still afoot scrambled to either side of the street, out of Raven's line of fire.

A bolt whizzed overhead, forcing Alen to his back. "Raven!" he shouted, his finger pointing off to their left where a bounty hunter clad in boiled leather mail stood behind a millhouse, taking aim from its corner with a crossbow trained on them.

Raven fired several blasts through the corner of the stone structure where the hunter's body should have been in relation to his head peeking around the corner. Raven shifted aim elsewhere as the crossbow clanged upon the street, the hunter's still corpse slipping to the ground. His aim shifted further east along the avenue, striking targets further afield. His next shot took a Benotrist guard in the leg whilst crossing the street, knocking him from his feet. His second took a bounty hunter in the chest as he rushed toward their position.

"They're moving off the stables!" Alen shouted excitedly. Raven turned about, looking where the ocran stables rested just east of the auction grounds.

"It's about time," Raven growled, taking aim as two dozen Benotrist soldiers flooded into the street from the stables.

*****

"They're moving," Cronus observed as the guards posted around the stables hurried off. Galen stood opposite him, each standing at the corner of two storage houses on opposing sides of the street near the waterfront. Galen stole a peek around the corner, watching most of the Benotrists clear away, rushing north between the stables. The port's central stables consisted of a circular training pen with a stone wall running along its perimeter and with a rectangular-shaped stable running southward from it, containing scores of stalls. An even longer stable ran north to south, facing the training pen and lesser stable with a wide pathway between them.

Cronus was positioned due south with a clear view between the stables. Kendra had just come to his side, catching her breath as she raced along the waterfront from the granary she had set ablaze, further drawing the Benotrists' attention from their true target. The auction grounds rested to the immediate west of the stables, further complicating their plans.

They needed time to seize five mounts, saddle them, and be on their way, all the while being targeted by the hundreds of Benotrists, mercenaries, man hunters, and overzealous citizens who flooded the port. Tosha had ordered every mount unsaddled and kept under guard or removed from Axenville altogether. Every ship was ordered out of port, hindering any attempt to flee in the event Raven slipped his bonds.

Bursts of laser flashed above the rooftops off their right, followed by the cries of wounded and dying men. Smoke drifted overhead, pressed by an easterly gale, casting an ominous pall above. Cronus counted three guards still lingering between the stables. "Psst," he called out to Kendra over his left shoulder. She looked expectantly as he lifted three fingers before touching his hand to his chest, signaling his intent. She nodded, comprehending his plan.

Cronus and Galen quickly crossed the avenue, taking up position along the south wall of the shorter stable. Kendra stepped into the clear, brandishing a bow in her left hand and notching an arrow with her right. She fixed her aim on the nearest soldier who stood post in the causeway between the stables. The soldier's eyes were fixed northward, in the direction where his comrades had rushed off to.

Kendra loosed her arrow, drawing a second from her quiver as the first one flew. The soldier cried out, the arrow embedding in his anus. He turned, his face contorted in rage as his eyes found Kendra. She smiled, never growing tired of her preferred target area: an armored opponent's backside.

"Argh!" the Benotrist howled, limping toward her with blade raised and the arrow protruding from his posterior, his comrades joining the fight. Kendra loosed her second arrow, the soldier knocking it away with his shield as her third struck above the greaves of the fellow to his left, piercing his naked thigh. The fellow kept his feet, though slowed by the wound, the third soldier outpacing his injured comrades.

Cronus held his sword at the ready, his back pressed against the wall of the stable as the three Benotrists passed, oblivious to his presence with their eyes fixed on Kendra. No sooner had they passed than he closed swiftly behind them, taking the one with the wounded thigh, chopping his knee. Galen moved likewise, driving his dagger into the neck of the other wounded soldier. Kendra loosed another arrow at the lead soldier. He knocked it away with his shield, closing upon her as she forsook her bow for steel. "Argh!" he shouted, thrusting his blade as he drew nigh.

Kendra blocked the blow, twisting away as he pressed his attack. Cronus was upon him before his second thrust, chopping the back of his knee. Kendra stepped around his stumbling feet, bringing her sword down upon his neck, nearly severing head from body as it dangled by the barest of tissue.

"Come. We haven't time to spare!" Cronus shouted, racing back to the stables as Galen finished the first soldier Cronus had crippled, pinning him to the ground with a knee to his back, driving his dagger between his plates of mail. Galen gained his feet as his friends passed, following them as people started flooding into the street from the auction grounds.

*****

Raven struggled picking out targets amid the chaos below. The surrounding streets were filled with people fleeing every which way, foiling the Benotrists' attempts to close upon him in any organized fashion, yet it foiled him trying to find them in the crowd. He spotted the familiar gray mail and helm exiting the auction grounds, a soldier whose frame was obscured by several women in front of him. Raven waited for them to break one way or another. Two broke left and the other right as they stepped onto the street, leaving Raven a clear shot. His laser took the soldier in the center of his chest, dropping him in the street, as those nearest him broke further in panic.

"Cronus!" Alen shouted excitedly, pointing to their right, as their three comrades rode into the street from the direction of the stables with two other ocran in tow.

"It's about time," Raven grunted, stepping back from the south side of the roof. Alen waved Cronus to the north side of the building as Raven fired discriminatingly, clearing the adjoining streets.

Cronus swerved through the serried streets, forcing panicked citizens out of his path, holding his reins in his right hand and those of the trailing mount in his left. They crossed over the first street slightly west of Raven's position before turning on the street that ran behind his position. A bounty hunter in boiled leather brandishing a shortsword recognized Galen as they turned onto the street. The fellow broke from the shadows for the minstrel's bounty.

Cronus almost released his own reins, planning to draw his sword as the fellow ran toward them, before laser fire struck him in the back, exiting his gut and striking the ground in front of him. Cronus sighed with relief, finding Raven on the rooftop ahead. The bounty hunter fell to his knees, his hands flying to his gaping wound before Cronus's mount trampled him underfoot.

"Jump!" Raven ordered Alen, firing up the street as Cronus and the others stopped below them. Alen stood warily upon the low precipice, staring down at the mount below as if he was perched upon a mountaintop. "Jump, or I'll throw you!" Raven barked, squeezing off another shot, dropping a crossbowman peering around a corner two blocks to their west. Alen sat down, easing his legs over the edge before dropping below, his rump hitting the saddle. He held on, gaining his bearing as Kendra tossed him the reins.

"Your turn, Rav!" Cronus shouted, drawing Raven's mount close to the wall.

"All right. I'm coming," Raven growled, holstering his pistol as he neared the edge. He stopped, thinking it looked farther down than he remembered. Deciding there was no way he was going to jump that far down without breaking something, he sat down, easing himself off.

Cronus winced as Raven missed the saddle completely, hitting the ground in an unforgiving thud. *How could he miss?* Cronus shook his head as Raven's cursing took its expected course.

"#@%&" Raven spewed invectives, gaining his feet while painfully climbing into the saddle.

"You all right?" Cronus asked, keeping an eye on the people spilling into the street.

"Feels like I broke my ass!"

"Is that even possible?" Cronus gave him a look.

"Apparently so." Raven snorted.

Cronus shook his head, biting a smile as he kicked his heels, urging his mount onward.

*****

They raced through the winding streets and narrow alleyways, knocking people aside. Cronus led their motley band, leaning sharply into each turn as the sound of their hooves striking stone echoed through the air. "Raven!" he shouted over his shoulder, lifting his sword to a rooftop ahead off their right, where an archer stood, leveling a notched arrow. *Zip!* Blue laser passed overhead, striking the edge of the structure below his feet. The archer dropped, the edge of the roof giving way beneath him, his arrow loosed harmlessly awry. Fragments of stone, mortar, and slate showered below as they swerved through the debris. They turned the next corner with the open countryside ahead. Kendra pushed up ahead of Cronus, leading them toward the coastal road, which skirted the shoreline, winding through the vineyards and rolling hills that stretched to the horizon. They pushed on, leaving Axenville behind, smoke billowing over its tortured sky.

*****

They rode apace, the late-day sun shining off the calm waters off their right as the green hills and lush vineyards yielded to rolling waves of golden grass. Cronus pulled back on his reins, easing his ocran to a halt as the others filed in around him. Raven leaned forward in his saddle, resting a forearm on the pommel as he stared ahead, his eyes fixed to a small fishing port along the horizon.

"Let's hope they have some boats in port," Raven said.

"They should," Kendra opined. "The princess only ordered the ships away at Axenville. These smaller villages were of little consequence and too far off to be bothered with."

"Maybe not." Cronus narrowed his eyes as a dozen riders rode out to meet them, their familiar gray helms and mail passing through the high grass like the dorsal fins of a dorun. They fanned out to either side of the coastal road that cut between the tall, grassy fields. They were dispatched to guard the coastal road east of Axenville and return by midday before happening upon Cronus's group and recognizing the Earther from afar.

"Take them!" their commander of flax ordered, drawing his sword and rushing forth, his ocran cutting through the high grass like a ship breaking a golden surf. Cronus drew his sword, his mount rearing into the air, directing Alen and Kendra to the left and Galen to the right. Raven snorted as Galen drew near, wondering if Cronus would mind if an errant laser blast found a home in the minstrel's skull.

"Fare thee well, Commander Kenti. May the foe again fall to your fell hand, and we shall sing of the glory—"

"Shut up, minstrel, and get your ass where it belongs! I should shoot you for just talking like that!" Raven growled.

"My dear Captain Raven, let us set aside our petty divisions. I regret the misunderstanding when we were first introduced. As native Torries, Commander Kenti and I have come to an accord. Perhaps you and I—"

"Only an idiot would trust you twice, and I ain't an idiot!" Raven snorted.

"My dear Captain Raven, I never said you weren't," Galen said with a mock bow before riding off to the right.

"Hey!" Raven growled after Galen rode off, slow to recognize the insult.

"Let him go, Rav. We have larger matters to attend." Cronus lifted his chin toward the approaching riders drawing near.

"I know. I see them," he said, dismissing the gravity of the threat. "Just how many of these clowns do we have to kill to escape this craphole country?"

"Apparently, twelve more." Cronus's mount reared again into the air as he drew his sword, charging forth through the grassy golden sea.

"All right, General Custer," Raven mumbled, joining Cronus's mad charge and hoping it didn't cost them their scalps.

Kendra, Alen, and Galen followed Cronus and Raven across the grassy sea, meeting the Benotrist cavalry. Laser fire spewed forth, striking the Benotrists' center mount, dropping the animal with several shots to its breast, forelegs, and neck. Its head dipped before rolling over, throwing its rider. Those to either side angled away, their ocran frightened by the strange light.

Kendra dropped her reins at full gallop, notching an arrow and releasing the shaft as the enemy drew close, her shaft embedding in a rider's right arm. She notched a second before the first had struck, shifting her aim leftward to the next rider in the line. Her arrow struck the ocran's neck as she grabbed her reins, swerving between the two she had struck.

Alen held tight to the reins with his left hand, gripping his sword in his right. He was new to the saddle and the sword, trusting in his courage and desperation to carry him through. The soldiers opposite him closed swiftly upon his flanks, squeezing him between them with blades leveled to deliver a crippling blow. A burst of azure light flashed brightly before him, piercing the shield of the soldier off his right before passing on, burning a cavity through his innards. The soldier slipped from the saddle, his body tumbling in the high grass, his mount veering off. Alen shifted his sword to his left, his blade meeting the steel of his other attacker. The clang of steel echoed over the din as he passed on, struggling to circle about as more laser fire riddled the fellow and his mount before he could circle back on him.

Cronus cursed his choice of mount, the obstinate beast fighting his every command, save for rearing, which the animal seemed to enjoy. Raven decimated the riders to their front, killing mounts and riders in a hail of laser fire. He caught sight of Alen off his left, Raven's laser fire dropping his immediate foes. Beyond Alen, he could see Kendra pass between the still mounted Benotrists. He broke from Raven's side, riding north to her aid.

Galen rode forth, brandishing an unfamiliar sword in his left hand. He lamented his recent misfortune, traveling the region to earn coin plying his trade, only to be waylaid by Benotrist soldiers falsely claiming him a spy. He escaped that danger only to run afoul the temperamental Earther, who desired his head on a spike. Now he rode into battle, facing trained cavalry with no hope to match their skill in the saddle or with a blade. He preferred using a dagger, which was of little use in a mounted charge.

Despite his misgivings, he pressed on with enough skill to meet his opponent's blade in full stride, the glancing blow denying the enemy an easy kill. Galen's poor grip proved disastrous, the blade flying from his grasp. His opponent circled quickly about; his eyes trained on Galen with expectant glee. Others closed from the south, catching him between them, each intent on claiming his head. He kicked his heels, spurring his ocran to a full gallop, swerving to dodge his opponent's hasty blow as he sped north. The others angled to their right, following him as he slipped behind Raven's mount, using the Earther as a shield.

Raven made a face as the minstrel circled behind him, stealing a glance around Raven's shoulder at the approaching riders. Raven shook his head disgustedly before riddling the approaching mounts with laser fire. The lead Benotrist mounts crumpled in the grass, taking their riders with them, the others veering off, abandoning the fight.

Kendra loosed another arrow, the shaft embedding in the left thigh of the warrior whose ocran she struck in the neck. The rider with the wounded arm circled about, charging her while holding desperately to his sword's hilt. Kendra discarded her bow, grabbing the reins as the soldier drew near. She bit a smile as a shadow passed behind her foe, turning her mount to the right to keep his eyes on her as Cronus drove his sword into his side. The fellow cried out as Cronus twisted his blade in his innards. She saw laser flashing behind them, striking targets farther afield as what remained of the enemy fled.

Cronus jabbed the Benotrist with two more quick thrusts before chopping his hand and snagging the collar of his mail, pulling him from the saddle. The soldier writhed upon the ground, twisting in agony with his arms pressed to his wounds. Cronus quickly scanned the field, seeing the enemy slain or fled and Raven, Galen, and Alen riding to meet them. He dismounted, delivering a fatal blow to the dying soldier, ending his torment. Unlike Tyro's minions, he took no pleasure in the suffering of his enemies, though he would make an exception for Kriton.

"Mount up, Cronus. The way looks clear," Raven said, riding up beside him as the others filed in around them. "Let's hope there's a ship still in port," he added, scrubbing his face with his hand, looking off to the fishing village to the east.

"Cronus, look!" Kendra called his attention to the west, her face ashen. The others followed her eyes westward, where scores of mounted soldiers paraded along the horizon.

"Wait," Cronus said as Raven drew his pistol. Centered amid their ranks, a soldier held aloft a blue flag, its rich folds full with the wind. Raven pressed the Scope Up switch on his pistol, scanning the line of cavalry in detail, sweeping their line until stopping at its center. There she sat beside the blue banner, her ebony hair lifting in the breeze.

"Tosha." Raven shook his head.

"Tosha? She doesn't give up. I wonder what she has to say," Cronus asked, climbing back in the saddle, turning his ocran about, his eyes narrow beneath the midday sun.

"Whatever it is, I ain't listening. We've said all there is to say," Raven lied, not caring to admit what the others already knew.

"What harm is there in speaking with her?" Kendra asked.

"You don't know her like I do, so butt out!" he growled. "Whatever she wants, she doesn't have the leverage to get it, not now. And if she sends her little detachment at us, I'll cut them down at this range."

"Rav, let me see." Cronus held out his hand as Raven handed him his pistol. Cronus used the scope, scanning the Benotrist cavalry. They dressed their line in good order but seemed content to hold their position. He wondered if they had another force attempting to circle north, cutting their retreat while this force held them in place.

The grasslands ended just north, stopping short of the rolling hills that stretched endlessly beyond. They couldn't have circumvented their position in so short a time since they rode apace upon leaving Axenville. His answer came as Tosha rode forth alone, her countenance betraying little of her intent. "Here she comes, and she appears to be alone," Cronus said, giving Raven back his pistol.

"Alone?" Raven made a face, taking another scan through his scope. "What's she up to?"

"Are you a dolt?" Kendra rolled her eyes. "She desires to speak with you, and if she is alone, she is placing her life in your hands. A woman would not do so unless she had something of great import to say."

"Go see what she wants, Rav," Cronus said.

"What if it's a trap?" Raven countered.

"What's she going to do, beat you up?" Cronus laughed, stealing Raven's favorite line.

"She just might." Raven snorted, kicking his heels, speeding off to meet her.

*****

She stopped mid distance, waiting patiently as he drew near, her countenance a mask of indifference, though her heart pounded emphatically. Her thoughts were a maelstrom of regret, uncertainty, and trepidation. Why was Raven so difficult? Why did he manifest such irrationality in her? Why did he rule her heart? She suddenly felt the wind upon her face, bringing her thoughts to the task at hand as he pulled up before her. They stared at each other for a time, each with a thousand things to say and no voice to speak them. Tosha was weary of harsh rebukes and barbed words but was too angry to so easily forgive him.

"You look better than last I saw you." Tosha forced a smile.

"Thanks" was all Raven could think to say.

"Raven, I..." she started before closing her mouth, uncertain of where to begin.

"What do you want, Tosh? Just give up this pointless chase. You can't stop—"

"I have ordered my men to stand down. They will not pursue you or the others. You are free to leave," she said firmly.

"Then why are you here? And what's to stop me from taking you with me? Your men can't help you from that far away."

"No, they could not, but I have reassured them that you shall not harm or detain me."

"I won't, huh? How do you figure that?"

"You've never hurt me, Raven. And you shall not take me by force." Her unwavering confidence seemed out of place.

"And why is that?" he asked, unnerved by her cryptic tone.

"Because"—she eased her ocran up beside his—"you protect the ones you love."

"How do you know I love you?"

"I know, but I wasn't speaking of me," she said, touching a hand to her stomach.

His eyes shot to her stomach. "You're—"

"With child, Raven, our child," she answered evenly, attempting to gauge his reaction.

"We were together only once, at Fera." He tried to recall the time frame in his head.

"Our wedding night," she affirmed.

"How long have you known?" His voice was harsher than expected.

"Just after you captured me, I missed my cycle, and then I knew. You do not seem pleased." She could not hide her disappointment.

"Not pleased? You knew all this time, and you didn't tell me until now?" he growled.

"Raven, I—" She was taken aback by his anger.

"All the days of hard riding could have cost you the baby, not to mention me chaining you up each night to keep you from escaping. Do you know why I did that? It was to keep you from running off and getting yourself killed in the wild or slain by bandits before you could ever find your father's men. All the while, you were more vulnerable than I believed!"

"You do care." She smiled, her heart mending with his concern.

"Of course, I care. What do you take me for? But you obviously don't!"

"I don't?"

"You should have stayed at your father's castle instead of traipsing across the continent looking for me. At least there, you and the baby would have been safe." He couldn't help but think of every harsh word he had spoken to her or how roughly he had treated her throughout their arduous trek. Any stress upon her threatened their child's life, and he hated himself for it.

"But then I wouldn't have been with you." She smiled, tilting her head with an innocence that did not fit her character.

"You're not with me now," he argued.

"I can be," she offered.

"You'd come with me?"

"No, you could come with me," she countered. "Cronus can lead the others across the lake. The way is clear for them now, and Torry North is but a short journey once they reach the crossroads."

"I'm not going with you, Tosh. Staying any longer in your father's realm is like petting a viper. You could come with me, though. We could raise our baby together on the *Stenox* and sail the world." He smiled.

"Raven, I…I can't. I thought you understood. I must have the baby in Bansoch. It is my duty as second guardian of the Sisterhood. I will be shamed if you are absent upon my return and even more so when I give birth. If my honor means anything to you, you must come," she pleaded.

"That's not fair, Tosh. You went ahead with all these plans without asking me, and now you want to guilt me into following you back to Amazon land where I'd be nothing more than a glorified slave?"

"A slave?" she challenged darkly. "You are a royal consort! No man on my mother's isle is so highly placed. It is an honor I bestowed upon you above any other. I spent my life refusing the offered suitors of nearly *every* house in my mother's and father's realms. It was my place to choose whom I wished, and I chose you, and I would not have done so if I thought you didn't feel the same.

"You desired me the first time your eyes fell upon me in that foul cell on Molten Isle. I knew that look that passed your eyes when you rescued me. It is a look a woman can sense and a man cannot hide. You desired me, and I desired you. After that moment, the fates would have it no other way. I simply accelerated our courtship, nothing more."

"Accelerated? You skipped the whole thing and went right to the wedding and bedding without even telling me!"

"I could hardly wait upon you to arrange our nuptials. You know absolutely *nothing* about women!" She narrowed her eyes.

"Obviously not since the one I married drugs me, kicks me, bites me, screams at me, and has me beaten up by every drunk in Axenville!"

"You stubborn…"

*****

Cronus sighed as he looked on, tiredly observing their argument from afar.

"Do they ever stop arguing?" Kendra asked.

"No. It's been like this for a thousand leagues." Cronus sighed.

"Surely you jest?" Galen said, curious why the princess chose Raven of all people as her consort.

"A thousand leagues," Alen affirmed, meaning the longest thousand leagues any two men had ever taken.

*****

They stared at each other in silence, their anger finally extinguished.

"If you do not return with me, then you forsake your child." Tosha sighed.

"I won't forsake our child." Raven scrubbed his face with his hands.

"Then you will come with me?"

"No. We part ways today, and when the baby comes, I'll be there."

"You shall be there? I don't understand."

"I need to return Cronus to Leanna. I promised her, and I will see it done. I have come too far to not see it through. I am tempted to take you with me to keep you safe, but my path is more dangerous than your return would be. Go back to Axenville and have a carriage take you north. No more time in the saddle after today."

"Do you think yourself my master?" she challenged, her spine straightening as she lifted her chin, indignant with his treating her like a child.

"I'm your husband, Tosha, unless you've forgotten. That's what husbands do where I'm from. They protect their wives. Go home, and I'll be there before you give birth."

"Do you so avow?" she asked.

"I promise." He reached out his hand to her face, hooking her hair behind her ear, losing himself in her golden eyes.

"I shall hold you to it," she whispered, pressing her lips to his. The breeze swept off the lake, lifting her hair in the summer wind as he returned her kiss. They held their embrace for an eternal moment before their ocran shifted apart. With that, he regarded her for a time and bade his farewell. She watched as he rode off, her moistened eyes holding firm lest they burst. Her eyes followed him as he returned to his comrades before continuing on to the fishing port.

CHAPTER 13

Brokov sat the captain's chair, staring out of the viewport of the bridge as the Troan coastline kissed the horizon. At this distance, it was but a narrow sliver of gray and green with the clear sky above and the ocean blue below. He templed his fingers neath his chin, deep in thought, as the ship cut the lapping waves.

"Twenty-four minutes to port," Kato affirmed, sitting on the helm off Brokov's right.

"Very well. Full ahead."

"You certain, Brokov?" Kato asked. "The last ping on Raven's transmitter places him on the eastern edge of Lake Veneba. He won't reach Tro for several days at best."

They had been monitoring Raven's movements since the day they disembarked at Tinsay so long ago, following his painstakingly slow progress across Northern Arax. Leanna stared at the monitoring screen for hours on end every day, her eyes never leaving that single ping that displayed Raven's location on the map. All her hopes rested on the knowledge that Cronus was with him. Lorken told her that they were together when he left them far east of Fera, but anything could have happened since.

As for the rest of the crew, they were restless aboard the confines of the ship. They had not set ashore since Tinsay and were climbing the walls. They shadowed Raven's movement off shore throughout his trek, waiting in position if he ever broke toward the coast. The fact that Raven never broke north to the Benotrist shoreline coincided with his much slower progress, which indicated he and Cronus lost their magantors at some point.

"I'm certain, Kato. It is best to test the waters at Tro before Raven arrives."

"We were in good standing with Magistrate Adine when last we departed Tro," Kato said.

"Things change, Kato. Most cities in Arax are politically volatile. Magistrates change at the whim of their masters. Klen Adine is no different and must balance the differing agendas of Tro's ruling families."

"Even if we receive a cold welcome, we shouldn't be in port long if Raven keeps his current pace."

"If he keeps his current pace," Brokov said sourly. There were many times when his progress stopped for days at a time, the last being when Raven reached the north side of Lake Veneba.

"It would've been easier if we had stayed with plan A instead of plan B," Kato said, regarding their original plan to meet them off the Benotrist coast north of Fera.

"Plan A was Tosha doing as she promised and freeing Cronus. Forget plan B. We're now on plan X, Y, or Z."

*****

Tro Harbor rested at the mouth of the Flen, straddling the opposite banks of the river. The city arced around the Troan Bay. The entrance of the bay narrowed severely to half the width of its widest part. The port city lined the opposite shores of the inlet with a few small, rocky islands dotting its center. The port rested forty leagues east of the confluence of the Veneba and Flen Rivers, where the trading hub of Gotto rested, Tro's oldest ally and sister city.

Tro was the largest and deepest of all Araxan ports. Ships flagged under all the realms of Arax traversed its tranquil waters. Unlike other independent ports that dotted the coastlines of Arax, Tro did not fall under the dominion of pirate influence, a fact that at times brought her into conflict with notorious buccaneers, such as Monsoon. Such individuals could only harry Troan trade routes, unable to permanently suppress the strength of a harbor the size of Tro.

Tro had built its own navy and a well-trained small army. It also generated enough wealth to hire small private armies whenever the need arose. The wealth of its merchants far exceeded that of their contemporaries and that of some kings. It was these few men who were the heads of the five ruling families, forming Tro's ruling plutocracy.

The ruling families controlled the ottein and slave trade along the eastern coast of Arax and as far inland as Notsu and Bacel. They controlled the iron and gold mines southwest of the city and similar holdings along the coastline. They arranged exclusive trade routes with Gotto, which provided the timber and livestock the city depended on at below market rates in exchange for trading one another's goods further inland and along the coast.

The ruling families of each city had intermarried over the centuries, further cementing their alliance through blood. The ruling families of Tro appointed Harbor Magistrate Klen Adine, who oversaw all bureaucratic functions of the city.

Klen Adine was drawn from his inner sanctum in the harbor's central forum to a great commotion. He smoothed the rich folds of his crimson robes as he passed between the towering pillars that lined each face of the city forum. Resting upon the southern shore of the Troan Bay, the city forum was a massive marble structure with twenty towering pillars, each the height of five men, lining its sides. Lesser stone structures surrounded the great edifice, forming the heart of the central district of Tro.

With glimmering stone wharves along the immediate shoreline, ships could dock close to the city forum, but only the most prestigious were afforded such curtesy. Most ships were docked further west or along the north shore, where lesser piers were built to receive them.

Klen Adine was young as far as magistrates went, having attained his post on his twenty-fourth year and holding it for ten years since. His narrow, even-set face was strikingly handsome with sea-blue eyes and rich dark hair that could make a maiden swoon. But Klen's charmless manner and reserved nature were equally off-putting to the fairer sex. He was entirely humorless and thoroughly efficient, which contrasted with his charismatic but carelessly corrupt predecessor, who met a ghastly end at the hands of the ruling families. Klen was promptly promoted from a lesser post for possessing the very attributes that his predecessor lacked. He retained his post by keeping the ruling families' favor ever since.

Klen followed the excited gestures of the populace lining the streets below, each pointing to the center of the bay where the morning sun shone off the shimmering hull of the *Stenox*. Klen sighed, releasing a tired breath, dreading the Earthers' return for a myriad of reasons. He had choice words to share with Raven and ordered his attendants to escort him to the forum once they docked. He wasn't surprised when the *Stenox* turned hard to port, heading straight for the central wharves that were designated for dignitaries instead of the lesser piers that suited their station. He shook his head with their presumption, knowing full well they took whichever liberties they pleased.

*****

Leanna stood behind the low wall of the third deck, her eyes wide with wonder as the *Stenox* sailed the tranquil waters of Tro. A flock of soren birds coursed overhead, their squawks echoing through the crisp morning air. The salty smell of the ocean filled her lungs as she stared out across the bay. The city surrounded them with stone structures and wooden edifices lining the shores of the bay.

She reflected on the wonders she had beheld since coming aboard the *Stenox* on that fateful night in Central City. Save for a journey to Cagan Harbor with her father when she was a child, she had never ventured from her home city. Now in the space of a few months, she had sailed half the world. Few cities matched the splendor of old Cagia, yet Tro surpassed that ancient port in size and wealth.

Upon entering the port, her eyes were instantly drawn to a massive statue rising from a small, rocky isle in the center of the bay. The legs of the stone giant straddled the expanse of the isle, rising to a height fifteen times that of a man. It was cast in the visage of a warrior with a broad shield in his left hand and a sword in his right, outstretched toward the mouth of the bay. Its face was fixed to the open sea with obsidian centered in its sockets surrounded by rings of sapphires forming the irises of its giant eyes. The morning sun shone upon the giant's face, illuminating its jeweled eyes as if they were alive.

"The Sentinel of Tro," Arsenc affirmed, standing at her side as she craned her neck, staring up at its towering form as the *Stenox* turned to port, skirting the face of the isle. Leanna knew Brokov and Kato sailed close to the statue to gift her an optimal view of the famed landmark. Even those accustomed to such wonders shrank before the majesty of the ancient statue. A sudden sadness overtook her at that moment, her moist eyes watering at their corners. "Leanna?" Arsenc asked, touching a hand to her shoulder.

"'Tis nothing," she lied, regarding him with a forced smile.

"I know," he reassured her, reading her mind. "I miss him also." Cronus often spoke of the Sentinel of Tro, wishing to see it one day as his brother had in Raven's company. Leanna never believed it would be her eyes to behold it first.

After turning hard to port, the *Stenox* sped toward the massive stone buildings that dominated Tro's central district. The wide stone wharves ahead were crowded with excited onlookers, who gazed with wonder at the alien vessel. Soldiers in silver mail over white tunics ordered the people back as others paraded along the wharves to greet the *Stenox* in disciplined ranks. The *Stenox* slowed as it neared the wharf, easing to port as its starboard hull touched the stone lip of the dock.

Brokov and Kato exited the bridge, stepping on the aft of the second deck as Zem stepped onto the stern of the first deck, his powerful metallic arms crossed over his large chest, standing guard, his mere presence a warning to any fool who thought to attack.

"Lorken has command," Brokov said, testing the grip of his pistol while adjusting his holster. "You know the deal."

"Aye. If you fail to make contact within the hour, we flatten the city." Kato shrugged as if it was a trivial matter.

"Yes, but let us hope it won't come to that. Arsenc, are you with me?" Brokov asked, staring up at the third deck where the Torry stood.

"Aye," Arsenc answered, mimicking their strange speech. He and Brokov descended to the first deck and stepped onto the wharf, where they were greeted by a harbor official attired in an ankle-length emerald tunic and gray cape.

"We wish to treat with the harbor magistrate. Does Klen Adine still hold that post?"

"He does. Magistrate Adine awaits you at the harbor forum. I am to escort you hither," the official declared.

"Lead on."

*****

Klen Adine was mildly surprised to see Brokov ushered into his presence instead of Raven. Of course, considering the reports he had received of late, he should not have been. His spies sent word of strange happenings along the Benotrist border. Even stranger was the news that a band of criminals had raided the Black Castle and escaped. Large bounties were placed upon their heads, sums so vast that they drew every man hunter in eastern Arax to Tro. Klen recognized three names listed on the bounty: Raven, Lorken, and the brother of Cordi Kenti. The man accompanying Brokov was unfamiliar but obviously Araxan.

"Magistrate Adine, I present the Earther Brokov and Arsenc Ottin, Torry second commander of unit." His aide bowed before Klen dismissed him. Klen sat behind a large wooden table with various parchments spread across its surface. He waved an open hand to two chairs opposite him, his guests taking the offered seats.

"Brokov, it is odd to treat with you. I must usually suffer the pleasure of your illustrious captain," Klen said dryly.

"Good fortune shines on you, Klen. You get me instead of Raven."

"Yes, my good fortune." He sighed. "As for your captain, is there a reason he did not attend this meet?" Klen reminded Brokov of an attorney in the Space Fleet JAG Corp who asked a question he secretly knew the answer to.

"He would if he were here," Brokov said, deciding to try the honest approach, as Klen had an uncanny way of finding the truth in the most convincing of lies.

"I surmised as much," Klen said, pushing a parchment across the table toward him. Brokov took hold of the wrinkled paper, turning it around, Arsenc leaning close to look as well. At the bottom of the parchment, in bold Araxan script, were the words *Raven the Earther*, followed by the word *bounty*.

Above the script was a picture that was supposed to be of Raven. The picture was a grotesque caricature of what he assumed was Raven. The face had floppy massive ears, an expansive forehead, bucked teeth, a flat large nose, and two very narrow eyes. *They got the eyes right.* Brokov snickered, keeping the thought to himself. *That's not Raven,* Arsenc thought, making a face.

"A striking resemblance. I think they truly captured his likeness." Brokov couldn't contain his smile, tossing the parchment back on the table.

"We can debate the creative skills of the imperial artist that produced that parchment, but it is Raven's name upon it. I have similar ones for Lorken, a Torry named Cronus Kenti, a Yatin Elite named Yeltor, and an escaped royal slave," Klen said, his fingers tapping each parchment of bounty as he mentioned their names. Brokov noted that Klen did not mention Terin among the wanted and feared he had been captured or slain. "Which leads me to wonder your purpose here, Brokov."

"Am I speaking to our friend or the magistrate of Tro?" Brokov asked, gauging Klen's response.

Klen would hardly consign their relationship as friendship but held some fondness for the Earthers. Raven was difficult to reason with at times and was wholly unsuited to treat with those in authority, though Klen seemed to manage as well as any. Brokov was far easier to treat with, as he was knowledgeable, intelligent, and well-spoken. The opinion of the ruling families, however, differed greatly on the matter of the Earthers.

"Tro is a major port of call. Our first priority is following up on our last visit," Brokov said.

"Your last visit?" Klen asked curiously.

"Yes. We successfully expelled the pirate fleet from Tro's waters and secured your trade routes to points south."

"Successful is a generous estimate," Klen said dryly.

"Do they still harry your merchant fleets or raid your territories?"

"In some measure, they still do," Klen countered.

"Other than singular raiders? How many of your ships have been assailed by multiple pirate vessels?" Brokov knew well that answer. You could never permanently squash all attempts of thievery. The combined mercenary forces employed by Tro had decimated the pirate fleets, slain countless buccaneer captains, and sunk scores of ships. The one failure of the campaign was the pirate admiral Monsson's escape.

"Point taken." Klen inclined his head, acknowledging that fact.

"And our one failure in that campaign can now—" Brokov continued before Klen interjected.

"Monsoon," Klen answered. "We received word of his capture some time ago. You captured him, did you not?"

"Yes," Brokov answered.

"And delivered him to the Benotrist emperor," Klen stated.

"Your sources are right again."

"And yet Raven and Lorken are wanted by the Benotrist emperor."

"Apparently so."

"It never takes Raven long to make enemies out of would-be friends," Klen said evenly.

"That wasn't his fault. He journeyed to Fera in good faith and was betrayed by his host."

"And I am to assume Raven is guiltless in the entire affair?" Klen raised a skeptical brow.

"It is Raven we are talking about." Brokov shrugged, conceding the point.

"Well, with Monsoon's capture, I can fully retire your commission, as he was the final objective in our campaign," Klen said. "But since you chose to deliver him into Tyro's hands rather than our own, I cannot reward you for his bounty."

"We expected such. We have other business to attend in the south, but if you have further need of our unique services, we are willing to hear them."

"I have no need to keep you from your mission to the Ape Empire," Klen said. Brokov shook his head, not at all surprised that Klen's spies knew about Argos as well. Was Klen revealing such knowledge to impress him or to let him know that they couldn't hide anything without him finding out? "Which brings us again to Raven. He is not with you, is he?"

"What made you believe that?" Brokov wondered how Klen had guessed correctly of Raven's absence.

"With man hunters from as far away as Barbeario, Varabis, and Cesa arriving daily in Tro to claim his bounty, I surmised that he was somewhere other than on your ship. The last reports put him east of Fera, heading in this general direction. Of course, he could break toward Bedo or double back to Torry North once he clears the Plate Mountains."

"Raven is not with us." Brokov shrugged, conceding the point.

"And I surmise that if you are here, he is heading this way," Klen stated.

"Perhaps." Brokov shrugged.

"And when he arrives, his presence will set off a battle in the streets, drawing every man hunter in Tro to claim their prize."

"If they're foolish enough to try," Brokov said darkly.

"The bounty is five hundred thousand certras." Klen gave him a face.

"Yes. I saw that on the parchment." Brokov sighed. "At that price, even we might be tempted. What do you say, Klen, five hundred thousand split two ways? You can give up your position, and we can go in as equal partners, maybe purchase a small isle, open a resort that caters to wealthy travelers. We can lounge on the beach surrounded by hundreds of beautiful women."

Klen would've smiled if he had a sense of humor. "Yes, as grand as those plans sound, I would just as soon have you collect Raven and be gone *before* you visit such carnage upon this port."

"We are of agreement on that matter, but you might wish to give that same speech to those who might attack us."

"That would be my preference as well, but things are more complicated since your last visit."

"Different? How?"

"It is not for me to speak of. Perhaps our mutual associate might further elaborate."

Kaly, Brokov mused. Kaly was a proprietor of several establishments that some considered unsavory. He often acted as the go-between, contracting swords for hire at the behest of Klen Adine and the various heads of the ruling families. Kaly was the one to contact the *Stenox* on behalf of the Troan council to combat the pirate lord Monsoon. Kaly was also the Earthers' strongest ally in Tro, and Brokov counted him as a friend.

"I will speak with...our mutual associate after I leave here," Brokov answered, deep in thought.

"Very well. The sooner, the better. He should enlighten you on several delicate matters." Klen's dry tone was as cryptic as he could manage.

*****

Brokov and Arsenc returned to the *Stenox* as swiftly as they could. Klen ordered his men to escort them to the wharf, keeping the populace from their route of travel. Stepping aboard, Brokov ordered everyone belowdecks. With the harbor teeming with bounty hunters, he decided it was best not to gift them any easy targets. Even if they weren't wanted, each of them held close association with one who was.

"Where to next?" Kato asked, following him onto the bridge.

"North side of the harbor," Brokov said, taking his seat in the captain's chair.

"Kaly?"

"Yep. Try to park as close as possible."

"Aye, aye, Captain," Kato said, humoring him with a little seafaring jargon as the *Stenox* pulled away from the wharf. Within minutes, they sped across the Troan Bay, closing swiftly upon the wooden docks that lined the waterfront of the north shore. Scores of vessels were moored along the wharves—merchant ships, slavers, privateers, and fishing cogs.

The merchant and slaving vessels were moored sans cargo, as all tradable goods and slaves with the sole exception of fish were regulated by the ruling families. All slaves were exchanged at the central slaving plaza on the south shore, the ruling families receiving a percentage on every chattel bought or sold. A similar exchange was applied to all tradable goods exchanged at the merchant plaza, also centered on the south shore.

Ships would unload their cargo on the designated loading wharves. If the ship intended to make a port of call longer than a day, it would have to moor empty at a wharf on the north shore of the bay. The rich estates of the ruling families rested further inland, upon the hillsides that ringed the bay, though each was positioned on the southern half of the bay, consigning the northern lands for the lesser merchants, trade guilds, and commoners of Tro.

Brokov eyed a massive structure overshadowing the docks ahead as the *Stenox* drew close. The structure rested a street behind the waterfront, constructed of thick timbers weathered by the salty air. The structure was nearly thirty-five yards abreast and ten high with a forward-slanting slate roof. The swinging front double doors of the establishment could be seen from afar, as no other structure separated the edifice from the waterfront. A large sign rested above the doors with the name of the establishment painted on its face: the Moorn. Those loitering upon the wharf stepped back as the *Stenox* turned to port, easing its starboard side to the lip of the wharf.

*****

Brokov stepped onto the wharf flanked by Argos and Zem with Arsenc close behind, leaving Lorken and Kato to safeguard the ship.

The northern docks of Tro were a gathering point for unsavory characters, and Brokov knew it was wise to bring the muscle. Brokov was no small man, far larger, in fact, than any Araxan human, but why exert himself in a potential scuffle when he had Argos's and Zem's services at hand? If Raven were in his place, such a thought wouldn't have crossed his obstinate skull.

The guards posted at the front of the Moorn thought to block their entry but wisely stepped aside. Argos patted the fellow on the head as they passed as if he was a child. Bright sunlight gave way to the dim interior. As their vision adjusted to the darker surroundings, they could see the outline of the main floor as lanterns affixed to the walls lining the periphery or hung from the ceiling lightened the room.

Spread across the open floor were nearly a hundred small tables filled with patrons in varying states of inebriation. A large staircase encircled the main room, leading to an upper floor. The center of the upper level was open with a balcony overlooking the main floor below and guest rooms lining its outer walls. A bar ran three-fourths the length of the back wall with several barkeeps serving customers crowding along its length. Brief-skirted serving girls hustled about, serving food and drinks to the boisterous customers.

Though the scene resembled a drunken rabble, there were many man hunters in the crowd sober enough to recognize who had just stepped into their midst. Every eye instantly went to them. Brokov's eyes swept the room, looking for any oddity or sudden movement in the sea of faces. Satisfied with what he saw, he took a step toward the bar. A surly, half-inebriated fellow with greasy, unkempt hair gained his feet as they passed. Brandishing a double-bladed ax, the fellow swung, attempting to bury it into Zem's head. The ax struck true but broke upon Zem's head like clay hitting steel. The ax's head snapped off, leaving nary a scratch on Zem's metallic skull.

The man's eyes drew wide in drunken disbelief, as the blow counted for naught. The man's attempt did not escape Zem's attention. He had allowed the attack to proceed out of curiosity. Zem would never have admitted such, but he took great pleasure in the Araxan humans' reactions to his near indestructability. Brokov didn't flinch as Zem tossed the poor wretch through the front doors with a flick of his wrist, the man screaming as he soared through the air before landing painfully on the street. There were no other objections to their presence as they continued on to the bar, patrons clearing away as they advanced.

A barkeep Brokov didn't recognize greeted them with all the warmth of an ice block. He simply snorted, regarding them with more derision than awe. "You're scaring off our customers," the barkeep said.

"Then your customers shouldn't be playing with axes when they're drunk. They almost gave my friend here a headache," Brokov said, jerking a thumb toward Zem.

"What spirits do you favor?" the barkeep asked, figuring they wouldn't be leaving unless of their own accord.

"As good as a drink sounds. We need to speak with Kaly," Brokov explained.

"Kaly's busy," the barkeep unwisely said.

"Arg." Brokov sighed. Argos reached a furry hand over the counter, snatching the fellow about the throat, dragging him over the bar.

"The...the back room!" he squawked, pointing demonstratively past the end of the bar, where a closed door rested at the end of the wall.

*****

Zem and Argos guarded the door as Brokov and Arsenc stepped within the elaborately furnished room. The chamber was alit by two lanterns descending from the ceiling, illuminating richly detailed, erotic murals decorating the walls. Spread across the floor were finely woven rugs and dozens of Calnesian cushions. In the center of the room, upon a large cushion, was a half-naked man with a goblet of wine in each hand and a scantily clad woman under each arm. The startled fellow quickly recovered from their intrusion, regarding Brokov with a knowing grin.

"Brokov, aren't you a sight." The fellow smiled, his light-green eyes sparkling with amusement. Arsenc could easily discern the fellow's easy nature and understood the Earthers' fondness for him. The man had a boyishly handsome face that failed to match his years with a lithe, average build and long dark hair.

"Kaly." Brokov nodded. "My friend here is Arsenc Ottin," he introduced.

"Arsenc, a friend of this man is a friend to me." Kaly regarded him with a raised goblet. "Girls, if you please." The young serving wenches gathered their clothes and stepped without, gifting Arsenc a flirtatious wink as they passed. "So what brings you back to my fair City?" Kaly asked as he gained his feet with naught but a loin garment covering his vitals.

"We're waiting for Raven, but it might be a few days until he arrives."

"I've heard the rumors, if they can be believed. Did he truly lead a raid on the Black Castle?" Kaly asked.

"Among other things." Brokov sighed. "You know Raven well enough. I'm certain he found more than one way to antagonize the Benotrist emperor."

"Considering the bounty on his head, I tend to agree."

"Yes, we've seen that also. Klen kindly pointed it out to us," Brokov said, remarking on the impressive reward.

"Anyone looking to collect will certainly earn their prize," Kaly opined, regarding the danger in confronting Raven, "which leads me to believe a savvier man hunter would seek out the same reward for the lesser prey."

Brokov knew he meant Cronus, the Yatin, and the slave. But if they were with Raven, claiming their bounty would be just as dangerous. "You have other news we should know?" Brokov asked.

"Yes. Your presence here will sit poorly with certain houses of the ruling families."

"Why?" Arsenc asked.

"Can your friend be trusted?" Kaly inclined his head toward Arsenc as he looked Brokov in the eye.

"He has forsaken all to join us on our quest to free his friend."

"His friend?" Kaly lifted a curious brow.

"Cronus Kenti, Cordi's brother," Brokov said.

The mention of Cordi soured Kaly's mood. He was fond of the young Torry and regretted his loss. He had never had the pleasure of knowing Cronus, but if he was Cordi's brother, it was enough for him to count him a friend. And if Arsenc considered Cronus such a friend as well, then perhaps they were fellow travelers.

"So be it," Kaly conceded. "Lorken has offended House Talana and House Maiyan. They seek his blood, but fear of your weapons stays their hands."

"How has he offended them?" Brokov asked suspiciously.

"Upon your last visit, Lorken soiled the virtue of a young maiden who shared his affection. They met in secret, hiding their affair with great success. The maiden happened to be Jenna Talana, daughter of Marcus Talana, the patriarch of House Talana. She was promised to Orvis Maiyan, son of Ortus Maiyan, patriarch of House Maiyan."

How could Lorken be so foolish to pursue the daughter of one of Tro's ruling patriarchs? Brokov thought. "If they were successful in keeping their affair secret, then how—" Brokov began to ask.

"The evidence of their transgression only came to light *after* Jenna gave birth to three children. One died on the birthing bed, terribly deformed, but a son and daughter survived. The boy's distinct coloring and size remove any doubt of his parentage," Kaly explained.

"Crap." Brokov sighed. Things had suddenly become very complicated.

"That's not all," Kaly said.

"Go on," Brokov said, though he really didn't want to know.

"There are more than man hunters here seeking Raven's bounty. Hundreds of Benotrist-hired mercenaries have been filtering in over this past year, likely building a cabal of Tyro loyalists in our midst. With your sudden appearance, we must be mindful of their intent. They appear to be led by a Benotrist Elite named Hossen Grell."

"Hossen Grell," Brokov said. The name sounded familiar, but he couldn't picture the face.

"He is a native to the lone hills with the unique features of those born there, a beard and rotund belly. He is a renowned mercenary with political contacts throughout eastern Arax. He has sworn loyalty to the Benotrist throne," Kaly said.

"Well, this just gets better and better." Brokov wanted to kick something.

"I suggest not telling Lorken of his progeny until Raven arrives. If things with Marcus Talana turn sour, you can depart Tro without having to wait for him. As for Raven, what do you need from me?" Kaly offered.

CHAPTER 14

The city of Gotto rested at the confluence of the Veneba and Flen Rivers. Its founders first settled between the two rivers, building a strong wall on its west side, guarding its only land-facing direction. Over the centuries, the city grew, its population covering both banks of the rivers and extending downstream. The city's wealth grew exponentially with its partnership with Tro.

Unlike the vast territories of Torry North, which were dotted with small farms worked by free landowners, the approaches of Gotto contained vast tracts of arable land owned by a few wealthy landowners and worked by small armies of slaves. Only wealthy landowners could afford the small private armies that protected their interests from roving bandits and barbarians who peopled the lawless regions surrounding them. Small landowners and freeholds were quickly squashed—absorbed by larger estates or driven out by bandits.

Gotto enlisted a small army to safeguard the city proper and patrol the roads east of Tro that paralleled either banks of the lower Flen. Like its contemporary cities, Gotto's central district contained large stone structures for its city forum, magistrate, and warehouses while the private dwellings along its circumference were constructed of timber.

Cronus stood upon the bow of the small merchant galley as Gotto came into view, straddling the banks of the Veneba. Smaller dwellings and newer structures lined the northeast bank while the older yet larger structures lined the southwest bank. He drew the hood of his cloak over his head as the river passed within the city proper, hoping to conceal his face from any who might recognize him. Raven remained belowdecks, miserably enduring the voyage, keeping out of sight and complaining to no end. Cronus felt sorry for his friend and knew his fellow Earthers would find his discomfort humorous. Unfortunately, Raven couldn't come on deck without being recognized.

"Has the captain agreed to take us to Tro?" Kendra asked, standing beside him as the bow cut the lazy waves lapping the hull.

"Reluctantly. He wasn't pleased that most of his payment won't be delivered until we reach Tro." Cronus sighed, weary of it all. They were so close now that every day seemed to stretch painfully.

"And what if Raven's friends fail to meet us?" she asked warily.

Cronus wouldn't allow his mind to explore that dark possibility. "They are likely to be there as anywhere." He failed to mention that the *Stenox* was shadowing Raven's tracker. They would be there unless the tracker was faulty or unless they met with some misfortune. Either possibility was remote, but if true—no, he had to keep faith.

"Cronus!" Kendra suddenly said as a rope lifted from the water, bearing a mass of woven netting stretching the breadth of the river. The massive weight was pulled by vast winches upon either bank, the cables wound around great gears built into flat stone foundations. Teams of moglo beasts pulled the great winches, raising the netting, blocking their path.

"Fetch Raven, but do so quietly!" he whispered as archers armed with pitch and flaming arrows lined each bank of the river. Kendra stepped away as Galen and Alen came to Cronus's opposite shoulder, wondering what course of action Cronus planned to take, before the captain's voice echoed over the deck.

"Reverse oars!" he bellowed, and the crew belowdecks instantly reversed course, fighting the current and their momentum.

"How did they know?" Alen asked, his voice laced with fright, wondering how they were discovered.

"Magantors flying overhead, most likely. Could be Benotrists, man hunters, or both," Cronus said quietly, making no sudden movement. The bowmen on the riverbanks were some distance off, but he didn't wish them to react to any movement until Raven came above deck.

"Turn hard to starboard!" the captain ordered, as the right bank was slightly closer than the left. Raven climbed the narrow steps that led from the lower hold, wasting little time scanning the river before stepping to Cronus's side.

"It is them!" men along the riverbanks shouted, pointing excitedly once Raven emerged from the lower hold. The archers loosed their flaming arrows as catapults hurled balls of pitch.

"Tell the captain hard to port!" Raven growled, regretting what he was about to do.

"Raven, the net!" Cronus pointed out the obstacle running the breadth of the river.

"I know. Just do it!" Raven repeated, drawing his pistol and aiming at the part of the rope holding the net directly to their front. Bright emerald light spewed from the barrel in an unbroken stream as he dropped his aim. The laser cut the net down the center before Raven released the trigger. Any longer would have burned out the core of the laser, as continuous streams were intended only as a last resort.

"Hard to port!" the captain bellowed as the net dropped away like parchment torn in half. The helmsman spun the wheel, turning the rudder as an arrow whizzed past, the heat of its flame briefly warming his cheek.

The bow of the ship turned as a projectile of pitch struck the starboard hull, followed by flaming arrows igniting the material that clung to the sea-worn timbers. Cronus lifted his bow, notching an arrow, taking aim over the bulwark at the closest archer in sight. The quiet whoosh of the bowstring echoed dully through the din as his arrow sped to target, taking an archer in the lower belly.

Kendra followed in kind, picking the nearest target and loosing her arrow, the shaft hitting a catapult crewman in the shoulder. Raven's pistol had recovered, and he spewed laser blasts across the riverbank as the ship passed through the gaping hole where the net was strung along their path. The crew cheered as the ship cleared the obstacle until the torn net caught in the rudder, pulling the stern of the vessel toward the riverbank.

Their attackers raced south along the bank, stopping every few paces to fire an arrow before continuing on, pelting the ship. One shaft found a mark in the helmsman's neck, his body slumping over the wheel, jerking the ship, and the others struggled to keep their feet. Once steady, Cronus found another target, taking a free sword in the inner thigh, just below the hem of his tunic, the man stumbling briefly before the loss of blood sent him to his knees.

Raven fired over the bulwark, exposing little below his nose, dropping several archers in quick order. They ignored the archers on the opposite bank, as their accuracy waned with distance. Smoke started billowing from the festering flames as pitch coated larger swaths of the outer hull and upper masts. The captain ordered his crew to douse the flames before two arrows struck his chest. He slipped to the deck with smoke stinging his lungs.

"Well, this sucks." Raven snorted, ducking his head, an arrow just missing his scalp.

"I believe your crude summation aptly describes our dire situation," Galen said, huddling behind the bulwark.

"Shut up, minstrel!" Raven growled.

Their attackers fixed their aim to wherever they ducked, waiting for them to lift their heads before loosing a shaft. Cronus crawled further toward the stern, keeping his silhouette below the bulwark. The task was much harder due to the archers' placement upon the embankment, granting them a higher view. As soon as Cronus had crawled some distance, Raven pointed his pistol blindly over the bulwark, spraying laser fire in their attackers' general direction, keeping their heads down.

Cronus stole a glance, gained his feet, and fired an arrow. The hurried shot found a home in an archer's left arm as Cronus ducked back below the bulwark. He stole a glance across the ship, spying several crewmen strewn upon the deck, feathered with arrows. A few still moved, writhing in pain. Others gathered behind whatever cover they could find, most forsaking sacks used to douse the flames for swords with the ship drifting closer to shore.

Wisps of smoke, black and gray, drifted over the ship, flames licking the darkening timbers. He shook the hellish visage from his mind before the fires claimed him. They had to get off the ship. With the captain down, many of the merchant crew looked to Cronus, as there were few warriors among them. "Pass the word! We take the bank on my command!" he shouted over the din, his eyes locked to the nearest mate. The fellow nodded, holding a shortsword, crouching behind the forecastle, relaying the command to those around him.

Zip! Zip! Zip! Laser fire spewed from high upon the embankment, striking their attackers from behind. The cries of the wounded mixed with the clash of steel as scores of soldiers swarmed the archers and free swords. Raven dared a glance, peering over the bulwark, his eyes waiting for wisps of smoke to clear to see afield. There, high on the embankment, stood Zem and Kato with laser rifles tucked to their shoulders, blasting targets at will. It was the most beautiful thing he had ever seen.

The ship's crew quickly forsook their blades for sackcloth to douse the flames, hoping to salvage their vessel as their attackers were overwhelmed. Scores of soldiers bearing the sigil of the city guard, two rivers on a field of gray, swarmed past Zem and Kato, slaying the attackers as Zem shifted his aim to the opposite bank. Within minutes, the enemy were subdued, and the ship was saved. Raven, Cronus, and the others gained the shore. Raven trudged up the embankment to his friends awaiting him above.

"You big, lovable hunk of tin!" Raven shouted happily, throwing his arms around Zem, giving him the biggest hug he had ever given.

"My exoskeleton is forged from pure Trundusium, far stronger than tin," Zem said, offended by Raven's endearment.

"Ah, shut up you big lug." Raven laughed, slapping Zem on the back before turning to Kato, lifting him off the ground, squeezing the air from his lungs.

"Ra-Rav-Raven, I can't...breathe." He coughed as Raven set him down and ruffled his head.

"Where did you find all the reinforcements?" Raven finally asked, wondering how they enlisted the aid of the city garrison.

"Kaly sent one of his close associates with us who is in good graces with the magistrate of Gotto. We were awaiting your arrival when we heard the sounds of your battle," Kato explained as his eyes shifted to Cronus. "Someone very beautiful awaits you in Tro, Cronus." He grinned like an idiot.

Cronus felt the burdens of his heart fall away, a sole tear of unadulterated joy squeezing from his eye.

*****

She waited in the engineering room, standing over Brokov's shoulder, her blue eyes fixed intently on the sonar. She followed the red light moving across the emerald screen, drawing ever closer.

"Is that them?" Leanna asked, though she knew the answer, needing his reassurance that it was so.

"It's them, Leanna." Brokov gifted her a smile as he looked over his shoulder. Kato and Zem departed aboard the *Atlantis* two days ago, deciding to await Raven at Gotto. Kaly had advised sending a small team, allowing him to use his friendship with the magistrate of Gotto to aid them, while leaving the *Stenox* and the attention it drew at Tro. They received the joyous news that Raven and Cronus reached Gotto in good health and in a larger company than the submersible could ferry in one trip. Zem remained at Gotto with some of Raven's party while Kato returned with Raven, Cronus, a wounded merchant captain, and the escaped slave who fled Fera in their company.

Leanna chewed her lower lip, her eyes fixed longingly as the red light drew ever closer, her heart nearly pounding from her chest. "You look beautiful, Leanna," Brokov commented, knowing her thoughts of self-doubt. He wondered why women always questioned their worth and appearance, even when they were as fetching as her. Leanna regarded him with moist eyes blurring her vision.

Upon confirming Cronus's safety, Brokov ordered her to the fresher. Upon stepping from the shower and donning the robe he provided her, she proceeded to her cabin to dress. There, awaiting her upon her bunk, was a shimmering blue calnesian gown with billowing long sleeves, tight bodice, and flowing skirt. It was the dress of a highborn lady or princess and must have cost a small fortune. A pair of lady's slippers and silver hairpins lay beside the garment. She stood frozen in place, staring at the lovely garment, as Lorken leaned against the open doorway.

"He would be pleased to see you in it."

"How...where..." she struggled to ask.

"We gave Kaly the coin, and he guessed your size. Now get dressed before Cronus arrives," Lorken ordered before closing the door.

She donned the lovely outfit, fixed her hair, and joined Brokov in the engineering room. She could hear the pounding of her heart as the display indicated the *Atlantis* clearing the mouth of the Flen, entering the bay. With the crew shorthanded, Lorken positioned the *Stenox* in the center of harbor, far afield of any potential foe.

*****

"Preparing to dock," Kato said into the comm.

"Magnetic seal open. Proceed to dock," Lorken's voice echoed.

Kato maneuvered the *Atlantis* beneath the *Stenox*, guiding it into position below the hull. Alen sat in the weapons chair, staring through the slanted portal at the murky water ahead, his eyes wide with wonder. The first Earther he encountered was Ben Thorton. The man's cold demeanor and otherworldly nature frightened Alen to his core. Raven and Lorken seemed equally threatening when he served at Tyro's table. In time, he came to know them and grew fond of them, awed by their unique nature and powerful weapons. Raven, though, spoke sparingly of their vessels, never explaining their bewildering power. Alen sat numbly behind the console, beguiled by the vast array of lighted panels and strange switches, which Kato sagely advised him *not* to touch.

Raven sat the captain's chair while Cronus huddled behind him, watching over the stricken merchant captain. They snapped the arrows embedded in his chest to fit him through the sub hatch but kept the shaft stubs in place to prevent blood loss. "Magnetic seal closed," Kato affirmed, the *Atlantis* locking into the hull of the *Stenox*.

The hatch opened above Raven's head as Cronus hoisted the wounded captain into his arms, passing him to Raven. Brokov stood above, his legs straddling the hatch as Raven lifted the merchant captain to him. Brokov sighed with relief upon seeing his friend but swore off such pleasantries as he carried their visitor to the first crew cabin, attending to his wounds. Raven was the first to emerge from the submersible, finding Lorken standing at the console.

"Welcome home, buddy." Lorken grinned, embracing his friend.

"Thanks, pal." Raven hugged him back, thankful to be back and ending his long journey. Cronus climbed out next, greeting Lorken in kind.

"You look better since the last time I saw you," Lorken said, noting his restored color and fuller cheeks. He wasn't completely restored, but months of even the barest nourishment helped him recover much of his luster and weight.

"Thank you," Cronus said, embracing his friend, though his eyes searched the cabin in vain for the one person he most longed to see.

"She's waiting for you outside." Lorken smiled, pushing him toward the door. Cronus regarded both of them briefly before hurrying without. He hadn't the words to convey the gratitude of his heart.

No sooner had Alen climbed out than Kato sealed the hatch and released the magnetic lock, guiding the *Atlantis* beneath the hull to collect the others.

*****

Cronus took a deep breath before passing through the door, uncertain of her reception. He was not the man he was when he bade her farewell at Central City. He felt broken, tired, and so very old, a dim relic of his former glory. He was battle-scarred and worn and wondered how a woman so beautiful could ever love him. *No!*

259

he thought defiantly, shaking such defeatism from his mind, and stepped into the open air onto the stern. His heart froze.

She stood before him, beauteous and ethereal. Was she real? Her golden hair was swept high upon her head, silver pins dividing its lustrous folds. Her flowing gown matched the azure hue of her sparkling eyes. He saw nothing of the Troan Bay surrounding her in panoramic splendor or the giant sentinel towering over the center of the harbor. He did not note the clear sky above or the song of sea-birds echoing over the lapping waves. He was drawn entirely into her eyes, losing himself in their timeless beauty.

"Cronus," she whispered, her voice failing her as she wept, rushing into his arms. She wrapped her arms around him, hugging him fiercely, pressing her head to his chest. She could not see his unkempt hair, his scars, or his battered flesh. To her, he had never looked as handsome as now, standing upon the deck of the *Stenox* with his dark hair lifting in the breeze and his green eyes staring at her with eternal love. Had any sight her eyes ever beheld been so grand?

They stayed in their embrace, their eyes closed as they held each other tightly, fearing to let go. No words were spoken, the silence filled only with the beating of their hearts. Her tears drenched his chest, soaking the coarse gray tunic he wore since Axenville. He forsook his battered mail in Gotto, bringing only his sword and the clothes on his back.

"I can't stop crying." She laughed through her tears, keeping her head pressed to his chest. He lifted her chin, staring intently into her eyes before wiping her tears with both of his hands upon her cheeks. Then he kissed her, crushing his lips to hers. There, upon the *Stenox* in the center of the Troan Bay, Cronus's heart was made whole.

*****

"Hand me the long blue one at the end!" Brokov commanded, staring through the optic strapped to his right eye as the merchant captain's still form lay upon the bunk. The optic revealed the internal organs and wounds in three-dimensional clarity, instructing him in clear detail how to restore the damaged tissue. Alen reached for the instrument indicated, handing it to Brokov. Fortunately, the Earther had laid the instruments upon the opposite bunk, briefly explaining their significance before they began.

No sooner had Alen stepped onto the *Stenox* than Brokov quickly entered the room and asked for his assistance. He observed his strange surroundings as Brokov applied the device to the captain's wounds. Flameless light illuminated the small cabin, far brighter than a hundred torches. How the Earthers conjured such magic he could only guess.

"Hand me the silver one with the round end," Brokov said, handing the blue one back to him. Alen handed the instrument over as Brokov tossed the two bloody arrow shafts on the floor. Brokov pressed the round silver bulb into the merchant captain's wounds for a few seconds before withdrawing the device and covering the man's naked chest with a blanket.

"Come. Let him rest," Brokov said, collecting his instruments, ushering Alen out. He had spent much of the time at sea since leaving Raven and Lorken at Tinsay completing the construction of these surgical instruments. His first test was restoring Arsenc's wounded leg. He responded well, showing no lingering impairment. The instruments were even able to genetically renew his scarred skin tissue, leaving no trace of the wound. This current test, however, proved even more fruitful, allowing him to mend, cleanse, and restore a punctured lung.

Fortunately for the patient, both arrows missed his heart and vital arteries, or he would have expired long before reaching the *Stenox*. He planned to test the instruments' ability to regenerate damaged or missing organs or limbs by coding a subject's DNA. There was no reason why it couldn't be done. He had managed to make three sets of the equipment, so they might take one in the field on their next extended foray ashore. The last set he constructed was more compact without the excess instruments.

*****

Arsenc waited within for a time, allowing Cronus and Leanna a period of privacy before stepping onto the stern to greet them. He was greeted by bright sunlight as he emerged onto the open deck with the serene visage of Cronus and Leanna sharing an embrace. They stood upon the deck unmoving, holding each other as the world passed around them. He smiled at the sight. If ever two people belonged with each other, it was Cronus and Leanna. They were equally brave, attractive, and true, true to their selves and to each other. He waited patiently for them to finally part before they noticed him standing near the doorway.

"Arsenc." Cronus smiled, waving him hither before bringing him into their embrace.

"You survived. Beyond all hope, you survived," Arsenc repeated as they parted.

"I had help." Cronus's smile eased with gratitude. "I have friends. I have friends far greater than any man can boast"—he placed a hand upon Arsenc's shoulder—"and a woman far better than I deserve," he finished, squeezing Leanna's shoulder tenderly.

"You have friendships that you have earned," Arsenc affirmed.

"And a woman who loves you for the man you are, not for the shortcomings that you falsely claim," Leanna added, hugging him again.

"What now?" Arsenc finally asked, wondering their course of action.

"We go home," Cronus answered with certainty. "We ride west to Corell. Once there, I intend to fulfill a promise I made to a beautiful woman before leaving for Rego." He regarded Leanna, recalling his vow to wed upon his return.

"A promise I shall hold you to," she reproached playfully.

"Have you told Raven of your plans? The others assume we shall be continuing on with them," Arsenc asked.

"I thought Raven understood my intentions, though we never spoke of it," Cronus reflected. They spent every moment of their journey trying to survive and escape that little thought was given to what would follow once they reached Tro.

"Must we return so soon?" Leanna asked, wondering how safe the road west would be with bandits, slavers, and the ever-pressing threat from the north.

"I must return. The enemy shall renew their attack upon our kingdom, and I intend to meet them. I have sworn my sword to the defense of the Torry realms, and I shall keep my oath," Cronus avowed.

Haven't you sacrificed enough? Leanna thought sadly. What more could one man do? What measure was one man weighed against the scales of millions? But despite her misgivings, Leanna would honor his wishes. "Raven will understand. He is a good friend," she assured him. "When I discovered you had been taken, I hurried into the rain, distraught over your capture. I was standing upon the Tarelian Bridge with the rain in my eyes when I saw the *Stenox* moored along the bank of the Stlen. I thanked the fates that it was still in Central City.

"I rushed to find Raven, explaining what had transpired and pleading for his help. He simply said, 'We'll get him.' Such a small phrase, implausible for a person of reason to believe, but it lifted my heart, and at that critical moment, it gifted me the one thing I needed most: *hope*. Yet deep within my heart, doubts clouded my joy, for how could he possibly find you and free you before you met a terrible end? Seeing you this day, so very handsome and brave, proved my doubts false and Raven's simple words true. He *got you*."

"Some men have great wealth or power, but I have great friends." Cronus smiled humbly.

*****

All Raven wanted to do was eat, have a long, hot shower, climb into his bunk, and sleep. He smelled so foul that he no longer noticed any stench not his own. But all those small indulgences were set aside by other matters requiring his attention. Kato was en route to Gotto to fetch Zem, Kendra, and that rotten minstrel. He gave serious thought of taking the foul vermin out to sea and tossing him overboard. The idea warmed his heart as he envisioned Galen gasping for life as he bobbed amid the mounting waves. *Nah, Cronus wouldn't forgive me for killing the varmint,* he thought sourly, remembering Cronus's high moral character, which hindered his sadistic pleasure. Somehow, Cronus brought out the good in him, even when he wasn't around.

"Are you listening to me?" Argos growled, knowing Raven had ignored everything he had said.

"Huh?" Raven cleared his head, realizing he stood in the weapons room but not remembering how he got there.

"I asked, when can we depart for Gregok now that you've rescued your friend?" Argos snorted.

"As soon as Kato gets back, we can be on our way, big guy." Raven slapped him on the shoulder. Argos's natural reaction would have been to smack someone upside the head for touching his shoulder, but his time among the Earthers had adjusted him to their friendly mannerisms. "Since we haven't been in port for a while, I should probably pay a visit to Klen and Kaly before we leave," Raven said.

"You sure that's a good idea?" Argos asked.

"What do you mean?"

"Every time you step ashore, you get caught up in some dimwit scheme that delays our progress."

"What are you talking about, Arg? The only delay was getting Cronus."

"What did wedding Tyro's daughter have to do with rescuing Cronus?" He snorted.

"That wasn't my fault. I didn't know that until it was over!" Raven protested.

"How about Varabis? When you went ashore to purchase a cask of ale, you managed to start a tavern brawl, burn down a city block, and cause a riot between the three largest private militias in the city."

"I was just there when all that went down. I didn't start any of it."

Lorken overheard much of the conversation from the engineering room through the open doorway between them. "Don't forget about the incident on Europa Lunar Station Six in Solar System

Prime!" he shouted, adding to the conversation, recalling their adventures in Space Fleet before crashing on Arax.

"That wasn't my fault either!" Raven shouted back.

"Tell that to the crew of the Stalingrad when our shore leave was cancelled and we were permanently banned from the base," Lorken shouted back.

"That wasn't my fault either!" Raven again parroted his denial, sounding more like a criminal declaring his innocence.

"And what about your last port of call in Milito, when—"

"I get the idea, Arg! All right. I'll be careful not to cause a ruckus when I go ashore." Argos snorted, shaking his head at Raven's false promise.

*****

"I must commend your timely intervention, Lieutenant Zem," Galen praised as they waited near the riverbank where the ambush occurred. Zem stood careful watch as Kendra and Galen waited beside him. When asked his name, he replied with his Space Fleet rank and name. He provided his rank as a matter of protocol, but the subject clearly irritated Zem for reasons the Araxans couldn't ascertain. Had they not crashed on Arax, Zem was poised for a rapid promotion through the ranks. His accidental exile to this forsaken backwater of the galaxy ensured the permanency of his low rank.

"Our intervention was executed with extreme efficiency. You are correct in your assessment, Galen," Zem said proudly, clearly pleased with the minstrel's keen observation.

"It was splendidly done. I must inquire about your previous altercations with similar unsavory elements of our fair land," Galen asked, eager to ingratiate himself with the powerful Earther.

"I have intervened numerous times at the behest of my shipmates since our arrival on your Class T planet. There was the incident at Teris when…" Zem droned on, regaling the minstrel with tales of his great strength, marksmanship, and intellect or, as Raven was likely to say, "his overall awesomeness."

Kendra rolled her eyes, tiring quickly of their banter. The nostalgia of finally meeting the metallic creature quickly waned as he opened his mouth. She didn't know who was more annoying, the pompous minstrel or the boastful Zem. They stood upon the embankment as the wounded were gathered further upstream. Hundreds of people worked furiously in clearing the dead and repairing the damage wrought. The time passed painfully slow as she awaited Kato's return. Just as Zem recounted what seemed his one hundredth tale, the *Atlantis* broke the surface.

*****

The return to the *Stenox* was equally mystifying and tiresome, as Galen and Zem's banter vied with the wonder of the vessel. Kendra sat at the weapons seat across from Kato, and Zem sat the captain's seat with the minstrel seated in the rear.

"The wonders of your vessel exceed the majesty of the royal palace of Corell or the timeless beauty of El-Orva," Galen marveled.

"Of course. The *Atlantis* can reach a depth of thirty thousand feet with complete hull integrity. It can achieve maximum velocity of two hundred knots subsurface." Zem continued at length, detailing the schematics and capabilities of the submersible.

Kato looked over at Kendra and wordlessly mouthed his apology, which drew a smile. "I haven't seen Zem this talkative since our last visit to Linkortus," he whispered.

"And Galen hasn't shut his mouth since Axenville." She rolled her eyes.

"Raven is difficult enough to suffer over short distances. How did you manage both of them?" Kato asked, feeling sorry for the poor girl.

"Raven is a pleasure to endure compared to him," she said lowly, nodding her head to the rear of the sub where Galen sat.

"You needn't speak lowly. My superior hearing can detect the slightest mumblings of your organics," Zem interrupted.

Kendra couldn't tell if Zem was offended or not. Raven had warned her about his metallic friend's unique sensibilities, but nothing could have prepared her for his domineering personality. As Raven had told her, "Zem is one of a kind." Of course, the same could be said of Raven and Kato. They were as unalike to one another as they were to native Araxans.

Raven was rough, coarse of speech, and physically imposing. Kato was diminutive by compare, thoughtful, well-spoken, and highly intelligent. His quiet voice put her at ease and contrasted with Zem's deep, metallic timber or Raven's coarse tongue. Even Raven's casual banter sounded like cursing.

"Raven spoke about your intervention in Axenville. Why did you help him?" Kato asked, his eyes fixed on the sonar, guiding the *Atlantis* beneath the river.

"Had he his weapon earlier, I would have helped him sooner. For without it, we would not have escaped. As far as *why* I helped him at all, it was quite simple. The magistrate of Axenville was likely to be supplanted. The port's ruling oligarchs were colluding with the Benotrist regional governor, who planned to annex Axenville. Much of Tyro's eastern expansion has been conducted in similar fashion. Why resist and risk annihilation when the Benotrists will guarantee the property rights of the richest citizens and fill their purses? If the lesser citizens suffer, so be it. Wherever this expansion has been similarly executed, the former magistrates have mysteriously disappeared. Such would have been my fate had I remained."

"So you hitched your wagon to our train."

"Wagon? Train?" She made a face.

"Never mind. The point is that you are with us now."

"So it would seem."

"We all have to agree before taking on new shipmates, but you'll have my vote." Kato smiled.

"Thank you." She smiled too, liking at least one of her new shipmates.

*****

No sooner had Raven stepped outside on the first deck than Leanna rushed into his arms, embracing him tightly and planting kisses upon his cheek as Cronus and Arsenc waited a few paces back. "You did it," she cried joyfully, pulling back as her moist blue eyes stared up at him, his large form blurry in her watery vision.

"We did it." He smiled before casting a glance over her shoulder to his friend. "You better marry this girl soon, Cronus. She's waited long enough."

"I promised that I would upon my return. That's a promise I mean to keep." Cronus smiled.

"We can do it right here in Tro or our next port of call," Raven offered. Their next stop would be Torn Harbor in the heart of the Ape Coast. Raven couldn't fail to notice Cronus averting his stare at the mention of their next port of call.

"Raven, I mean to return to Torry North before you lift anchor." Cronus sighed, regarding his friend with a heavy heart.

"The road to Corell is dangerous. Why not wait until I can drop you off somewhere safer like Cagan? Or better yet, stay with us. We could use more crewmates that we trust," Raven offered almost desperately, trying to convince his friend to stay.

"I am sworn to the Torry throne, my friend. You know this. What worth is a man's word when he casts aside a sacred vow?"

"I think your sacrifice at Tuft's Mountain and your suffering at Fera complete your vow," Raven countered.

"Raven, I owe you more than a man can repay in a lifetime, but the debt does not absolve me of my oath."

"You don't owe me anything, Cronus. I still owe you at least one more if we're keeping count. But if you're hell-bent on heading west, at least wait another day or so until I can hire you a proper escort to accompany you to Corell."

"Raven, I couldn't accept such a costly—" Cronus protested until Raven interjected.

"You're not going alone, Cronus! I'll have Kaly make the arrangements. Consider it my wedding gift to you both."

"Thank you, Raven." Leanna kissed his cheek again as Cronus regarded him with deep gratitude.

"No man has better friends," Cronus said, his voice tightening in his throat, placing a hand to Arsenc's shoulder and staring gratefully at Raven.

*****

"You should've told me this days ago!" Lorken demanded, staring down Brokov as they stood on the bridge.

"If I told you then, you would've run off and confronted Marcus Talana while we were stuck waiting for Raven. Now we can formulate a plan without that burden over our heads," Brokov reasoned.

"You think I would've done anything so foolish? I know when to act and when to wait. You should've trusted me to know the difference."

Raven stood between them with his foot resting on the captain's chair and an elbow upon his knee. Brokov finally revealed that Lorken fathered twin children on the daughter of Marcus Talana. The news struck Lorken like a boulder to the head. He was smitten with Jenna Talana for a time before she abruptly ended their affair, not realizing she was already pregnant with his child.

By the time she was aware of her condition, the *Stenox* had left port, leaving her at her father's mercy. When she finally delivered the children, their paternity was painfully obvious. Equally furious was Ortus Maiyan, whose heir, Orvis, was betrothed to the lady Jenna. Now they incurred the wrath of two of the five ruling families of Tro.

The *Atlantis* had just returned with Kendra and Galen brought aboard when Brokov asked Raven and Lorken to the bridge to discuss the matter. It went over as well as a kick to the groin. Lorken shook his head in disgust before stepping toward the door.

"Where you going?" Brokov asked, fearing the answer.

"To see Jenna. What more do I have to wait for?" Lorken snorted.

"Before you go rushing off, you might want to plan a few contingencies in case things go south," Raven advised.

"You would know."

"What's that supposed to mean?" Raven asked with a hurt look.

"You really need to ask?" Lorken snorted.

"All I'm saying is to be careful. The girl's father may try to kill you. You also have the girl's feelings to consider. Women can be a little sensitive when it comes to these things," Raven tried to explain.

"If I'm going to take advise about women, it certainly isn't going to be from you!"

"What's that supposed to mean?"

"How's your marriage working out for you?" Lorken drove home his point.

"It's fine," Raven said defensively. "Just a few problems with the in-laws, is all."

"Let me know when those little problems are resolved, because I'd like that bounty your father in-law put on my head lifted."

"That cuts deep," Raven lamented.

"I'm sure." Lorken rolled his eyes, knowing Raven had all the sensitivity of a rock.

"Lorken, just give us one hour to bring everyone up to speed, plan a few contingencies, and vote on our new crewmates. Then you can proceed to contact Jenna with everyone focused on covering your back," Brokov said diplomatically.

"One hour." Lorken lifted a single finger to emphasize his point.

*****

Raven didn't remember when they had crammed so many people into the dining cabin. Zem and Argos stood farther back, standing along the wall opposite the door, each taking up too much space. Cronus and Leanna sat at the table with Kato, Alen, and Brokov. Kendra stood nearest the door beside Lorken while Raven and Galen stood at opposite ends of the table, the minstrel wisely placing himself as far from Raven as possible. Brokov commenced the discussion, retelling their operations since departing Tinsay.

"Kaly's contacts have informed him of intense Benotrist activity all along the border from the Plate Mountain range to the northern approaches of Lake Veneba," Brokov explained.

"I can verify his spies' assessment. The Benotrist regional governors have purchased large amounts of provisions from all the bordering holdfasts and estates, driving up the price of essential goods," Kendra said, leaning against the doorway with her arms crossed.

"Kaly seems to think a Benotrist invasion is eminent. His spies reported a Benotrist legion marching south from Nisin, staging somewhere between the Plate foothills and the western shores of Lake Veneba," Brokov added.

"We saw columns of troops moving south just before we reached Axenville. That would corroborate Kaly's assessment," Cronus added.

"They could just be reinforcing their border," Argos said.

"Possibly, but unlikely." Brokov scrubbed his chin with his hand, depressing a switch near his elbow. The surface of the table was soon alit, its silver surface transforming into a luminous map of northeastern Arax in stark detail. Galen, Kendra, and Alen stared in awe as the waterways, lakes, and ocean shimmered like rippling waves as if alive. The forests that circled the Plate Mountains were flush, as if sunlight reflected off their emerald leaves. The Plate Mountains, the Lone Hills, and the Ape Hills rose above the map like jagged rock.

Every detail sprang to life. It seemed so lifelike that if they stretched their hands over the cities and palaces that dotted the map, they might slay thousands by pressing their palm down upon the world, like an omnipotent being exercising its will upon the wee mortals below.

"The likely target of a single legion would be the crossroads of Bacel and Notsu, which straddle the vital arteries connecting Corell to Tro and Nisin to points south. It could be used as a staging point for an assault upon Tro or an invasion of Torry North," Brokov added, moving a luminous marker over the map to the points indicated.

"That makes the road to Corell even more dangerous, Cronus. You sure you want to chance it?" Raven asked, hoping Cronus might change his mind.

"A small party can outpace a lumbering army," Cronus assured him, knowing any invasion hadn't yet started but emphasizing the need to leave Tro as soon as possible.

"All right," Raven relented, figuring that once Cronus made up his mind, there was no turning him back. "You best be leaving soon. I'll see how many men Kaly can spare for your escort."

"Ride fast and avoid setting camp outside villages or cities when possible. Once you reach Gotto, see if you can join a caravan. There's safety in large numbers," Brokov advised.

"My thanks," Cronus said politely, though he already knew what Brokov advised.

"Maybe some of us should go with them," Kato offered. "Zem and I could provide ample protection, at least as far as the Torry border."

"My gratitude, Kato, but you all have done more than enough to see me home. I can undertake this last leg of the journey. I am familiar with the road from Notsu to Corell. Besides, you have commitments to attend in the Ape Empire." Cronus regarded Argos respectfully.

"Yes. General Matuzak has need of your services," Argos affirmed in his deep voice.

"Cronus is right, Kato. Kaly's escort should see them safely to the border. We've held up with a skeleton crew but can ill afford losing you and Zem for any length of time, which brings us to the next matter. We took a vote before calling all of you in and have decided to bring Alen and Kendra on as permanent crew," Raven offered.

"Truly?" Kendra said, regarding Brokov and Raven curiously. Raven had mentioned such a possibility on their journey here, but she wasn't certain of his commitment.

"You had my back when it counted most. I'd have to wait to find out with someone else. Besides, you are skilled with a bow and sword, have good tracking skills, and are familiar with the lay of the land throughout eastern Arax," Raven said.

"And given your aptitude, you should adapt fairly well learning our ship and equipment," Brokov added.

"I accept," Kendra said gratefully. Alen, however, shrunk sheepishly in his seat, his eyes lowered to the center of the table.

"Alen?" Raven asked, reading his poor body language.

"I...I am honored by your acceptance and grateful that you count me among your friends, Raven, but...but I must go with Cronus. If the Torry realm stands against Tyro, I must stand with them. I have little to offer but will give the Torry cause all that I have."

"Do you know what you're giving up, Alen?" Raven asked. "You can earn an equal share of our earnings. You can gain wealth beyond your wildest dreams. We'll teach you to use our weapons, and you'll never suffer abuse by the likes of those Benotrist scum ever again. You would give all that up?" Raven asked, shaking his head over his ruined plan of having a full crew. He had harbored hope that Cronus and Leanna would stay on, though neither had ever alluded to such a notion. If Cronus stayed, then Arsenc was likely to stay as well. Now they all planned to ride for Corell and certain doom.

"You'll die," Lorken said dismissively, impatient to end this meeting and pay a not-so-subtle visit to Marcus Talana. "Tyro has fresh levies ready to throw at Torry North. You have little hope to stop them, and I doubt they'll fall for another trick like Bode pulled off at Tuft's Mountain."

"Perhaps not, but we will fight nonetheless," Arsenc retorted, staring down Lorken from across the table.

"Lorken means no offense, Arsenc." Cronus placed a calming hand upon his shoulder before regarding Lorken. "Only the fates truly know if our cause is lost, but we have sworn our lives to the defense of our kingdom. We must go. If I perish or live to be an old man, I shall never forget what each of you has done to deliver me from the bowels of that foul place, you and Raven most of all, Lorken."

"You're welcome." Lorken sighed, regretting his harsh words.

"What are we even talking about?" Kato shook his head. "We know what Tyro is, and we sit here ignoring the obvious and questioning Cronus's wisdom for returning to defend his home when we should be joining him, everything else be damned!"

"Easy, Kato. We made other promises long before this war started," Raven said.

"To General Matuzak and the Ape Empire, I know," Kato said, casting his eyes to Argos's imposing form. "Arg, what profit does your general gain if we go to him while Tyro conquers the rest of Arax? Can your empire stand against a world united under Tyro's banners?"

"It will take more time than our visit to Gregok for Tyro to conquer everything," Raven argued.

"Are you willing to take that risk?" Kato asked.

"It's not our fight," Raven countered.

"It's been our fight since Thorton joined with Tyro. We must balance the scales to give the Torries a fighting chance," Kato said.

"Don't talk to me about balancing the scales, Kato. I just crossed the continent, leaving hundreds, if not thousands, of Benotrist and gargoyle corpses along the way. We've done more than our fair share. And forgive me if I don't give a damn about a pompous kingdom that favors the dignity of a foreign princess over the life of their own hero!" Raven growled.

Cronus made a face, confused by Raven's words. Seeing the confusion on his face, Leanna whispered in his ear, explaining that Raven had first rescued Tosha to trade her for him over the protest of Minister Antillius. Cronus never knew. Neither Raven nor Tosha mentioned anything of such an exchange. By the time they reached Fera, Raven had changed tactics and agreed to Tosha's plan to free Cronus. He shook his head, amazed by the lengths Raven took to set him free.

"Your friends." Leanna smiled, running her hand along Cronus's arm as she regarded the faces gathered in the small room. She had come to love them dearly during the time she spent on the *Stenox* since that fateful night in Central City.

"There were countless times in our own history, Raven, where evil men were left unchecked because good men did nothing." Kato sighed.

"Interventionists have been using that line for centuries, Kato. This ain't Earth, and we ain't the Peace Corps. We're going to Torn Harbor to see General Matuzak as we promised. Once that is complete, we'll see about Thorton, or you can go off and join the Torry army if you like," Raven said.

"Maybe I will." Kato stiffened.

"And we would welcome your company, my brave fellow," Galen said.

"Shut up, minstrel!" Raven pointed threateningly at Galen. "I never wanted you aboard my ship, and I sure as hell don't need you goading my friends into joining you. Just keep your miserable mouth shut until your carcass is safely on the road to Corell." If Galen was offended, he showed it not, but the others were startled by Raven's ire.

"Enough," Brokov said, steering the conversation to the task at hand before Raven decided to kill Galen right then and there. "Cronus and his party will depart as soon as we arrange an escort with Kaly. Just be ready to depart by morning."

*****

Lorken marched through the wide-set streets of Tro's southern district like a storm moving across the sea. His eyes narrowed in barely restrained rage, and nervous citizens stepped out of his path. Wealthy merchants in richly colored robes cowered behind their servants as the large Earther passed, fearing to look but too curious not to. The private dwellings of Tro's wealthiest merchants lined either side of the street, their stone masonry walls far superior to the simple wooden homes where the lesser gentry and tradesmen dwelled but less by far than the spacious estates of the ruling families, which rested further ahead atop the small hills overlooking the Troan Bay.

Raven tried to join him, not wishing his friend to confront Marcus Talana alone, but Lorken warned him off. He was not in the mood to suffer anyone's presence and would do this on his own. Raven told him he had two hours before the cavalry would be sent after him. Though the others feared for his safety, Lorken didn't care. In fact, he wished Marcus Talana would try something so he could unleash hell upon the arrogant oligarch. His thoughts swung between his rage at Marcus Talana and his concern for Jenna.

He remembered well the day they arrived on Arax, six survivors stranded upon a far-off planet. The only women in their small company had perished with the others as they crashed on Arax. The thought of being trapped on an alien world for the rest of his days with no female companionship consumed his fears until they discovered that Arax had an indigenous human population. They happened to set down on the only other world where humans dwelled.

Since the first exploration vessels set out from Solar System Prime two hundred years ago, they had discovered only one life-supporting planet, the Aurelian home world. Other than that hostile race, they were met with endless discoveries of lifeless planets. The only hope of mankind to establish permanence in the greater universe was to terraform lifeless worlds into Earthlike habitats for human colonization. Such expansion was perceived as a threat by the Aurelians and triggered the interstellar wars.

After defeating the Aurelians, Space Fleet shifted its emphasis to deep-space exploration, searching for suitable worlds to terraform. Their mission met with disaster, as their vessel passed through an anomaly, catapulting them to unknown space and to the surface of Arax. With their spacecraft broken and much of their crew dead, they emerged from the wreckage on this strange new world with no ability to return to their own.

The humans of Arax were strikingly similar to those of Earth, save for unique differences. They were of one race, a sort of amalgamation of the races of Earth, with olive skin that varied only slightly in its hue among individuals. Save for a few inhabitants native of the Lone Hills, Araxans had no facial hair and little hair upon their bodies. They were smaller and slighter of build and kept much of their youthful appearance in old age. They were swift of foot and strong in endurance, and despite the uniformity of their flesh, they possessed a striking diversity in the color of their hair and eyes.

Despite the differing characteristics between the humans of Earth and Arax, the similarities outweighed them, the most significant of which was their sexual compatibility. Lorken reflected on the day he first met the lady Jenna Talana along the wharves of the Troan Bay. He was smitten by her striking beauty and playful nature. She boldly approached him, inquisitive of his strange attire and peculiar physical characteristics. His attraction was reciprocated, as she was drawn to his easy charm, strength, and confidence. He was unlike any man she ever knew, and she brazenly sought his favor. Their courtship constituted his fondest memories.

And then it ended. They had always met in secret, and when she failed to show, he was met by her maidservant. The girl presented him a parchment penned in her hand, telling him that she no longer desired to see him. Lorken's overtures were rebuffed, and when the *Stenox* departed Tro, he closed his heart and didn't look back, believing that she had rejected him. Now he knew otherwise. Her father likely discovered their dalliance, forcing her to end the affair. He thought she betrayed him, and yet all this time, she carried his child—no, his children. He wondered how her father received such news and how he treated her.

The wide-set street widened even further as he ascended the hill. The wealth of Tro could be evidenced by the quality of its streets and causeways. Ahead, the streets were laid out with layers of ground rock, soil, gravel, and an exotic epoxy of volcanic material akin to concrete. The topmost layer consisted of tightly placed flat stones fused together by the strange epoxy and polished smooth. The construction was the work of thousands of slaves and skilled masons over many years.

The way ahead opened considerably, as the domiciles of the merchant class gave way to the spacious estates of the city's ruling families, each laying claim to a separate hill overlooking the bay. There on the hill ahead rested the estate of House Talana, a vast dwelling that sat on the hilltop like a crown upon a mountain. Manicured palace greens surrounded the estate, tended by a small army of slaves.

A stone wall the height of two men circled the estate and manned by guards in resplendent green tunics and golden capes, the colors of House Talana. Sunlight reflected off their polished steel breastplates, greaves, and helms. The outer wall consisted of six small watchtowers with covered canopies to protect the guards from the elements.

Lorken drew the attention of the men manning the watchtowers as he ascended the hill. He could see them scurrying along the walls, taking up position and no doubt alerting their master of his approach. The road led straight to a massive iron gate on the north face of the stone wall. Lorken was met by a closed gate and a dozen archers lining the wall above, their arrows trained upon him as a dozen guards stood post behind the bars of the gate with swords drawn.

"I'm here to speak with Marcus Talana!" Lorken declared, his eyes scanning their faces for any hint of trouble. The guards with their swords did not concern him since they were behind the gate and appeared to have drawn them out of fear rather than for some hostile intent. The archers above presented the greater threat. He was well within their "Can't miss" range, their faces obscured by their drawn bows.

"For what purpose do you seek an audience with Master Talana?" said a guard with braided silver cords gracing the shoulders of his green tunic, marking him a commander of flax or a similar-sized element.

"He knows my purpose, but if he asks, tell him I've come to claim what is mine."

Lorken waited for a torturous amount of time for the guard to hurry off and return. He received his answer when the guard opened the gate, signaling him forth. He was glad they didn't ask for him to hand over his weapon. He would never allow that and guessed they were told likewise. Marcus Talana was many things, but a fool wasn't one of them. He knew that if Lorken meant him harm, his guards and small palace would count for naught.

The grounds of the estate were a myriad of exotic gardens, manicured greens, and tropical frolog trees, their high branches bending in the breeze. The estate resembled a small fortress with towers and battlements around its periphery.

The guard led him to the front entry, where a young male slave greeted them. The slave wore a brief white calnesian tunic and finely woven sandals, his rich attire a demonstration of his master's wealth. Lorken noted the thin silver collar circling the boy's neck. The slave didn't seem ashamed by this degradation, smiling politely as he ushered him within.

*****

Marcus Talana awaited his guest in the central atrium of his spacious estate. Long columns circled the inner chamber with a large fountain centered below its open roof. Marcus Talana stood in front of said fountain, burgundy robes covering his ankle-length emerald tunic. He clasped his hands behind him, standing statue still, his steel-blue eyes narrowed to receive the Earther.

Marcus Talana would have preferred to deal with the Earther as he did with others who dared offend his house: by claiming his head and adorning the outer gate with his severed crown. Unfortunately, his daughter chose to soil her virtue with a man far too dangerous for such action. Any false move could bring the wrath of the detestable Earthers down upon his house.

He had far more to lose than the honor of his house. He had three sons to consider. As head of an ancient house of Tro, he was entrusted to see to its prosperity and continuance long after his death. His daughter's indiscretion did more than damage the prestige of his house. It offended House Maiyan and ruined any hope of joining their houses for another generation, as Ortis Maiyan had no daughter to wed a son of House Talana.

When he first discovered his daughter's association with the Earther Lorken, he confined her to her chamber and ordered her handmaid to meet the Earther in her place, informing him that their dalliance was at its end. Only later did he discover that his intervention was too late, as she was with child. Arranging his daughter's nuptials to House Maiyan was difficult if she was soiled, impossible if she carried another man's child, for the shame would be known by all.

"Master," his slave greeted, bowing low as he entered the atrium with the commander of the outer gate and the Earther trailing him.

"Rise, Lania. You and the commander may wait without while I speak with our *esteemed* guest."

"Yes, Master." The slave again bowed and withdrew, leaving his master alone with the dangerous Earther.

Lorken regarded the scene with disgust, seeing a man forced to abase himself in such a way. Household slaves were chosen for their attractiveness and docility or were bred to nurture such attributes.

Lorken shook his head and stepped forth. "Marcus Talana," he said stopping a few paces before the patriarch of House Talana.

The man stood a head shorter than him with black hair draping below his shoulders and even-set icy-blue eyes that appeared nonplused by his towering form. If Marcus Talana was afraid, neither his demeanor nor actions demonstrated it.

"I am he. And you are Lorken, an Earther from the *Stenox*," Marcus stated.

"That's me," Lorken answered. The two men had never met. The only dealings the ruling families had with the Earthers was through their proxy, Magistrate Adine. It was Klen Adine who commissioned Raven and the *Stenox* to hunt down the fleet of the pirate lord Monsoon. It was their presence in Tro at that time that led to the fateful meeting between Lorken and the lady Jenna.

"I assume you have come here upon certain…rumors," Marcus said, his stony face a mask of indifference.

"I have."

"What have you been told?"

"That Jenna bore my children."

Marcus wanted to curl his lips at Lorken's familiar use of his daughter's name but held his distaste in check. "If you find the rumor true, what are your intentions?"

"That depends on Jenna. I'll have her hand in marriage if she will accept."

"Marriage?" Marcus lifted a brow above an icy-blue eye.

"Yes. I would claim my children, as is my right as their father."

"Your right? What right has a thief to the usury gained from stolen wealth?"

"Thief? I did not take her by force. She chose me just as I chose her!" Lorken growled, refuting the lie.

"Chose you? She had no right to gift her maidenhood that belonged to another. You have both shamed my house with your torrid affair," Marcus sneered.

"Why would you force your daughter to wed against her will? You can't force her to love another."

"Love?" Marcus said incredulously. "You misplace that ambiguous lie of dreamers and poets with duty and propriety. Love is irrelevant in the affairs of state and the empires of blood. Her worth to this household counts for naught with her tainted womb, which has offended the honor of this house."

"What does a slaver know of honor?" Lorken challenged.

"You question my honor on the possession of slaves?"

"I question anyone's honor if they sell, buy, or own another being. You have no authority to question my morals or honor!"

"And this strange land you hail from, there are no slaves there?"

"We outlawed such barbarity hundreds of years ago."

"You consider the subjugation of our lessers barbaric?"

"Your lessers?"

"Yes. There is a hierarchy in all things, and men are no different. There are those born to serve and those born to be served."

"Our coming to your world disproves that notion. We serve no one, and no one serves us."

"Which only proves you unsuitable to wield the power you possess. Had anyone else tainted my daughter, they would have been swiftly dealt with, but your involvement requires a more...deft approach."

At least Marcus Talana was wiser than Tyro in respecting the power the Earthers wielded, but Lorken grew weary of this game. "If you have a suggestion about resolving our problem, then spit it out!" He snorted. *I'm sounding more like Raven every day,* he thought sourly.

"Spit it out? Oh yes, one of your coarse expressions that reveals your true nature. You project the trappings of civilization, but they are mere dressings to conceal the barbarian beneath." Marcus smiled with condescension.

"What do want?" Lorken cut the chase.

"Since you justify the defilement of my daughter by invoking the absurdity you call love, that ambiguous lie peddled by poets and singers, I shall put your lie to the test."

"Speak plainly so I can understand what the hell you're babbling about!" Lorken growled, his patience wearing thin.

"Your children I give to you. The girl is quite lovely, the visage of her mother. The boy, well, his paternal parentage is without doubt. As for their mother, we shall see." His last words rang ominously.

Lorken backed a step as a dozen guards entered the atrium from his left, escorting a veiled woman wearing a long sand-colored gown. They ushered her before Marcus and withdrew to the perimeter of the chamber. Marcus lifted the woman's veil. "Jenna," Lorken said, stepping near before Marcus lifted a hand, cautioning him to remain where he stood.

Jenna shook slightly, training her blue eyes to her folded hands, which were concealed within the folds of the long sleeves of her gown. Her ebony hair was sheared, her meek demeanor belying her vivacious nature. Lorken could well imagine the suffering she had endured since he saw her last. The woman he fell in love with was now hidden beneath this icy shell. Until he could remove her from her father's influence, he had little hope of seeing that woman ever again.

"My children?" Lorken asked.

"In time," Marcus said with a false smile. "I shall have them sent to your vessel by nightfall."

"And Jenna?"

"That is another matter altogether," Marcus answered cryptically, as if privy to some mystery he longed to share.

"What matter?"

"Before I relent to your union, you must pass a test of your... devotion."

"What test?" he growled.

"As I have already explained to my faithless offspring, she is no longer my daughter. I rescind all titles and privileges our noble house has bestowed upon her since birth. But as she remains under my dominion, her life is mine to give, take, or *end*. Since she chose to forsake her familial duty for the carnal pleasures you shamelessly offered, I will test if her faith in you was well-placed. I will sell her to you if you are so inclined. She may serve as you desire, perhaps as a chamber slave, a scullery maid, or a bed slave if you desire. She can serve however you wish. 'Tis a boon to any man's prestige having a former lady of House Talana as his personal trophy to do with as he pleases."

"What kind of fiend do you take me for?"

"It matters not what I take you for, Earther. It matters only to Jenna. I offer her to you. Her fate rests in your tender mercy, her joys or sorrows dependent on your honor. I place her at your mercy, a fitting punishment for her false faith in your character if she chose poorly."

"I'll take her," Lorken affirmed, "not as my slave but my wife, if she'll have me. Either way, she will be free of you." Jenna braved a glance, her moistened eyes regarding him with a mix of surprise and joy.

"Before you claim your prize, there is a matter of payment," Marcus said, his narrowed blue eyes fixed to Lorken's brown.

"Name your price."

"Twenty thousand certras."

"Twenty thousand?" Lorken lifted an eyebrow at the dazzling sum.

"Twenty thousand, no less. Of course, if you choose not to meet the price, I am certain another buyer might be found, perhaps Orvis Maiyan. Perhaps having his former betrothed as a house slave instead of his wife can restore his tainted honor." Jenna looked at her father, horrified that he would suggest such a possibility. Would he truly sell her? Had her offense wounded him so deeply that he would cast her into oblivion?

"You'll have your coin, Talana."

"Excellent. Perhaps Jenna's faith in you was not misplaced. Return to your ship and arrange payment. I shall give you by night-fall to gather the sum. My agent shall meet you at your ship. Once payment is received, I shall deliver her and her children to you."

Lorken agreed, giving Jenna a reassuring smile. "Be strong," he whispered, touching a hand to her face before turning to leave.

*****

> He blew a kiss across the still water
> He took my hand as we walked along
> He vowed to return from war if it took him
> He vowed to return and hear my fair song

He came to me across the still water
He returned to me from journey so long
He took my hand in his as he kissed me
He promised his love as I sang him this song

Leanna's voice soothed Cronus's mending heart as he leaned against the rail of the first deck, which circled the stern, his arms wrapped protectively around her, her back pressing against his chest. The late-day sun reflected off the calm, lapping waves as they stared out across the bay. There in the distance, where the Flen fed into the bay, was their way home.

The waning sun shone upon the silhouette of the Flen River Bridge, which straddled the jagged high banks of the Flen, connecting the halves of the city. The bridge rested a fair distance upstream, towering above its nearest landmarks, its ancient stone towers and high arches a tribute to the men who built it ages ago. The stone bridge spanning the powerful Flen rivaled the incredible works that surrounded the bay. Soon, they would cross over that bridge on their journey west. Leanna closed her eyes, leaning her head against his warm chest.

Their fellow Torries were gathered around them, along with Alen, Kendra, and Kato. They were moved by Leanna's gentle melody of courtly love that was pure and selfless.

"That was nice, Leanna. How about a song from my world?" Kato offered.

"Of course. That would be lovely." Leanna smiled with her eyes still closed, enjoying Cronus's embrace.

"Zem, can you turn on the amp with selection 436?" he said into his comm.

"Why?" Zem asked with a measure of annoyance. He sat post in the engineering room, checking the ship's diagnostics.

"I want to play a song for our guests," Kato said, annoyed for having to explain himself.

"If you want to impress upon them our advance culture, selection 914 would be more appropriate," Zem advised.

"I'm not going to play 'Anchors Aweigh'! Just plug in 436," Kato said, indicating "December 1963" by Frankie Valli and the Four Seasons.

"Idiot," Zem mumbled as he loaded the requested sequence, and the ship played the music off the stern.

Kato sang, his voice in sync with the music emitting from the amplifier. Passersby near the stone wharves looked on with curiosity at the strange music coming from the Earthers' vessel. Most found the melody strangely pleasant despite its alien origin.

Alen listened attentively, drawn to the music's calming allure, the song reflecting the Earthers' carefree nature. The one thing that the Earthers shared was an apparent lack of fear or worry, as if their greatest travails were but mere annoyances. They discounted Tyro's might as inconsequential and made sport of the bounty placed on their heads. Even when Raven was chained and caged in Axenville, the Earther never lacked for confidence that they would escape, belittling their captors with his flippant tongue. They were completely unlike his own people, who suffered in slavery, bred to be weak, and captive to their fears.

He reflected on something that Cronus had told him during their journey: "Men are men. Their minds are dulled or sharpened by the company they hold or the treatment they receive." What hope had he to be any more than a slave when born a Menotrist in Tyro's realm? But now he was set free by whatever forces that guided the fates of men. He stood upon the deck of an alien vessel surrounded by men and creatures better than himself, but they were men who raised him up, making him better than he was. They were unlike his former masters, who profited from his weakness.

Brokov's wondrous healing instrument had removed the scars of the brand marking him a royal slave. Kato's music made him reconsider joining the Earthers. What possibilities awaited him if he joined their crew? Adventure and freedom were enticing to one born a slave. But alas, he had to make his life count for more than his own comfort. If the fates set him free, then it was for a reason, and that reason was to fight with all he possessed to free his people.

"Such a spirited melody, my friend. Perhaps I might share one of my own had I not lost my mandolin during our flight from Axenville," Galen said as Kato finished the last verse.

"Torturing our ears is the last thing we need, minstrel. How about something better, Kato, like 1174?" Raven interrupted, overlooking them from the second deck with his forearms resting on the railing above.

"'The Streets of Laredo'?" Kato made a face. "No one wants to hear about a dying cowboy, Rav."

"Kato," Leanna said with pleading eyes, paining him with guilt as she looked up at Raven's disappointed face.

"Oh, all right," Kato groaned. "Zem, give me 1174," he said into the comm.

"Again? We just played that relic last year," Zem voiced his annoyance.

"Just humor him, Zem." Kato sighed as the music started emitting through the amp, the mournful melody echoing across the ship as Kato began to sing.

> As I walked out in the streets of Laredo
> As I walked out in Laredo one day
> I spied a young cowboy all dressed in white linen
> Dressed in white linen and cold as the clay

Raven listened as Kato sang the familiar tune, the words bringing back fond memories of home, of his family gathered around a campfire while his sisters and grandfather sang that tune and many others. His brothers would argue and wrestle. His father would tell tales of ghosts and adventure while his mother ferried food and hot drinks from their cabin. He doubted if he would ever see them again, wondering what they were doing this very minute. Were they looking up at the same stars, wondering his fate?

He could see Lorken stepping to his side through his periphery, standing there with his arms crossed, awaiting Jenna. Lorken had gathered all the wealth he had accumulated since their arrival on Arax to meet Marcus Talana's price. Even that was not enough, and the others gladly gave of their shares to reach the amount. Raven straightened, slapping Lorken on the back.

"Good luck, buddy," he said, noticing a large party marching toward the *Stenox* along the wharves led by a flagbearer hoisting the colors of House Talana. Behind him marched a company of soldiers in columns of two, escorting a litter born by eight slaves with drapes concealing its occupants. The group stopped at the end of the *Stenox*'s long stone wharf while two of their party approached the vessel. One was a guard wearing a green tunic and gold cape. The other was older with silver hair and attired in the long emerald robe denoting a position of authority.

"I am Valeus Torenta, steward of House Talana," the elder man stated, standing impassively with his hands folded politely before him.

"Go on. I'm listening," Lorken said, stepping to the starboard rail of the second deck, which faced the wharf. Valeus Torenta's eyes shifted, studying Lorken's dark form above. If the man feared him, he showed it not.

"And you are the Earther Lorken, I assume?"

"Yep," Lorken answered bluntly.

"Very well. Let us proceed and conclude this matter," the steward stated, signaling the slaves bearing the litter forward. The slaves carried the litter to the midpoint along the wharf, setting it down before kneeling as the steward drew back the curtain, helping the woman within onto the pier. She was veiled and wore an ankle-length tan-hued shift.

The simple garment poorly concealed her charms, and even from afar, Lorken knew it was Jenna. Two other women followed, stepping from the litter, each holding an infant. Their brief garments and collars marked them slaves of House Talana.

Within moments, Lorken had stepped onto the pier, carrying a heavy chest, setting it down at Valeus's feet. He lifted the lid, tossing it aside, revealing the gold coins piled therein. It was a significant fortune, far greater than Jenna's betrothal to House Maiyan would have profited her sire.

"Here's your master's blood money. Remove her veil so I can see what I'm buying!" Lorken growled. Valeus Torenta did not respond to Lorken's snide rebuke of Marcus Talana. He was wise enough to know the Earthers were beyond correction, and throwing insults or taking offense to those cast achieved nothing. He simply lifted the cowl behind Jenna's head and gently removed her veil.

She stood statue still, her dark hair unbound and her eyes downcast, shamed by this whole affair. Lorken strode forth, his heavy boots pounding the pier before stopping before her. He lifted her chin, forcing her blue eyes to his. He could lose himself in those beautiful eyes, eyes that reflected the intelligence of the woman to whom they belonged. He had so much to say and ask of her, but not until she was safely aboard.

"Take the children aboard while I finish this business with your father." Jenna lifted her hands, revealing the manacles connecting her wrists. It was then he noticed a glint of metal peeking at the top of her gown. He pushed the edge of the garment slightly down, revealing an iron collar locked around her throat. "What is this?" he growled, turning on Valeus with a murderous glare.

The steward backed a step as he saw several more Earthers emptying out of their vessel with their hands on their weapons. He raised an open hand, cautioning his own men to remain still. Any sudden movement could easily erupt in bloodshed, which would not serve his master's interests.

"Master Talana has decreed that the status of the lady Jenna shall be determined by yourself upon delivery of payment," Valeus quickly explained.

"I already told him that I'm purchasing her freedom, not buying a slave. Unlock her manacles and take that damn thing off her neck!"

Valeus complied, not taking pleasure in Jenna's suffering from the start but following his master's wishes, as was his duty. "My lady." Valeus bowed his head, granting Jenna the respect he had always shown her. He wished to say more to her, to offer his regrets for her poor treatment, but it was not his place to question Marcus's will. He was thankful that the Earther seemed protective of her, for he had feared to consign her to a life of cruel bondage. Jenna gifted him an appreciative glance before Lorken drew her away. "The children." Valeus ordered the servant girls hither. They set one infant in Jenna's arms while Leanna hurried forth, offering to help with the other.

"Jenna, I am Leanna. Let me help you aboard."

*****

After dealing with Valeus, Lorken found Jenna and Leanna in the second crew cabin, tending to the children. Jenna rose quickly from the lower bunk with their daughter in her arms. Her heart pounded as she stared up into his powerful brown eyes. She found his raw masculine power attractive and frightening at the same time. He was unlike any man she had ever known and knew after their first meeting that she could never desire another.

"Are you all right?" he asked, squeezing her slender shoulders.

"Did you mean what you told my father and Valeus?" she asked, her voice firmer than her fragile heart. "I am not a slave?"

"Never!" he affirmed, placing a kiss to her forehead. "You are free, free to leave and live anywhere you desire or free to live with me as my wife."

"You still want me?" She smiled, her watery eyes betraying her fragile state. She loathed feeling so weak.

"I've always wanted you. I only stayed away when I thought that was your wish."

"That was my father's doing. He forbade me seeing you and sent my servant to tell you I wished not to see you. By the time I realized what he had done, the *Stenox* had left port, and I remained behind. I soon discovered that I carried your child," she explained.

"I know. It's over now, Jenna. You are safe. But you still haven't answered my question," he said, easing to his knee as he took her hands gently into his, staring into her blue eyes. "Will you be my wife?"

She was taken aback by his act of humility, kneeling before her, which was out of character. She was ignorant of the Earther custom of courtship but quickly guessed its significance. "I will." She smiled, tears squeezing from her eyes as he gained his feet, kissing her fiercely as she held their daughter to her breast.

Leanna sat upon the bunk opposite them, holding the boy as she watched their affection. It was a side of Lorken she hadn't seen. She wondered at times if the Earthers were different in this regard, copulating with the carefree indifference they demonstrated in all their other interactions. She was happy for Jenna and jealous as well, for she longed for the day to bear Cronus's child.

"Do you care to meet your daughter?" Jenna asked, lifting the girl in her arms toward him. Lorken took the child gently in his arms as if she would break. The girl rested peacefully, her tiny face nestled between the folds of her blanket. It was almost surreal, standing upon an alien world holding his child born of an alien mother. The girl looked the image of Jenna, without a trace of his shape or color, but she was his nonetheless.

"What is her name?"

"I…I haven't yet named them."

"Hmm. How about Lara, after your mother?" he offered. Her mother loved her dearly and had begged her father to show Jenna mercy, but he refused.

"Thank you. Lara it is." She smiled, kissing the baby's head.

"What of your son, Lorken?" Leanna asked.

Lorken handed Lara back to her mother before lifting the boy from Leanna's arms. The boy's face and coloring were entirely his own. Strangely, the boy looked nothing like his mother. Whether the children's physical characteristics were happenstance or the result of a genetic quirk of their alien coupling, he could only guess. Brokov would be certain to examine the children more carefully to see if the others could expect a similar result once they decided to have children.

"John," he said, naming the boy after his own father.

*****

Klen Adine sighed, tiredly waiting for the steward of House Talana to leave the vicinity of the *Stenox*. He observed the exchange from the end of the wharf, his men providing a visible presence to deter hostilities between House Talana and the Earthers. He ordered more than one hundred soldiers of the harbor garrison to stand post around the *Stenox*. Once the Talana delegation departed, he approached the vessel.

*****

"It's been a long time, Klen. What brings you out of your hole?" Raven asked, standing on the bridge with his right hand resting on his holstered pistol. Zem and Brokov joined them on the bridge as Klen stood before them, his hands tucked within the sleeves of his robe. His studious blue eyes regarded them carefully. He came aboard alone, trusting no ears other than his own.

"I see you survived your journey through the Benotrist heartland with all your limbs attached," Klen said dryly.

"Just a leisurely stroll through the countryside, Klen. It was quite relaxing. You should try it sometime," Raven said.

"I'm sure." Klen sighed. "Your antics seem to have incensed the Benotrist emperor. You are aware of the bounty upon your head, as well as on Lorken, Cronus Kenti, and an escaped Menotrist slave that you are harboring on your vessel?"

"If Tyro's hell-bent on collecting our bounty, he's welcome to try." Raven shrugged.

"The Benotrist emperor need not confront you himself or risk his own men with your bounty so high. Word has spread far and wide of your bounty. Mercenaries and free swords from all eastern Arax are converging on our fair port, hoping to gain their fortune on your capture or death, though I doubt they'll chance the former. Perhaps their ambitions are of little concern to you, but any altercation will certainly endanger the populace of Tro."

"We'll be gone before they arrive," Raven said, dismissing the threat.

"They're already here."

"When?" Raven asked.

"When?" Klen lifted an eyebrow, wondering the limit to Raven's naivety. "Mercenaries and man hunters have been trickling into port since your bounty was issued. But of greater concern is the sudden arrival of hundreds of mercenaries this very day, whose origin is clearly Benotrist, though they mask it well."

"Why hasn't Kaly warned us?" Brokov asked.

"Why do you surmise I am here?" Klen answered. "Kaly is being watched. Over three dozens of the new arrivals have staged themselves throughout the Moorn. He contacted me through one of our go-betweens. Under our usual dealings, I would simply wait for you to come to me, but I lack the time for such convenience. You must hasten your departure from Tro."

"We're still waiting for Kaly to provide an escort for Cronus," Raven countered.

"He has made arrangements, which is another reason for my subterfuge. He has contracted six warriors for this task. They will receive your friends with an additional five mounts in tow, one for each. They will meet you at the faxet stables before dawn. Kaly suggests you deliver your comrades with as much stealth as you can provide. Your undersea vessels would be most effective in this endeavor," Klen advised.

"Only six warriors for an escort?" Raven asked.

"Would you prefer a larger escort whose loyalty is in question or a smaller group you can trust? Kaly chose the latter, selecting only those he trusted with your friends' safety. He might have found more if time allowed, but as you well know, we must make do with what we have, not what we wish it to be."

"We know. We're just not happy about it. You mentioned a hundred Benotrist mercenaries in the city. You placed three dozen at the Moorn. What about the rest?" Raven asked.

"Most are at the Lady's Favor at the behest of Hossen Grell. He holds the favor of Orvis Maiyan, whom—"

"Yeah, we know all about him. He's not one of our biggest fans since Lorken took his girl." Raven snorted.

Fan? Klen thought to ask the meaning but decided against it. It was likely one of those many references the Earthers were prone to use that made sense only to them. He was surprised he understood half of what they said. "Yes, he is most displeased with your presence in our port and has rashly aligned himself with a known Benotrist agent."

"The Lady's Favor, huh." Raven scrubbed his chin with his hand. The Lady's Favor was a tavern nearly of a size to the Moorn resting further west and south along the waterfront. "All right. Get word to Kaly that we'll get Cronus to the stables before dawn."

*****

They said their farewells aboard the *Stenox*, wondering when or if they would meet again. Brokov slipped into the pilot's seat of the *Atlantis* as Arsenc sat beside him in the weapons seat. Galen and Alen sat in the rear compartment, awaiting Leanna to squeeze in between them. She stood in the diving room, as she and Cronus saved their last farewell for Raven.

"Thank you," she said, kissing his cheek as tears squeezed from her eyes. "You kept your promise." She recalled that night so long ago when he promised to return Cronus to her.

"I got him out. Now it's your job to keep him from wandering off again." Raven gave Cronus a gentle shove.

"I shall keep him close." Leanna slipped her hand through Cronus's arm, drawing him to her.

"Am I your prisoner now?" Cronus smiled, looking into her blue eyes.

"Yes, and I am a watchful jailer." She touched a finger to his nose.

"At least she's prettier than the last one," Raven quipped.

Cronus couldn't disagree. He regarded her briefly before returning his gaze to Raven. "Thank you, Rav, for everything."

Raven nodded, bereft of words. He simply wrapped his arms around him, embracing his friend. "Take care, buddy." He offered a pained smile, hating to see him go. He kissed Leanna on the forehead and helped them through the hatchway to the sub. Leanna squeezed in the back, and Cronus entered last, sitting in the captain's seat. He looked up at Raven through the open hatch, placing his fist to his heart. Raven returned the gesture and sealed the hatch.

*****

The *Atlantis* surfaced within a shallow cove north of the mouth of the Flen River. The small inlet was little used with its shallows hindering most vessels from mooring therein. Using the cover of the predawn night, Brokov drew as close to the shore as possible before surfacing. A cursory sensor sweep of the shoreline found no prying eyes save for two of Kaly's men, who awaited them as planned.

Cronus opened the top hatch, peering carefully over the lip of the opening as waves lapped gently against the hull. His head looked as if he was rising from the sea because of the vessel's low silhouette. Within moments, they had climbed out, making their way to a nearby stable where their mounts were saddled and waiting.

"They're ashore. Ready second team. Set my ETA at one hundred fifty seconds," Brokov spoke into the comm, pressing the Hatch Closed switch on the console.

"Received," Raven's voice answered back.

*****

The Lady's Favor sat upon the waterfront, mid distance between the mouth of the Flen and the Moorn. It served lesser clientele, resting at the water's edge where the more unsavory crews docked. The structure was of similar construct to the Moorn with an open main floor and a bar running along its back wall. A wide stair circled the periphery, leading to the second floor with rooms lining its outer walls and a balcony circling its center, overlooking the main floor below.

The Lady's Favor required a strong owner to manage its raucous crowd. The previous owner managed well enough but was overwhelmed as numerous Benotrist mercenaries flooded his establishment. Orvis Maiyan purchased the tavern, relieving its owner of its growing burden. Orvis Maiyan purchased the Favor to facilitate a gathering point for like-minded contemporaries, those holding a mutual dislike of the Earthers. The dislike extended to those allied with the Earthers and even those who associated with them in any capacity.

Since the *Stenox* sailed into port, the Lady's Favor was filled with hundreds of mercenaries and man hunters at any given time. In the predawn hours, when most of Tro's citizens were yet asleep, sizable crowds still lingered throughout the main floor of the tavern. The patrons spent countless hours plotting their moves against the Earthers. They were divided into dozens of disparate groups, the most notable of which was the Benotrist contingent led by Hossen Grell. Hossen sat at a large table at the back-left corner of the main floor, surrounded by sycophants who gathered about.

"The Earthers are up to some mischief, Hossen. They met at length with Magistrate Adine last eve after receiving a delegation from House Talana," whispered the fellow seated to his immediate left.

"They have recovered their captain. My men have seen him upon their ship," another said.

Hossen pursed his lips, unfazed by the news. His own spies told him of the failed ambush at Gotto yester morn and that Raven, Cronus, Alen, and a female warrior departed Gotto via one of the Earthers' damnable undersea vessels. His other sources confirmed that Marcus Talana had sold his daughter to the Earther Lorken after defiling her virtue.

He should've hung the girl for her treason, he thought sourly, pondering his dwindling options. Tyro sent him to Tro to build a network of support within the vital trading hub, a network intended to sway the ruling oligarchs to align themselves with the Benotrist Empire or, if not, to undermine the city's defenses when he decided to seize the harbor. Hossen was well ahead of schedule, constructing a formidable network within Tro when Tyro's edict shifted priorities to the capture of the fugitives from Fera and the other Earthers.

Somehow, Raven had managed to cross the continent while evading Tyro's pursuit. Now that he reached the *Stenox*, the task of capturing him was nigh impossible. That damn vessel currently sat in the middle of the bay, rendering any hope of sneaking up on them pointless. He needed them to set ashore. Cronus Kenti was another matter. His spies in the Moorn reported that the Torries planned to disembark at Tro and return to Torry North. If Cronus chose such a path, Tyro had other agents to deal with him.

Despite his success in building a viable network of Benotrist support in Tro, Hossen needed to capture or kill at least one of the fugitives Tyro sought to strengthen his position at court. Being a native of the Lone Hills, Hossen Grell was ever mindful of the distrust his fellow Benotrist Elite harbored. Tyro recruited dozens of foreigners to his Elite, gathering men of unique skills to his service. Such endeavors did not curry favor with Benotrist and gargoyle nativists, who distrusted those not of their blood.

"We need them to set ashore," Hossen said, raking his fingers through his dark beard.

"How?" one of the others asked.

"By threatening something or someone they value," another answered.

"The Moorn," Colbe Denarv declared, a Benotrist free sword and native of Mordicay. "We strike come the dawn. Gather your men. We shall set it ablaze and guard its exit points!"

"Perhaps." Hossen pretended to consider the ridiculous notion, knowing a flat refusal would only fuel Colbe's desire to do so. By considering it with a mere perhaps, he intended to interject before another fool seconded the notion. Things could easily get out of hand if one was not careful, and Tyro brought Hossen Grell into his service because he was *very careful* and brilliant in his political maneuverings.

"Your plan has merit, but a fire and an attack upon the Moorn is a bit much. The fire might spread, and all of Tro would hold us to account. But a fire alone might draw the Earthers ashore to help their friends, a fire whose origin need not be known until we have claimed our prize. I care not to incur Tro's wrath for anything less than an Earther's head."

Creak! The sound of Zem's heavy boots on the floor's timbers echoed audibly across the tavern. A hundred pairs of eyes drew instantly to the doorway as the towering creature stood before them, his luminous blue eyes sweeping the assemblage for the slightest threat. All the voices clambering to act against the Earthers grew predictably silent.

"Hossen Grell!" Raven called out, stepping around Zem. He didn't expect the fool to answer back, but nervous eyes were bound to point him out. Besides, any portly men with beards were a rare sight on Arax. There shouldn't be more than a dozen in the entire port. "I see you." Raven shrugged, his dark eyes finding Hossen across the room.

Hossen ducked below the table as laser streamed across the tavern. He paused beneath the table, collecting his wits as bodies dropped around him. Another blast pierced the table, grazing his shoulder. We wasted no time crawling behind the bar, keeping low enough to conceal his movement.

Zem's and Raven's fire abated as the Benotrists gathered about the back corner. Tables littered the floor, smoke drifting above mortal wounds. Dozens fled through the exit at the back right corner. Some were huddled behind tables, and others were crowded along the periphery, keeping to the shadows. Dozens more stood where they were, wielding whichever weapon their hands found.

"Murderer!" one fellow shouted.

"Killing those who plot against me ain't murder. It's just good sense," Raven retorted, taking a step further into the tavern. *Zip!* Raven's aim found an archer drawing his bow on the floor above. The blast took him through the chest, his body forcing him over the rail that circled above. His body dropped, smashing a table below, and all hell broke loose.

A fellow rushed from their immediate left, Zem catching his chest with the back of his hand, sending the man sailing across the tavern and through the far wall. Raven hurried a few shots, seeking archers in the crowd as others lumbered forth, hoping to claim his bounty. *Zip! Zip! Zip!* His laser cut down those nearest them before shifting further afield.

He caught sight of Zem tossing another unfortunate wretch aside before embedding his fist in a third man's head. Zem holstered his pistol, using his free hand to pry the shattered skull from his left. Raven's aim found an arm cocked back in the crowd, brandishing a dagger. He fired through the man who obscured his target, the blast piercing both men, the dagger clanging off the floor.

Zem moved among the crowd, tossing men aside like broken toys. A dozen men closed upon him, hoping to topple the metallic giant. He brought his fist down one fellow's spine, snapping his back. He caught another's errant punch, crushing the man's fist within his own before hoisting him in the air. He swung the man about his head, using him as a club, smashing those crowding around him before tossing him over his head, the man's body passing through the front wall of the Favor.

"Showoff!" Raven grunted, firing into the crowd, rethinking Argos's suggestion to simply blow this tavern to kindling and saving the bother.

*****

"It's time," Vade Cavelle said, leading their small party from the stables onto the Tel-Ro, the main avenue that circled the port. The Troan free sword was one of Kaly's most trusted associates. He held his word as sacred. Where most free swords would have forsook their duty and turned Cronus and Alen over for their bounty, Vade Cavelle would not after giving his word to Kaly to escort them to Torry North. He and his five companions vowed to see them safely through. They were similarly attired in dull-brown tunics and well-worn mail, greaves, and helms with their shields slung over their backs, giving the visage of simple-armed travelers.

"How far to the bridge?" Cronus asked, drawing up alongside Vade, similarly outfitted as the others.

"A few moments," he said, keeping his small company to the side of the avenue as men passed in the opposite direction. Laser fire illuminated the harbor sky off their east. The sound of frantic cries rang out in the night air, proof of the Earthers' assault on the Favor, drawing most eyes away from their path. Men rushed past them, brandishing swords and crossbows, traveling to the sound of battle. Others fled in the opposite direction in disorder, fleeing the carnage.

*****

Hosen Grell crept along the back of the bar, keeping his head down as the shouts of dying men echoed through the fetid air.

Crack!

Hossen looked up sharply as a body struck the wall above. His panicked eyes drew wide as the broken corpse slipped from the wall, dropping like a heavy stone. He shifted away as the body struck the back edge of the bar before smashing into the floor, a hand's width from his face.

Across the main floor, Zem snatched another fellow by the scruff of his neck, tossing him through the air like a loaf of stale bread. The miserable wretch met the wall above the bar headfirst. The sound of his snapping neck echoed dully over the din, his head breaking a large hole in the wall, leaving his feet dangling out of the crevice of broken timbers.

Hossen waited with bated breath, hoping the second body would not fall on him. His plans of attacking the Earthers were abandoned. His new plan was to live. He wasted no more time gaining his knees, crawling for the exit. Fortunately, the backdoor was open, but it rested a few paces beyond the end of the bar with several bodies littering his path. He would have to expose himself to the Earthers' laser fire to cross that deadly space. He waited to gain his breath and launched himself toward the door, passing through the exit as a laser blast struck behind him.

The door led to the back alley, where several bodies were strewn across the pathway, feathered with arrows. He cleared the doorway as a shaft shot from the dark, grazing his chest. He jumped back as another struck where he last stood. Craning his neck, he could make out a silhouette at the east corner of the structure behind the Lady's Favor. He took a tentative step before jumping back as another arrow passed empty air where he had intended to venture. He burst across the alleyway just after the arrow passed, reaching the corner of the adjacent dwelling, another arrow missing his leg.

Kendra cursed her aim as the shadow escaped her.

*****

"Argh!" a Benotrist mercenary cried out as Raven placed three blasts in his back as he attempted to crawl away. He shifted aim to another with a dagger raised in his left hand, striking the fellow in the throat, the blast nearly separating head from neck, the dagger falling harmlessly from lifeless fingers. Raven shook his head as Zem kept his pistol holstered, engaging the drunken rabble hand to hand.

The large metal bully grabbed hold of an outstretched arm, twisting its owner to the floor before pressing a boot to his head and pulling the arm from its socket. The poor fellow's screams rent the air as Zem jerked the limb free. He hoisted the severed append-age, blood draining from its end, and swung it like a club, knock-ing another upside the head. "That's just sick." Raven winced. Zem seemed to be enjoying himself way too much.

Zem paused as what remained of the crowd drew back, their vigor waning with the futility of facing the Earthers' fury. Three dozen corpses littered the tavern floor besides the few Zem threw into the walls. A dozen others nursed broken limbs or fractured skulls, writhing on the floor in agony.

"All right, big fella, let's get out of here," Raven said as they backed away, hoping their diversion bought Cronus time to slip away unnoticed.

*****

"They're moving," Brokov said into the comm, following their progress through the scanner on the bridge.

"Moving to extraction point," Lorken answered back, steering the *Spectre* into position along the wharves.

Argos stood over Brokov's shoulder as he sat on the helm, his thick arms crossed, struggling to make sense of the silhouettes moving across the gray screen. The *Stenox* rested on the west end of the harbor, its stern some five hundred meters from the mouth of the Flen with the Lady's Favor resting off its port side bow.

"Which one is Raven?" Argos asked, confusing the heat signatures on the screen that seemed to blend together.

"The red signatures are Raven, Zem, and Kendra. The green are everyone else." Brokov tapped the screen, pointing out Zem's and Raven's larger silhouettes as they exited the front of the tavern and Kendra's smaller signature moving to join them from the street farther back.

"What are those?" Argos asked as several green shapes approached from the west side of the Lady's Favor, seeming to close in on Zem's and Raven's backsides as they moved east along the wharves.

"Those are trouble," Brokov answered dryly. "Lorken, our boys have company approaching their backside," he spoke into the comm.

"I see 'em," Lorken answered.

The *Spectre* surfaced shy of its rendezvous point, its lasers cutting across the wharves off Raven and Zem's right. Raven craned his neck, following the laser to its target behind them. The blasts struck the mob of pursuers, riddling their serried ranks, dropping several at once. Several tripped over their fellows who dropped in front of them. Before gaining their feet, they found themselves alone as their surviving comrades broke off, running for their lives. Kendra cut across an alleyway, converging with her comrades as the *Spectre* pulled up alongside the nearest wharf.

"Good work, kid," Raven greeted her as the top hatch of the sub slid open.

"I think Hosen escaped," she lamented.

"Maybe, but we bought Cronus the diversion he needs to slip across the bridge," Raven said.

*****

Cronus's small company traversed the wide-set avenue, the breaking dawn playing off the white stone walls of the granaries that lined either side of the Tel-Ro. The empty street would soon be bustling with vendors selling their wares. They spied a few curious souls watching as they passed before going about their business. The Tel-Ro was the central causeway of Tro Harbor, shadowing the waterfront as it circled the city. It ran in a continuous arc from the northern mouth of the bay to the west, passing over the Flen River Bridge before circling back to the southern mouth of the bay. The elevation ahead rose steadily as they neared the Flen, the Tel-Ro widening as the bridge drew close.

The Flen River Bridge spanned the banks of the ancient river, stretching seven hundred meters across. The stone bridge was constructed with a series of arches with alternating rectangular stones running lengthwise and across to strengthen its massive supports. The centermost arches rested on a stone isle in the middle of the river. The massive work was a wonder to behold, constructed of gray stone arches and red stone running the length of its upper surface. Two watchtowers guarded each end with massive battlements overlooking those passing over the vital causeway, though it was only manned during moments of crises.

Cronus stared up at the red stone bulwarks that towered above like ageless sentinels. The bridge spanned fifteen meters in width, allowing a number of their party to ride abreast. Cronus drew up alongside Vade Cavelle as they crossed onto the north end of the bridge.

"Is it usually this sparse?" he asked warily.

"Some days, yes, but not for this early hour," Vade said, though he also kept a wary eye.

Leanna eased her mount up beside Cronus's left, her curious gaze drawn to her left as the rising sun broke upon the bay, its golden rays reflecting off the tranquil waters. The bridge rose some twenty-two meters above the surface, allowing Leanna to survey the harbor in panoramic wonder. Patches of mist still lingered at the mouth of the bay and the base of the sentinel as if the great statue was rising through the clouds. She could see several ships traversing the harbor, making haste for the open sea, their tall masts full with the morning wind. Flocks of lumar birds passed over the harbor, their wingtips kissing the surf as their squawks echoed dully in the distance.

She could see the silver-blue hull of the *Stenox* resting in the center of the bay. She thought of her time aboard the vessel and the friendship the Earthers had shown her. Cronus followed her gaze to the *Stenox*, guessing her thoughts. "That was your home for some time now," he said.

She turned to him, reaching out her hand to his as they rode. "You are my home. The *Stenox* was merely where I slept. But yes, I shall miss them. They are true friends, Cronus, and I am proud of you for knowing them," she said, squeezing his hand.

"Raven was right." He sighed.

"How so?"

"He said I was lucky to have you."

"Of course, you are." She smiled.

"This is where you say that you are lucky to have me as well." He lifted an expectant brow over his green eye.

"Not true. You are a very troublesome boy. You are constantly in danger and managed to get yourself captured, worrying me to death. With any other man, I would have already been wed and had him well-trained," she said in all seriousness before laughing. Oh, how he loved hearing her laugh.

"Well, let's go home and wed, but I doubt you'll ever train me."

"Fair enough." She smiled, knowing he was hopelessly hers in every way. She had missed their playful banter, and with every moment together, she could see his old self returning.

An unsettling disquiet took hold of Cronus's mind as they neared the center of the bridge. It was a sensation he last felt upon the battlements of Fera, as if he was being watched by malevolent eyes. He slowly craned his neck, taking a furtive scan behind him. Nothing appeared amiss, but his instincts warned him otherwise.

"Who are they?" he heard Leanna ask, and his eyes returned ahead where a dozen riders approached from the south end of the bridge. Vade drew back his reins, easing his mount to a halt as the others did likewise. From a distance, he couldn't make out their faces, but they were uniformly attired in nondescript gray tunics, mail, and greaves. Though they bore no adornments of rank or realm, they were clearly Benotrist. One in the Benotrist party stood apart from his comrades, a gargoyle of unusual size with crimson eyes that fixed on Cronus as if the distance between them was but a breath away.

"Kriton." The name escaped Cronus's lips like poison.

"Who is Kriton?" Leanna asked guardedly.

"Stay behind me!" Cronus commanded, fixing his shield over his left forearm and drawing his sword with his right.

"Others approaching behind us!" one of their escort called out. Vade looked back, spotting a half dozen riders approaching from the north end of the bridge, cutting their escape.

"Who is Kriton?" Leanna asked again, fear rising in her throat.

"The keeper of the dungeon of Fera," Alen answered weakly. Leanna regarded his shaking hands as she stared behind her where he sat on his mount.

*****

"Kenti is mine. The others, do with as you will," Kriton hissed, his feral gaze fixed intently upon his prey.

"The slave is the only other rich bounty. The others are worthless," the Benotrist to his left complained.

Kriton turned his murderous glare to the Benotrist mercenary, the man suddenly cognizant of his overstep. Long had Kriton dreamed of this day, the day he would impale Cronus's heart with his sword and feast on his wretched flesh. The Torry escaped his cell and drove him from the battlements of Fera. He slipped his grasp at the proctor's holdfast, and he missed him by mere days at Axenville.

Once Cronus reached the *Stenox*, he feared he had lost him forever. His only hope was Cronus's desire to return to his native realm. He guessed correctly, figuring Cronus to commandeer ocran through the Troan Kaly, whose resources were all placed on the northern half of the city. Cronus wouldn't risk traveling west on the north side of the Flen, which meant he would have to cross this bridge.

He traveled to Tro alone upon his magantor, sending his large cohort ahead on ocran. Once he reached the eastern port, he gathered a number of Benotrist mercenaries to him, convincing them to forsake the bounty on the Earthers for the easier prey.

Since Fera, Cronus plagued his waking thoughts, driving Kriton with an all-consuming fire. He had to finish him here or be driven to madness. His arduous pursuit across the northern steppes and endless forests brought him to this pinnacle moment. Just ahead on the bridge was the catalyst of all his suffering: Kenti.

"Kai-Shorum!" Kriton hissed, raising his sword as he kicked his heels, driving his ocran forth, sunlight reflecting off his helm and shield.

Cronus's mount charged across the bridge, its hooves sounding off the surface like thunderclaps. A northerly gale pressed upon his face, lifting his black mane behind his helm, trailing him like a dark flame. Before him rode the source of all his torment, the defiler of his soldiers and the ghastly nexus of his every nightmare. He would have Kriton this day or die in the attempt. When last they met, Cronus was weak and sickly, a shadow of his present self. Let the vermin test him restored and unchained.

Cronus couldn't hear the shouts of his comrades following in his wake or the war cries of his foes rushing to meet him. He could only hear the beating of his heart as he drove upon Kriton, his green eyes fixed to the gargoyle's red. Kriton sucked the slather from his fangs, his feral countenance contorted in abject rage. "KENTI!" he screamed, driving headlong toward his foe.

They raced across the bridge, driving upon one another like comets colliding in a midnight sky. Cronus released his reins just before impact, lifting his shield to meet Kriton's deadly slash, his sword arm countering, striking Kriton's reins, severing them with a single blow.

Kriton cursed as his tenuous hold on the unfamiliar ocran slipped away with his severed reins. Another hasty blow glanced off Cronus's shield as the Torry backed away, the thrust meeting mostly empty air. The hurried blow cost Kriton his balance, his momentum nearly pulling him from his saddle.

Cronus tried to maneuver his mount behind Kriton's ocran, but the obstinate beast was slow to respond to its unfamiliar master. Cronus took what Kriton offered him, jabbing his blade into the hindquarter of Kriton's ocran, the quick thrust causing the beast to jerk suddenly, shifting to the edge of the bridge. Cronus had turned his mount to press his attack when the sound of Kriton's men echoed over the din, distracting him from his prey. "Argh!" the Benotrists shouted, racing across the bridge with their swords raised.

Two arrows passed overhead, striking one ocran in the throat, causing the beast to stagger as the other fell harmlessly astray. *Zip!* An intense green flash burst amid the Benotrists, temporarily blinding friend and foe alike. Cronus closed his eyes as the flashes continued, the wrenching screams of the Benotrists piercing his ears.

When Cronus's vision cleared, he took a furtive glance, spying a Benotrist corpse sitting on a saddle sans a head, as if the flesh above its shoulders had melted away. Another Benotrist lay upon the bridge with his left arm and much of his chest missing.

"Earth scum!" Kriton hissed, staring out to the bay where the *Stenox* sat, spewing its cowardly fire upon his men.

"Cronus!" Leanna's voice cried out, causing him to look back where he had left her. She ambled her ocran closer to him, brandishing a sword that her mount was conveniently outfitted with. Arsenc drew his mount up beside hers, guarding her as best as he could as their escort rushed forth to aid Cronus or back to guard their rear.

"Arsenc, keep her there!" Cronus cried out, hoping to protect her from herself.

"Your woman?" Kriton snarled, his clawed digits reaching for the severed ends of his reins, his eyes shifting between Cronus and Leanna, suddenly realizing her significance. "Leanna!" he hissed, drawing Cronus's ire. "That is her name, the one that you called to in your dreams." Kriton's voice carried the threat and malice of his unspoken words. He would defile her after slaying Cronus and then toss her broken corpse into the bay.

"AGGHH!" Cronus shouted, charging forth, driving his mount into Kriton's flank, pushing him to the edge of the bridge. Kriton forsook his reins, lifting his shield as Cronus struck at him with unnatural strength. Cronus pressed his attack, hacking away at Kriton's shield as if cutting a tree. Kriton snarled, hissing his frustration as he attempted a counterstrike to stay Cronus's fury.

Kriton's shield arm was twisted across his body, guarding his right flank as he swung his blade in his right claw. The hasty blow missed as Cronus slammed his shield into Kriton's, driving him backward from the saddle. Kriton's back struck the rail of the bridge, his momentum carrying him over the side.

Kriton fell headlong through the air, his crimson eyes frantic as the watery surface drew closer with his descent. He released his sword and shield, attempting to spread his wings to break his fall, but the weight of his mail, greaves, and helm and the speed of his descent hindered the effort. *Splash!* Cronus stared over the edge of the bridge as Kriton slipped beneath the surface, sparing little more than a glance before returning to the fight.

*****

"What do we have?" Raven barked into the comm as he climbed through the hatch and into the *Stenox*.

"Trouble on the bridge," Brokov answered back through the comm.

"What kind of trouble? Is the helm malfunctioning?"

"Not that bridge, Rav. The bridge over the Flen," Brokov explained. "Idiot," he mumbled after cutting the feed.

"On our way!" Raven said. "Zem, relieve Kato in the weapons room," he ordered as Zem emerged from the *Spectre*.

"I'll relieve him," Lorken said, following Zem and Kendra through the hatch.

"All right," Raven said before rushing down the corridor of the first deck. Stepping onto the stern, he was met by another blast of the ship's laser banks firing overhead, their long beams striking targets on the bridge. "Crap!" he growled, knowing Cronus had run into trouble. From this distance, he could see men scurrying along the top of the bridge. He quickly climbed the ladder to the second deck, rushing onto the bridge.

*****

Vade Cavelle maneuvered his ocran, guarding Cronus's back as he engaged Kriton, matching blows with an onrushing Benotrist. Two of his comrades closed alongside him while the others guarded their rear. Their disadvantage at the outset shifted with the Earthers' intervention, their deadly weapon decimating the Benotrist mercenaries to their front.

Lasers flashed behind them, striking those approaching from the north end of the bridge. One beam took an ocran in the head, obliterating everything above its neck, its body dropping, throwing its rider. The screams of dying and frightened men echoed in Vade Cavelle's ears. The surviving Benotrists forsook the fight, fleeing for their lives. The Benotrist directly before him could not disengage without Vade striking his backside, so he kept exchanging blows until Cronus circled behind him, thrusting his blade into his back.

Vade knocked the stricken foe from the saddle before taking stock. Several Benotrists retreated across the south end of the bridge, leaving most of their comrades behind. Several bodies were strewn across the bridge, each dismembered in some grizzly fashion with smoke drifting above sundered flesh. A few riderless ocran hurried off, their bloody saddles evidence of their masters' fates.

Cronus spurred his mount past Vade, returning to Leanna, where she waited but a few paces behind. He noticed Arsenc and Alen guarding her flanks. He spotted Galen farther off and afoot, moving among the stricken Benotrists, who attacked from the north. Galen slit their throats, whether they were wounded or still, making certain of them. Vade's men guarded their rear, chasing off the enemy, who fled north.

"Cronus," Leanna said, touching a hand to his face as he drew alongside her, confirming with her hand and eyes that he was unharmed. It was the first time she had seen men die by his hand.

"Are you well?" Cronus asked, taking her measure. He could see her arms shaking, though she tried to still their quiver.

"Yes," she said hurriedly, knowing they hadn't the time for more words than that.

"We have to move," Cronus said, riding past them to gather Galen and the others.

*****

The cold water engulfed him, the weight of his armor forcing him to the river's depth. His waning breath escaped his lips, his clawed fingers pulling desperately at his mail, working it free. He thrashed violently as the cumbersome ballast caught on his wing before casting it off. Wrapping his wings tightly to his side, Kriton pushed to the surface. He swam toward the light, his limbs taxed with the weight of the burdensome greaves and belt.

He broke the surface downstream, his lungs drinking the fresh air none too soon, emerging where the swift current carried him far below the bridge. Kriton kept low in the water lest his foes find him helpless upon the river. It would take the Earthers naught but a simple blast of their foul weapon to end him. He moved carefully through the current, moving only enough to stay afloat as he drifted toward the southern bank of the river, where it met the mouth of the bay.

"Kenti!" he snarled in a guttural hiss, his crimson eyes affixed to the top of the bridge, where his prey again eluded him.

*****

Cronus's small group made their way across the bridge, passing the macabre remains of their fallen foe. Cronus asked Leanna to shield her eyes, but she scoffed at such sensibilities and steeled her mind to the ghastly sights. He could not protect her from the war and the battles to come, and she needed to be unfazed by its brutality. She passed a corpse with a terrible cavity cut through its chest as wide as a fist. The fellow's still form stared to the heavens with dead eyes and slackened jaw. She felt no pity for the man for his ill intentions toward them. Her only regret was that she hadn't slain him herself.

"A gruesome sight, my lady, one unsuited for your fair eyes," Galen said, riding at her side.

"You are kind to protect me from the harshness of our world, minstrel, but I am not a frail flower to be admired, protected, and displayed until my petals are plucked or I wilt with age. These men intended malice upon us, as they received. I am merely seeing them in their rightful state, dead, for even carka birds have to eat."

"And so they shall, Lady Leanna." Galen bowed, knowing he should've expected no less from the woman who claimed Cronus's heart.

They followed the Tel-Ro as it meandered south of the bridge, angling sharply eastward before crossing the Gotto causeway. They were met at the junction of the two main thoroughfares by a fellow masked in a flowing long cloak, his head concealed beneath its cowl. Vade and Cronus were met by the fellow's outstretched hands as they rode forth to confront him.

"Hold, Cronus," a familiar voice called out, stopping him mid-stride. He lifted his cowl enough to reveal his face before dropping it back into place.

"Kato?" Cronus asked, wondering his purpose.

"We decided to go with plan B." The Earther smiled. "I'll need to share a mount with one of you, and we can be on our way."

Plan B? Cronus thought to ask the reference but thought better of it. It was likely another Earther phrase that only made sense to them, though he could guess its meaning.

*****

"Plan B?" Raven growled, overlooking the Troan Bay from the bridge of the *Stenox*.

"It's his choice, Rav. What are we supposed to do, chain him to the hull?" Brokov countered, sitting the helm.

"Does he even have a tracker?" he asked.

"I didn't have time. Hell, I haven't even removed yours yet."

"Wonderful." He snorted. "How are we supposed to know where he is or if he's alive?"

"We don't, but we'll be at Gregok for quite a while from what Argos claims. Kato will escort Cronus as far as Notsu and then head straight for the Ape Empire. We'll ask General Matuzak to have his troops at the border to keep a lookout for him."

"We can't stay in the Ape Empire indefinitely, waiting for him to show himself. I have business in the west in the coming months," Raven said, his thoughts consumed by Tosha and his promise to return for the birth of their child.

"What business would that be?" Brokov asked as the *Stenox* passed below the Sentinel of Tro, skirting south of its rocky isle.

"I'll tell you later," Raven said with all the charm of an old grump.

"Tosha, huh?" Brokov correctly guessed by the sour look Raven gave him. She seemed nice enough when she was aboard the *Stenox*. Raven must have brought out the worst in her, Brokov surmised. Knowing his friend's history with women, he wasn't surprised.

Zip! A blast of laser issued from the bow, streaming south across the bay, striking the upper masts of a galley anchored along the stone wharves allotted to the ruling families of Tro. The beam ran the length of the upper riggings, cutting them in two, their upper half collapsing upon the lower. Men scurried along her laden decks, hurrying down the gangplanks to flee the stricken vessel. "What was that?" Raven barked, wondering what threat the ship posed.

Brokov scanned the waterfront, examining the vessel in question, quickly realizing the motive of the attack. The rich green-and-gold sails of House Talana indicated the vessel's loyalties. The ship was a massive merchant galley with double rows of oars, a large forecastle, and a sea maiden cast in silver adorning its bow. "It's the *Lady Talana*," Brokov cursed.

"Lorken!" Raven growled into the comm, trying to hail his friend as a second beam sped across the water, striking along the hull of the ship.

"Forget the override, Rav. I disabled it," Lorken growled back as the laser continued along the ship's hull, stopping amidships, sealing its fate as it started to list. The *Lady Talana* was the flagship of House Talana and Marcus Talana's pride and joy. Such an affront meant the direst of repercussions, and the *Stenox* wouldn't likely be welcome in Tro for some time.

"You still got control of the helm?" Raven asked Brokov.

"Yes."

"Then let's get of here before he blows up something else."

The *Stenox* sped through the mouth of the bay, leaving scores of dead Benotrists littering the north shore and across the Flen River Bridge and a merchant galley sinking along the south shore. Lorken surrendered the laser controls, having avenged Jenna's honor. Raven didn't blame him, knowing he would have done the same. With Lorken's rash action and the bounty on their heads, they would have to lay low for a while.

Raven leaned back in the captain's chair with his feet resting on the console in front of him, the Troan coastline shrinking in the distance. He had more thoughts than his tired mind could sort. The only clear thought he could muster was concern for his friends traveling the dangerous road west. "Good luck, Cronus," he said tiredly.

"Here. This is for you," Brokov said, handing him a rolled parchment. Raven unrolled the crinkled paper, scowling as he read his wanted poster. It had a picture of a hideous face with his name at the bottom titled Raven the Earther. He crumpled the paper into a ball and tossed it at Brokov's head. "Don't worry, Rav, we made plenty of copies." Brokov grinned.

CHAPTER 15

The journey from Gotto to the crossroads passed without incident, to Cronus's relief. The well-traveled trade route connecting Tro to the eastern continent's inner markets was replete with inns, wells, and villages along its length. The road meandered the Teteran divide, passing between sparsely paced copses of tulac and lupec trees and offering few places for highway men to spring a trap.

Cronus was familiar with the road, having traveled east of Notsu at times, though never attaining Tro. He followed Vade Cavelle's lead, the man's knowledge of the area far exceeding his own. He understood why Kaly chose him for this task. He was quiet but competent with a sense of honor and duty that was rare for a free sword.

"We must be drawing near the crossroads," Kato said, drawing his mount up beside him.

"A few leagues I would guess," Cronus said, regarding his friend, thankful for his company. Once they set out from Tro, Kato feared they might be assailed by large numbers of raiders or Thorton's gun, but the path was remarkably uneventful. The only difficulty was finding Kato a spare mount, which they accomplished once they reached Gotto. Until then, he shared Alen's ocran.

"Once we attain Notsu, we'll have to take stock of the situation to the west. If the road appears clear, I shall start for the Ape Empire," Kato said. He had forsaken the cloak that concealed his identity since departing Gotto. Enough strangers had seen him on the road to spread word about an Earther. His safest route was south along the Lone Hills before breaking southeast toward the Talon Pass.

"I am honored that you saw us safely to Notsu. Truly honored, Kato." Cronus regarded him.

"You are a good man, Cronus Kenti. We could do no less than see you safely home. Raven brought you most of the way. The least I can do is finish what he started."

"HOLD!" The shouted command rang out up ahead with dozens of mounted soldiers in polished steel mail over white tunics emerging from a copse of trees from either side of the road.

"Wait." Cronus lifted an open palm, staying Kato's hand as the Earther went to draw his pistol. "They're Torry."

*****

King Lore released a heavy sigh, his eyes affixed to the map rolled out upon the table. The council of Notsu provided him richly furnished apartments on the manse of Tevlan Nosuc, the wealthiest merchant in the city's ruling council. The Torry king cared little for the rich trappings, attentive servants, or comfortable bed he slept upon. His thoughts were elsewhere, focused on the unknowns that lay north of Bacel and the Kregmarin plateau.

His magantors sighted columns of Benotrist infantry marching south along the Kregin Gap. The Benotrists were human and suffered the same limitations as his own army, but they were equally heavily armed, and he would fare poorly in a conflict with a full legion. His true concern was the gargoyles. They could outmaneuver his slower troops and cut his axis of supply and retreat.

"Our latest patrols place thousands of Benotrist infantry assembled here, along the Upper Vena," General Morton, commander of the 5th Torry Army, said, running his fore digit along the map.

"That puts them ten days march from Bacel," Lore surmised.

"At most, sire. Perhaps less if they are properly motivated."

"No, they will have to cross the plain of Kregmarin. It is barren and inhospitable. Even the fleetest of soldiers could not traverse that land in less than eight days. Have your men scouted the northern approaches of Bacel, as I requested?" the king asked.

"They have, sire. The most suitable placement for our purposes is here," Morton said, stopping his finger at the southern end of the Kregmarin Plain.

King Lore examined the position in detail. As king of Torry North, he was quite familiar with the terrain bordering his realm, as well as the lands of his neighbors. The position General Morton indicated was a cluster of several hills along the southern edge of the Kregmarin Plain, a position the Benotrists could only reach after a long march across the barren plain, suffering the privations that the land would extract. The Torries would hold the high ground, and the Benotrists would be taxed by their arduous trek.

"What of water?" Lore asked.

"There are three watering points here, here, and here," Morton pointed out. That news was better than expected, as Morton originally believed the entire plain was barren of such watering points. "I have ordered the digging of four more should you decide to hold the enemy there or to poison all the points should we not. The position holds a commanding view north and west for countless leagues. The lands further east are a mix of grasslands, forests, and jagged canyons with dense marshes that stretch along the southern approaches of Lake Veneba."

"Strange land with arid plains, grasslands, and marshes in such proximity." Lore shook his head.

"Yes, but to our benefit, it appears," Morton said.

"It would appear so. Is this the place you would position the army, General?" Lore knew Morton would prefer to withdraw to Corell than venture this far afield, but he needed to at least attempt to safeguard his allies. They couldn't afford Bacel and Notsu falling into Tyro's lap without even a fight.

"If I must defend the crossroads, then yes, that is the place I would do so. But I am wary of what awaits us if that is the course we choose."

"If Tyro sends one or even two legions at us, we can always bloody them and withdraw, stretching their supply trains while our cavalry slash and burn their lines of communication," Lore advised.

"What if they attack with more, sire?"

King Lore took a deep breath, his eyes playing across the end of the map, which only depicted the lands between the Kregin Gap and the crossroads. "Terin and Yeltor reported seeing between three and five gargoyle legions mustered at Fera. General Yonig leads three to four more in his Yatin Campaign. I can ill conceive Tyro risking a third front in the east to match the scale of the other two."

"Those legions at Fera could just as easily march here as well as Rego," Morton argued.

"Aye, they could, though Rego seems the likelier target." Lore sighed.

"I have studied Tyro's tactics throughout his conquests, sire. He never repeats an unsuccessful attack. If one route is blocked, he finds another."

"Not at Mordicay. He failed twice assaulting the harbor and succeeded on his third," Lore corrected him.

"No. He failed on the first attempt with a frontal assault. His second was with spies setting fires before an assault on the main gate. On the third attempt, he attacked at night and by sea, landing his men upon the wharves under the cover of darkness. That was also the only time he attacked a position more than once. Each other time, he bypassed a fixed point for more fertile targets."

"He could similarly assail Rego by different means, General. He could send a legion further west, sweeping around the Mote Mountains, enveloping Rego from the south while his main body assaults along Tuft's Gap. And I doubt they would fall for Bode's trap a second time."

"Perhaps. I wouldn't be surprised if they attempt a full crossing of the Plate Mountains, sending one or two legions at our heartland while our armies are guarding the passes east and west," Morton contemplated, that dark possibility torturing his waking thoughts.

"Our scouts would discover such a movement," Lore said, dismissing the possibility.

Since the Sadden Wars, the Torry realm had expelled the gargoyles from their original nesting grounds along the Plate and positioned the bulk of their magantors along observation points throughout the mountain range to guard against gargoyle incursions. The gargoyles would lose half their numbers in any hasty crossing and reach the other side disorganized, scattered, and easily destroyed in detail. Of course, it was the Torries' early success in driving the gargoyles out of the Plate Mountains that led them to align with Tyro and conquer the Menotrist Empire, establishing their new empire, which threatened Torry North now.

"Sire." Minister Monsh's apprentice, Aldo, entered the chamber and bowed, the hem of his long golden tunic dusting the finely woven carpets.

"Yes, Aldo," Lore said as the two men regarded the young scribe.

"Sire, Chief Minister Monsh sent me ahead to inform you that he waits on the estate grounds with Commander Connly and a dozen travelers of interest," Aldo explained.

"Did the chief minister speak to the nature of these *travelers?*" General Morton asked irritably.

"Yes, Commander of Army Morton. One is an Earther, and another claims to be Commander of Unit Cronus Kenti. Commander Connly has verified the identity of the latter claimant."

"Send them in and fetch Yeltor. He should also verify Commander Kenti," King Lore ordered.

*****

Cronus paused before the archway, taking a deep breath as he followed the chief minister within. Kato, Leanna, Galen Vade, and Alen followed in kind, flanked by a dozen members of the King's Elite dressed in their distinct silver breastplates, greaves, and helms over sea-blue tunics. Cronus and the others surrendered their swords, though strangely, they allowed Kato to retain his pistol.

The spacious chamber was alit with basin torches throughout. Finely woven tapestries hung from the stone walls with ornate furnishings throughout. They were met by two men standing in the center of the room, one attired in silver breast armor and greaves over white tunic with four corded braids wound around his shoulders, signifying his rank as commander of army. The second man wore the same armor over a blue tunic. Cronus recognized the face, though he had never spoken with him before.

"Sire." Cronus knelt, recognizing his king, and the others followed his obeisance. Even Kato took a knee, demonstrating his deep respect for royal protocol.

"Arise!" Lore greeted, eager to hear their tale.

"Sire, I am—"

"Cronus Kenti?" Lore asked, confirming what he already knew.

"Yes, my king." Cronus released a relived sigh.

"I feared to never treat with you, Commander Kenti. I am thankful to be wrong. Your bravery and fell deeds at Tuft's Mountain have not escaped the knowledge of the realm."

"My thanks for your words, King Lore, but my men deserve the greater praise. I alone stand before you, as they have perished to a man, save for the wretched few who suffer a bondage worse than a thousand deaths."

"A good commander laments the loss of his men. A good commander values the lives of his men. A great commander performs his duty despite his strong feelings for his comrades. You did your duty, Commander, and stand before me while they do not by mere happenstance, not upon any failing of your own. As for your men, I shall do right by their kin and their memory."

"You have my deepest gratitude, sire."

"Nay. Your bravery and sacrifice are the virtues for which I am grateful, Cronus, though those virtues are not those that instill such loyalty in your friends. I ask myself, why would a young Torry scribe and two Earthers risk their lives venturing to the Black Castle, the very heart of Tyro's power, for *you*? Why? Why would they place your life above their own?" Lore asked, shifting his gaze to Kato, examining him with an inquisitive eye. The Earther didn't match Terin's description of Lorken or Raven, but perhaps the lad was mistaken.

"They went because I asked them, sire," Leanna spoke, slipping her hand into Cronus's.

"You asked, and they acquiesced?" Lore lifted a bemused brow. "Beautiful women have moved men to act through the ages, but not in this, my lady Leanna." Leanna blushed. The king knew her name and so much more, as if privy to their thoughts.

"Raven and Lorken went because we don't abandon our friends to such a fate, King Lore," Kato firmly declared.

"You are not Raven or Lorken?" Lore asked. "Yet it is they that went to Fera. How come you're in Cronus's company while they are not?"

"We left them at Tro. I came along to safeguard Cronus and Leanna to Notsu," Kato explained.

"And your name?" General Morton asked suspiciously.

"Kato. As you can see, I am an Earther as well."

Something the king said finally struck Cronus. "Sire, how did you know that it was Terin, Raven, and Lorken that traveled to Fera?"

A smile eased across the king's lips, as if he was waiting for Cronus to finally ask. "A certain fair-haired young scribe returned from Fera, telling wondrous tales of your escape."

"Terin!" Leanna gasped.

"He...he lives?" Cronus asked. He had steeled his heart throughout their trek, fearing the worst, but the king's merriment melted his pessimism.

"We have much to discuss. General Morton, please see to your army as we discussed while I converse with our guests."

"Yes, Majesty." General Morton bowed and withdrew.

*****

The king entertained his visitors through much of the evening, telling of Terin's adventures since their parting at Fera and his appointment to the King's High Elite. Cronus was thankful Terin survived and was surprised by his placement in the king's service. Arsenc remarked that Terin was miscast as a scribe anyway, and the king could not refute that assessment. Kato spoke on the Earthers' actions as they shadowed Cronus and Raven's trek across the continent, though he spoke not of how they were able to track them. The less the royal houses of Arax knew of their extensive powers, the better.

"Where does the road lead you from here?" the king asked.

"South and east, King Lore, to the Ape Empire, where my friends shall be waiting," Kato explained.

"And your escort?" Lore shifted his eyes to Vade Cavelle, who spoke not a word throughout the night and sat quietly beside Arsenc.

"We must return to Tro, King Lore," Vade answered.

"You may leave and attend your men, Vade Cavelle. My steward has seen to their lodging. Please stay the night in this fair city before returning to Tro. You have earned my gratitude for safeguarding my people and delivering them into my keeping."

"It was my honor, King Lore." Vade bowed and stepped without.

"As for our Earth friend, please accept a flax of Torry cavalry to guide you to the Talon Pass," Lore offered.

"I could manage well enough alone, but I will not turn away your gracious offer," Kato said.

"Very well, Kato. Chief Minister Monsh shall ask Commander Connly to select a suitable escort from his command."

"I shall see to it, sire." Eli Monsh regarded him with a tilt of his head.

Cronus continued with his tale, telling the king of all that transpired from his first encounter with Terin on the road to Central City to his trek across the northern expanse of the Benotrist Empire. He omitted much of his men's suffering and fate, wishing to spare Leanna such macabre details. The king sagely listened, piecing together his telling with Terin's version of events. King Lore asked Cronus to pause as he reached the point where Alen fought in the Pit and joined them in their flight from Fera.

"To what purpose shall you direct your freedom, Alen?" the king asked. Alen had not spoken a word throughout the evening, simply sitting beside Cronus within the circle of chairs that the king had arranged as they spoke. His face flushed crimson as the king addressed him, his eyes trained to the floor. One simply did not speak so informally with royalty in the Benotrist Empire, to which he was accustomed. He dared a glance, lifting his eyes to the king's. King Lore's steel-gray eyes were a strange mixture of terrifying power and genuine kindness.

"I wish to help those who fight against Tyro in any way that I can, King Lore. My sword arm is weak, but I shall serve wherever you have need of me."

"Your sword arm we shall strengthen, but your knowledge of Fera and its layout may prove invaluable if we ever take the offensive. For now, I shall send you to Corell to my daughter, the princess Corry. I shall attest to your placement with Commander Nevias as a messenger. It is a simple yet important duty, in which you should excel until we find better use for your skills," Lore offered. A garrison messenger at Corell would traverse the palace, ferrying messages from one point to another. During a siege, the task was even more arduous, as commands were often relayed by word of mouth as much as horns or signals.

"Thank you, King Lore." Alen bowed.

The king allowed Cronus to finish his tale, which concluded with their arrival at Notsu. He was most concerned with the Benotrist troop movements along the north-south road that rested between Lake Veneba and the eastern foothills of the Plate. Cronus reported seeing large columns of Benotrist infantry moving south along that route.

"Did you recognize any markings?" Lore asked.

"A gray hammer on a field of red of the 8th Benotrist Legion, sire," Cronus answered.

"They were garrisoned at Nisin by our recent reports, sire," the chief minister interjected.

"It seems Tyro is deploying his forces forward, which is not unexpected," Lore said.

"Does the army plan to march north to engage them, sire, or hold position here?" Arsenc asked, forgetting himself and the boldness of his question.

"The movements and actions of our armies do not fall under your purview at this time, Commander Ottin," the chief minister admonished.

"My apologies, sire, but I…" The words tangled in his throat.

"Go on, Arsenc," King Lore commanded.

"I was not in the field at Tuft's Mountain, sire. I was waylaid, as my unit was slain. Of our number, only Cronus and I survived. If there is to be a battle here, I wish to fight beside my countrymen even if I must serve as a foot soldier."

"Is not your place with Commander Kenti?" Lore asked.

"Our unit is destroyed, sire. If Cronus is given another, it would be some time before it is ready for battle. Please, sire, let me redeem my honor and take my rightful place in the line of battle," Arsenc pleaded.

"If you are so moved, then I shall welcome you by my side. You will stand with my royal guard, along with another fellow whom Cronus and Alen encountered, if ever so briefly," Lore said as Aldo stood at the door with Yeltor beside him. The king beckoned him hither, Cronus's curious eyes giving way to recognition.

"I know you," Cronus said, trying to place the face until he recalled where he saw him before. "Fera. You were on th—Yeltor?" he asked, recalling the name.

"Cronus." Yeltor smiled, tilting his head toward Alen, recognizing them in kind.

"How? How are you here?" Cronus asked, wondering why the Yatin Elite now served the Torry throne, as evidenced by his tunic and armor.

"It is another tale, which Yeltor will share with you once you retire to your chambers. For now, let us conclude our visit. Aldo, if you would escort our guests to my steward. He shall see you to your chambers." As they gained their feet to depart, Lore asked Cronus and Leanna to stay, waiting for the others to leave until only he, Minister Monsh, Cronus, and Leanna remained.

"Sire?" Cronus asked, wondering his king's purpose.

"I am sending you on to Corell in the company of Minister Veda, Chief Minister Monsh's apprentice, Aldo, and a number of my personal retainers. I have prepared a writ naming you to my Elite, where you shall serve from this day forth. Kneel, Commander Kenti," Lore commanded, standing in the center of the chamber. Cronus was taken aback, moved by the honor the king bestowed upon him. He knelt before his king as the monarch's steel-gray eyes appraised him.

"I am placing you in my High Elite, Cronus, for your great service to the realm and the high nature of your character. When I asked why your friends would risk their lives to save you, I hoped to glean an inkling of their motive. I needn't look further than their eyes to know how they regard you. Arsenc risked treason for desertion in order to partake in your rescue. The Earthers were willing to wage war with the Sisterhood to affect your release. Terin risked his life and perhaps the fate of the realm to free you. Different men of differing stations, each risking their place in the world and their very lives to free one man, the man who kneels before me this night.

"Men would never risk so much for a man of low character, whose loyalty was cheaply won. These men see you as more than a friend or comrade in arms. They see you as their *brother*. For this reason, above all others, I name you to the King's High Elite. Rise, King's Elite Cronus Kenti!" Lore commanded, helping him to his feet.

"Sire, I am honored," he said weakly, overcome with emotion and the faith Lore placed in him.

"When I learned of your sacrifice and contribution to our victory at Tuft's Mountain, I planned to so name you to my Elite if you were ever to escape from Fera. You have earned your place, Cronus." Lore placed a hand to his shoulder.

"Though you are named to the King's High Elite, you must first suffer the tutelage of Torg Vantel. It is to him that you are to report when you reach Corell," Chief Minister Monsh added. After the privations of his ordeal, Torg Vantel's harsh training should seem a comfort by compare, but experience taught Cronus to never make such base assumptions.

Tears slipped along Leanna's cheek, her heart bursting with pride. She was further dismayed as the king stepped near, wiping her tears with his fingers. "You are rightly proud of your future husband. He, too, is proud of you, Leanna." The king gifted her a smile. "A true Torry woman fights for those she loves. You placed your life in the hands of the Earthers to seek Cronus's freedom. You chose wisely. If you are equally wise, Cronus, you shall wed her upon your return," Lore said, directing his steely gaze to Cronus.

BENJAMIN SANFORD

"That is a vow I shall keep, sire," Cronus affirmed, taking Leanna's hand.

"And a vow I shall hold him to." Leanna smiled.

*****

"Kal, king of ancient times…" Galen's voice rang out in the warm evening air as he sang the ode of the ancient monarch. They sat upon the veranda of the manse of Tevlan Nosuc, overlooking the sand-and-stone structures that lined the streets of Notsu. Galen leaned against the stone wall that ran the length of the open balcony, his slender fingers plucking the strings of the mandolin he acquired at Gotto, replacing his instrument he lost at Axenville. The others gathered about, listening as the words of the ballad kindled their imaginings of that long-ago-fallen realm.

The servants of House Nosuc attended to them as honored guests of the Torry king, offering them food and drink. Alen refused the offerings as he noted the slave collar affixed to the throat of a serving girl, caring not to partake. The girl smiled shyly and moved on.

"You should eat," Arsenc said, sitting beside the former slave upon a cushioned settee.

"I did not escape slavery to be served in kind," Alen answered bitterly.

"The girl's bondage will remain whether you partake or not," Arsenc opined.

"You would not feel so if you were ever enslaved," Alen retorted.

"I needn't suffer abuse to know that it is horrid. We can only press forward toward the greater good," Arsenc added.

"The greater good?" Alen asked, not liking his callous disregard of the girl's plight.

"Slavery exists throughout the world, Alen. Even in Torry North, we hold slaves, though the practice is restricted to criminals and debtors. It is tolerable if restricted, though we must be mindful of its festering nature. Either way, we cannot abandon our allies, who cling to it, lest we face Tyro alone. He is the greater threat. The oli-

324

garchs of Notsu hold a few thousand slaves. Tyro holds *millions* in bondage."

"I cannot abide slavery in any form." Alen shook his head.

"I understand," Arsenc relented, leaving his friend to his sorrow.

Yeltor sat between Cronus and Kato, telling the adventures he shared with Terin. It was strange that Yeltor and Terin's greatest troubles arose once they escaped Benotrist lands. The siege of Telfer seemed a horrendous affair. Yeltor spoke despairingly of his people's plight. He alluded to the cruelty the gargoyles administered, omitting the goriest details for the sake of Leanna, who sat beside Cronus. His telling of Terin's fell deeds drew Cronus's admiration as he recalled Terin's bold stand in the streets of Costelin. Now his prowess shined all the brighter, repelling gargoyles in the hundreds.

"When you see Terin, send him my regard." Yeltor sighed.

"I shall. Tell me, Yeltor, you are a Yatin Elite, yet you serve King Lore," Cronus asked curiously.

"I am banished from Yatin by imperial decree for my failure in rescuing my prince."

"Your emperor judges harshly," Leanna said, wondering what more Yeltor could have done to save his prince.

"He judges failure, and I failed. Such is my fate. I followed the Yatin minister to Corell, and your king offered me a place at his side. I have pledged my sword to him and shall follow him into battle to restore my honor."

"Your honor was never in doubt, Yeltor, only the wisdom of your emperor," Kato said. Of all the Earthers, Kato understood the Araxan code of honor the most by his own upbringing in Nagano. The others scoffed at the flowered courtesies and kneeling of vassals to their kings, whereas Kato accepted such norms as the proper acknowledgment of feudal authority.

But like his Earther brethren, he rightly questioned unjust rulers. The respect offered to kings required equal respect and fair treatment in return. When such reciprocity was broken, so were the bonds that bound the governed to their sovereign. The Yatin emperor was a fool who was unfit to rule and would likely bring ruin to his realm.

"My honor cannot be restored until I prove my vows to King Lore on the field of battle. Only then shall my words sworn to him have merit."

"The battle you seek may not happen for a time or in this place," Kato said.

"No." Yeltor shook his head. "War is coming to this land. Before our arrival, the trade routes were nearly severed, caravans beset by bandits and marauders. The Torry cavalry have secured the routes to Gotto, Corell, and points south. Their advent has unmasked the obvious loyalties of these bandits who serve Tyro. We have reduced the marauders, slaying hundreds with counter raids and ambushes, yet their leader continues to evade us."

"Their leader?" Cronus asked.

"He parades as a brigand, though we know him to be far more. His name is Sar Culosk, a Benotrist commander with a distinct scar running from his left ear to the corner of his mouth. He is a vicious, cunning warrior, who leads a sizable cavalry contingent. At first, he attacked merchant caravans, capturing them. He would lead them far off the traveled causeways, slaying man and beast alike and burning their wares and remains. The people of Notsu believed the disappearances were the result of restless spirits plaguing the countryside.

"Eventually, Sar Culosk expanded his range, no longer bothering to conceal the evidence of his crimes. The merchants hired more free swords to guard their wealth to some effect. Once King Lore arrived, leading his great host, he ordered much of his cavalry to hunt down these marauders, uncovering their true loyalties. Commander Connly's cavalry has destroyed hundreds of the brigands, but Sar Culosk yet evades them," Yeltor explained.

"Hired brigands do not prelude a military incursion," Kato countered.

"No, Kato. It is Tyro's way," Cronus said, recalling the gargoyle raiders that plagued the Wid River Valley prior to the battle of Tuft's Mountain. "The Benotrists have expanded their empire across Northern Arax by destabilizing lands prior to their invasion, oftentimes convincing their would-be conquests to join them for protection from the very elements the Benotrist set in motion."

"True." Yeltor sighed. "The ruling councils of Bacel and Notsu received overtures from Tyro, offering his protection if they allied with him."

"Was it so when Tyro invaded your homeland?" Leanna asked.

"No. His attack upon our frontier took us by surprise," Yeltor said.

"The lay of the land dictates the deviation from Tyro's preferred approach, most likely," Cronus added. The narrow border shared between Yatin and the Benotrist Empire likely forced a surprise attack. Any overtures of union would have alerted the Yatins to strengthen their border and marshal their forces.

"Perhaps, but we can be certain that Tyro's eye is fixed to Bacel and Notsu. It is here that the hammer shall fall. Though we have curtailed the Benotrist raiders, Sar Culosk is still at large, and you should be mindful of him as you journey home," Yeltor warned.

Cronus scrubbed his chin with his hand, his thoughts on Yeltor's warning. He intended to travel swiftly, using speed to limit their exposure, but now it seemed they would be traveling with a large contingent of the king's retainers. It was a trade-off; a larger group was slower but offered safety in numbers.

"The road to Corell is open and far calmer than the paths we have traveled," Leanna said, touching a hand to Cronus's arm.

*****

The following day saw them depart. Kato left just after sunrise, bidding his farewell before joining a column of Torry cavalry out the south gate of the city. His personal escort would break off further south, guiding him to the Talon Pass.

The others waited until midday for the king's retinue to gather themselves for the journey back to Corell. Besides Minister Veda and the scribe Aldo, they were also joined by Minister Veda's scribe Merith and a dozen Notsuan merchants and their households, along with a score of the king's attendants. A full unit of Commander Connly's cavalry provided escort.

"Would the lady Celen care to ride in the carriage, Commander Kenti?" Minister Veda offered, standing before the open door of his coach, which waited in the middle of the central road that ran east and west through the city. A dozen carriages of varying design lined the avenue, each manned by two drivers and two to four footmen.

Cronus stood alongside the trade minister's carriage with his ocran's reins in hand and his comrades gathered about. "You are most generous, Minister Veda. My betrothed would be happy to accept your kindness," Cronus said, regarding Leanna, who stood at his side.

"You are most kind, Minister Veda, but my place is beside Cronus. I will ride." She gifted the minister a sincere smile and Cronus a scolding look.

"Of course, my lady. If you decide otherwise, then you are welcome to join us. Scribes, please step within!" the minister commanded, and Aldo and Merith lifted the hems of their tunics and climbed into the covered carriage. The minister followed as the footmen closed the door.

"You're not getting rid of me that easily," Leanna admonished.

"The carriage looks quite comfortable, Leanna. I don't want you to become saddle sore. It's still a long journey to Corell," Cronus reasoned.

"My rump can handle it. Besides, we've spent enough time apart," she said, placing her foot in her stirrup and climbing onto her mount, the movement pushing the skirt of her tunic up her thighs as she straddled the ocran. Galen and Alen did likewise as Arsenc approached to see them off.

"Take care of her." Arsenc lifted his chin toward Leanna as he embraced his friend.

"I'll keep her close." Cronus smiled, though the gesture didn't reach his eyes. He didn't like parting from his friend. "I'll see to her safety. You see to yours."

"Farewell, Cronus." Arsenc gifted a pained smile in return.

"Fare thee well also, my friend, and thank you…for everything." Cronus embraced him one last time before climbing into the saddle as their caravan started to move.

The others waved farewell, following the retinue toward the west gate. King Lore, Chief Minister Monsh, and General Morton awaited them upon the steps of the city forum, the soldiers and retainers in the column bowing their heads as they passed.

"It is time, General," Lore commanded as the column passed from sight toward the west.

"As you command, sire." Morton bowed before seeing to his men.

CHAPTER 16

The long columns of infantry stretched to the horizon, their sandaled feet kicking up clouds of dust above the arid plain. The stifling heat of late summer weighed their armor like burdensome stone. Arsenc removed his helm, letting the air cool his scalp as he rode alongside the Torry infantry. Despite their white tunics soiled in sweat and their armor dulled with use, they marched forth in good order, their focus on the task ahead.

Arsenc wiped the sweat from his brow before replacing his helm and riding ahead to rejoin the royal guard, their sea-blue tunics standing out among the line of white. Drawing up beside Yeltor, he noticed King Lore further ahead on foot, leading his mount alongside the formation, conversing with soldiers in the ranks.

"What is he doing?" Arsenc asked curiously, slowing his mount to match the easy gait of the others.

"He travels afoot at times to converse with the men. He does so several times a day since we departed Corell," Yeltor explained.

"For what purpose? What information could he glean that he doesn't already know?"

"He asks about their homes and loved ones, their plans for the future, how their training has progressed," Yeltor said.

"Truly?" Arsenc was taken aback. King Lore was known for taking a keen interest in the lives of his closest servants and retainers, but he thought it nothing more than polite banter. The king, however, seemed genuinely interested in what the soldiers had to say. Here was the king of the Torry realms, walking beside his men on a dusty road, wearing a polished helm that weighed upon him with equal discomfort as they suffered. It was not a mere idle stroll where the king dismounted for a brief time before returning to his saddle. King Lore marched half the day, moving along the line of march, conversing with countless numbers of soldiers.

"From where do you hail, soldier?" King Lore asked another troop marching beside the first he spoke with.

"The Talsorn Valley, sire," the soldier answered, his young heart pounding, not believing the king was speaking with him so informally.

"Talsorn Valley," Lore mused aloud as if recalling some detail that he could impress upon the soldier about his home region. "Do you know a fellow by the name Corlis Elantor?"

"Yes, sire," the young lad said excitedly. "He owns a vineyard along the upper valley. I spent a summer in his employ during my twelfth year. I would have worked other years, but my father required my help tending our fields. He was very kind and told wondrous tales, though we couldn't tell if they were true."

"Corlis tended to exaggerate when repeating a tale, no doubt." The king laughed.

"How do you know, sire?" the lad asked.

"Oh, he was one of many who fought by my side during the Sadden Wars. He would take delight in the silliest of things, whether it was observing the amorous affections of two heated moglos or pointing out the flatulence of our comrades after he laced their food with poka spice." Lore laughed at the memory.

"He yet favors such antics, sire," the lad said, the soldiers around them sharing a laugh.

After a time, the king moved on, striking up conversations with others further ahead before taking to the saddle, joining Arsenc as they rode alongside the column with a dozen of the King's Elite guarding their flanks.

"How fares your journey, Commander Ottin?" King Lore asked.

"I am honored to ride beside you, sire."

"So you have said, but that was not what I asked. You are riding to war with men not of your unit. Your friends are elsewhere, and you are uncertain of your place in battle."

"My friends are safe, sire, and shall remain so should we win the day. My place is where you choose it to be, sire."

"And I place you in my royal guard, where your loyalty and sword shall prove most useful."

"My loyalty, sire?" Arsenc made a face.

"Your loyalty. You forsook a likely promotion after recovering from your wound and the capture of your commander in order to aid in his rescue. What qualities does Commander Kenti possess to instill such devotion in his friends?"

"He is my friend and commander, sire. We have traveled the breadth of the realms in your service, guarding each other's back. He is as close to a brother as a man can have. And…and I couldn't bear the thought of him suffering such a fate," Arsenc reflected.

"Young Caleph shares your sentiment, Arsenc."

"Terin is much like him," Arsenc confessed.

"As are you and Yeltor and your Earth friends."

"Sire?" He wondered the king's meaning.

"Heroes," Lore stated firmly, as if recalling another time and another group of men.

"We're not heroes, sire. Our only intentions were survival and duty. We were—"

"Our actions define us as heroes or cowards, not our intentions. Such is the nature of war, Arsenc, men marching beside their comrades into walls of spears and under rains of arrows, refusing to relent so as not to shame themselves before their brothers. For every man who shirks his duty and abandons his post, a hundred stand their ground. What more can a hero be than a man who risks his life for country and friend in spite of the obvious fear that strikes at us all? You fought beside heroes, Arsenc. Your former unit died nearly to a man in defense of our people. The paths *of war and heroes* are forever intertwined."

"If war creates heroes, I would forsake the appellation for peace." Arsenc sighed heavily.

"War does not create heroes. It merely reveals them. They are not measured by the greatest of deeds but by the simple willingness to do their part. I am marching north in their company," Lore said, sweeping his open right hand over the column of soldiers.

"War reveals the worst of us as well, sire." Arsenc reflected on the cruelties he had witnessed.

"Such is its nature, exposing our weakness and fortifying our strengths until one triumphs over the other. When the battle draws nigh, I am certain which will gain dominion in you, Arsenc."

*****

Kato tucked the butt of his laser rifle into his shoulder, fixing one of the retreating riders in his sights. His breath ceased, steadying his barrel as he squeezed the trigger. *Zip!* The flash of blue laser struck the fellow in the small of the back. He shifted aim as the body tumbled from the saddle. *Zip!* The second flash took the next rider in the left shoulder, burning a hole through his socket, his shield slipping from his limp fingers. Kato fired again, striking the man's ocran in the hind quarters, the blast burning the length of the beast's body. The ocran faltered, dropping dead in the grass, throwing its rider.

The Torry cavalry rode passed Kato, chasing their quarry across the grassy vale as the Benotrist raiders broke for a copse of torbin trees covering the crest of the hillside ahead. A few remained beside the Earther along the opposing ridge, their eyes wide with wonder as he dropped their foes with his strange weapon. He hurried his shots as they drew near the trees, his errant shots striking enough to drop three more from their saddles. The Torries pursuing them made quick work of those afoot.

Laser fire followed the others into the trees, taking another as they passed under the shade of the high-needled boughs of the torbins. "Let us skirt to the left and see if they emerge from the other side," Kato said, kicking his heels, urging his ocran down the grassy slope.

And so it went for the past two days when their column encountered a Benotrist raiding party numbering eighty riders. The Benotrists' attempt to ambush the Torry cavalry met with disaster, as the savvy Torry riders were familiar with such tactics. Kato's presence simply guaranteed the result, his laser fire decimating the Benotrist ranks as they fled east, leaving half their men dead or dying behind them. Kato put off his journey, pursuing the enemy riders ever eastward, thinning their ranks. What were a few days added to Kato's journey when his gun hand greatly aided his Torry friends?

Northeast of Bacel

The scouting party raised a trail of dust along the arid plain, drawing closer as Commander Connly sat on his mount along a gentle rise south of the approaching riders. The Torry cavalry commander's discerning green eyes followed the men as they swept across the loose-packed soil of the Kregmarin Plain. He was tasked by King Lore to scout the northern, southern, and eastern approaches of the crossroads for enemy activity and to engage and eliminate enemy raiders wherever they were found. His priority target since arriving at Bacel was the Benotrist raider Sar Culosk.

The scouting party raced up the gentle rise, their black capes rippling in their wake as they drew near. Connly could see the crest of the 2nd Torry Cavalry emblazoned upon their breastplates, a silver ocran rearing into the air upon a field of green.

"Commander," the lead scout greeted, thrusting his right fist to his breast.

"Report!" Connly commanded.

"Enemy cavalry to our east, just over the next ridge. Sar Culosk appears among them."

"How many?" Connly asked.

"Fifty to sixty riders, Commander."

Connly's eyes tightened, his mind running the numbers in is head. He had sent one hundred riders south of Notsu some days ago to scout for enemy raiders threatening the southern approaches of Notsu and Bacel and to escort the Earther to the Talon Pass. He had sent another fifty riders to scout the east road toward Gotto. Fifty more guarded the supply caravans northward to reinforce the army at Kregmarin.

Another two hundred were detailed to various duties, leaving him four hundred riders along the gentle rise, awaiting his command. He planned to continue north and east, skirting the edge of the Hotchen Forest that bordered the Kregmarin Plain, but the sudden appearance of Sar Culosk seemed too good an opportunity to pass up.

"Eastward!" Connly commanded. "We shall end the Benotrist raiders by nightfall!"

"East!" The men echoed the order, charging down the gentle rise, their four hundred mounts raising billowing clouds in their wake.

*****

"Packaww!" The magantor's screech echoed through the clear sky, its rider scouting the lands below for sign of the enemy. He could discern the southern foothills of the Plate Mountains far to his northwest, their forest-clad slopes forming an emerald line along the horizon where they met the Kregmarin Plain, which stretched endlessly south and east. The Torry scout pressed northward, his comrade drawing close upon his right flank, their magantors' wingtips an arm's length apart.

The pair continued apace, their eyes scanning for countless leagues for any sign of Benotrist or gargoyle movements, but the lands below appeared as empty as the sky. They had been patrolling these lands for days, ever watchful for sign of the enemy as the army marched to the crossroads. Now that the army had left the crossroads for Kregmarin, their patrols intensified.

General Morton wanted constant surveillance to the east and west, fearing the enemy could send a gargoyle legion around his flanks. The open plain to his west was easily scouted, and his magantors had found nothing of note throughout the campaign. A few magantors could cover the open ground in large sweeps in a single patrol.

The lands east of Kregmarin were more problematic, as the Hotchen Forest pressed close upon their flank. The Torries concentrated their cavalry to the east to patrol the terrain that a magantor could ill discern from their airy heights. Most of the magantor patrols were concentrated along the northern end of Kregmarin, where Benotrist infantry were spotted moving south, bearing the sigil of the 11th Benotrist Legion, crossed silver daggers upon a field of black. Torry scouts had engaged Benotrist magantors above the enemy legion, slaying two Benotrist magantors and driving off the rest. That engagement had been days ago, and the Torry magantors roamed the skies uncontested.

The two scouts circled about, starting back to their base as a small line of winged forms dotted the northern horizon. They counted a half dozen in total, their forms coming into focus as they drew near, the dark feathers of the great avian and the golden-hued tunics of their riders indicated their Benotrist origin.

The Torry scouts sped south, outpacing the Benotrist magantors. The enemy mounts carried two riders per mount, a driver and an archer. They were not meant to scout the terrain but to contest the dominion of the sky. Their extra rider prevented them from overtaking the lighter-burdened Torry magantors.

Two days hence

King Lore stood before the open map upon the table in his pavilion. General Morton, Commander Tulisk of the Notsuan contingent, Commander Bolis of the Bacel contingent, and the Torry magantor commander Dar Valen all gathered around the table. They marched in good order for many days, nearing the southern edge of the Kregmarin Plain. They were a good day's march from reaching their intended position, a series of small hills from which to best receive the Benotrist legion, which was finally marching from the Kregin Gap to meet them.

"My scouts have spied the enemy legion some five days north of us, sire, approximately here," Commander Valen said, touching a finger to the north center of the Kregmarin Plain.

"When shall we be in position to receive them?" Lore asked.

"By midday on the morrow. The 9th and 10th Telnics have already begun construction of palisades covering the forward slopes of the centermost hills. Our forward elements that I have sent ahead days ago have dug out two more wells, giving us at present six operational watering points," General Morton explained.

King Lore couldn't help the doubt creeping on his thoughts, a constant reminder of the stakes of the coming battle should he fail. "What of the western approaches here?" Lore asked, waving an open hand over the barren plains that ran the length of their left flank.

"Our scouts have spotted no troop presence throughout the area, sire, but the Benotrists have concentrated their magantor patrols there, chasing off our scouts. I responded, sending the bulk of our war birds to drive them off. We lost three magantors yester morn to the enemy's five," Commander Valen said.

"Did your scouts find anything of note after driving them off?" Morton asked.

"Nothing." Valen shook his head, dismayed that the enemy would contest the skies over terrain their army had no intention to cross.

"Then what explains their presence if not to mask their intent?" Commander Bolos asked irritably.

"Only a gargoyle legion could attempt to cross that region with necessary haste to confound us. Before we meet the Benotrist legion marching toward us, we must make certain of our flanks. If the enemy contests the skies to our west, then we must reinforce our patrols there," King Lore affirmed, fixing his gray eyes to Commander Valen.

"I have doubled all patrols to the west with two riders per mount with orders to engage the enemy should they meet," Commander Valen assured.

"Very well. See to your men, Commanders. We move at first light," the king said.

Three days hence

Arsenc looked northward across the barren plain from the hillside of their palisade. The heat of the late-summer sun pressed heavily upon them as the men dug trench lines around the surrounding hills. Arsenc took a drink from his water pouch before grabbing hold of his spade to finish his section of the palisade. No soldier was above the menial task, as he spied commanders of unit and telnic with spades in hand, moving dirt, as well as the king's royal guard and High Elite.

The army had been in place for two days, preparing defensive positions. With the enemy still two days off, they continued to improve their defenses. General Morton ordered caravans to ferry wooden stakes from Torry North at the outset of the campaign. The men put them to good use, driving them into the forward slopes of the hillside, their sharpened points jutting outward in front of the palisades.

"Packaww! Packaww!" a magantor screamed overhead, its shadow passing over the hillside as it continued east. Arsenc felt a tinge of jealousy, as Cronus, Yeltor, and even Terin had ridden upon the wondrous birds. Every day, he dreamed to fly a magantor, soaring above the land with the wind upon his face. *Someday*, Arsenc thought as the golden-feathered avian passed from sight.

Just before nightfall, two flax of cavalry entered the perimeter, their lathered mounts evidence of the urgency of their mission. Their commander was quickly ushered to the king's pavilion.

*****

"We hold our ground, sire," General Morton declared firmly as the commanders gathered in the king's pavilion. The cavalry commander of flax stood rigidly beside the general, his grim report sending the war council in disarray. Commander Connly's cavalry had spotted the Benotrist raider Sar Culosk some days ago, chasing him eastward before slaying the rogue and most of his cavalry contingent. Their pursuit had led them far afield, leaving King Lore's right flank blind. The king's greatest fear was realized as a gargoyle legion emerged from the forest to the northeast and was within a day's march away.

"If we hold position here, the gargoyle legion could bypass us for Bacel. Four telnics of the Bacelian garrison are here with me. Our city would be near defenseless," Commander Bolis lamented.

"If you forced-marched for Bacel, you would be pressed to beat the gargoyles to your city gates. You'd more likely be caught in the open, your four thousand men surrounded by their fifty thousand," Morton countered.

"Or stay here and face one hundred thousand," Bolis argued, regarding the Benotrist legion a day's march to their north.

"We face them regardless," Morton said. "The Benotrist legion is comprised of humans, and they suffer the same limitations as we. We hold the only water source for countless leagues, and they have marched for many days across the Kregmarin to reach us. They either carry their water or have it ferried south. Even a hundred caravans couldn't adequately supply their needs.

"They can ill afford to circumvent our position and suffer five days of further privations reaching the crossroads. Half their army would drop dead in the heat. We hold the only watering points for leagues. They must attain this position. Nor could they allow us to remain here, cutting their tenuous supply trains. No, they must force battle here."

"But it is our cities that shall suffer if we fail," Commander Tulisk lamented.

"Torry North shall suffer no less should we fail. All of our lands east of Corell lie defenseless if we should fall," General Morton retorted.

"Commander Ploven." King Lore beckoned the commander of flax hither.

"Yes, sire."

"Where is Commander Connly's cavalry at present?"

"Between the gargoyle legion and your position here, sire. He is currently harassing the enemy's flanks and slaying any stragglers or small patrols they have sent forth while he awaits your orders," Commander Ploven explained.

"The gargoyle legion you encountered, what markings did their banners bear?" Morton asked.

"A gray ax with crimson stained upon its blade on a field of black," Ploven detailed.

"The 4th Gargoyle Legion," Morton said, recalling the markings. He was well-versed in the sigils of Tyro's legions. The Fourth Legion was last rumored to be in the western provinces. He recalled Terin's report of the gargoyle legions gathered at Fera, and his description of the sigils he observed matched those of the 4th, 5th, 6th, and 7th Gargoyle Legions.

If true, then what explained the 4th Legion's sudden appearance this far west? Had they forced-marched across the breadth of Northern Arax in so short a time? Were the other legions nearby as well? Or was Terin mistaken in what he saw at Fera?

"My city must be warned," Commander Tulisk insisted. Like Commander Bolis, he had come here with five telnics of Notsu's army, leaving a skeletal force to garrison the city.

"I shall send a magantor to Bacel and Notsu with the king's leave," Commander Valen offered, looking to the king for guidance.

"See it done, Commander," Lore said, his gray eyes returning to the map upon the table. He would have preferred to unleash his cavalry upon the lines of communication of the Benotrist legion, cutting their tenuous water supply and crippling their advance. The water supplies upon the Kregmarin were as much a hindrance to his cavalry as to the enemy.

"Commander Ploven, inform Commander Connly to concentrate his force to our southeast. Slow the gargoyle advance where practical, but do not risk his men or ocran needlessly," King Lore commanded.

"Yes, sire." Ploven bowed.

"Our course forward, sire?" Morton asked. It was far too late to withdraw in good order, and the crossroads were a poorer place to make a stand. If it were his decision, he would withdraw to Corell and let the enemy break themselves upon its ancient walls, but the time for such a move had passed.

"We hold our ground!" Lore declared.

Two days hence

Arsenc gazed north as the banners of the 11th Benotrist Legion graced the horizon, their crossed silver daggers on a field of black visible from the hillside. From afar, the mass of infantry carpeted the land, their golden tunics and bronze helms matching the hue of the sun above. By dusk, they set camp before the hillsides of the Torry position, just beyond archer range. Their weary troops put spades to dirt as the sun slipped neath the western sky, ensuring little rest for the haggard legion. They suffered the beating sun and lack of water throughout their trek, leaving four thousand of their comrades dead along the arid plain. Their supplies couldn't keep pace with their consumption, and their commander couldn't risk delay in driving the Torries from their path.

By the following morn, the 4th Gargoyle Legion approached from the east, their own numbers thinned from their harsh crossing by nearly three thousand, yet such losses did little to slow their pace. They merely fed upon their fallen comrades, considering them weaklings unfit for the legion.

King Lore stood upon the centermost of the hills, facing the 11th Benotrist Legion, his gray eyes surveying the length of their lines. The Benotrists hastily constructed a siege trench in front of an earthen palisade running the length of their formation. He counted between forty to fifty thousand men, which was the approximate number for one of Tyro's legions. He was uncertain of their losses throughout their forced march, but their logistics would have been put upon supporting such a force.

The two legions gave the enemy nearly one hundred thousand troops to throw at him. The twenty thousand men of the 5th Torry Army combined with the nine thousand troops provided by Bacel and Notsu still left him outnumbered three to one. General Morton stood at his side, his eyes sweeping the impressive force arrayed against them.

"Keep extra vigil tonight, General," Lore warned.

"I have already done so, sire, and shall repeat the command to emphasize its import," Morton said, assuaging the king's worry. The king was familiar with the gargoyle tactics during the Sadden Wars and their proclivity for night assaults.

"Very good. Shift all of our archers to our right."

"I have already done so, sire," Morton said, having given the order as soon as the 4th Legion set camp to their east. Arrows were most effective against the lightly clad gargoyles than the heavier-armored Benotrists, and they needed every arrow to count if they wished to bleed the enemy to their fullest.

*****

"Kai-Shorum!" The piercing screams rent the night air as gargoyles sounded their war cries. Even the bravest of souls wavered as the high shrills echoed in the dark still air.

"To arms!" The cry went out through the Notsuan ranks as men were roused from their slumber to stand to post. Gargoyles swarmed over the palisades, clearing the sharpened pikes that protruded their forward slopes. The Notsuan fore ranks met their ascent with interlocked shields and leveled spears. The rear formations were not as prepared, as their ranks were slow to form, still stirring from their sleep. Scores of gargoyles flew over the front ranks, taxing their wings to reach the Torry rear and center. They descended amid the disorder of waking troops, their curved blades striking out at any Notsuans they happened upon.

Arsenc was roused from his sleep as Yeltor shook his arm. They quickly donned their helms as the surrounding cookfires flickered with soldiers passing in front of their waning flames. They found the king nearby, fully clad and mounted as the sound of battle echoed over the eastern hills, where the men of Notsu guarded their right flank.

"To me!" King Lore shouted over the din, drawing his sword and urging his ocran into the fray. He named his mount Stormrider with its black coat and the lines of gold running the length of its sides. The faithful beast carried the king swiftly through the encampment with a dozen Torry Elite hurrying to keep pace. Arsenc and

Yeltor attained their mounts and rode off to join the king with a telnic of Torry infantry hurrying afoot.

"Hold position!" Commander Tulisk ordered as his center wavered with thousands of gargoyles swarming over their palisades, driving them back. "Reserves forward!" he said, commanding fresh troops to his center, their shields interlocked overhead to protect their heads from enemy dropping upon them in the dark.

Torry archers fired at will upon the gargoyles pressing the front, their hurried shots unable to miss in the serried ranks. The forward wall of Notsuan spears met the hurried charge, skewering hundreds of gargoyles upon the eastern hillside, and yet they pressed on, their crimson eyes ablaze with heated fury. They slaughtered countless numbers, and more filled the breach, crawling over their fallen with fangs gnashing and blades raised.

Other than a small circular shield, the gargoyles wore no armor, forsaking protection for speed and flight. Those that landed in the rear wreaked havoc upon the sleepy and surprised men until Notsuan and Torry soldiers cut them down.

The gargoyle assault fractured in the dark, denigrating in a chaotic melee as units stumbled into one another. Thousands swarmed over the palisades, crushing their comrades underneath. Countless others sprang into the air, struggling to gain lift and pass over the enemy's fore ranks.

Arsenc followed his king up the near slope of the eastern hill, guiding his mount through the melee of men and gargoyles battling in their midst. Outstretching his sword in his right hand, he lopped a gargoyle head that landed just ahead, the creature's body crumbling in his wake as he passed. The dim glare of cookfires and the waning moonlight provided the only illumination as men struggled to find their way in the chaos. He caught sight of Yeltor off his left, charging through a small cluster of gargoyles that banded together, his ocran knocking them aside with Torry infantry rushing in to finish them.

"Kai-Shorum!" Gargoyle battle cries echoed further ahead, ascending the west slope of the hill. Arsenc pushed his mount to keep pace with King Lore, who charged apace, forcing his personal guard to match his gait. Breaking the crest of the hill, they were visited by the hellish vision of men and gargoyles battling desperately in each direction, fighting with swords, fangs, and bare hands.

"Column to the left and right! Smite the enemy wherever you find them!" King Lore shouted, splitting his trailing force to either flank. The Torry infantry poured over the crest of the hill, falling upon any gargoyles that set down behind the Notsuan front.

Arsenc broke left, pushing his mount along the side of the hill, swinging his sword judiciously, taking a gargoyle's sword arm at the elbow and another in the back as he rode apace. Arrows spewed from the hillside above, passing over the Notsuan soldiers holding the front and riddling the tightly packed gargoyle ranks swarming the palisades. The sounds of battle echoed far afield, their sources obscured in the dark of night.

Arsenc followed his comrades to the northern bend of the hillside, cutting a path through the gargoyles that set down in their path. Their small cavalry charge stunned the surviving gargoyles before the Torry infantry swept over the crest of the hill, crushing what remained. Soldiers fell upon the lightly armed creatures, hacking wings, limbs, and skulls with prejudice.

Arsenc flinched, drawing to his left as a dim shadow crossed the face of the waning moon. He shifted his shield overhead, holding his sword at the ready as a gargoyle swept from above. The weight of the creature nearly took him from the saddle as its body met his shield. Arsenc thrust his blade blindly upward, feeling it sink into the creature's flesh, blood running the length of his sword, soaking his arm. He twisted the blade before jabbing repeatedly with hurried thrusts, and the creature clawed desperately at his shield and helm before slipping away.

Yeltor lopped another gargoyle head, guarding Arsenc's left as the next wave of gargoyles settled in their midst. The new arrivals fared poorly, met by the ready blades of Torry infantry rushing to greet them. The hapless creatures broke upon the disciplined cohorts of interlocked shields and ordered ranks.

The battle continued through the night until the final vestiges of the gargoyle assault withered under rains of arrows and thrusting spears, unable to break the disciplined human ranks.

*****

The rising sun broke the horizon, revealing the carnage wrought upon the eastern hill. Thousands of corpses were piled in heaps along the palisades, their stench festering with the rising sun. Thousands more littered the slopes of the hillside, their bodies twisted in unnatural angles, feathered with arrows or hacked to pieces. Wounded men lingered in agony, suffering mortal blows yet staying their inevitable fate.

Others were carried to the healing tents in the center of the encampment to be tended by the Matrons who accompanied the army. The women stood post outside their pavilion in their distinct red gowns, waiting expectantly for each patient. The initial trickle of wounded men quickly cascaded into hundreds, overwhelming the healers.

King Lore stood upon the east hill, surveying the carnage wrought by their first engagement. Further east, he observed the banners of the 4th Legion where the gargoyles were reconstituting their own battered force. The earliest reports were two thousand dead and wounded of their own number, most of them men of Notsu. Commander Tulisk stood beside him, his dented helm and blood-stained tunic symbolic of his battered army.

"We must burn the dead lest disease claim more men than enemy swords," King Lore advised.

"I have set my men to the task, but there are too many to gather," Tulisk muttered bitterly. He estimated the gargoyle casualties four times their own but took little solace in the exchange, as the likeliest path to victory was winnowing the enemy upon these hills with their blood. How many of his men must be sacrificed to achieve such an end?

HAROOM! The sound of horns echoed over the hilltops, drawing their tired eyes to the north. "To ARMS!" men shouted, relaying the alarm.

*****

King Lore reached the center hill of the Torry formation, over-looking the Kregmarin Plain, as the 11th Benotrist Legion formed in ordered ranks below. The rising sun shone off their helms and spear tips like thousands of flickering stars. They marched forth with their square bronze shields interlocked as they drew near. General Morton shifted a thousand archers from his right flank to reinforce the center. The 5th Torry Army brought a dozen trebuchets to Kregmarin, and General Morton positioned them behind his center. The contingents from Bacel and Notsu brought half a score as well, their crews standing post, guarding the Torry flanks.

"Fire!" General Morton ordered. Balls of flame hurled over the Torry front, striking the Benotrists below as the trebuchet crews released their flaming missiles, opening holes in the enemy ranks. The projectiles splashed upon contact, spreading their gelatinous flames for several paces. Men screamed, their tunics catching fire with flames coursing over their flesh. The crews intermixed small boulders, caving holes through the serried ranks, dropping a dozen men with each strike.

"KAI-SHORUM!" the Benotrists shouted, charging up the slopes, their war cries echoing over the din like distant thunder. Torry soldiers awaited them behind their palisades, their spears leveled above the wall of dirt and protruding pikes. The Benotrist fore ranks huddled behind the forward slopes of the palisades, struggling to negotiate the well-built obstacle, as Torry spears jabbed at them whenever they lowered their shields. Arrows spewed overhead, striking those further afield but with less effect than against the gargoyles.

Some Benotrists worked their way between the protruding pikes to little effect, catching spear thrusts whenever they lowered their shields to climb. The outnumbered Torries used their position to great effect, cutting down any Benotrists who attained the palisades. Hundreds of Benotrists perished at the outset, their corpses hindering those who followed.

King Lore surveyed the battle, his gray eyes sweeping the length of the Benotrist line within his view. From his position, the Benotrist assault extended the width of several of the small hills, wrapping around their west flank, where the Bacel contingent guarded their left. He wondered why the enemy threw themselves into the teeth of his defense rather than circle to his rear. Despite this folly, the Benotrist legion outnumbered his force nearly two to one.

The battle raged throughout the morn, the Benotrists gaining footholds in several places along the line, their ranks thicker than the Torry front. General Morton deployed his reserves wherever the Benotrists attained a hold, driving them back. Balls of flame hurled overhead, wreaking havoc in the serried ranks gathered below. The smell of burning flesh drifted in the air, melding with the screams of wounded and dying men.

Arsenc and Yeltor remained at the king's side amid the royal guard and King's Elite, waiting to join the battle. Though weary from battling through the night, standing idly by as their comrades fought below was torturous. The battle continued, the Benotrists throwing themselves upon the Torry palisades for little gain. Though thousands lay dead upon the hillsides, the battle appeared controlled and orderly from afar, contrasting the chaos of the previous night.

By midday, the Benotrists signaled retreat, their soldiers leaving four thousand casualties behind. The Torries suffered a tenth of that number. Hundreds more of the enemy succumbed to the heat, unable to replenish their water during the battle. The Torry soldiers emerged from their positions, slaying the enemy wounded left behind, abandoning all pretense of civility, granting the Benotrists the same mercy they offered others.

The following night

The gargoyles renewed their assault, striking in force on the Torry rear, driving deep into the Torry center before being turned back. By daybreak, the Torries remained firmly entrenched upon the hillsides, though weary from nearly two days of continuous battle. The Benotrists remained in place to their direct front with no apparent intention to repeat their ruinous assault from the day before. By late day, two magantors returned from their deep patrol minus their four comrades. King Lore called a war council after the scouts relayed their grim report. Commanders Bolis, Tulisk, and Valen and General Morton gathered about the map table in his pavilion as the magantor scouts shared their discoveries.

"Our patrol set out at first light to our northwest before sweeping east along the upper Kregmarin. We came upon large columns of Benotrist infantry marching south here and here." The scout pointed out upon the map.

"Infantry? How many? Did you see any sigils to identify them?" General Morton hurriedly asked.

The scouts shook their heads. "We were set upon by a dozen enemy magantors as soon as we discovered them. Our commander was slain, along with three others, while we battled in the sky. We slew several of their number in the exchange. We broke off as quickly as we could to relay our findings. We couldn't get close enough to identify their markings but counted numerous telnics moving south, at least ten to fifteen as we could see," the first scout said.

Morton's face paled, his greatest fear coming to fruition. Ten to fifteen telnics wouldn't be marching south across the Kregmarin alone. There was power behind them, at least a full legion, perhaps more. Their location meant they would be upon them in two days at most.

"We must withdraw!" Commander Tulisk insisted, knowing any delay meant being surrounded.

"As I have explained at length, Commander, the time to withdraw has passed. We must hold at all cost. We hold the high ground and the only water source for countless leagues. The Benotrists cannot bypass us and leave us in their rear unguarded. Any force left to deal with us would suffer from lack of water or require massive logistical support just to stay alive in this blistering heat. We have lost two hundred men in recent days to heat alone, and our men have been given water and rest. What condition is the enemy in?" Morton countered.

"If we stay here, upon these rocks, we shall perish to a man!" Tulisk declared.

"And where shall we go? Your cities cannot withstand the forces marching against them. Our numbers will count for naught on even ground. I have long counseled withdrawing all of our forces to Corell, where we could defend the white walls against ten legions with the men we have here. Even if we left now, we wouldn't reach the approaches of Bacel before the gargoyles would be upon us," Morton said.

"We fight them here or at our doorstep. At least here, we can make the bastards pay dearly for our blood!" Commander Bolis resigned himself to his fate, knowing retreat was no longer an option.

"Commander?" King Lore regarded Tulisk.

"So be it. We stand our ground," the Notsuan commander relented.

One day hence

The 11th Benotrist Legion renewed their assault, shifting further west, testing the Bacelian troops guarding the Torry flank. The battle waged throughout the morn with results similar to their first engagement. General Morton shifted several telnics to counter any breaks in the line. The Benotrists should have fared better, but they suffered in the intense heat, driven by a desperation that Morton did not understand. The Benotrists withdrew by midday, leaving three thousand casualties behind. The Bacelians suffered almost a third of that while the Benotrists lost another thousand to dehydration.

Before sundown, a column of dust lifted along the western horizon, raising the Torries' alarm until the banners of the 2nd Torry

Cavalry appeared at the head of a vast host. Commander Connly had arrived, leading nearly three hundred of his mounts.

*****

King Lore called his war council, once again relaying grim tidings. Commander Connly stood at his side, his hard green eyes masking his exhausted state. His men rode for days, slaying Sar Culosk and his cavalry contingent far to the east. Their return journey was no less perilous with gargoyles blocking their direct path.

"Sire?" Connly asked, begging leave to begin.

"Go on, Commander." Lore sighed.

"At the outset of the army's deployment at Kregmarin, we came upon the last remnants of the Benotrist raiders that have plagued the trade routes of Bacel and Notsu. We spotted their leader, Sar Culosk, among them and gave chase. He led us many leagues to our direct east before we overtook him, slaying his host to a man. Unfortunately, our pursuit left us blind to the 4th Gargoyle Legion that emerged from the Hotchen Forest to the northeast. By the time that we were aware of our folly, I dispatched a small contingent to race ahead to warn you of the threat. When they never returned, I could only surmise their fate.

"Before we began to circumvent the 4th Legion, we discovered a sizable gargoyle caravan heading due west for the Kregmarin. We assaulted the caravan, seizing its supplies bound for the Benotrist legion to our north. Among the spoils were countless wagons bearing vats of water. Tyro had prepositioned these supplies long ago in the forest of Hotchen to ease his troops crossing this hostile land. I lacked the men to commandeer their wagons and ordered them destroyed after watering our mounts and filling our satchels."

"That explains the Benotrists' desperation for assaulting our positions," Morton said.

"They need our water," Connly answered.

"It is hard to believe Tyro would risk his campaign on such a tenuous source of water," Commander Bolis said.

"He didn't," Connly added. "The Benotrists were to be supported by vans of supplies following each legion, but the 11th Legion's supply trains have been delayed. The Kregmarin is quite unforgiving to heavily laden wagons. The Benotrist supply trains are at least several days off, even trailing the 8th Benotrist Legion that has marched past them."

"The Eighth Legion?" Morton asked.

"Yes, a gray hammer on a field of red. Our patrols spotted their banners at the head of their vast host," Connly affirmed.

"You have spoken what we already know, save for the enemy's tenuous water supply, which is to our benefit. Yet your countenance seems much pained. What ails you, Commander Connly?" General Morton asked.

"The 8th and 11th Benotrist and the 4th Gargoyle Legions are not alone. We have found at least two other gargoyle legions following some distance behind the Fourth. One bears a fractured white skull on a field of gray, and the other a black whip and gray chain upon a field of green."

They were the sigils of the 6th and 7th Gargoyle Legions, confirming Morton's suspicion that they were the very same legions Terin witnessed at Fera. That left them facing five legions with no hope to withdraw. The outcome was no longer in doubt, a fact that did not escape the commanders gathered in the king's pavilion. King Lore noticed Morton's solemn demeanor. His general had long counseled against this campaign from the outset but faithfully followed Lore's command despite such misgivings.

"General?" Lore asked, wishing to know his thoughts.

"The chance of our death in this campaign was always a possibility. Now it is a certainty. I am resigned to this fate and shall bleed the enemy to my utmost. The men, however, may react differently. Soldiers always face the possibility of death in battle. Few, however, face its certainty before the first arrow is loosed."

"You fear they shall forsake their duty?" Lore asked.

"Perhaps. Perhaps not. I have trained these soldiers, and they have fought bravely. But they are still men, and all men have a breaking point." Lore considered Morton's misgivings. The lives of these men were now likely forfeit because of his decision, his mistake. He was the king, and his men followed him loyally, trusting him with their lives, and he failed them.

"All is not lost, sire," Connly said, lifting his chin defiantly.

"Commander?" Lore asked curiously for his explanation.

"The enemy far outnumbers us, this is true, but their numbers are a weakness. Their supply trains are tenuous at best. Grant me leave to harry their caravans and cut their water supply, and their numbers will wilt in this blistering sun. Let them test our strength with parched throats. They'll die halfway up the hillsides."

"Your plan has merit as far as the Benotrists are concerned, but the gargoyles are far more resilient," Morton said.

"Even gargoyles need water, General," Connly added.

"You have my leave to try, Commander. How soon can you depart?" Lore asked.

"Come first light, sire. My men and ocran need a night's rest. I have sent a flax south to gather the units I dispatched."

"Very well," Lore affirmed before shifting his eyes to Commander Valen. "How many magantors have you, Commander?"

"Thirteen, sire."

"Dispatch messengers to Bacel, Notsu, and Corell. Let them begin preparations in the event we fail. I also want poisoners positioned at each well. If we are overwhelmed, we'll leave them no source of water."

Two days hence

The Torries and their allies awoke to the sight of the 6th Gargoyle Legion encamped south and east, its banners lifting in the warm breeze, a fractured white skull upon a field of gray. The 4th Gargoyle Legion had spent the past days reconstituting their telnics after suffering heavy losses in the previous engagements.

By last evening, the banners of the 7th Gargoyle Legion paraded along the southern horizon, a black whip and gray chain upon a field of green. They marched in good order, skirting the 6th Legion before taking up position to the southwest.

By the following morn, the Torries discovered another gargoyle legion encamped to their west, their banners displaying a black-mailed fist upon a field of white, the sigil of the 5th Gargoyle Legion. By day's end, the lead cohorts of the 8th Benotrist Legion broke the northern horizon.

Arsenc gazed with fell acceptance at the vast host carpeting the Kregmarin Plain. Had the enemy wood for cookfires, they would've spread to the horizon in each direction like the stars in the heavens. What hope had they against such an army? None, it appeared. Commander Connly had miscounted the enemy by a legion, for six now surrounded them, ringing the small hills, preventing any escape.

"They'll attack on the morn," Yeltor said, standing at his side, his dark eyes staring at the enemy with the same resignation.

"Aye," Arsenc agreed. The enemy couldn't wait any longer upon the arid plain. Any delay would cost them more casualties from the heat than a frontal attack would incur.

*****

The morning sun broke upon the Kregmarin, drawing away the dark like a giant curtain, revealing the enemy host arrayed for battle. The sun shone upon the Benotrists' helms and armor with dazzling brilliance, forcing the Torries to narrow their eyes from its blinding glare. From afar, the Torries could not see the weary faces of their foes. Their lead elements had arrived before sunset and spent much of the night waiting for their following telnics to reach the battle and align in formation. Nor could the Torries see the thousands of dead soldiers littering the Kregmarin Plain, having succumbed to heat and exhaustion throughout their trek.

The 11th Benotrist Legion aligned to the right of the 8th Benotrist Legion, facing the northwest perimeter of the Torry defenses that ringed the cluster of hills. The 8th Legion faced the northeast portion of the Torry perimeter, joining their left flank with the 4th Gargoyle Legion, which guarded the east. The legions stood statue still, facing the defenders with grim discipline. Their eyes were fixed on the Torries, Bacelians, and Notsuans upon the hilltops.

They waited expectantly for what seemed an eternity until a blast of horns echoed over the battlefield. The Benotrists and gargoyles drew their swords, banging the flat of their blades on their shields, the deafening sound echoing like thunderclaps, heralding their commander's advent.

He rode between the Benotrist legions upon a crimson ocran, whose coat was akin to bloodstained cloth, its silver horns jutting fiercely from its wide-set skull. He wore a golden cuirass over a black tunic with golden greaves and gauntlets and a bright-red cape lifting in the morning breeze. He stared intently through the empty eye sockets of an ape skull affixed to his helm, like glowing embers in a lifeless void.

Two dozen of the emperor's Elite preceded him in columns of two, guarding their captain as he galloped forth, accompanied by a standard bearer hoisting the blue flag of truce. He stopped short at the base of the center hill, his unnerving gaze sweeping the length of the Torry ranks lining the slopes above, the dark countenance of his grotesque mask unsettling the hearts of the weary defenders.

His sweeping gaze stopped atop the hill above where the banners of House Lore stood proudly in the morning air, a golden crown upon a field of white. There, upon the hillside, he found King Lore astride his ocran, dressed in bright silver helm and armor over a sea-blue tunic. He outstretched his right arm, boldly pointing his forefinger to the Torry king.

"I call upon you, King Lore! Come forth! Meet me here betwixt our armies, your sword to mine. Let our soldiers bear witness to your bravery should you accept or your cowardice if you decline!" his voice thundered, challenging the Torry king.

Lore eased Stormrider forward, the faithful ocran responsive to the king's slightest command. "Who is he that speaks so bold?" Lore asked, his strong voice matching the timber of his challenger.

The man lifted his helm, revealing a handsome young face with a wide grin that failed to reach his dark, cold eyes. "I am Morac, son of Morca, first of the Imperial Elite, keeper of the Golden Sword, anointed to lead these gathered legions in the conquest of your king-dom! Come forth! Meet me here, your skill and blade against my own!"

Yeltor broke from the ranks, easing his mount up beside the king. "Sire, you must not go. No common blade can match his sword."

Lore released a measured breath, his heart pounding with the folly of his decision to bring his army to this fell place. His soldiers' lives were forfeit by his action. Now he could only ask that they sell their lives dearly, bleeding the enemy to their utmost. Would they do so if their king refused Morac's challenge? Courage and cow-ardice were contagious emotions, feeding upon themselves within any group. He lifted his gray eyes to the heavens, regarding the clear morning sky in all its beauty. It was such a contrast to the grim vis-age below. Lore returned his eyes to his challenger as he removed his helm, freeing his black mane that was partly silver with age.

"I hold no magic sword to match your blade, son of Morca. The flower of my youth has long dimmed, and my sword arm has grown stiff with ill use, yet I accept your challenge, invader from the north!" he answered in kind, easing his mount down the slope of the hill to level ground.

Morac waited some paces north, greeting the venerable mon-arch with mocking disdain. "I expected a grander visage of the royal Torry line. The legends of your great renown fail to match what I see before me, King Lore. King of Torry, or king of *thralls?*" Morac sneered.

"King of men, true men who honor their people and *realm*, men who protect the weak and defy the wicked. They are far more than the likes of you, Morac, slaver, killer, betrayer of mankind. Your people have forsaken the brotherhood of men for gargoyles. You are accursed. And if this day brings you victory, you shall be nothing more than a king of *bones*."

"We shall see!" Morac smiled falsely, donning his helm.

Lore donned his helm, briefly facing his men lining the hillside above. "Let us sell our lives dearly this day, my brave fellows. If we shall fall this day, our loved ones will face this host that stands before us. Let us purchase them a fighting chance by slaying as many as our swords and spears can claim. Victory or death!" Lore declared before their brave assemblage, rearing his ocran into the air. Stormrider was aptly named with streaks of gold running the length of his black coat, like lightning in a tumult sky. The beast snorted defiantly, its fore legs clopping the soil as the Torry ranks echoed their sovereign's defiant chant.

"VICTORY OR DEATH!" they shouted, their chants repeated by those further afield. Those beyond earshot of Lore's command knew little of what had transpired but followed the spirit of their fellows.

Stormrider thundered forth, kicking dust as he closed upon Morac's blood-hued mount. Lore hoisted his sword, sunlight playing off its steel, as Morac rushed to meet his charge. Morac's golden sword alit with a fiery glow as the sun shone upon its face, his red cape trailing him like a flame. Stormrider lowered his head, leveling his silver horns to his foe, and Morac's crimson mount did likewise. Nary an utterance escaped the lips of the armies, their deafening silence magnifying every sound of the combatants.

Morac's fiery gaze met Lore's steel-gray eyes as they drew near, reading the king's intent in his unyielding countenance. The king meant to slam his beast into his own, likely killing them both, choosing suicide over certain defeat. Morac shifted left, denying the Torry king his sacrifice but exposing his own mount's flank, Stormrider's right horn grazing his ocran's hindquarter.

Morac forsook his reins, shifting his shield in his left across his body while reaching out with his sword arm, striking at Stormrider's head as the beast's horn grazed his mount. The errant swing struck Stormrider's right horn before passing through its muzzle.

Morac's ocran bounded away, its hind legs kicking from the sting of Stormrider's horn. Stormrider bucked violently, the sight of his severed muzzle and horn falling away causing the beast to panic. The pain drove the beast to utter madness as he thrashed about, throwing his master from his saddle before scattering off.

Lore tumbled in the dirt, losing his helm and shield somewhere in the chaos. A thousand Torry hearts nearly stopped as their king struck the ground. The stunned monarch slowly gained his senses, staggering to his feet as Morac circled about, kicking his heels, urging his mount forward. Morac smiled as his ocran lowered its head, leveling its horns as it drew close. Visions of his ocran skewering the Torry king played genially before him, clouding his periphery as ten thousand voices shouted in warning.

Lore stood his ground, brandishing his sword with both hands to receive the beast's charge, his dark mane lifting in the wind. The Torry king forsook all hope, knowing these breaths would be his last, but his men needed to see his courage and match his ferocity for the battle to come. At fifteen paces, he could see the light reflecting off Morac's cruel eyes as the Benotrist warrior drove his beast feverishly on. At ten paces, a dark blur struck from Morac's right, lifting him from the saddle, his ocran buckling.

The Torries upon the hillside cheered as Stormrider drove his remaining horn into the ribs of Morac's beast, blood issuing from the mortal wound in a brighter hue than the beast's crimson coat. Stormrider withdrew his horn, leaving the beast stumbling as it staggered off before dropping dead in the dirt.

Morac gained his feet as Lore strode forth across the dusty ground, his sandaled boots pounding the soil as he swiftly closed on his stunned foe. Morac retained his shield and sword, bringing the circular steel up in time to receive Lore's blade, the emphatic blow nearly driving him to his knees. Morac blindly swung his blade where the king should have been as his shield shook in his hand.

Lore dodged the errant blow, bringing his sword up aside Morac's head, the strike denting his helm above his right ear. Morac screamed aloud, pain jarring his brain. He thrust his blade forward, driving Lore back before gaining his senses. With blood oozing from his ear, dripping down his arm, he swung again, his blade alit with unworldly light.

Lore instinctively brought his sword to match the blow, betrayed by his trained reactions. He knew well the power of Morac's blade but was too late to correct his mistake. *Crack!* Lore's sword broke asunder as the golden blade met its strong steel. The Torries upon the hillside stood silent as their king stood helpless.

Lore did not frown or flee but stared defiantly into Morac's cruel eyes as the Benotrist Elite swung again, his blade taking Lore at the neck. The king's head rolled to the ground, his gray eyes alive for a brief moment, watching his own body fall lifelessly to the ground before his eyes grew dim, his soul fading away.

The battlefield grew deafly still as both armies watched Morac grasp King Lore's severed head and hold it aloft, declaring his victory. Morac threw his bloody trophy to the dirt and raised his arms in triumph. "Are there any more among you brave enough to challenge me?" he shouted, mocking the Torry soldiers with utter contempt. He noticed a chorus of hopeful gasps coursing the Torry ranks above, contrasting the shouts of warning from his own men behind him.

The Sword of the Sun burned his hand, urging him to act. He fought the blade's power, subjugating its will to his own. He was the blade's master, not its slave, but the sword persisted, forcing him to turn about. Morac's eyes drew wide as Stormrider charged him with his left horn leveled upon him, blood and gore caked along its silver length. His eyes were ablaze in unnatural rage, blood issuing from its severed muzzle. The beast drew near to avenge its master and slay the man who maimed him.

Morac yielded to the will of the blade, delivering a measured strike as he jumped clear. The blow sliced through the ocran's neck, killing the beast, its head dangling from its body by the thinnest strands of flesh. Stormrider's body continued beyond Morac for several paces before dropping dead.

Morac recovered his senses and stormed toward the fallen beast before hacking Stormrider's head with his sword in heated fury, the ocran's blood spraying his tunic, arms, and helm, speckling the white bones of the ape skull that covered his face.

"Argh!" Morac shouted, his countenance contorted in maddened rage, venting his anger until it was spent, leaving the ocran's carcass in a disordered state. The ocran's blood seemed to dim the blade's aura, its fiery glow abating with its master's rage. Morac caught his breath, his chest heaving as he stood, drenched in blood with his sword in hand.

His gaze swept the hillsides above, surveying the Torries entrenched behind their palisades, their spear tips and shields resplendent in the morning light. "KAI-SHORUM!" he shouted, lifting his sword toward the enemy above, its fiery glow returning as the sun played along its ancient metal, burning away the blood caked upon its blade.

"KAI-SHORUM!" The Benotrists and gargoyles echoed his battle cry, their voices echoing over the battlefield like the hissing of a violent wind.

Morac's battle cry was greeted by a hail of arrows, the shafts raining down upon him but missing their mark as he ran to join his approaching legions. The Benotrists surged forth like the rising tide, sweeping toward the northern slopes of the hillsides like waves breaking upon the shore.

"KAI-SHORUM!" the gargoyles chanted, pressing their attack from the east, south, and west. While the Benotrists held to disciplined formations with interlocking shields, the gargoyles swarmed the hillsides in battle frenzy.

"Shift all archers to our flanks and rear. Leave *none* to our front!" General Morton commanded.

"Aye, General," Commander Venitie replied, issuing the order. The archers were most effective against the poorly armored gargoyles than the Benotrists, and every arrow needed to count.

The gargoyles attained the hillsides before their slower Benotrist comrades, swarming over the palisades like insects upon a hive. To the east, the 4th Gargoyle Legion and the better part of the 6th Legion carpeted the plain like a dark wave cresting the hillside. Venitie's bowmen greeted them in kind, dropping hundreds with each volley. The archers needn't even aim, unable to miss, their shafts disappearing in the endless mass. Commander Tulisk committed what few reserves he had, joining his Notsuan soldiers in the foremost ranks.

Gargoyles crawled over the palisades, exposing their legs and bellis to spear trusts. Others managed to fly over the defenses, setting down in the enemy rear, exhausted and spent. Torry reserves rushed down the hillsides to slay them as they landed. The Notsuan soldiers slaughtered hundreds of gargoyles along the eastern palisades, their corpses piling along the front, allowing those who followed to use the carcasses to more easily attain the defenses.

Soldiers jabbed at the gargoyles between their pikes and shields, taking whatever flesh was offered before black-clawed hands grabbed hold of them, dragging them clear of their comrades, where they were set upon by the gargoyle swarm, each stabbing and biting their helpless prey. Arrows spewed overhead, dropping gargoyles in the thousands, but did naught to stem the tide. Tens of thousands rushed the hillsides, swarming over the defenses.

Commander Tulisk blocked a sword arcing overhead, driving his sword into the gargoyle's belly before twisting it free. The creature wailed, thrashing about as it landed upon his shield. He twisted his shield, shifting the creature's weight as it slid to the ground, its snapping teeth dropping near his sandaled boot. The soldier nearest him drove his sword into the creature's neck, finishing it. He lifted his shield as another swept down from above, swinging its curved blade, the blow glancing off his shield. Another soldier drove a spear into the gargoyle's belly, jerking it free to stab him again.

Commander Tulisk stepped clear as the foul wretch tumbled to the ground, its curdling scream paining his ears. Tulsik finished the creature, stealing a glance to survey his surroundings. He couldn't see far afield, as gargoyles swarmed his entire line, blocking his line of sight and even the sun. Only the shouts of men in the distance hinted that they still resisted.

A soldier some paces away tumbled to his knees, a spear protruding from his neck. He fell face to the dirt, revealing the offending gargoyle behind him. The creature grinned demonically, its glowing crimson eyes fixed upon Tulisk. Tulisk's blood ran cold as the creature sprang forth, its wings spread and fangs glistening. Tulisk lifted his shield to receive the blow before a terrible weight struck his back, driving him into the ground.

He couldn't see with his head pressed into the dirt as he struggled to gain his feet. A sudden pain struck his right leg as a blade hacked at the back of his knee. He felt fangs tear into his shoulders and ribs as several creatures swarmed over him, eating him alive.

*****

The 7th Gargoyle Legion and the better part of the 6th assailed the southern slopes, their numbers alone nearly double the total of the Torries and their allies combined. General Morton positioned 1,800 of his 3,000 bowmen along his southern flank, where they awaited the coming storm upon the rocky slopes. Morton deployed only six telnics of infantry along the south-facing palisades, precious few against the eighty telnics the gargoyles threw against them.

"FIRE AT WILL!" The command echoed along the line as the dark mass drew near. Archers took hurried aim, notching arrows as soon as the last one was loosed. Balls of flame arced overhead, finding targets with ease in the enemy's serried ranks. Thousands of gargoyles fell to the withering fire before the first ranks came to blows. The first to attain the palisades fared just as poorly, torn apart by Torry swords and spears. Hundreds fell at the palisades before those that followed forsook such folly, taking flight and setting down in the Torry rear, exhausted but facing less resistance.

The Bacelians upon the western slopes fared little better, facing the 5th Gargoyle Legion, supported by only six hundred of Venitie's bowmen and a small reserve of two Torry telnics to their rear.

*****

General Morton waited upon the northern slope as the 8th and 11th Benotrist Legions broke upon the hillsides, their countless numbers overwhelming his vision. Trebuchets lobbed head-sized boulders into the sea of glistening armor to great effect, each tearing visible fissures in the Benotrist ranks. The Benotrists struggled up the shallow slopes, weighed by their armor, thirst, and heat while suffering the withering ballista fire and Torry spears holding them at bay. Morton surveyed his lines for some distance east and west. His lines held for now, but it was only a matter of time before they broke.

The Torries made quick work of those attempting to scale their defenses. He spied a Torry spear gutting a Benotrist climbing atop the palisade. The cries of dying men echoed grimly along the line as hundreds of Benotrists were pressed against the palisades, crushed by their comrades pushing upon them from their rear. Some Torries climbed atop the trench line, jabbing the helpless fore ranks of Benotrists, who couldn't raise a hand in their own defense, pressed by all sides as they were.

Torry spearmen made measured thrusts, killing the enemy with methodical ease before being cut down by enemy archers. Further west, dozens of Benotrists broke through, driving the Torries from their trench before Morton ordered a unit of reserves forward to fill the breach.

Arsenc and Yeltor held firm, waiting beside General Morton as the battle raged below. An occasional Benotrist arrow struck the ground nearby but to little effect. Their own ballista answered in kind, raining boulders and fire upon the congested enemy. The Benotrists suffered enormous casualties as thousands lay dead or dying upon the barren plain and along the palisades. A pair of magantors fought in the distance, their riders releasing arrows upon one another as they passed.

Arsenc's eyes returned to the battle below as a fiery sword swept through a section of palisade, its blade alit with a blinding glow. "Morac," he whispered, struck by the power wielded by the blade's master. A few strokes gashed a widening hole in the palisade. Morac passed through the breach, his slashing blade cutting through Torry shields and swords like brittle sticks. Scores of Benotrists followed in his wake, their steady stream bleeding into a festering swarm.

"FORWARD!" General Morton ordered several units of reserves into the breach. Torry soldiers rushed down the hillsides with shields raised and spears levelled. They tore into the Benotrists, cutting down their disordered ranks but faring poorly against the Sword of the Sun as Morac broke their counterattack.

A half dozen spears closed upon Morac as he drove his sword through an upraised shield, piercing a Torry's chest before withdrawing his blood-soaked blade. He turned sharply toward his attackers, swinging his blade in a wide arc, snapping spears like twigs before cutting again, slicing a shield in half. The cloven metal fell to the dirt with an arm still attached. Another swipe took the next foe at the shoulder, slicing his arm and cutting a fatal gash across his chest. He took another at the hip, splitting him in half. His blade met a hasty swing, breaking the man's blade asunder before driving his sword into his chest.

Scores of Benotrists poured through the breach, swarming to either side of Morac and stopping the Torry counterattack cold. The Torries shifted their ballista to the break in their line, flame and stone blunting the Benotrist incursion. Morac continued up the rise, cutting his way to the Torry general standing upon the hillside above, surrounded by a dozen Torry Elite in their distinct blue tunics and silver helms.

Yeltor dodged an errant thrust, taking a Benotrist at the knee as Arsenc finished him, finding the gap in his neck between his helm and breastplate. Arsenc retrieved his blade, blocking another strike as Yeltor maneuvered behind his attacker, cutting him down before spinning to meet the next foe. Arsenc turned as a Benotrist approached Yeltor's right whilst he was engaged. The soldier wore two braided cords upon each shoulder, marking him a commander of unit. Such men were promoted through the Benotrist ranks through savagery and cunning.

He met the fellow's ardent swing with his shield, driving his sword into the man's flank. The Benotrist commander blocked the thrust with his own shield before striking again. Arsenc could see Yeltor in his periphery striking down his opponent off his left and took a step to his right, drawing his opponent's view away from Yeltor. He received the Benotrist's blow upon his shield, dropping to his knees while delivering his counterstrike to the fellow's ankle.

The blade struck true, snapping bone, the Benotrist releasing an anguished scream. Yeltor closed upon the Benotrist commander, driving his sword into his back just as Arsenc struck his ankle. He fell in the dirt, his ankle broken and lung pierced.

They had little reprieve to gain their bearing or breath, as more Benotrists swarmed the hillside. Horns sounded over the din, heralding differing commands as the battle disintegrated into chaos. The Torry standards fell amid the fray as General Morton met his end, overtaken by Morac's vanguard. Yeltor cut down another foe as Arsenc guarded his flank. An arrow whizzed past, grazing his helm as sparks sprayed from clashing blades. Yeltor shifted his shield to his opponent's blade, freeing his sword. He jabbed repeatedly with uncanny speed, taking his opponent off guard, his hurried thrusts finding flesh several times along the fellow's side. He pushed him aside, catching sight of the Golden Sword alit with a fiery glow arcing overhead. His instincts betrayed him, raising his shield to stay the blow.

Morac smiled, his sword cutting through the upraised shield like stale bread. *The fools never learn.* He grinned as Yeltor's shield split in half, severing his left arm at the wrist. Yeltor had realized his folly as soon as he lifted his shield. He could do naught but receive the blow, knowing the cost of his mistake. Waiting for the blade to pass, he drove forward, throwing himself into Morac's chest, trying to knock the Benotrist warrior from his feet. Morac shifted his shield between them as Yeltor stumbled forth with Morac's sword arm pinned between them.

Blood oozed from the stump of Yeltor's left wrist, smearing across the surface of Morac's shield as he struggled to drive the Benotrist warrior from his feet. Morac stepped back with his right foot, gaining leverage to keep his feet. The sword's heat bathed his palm, guiding him to act in accordance to its will. Morac hesitated, leaning to his own strength to drive his crippled foe backward before relenting. Pulling the sword further left across his body and below his shield, he slashed low, the arc taking Yeltor below his right knee. Yeltor tumbled over like a stricken porian. Morac wasted little time driving his blade into Yeltor's chest, ignoring his sword's urging to not do so.

"Argh!" Morac screamed, his left leg crumpling, driving him to the ground. Arsenc stood over the Benotrist champion, Morac's blood staining his blade. Morac lay sprawled upon the ground, a severe gash cut into his left leg below his knee, where Arsenc struck, denting his greaves, the blow breaking his leg. Arsenc swung his blade down upon Morac, avenging his king, his general, and his friend.

Morac had little time to react, the hilt of his sword forcing his hand to lift the blade accordingly, blocking Arsenc's emphatic blow. Arsenc's sword shattered as it met the golden blade. His eyes drew wide, his rage abating with dismay as Morac reached up, driving his sword into his gut. Morac's eyes drew wide as Arsenc slipped further down upon the blade, his sword hand reaching for a dagger from his hip, struggling to reach out and slice Morac's throat.

Morac cursed as Arsenc clawed his way down the Golden Sword, his innards afire as the metal gored him, drawing perilously close. Morac lay helpless to stay his fate, the sword trapped inside his dying enemy as the knife drew perilously close. He winced, unable to look, as death was but inches away. Arsenc slid further down the blade, finally close enough to end Morac's life, when mailed fists grabbed hold of him from behind, dragging him off Morac's outstretched blade. Benotrist soldiers pulled him away before throwing him down and hacking him to pieces.

Yeltor's eyes grew dim as he beheld Arsenc's fate, his own blood pooling beneath him. "We failed," he whispered, his life fading on that barren hillside upon the desolate plain. He closed his eyes, swords thrusting into him from all sides.

Morac was helped to his feet, supported by men under either shoulder as his left leg swelled in agony. "Victory is ours, emperor's Elite," they assured him as he glanced in each direction, where gargoyles swept over the hillsides to his east, south, and west while Benotrists swarmed the palisades along the northern slopes. Tens of thousands lay dead or dying, ringing the hills in wretched heaps. Cries of wounded men and gargoyles rent the air, echoing over the din in a haunted chorus. Gargoyles feasted on the fallen, slather dripping from their expectant fangs as they tore into the flesh of their victims, living or dead.

Torry archers loosed their arrows in hurried frenzy, struggling to empty their quivers as the enemy swept over the hillsides. The trebuchets grew silent, their crews slaughtered by Benotrists rushing up the northern slopes and gargoyles taking them from behind.

Thousands of gargoyles swept into the Torry encampment, slaughtering the wounded gathered around the healing tents and the Matrons attending them. No quarter was asked for, and none given. The battle degenerated into mindless slaughter, continuing to midday until every defender was slain. It would take days to count the dead, and Morac's legions suffered far more than their foes. Morac cared naught, for he had more reserves to call upon, and Corell had but a pittance.

"Kai-Shorum!" a soldier cried out as the battle waned.

"Kai-Shorum!" another answered in kind before others took up the call.

"Kai-Shorum!" The dreadful chant echoed over the hillsides in a deafening chorus, heralding their victory across the Kregmarin Plain.

CHAPTER 17

"Another drink, friend?" the barkeep asked, the light of the tavern lamp reflecting off his curious gray eyes.

"I shall," Cronus said, pushing their cups across the bar as Leanna stood at his side.

The barkeep topped their rims with Bedoan ale, sliding them back across the bar, regarding them with a curious eye. The tavern was oft filled with strangers from far-off lands, traversing the main thoroughfare connecting Notsu and Corell. He could tell by their manner and look that Cronus was a Torry, which was not out of place since they were well within the Torry border, some thirty leagues east of Corell. What piqued his interest was Cronus's bearing, which was likely a warrior of some rank.

"You're a soldier?" the barkeep asked.

"Am I so transparent?" Cronus shook his head.

"Aye." The barkeep grinned. "I can spot a soldier of Torry North even if I were blind. The name is Gregarn Kress, though others call me Garn. And yours, lad?"

Cronus hesitated, sharing a look with Leanna as she squeezed his hand. "Cronus. Cronus Kenti," he answered, reluctant to give his name but sensing Garn's honest nature. Besides, they were well within Torry North, and he doubted agents of Tyro dared venture there so brazenly.

"I gather you do not wish your name bandied about for all to hear. You needn't worry, lad. I'll keep it to myself."

"My thanks," Cronus said, partaking his drink. It was a long time since he was called lad. The barkeep must've been older than he appeared. He was a strongly built fellow some inches shy of Cronus's stature with discerning gray eyes and enough silver in his blond mane to indicate his advanced years.

"'Tis the least I can do for a fellow Torry soldier."

"You served?" Leanna asked.

"That I did, my lady. Sixteen years in service to the Torry throne until a broken leg ended my usefulness." He shrugged, no trace of bitterness in his tone.

"After sixteen years of leal service, you were cast out?" Leanna asked ashamedly.

"Hardly cast out, my lady. King Lore does not treat his soldiers with callous disdain. No, I was gifted a generous sum for my service, which I used to purchase this fine establishment," Garn said, turning to retrieve a sword hanging on the wall behind him. Cronus had noticed the weapon prominently displayed when they first entered the tavern, wondering if it was for display or served a functional purpose. Garn laid it across the bar between them. "Three campaigns and countless skirmishes have I faced with that blade in hand." Garn patted the blade, offering Cronus to test its worth.

Cronus released Leanna's hand, taking hold of the sword, running a finger carefully along its edge. "Still quite sharp."

"I haven't much use for a dull blade." Garn snorted.

"You still find need of it?" Leanna asked.

"On occasion, my lady." Garn smiled.

"Leanna," she offered her name, extending a hand in greeting.

"Leanna." He bowed, kissing her hand.

"Perhaps you shall have need of your sword again," she said.

"The war." Garn nodded. "You may be right. If the minions of Tyro dare come this way, this blade shall meet them. My leg may have betrayed me, but I still have two hands to wield it." Cronus smiled at the familiar determined bluster that came naturally to old soldiers. "Of course, I may have need of it sooner if the outlaws raiding the Covar Province venture this far north."

"Raiders?" Cronus's ears perked.

"Aye. They have sacked several villages and countless farms south of here. Some reports claim they are slavers. Others believe them to be of Naybin origin. Perhaps they are both."

"Naybins?" Cronus asked. "This far north?"

"Evil tidings, indeed," Garn added. "But I know the men who claim the raiders are Naybin. They are well-traveled and know of such things. The question, Cronus, is, why would Naybin soldiers raid our homeland with the garrison of Corell to our west and the 5th Army at Notsu to our east?"

"What happened to the villages they raided?" Leanna asked.

Garn sighed, pouring himself a drink, downing his cup and setting it forcefully upon the bar. "What did not happen to them is the more appropriate question, my dear lady." He regarded her with a pained look.

"Any survivors?" Cronus asked.

"Few. Livestock and those who resisted were slain. All structures burned to the ground, and those who surrendered were given over to slave traders in league with the raiders. Some of the cruelties visited upon our people I shall not speak of in the lady's presence."

Cronus slipped his fingers around Leanna's, squeezing her hand. They hoped to attain Corell without incident. Their journey from Notsu progressed without duress, save for the drudgery of the open road. Minister Veda's caravan was laden with baggage and provisions, reducing their rate of travel by half. Cronus thought of riding ahead with their small party, but Leanna advised him to remain with the larger group.

Their caravan had set camp just outside of Torune, a modest village resting thirty leagues east of Corell. The village elders received Minister Veda with all the pomp and ceremony they could offer, including the finest lodging their only inn had to offer. Many of their party broke from the larger group to visit the tavern for a quiet ale and a hearty meal.

Galen stood near the hearth along the opposing wall, entertaining the tavern patrons with ballads on his mandolin. Alen sat alone at a corner table, waiting for his friends as a serving wench hurried off to fetch their meal. The half-empty tavern was filling with the waning light of day. The crowd lacked the tavern's usual boisterous clientele, as most were retainers and servants of the Torry crown.

"Your party is heading west?" Garn asked.

"Corell," Cronus said. It was no secret.

"Then keep together. Double your sentries at night, and be wary of strangers," Garn advised.

"We shall."

"Of course, all my fretting might be for naught. I've heard rumors of the 1st Torry Cavalry moving south, at least three unit-sized elements, likely Tevlin's command, if the rumors are true," Garn added.

"A charging golden ocran on a field of gray?" Cronus asked, recalling the sigil of the 1st Torry Cavalry.

"Aye."

"They were based along the western border last I remember," Cronus thought aloud.

"Many strange happenings. Such is war, Cronus," Garn said, again filling Cronus's cup as well as his own. "No charge for this drink," Garn offered, lifting his cup in the air. "To our fellow soldiers facing the enemy whilst we sit safely here."

"To our soldiers," Cronus said, downing the cup.

"One would think Tyro a madman for continuing his war after the slaughter at Tuft's Mountain. I hear tell we slew four legions. Did I hear correctly?" Garn asked.

"True. But Tyro has many more to throw at us and will not repeat such a blunder."

"To the Torries who fought at Tuft's Mountain." Garn again filled their cups.

Leanna could see the pain in Cronus's eyes as he thought of his men. She thought to intercede before Cronus spoke, staying her hand. "To our friends who fought at Tuft's Mountain." Cronus lifted his cup.

*****

They set out at first light, breaking camp in good order as Minister Veda called for Cronus to attend him. The trade minister rode an ocran this morning, forgoing his carriage for the first time during their journey. He ordered his apprentice, Merith, to attend to his various duties as his scribe. Minister Veda and Cronus rode ahead of the column with their cavalry escort guarding their flanks some distance away along the open farmlands that stretched endlessly to the horizon.

"You were missed last evening, King's Elite Kenti. The village elders were anxious to meet the hero of Tuft's Mountain," Minister Veda said with an air of respect for Cronus's bravery.

"My men were heroes, Minister Veda. I am simply a survivor." Cronus sighed.

"I am not a warrior, so I know not of such things, but I know of your fell deeds, Cronus. I have committed my life to service to the crown in the furtherance of trade and commerce to strengthen our kingdoms. I believe such efforts far exceed the wielding of a sword, as the gold I have brought to our treasury helps pay for our armies. But gold cannot purchase courage, and for this, I commend you."

"My gratitude, Minister."

"When we attain Corell, the princess shall require your audience. Be mindful of the protocols of court when—"

"I am aware, Minister."

"Very well. Your friend Terin seemed ill-prepared for such a meet. That is why I ask."

"Terin." Cronus smiled, shaking his head.

"Yes, Terin. He was first introduced to the court under false pretense, though not of his own doing."

"False pretense?"

"Yes. I was told he was a scribe and apprentice to Minister Antillius. I was aghast that one so poorly cultured would be so highly placed. I was unaware of King Lore's alternate plan for the boy's placement. Had I known the boy's parentage, I might have been less surprised by his ascension."

"Parentage?" Cronus made a face. Minister Veda lifted a curious brow, noting Cronus's ignorance of his friend's origin. "What of his parentage, Minister?" Cronus pushed.

"If his father is who I believe he is, then our young friend carries a rich bloodline indeed."

"His father was of high birth?" Cronus failed to recall a great house bearing the name Caleph. In fact, he couldn't recall any of that name in any house, great or small.

"Who said anything about his father?" Minister Veda said with a tight smile. It was obvious that Cronus was ignorant of Terin's origin, which led Veda to suspect that even Terin was ignorant of his lineage as well.

"His mother, then. What of her?" Cronus asked, tired of the minister's senseless subterfuge.

"'Tis mere speculation on my part, King's Elite. I don't think it is my place to offer you unfounded theories."

"But you already have, Minister."

"So I have. Very well. Let me begin at the start. It was many years ago, during the reign of King Lorm, when I first attained the post of king's minister..."

Four days hence

"Umph!" Terin grunted, hitting the ground for what seemed the thousandth time. His weary muscles failed to respond to the urgency his mind asked of them as he struggled to gain his feet. His opponent stood several paces off, gifting him time to collect himself.

"Attack, Lucas!" Torg Vantel admonished Terin's opponent for granting him such reprieve. Lucas acknowledged Torg with a reluctant nod before grabbing hold of Terin from behind, wrestling him to the ground. Lucas was the fiercest grappler in the King's Elite, and Terin struggled mightily to hold his ground.

Whenever Lucas took pity on him, Torg ordered him to continue, beating any pride Terin retained from his humbled flesh. To Terin's credit, he uttered no complaint and fought to his utmost.

His father had schooled him in many forms of combat, including bare hand, but no such training could have availed a foe as skilled as Lucas.

"The enemy shall grant you no mercy, so we train without it!" Torg's deep voice echoed as Lucas squeezed Terin's neck. Terin struggled mightily as the world dimmed. He lost track of time as his vision faded, drowning in a darkened void. The next thing he felt was the sand beneath him as he lay upon his back. The bright sky above came into focus as his eyes fluttered open. He stared skyward through the opening in the courtyard overhead as the tall white walls circled into the heavens, meeting the blue sky above.

The sound of hooves clopping stone echoed dully in his ears. Hundreds of voices sounded all around him as the central courtyard bustled with activity. He had spent the better part of the past ten days in the wrestling pit of the courtyard, far below the training arena nearer the roof. The fighting pit rested off the side of the central courtyard, filled with sand to ease the falls one suffered under Torg Vantel's tutelage. The rest of the courtyard floor was covered in fitted stone.

A small corral rested opposite the fighting pit. A large tunnel ran north to the main gate while several smaller tunnels jutted in various directions, the most prominent of which led straight east to the palace stables. Another wide tunnel led to the palace warehouses along the west wall. Wagons and ocran traversed this vital thoroughfare throughout the day, providing Corell the logistical support a palace of its size required.

The main tunnel, running north to the main gate, was guarded by a series of smaller gates along its length. During a siege, these would be sealed, providing additional layers to the palace's defense. Archer slits ran the length of the tunnel along its ceiling, allowing bowmen to whittle any enemy breaching the main gate.

"Are you going to lie there all day or say hello?" a familiar voice called out to him.

Terin rolled to his knees, curiosity overcoming his aching muscles as he gained his feet, brushing sand from his naked chest and limbs. There before him sat a man on an ocran. He screwed his eyes as the fellow's countenance came into focus. "Cronus?" he questioned, disbelieving his tired eyes.

"It's me, Terin." Cronus smiled, leaning forward in the saddle with his hands upon the pommel. There he sat, the luster returned to his dark mane and handsome face. His body was filled out to its former glory, his sturdy attire matching his restored countenance. He was the Cronus of old, appearing much the same as when he last saw him at Rego, not the emaciated stranger he beheld at Fera.

"Cronus!" Terin shouted happily, finally certain that he was, in fact, alive and not an apparition. Terin rushed to meet his friend, forgetting his fellow Elite and Torg, who surrounded him in the fighting pit. He bounded over the low stone wall that separated the training area from the courtyard proper as Cronus dismounted to embrace his long-lost friend. "You're alive!" Terin repeated happily, overcome with emotion.

"He lives much thanks to you," another familiar voice said as Terin finally took note of the column passing through the courtyard. Scores of Torry cavalry and courtesans paraded past, stretching endlessly along the north tunnel before emptying into the courtyard. The cavalry broke left, proceeding to the stables, while the rest of Cronus's companions posted in the courtyard.

Terin broke from Cronus's embrace just as Leanna stepped near, placing a kiss upon his cheek. He thought to embrace her as well, but the grime and sweat on his naked chest gave him pause. He stood nearly naked, save for the dark-tan training kilt wrapped around his waist. Leanna held no such compunction, drawing him to her in a fierce embrace, caring not if he soiled her tunic.

"He escaped." Terin almost wept. He had feared for Cronus's safety since their flight from Fera. Not a night went by without Terin wondering his fate.

"*They* escaped," she corrected him as he spied Alen sitting on his mount beside her.

"Alen?"

"It is well to see you, Terin." Alen regarded him.

"Raven and Lorken?" Terin asked, his eyes shifting along the column to see if they were among them.

"Safe aboard the *Stenox* and sailing toward the Ape Empire." Cronus smiled. Terin shook his head, overcome with joy.

"Terin!" Torg Vantel echoed, his stern tone reminding Terin of his duty.

Terin winced, knowing Master Vantel did not take interruptions to his regimen lightly. "Master Vantel, this is my friend, Commander of Unit Cronus Kenti," he said, backing a step to address Torg, waving an open hand toward Cronus. Torg stepped over the low wall of the pit to meet the hero of Tuft's Mountain. He would admonish Terin later for stopping his training unbidden but understood the boy forgetting himself with the return of his friend.

"Master Vantel." Cronus bowed his head politely. He had met the grizzled commander of the Elite on several occasions but doubted if Torg remembered him in the sea of faces that he occupied at those times.

"Your legend precedes you, Commander. The King's Elite honors your deeds at Tuft's Mountain," Torg said, offering his hand, as they clasped forearms. To receive such a gesture from Torg Vantel was the greatest of honors any Torry soldier could aspire. Torg could see the worth in Cronus's eyes. They were the weary eyes of a warrior who had seen battle and lost comrades dear to him. They were eyes bereft of the prideful arrogance akin to summer soldiers and green warriors. It spoke well of Terin to count such a man among his closest friends.

The soldiers milling about stood statue still as a royal carriage emerged from the north tunnel, stopping in the center of the courtyard just behind Cronus. A footman climbed down from the back of the coach clad in a scarlet tunic. He quickly opened the door and bowed as Minister Veda stepped without, accompanied by Merith and Aldo. The trade minister quickly recognized Torg standing amid Cronus's small entourage.

"Master Vantel." Veda bowed, acknowledging Torg with the deepest reverence.

"Minister Veda." Torg tilted his head in kind, regarding Veda with mutual respect. As commander of the King's Elite and master of arms, Torg was second only to the royal line. His word was law, even over the chief minister, the generals of the realm, the regents of Cagan and Central City, and the provincial governors of the realm. Torg, however, restricted his authority to those duties that he was primarily charged: the Elite and the readiness of the palace garrison.

"I require an audience with Her Highness, Princess Corry, and yourself, if you would be so kind, Master Vantel," Veda said with deep reverence.

"Very well. I assume it entails matters of state as well as the fortunate return of Commander Kenti?" Torg regarded Cronus and his comrades.

"Indeed. If you and your friends would follow me, Commander Kenti," Veda instructed.

*****

Terin stood post beside the throne attired in a clean white tunic and silver breastplate and greaves, his eyes fixed straight ahead with practiced discipline. Torg had dismissed him to bathe and present himself to the princess as Minister Veda led his friends from the courtyard. He was eager to speak with Cronus and hear how he escaped Tyro's realm. He wondered if Raven led them to the northern coastline as they had planned or if they escaped by other means. He noticed the stranger in their group, the lanky fellow with the sharp nose, and wondered when he had joined them. Mostly, he wished to hear their tales in a private chamber beside a warm hearth rather than the formal rigidness of court.

Torg stood upon the opposite side of the throne, standing at the princess's right with a dozen members of the King's Elite forming a semicircle behind them in their distinctive azure tunics and winged helms. "Minister Veda!" the court herald proclaimed as the minister of trade entered the vast chamber, his burgundy robes swirling at his feet as he strode proudly forth. His scribe Merith accompanied him, followed by Cronus, Alen, Leanna, and Galen.

The small group approached the dais and knelt in unison before Corry gave them leave to rise. They were still attired in their traveling clothes—Cronus in a knee-length brown tunic and Leanna in similar gray. Once she was told of their arrival, Princess Corry ordered them hither, forgoing the usual protocol for visitors to be bathed and properly attired before they were presented at court. Terin barely had time to catch his breath as he stripped his training garb, jumped into a cold bathing pool near the training pit, and climbed out and dressed in a matter of moments before hurrying off to the throne room, as he was ordered.

"Minister Veda, we welcome your return to Corell," Corry greeted with practiced grace.

"Highness, I return at your father's behest to relay tidings pertinent to the realm and in the company of these fellow travelers, whose return is of interest to the throne."

"The enemy advances upon the Kregmarin, and the king's decision to meet them in battle is known to us, Minister Veda. We have received the king's missives from our magantor scouts some days ago. If you wish to relay the king's orders for the preparedness of the realm and the evacuation of Notsu and Bacel, I invite you to council upon the conclusion of this audience," Corry explained.

"That shall suffice, Highness." Veda bowed, stepping aside as Cronus and Leanna were beckoned forth. Merith followed his master, stepping back as his eyes met Terin's standing beside the throne, his face a mask of trained indifference as he guarded the princess. He wondered if the crown's new favorite son held him in poor regard for his prudish behavior toward him when they first met.

Minister Veda had instructed him to not speak of Terin's suitability to his new position. There was more to Terin's lineage than what he knew. He was certain that Minister Veda was privy to some vital information on the farm boy's mysterious significance but would not convey such knowledge with his curious apprentice. His natural dislike for Terin was only compounded by Aldo's apparent friendship with the crown's champion. Merith wisely averted his eyes and kept his thoughts to himself.

"Highness," Cronus and Leanna greeted in unison as they stepped forth, stopping short of the dais. Corry rose from the high throne, which she sat in her father's place, smoothing the folds of her silver gown as she descended the steps to the floor below. She motioned Terin to follow as she stopped before Leanna, touching a hand to Leanna's cheek.

"You found him." Corry smiled, her eyes studiously appraising the man beside her.

"I have thanks to Raven and Lorken and the wonderful boy who guards you." Leanna smiled at Terin. She had feared for him since they heard of his separation from the others, worried that he was taken or slain.

"We are fortunate that both of these Torry sons are returned to us to serve the realm," Corry said, caring not to acknowledge Raven's contribution to their efforts. If she never again made his acquaintance, she would consider herself fortunate. "Commander Cronus Kenti," Corry greeted him, testing his name upon her lips as she regarded him. He matched the visage that Leanna and Terin each described, though Terin spoke of his strength and courage, whereas Leanna admired his handsome face and kind green eyes.

"Princess." Cronus again bowed his head.

"Your betrothed and friends speak well of you, Commander. I fear you shall be burdened by such lofty expectations. My father wrote that he was sending Minister Veda to Corell with a special visitor whom he had placed in the King's Elite. He did not reveal your name and intended to surprise me. There is no choice worthier than the hero of Tuft's Mountain to serve in the King's Elite. I am certain Master Vantel will gladly accept your service."

Corry turned, gifting the master of arms a flirtatious wink. Torg snorted, regarding Corry with a tilt of his head. Torg rarely demonstrated his pleasure with anything more than a snort and a nod, and that was all she expected. "And who are your companions?" Corry inquired, regarding Alen and Galen, who waited behind them.

"Alen aided us in our escape from Fera." Cronus pointed him out as the former Menotrist slave bowed.

"Alen?" Corry lifted a curious brow, turning to Terin to confirm his identity, who confirmed with a polite bow of his head. "You were once slave to Princess Tosha and won your freedom in the champions' arena at Fera?" she asked, recalling Terin's tale of their escape.

"Raven won my freedom, Highness. I offered little—" Alen began to explain before she interrupted him.

"I am well aware of Captain Raven's actions in the arena and yours as well, Alen. Without you, he would not have been victorious. Terin speaks well of you and of your bravery during their escape. I welcome you to Corell."

"My gratitude, Highness." Alen bowed.

"And this is Galen, a minstrel who aided us in our escape from Axenville and remained with us since," Cronus said.

"Your Highness, I am bereft of words that describe your timeless beauty. I am honored to again visit Corell and my native realm." Galen graciously bowed.

"Again? You have visited Corell before?" Corry asked.

"Yes, Highness. It was three summers past. I was commissioned, along with a score of other musicians and singers, to perform at a festival celebrating the ascension of your minister of alchemy." Corry was not present during the mentioned gala, spending that season in Cagan. Even if she were, she doubted she would have remembered one face out of so many, though Galen's long face would have been difficult to forget.

"You must be weary and famished from your arduous journey. My stewards shall see you bathed, clothed, and fed. After, you shall join me in a less formal chamber. I am most eager to hear all of your adventures," Corry said.

*****

"Such is the state of our affairs at Notsu. I have returned with most of our people. Chief Minister Monsh retained a skeletal staff to attend his base needs. Save for a small cavalry contingent, he represents the only official Torry entity in Notsu. Should our armies be compromised north of the crossroads, he shall need to make a hasty departure," Minister Veda explained.

"Ill tidings indeed," Minister Thunn thought aloud.

Following Minister Veda's arrival, Princess Corry assembled her high council in her father's inner sanctum. Minister of trade, Lutius

Veda; minister of agriculture, Torlan Thunn; minister of Alchemy, Vergus Kalvar; commander of garrison, Nevias; and Master Vantel gathered about the long oval table with a map of Torry North and its eastern approaches rolled out across its surface. With Squid Antillius at Central City and Chief Minister Monsh at Notsu, Minister Veda assumed the post of high minister to the crown.

"King Lore was adamant that you take utmost care in securing Corell, Highness," Lutius counseled.

"Her Highness has done so since the king's departure, Minister Veda," Torg's rough voice answered.

"The garrison of Corell is fully mustered at ten telnics. Another twelve reserve telnics have mustered at Central City to fill the losses suffered by the 2nd and 3rd Armies at Tuft's Mountain. Another five telnics have mustered at Cropus." Nevias tapped the map where the northern city of Cropus rested at the Plate foothills.

"How goes the harvest order I issued, Minister Thunn?" Corry asked of her minister of agriculture.

"The order has been issued, Highness, but is met with misgivings. Many of our farmers have been called to military service, leaving their fields tended by their wives and children. Others are resistant to reap half of their yield long before the harvest season," he explained.

"Better half the harvest than none at all," Torg growled.

"Have your surrogates explained to them the necessity, Minister Thunn?" she asked. Corry knew her edict for all lands east of Corell to call in half their harvest would be unpopular. She issued the edict as a precaution in the event her father's army was flanked, leaving the Torry lands east of Corell undefended. If her father proved successful, then her decision would cost them much-needed yield, but Corry had planned for the worst, knowing a lesser yield was better than starvation if things turned out poorly.

"My subordinates have been most adamant in conveying your concerns, Highness, but farmers are a stubborn lot. Be as that may, the edict has been issued and is being adhered to," Minister Thunn assured.

"What is the status of General Bode and the refurbishment of the 3rd Army?" Minister Veda inquired, his eye fixed upon Central City's place upon the map. If things went poorly to their east, Bode's army represented the nearest relief force of significance available.

"General Bode has split his command, leaving several telnics at Central City to collect his reinforcements while the greater part has deployed nearer our western border," Nevias explained.

Torg understood Veda's concern on the disposition of the Torry armies. They were spread far too thin for his liking with the 2nd Army at Rego, the 3rd at Central City, and the 5th north at Kregmarin. The gargoyle incursion into Yatin and the precarious nature of the Macon Empire froze the 1st and 4th Armies at Cagan, preventing them from coming to their aid. The realm stood upon the precipice, the merest stumble able to send it into a dark abyss.

"Let us trust the fates to grant our king victory and return safely to Corell." Minister Veda's somber voice carried dully in the still air.

The torchlight reflected off Corry's blue eyes as she steeled her heart, guarding against the fear and weakness that her station could not abide. "We trust our wits and good sense, Minister Veda. The fates are fickle masters that are as likely to betray their supplicants as their detractors. We have much to attend in the coming days. Please see to your people. I am sure they are weary from their journey," she said, dismissing her council.

*****

Cronus tugged at the collar of his tunic. It was white, new, and briefer than he was accustomed. It was the formal garment of an untrained King's Elite with silver breastplate, arm guards, and greaves. Galen and Alen stood beside him in the outer corridor, modestly attired in similar ankle-length emerald tunics. Finely woven sandals peeked beneath the hems of their garments, each far more delicate than Cronus's sturdier footwear that laced along his calves. Cronus began to wonder if his promotion to the King's Elite was worth all this fuss. He felt woefully exposed yet overly dressed at the same time. He shared Raven's dislike of formal gatherings and galas, preferring the simpler things in life.

Terin stood beside him, clad in the same attire. He seemed at ease, obviously accustomed to such formal dress and protocol. They had little time to speak, as Cronus and the others were ushered from the throne room, bathed, dressed, and escorted to this place, where they were ordered to wait.

"Do you often guard the princess?" Cronus asked curiously.

"Part of each day, but I spend most of my time in Master Vantel's company, just as you shall." Terin smiled, eager for his friend to share in his torment.

"Are you happy to see me or pleased to share your misery?" Cronus lifted a brow.

"I am just relived you are safe. After we were separated at Fera, I feared you were captured, or worse."

"Nothing is worse than capture, not even death." Cronus thought of his men suffering in that vile place.

Terin had seen enough of the gargoyles atrocities in Yatin to know the truth of that. "It is good to see you, Cronus." He offered, grateful to see his friend once more.

"You as well, Terin. You have come far since that day we first met on the road to Central City. Your father must be proud of the man his son has become." Cronus placed a hand upon his shoulder.

"Thank you, Cronus. I am also glad to have another to train with to share in Master Vantel's instruction," Terin confessed.

"I knew it." Cronus grinned, nudging him.

"Come. The princess awaits," Terin said, leading them further along the corridor.

"What of Leanna? We were separated—"

"She is with the princess," Terin answered. He was told to escort them to Corry's private sanctum. It was she who ordered her stewards to see that they were bathed and correctly attired.

They traversed several long corridors, light filtering through small archways above, illuminating the white stone walls. Soldiers in golden tunics and polished steel armor with silver wings extending from their helms stood post along the passageway. Torry Elite clad in their distinct blue tunics stood post on either side of an open archway at the end of the corridor. The glow of torchlight filtered without, casting a dull shadow upon the wall ahead. The guards regarded Terin briefly, allowing him to pass, as he was expected, the others following his lead.

Upon entering the enclosed chamber, Cronus's eyes were drawn to a large hearth centered upon the opposite wall with a half dozen high-backed chairs facing it in a half circle. Two figures stood before the hearth, their shapely, feminine forms silhouetted by the crackling flames.

"Highness," Terin said, stepping forth to kneel before she indicated him to remain afoot.

"Welcome to Corell, gentlemen," Corry greeted them. "Please sit," she added, spreading her hands to the empty chairs around her. "You as well, Terin," she whispered, indicating the chair to her right, nearest the hearth.

Cronus took one step forth before his eyes came into focus, recognizing the woman standing beside the princess. Leanna stood before him, attired in a flowing emerald calnesian gown that matched the hue of his eyes. The gown had long, voluminous sleeves and swirling skirts that pooled at her feet. The firelight shone off the rich folds of her golden hair.

Her beauty took his breath and his tongue as he stood before her, bereft of voice. Leanna regarded him in kind, taking in the sight of his masculine form attired in the tunic and shining armor of a King's Elite. The brief garment displayed his toned, muscled limbs, which brought her delight and him embarrassment, though he would show it not.

"Your lady, Cronus," Princess Corry admonished, drawing him from his boyish stupor. Corry smiled to herself as Cronus took Leanna's hand and led her to their seats opposite her and Terin. Galen and Alen assumed the center seats after the princess greeted them in turn. "Now shall we commence with your adventures?" Corry asked, eager to hear all that transpired after their escape from Fera.

Leanna squeezed Cronus's hand, offering him her support as he retold his grim tale and harrowing ordeal from his capture at Tuft's

Mountain to Raven's timely rescue when all hope seemed lost. Corry grudgingly acknowledged the Earther's usefulness, though she was loathe to do so. Much of this part of Cronus's tale was unknown to them, as he had never had the chance to speak of it to Terin before they were separated after their escape.

Cronus omitted much of the horror his men suffered in the dungeon of the Black Castle. Such were the things of nightmares and not for the ears of women. It was enough that Leanna knew more than he cared for her to know, and what she didn't, she could easily guess.

The tone of Cronus's telling noticeably shifted when he reached the part where they escaped Fera. His pained, monotone voice came alive and animated as he told of their first night in the wilds and Lorken breaking off on his own. He continued with the loss of their magantors, using greater detail in describing the gragglogg attacks and their adventures thereafter. He spoke of Raven and Tosha's strange interactions and constant bickering mixed with moments of affection.

"Why would she wed such a man?" Corry thought aloud.

"He saved her life, Highness," Leanna said in Raven's defense.

And Terin saved hers. Corry would speak no more of Captain Raven. If Tosha wished to bind herself to such a ruffian, then she was a fool. "Please continue, Cronus," Corry said.

Cronus spoke of their strange journey along the Benotrist frontier and their troubles at Axenville. He minimized Galen's roguish behavior, giving the minstrel the benefit of the doubt for the aid he rendered during their escape. Corry was taken aback by the length of his journey and the dangers that threatened them throughout. Their trials continued even after reaching Tro, where they were beset by agents of Tyro. His description of Kriton lifted the hairs on Terin's neck.

"Did the creature die in the fall from the bridge?" Corry asked.

"I know not his fate, only that he struck the surface. Whether he resurfaced or not, I had not the time to be certain whilst the battle raged," Cronus explained. He loathed the idea of facing that vile creature again and hoped he met his end in the Flen.

The rest of his tale was uneventful, save for their meeting with Corry's father at Notsu and the disquieting rumors of Naybin raiders harassing their southern provinces. At the conclusion of his tale, the chamber grew quiet for a time. 'Twas an unbelievable tale that if spoken by another, it would have been dismissed as a fanciful yarn. But Cronus spoke not as a hero but a survivor, for only their collective wits, courage, and dumb luck allowed them to escape.

"And I believed Terin's tale to have no equal. You have proven my assumption false," Corry finally said, breaking the eerie silence.

"I have yet to hear his tale from his own lips, though Yeltor spoke at length of their adventures. Perhaps he should begin at Tuft's Mountain. I would hear of his rescue of Her Highness at Molten Isle and all that followed," Cronus said.

And so Terin relayed his tale with Leanna and the princess interrupting whenever their knowledge exceeded his own. After Terin finished, Corry asked Galen and Alen to share their histories. Alen required much prodding, his servile upbringing reflected in his quiet voice and downcast eyes. Corry felt such pity for the former slave. Her father's missive suggested she find a place for him in court. He thought the boy could serve as a palace messenger. He was slight of build and swift of foot, which suited him to the task.

"Do you wish to serve as a palace messenger, Alen?" the princess asked.

"I...I would be honored, Highness," Alen stammered, hopeful to find a place and purpose in this strange land.

"Very well. On the morrow, you shall report to Commander Nevias, the commander of the garrison of Corell. It is in his service you shall serve."

Galen then spoke at length of his sordid past, though to hear him speak it, one would assume he was the arbiter of culture and stately virtues. He was a master of overstating his accomplishments and omitting his faults. Yet his flowery speech and respectful decorum suited him to the royal court.

"Have you written a ballad of your adventures, minstrel?" Corry asked.

"I am constructing a tome of sonnets and ballads of Commander Kenti's valiant escape from Fera, his daring flight across the Benotrist heartland, and his brave rescue of his comrades at Axenville, where I earned the favor of his esteemed company. Now we are kindred spirits, returning to our native realm in the hour of its gravest peril. Should Your Highness deem myself worthy, I shall gladly sing in this private sanctum or the great keep for all to hear," Galen explained, standing from his seat and bowing deeply, sweeping a hand across his waist in esteemed reverence.

"Perhaps on the morrow, minstrel. For now, let us partake of the king's table. You must be famished from your travels, and I have ordered food prepared in your honor," Corry said, ordering them to retire to the royal dining chamber.

Three days hence

The morning found Cronus and Terin in the training arena, exchanging blows with blunted swords. Torg Vantel had drilled Cronus without cease since the morn after his arrival. Cronus was surprised by Terin's swordsmanship. Was Terin always this skilled, or had Torg's instruction manifest such change? Terin's father also trained him, as Terin repeatedly claimed. Cronus was a skilled swordsman, perhaps the finest in the Ninth Telnic, but he struggled to hold his own against his young friend despite his greater size and reach.

He backed a step in the loose sand as Terin pressed his attack, thrusting his blade toward Cronus's stomach. Cronus jumped further back, slapping Terin's blade with the flat of his shield. Terin stumbled briefly, stopping as Cronus's sword touched his throat. "Dead," Torg stated flatly, acknowledging Cronus's victory. "AGAIN!"

And so it went. They lost count of the number of times they *died* at the other's hand. They fought each other and together in pairs or threes, challenging their fellow Elite in mock battle. They fought without cease, their brains numb to thought and honed to react on instinct. At times, Torg drew Terin aside, giving specific instruction on the use of his sword and the unique skills that such a weapon required. Strength and arcing blows were of no consequence to such a blade. A sword that could slice through shields and blades like brittle parchment required only small movements to break blades and slay foes. Anything more was wasted motion.

"Two strokes!" Torg emphasized, holding the first two digits of his right hand in the air. "Split and thrust! Split their blade, and thrust for the kill!" And so Terin did, attacking stick dummies in rapid succession. Such tactics were most useful against common blades and required speed and precision to maximize lethality and minimize exposure. His intense training with blunted swords prepared him to battle Morac should such a time arise. In such a battle, Terin would hold the lesser sword and would need swordsmanship to hold his ground.

Cronus and Terin would finish each day exhausted and spent. Little time was left to them to bathe, eat, and sleep before repeating the process the next day. They saw little of their comrades. Alen was busy running messages throughout the garrison at the behest of Commander Nevias. Galen was a guest of the crown, entertaining the court with ballads and songs. Leanna attended Princess Corry as a maiden of the court. The princess grew quite fond of her, and together, they often viewed Cronus and Terin's training sessions.

By midday, a pair of magantors appeared in the eastern sky, their riders the harbingers of ill tidings. They were ushered to the throne room upon landing, bearing news of the king. Corry sat on her father's throne, her blue eyes following the magantor scouts as they approached the dais and knelt. She commanded them to rise, observing their haggard faces and soiled garments. Their tunics were bloodstained and armor dented and dull. They appeared to have flown without cease, forgoing their base necessities to attain Corell. She struggled to suppress the whispers of her heart, where her darkest fears dwelled. Something was terribly amiss.

"Speak!" the princess commanded.

"Highness, we have journeyed from the Kregmarin Plain upon order of the king to inform Your Highness on the disposition of the 5th Army." One of the scouts bowed with hurried grace.

"Then speak," she commanded evenly, tired of the needless formality.

"King Lore and the 5th Army have held position upon a ring of small hills along the southern Kregmarin against two legions, one Benotrist and another gargoyle. They have inflicted heavy losses upon the enemy through several days of battle. Alas, the two legions were but the vanguard of a larger invasion. No less than five legions have surrounded our army, cutting their route of escape and trapping them therein.

"King Lore ordered most of our contingent to raid the Benotrists' tenuous water supplies while a few of us were sent hither to inform Your Highness of the army's dire position. Others were sent to Notsu and Bacel to warn them of our dire state and to prepare their people for siege or flight. With much of Notsu's and Bacel's armies alongside our own, they have little choice but to flee. We were set upon by Benotrist magantors once we departed, slaying one of our company. We fought our way free before passing on to Corell," the scout finished, his grim tale draining the blood from Corry's face.

"Does my father live?" she asked solemnly.

The scouts shifted nervously, unsure of their answer. "We know not his fate, Highness, only that he was beset upon our departure. The army was dug in behind good entrenchments upon high ground of their choosing."

But surrounded by many times their number, she thought sourly. Corry dismissed the scouts and called her war council.

CHAPTER 18

He stared southward with rapacious eyes, his gaze fixed upon the sprawling city before them. Bacel rested north and east of the fabled crossroads with thick-built walls circling its outermost perimeter the height of four men. The walls were crafted with gray stone with jagged bulwarks jutting from the battlements above. They were walls built to protect the city from the armies of men and wholly unsuited against gargoyles. White spirals and copper domes towered behind the outer walls, silhouetted against the midday sky.

Morac's eyes swept the length of the city's north wall. The Council of Bacel had refused his generous offer of sparing the city his full wrath. He merely asked for total submission in exchange for their miserable lives, but they dismissed his offer, thus sealing their fate.

Morac winced as he shifted in the saddle, pain running north of his left leg, which dangled miserably with splints tied to either side. His healer advised that he rest in a wagon, but he dismissed such frivolity. No troops would respect a commander who clung to such comforts. Nay, he would oversee the destruction of Bacel from his mount and add the tittle of lord to his retinue of appellations. The 7th and 5th Gargoyle Legions surrounded the hapless city whilst the remaining legions were elsewhere, attending equally pressing aims.

"Emperor's Chosen, we await your commandsss," General Concaka, commander of the 5th Legion, hissed, sitting on an uneasy mount at Morac's side. Morac was flanked by both of his legion commanders, Vaginak to his right and Concaka his left. Each gargoyle was visibly discomforted by riding an ocran, as the beasts were naturally unnerved by the foul creatures, but Morac wished his commanders to possess greater mobility on the battlefield.

The gargoyle generals were equally despondent over the casualties their legions suffered throughout this campaign. The 5th Legion lost over eight thousand throughout the campaign while the 7th lost eleven thousand. The other legions fared as poorly or worse with the 4th Legion losing nearly seventeen telnics. The Benotrists legions suffered over twenty-three thousand between them. Nine thousand of the Benotrist casualties perished from heat, fatigue, and disease, suffering the privations of the Kregmarin Plain. The lack of water killed nearly as many men as Torry swords.

After suffering countless casualties attaining the Torries' defenses so determinedly, they discovered all the wells poisoned. Morac cursed Lore for such treachery, swearing to avenge his men who died of thirst after the battle was finished. All they gained was a pile of barren rocks. Nay, he reminded himself, they gained far more in the reduction of the Torry ranks. Lore foolishly extended his neck, and Morac struck it off. The Torry heartland was now open to his legions, and he would gladly exchange his lost men over and over again for that.

"Let it begin," Morac said, his monotone voice barely above a whisper.

*****

"Kai-Shorum!" Gargoyle war cries echoed through the still air, unnerving the men holding the walls as their dark forms dotted the sky.

"To arms!" men shouted, calling every able man to the battlements as the enemy drew nigh. Archers loosed their arrows in the thick gargoyle ranks, forsaking aim for volume, as they could hardly miss. The stricken tumbled midflight, dropping to the ground, short of the walls. The gargoyles enveloped Bacel, assailing the city from each direction.

With most of their soldiers slain at Kregmarin, the city conscripted every able man to hold the walls. Few had time to flee the city before the first gargoyle cohorts were upon them, slaughtering those who ventured beyond the city gates. Minister Fugoc warned his people of the fate of those who submitted to Tyro's tyranny. Death was a mercy to such a fate, and the city chose to fight to the death.

The lead gargoyle ranks set down upon the battlements, slashing desperately with their curved blades at the walls of spears and swords that met them. They fared poorly in the exchange, the defenders driving them from the ramparts, their bodies slipping over the outer walls to the ground below. The jagged gray walls lacked the height to tax the gargoyles' strength as the following ranks passed overhead, setting down behind the wall and within the city proper.

The men holding the walls fought to their utmost, driving spears into the gargoyles' unprotected flesh. Archers took aim behind them, releasing their volleys at a fevered pace. But their stern defense quickly yielded as more gargoyles set down behind them, upon them, and beside them.

Soldiers drove their swords into gargoyle bellies as others tackled them from behind, driving them to the wall's stone causeways while others stabbed them repeatedly. Others were cast from the battlements, their hurried screams echoing over the din. Gargoyles swarmed the narrow streets of the city like a raging stream flooding its banks. Men fought desperately, guarding their streets and homes until they were surrounded and cut to pieces. Gargoyles smashed in doorways, slaughtering anyone they found therein, dragging them into the streets where they feasted on their flesh.

Half the women and children had fled Bacel at the outset of the Kregmarin campaign, but thousands yet remained. Many huddled helplessly in their homes as their men guarded them with sword and shield. Others took up arms beside their men, unwilling to die like chattel. Others killed themselves and their kin, fearing to be taken alive by such creatures. Spirals of billowing smoke twisted above the dying city as fires raged unchecked.

The battle swiftly descended to hapless slaughter as the soldiers holding the walls were swept aside. The gargoyles drove into the heart of the city, converging upon the forum of Bacel like corka fish swarming a wounded Worken. They found the great structure vacant, as every official and soldier died holding the outer walls.

With their anticipated bloodlust denied, the creatures vented their fury upon the ancient edifice. Hundreds took up hammers, smashing the columns supporting the structure.

The cries of the wounded drifted mournfully above the din as the slaughter continued into the night. A thunderous crash echoed through the dying city as the city forum finally collapsed, spewing clouds of powdered dust throughout the heart of Bacel. By the following morn, the city was dead, its crumbling walls and broken dwellings charred and lifeless, like the skeletal remains of a mammoth beast laid bare in the morning sun.

Morac entered the city, passing through the sundered gate that twisted ajar as if torn apart by the hands of a giant. Leading his contingent of aides and fellow Elite, he rode through the bloodstained streets, navigating the piles of corpses and debris. The smell of burnt flesh hung in the fetid air, offending the senses, while the soulless eyes of the dead stared hauntingly forward. Morac dismissed the carnage and ruins, sparing the victims of his slaughter little heed.

They proceeded to the toppled remains of the city forum, where towering columns once stood but were now merely rubble. Several dozen pikes were driven into the ground, circling the debris with severed heads atop them. Sightless eyes and slackened jaws graced their pallid features as their heads faced outward as if guarding the ruins with their fallen spirits. The heads were those of the ruling council of Bacel that Morac's soldiers could identify, but they depended upon the frightened testimony of the few captives they kept alive long enough to be certain.

Morac's eyes studiously observed the head nearest him, finding macabre fascination with the fellow's gaunt features and pierced ears. The fellow was obviously a pampered oligarch of some standing. He held only contempt for such perfumed dandies. Such weaklings would learn their proper place in a world ordered by Tyro. Let the realms of the south tremble before his legions. Let them fight in vain or abase themselves before his majesty—submission or death. His campaign had just begun, and he claimed the 5th Torry Army, the Torry king, and Bacel.

"Lord Morac," Borgan declared, acknowledging him with his newest appellation, the proper tittle given to any regent or conqueror of a city. The Benotrist warrior Borgan ranked eighth among Tyro's Elite and acted as Morac's vice commander as the next ranking member of the Imperial Elite. He was boisterous and loud spoken with chiseled features and even-set gray eyes framed by his dark-brown mane.

Lord, Morac thought amusedly. He was now lord of Bacel, a city of rubble and bones where no living thing now dwelled. He would topple every edifice and sow the ground with salt so nothing would ever grow there again. Let his lordship be a reminder of what awaited those who defied his rightful dominion. Morac nodded, allowing Borgan to commence.

"Behold, my fellows, our commander who stands before you, bathed in glory and conquest. He is Morac, son of Morca, keeper of the golden blade, highest among the Emperor's Elite, and anointed to lead our legions in the conquest of the Torry realms. This day, he claims dominion of Bacel and the tittle of lord, as is his right!" Borgan declared to thunderous cheers.

Siege of Notsu
Two days hence

The people of Notsu awoke to the sight of the 6th Gargoyle Legion encamped to their south and west, their banners with a fractured white skull upon a field of gray blowing strongly in the summer breeze. By late day, the banners of the 11th Benotrist Legion could be seen to the north and east, bearing their sigil of crossed silver daggers on a field of black.

Many of the wealthier populace had already fled, stealing away once word reached Notsu of the defeat at Kregmarin. Only those escaping on ocran had any hope of outracing the enemy, as Morac had ordered the 6th Legion south and west to block the roads to Torry North and points south. The 6th Legion swept wide around

Notsu, slaughtering many of those attempting to flee before closing upon the doomed city.

With the setting sun, the people of Notsu gazed with laden hearts at the campfires dotting the horizon. With certain death waiting at their door, they could naught but wait, surrounded, friendless, and forlorn of hope. The enemy held at a distance, giving no inclination of their intent. There was no askance of parlay or demand of surrender, only an eerie silence that unnerved the bravest of Notsu's defenders. With barely two telnics of the city garrison able to man the walls, the city had no hope of repelling the feeblest of attacks.

Prior to the defeat at Kregmarin, the ruling council had ordered the city's cavalry contingent and a telnic of soldiers to reposition to the western holdfast of Surlone, nearer the Torry border, with much of the city's treasury and hundreds of women and children of the wealthier oligarchs. Word was sent, ordering those forces to flee further west to Torry North, regardless of Notsu's fate.

The following morn, a small detachment of Benotrist cavalry approached the north gate of the city under the blue flag of truce, offering parlay.

*****

The north gate of Notsu opened as the representatives of the ruling council rode forth with the agreed upon escort to meet the Benotrist commander mid distance between their lines. There ahead, upon a shallow rise, stood a dozen Benotrist cavalry beneath a banner bearing a golden sword upon a field of black. Minister Niotic released a measured breath, his heart pounding with trepidation as he drew nearer the Benotrist emissaries. His fellow council members followed in kind, despondent over their dire state.

The Benotrists were similarly clad in golden armor over blood-red tunics with a sun and moon emblazoned upon their breastplates divided by a sword with a whip woven along its length, the sigil of Tyro's Elite. Niotic reflected on the blatant disparity of their meager ten-man escort to the finest warriors of the Benotrist Empire. Of course, if they truly intended them harm, they could easily overwhelm Notsu's lightly guarded walls.

The mere askance of parlay proved the Benotrists desired to seize the city intact, either for logistical purposes or to spare their legions further casualties. Every soldier spent sacking Notsu was one less to assail Corell. Minister Niotic stopped short of the Benotrists, who received him in a semicircle while his fellow council members drew up beside him, their guards holding at their rear and flanks.

A Benotrist warrior ambled his mount forward of the others from the center of their line. Unlike the others, he wore a long black tunic that draped below his knees over black breeches and golden armor. A blood-red cape draped his shoulders, and fierce dark eyes stared through the sockets of an ape skull affixed to his helm, projecting malice and spite meant to unnerve them. The warrior removed his helm, revealing a strangely handsome face that did not match his cruel lips and the dangerous look that passed his eyes.

"Ministers, I am Morac, first among Emperor Tyro's Elite, keeper of the golden sword, general of the legions arrayed before you, and lord of Bacel," Morac said, greeting them with false pleasantry.

"I am Niotic, chief minister of Notsu. These are four of my fellow ministers—Purbis, Vabian, Voran, and Jorlu." Niotic waved an open hand to either side, regarding his fellow emissaries.

"Very well, Niotic. You have answered my parlay, which leads me to believe you are men of reason, perhaps more so than the men of Bacel," Morac began.

"Bacel has been taken?" Minister Vabian asked, taken aback by Morac claiming lordship of the city. The Notsu delegation noticed an amused sneer on the lips of the Benotrist warriors facing them, as if privy to a pun to which they were unaware.

"Bacel refused my generosity. Therefore, Bacel is no more. If you happen to visit your sister city, you shall find ash and rubble. No living thing dwells there. Her walls are smashed, buildings burnt or toppled, and the city forum reduced to a pile of debris. We have sown salt in her soil so nothing shall grow there again. Such is the fate of those who refuse me," Morac said, taking delight in the look that passed their collective faces.

"What of the people?" Minister Vabian asked.

Morac leaned forward in the saddle, fixing the minister with an unnerving stare. "Sword and flame," Morac whispered, his words laced with venom.

"Yet you claim lordship of a city that is no more?" Niotic asked.

"I *am* lord of Bacel, as is my right by conquest," he affirmed.

"A lord of bones and ash!" Vabian put voice to his thoughts.

"But lord all the same." Morac's false smile tightened.

"You asked for parlay, Lord Morac. I assume it is for more than prideful bluster?" Niotic asked, weary of Morac's boasts.

"Patience, Minister Niotic. We need not be enemies. I am willing to overlook your dalliance with the former Torry king. You lost most of your soldiers at Kregmarin for the benefit of your Torry masters. There is little profit in casting good coin after bad. The choice is yours, Ministers. Open your gates to my legions and submit to Tyro's dominion. Submit and your lives and families shall be spared, your property and wealth protected, though subject to taxation and oversight as vassals of the empire. You may even retain your posts as regents of Notsu—subject to my authority, of course. Or," Morac continued, drawing out the word to emphasize what would follow, "I can set my legions upon your city. Let the ruins of Bacel speak to my mercy."

Minister Niotic sighed, his heart heavy with defeat. They were surrounded and hopelessly outnumbered with no allies left to call upon. King Lore was dead and with him the only Torry army for hundreds of leagues. Two of every three of their soldiers died at Kregmarin. Though many of their women and children escaped to Torry North, Tro, and points south, most still remained. Were their lives worth what little damage they might inflict upon Morac's legions if they resisted?

"And we are to trust your word? We know well the fate of those who surrendered to your legions in Yatin and the tribes of Menotrists and Venotrists who have fallen under Tyro's yoke. Death is a sweeter mercy than to live as them," Minister Vabian snarled, his thoughts on the son and brother lost at Kregmarin.

"The choice is yours, Ministers. You have until midday to decide."

"You will have our answer," Niotic said.

"Of course," Morac said. "Though I have one specific condition that you must meet."

"And that is?" Niotic asked warily.

"Bring me the head of Minister Vabian."

*****

The head of Vabian was delivered to Morac as the gates of the city opened to receive his legions. The city garrison was ordered without, forced to join Morac's invasion of Torry North, and replaced by a Benotrist garrison force, whose loyalty was beyond reproach.

Morac discovered through his spies that the Torry chief minister Eli Monsh fled the city after the battle of Kregmarin. He had hoped to snare several members of Lore's inner circle during his campaign, but his net came up empty. He found the city granaries only half full, further straining his tenuous supply trains. He immediately ordered the 6th Gargoyle Legion west toward Corell with the other legions to follow as soon as they were able.

He moved stiffly around his chamber, hobbled by his broken leg, which he concealed beneath an ankle-length tunic. The wound was slowly healing, and he struggled to keep his condition hidden from enemy spies. The next morn, he was greeted by a familiar face as a gargoyle of large stature entered his temporary quarters at Notsu.

"Kriton," Morac said, greeting his comrade.

CHAPTER 19

She stood upon the battlement of an east-facing turret, her slender arms folded within the sleeves of her dress as she stared east, her eyes fixed to the horizon. The folds of her golden hair lifted in the evening breeze as her thoughts lingered on what lay beyond. Corry received no word on her father's fate since the messengers arrived bearing news that the army was hopelessly surrounded north of the crossroads. She found herself upon the battlements every evening, staring to the east, as if the answer carried on the wind. She steeled her heart to the dark possibilities preying on her conscious.

"Are you cold, Highness?" Terin's voice called out, drawing her attention to the young warrior standing behind her.

"I am well," she said, indifferent to the chill of the late-summer air. She took a moment to regard him as he stood with shoulders back, wearing a simple sand-colored tunic and sandals with his wondrous sword upon his hip. She found Terin's company strangely soothing, distracting her laden mind from its profound loneliness.

He found her each night upon the battlement after spending his day suffering Torg's harsh training. He had always cut an attractive build, having toiled on his father's farm, but now his muscles were sharply defined, a testament to Torg's merciless regimen. Whenever his duties to Torg ended, he bathed and reported to the princess to fulfill his duty as her protector.

"Stand," she commanded as he started to kneel, motioning him hither. He smiled, stepping to her side. They were not in the formal setting of the court, and though she enjoyed his deference at first, now it felt odd expecting it of him. He was more than her protector and servant; he was her friend. He was her…

"Cronus sends his regards," Terin said, distracting her thought.

"Oh, how goes his training?" she asked, shaking that final thought from her mind.

"Far better than mine, I am ashamed to say."

"You are a poor liar, Terin Caleph." She gifted him a smile, knowing what a poor liar he was. "You wield a sword as well as any other. I have seen you train."

"You are kind, Highness, but I doubt to ever be Cronus's equal. He wields a sword nearly as well as Master Vantel."

She could see through the lie, knowing Terin to flatter his friend to prove Cronus's worth in her eyes. She observed their mock battles in the arena and found them equally matched. Her father chose wisely in placing Cronus in the King's Elite.

"You need not boast Cronus's worth to me, Terin. I am very fond of him, as well as his lady," she said, having spent the better part of her day in Leanna's company.

"I do not boast on his behalf, Highness. Cronus is a far better swordsman than I," Terin confessed.

"If you insist, Terin, but you are still the crown's champion, and to you falls the burden that that tittle demands."

"And I hope to not fail in the measure." He sighed, not at all confident in the faith she placed in him.

"We each must uphold the trust placed in us by others, Terin. My father placed me upon the throne in his and my brother's absence. I must rule with wisdom equal to his own. Should I fail, then our kingdom shall suffer for my foolishness."

"That is different, Highness. You have been prepared to rule all your life with the finest tutors in all matters of the realm. You are kind, fair, and intelligent, far more than you give yourself credit. Your father trusted you for your ability, not out of loyalty to his daughter."

She was thankful her blush was hidden in the dim light. She never tired of Terin's flattery. Men rarely valued intelligence in a woman, unable to see beyond a comely face or feminine charm. Though she favored his admiration, she could hardly allow him to know its effect. "As you have been prepared for the role appointed you," she countered.

"I have only been training since arriving—" he began before she interrupted.

"You have been prepared since birth, Terin, though you knew it not. How many farm boys are taught the sword as you have been or taught to read and write? Almost none. Your father trained you in all arts of warfare. Did you truly believe your training was the equal to a regular citizen warrior? Most of our soldiers are farmers first and soldiers second. And your mother, she taught you more than to read and write. She taught you the history and geography of the realm, did she not?" His sheepish response confirmed her claim.

"You see, Terin, you have been well-schooled for the task appointed you. Your adventures since leaving your home have further prepared you, forcing you to bond with your sword, truly claiming its power as prophecy foretold."

It was his turn to blush, taken aback by her flattery. With such trust placed in him, he feared nothing more than failing her. Much of the prophecy that the king and Squid spoke of was beyond him. Even El Anthar, the Jenaii king, believed Terin was destined to fulfill some grand purpose.

"Have you eaten?" Corry asked, knowing full well that he hurried to bathe and present himself, forgoing such necessities so as not to keep her waiting.

"I can fetch something before bed," he said, ignoring his hunger.

"Come. I shall have food brought to my private sanctum. Galen has written several ballads he wishes to perform. Leanna and Cronus shall join us there," she offered, slipping her hand through his elbow, allowing him to escort her.

*****

> With sword and flame
> He wields in hand
> Below the airy peak he stands
> Warrior born

Battle forged
With cunning smites
Gargoyle horde

Torry born
Torry bred
Commander of unit led

Upon Tuft's Mountain
Woe to those who stand
Upon her slopes in numbers grand
Against a foe spawned of hate
Of untold legions in numbers great

Four legions upon the grassy sea thus came
With blood-red eyes and banners same
Kai-Shorum!
Their shouts then rang
Evil chants their voices sang

Across the fields few did ride
To set ablaze the evil tide
Fires set by his fell hand
Swept the scourge from blessed land

Torry born
Legend forged
Kenti! Kenti!
All the realm proclaim
Heralding their savior's name

Galen bowed once finished, the dim torchlight playing off the shimmering folds of his emerald robe. The others were seated before him in cushioned large stools. Cronus received the praise reluctantly, the memories bitter in his mind. Others were lauding his heroics as the stuff of legend. He knew better. His fell deeds and survival were the result of brave men helping him and dumb luck. But Galen wrote the ballad in his honor, and it was rude to disparage his effort. He would implore him, however, to include his comrades, placing their contribution equal to his own.

"That was beautiful," Princess Corry said approvingly.

"Shall I sing another, Highness? I have several more that—"

"The ballads are quite good, Galen. However, Cronus and Terin must retire, I am afraid. The evening grows late, and Master Vantel requires their full measure well before sunrise," Corry explained.

"Of course, Highness." Galen bowed again, preparing to leave when a servant girl hurriedly entered the chamber, kneeling before the princess.

"Telana," Corry greeted her, ordering her to rise.

"Highness, Commander Nevias waits without," the girl said.

"Send him in."

The girl curtsied before stepping without. Commander Nevias entered soon after, stopping to kneel as the princess waved him to forgo such curtesy.

"Highness, Commander Dar Valen has returned."

"Does he bring news of my father?" she asked evenly, struggling to quell her pounding heart. Dar Valen was the high commander of all Torry magantor forces. He was supposed to be with her father, supporting the army and scouting the enemy, his return to Corell boding ill for the Torry king.

"He does." Nevias's tone betrayed the awful truth.

"Fetch Master Vantel and Minister Veda. We shall convene in the king's inner sanctum," she ordered.

*****

"Wait here," the princess commanded Terin, ordering him to stand post outside the chamber. Torchlight filtered through the white stone archway of the council chamber. Royal guards stood to either side, brandishing shields in their left hands and spears in their right, crossing their spears over their shields as the princess passed within.

Unsure of where to stand, Terin stepped several paces away, standing along the wall and striking a similar pose as the palace guards. His thoughts were on the princess. He had escorted her hither, following her quick pace through the passageways of Corell. The news of Commander Valen's return likely confirmed her worst fears of her father's fate. She spoke not a word, her quickened pace and rigid posture belying her pounding heart.

The sound of sandals upon stone drew his eye to his left, along the corridor where Minister Veda's proud carriage approached with Merith and Aldo following dutifully behind, their hands tucked within the sleeves of their sun-colored tunics.

"Minister Veda." Terin bowed his head, greeting the minister of trade as he drew near.

"Champion Caleph." Minister Veda regarded him with a practiced greeting, stopping in front of Terin. "Merith and Aldo, wait here while I treat with the council," he ordered the two scribes before passing within.

"It is well to see you, Terin. How goes your training?" Aldo asked with genuine interest.

"I have sore muscles that I did not know I had." Terin smiled in all honesty.

"I am certain you shall overcome your discomfort." Aldo grinned.

"Merith," Terin greeted the other scribe. They shared a general dislike, but Terin wished to forswear their grievance if they could. Merith's superior air had dimmed as late since Terin's ascension. He could hardly consider Terin an uncultured peasant when the king conferred upon him the appellation of Champion of the Realm, a title created from ancient prophecy and left vacant for centuries until granted to Terin.

Of course, he didn't have to be pleased with this upstart's rapid ascension. He still wondered how the fabled Sword of Light fell into the hands of a farmer's son or how Terin managed to rescue Princess Corry, befriend the hero of Tuft's Mountain, and escape the Black Castle. With every deed, his legend grew, supplanting all others.

Merith had spent countless years laboring as Minister Veda's apprentice to attain position in the royal court. His grandsire was lord regent of Turlis, which guarded the southwestern border of Torry North. He could trace his rich bloodline to King Cot, whose daughter wed the regent of Turlis, yet his blood and accomplishment counted for naught when weighed against this jumped-up peasant. Minister Veda warned him to tread with caution in treating with Terin. The minister was privy to certain knowledge of Terin's heritage, which indicated he was more than he seemed.

"Terin, if you might forgive the asperity with which I treated you upon our first meet," Merith said with as much humility as he could suffer.

"No need to forgive if we are friends," Terin offered, extending his arm.

Merith was taken aback, unaccustomed to such gestures. He was too well-bred for such affinity but relented. If he was to gain a measure of civility with this stranger who had upset the balance of the royal court, he might as well lower himself by partaking in the informal greeting as they clasped forearms.

*****

"Highness." Dar Valen bowed as Corry entered the chamber. He stood beside Torg Vantel on the opposing wall with an oval-shaped table between them. A map of northwestern Arax was already unfurled across the wooden table with stones set to each corner to keep it flat. Commander Nevias and Minister Veda proceeded her, stepping to either side as they gathered about the table.

"Commander Valen, you have word of my father?" Corry asked, forgoing the pleasantries.

Dar Valen released a tired sigh. He was battle worn and saddle sore. His weathered cloak was torn and ragged, his tunic was bloodstained, and breastplate was dented. His tired eyes were sunken and bloodshot, a testament to his arduous journey. Whatever had befallen him since Kregmarin left visible scars on his beleaguered countenance.

"The 5th Army is gone. The enemy overwhelmed their position. If the king lives, he is most certainly a captive. My scouts observed the battle from afar, and our attempts to draw near were fiercely met. We suffered heavy casualties, forcing us eastward. We circled south around the enemy, fighting our way free over the days that followed," Dar said.

She felt his words rend her heart. Her throat tightened, strangling her voice in those tightening narrows. Once she knew that he was surrounded, she clung to the thinnest of hopes, but now those slender strands were severed. The chamber felt suddenly cold, though she stood numbly indifferent as the chill coursed her flesh.

"Princess." Torg Vantel circled the table, coming to her side. He placed his meaty hand upon her right shoulder, steadying her. Her blue eyes met his steely gray, regarding the craggy commander of the Elite. He was more a grandfather than a sworn sword, and oh, how she loved him. Corry patted his hand with her left, reassuring him.

"I shall shed tears when time permits, Master Vantel. Let us proceed," she said, stepping closer to the table. "Continue, Commander Valen."

Dar Valen relayed his harrowing tale, describing his final night with King Lore and his orders to raid the Benotrist supply trains along the central Kregmarin Plain. They destroyed much of the Benotrist water supply being ferried along that sparse and barren land, further strangling the troops surrounding the king. They were eventually driven off by enemy magantors.

Upon their return to the king, they observed the enemy assault overwhelming the Torry position from all sides. Benotrist magantors blocked their advance, sweeping the western sky and driving them east. They lost a dozen war birds while felling an equal number of the enemy. The days that followed saw their numbers dwindle, harried by Benotrist magantors and gargoyles with few safe lands to set down.

"We avoided the crossroads, uncertain of Notsu's or Bacel's loyalty with the destruction of our army. We came upon a contingent of Torry cavalry somewhere along this line." Dar ran a finger along the map, south of Notsu.

"How many?" Torg asked.

"Nigh a hundred. They were moving south and west to rendezvous with Commander Connly. It appears our cavalry survived the battle."

"What are Connly's intentions?" Commander Nevias asked.

"First is to consolidate his forces. They were spread into several subgroups prior to the battle, scouting the approaches to Kregmarin and the crossroads. I have no inclination to his plans beyond that," Dar answered.

"Were their eyes shut when the enemy surrounded our king?" Minister Veda accused, voicing the question they were all thinking.

"I was with our king at the outset. Commander Connly was responsible for scouting the swamps, forests, and rugged terrain north and east of Kregmarin. He was also tasked with destroying any enemy cavalry he came upon, which he did to the detriment of us all. The enemy cavalry drew him far enough east to allow a gargoyle legion to advance upon our east flank unseen. As soon as our magantors spotted the enemy, it was too late to withdraw.

"The king held the high ground against the Benotrist legion to his front and the gargoyle legion to his right. He bled the enemy to great effect until we discovered the other legions approaching. King Lore decided to attack the enemy's weakness, their water. The Benotrists left thousands dead during the crossing of the Kregmarin and even more as they waited in position to our direct north. Their water shortages forced them into battle before they were ready.

"The army had slain thousands when last I departed the king. By then, we were hopelessly surrounded with the other legions joining the siege. By that time, Connly was tasked with raiding the enemy supply trains wherever he could find them," Dar further explained.

"And the king remained? Why? He could have taken flight with you," Minister Veda asked curiously.

"King Lore would never abandon his men, nor would he surrender!" Dar said indignantly.

"No, he would not," Torg said with a voice far too quiet for the old warrior. "So he remained, bleeding the enemy to his end."

Corry could see it now, her father standing on a hillside upon that barren plain, facing overwhelming numbers yet fighting to his last, giving his last drop of blood to thin the enemy ranks knowing that each one he slew was one less to threaten Corell and her. He sacrificed himself so that she might prevail. She wanted nothing more than to retire to her private chambers and weep, to ease the burden of her broken heart, but she had no such luxury. Until her brother returned to claim his throne, the weight of the crown fell to her.

"Minister Veda, I name you chief minister until Chief Minister Monsh or Minister Antillius return," she declared. Eli Monsh was last reported at Notsu, though his current whereabouts were unknown. Squid Antillius was at Central City, preparing to take up post as the king's ambassador to Bansoch. Corry had ordered him recalled some time ago, but she received no word on his return or whereabouts.

"As you command, Highness." Lutius Veda bowed.

"Your first act is to order the evacuation of all our people east of Corell that dwell within thirty leagues of the road to Notsu. That is the likeliest path of the gargoyle and Benotrist legions," she said, eyeing the map carefully.

"It shall be done, Highness," Lutius answered, though it was likely too late for those living nearest the border.

"I don't want them brought here. Move them far west of Corell and off the main causeway. I want the road clear for General Bode. His army should already be en route," she said.

"He is still at Central City, reconstituting his army," Torg said.

"He was ordered hither days ago. Why does he tarry?" Nevias asked irritably.

"How long did it take you to muster the garrison of Corell?" Torg countered.

Nevias withdrew his accusation, for even now, the muster was not completely filled. Vassals sworn to Corell were spread far across the eastern Torry realm. General Bode's army suffered many casualties at Tuft's Mountain and was repositioned to Central City and then to the Torry's western border only to be ordered back to Central City to reconstitute and march for Corell. Bode's 3rd Army was further burdened by the integration of thousands of reserves to replenish his losses at Tuft's.

"The enemy shall strike Corell with all their might. We must hold until General Bodes arrives. I want our food stores fully supplied. Remove anyone not able to wield a sword or draw a bow. Every man or woman who remains must stand to post," Corry commanded. Torg regarded her proudly. She was truly her father's kin, resolute and unyielding. "How many cavalry have we in the palace?" she asked.

"A hundred mounts, Highness," Nevias answered, curious with her inquiry.

"Use them to spread word of our evacuation and prepare quarters for them at Besos," she said, tapping the map thirty leagues west of Corell, where the holdfast of Besos rested along the east-west road. "They shall be of more use in a siege, raiding the enemy's lines of supply, than trapped here," she added. There was also the additional benefit of not having to feed the ocran from the palace stores during the siege.

"Highness, perhaps we should rethink such a hasty—" Lutius began before she interjected.

"We prepare for siege and must sell our lives dearly if the enemy means to storm our walls. Anything less than our full measure shall be our endless shame. Make no mistake, Minister Veda. The hammer shall fall here, and we must plan accordingly and for the worst possible eventualities." Lutius bowed, respecting her steely resolve. "How many arrows have we fletched?" she asked.

"One hundred and forty thousand, Highness," Nevias said.

"And ballistae munitions?" she asked.

"Three thousand, which is as much as we can store," Torg said.

"I want the garrison committed to constructing bows and fletching arrows."

"It shall be done, Highness," Nevias assured.

And so it begins, she thought, her blue eyes focused on Notsu and Bacel upon the map before drifting north, where the Kregmarin Plain rested. "See to your men, Commander Valen," she said, concluding her council. Lutius, Nevias, and Dar bowed before stepping without, leaving Torg alone with the princess. She rested her hands upon the flat of the table as if the world weighed upon her. Torg stood beside her, his stoic countenance betraying nothing of the turmoil raging within.

"How do you do it, Torg?" the princess asked, her throat tightening with emotion.

"Loss is a part of life, Corry. You know that as well as anyone."

"Then life is cruel."

He touched her shoulder, turning her about and lifting her chin, her watered eyes meeting his cool gray. The old warrior's heart had never felt more brittle, staring into those sad blue pools. She was like a granddaughter to him, and he cherished her so. He took her in his arms and held her as she wept. The sorrows she fiercely guarded poured forth like a breaking dam. She cried until her tears ran dry, holding tightly to his chest until fatigue claimed her waning strength.

"Thank you, Torg." She smiled weakly, pulling briefly away as she regarded the craggy master of arms.

"I weep for him as well, my dear." A rare, gentle smile passed his lips as he thought of King Lore.

"I may be alone, Torg, but you are not. TELL HIM. Tell him before it is too late and regret plagues the days left to you. Do not let your pride rob you of your joy."

"You know?" He lifted a curious brow.

"Yes, and so should he."

"His burdens are many, and I will not further his load, not now anyway."

"It is not a burden, Torg. He is a wonderful boy, a fine warrior, and a better man. Tell him before it is too late."

"Very well, but not tonight," he relented, knowing he could never deny her when she used those disarming eyes of hers.

CHAPTER 20

Haroom! The sound of horns echoed through the palace, jarring him awake. Terin stumbled from his bed, donning his tunic and sandals and fixing his sword belt around his waist as the horns sounded again, thundering through the bowels of the palace, calling the garrison to arms. Cronus was already out the door of their barrack, his breastplate, greaves, and helm in place.

Terin struggled to match his pace, rushing to keep within sight of Cronus as they traversed the narrow corridors that led to the upper battlements above. They ran apace through the corridors and stairwells with dozens of others crowding the passageways, hindering their ascent.

Within minutes, they passed through the final archway that emptied onto the causeway behind the inner battlements. The morning sun broke upon Terin's face as he cleared the archway. He winced briefly against the glare before following Cronus up the stone steps to one of the north-facing turrets of the inner battlements.

They were greeted by the sight of hundreds of soldiers taking up position as they ascended the north turret, stepping onto the causeway of the inner battlement, overlooking the outer battlements below. Soldiers lining the ramparts pointed excitedly to the northeast, Terin's eyes following where they indicated. There, northeast of Corell, hundreds of dark-winged figures dotted the horizon—*gargoyles*.

Many days had passed since Commander Valen's arrival, heralding the news of the king's demise. Their magantor scouts had skirmished with Benotrist patrols along the eastern approaches of Corell, shielding the enemy advance. Thousands of people had flooded the palace in recent days, driven out of lands where the enemy advanced, relaying harrowing tales of gargoyle savagery. Many more failed to outpace the enemy as the gargoyles swept over the land like a foul tempest.

The princess ordered the survivors to continue their way west, not wishing to tax the palace's stores, which were needed for the siege. Men capable of wielding swords were allowed to remain to supplement Corell's auxiliaries. These hastily assembled volunteers numbered nearly two full telnics. Another three telnics were gathered from the surrounding holdfasts, which were deserted in the face of the overwhelming force arrayed against them. These five telnics joined the ten telnics of the palace garrison and the two thousand archers already assembled at Corell.

No word had reached Corry of the whereabouts of the 1st and 2nd Torry Cavalry or their commanders, Tevlin or Connly. Whether they lived or perished was beyond anyone's guess, and with the Benotrist magantors contesting the skies, they were blind to what awaited to the east.

"Over there!" Shouts rang out, men shifting their gaze to the northwest, where more gargoyles took up position. Cronus narrowed his eyes, struggling to ascertain their numbers from this great distance, but he could only guess their visible strength in the hundreds. Doubtless, many thousands waited beyond. "They're establishing a perimeter," Cronus thought aloud. "Come. Master Vantel will expect us at Zar Crest." He pointed to the nearest observation platform jutting above the inner keep.

*****

Corry rested her hands upon the rampart of Zar Crest, overlooking the enemy taking up position along the breadth of their northern horizon. With each passing moment, another group seemed to appear somewhere along a wide arc that ran from their northeast to their direct west. The lookouts atop the Tower of Celenia spotted another large contingent southeast, just beyond the sight of those manning the lower battlements.

"Our lookouts have spotted a sizable element straddling the road west, just short of the forest," Commander Nevias informed her.

"I do not see Benotrist magantors," Corry observed.

"Nor do I. They seem to be concentrated to our east, or so Commander Valen reports."

"I want his birds in the sky posthaste. Have him scout our northern, western, and southern approaches and verify the legion that surrounds us!" she commanded.

"Alen!" Nevias called him forth.

"Commander," Alen said, stepping forward, clad in a simple tan tunic and thick-soled sandals, the uniform of a palace messenger, with a dagger sheathed upon his hip.

"Did you hear what the princess said?" Nevias asked, appraising the messenger with a discerning eye. Alen had earned the commander's trust since his placement in his service.

"Yes, Commander." Alen bowed nervously. He felt out of place among the commanders of rank, Royal Elite, and courtesans gathered upon the observation platform. The former slave could not help but feel intimidated standing freely among such a gathering, recalling his days of servitude in Tyro's court, toiling under the lash. But here, he stood as a free man, serving of his own volition. Nevias asked him to repeat the princess's command and sent him off to the magantor platforms, where Commander Valen was posted.

Torg stood at Nevias's side, his arms folded over his chest. While the others observed the enemy gathering along the horizon, Torg fixed his eye upon their own men, examining the placement of each unit and flax positioned along the battlements. It would be some time before the enemy assailed the palace, if at all, but they must be ready. Most of the garrison was recently mustered and unaccustomed to the lay of the castle. That needed to be fixed, and he would order Nevias to emphasize battle drills over the coming days until the men could attain their posts in their sleep.

"Master Vantel!" Cronus greeted, clearing the open stair that ascended the observation platform. Torg waved them hither, and Cronus and Terin stepped forth. Terin's eyes were drawn to the sights beyond, as the jagged ramparts overlooked most of the palace roof.

From these airy heights, the surrounding land shrank in the distance in panoramic splendor. Zar Crest rose imperiously above the inner keep with an open stair wrapped around its inner walls. Only Corell's towers exceeded its impressive height, their spiraling citadels piercing the sky above.

The platform of Zar Crest spanned nearly ten meters abreast with a gray stone floor and jagged white ramparts. The surfaces of the walkways and floors of the palace battlements and platforms had a rough stone surface to prevent slippage when wet with rain or soaked in blood. Besides Torg, Terin recognized Commander Nevias, Minister Thunn, and a dozen members of the Royal Elite in their distinct blue tunics and polished armor, along with several commanders of lesser rank. But most of all, he noticed the princess staring northward with her back to them.

"We'll forgo your lessons for today. I have another task for you to attend," Torg said. Corry turned, her blue eyes meeting Terin's as he received his orders. His training was nearly complete, though Torg never told his pupils how long their instruction would last or end. Whenever she asked the craggy taskmaster of Terin's progress, he would only snort and claim, "The boy has much to learn," though she could not miss the pride in his voice whenever he spoke of *the boy*. No matter Torg's natural pessimism with the readiness of his charges, she knew Terin was ready to take up his post as Champion of the Realm.

*****

"How many times did Master Vantel want us to do this?" Terin asked as they walked along the wide causeway that separated the outer ramparts from the walls of the inner battlements. The walkway ran the circumference of the castle, connecting each turret and wall throughout. At forty feet abreast, it was wide enough to quickly move soldiers from one side of the palace to the other. Soldiers stood watch at the outer battlements, overlooking the enemy now taking up position south and east of Corell. The initial alarm eventually waned, and Commander Nevias ordered most of his troops to stand down and resume their supplementary duties.

"Three more times," Cronus said, recalling Torg's instruction. He had tasked them to familiarize themselves with the layout of the castle, starting with walking the breadth of the inner battlements a dozen times over. Having completed that task, they moved on to the outer battlements. The morning was growing late, and Terin wondered what Torg would ask of them next and guessed he would want them to traverse the countless stairwells that led to the bowels of the massive fortress. He wondered at what point their legs would simply fall off.

"Seems like our thousandth lap," Terin said.

"Master Vantel wants us to be able to do this in our sleep," Cronus said. Terin hardly ever complained about the mundane tasks Torg assigned them, and Cronus wondered if his young friend was growing weary from their endless training. He was tired as well but hardly paid it mind.

No rigorous task could dim his spirit after suffering the hospitality of the dungeon of Fera. His muscles were taxed but growing strong, and he held Leanna in his arms at the end of every day. The princess allowed her to remain to serve as her lady-in-waiting after most women were removed to Besos and places further west.

Perhaps Terin's thoughts were on the whereabouts of Arsenc and Yeltor. Cronus remembered when Commander Valen brought word of the king's fate. They received no further news since that fateful night. Whatever fate that befell their comrades could only be surmised. Cronus doubted they survived, and part of him hoped that they did not rather than be taken captive. He well knew the gruesome fate of those captured by the Benotrists and their gargoyle comrades. He reflected sadly that if Arsenc had perished, he was the sole survivor of his unit. He shook the thought from his mind, fearing to dwell on their demise lest he weep.

Terin noticed his friend's sudden dour mood, knowing full well what brought about these brief somber moments that came over Cronus from time to time. "We may see them again, Cronus. We have overcome impossible odds more than once," he said.

"Improbable odds, perhaps, but not impossible, Terin. I was spared my fate by Raven's pistol and your sword. Even then, it was a close-run affair. Arsenc and Yeltor have no such advantage. We can hope that providence favors them if we wish, but if they were at Kregmarin with the king, they are as good as dead or worse."

"I fear for them, but not knowing is maddening enough." Terin sighed. Reports of happenings to their east were few and sketchy at best. What of the Torry cavalry? Commanders Connly and Tevlin's whereabouts were anyone's guess. They could all be dead as far as they knew. What of Chief Minister Monsh? Did he remain at Notsu, or did he escape? So much was uncertain.

Terin's gaze was suddenly drawn to the southwest, where the open farmlands met the edge of the Zaronan Forest. There, above the treetops, a pair of magantors swept overhead, driving hard for Corell. The cause of their urgency was soon revealed as a dozen Benotrist magantors emerged behind them, their riders loosing arrows as they drew near. A strong impulse took him, and Terin ran toward the open archway up ahead, passing under the raised portcullis beneath the inner battlements.

"Terin!" Cronus called out as he struggled to keep pace. Terin raced along the causeway of the inner palace, circumventing the opening of the inner courtyard, which rested some 160 feet below. He burst through the inner keep, racing up the stairwells to the uppermost levels, where the west-facing magantor platform jutted prominently from the palace wall. The palace guards posted through-out the inner keep seemed strangely indifferent as he sped through each door and passageway.

Terin burst into the magantor stable, finding the bird that bore him from Fera strangely saddled and waiting, as an attendant had prepared it for its new master. "Wait. You can't..." a young stable attendant protested as Terin pressed a palm to the bird's head. The magantor dipped its massive head, nudging Terin with its beak, acknowledging their kinship. Terin grasped its reins, drawing the bird out of its stall. The magantor stables were circular platforms with stalls lining their periphery and facing inward.

"Terin!" Cronus called out as he climbed into the saddle, guiding his bird through the entrance that led to the open platform without. Terin ignored his friend's call, his eyes transfixed, staring ahead and blind to everything, save for the task at hand.

Cronus followed after him through the archway, stopping midstride lest his momentum carry him over the lip of the open platform that jutted from the upper wall of the keep. He stared dumbstruck as the magantor bounded off the lip of the platform, its giant wings catching the air, soaring over the battlements below.

*****

"Look!" a soldier cried out as the approaching magantors came into view, closing desperately from the southwest. Corry stepped briskly across the command platform, her eyes fixed on the distance where the Torry magantor scouts came into view. Their movement seemed gauche and uncharacteristically slow, as if under duress. A moment later, the source of their affliction came into focus as a number of Benotrist magantors followed close behind. Even from afar, she could see arrows loosed upon them, most fluttering harmlessly in the wind.

The moments passed painfully as the magantors pressed on, sweeping beyond the forest and over the endless green fields separating the palace from the forest edge. She saw an arrow strike true, piercing a magantor's wing. "Packaww!" The great avian's scream echoed dully in the air, but it continued on. Scores of gargoyles clustered upon the fields below took flight, their clumsy wings unable to attain the speed or height of the far swifter magantors.

"Launch a magantor flax!" Corry commanded. If they wished to contest the skies of Corell, then she would oblige them.

"It seems someone already has," Nevias said as a dark-feathered avian swept over the outer wall, turning sharply to its left toward the fray. Torry magantors had golden, white, and light-gray feathers. Only one magantor was black in color.

"Terin." She gasped, her eyes finding him upon the beast as he shrank from sight, speeding off to aid their returning scouts.

Terin urged his mount onward, driven by a mysterious power coursing his flesh, a power he must obey but never comprehend. He drew near enough to see the strained faces of the Torry riders, their frantic eyes betraying their sorry state. The magantor to his left flew weakly, arrows piercing its left wing. The one off his right lingered farther back, blood staining its hind quarter, though Terin could not see the source of its terrible wound from afar. A Benotrist magantor drew up behind them with a rider and an archer. The archer rose up in the saddle, loosing an arrow. The Torry rider shifted, the arrow grazing his ear before fluttering away.

The archer ducked behind the rider, notching another arrow, his comrade pushing their war bird closer. The archer again rose up in the saddle, his eyes fixed upon his prey with rapacious glee, the Torry rider a mere stone's throw as he steadied his aim. *Whoosh!* The archer's eyes drew wide as another magantor swept overhead of their prey, coming straight toward them before dipping below their magantor's right wing, its rider brandishing a silver blade bathed in azure light.

The power of the sword coursed Terin's flesh as he swept overhead the Torry magantor, whose sole rider returned his stare, rooted in place with slackened jaw. The Torry had no time to ascertain if Terin was friend or foe as Terin swept overhead. Terin cleared the Torry magantor by the slimmest of margins before diving below the Benotrist war bird that trailed just behind. Hoisting his father's sword, he passed under the enemy's right wing, slicing the appendage clean off.

"Packaww!" the stricken bird screamed, tilting to its right before tumbling from the sky, its riders thrown clear, their frantic cries growing fainter through their descent. The trailing Benotrists struggled to comprehend what their eyes beheld as Terin's bird banked left, crossing the face of the nearest foe.

He dipped below the beak of his prey, his magantor tilting sharply to its right so as not to tangle its right wing with the other's claws as Terin brought his blade across the beast's neck before passing on. The magantor's head lifted from its neck before slipping free, tumbling to the distant ground as its lifeless body soared ever briefly before dropping in kind, its riders clinging to its corpse through its descent.

Corry stood spellbound upon Zar Crest as the battle unfolded before her in horrific splendor. Even from afar, she could see the riders of the second magantor tossed clear before its headless corpse smashed into the fields below, their bodies following with equal effect. Her heart went to her throat as Terin passed between two others, his sword glowing with its otherworldly light. "Where are our magantors?" she repeated, wondering when they would launch. No sooner had she asked than a dozen Torry war birds spewed from their platforms to join the fray.

*****

Terin shifted, leaning left, he and his bird following the will of the blade as an arrow whizzed past while he soared through the disordered formation. Several broke away, urging their birds to escape the madness of Terin's fell blade. Others remained, attempting to circle him to fire their arrows. One archer drew his bow as they drew near, Terin's chest resting in his line of sight. He released the shaft, his expectant eyes following its course.

Terin's sword came across his chest, splintering the arrow harmlessly away as his war bird passed under the offending magantor. He thrust his sword into the air, running its blade along the Benotrist war bird's belly, spilling its innards as he passed.

Another arrow whizzed past, grazing his magantor's neck as he turned sharply left. The bird dove headlong, avoiding another volley, the wind pressing Terin's face through the sudden descent. Scores of gargoyles swarmed over the fields below like small insects from these airy heights. He pulled up halfway through his descent, leveling out as he craned his neck, searching the sky above for his foes.

The Benotrist flax commander cursed the Torry interloper and his wretched sword that slaughtered his men and birds at will. Several of his men sped off, and their original prey was drawing farther away. He collected his remaining five mounts, forsaking the fleeing Torries, focusing their efforts on their true foe, the fair-haired warrior with the glowing sword. "Kai-Shorum!" he commanded, sweeping down after Terin.

Terin leveled out from his dive before angling southward. The Benotrist war birds swept downward, closing upon Terin as he circled about, meeting their charge with blade raised in defiance of their numbers. His mount sped forth, obedient to his will as the enemy drew nigh, sweeping down from above.

*****

"The fool," Corry whispered despondently as Terin drove headlong into the line of magantors. They swept down from the sky above, their war cries steeling their shaken courage. Corry winced as Terin passed from view, lost amid the enemy. Only the glow of his sword stood out among the cluster of men and fowl.

Another magantor tumbled from the melee, its riders flailing through their descent as they were thrown clear. The stricken beast fell vertically like a lifeless stone. Another moment passed before another rider was thrown from the melee, his limbs flailing helplessly through his descent. Corry's fears that the poor fellow was Terin eased as she followed the arc of his blade, still flashing amid the fray. She caught her breath as his magantor broke in the clear but cursed his idiocy as he circled back to reengage.

Terin slashed at a passing foe, severing the magantor's wingtip. The beast thrashed painfully, nearly throwing its riders as it scurried away. He brought his sword across his chest, knocking away another shaft before passing underneath the offender's beast to deliver a mortal blow. The Benotrist rider forced his mount into a dive, knowing Terin's intent.

Terin quickly realized his folly as the Benotrist magantor suddenly dropped, nearly knocking him from his saddle. Terin drove onward, unable to raise his blade as his magantor grazed the other's underside as it passed. Terin held tight, pressing his body flat to the magantor's back as the enemy bird passed overhead. The blow knocked his magantor off course as it passed. It jerked suddenly, struggling to right its course.

Terin held tight as the bird leveled out. No sooner had he lifted his eyes than another Benotrist war bird drew alongside him, its archer rising up in the saddle to loose a bolt. The Benotrist shifted his aim to the neck of Terin's magantor. They quickly learned that targeting Terin was folly due to the power of his sword. The archer smiled briefly, the distance too short to miss.

Whoosh! Massive talons snatched the archer from the saddle, snapping his bow and piercing his chest. A light-gray blur swept before Terin's eyes as a Torry magantor lifted the archer away before releasing him clear of his mount, his hapless screams fading through his descent. A second Torry magantor plucked the second rider, tossing him aside, his mount flying on without him.

The madness of the blade eased as Torry magantors swept the sky, allowing Terin to take stock of his surroundings. They were some distance from the palace with hundreds of gargoyles flooding the fields below, snarling futilely, unable to attain their altitude. He could see a few Benotrist magantors fleeing in the distance. The Torry magantor commander directed him back to the palace. Suddenly, Terin was unfamiliar with his magantor skills, as if his ordeal was naught but a dream, returning to the palace unsteady in the saddle.

*****

Terin's return to the palace was met with slackened jaws and awed whispers. Dar Valen's magantor had set down moments before his own, and the Torry commander passed his war bird off to an attendant. He awaited Terin as the Torry champion set down on the platform outcropping. Cronus waited farther back, at the stable entrance, observing the outstretched talons of Terin's magantor land upon the platform.

He had seen Terin's handiwork at Costelin and again at Fera, but what he just did defied all reason. He maneuvered the magantor far easier than any trained rider was capable. It was as if he and the beast were of one mind. The entire palace now witnessed his fell deed, removing any doubt of the king's judgment in conferring upon him the appellation of Champion of the Realm.

"Champion Caleph!" Dar Valen hailed as Terin set down, his magantor's talons scraping the platform's stone floor.

"Commander Valen." Terin struggled to recall his name as if waking from a dream. He struggled dismounting as if unfamiliar with the process.

"Are you well?" Dar Valen asked, steadying Terin as he staggered briefly.

"Terin," Cronus said, stepping near as others emerged from the stables, gathering round.

"I...I am fine," Terin answered weakly.

"Where did you learn to fly like that?" one of the riders asked. Not even the most experienced magantor handlers could maneuver a war bird so deftly.

"I..." Terin couldn't answer.

"You saved us, Champion," another fellow spoke. Terin recognized the faces of the riders. They were the ones beset by the enemy when he intervened.

"It...it was my honor," Terin acknowledged, uncomfortable with their praise and adulation.

"TERIN!" The unmistakable voice of Torg Vantel echoed from the stable archway as the grizzled warrior stormed across the open platform, where the surrounding lands stretched endlessly in the background. The others backed quickly away like a heard of douri as Torg entered their midst.

"Master Vantel." Terin bowed as Torg stopped but inches away.

"The princess summons you. She awaits in the throne room."

"I...wh..." Terin stumbled over his words, his mind still out of sorts, wondering why she demanded an audience in so formal a setting.

"Stop tripping over your tongue, boy, and do as you are bid!" Torg reprimanded, and Terin sheepishly bowed and hurried off. Cronus meant to follow when Torg commanded him to stay before turning his steel-gray eyes to Commander Valen. "Commander Nevias awaits you in the council chambers. Bring the scouts who have just returned. We shall hear their report firsthand."

"Aye, Master Vantel." Dar Valen bowed before ordering his scouts to follow him through the archway.

After the stable attendants cleared the platform, escorting the returning magantors to their stables, Cronus found himself alone with Torg, who stood on the flat stone outcropping. Torg seemed deep in thought, his steel-gray eyes fixed on the distant horizon where the open fields met the Zaronan Forest.

He had stood upon the platform so many times through his years of service to the crown but never truly seeing. The view was breathtaking and dangerous. A few steps to his left, right, or front and he could easily fall to his death. He could feel the tingling sensation run north of his ankles just standing in the center of the platform. A step in any direction would send that strange affliction to his chest and beyond.

At that moment, Cronus could see Torg's true age, the sunlight exposing the silver in his dark mane. It was then he realized that Torg was frightened, not for his own life but for Terin's. Perhaps Minister Veda's suspicions were true.

"What compelled Terin to undertake such a foolish act?" Torg asked, his eyes still fixed in the distance.

"The sword. There can be no other explanation." Cronus sighed, stepping beside Torg while looking to the distance in kind.

"The enemy will not attack tonight or anytime soon. Get some rest, and we'll continue with your training come sunrise." Torg sighed, leaving unsaid much of what he intended to say. Cronus bowed and withdrew before stopping midstride. His brain reproached him, cautioning him to move along, but his heart bade him stay.

"Whatever kinship you share with Terin, he deserves to know." Cronus stepped away before Torg could answer or reprimand him for taking such liberty. Torg respected Cronus far too much to ever scold him as he did Terin. Nor could he deny the truth of Cronus's perceptive words.

*****

Terin took a deep breath before entering the throne room. The guards appeared to be expecting him, allowing him to pass unchallenged. His mind was slowly clearing from the madness that the sword invoked, but the strain on his body was evident by his weary countenance and taxed posture. He was uncertain what to expect upon entering, expecting the princess to be upon the throne with a retinue of guards, courtesans, and retainers. The purpose of her summons weighed heavily on his mind, but it certainly boded ill.

The usually vibrant chamber was poorly lit and empty, save for the lone figure standing in its center. Corry received him with her slender arms folded over her silver gown, her blue eyes boring into him as he stepped nigh. "Stand," she commanded as he began to kneel, forgoing such protocol at this time.

"Highness," he acknowledged, suddenly wary of her cool demeanor.

"My father placed great trust in you, Terin Caleph. I have similarly committed to trust you and my father for so placing you in our service." Terin did not know how to answer or if there was even a question that she expected a response. "When you ventured to Fera to aid Cronus's rescue, I counseled against it but did not forbid it. You pledged your word and honored your promise. Now you are pledged to me."

"Have I failed—" he began to ask before she cut him off.

"By what authority did you decide to commandeer a magantor and fly off with such reckless abandon?" Her eyes narrowed with lethality.

"I...I—they needed help," he said, his answer sounding nothing like he intended.

"Your duty is to defend the palace, not risk your life and your sword for whatever adventure you care to explore. You ventured far from the palace walls. What if you were slain or captured? What if the enemy gained your precious sword to add to the blade they already possessed?" she asked. *What if you died?* she wanted to ask, but the very thought rent her heart.

"I am sorry, Highness. I—the sword calls to me, and...and I cannot refuse it," he said tiredly.

"Are you the blade's master or its slave?"

"It's not like that. It's—"

"It is like that, Terin. You must master the weapon, or it shall master you," she said, her voice softer now. For some strange reason, she couldn't bear to be angry with him.

"I shall do as you wish, Princess."

"You are no one's slave, Terin, or no *thing's* slave. You are stronger than that." She placed a hand to his cheek, her soft palm soothing his face. Staring into his eyes, she could easily discern the toll the sword claimed. She ordered him to rest and report to Torg come sunrise as she left to meet with her commanders.

*****

The commanders were already in a heated debate when Corry entered the council chamber, gathered about as the scouts pointed out their findings on the map rolled across the table.

"Highness." Torg's voice silenced them as she took her place at the table, waving them to remain standing.

"What have you?" she asked.

"Highness, these are the scouts that returned." Dar Valen waved an open hand, indicating the men to his immediate right and across the table from her.

"Your names?" she asked.

"I am Havis Darm, Highness," one said, his diminutive stature and fair hair a stark contrast to his comrade's lanky frame and coal-black mane.

"And Dalin Vors, Highness," the lanky-framed one confirmed.

"And you are the men who were harried by the enemy short of our walls?" she asked.

"Yes, Highness. If not for the king's champion, we would not have attained the palace," the one called Havis acknowledged gratefully.

"Yes, you may thank him when next you meet. Now what news have you?" she asked.

"Yes, Highness," Havis continued. "The gargoyles that surround Corell are of one legion. Their sigil is a fractured white skull upon a field of gray."

"The 6th Gargoyle Legion," Torg confirmed.

"They have spread their lines in a wide arc from the east, around the north, and concentrating heavily to our west, where they block the main road west. It is there where they are constructing palisades and trenches to waylay any reinforcements we might expect from Central City and points west. They are also concentrated to our south and east. We counted nearly eight telnics along this line." Havis ran a finger along the southeastern approaches of Corell. "We spotted several more telnics due south around…here." He ran his finger in a circle some leagues due south of Corell, far beyond where they were ordered to scout.

"It was there where the enemy magantor patrol struck us in force," the one called Dalin confirmed.

"Why would their magantors be concentrated to our south? We have no armies of consequence there," Gais Luven, commander of the north wall, asked.

"It is the likeliest route of our Jenaii allies," Commander Nevias said. Torg liked it not. Magantors were meant to stop other magantors from seeing what you did not wish them to see. What were they masking in the south?

"I doubt the Jenaii shall soon come to our aid. Our messengers to El-Orva have yet to return, and the Naybins are demonstrating in force along their border," Corry said, not willing to place false hope in a deliverance unlikely to appear. Their greatest hope lay in General Bode breaking the enemy line and reinforcing the palace before the rest of Tyro's legions arrived.

"Anything else of note?" Torg asked the two weary scouts.

"No, Master Vantel," they said in unison.

"Attend to your mounts and get some food and rest," he commanded.

"Our magantors are both badly wounded. The Matrons are seeing to their care," Havis explained.

"I will find other duties for you to attend until they recover. Dismissed," Commander Valen ordered. The men bowed and withdrew.

"What word have we from General Bode?" Corry asked as the scouts stepped without.

"Nothing since his last missive four days ago," Torg said, regarding the message that General Bode had recalled his telnics from the western border and was preparing to march to their aid.

"Commander Valen, I want you to take all but one flax of our remaining magantors north to Cropis," she said, tapping the northern stronghold that rested in the Plate foothills. Cropis was the central base and training ground of the Torry magantor cohorts and guarded against gargoyle incursions across the Plate. Its lord was Torgus Vantel, son of Torg. "Consolidate our magantors, and sweep the enemy war birds from the sky!" she commanded.

Six days hence

By late morn, long columns of gargoyle reinforcements were spotted by the lookouts atop the Tower of Celenia, drawing from the east like a massive serpent slithering across the land. The castle was again called to arms, and Torry soldiers took up position along the battlements as the enemy paraded along the horizon, circling to the south. By midday, the new arrivals began constructing defensive works around their encampments and unfurling their banners in the late-summer breeze, bearing the black-mailed fist upon a field of white, the sigil of the 5th Gargoyle Legion. The 5th Legion replaced the gargoyles holding the southern approaches of Corell, freeing them to strengthen the perimeter elsewhere.

*****

She leaned back against his chest as his arms wrapped protectively around her, drawing her tight. They stood upon the upper battlements, gazing as the setting sun slipped below the horizon.

She took comfort in his warmth in the cool night air. Leanna sighed as Cronus kissed the back of her head, the small affection meaning more to her than jewels or gold. She took solace in his company, savoring these precious moments.

They had so little time together, his duties occupying the greater part of his day. Each morning, he and Terin trained with Torg. Their remaining hours were spent standing post at different parts of the palace to familiarize themselves with each part's defense, function, and importance. That left the waning hours of each night to share with her.

The sound of axes and shovels echoed in the distance, carrying upon the wind as a constant reminder of the enemy's activity. There were two legions now arrayed against them, but Cronus noted that each was far below peak strength. Perhaps they were thinned by the battle at Kregmarin. He wondered how many more legions were en route and what strength they might have. These glum facts played cruelly on Cronus's mind. He regretted not sending Leanna away, far away from these wretched creatures that surrounded them.

"You're doing it again." Leanna sighed tiredly, resting the back of her head against his chest.

"I can't help wishing you were elsewhere, somewhere safer than here."

"To what end?"

"To what end? There are two legions surrounding the palace and more on their way. What hope have we? I am not prone to panic, nor do I easily frighten, but I can't bear to see you..." His voice trailed, unable to put words to his fears.

"To what end, my love?" she repeated. "To die sooner here or later at Central City is but a respite from the inevitable. And what life is there for me if you die here? To leave would gain me naught but a brief time to mourn you while awaiting my doom. I choose to stay with you, my love. We've spent precious time apart, and only a miracle unlooked for returned you to my arms. To send me away would only consign me to a torturous fate. Would you truly wish me to suffer so? I would rather spend my last days, however few or many they may be, with you."

"So be it." He sighed, holding her tight as he pressed his lips to the top of her head.

Two days hence

The afternoon found Terin standing post at Corell's main gate, centered on the castle's north wall. The massive gate rested at the end of the central tunnel that ran south toward the open courtyard. The gate itself spanned twenty meters abreast with a grated portcullis lowered over its face. Behind the portcullis were foot-thick wooden doors plated in iron, each ten meters wide, that opened inward. They were currently opened, affording the guardians of the gate to see through the grated portcullis.

To bar the gate for battle, the portcullis was lowered, and the two massive doors were closed and barred with a second gate descending from above. The second gate rested in front of the portcullis and the first gate. It was nearly ten inches thick and forged of solid iron and required massive winches to raise and lower it. Within the tunnel, nearest the gate, guards stood post upon a series of platforms that lined its length with battlements jutting from its sides, running the length of the tunnel. Through all its storied history, the walls of Corell were never breached.

Terin spent the better part of his time learning the intricate workings of the three parts of the gate. The grated portcullis was always lowered at night and throughout a siege, such as now. The doors that opened within remained open to afford the defenders a clear view of happenings without. They remained open throughout the day unless the enemy drew near. The larger solid iron gate rested in front of the portcullis and was nearly impossible to dent, let alone breach. It had stood unyielding for centuries. Archer holes also lined the tunnel, along with several other gates, further hindering any assaults through the heart of the palace. Terin could only marvel at the design and majesty of Corell, wondering how the men of the ancient Middle Kingdom ever created such a wonder.

Though he was the king's champion, Terin had not completed his formal training and, thus, did not wear the distinctive blue tunic and silver armor of the Elite. Nor was he clad in the polished steel armor and white tunic of a Torry warrior. He wore a simple tan tunic and nondescript armor. Corry desired that he dressed according to his new station, but Torg stated that he had not yet earned such a privilege. Terin truly did not care, only wishing to learn what was asked of him, and this day meant learning the operation and defense of the main gate.

Terin stared north through the grating of the portcullis at the gargoyle pickets positioned along the horizon. From level ground, it was difficult to guess their number. But even from afar, he counted hundreds aligned north of the gate.

"Harrumph!" an ocran snorted beside him, unnerved by the gargoyles' foul smell, which drifted over the battlefield. The guardians of the gate kept a mount saddled and ready at all times to quickly relay information to the palace interior in the event their signals would not swiftly suffice.

Terin sympathized with the soldiers guarding the gate, wondering how they dealt with the tedium of their duty. No sooner had he lamented their plight than his eye caught a gray blur passing before the gargoyle lines. His eyes slowly focused as the distant blur took shape. It was an ocran with a human rider, galloping apace as scores of gargoyles hurried in pursuit.

"Raise the gate!" Terin's voice echoed with an unnatural presence as he commandeered the nearby mount and drew his sword.

"We have orders not to raise the gate under any circumstance without..." the gate commander countered until Terin's terrible countenance silenced his protest. "Raise the gate!" he relented.

*****

Corry lingered on Zar Crest longer than she intended. The usual solace of the open air grew bitter with the gargoyle legions surrounding them. The foul creatures continued to tighten the noose, strengthening their lines as reinforcements arrived from the east. Most disturbing of all were the recent sightings of men clad in gold cloaks and tunics marshaling from the south under the banner of the 1st Naybin Army, a black hand upon a field of gray. So far, they numbered in the hundreds, but more were likely to follow. The Benotrist magantors were likely concentrated to the south to mask their approach. How such a force was able to journey north without notice of the Jenaii, one could only guess.

"Look yonder!" a soldier upon the inner battlements below shouted, drawing her eyes to the north, where a flax of cavalry appeared behind the gargoyle lines. By the gargoyles' frenzied reaction, they could guess the riders to be hostile to the enemy. The small cavalry contingent skirted the northern fringe of the enemy lines, drawing them away to the northeast.

"A strange tactic, but to what purpose?" Galen questioned, standing to her side.

"There." She pointed out as a single rider burst into view from the northwest, passing between a large gap in the gargoyle perimeter as the cavalry contingent continued north and east, drawing the enemy away. Their actions were now clearly discerned as a diversion to allow their comrade to slip through the enemy lines. Cory stepped closer to the rampart, resting her hands upon the jagged stone as her eyes fixed on the brave warrior racing toward the main gate with hundreds of gargoyles closing around him.

Her breathing eased as the man's gray ocran broke free, riding past the gargoyles' forward pickets. Terrible war cries echoed from the gargoyle masses with arrows spewing from their scattered ranks. Even from these airy heights, Corry could see the mounted warrior falter with several errant shafts striking him or his mount. The beast continued apace, driven by desperation with scores of gargoyles chasing him across the open fields.

"Order reinforcements to the main gate and raise the portcullis to receive him!" Corry commanded Nevias, who stood off her other shoulder.

"I believe it is too late, Highness." Galen sighed somberly as the ocran tumbled in the grass, trapping its rider beneath its heavy bulk.

A chorus of groans echoed along the battlements below as the Torry soldiers lining the walls bemoaned their comrade's fate. Nearly every eye was riveted to the desperate scene unfolding north of Corell. Just as all hope had forsaken their cause, another ocran burst into view, charging north across the fields from the castle gate.

The ocran was black as midnight, contrasting the bright aura of its fair-haired rider, whose unfastened helm tumbled from his head as he pressed northward to aid the fallen warrior. He galloped apace, leveling his sword to the gargoyles closing around the helpless warrior. "The fool." Corry gasped as the rider's blade alit with a luminous azure glow.

The gargoyles closed upon the downed ocran and the helpless warrior trapped beneath its carcass with rapacious glee, savoring the easy kill that lay before them. The warrior struggled futilely to free his left leg from beneath the mount or draw his sword, as its scabbard was equally pinned beneath his leg. He shifted his efforts to his dagger upon his right hip, freeing it as the hiss of a gargoyle drew his attention.

He craned his neck as the foul creature pressed near with its curved blade poised overhead. He lifted his dagger feebly to block the expectant blow, wanting nothing more than to close his eyes and accept his fate, but duty drove him to fight to his last, though hopeless was his cause.

The gargoyle snarled, sunlight playing off its white fangs as its sword started its descent. Neither the gargoyle nor the warrior heard the sound of hooves clapping the ground as a dark blur passed their periphery. An outstretched silver blade lopped the creature's head, the disjointed crown spinning above its neck, its lifeless eyes staring numbly as it fell.

Terin raced past the trapped warrior as the enemy closed upon them, driving into their scattered ranks. One creature sprang into the air, thrusting its wings as it glided forth to meet him. Terin swung true, splitting the gargoyle from shoulder to crotch before passing on. Another remained afoot, rushing forth with blade at the ready, and Terin's sword met the gargoyle's curved blade, splitting it like parchment before striking unprotected flesh. The creature writhed on the ground, its right arm severed at the shoulder and a large gash cut from its chest.

Corry stood spellbound, watching the foray unfold below. Terin roamed amid the gargoyle host, lopping heads and limbs at will, his sword dancing in his hand like a whip of lightning. Few stood their ground, swinging their blades futility as he cut them down. Others stood statue still, frozen in place, transfixed by the mysterious power emanating in their midst. The rest fled, mindless fear replacing nerve and bloodlust.

"CALEPH! CALEPH!" Torry soldiers cried out from the palace battlements as Terin swept the enemy from the field in a large arc around the fallen Torry. Gargoyle screams echoed over the din as the maddened blade struck true, chopping limbs and wings as he rode through their disordered ranks.

The wounded Torry struggled to free his trapped leg as the battle raged around him. He had lost track of his strange benefactor, who suddenly appeared from nowhere, slew his attacker, and rode off into the teeth of the enemy. He pulled frantically, desperate to free his limb as excruciating pain coursed his leg.

"Lower you head!"

He craned his neck, following the voice to a young man standing behind him, brandishing a silver sword emitting a bright azure light. "You." The soldier gasped, recognizing the man who had saved him. The soldier cringed as Terin stepped forth, bringing his blade down upon the ocran's carcass. The startled fellow expected the blade to strike him as Terin slashed away to either side of him.

"Come!" Terin shouted, hooking an arm underneath his shoulder, dragging him free. Only then did the soldier open his eyes, finding the ocran cut into thirds with only a small portion pinning his leg.

"ARGH!" he winced, becoming aware of the full damage to his leg.

Terin ignored his cry, hoisting the soldier over his saddle as he climbed up behind him. The soldier again cried out, his left knee severely swollen with a terrible gash running north of his ankle.

"Hold steady, friend!" Terin shouted, circling his mount around as gargoyle war cries echoed ominously near.

The soldier lay across the saddle in front of Terin like a sack of grain, his furtive eyes finally able to fully scan his surroundings. The retreating gargoyles quickly regrouped with hundreds more joining their cause. They rushed forth like a dark tide, their foremost ranks but twenty paces away.

"Where are the others?" the soldier excitedly asked, finding no one other than Terin to face the enemy.

"It's just us." Terin grunted, kicking his heels as they sped off toward the still open gate with the enemy close upon them.

Corry waited with bated breath, her eyes following Terin's mount across the open fields with hundreds of gargoyles in his wake. Arrows spewed from the battlements once he passed within the shadow of the palace, passing over his head and into the gargoyles' path. Dozens tumbled in the grass as Terin passed under the portcullis. They continued after their prey as he escaped beneath the lowering portcullis, blocking their advance.

Gargoyles could rarely be turned once they were roused with bloodlust and battle frenzy. Such emotions only dulled with futility and exhaustion. Their frenzy carried them perilously near the palace walls, where Torry archers picked them apart. More than two hundred littered the ground before they broke off their attack, staggering back to their lines.

Corry's fear turned to elation and then to cold anger. "I'll have words with Terin," she said to Torg, who stood statue still behind her, his countenance betraying little of his inner storm.

"So shall I!" he growled as she stepped away.

"Caleph! Caleph!" the garrison shouted, heralding the son of Jonas with due praise, their voices ringing from the highest battlements.

*****

"Will he live?" Terin asked the Matron who had stepped from the chamber where they attended the wounded soldier. He had waited in the outer corridor after they brought the wounded man to the infirmary.

"He should. His injuries seem confined to his left leg. He has lost a lot of blood, but not enough to close his eyes," the Matron replied. She had a kind voice and fair features with light-brown hair peeking from the hood of her red gown.

"Is he well enough to visit?" he asked.

"Yes, and he is asking to see you. Just be mindful that we are still tending his leg," she cautioned, waving an open hand toward the doorway.

Terin bowed politely and stepped within, finding the man he rescued upon a narrow bed with two Matrons still attending to his leg. The man's knee appeared swollen and discolored. A terrible open wound ran below his knee. The Matrons cleaned the wound and used delicate pincers to remove any foreign materials from his exposed flesh, discarding them on a small tray. Terin could see various pebbles, splinters, and a rather large arrowhead amid the recovered debris.

Once cleaned, the wound would be soaked with alcohol and tacra powder, which was ground from tree moss. Such measures proved effective to combat infection, and the Matron Guilds were well-schooled in such herb craft. Such precautions were even more necessary with gargoyles coating their arrowheads in feces and other foul material.

Once the wound was treated, the Matrons would stitch the tissue together as best they could. This would require a good many stitches. The soldier refused to cry out once he was in the ladies' presence, biting off his pain and putting on a good show for their sakes. Terin well understood and thought nothing worse than having the princess hear him whimper.

"It is you," the soldier greeted, his eyes lighting up as they found him at the doorway.

"Yes, it's me." Terin smiled, stepping around the Matrons who were attending the man's leg before stopping at his bedside, near his head.

"Jacin Tomac," the fellow offered, extending a weak hand.

"Terin Caleph," he answered, clasping Jacin's forearm. Despite his weakened state and matted long brown hair, Jacin was still a tall and hardy solider with handsome features. He reminded Terin of Cronus in his bearing and look.

"Thank you, Terin, for saving my life." Jacin winced again as the Matrons continued to pick debris from his leg.

"It was my honor. I have friends who fought at Kregmarin. I thought of them when I saw your mount fall." He couldn't save Arsenc or Yeltor, but he could save Jacin.

"We all had friends there." Jacin sighed, sadness compounding his weakened state. "You honor your friends with your courage, Terin. If ever I can walk again, I vow to return your favor."

"Others have helped me, Jacin, so that I might help you. You can favor me by helping someone in your path that might not be able to return the favor to you." He smiled, gently patting Jacin's shoulder.

"Only a son of the Torry realm would say such a thing." Jacin shook his head proudly.

"Where did you come from? And what is the urgency that drove you to attain Corell so desperately?" Terin had to ask.

"I am a commander of unit in Commander Connly's cavalry. I bring urgent news for the garrison," Jacin said as he followed Terin's eyes to the shoulder of his tunic. "My braids were removed in case I was taken by the enemy," he said, further explaining the absence of his insignia.

"Commander Connly? We haven't heard of his whereabouts in quite a while. Many thought he might have perished. Commander Valen reported meeting a contingent of his force some leagues west of Notsu."

"He lives, I assure you," Jacin affirmed.

"Terin," the distinct voice of Commander Nevias called out as he entered the chamber.

Terin stiffened and regarded the garrison commandeer as he stepped forth. "Commander, this is Commander of Unit Jacin Tomac. He brings word from Commander Connly."

"Very well. You are summoned to the throne room. Princess Corry awaits you there." Nevias pointed him toward the door, where an armed flax of royal guards awaited to escort him to his royal audience. He could tell by Nevias's curt tone that the summons was formal and quite serious.

"I hope you are soon well, Jacin," Terin said, bidding his new friend farewell before stepping without.

"Commander Tomac, I assume you have important news to report by the desperate ploy your comrades undertook to gain you access through the enemy's line," Nevias said, taking Terin's place at Jacin's side after dismissing the Matrons until he finished speaking.

"I do, Commander Nevias. Commander Connly's cavalry is three days' ride to our east. He sent us to inform the palace of the enemy's movement."

"We have seen their movement. The 6th and 5th Gargoyle Legions surround our walls as well as a trickling of Naybins to our east, though by their numbers, they appear lightly numbered for full legions." Nevias snorted.

"The gargoyle legions are lightly numbered due to their losses." Jacin coughed. "The Naybins are but a vanguard of seven telnics led by the Naybin champion, Dethine. He is less than a day's march to our south with his main body and at least fifty siege engines."

"No siege engine ever constructed can test the walls of Corell," Nevias said, dismissing the threat.

"Perhaps, but they will try nonetheless."

"Let them. What else do you have to report? Everything you have spoken is well-known or soon shall be."

"The main threat comes from the east. Four more legions are en route—two gargoyle and two human. They are led by Morac, first among Tyro's Elite. It is rumored that he wields a magical blade that he used to slay King Lore."

"The king is dead?" Nevias paled, Jacin's words finally confirming what they all believed but hadn't truly known.

"I fear it is so, Commander. He fell at Kregmarin, along with the 5th Army and many of our allies. Only our cavalry and magantors escaped the slaughter," Jacin said.

As Nevias digested the news, Jacin continued. "After Kregmarin, Morac's legions fell upon Bacel and Notsu. Bacel was completely destroyed, its people slaughtered. Notsu surrendered, avoiding Bacel's fate."

"Notsu surrendered?" Nevias could not conceal his disdain for such betrayal.

"They had little choice with most of their garrison slain at Kregmarin. The two telnics they offered Morac are little more than dregs."

"Two telnics that will be sent against our walls," Nevias said.

"True, but the better part of their cavalry rides with us, as well as another fifteen units of infantry that defend the holdfast of Besos," Jacin affirmed.

"And what of Connly? What are his intentions?"

"He continues what we have done since Kregmarin, harassing Morac's supply trains and eliminating any unit-sized or smaller detachments that separate from their main host. We have slaughtered thousands since Kregmarin, thinning Morac's ranks wherever we can."

"And Commander Tevlin?"

"His cavalry is using similar tactics to our south."

"How soon until the rest of Morac's legions are upon us?"

"The 7th Gargoyle Legion is perhaps two days east, and the 8th and 11th Benotrist Legions another four days behind them. The 4th Gargoyle Legion still lingers near the crossroads."

"Very well. The princess sends her gratitude for bringing this news, Commander." Nevias regarded Jacin before calling the Matrons to continue tending to his wounds.

*****

Terin took a deep breath before entering the throne room, fearing what reception he might receive. The vast chamber was alit as it had been during his first audience with King Lore. Only a dozen royal guards stood post along the walls, their winged helms casting their unique shadows upon the white stone floor. His eyes found Princess Corry upon her father's large throne, its massive size threatening to swallow her slender frame. Her fierce countenance quickly refuted such a notion as her cold blue eyes appraised him from afar.

He swallowed past the lump in his throat as he felt her heated gaze. He thought she might strike him dead with her glare alone. Torg stood to her right, his muscled arms crossed over his chest, projecting all the warmth of a winter gale, yet even he looked more forgiving than the princess. He found Cronus standing to her left, his easy smile the only comfort he was likely to receive. Terin stopped short of the dais and knelt with his head bowed. He remained there for an eternal moment as she appraised him until her anger cooled.

"Lift your eyes," she commanded, keeping him on his knees.

"Highness, you called for me?" he answered warily.

"What were your instructions at the gate?"

"I—to learn its workings and defense, Highness," he said, dreading the chastisement that was certain to follow.

"Who are you pledged to serve?" she asked.

"You, Your Highness."

"Did I not *forbid* you to leave the palace?"

"Ye-yes, Highness." He sighed, lowering his head in defeat.

"Look at me, Terin," she calmly ordered. He lifted his eyes back to hers. "You disobeyed my order, did you not?" Such a crime could be punished by death, but she doubted he knew that, as he was hopelessly naive.

"Forgive me, Highness. I...I just saw the rider beset by those gargoyles, and I...I had to—"

"To what?" she snapped, tiring of his stammering attempt to justify his idiocy. "To again venture far beyond our walls to save one man while risking your life and the sword you were chosen to carry? To venture where we cannot help you? Was that the aim of your witless plan? You have learned nothing of the burden you carry. How can I trust you to master your sword if you insist on being its slave?"

Terin paused, unable to answer her charge. How could he master a power he did not understand? It was one thing to make vows to do so in the calm of the throne room but another in the heat of battle when the sword calls to him.

"If it were a time of peace, I would have ordered you whipped for your disobedience, but the hour is late, and we are beyond that now. Remove your sword and place it upon the floor," she commanded. Terin hesitated briefly, taken aback by the coldness of her order. He relented, drawing the weapon and setting it carefully upon the floor in front of him. A sudden pang pierced his heart as he pushed the sword away, as if a part of him was sundered. He took a deep breath, attempting to quell his pounding heart.

"Your sword shall be returned after your punishment is served," Corry answered, noting the anguish permeating his countenance.

"Yes, Highness," he barely whispered.

Corry hated this. She hated to see him suffer, especially by her own hand, but what choice had she? His rashness reminded her so much of her father and brother. Her brother's rashness distracted him from his duty. It was his place to sit on the throne and order the defense of the realm, yet that task now fell to her. In the realm's darkest hour, where was he? In the south, seeking glory while Torry North burned.

Her father's rashness led him foolishly into the unknown, taking the better part of Torry North's might with him into oblivion. She held no power to stop such follies, as they were the decisions of the king and crown prince, but she had no such hindrance with Terin. She would cure his self-destructive leanings even if he hated her for it.

"Master Vantel shall see to your discipline," Corry said as Torg descended the dais.

"Come!" Torg growled, snagging Terin by the collar as he passed. Corry followed them with her eyes across the throne room until they stepped without.

"You disagree?" she asked, hearing Cronus sigh.

"It's not my place to question your decision, Highness."

Corry shifted to face him. "Speak freely, Cronus. You have earned as much for your bravery at Tuft's Mountain."

"You ask of Terin what he cannot give, Princess. The sword doesn't master him, at least as far as I have seen. It doesn't subvert his will. It only draws it out."

"That is even worse. You are claiming he is willfully disobeying my command?"

"No." Cronus sighed, struggling to put his thoughts to words. "The sword…the sword seems to know what Terin wants to do and makes him do it. That is different from willful disobedience. When he saw our magantor scouts assailed by the enemy, he wanted to help them. The sword simply made it happen. The sword is not mastering him. It is making him the master of his own desires."

She pursed her lips, her mind awash with the possibilities of Cronus's theory and its ramifications if true. Her father and King El Anthar suggested this theory as well. "You believe the sword urges him to claim what he desires?"

"More like *do* what he desires," Cronus clarified. "It's just my opinion, Highness. It doesn't mean I am right."

"If so, then if he desires gold, the sword would make him a thief? Or if he desires to kill, the sword would make him a murderer? Or if he desires a woman…" She stopped, not wishing to venture there.

"I don't think it works like that, Highness. Even if Terin desires gold or women or a particular *woman*"—she blushed as he emphasized the word—"it would not force him to act against his nature."

"If what you say is true, then he is doomed." She shook her head.

"Doomed?" He lifted an eyebrow.

"Once the enemy surrounds us in ever greater numbers and parades our captive people before our walls, subjecting them to unspeakable torment, what will Terin do?" she asked.

He needn't answer, knowing full well the validity of her words. "You are right." He sighed, scrubbing his chin with his hand.

"That is why he must learn to master the sword if I am correct or his desires if you are. Either way, we have much to do to ensure Terin survives long enough to achieve his destiny, whatever destiny that is. And if he fails, so do we."

"What can I do?" he asked.

"You are his friend, his best friend. Stay with him. Guide him. Guard his back when the madness of the blade takes him."

"I will."

*****

"Ugh!" Terin groaned, hoisting the buckets from the floor. They were filled with waste and urine, and he struggled not spilling their foul contents as he carried them to the base of the castle. He wished he was numb to the smell, but after hours of moving hundreds of buckets, the odor was as foul as when he began.

He wore a dark-brown tunic and threadbare sandals that were soiled from his labors. His arms ached from Torg's unique punishment, or was this task the princess's idea? He bitterly recalled how Torg dragged him in tow from the throne room, stripping him of his clothes for the rags he now wore and set him to work.

Unbeknownst to Terin, the lowly task was a personal favorite of Torg's to humble recruits. Because of Terin's accelerated training, he did not have the luxury to spend precious time breaking Terin's willful spirit. In times of peace, he would have ordered recruits to the King's Elite to perform this task for a moon's turn. When the princess left Terin's punishment to Torg, he gladly offered the boy up to this humiliating task.

To Terin's credit, he offered no complaint and carried out the chore as ordered. Torg reminded his young charge that the lowest servant carried out this necessary task every day and that all men should be mindful of the value of their service. In times of peace, Torg would oft order his Elite to perform various lowly tasks to instill in them a connection to the people they were sworn to protect.

"Your task is done. Bathe, don fresh garments, and retire to your chambers," Torg said as Terin cleared the last step upon his return from the base of the palace as the setting sun slipped toward the west.

"Yes, Master Vantel." Terin sighed wearily, bowed his head, and continued along the passageway to return the waste buckets to the sanitation chamber.

"Leave the buckets, Terin. I'll find someone else to return them. Go bathe yourself," Torg said.

"Thank you, Master Vantel." He bowed and stepped away.

Torg waited until Terin disappeared down the stairwell before picking up the buckets and returning them to their proper place himself. Seeing the commander of the Royal Elite unafraid to dirty his hands muted any protest from his lessers when they were so ordered.

Two days hence

By late morn, the 7th Gargoyle Legion was spotted by the lookouts atop the Tower of Celenia along the east road at the horizon's edge. They marched in good order, parading before the palace walls behind their emerald banner, a black whip with a gray chain woven along its length upon a field of green. By midday, they were well-positioned to the west, relieving the gargoyles of the 6th Legion that were placed there, freeing them to strengthen the northern portion of the perimeter.

Over the past three days, numerous elements of the 1st Naybin Army appeared along the eastern perimeter, their gold tunics and capes and human forms standing out among their gargoyle allies. By midday, they numbered at least seven telnics. The newest arrivals brought siege engines drawn by teams of moglos. The defenders watched curiously as the Naybins repositioned along the northern perimeter, aligning their siege engines with the main gate.

It was all as the Torry cavalry commander Tomac had claimed, including his apt description of the Nayborian warrior leading these cohorts named Dethine. The Naybin warrior paraded forward of his lines upon a golden ocran, which matched the coloring of his garb and hair, which trailed his helm in braided long locks.

"Men of Corell!" he shouted, his voice carrying upon the wind with unnatural clarity. "I am Dethine, son of Dethar and champion of greater Nayboria! I call upon you to send forth your champion, if there is any among you brave enough to claim the title!" He drew his sword and thrust it into the air, the blade igniting with a dull golden glow, bathing his arm in an otherworldly light. He galloped forth, stopping mid distance between his men and the palace walls. "Come forth, men of Corell! Test your mettle to *mine*! Is there any worthy of my CHALLENGE?" Dethine taunted.

"CALEPH!" a Torry soldier answered, standing post along the outer battlements above the main gate. "CALEPH! CALEPH!" Others took up the chant until it spread to the entire garrison, Terin's name reverberating across the palace walls.

Corry frowned, surveying the spectacle from the inner battlements with annoyance. Terin stood rigidly at her side, struggling to ignore his comrades' pleas. He could feel Corry's eyes upon him, warning him to not react to Dethine's challenge. His day of punishment was fresh in his mind, warning him to heed Corry's order to not act on impulse. Strangely, he felt no urgency to meet Dethine's challenge. Whether it was his will not to act or the sword's, he could only guess.

What did conflict him was the garrison heralding his name. To not heed their cry felt cowardly, but what choice had he? He dared not look at the princess, for her command was implicit. He was to remain at her side unless given leave to do so.

They had spoken little the past two days with an uncomfortable silence standing between them. He was withdrawn by her chastisement, and she by the confirmation of her father's demise. Jacin's information had proven to be true in all maters thus far, and she had no reason to doubt what he said of her father's fate. The manner of his death was still in doubt, but not his death itself.

Commander Connly had extracted the details of the king's death from several gargoyle captives, piecing together their varied testimonies before slitting their throats. They all agreed that Morac challenged her father to meet him in open combat in full view of both armies. Lore obliged, foolishly meeting Morac's golden blade. Only Terin's sword could match Morac's, and even then, she doubted the outcome. Her father fought bravely and died by Morac's hand.

She shook her head at such folly. She was adamant that that would *not* happen there. If Morac wished to test Terin's blade, he would have to come to him upon these walls if he dared. She would not let Terin repeat her father's mistake even if he hated her for it. *But does he hate me?* she wondered. *No,* she corrected herself. Hating her

443

was not in his nature. His pride was wounded, and he would come around in time—if they had time, that is.

"I hear the name Caleph! Is he your champion?" Dethine shouted. "If so, then send him forth if he is not craven!"

Cronus stood beside Terin, noticing his clenched fists and rigid stature as the Nayborian goaded him. Without preamble, he strode across the battlements onto the nearest turret where a trebuchet was positioned.

"CALEPH!" Dethine taunted, parading further forward, leveling his sword toward the north wall of the palace. "Come forth and fight if you dare! Or is the name Caleph merely the Torry appellation of cowardice?"

Thump! A fiery projectile arced over the palace walls. Dethine's ocran reared into the air as the object drew near like a falling star before striking the ground a few paces from his mount. Fire spread across the grass to his front, frightening his mount. It galloped away with Dethine barely holding on.

Cheers rang out along the palace walls as Dethine tumbled from the saddle in full view of his men. Corry looked at the offending trebuchet positioned upon the turret to her direct left. Her eyes found Cronus standing beside the trebuchet's crew, congratulating their handiwork that he no doubt ordered. She nodded her head as he caught her eye, acknowledging his shrewd act that silenced Dethine's tongue and spared Terin having to contend with the sword's will.

Three days hence

"To arms!" The cries rang out along the palace walls as the morning sun broke the eastern sky. Terin and Cronus ascended Zar Crest as the breaking dawn revealed the endless columns of gargoyles dotting the eastern sky. Terin spun about, scanning the surrounding firmament, where gargoyles drew near from each direction.

"There must be thousands!" Terin thought aloud.

"Tens of thousands," Cronus corrected, tightening the straps of his helm.

The gargoyles struggled mightily to attain level height with the palace walls, taxing their wings to their fullest as they took flight far afield. The builders of Corell constructed the walls of a height that gargoyles could not easily assail, only reaching its outer battlements exhausted and spent.

"What have we?" Nevias asked, stepping onto the crest with Corry and Torg following in his wake.

"Enemy approaching from each direction," one aide reported as the garrison commander surveyed his defenses.

*****

The first wave of gargoyles drew near the outer east wall, arrows spewing from the battlements, shredding the fore ranks under withering fire. Gargoyles tumbled from the sky, some dropping like heavy stones with arrows piercing their skulls. Others flailed, slowing their descent with arrows feathering their limbs and wings. Hundreds dropped from formation, nearly half of the first wave, as their brethren attained the outer battlements.

The wretched creatures were greeted with jabbing spears thrust between interlocked shields, driving them from the battlements with relative ease. Thousands of arrows passed overhead, striking the following wave. The second faltered as quickly as the first, their lightly armored ranks susceptible to Torry arrows. The defenders of the east wall awaited the third wave as the first waves struck the north and west walls with equal ferocity.

Torry bowmen loosed their volleys in a steady stream, thinning the enemy columns before they could set down. The third wave was thrown back at the east wall with a few clinging to the ramparts as the fourth wave followed. Hundreds succumbed to the archers' withering fire, yet the survivors pressed on. Several broke higher above their comrades, expending all their energy to attain elevation mere feet above the outer battlements. The maneuver further exposed their undersides to Torry spears and swords, but now their stricken bodies dropped upon the defenders below.

Some archers shifted their hurried volume to take careful aim at those breaking higher, hoping to strike them before they passed over the ramparts. Terin saw several arrows strike one creature as it passed over the battlements, its riddled corpse striking two soldiers standing upon the causeway that separated the inner and outer battlements. The force of the impact knocked them over. They staggered, gaining their feet, stunned from the blow but returning to battle as others passed overhead all along the walkway. Terin felt no urgency from his father's sword, his heart strangely serene as the battle unfolded in an orderly manner with the enemy unable to breach the walls. Had he mastered the will of the blade, or did it not consider the enemy a threat at this time?

A few gargoyles able to pass over the battlements set down on the walkway, untouched by arrows. They set down, the fire in their eyes dulled from exhaustion, easy prey for the Torries' fresh arms and sharp blades. "It's a slaughter," Terin said as hundreds of gargoyles were slain upon the battlements, the survivors offering little fight as they clung desperately to the outermost ramparts. Arrows rained overhead, decimating the waves that followed. After the sixth wave, the attack on the east wall faltered as gargoyle frenzy gave way to hopeless futility.

"They're breaking!" more than one soldier shouted as the gargoyles attacking the east wall broke off, returning whence they came. The Torries holding the outer battlements drove the few hangers-on from the ramparts, prodding them over the wall with repeated spear thrusts. Within moments, the attacks on the northern and western walls crumbled in kind. The attack on the southern wall stubbornly continued until Torry archers guarding the east wall added their fire to the archers positioned there. By the eighth wave, the southern attack broke, their survivors breaking, returning to the safety of their siege lines.

The gargoyles lost 4,500 dead and wounded on the walls of Corell. The Torries suffered thirty dead and as many wounded. Thus ended the first assault upon Corell.

*****

446

The Torries gathered the enemy dead into great piles and set them ablaze atop the battlements, but most were dropped through massive chutes to the base of the palace, where they were incinerated in vast crematories. Others ventured through the main gate but keeping close to the palace to gather the corpses that littered the grounds below the walls, setting them ablaze before disease took hold from the thousands of rotting bodies. They conducted this grizzly work, ever mindful of the enemy lines in the distance. Any sign of movement along the enemy ranks and the Torries would cease gathering the dead and hurry back through the main gate. They needn't fear enemy forays for now, as the gargoyles had no stomach to test Corell's walls again this day.

Two days hence

Thump! The stone ballista struck the palace wall above the main gate to little effect. The other Naybin trebuchets repeated the calibration, concentrating their aim upon the sections of wall above and beside the main gate. Torry arrow catapults responded in kind, their crews maneuvering them along the north wall of Corell. They flung shafts the length of a man for several hundred yards, the Naybin crews well within their range. With nearly a dozen large trebuchets aligned north of the main gate, the Torries had no lack of targets.

The remaining Nayborian siege engines were small stone throwers and arrow flingers that targeted personnel along the outer battlements. A Naybin soldier cried out as a shaft pierced his back, pinioning him to his trebuchet. His crewmates ignored their stricken friend as they hurried another shot. The Naybins used a standardized eight-pound round stone ballistae, allowing consistency with targeting. Any deviation in weight would affect variance in trajectory.

The Naybins had brought hundreds of said ballistae from Plou, which were properly weighed and constructed in their home quarries. Eventually, they would need to forge ballistae from local quarries, which risked dubious weighting. Any variance would risk their shots to land elsewhere from their previous shot. The Naybins needed to husband their shots, forcing them to concentrate their fire on a single point in the palace walls. Only repeated blows to the same point in the wall could cause significant damage. At their present location, the Nayborian crews were beyond the range of Torry longbows but exposed to Torry trebuchets and arrow catapults.

Thump! Thump! Two more ballistae struck the wall on either side of the gate, their crews hurriedly working as Torry catapults returned fire. And so it went throughout the coming days. Two trebuchets were struck with fire ballistae and dozens of crewmen slain while the Naybins hammered away at the wall around the gate.

Three days hence

The midday sun shone off their helms and shields like a million flickering stars as their endless columns stretched to the horizon. Torry lookouts atop the Tower of Celenia spotted the approaching legions by late morn, alerting the garrison of the expected dread. The vanguard of the 8th Legion had long since paraded before the walls of Corell as the main body continued their westward march. They moved into position along the northern perimeter, filing beside the Naybin contingent. They planted their standard to the Naybin right, a gray hammer upon a field of red.

A second standard was planted to the Naybins east, crossed silver daggers upon a field of black, the sigil of the 11th Benotrist Legion. The Torries upon the battlements watched with growing unease as the enemy ranks swelled throughout the day. While the gargoyle legions were thinned by their earlier engagements, the human Benotrist legions appeared mostly intact, perhaps in 80 percent strength. They had lost nearly as many men crossing the Kregmarin Plain than they did in battle.

Morac pulled back his reins, stopping his mount atop a small rise east of Corell, his fellow Elite filing in to either flank as he surveyed the palace from afar. Corell stood like a mountain of white upon a jade sea, its highest citadels jutting into the firmament like swords thrust into the air. He could discern a lone magantor silhouetted against the clear sky, circling the upper palace before setting down on a north-facing platform.

"Your prize, Lord Morac!" Borgon declared loudly for all to hear. Eighth among Tyro's Elite, he acted as Morac's second.

"Soon." Morac narrowed his eyes, not laying such claim until the palace was his, but it was tantalizingly close. With only its garrison to defend it, Corell would topple if properly pressed, not the reckless assault Commanders Maglakk and Concaka attempted several days past.

Morac tested his left leg, slipping it from the stirrup and straightening it painfully. The visible wound had healed, but the damage still persisted. The gruesome scar peeked beneath the folds of his black tunic and above his booted sandal. He chose to leave it in full view, leaving it as a symbol of his glorious victory at Kregmarin.

The wind lifted his dark mane above his bright-crimson cape, which rippled like the waves of a blood-red sea. Though similarly clad as his fellow Elite, he was set apart by the ape skull affixed to his helm, which was lifted above his brow, and the golden sword that rode on his left hip.

"Guyin," one of his brethren uttered, pointing out an approaching rider who galloped east along the edge of the columns of westbound infantry that passed behind them. The rider rode apace, only slowing as he neared the base of the small rise.

"What tidings, Guyin?" Morac asked as the Elite eased his mount to stop before him.

"Lord Morac." Guyin bowed. "The Torry garrison is strongly positioned within the palace. The Nayborians have fixed their siege engines along the northern perimeter. They are targeting the main gate with continuous fire. Their chieftain awaits you north of the palace."

"I'll meet with him and all legion commanders at my pavilion once it is erected. Have you found suitable ground for its placing?"

"North and east of the palace, just yonder." Guyin pointed out, his arm extended in the direction indicated.

"Very well. See to it."

"There is more, my lord," Guyin added.

"Speak of it!" Morac masked his annoyance with Guyin's melodrama.

"The Torry crown prince is not in command of the garrison." Guyin smiled as if privy to a grand mystery.

"Speak of it!" Morac snarled, causing Guyin to flinch.

"The princess Corry sits the Torry throne. It is she who commands their defense," he hurriedly answered.

"The princess..." Morac trailed, his mind alit with possibilities. He had wondered if she might be present. He was expecting her fool brother to return before the siege began to claim his birthright. Torry law required the crown prince to sit the throne before claiming kingship of the realm. 'Twas a daft formality but a rule nonetheless. Yet here the Torries awaited him, guarding their most precious asset, the great palace of Corell, with only a scant garrison to guard it and their princess.

Did Lorn believe defending the palace beneath his time? Did he not realize his kingdom was doomed if it fell? He hoped to catch the whelp in Corell, finishing the Torry realm in one fell swoop. So be it. He would merely finish Lorn at a later time. The princess, however, offered a tantalizing consolation. She was a prized flower whose petals he would take pleasure in plucking.

"My lord?" Guyin asked, drawing Morac from his thoughts.

"You have orders, Guyin," Morac said curtly before riding south, circling the palace to inspect the siege lines for himself.

*****

Cronus removed his helm, letting the fresh air cool his brow, observing the enemy below. The gargoyles of the 7th Legion worked furiously in building siegeworks and palisades along Corell's western approaches. From afar, they appeared as small insects burrowing from their nest in long black columns. He counted between thirty and forty telnics in their legion, though from afar, his estimation was little more than a guess. He had spent the better part of his day at the west wall at Torg's insistence, learning the workings of the palace defenses from each assignment he was given. The soldiers manning these walls could find their battle positions blindfolded, and Torg expected the King's Elite to react in kind to any post in the palace.

Commander Cors Balka was the west wall commander. He was a stick-thin man with penetrating brown eyes and an easy frown. Cronus found his cantankerous disposition even more dour than Torg's, if that was possible. Ironically, Cors Balka took a liking to Cronus in their short time together. They stood side by side along the outer battlements, surveying the enemy in the distance.

"What is your count, King's Elite?" Cors asked, his eyes narrowed with the late-day sun hitting him in the face.

"Thirty to forty telnics as far as I can tell, Commander, but I am not a King's Elite yet," Cronus corrected.

"Bah! You're more Elite than half who hold that rank, Cronus. Any soldier who did what you did at Tuft's Mountain is worthy of the title."

"You're too kind, Commander." Cronus shook his head, not believing himself worthy of such praise.

"I'm an ornery old ass, Kenti, at least that is the sentiment of my men. Better that than thinking me soft, I suppose," Cors quipped. Cronus tried not to laugh, but Cors Balka's blunt speech reminded him so much of Raven. Of course, Raven was a hopeless optimist where Cors was a dour pessimist, but their manner of speech was strangely similar.

"Cronus!" a familiar voice called out. Cronus backed a step from the rampart as Alen came running south along the walkway separating the inner and outer battlements, the sound of his sandals slapping the stone echoing audibly in the air.

"Alen," Cronus said, greeting his friend as the young Menotrist stopped in front of him.

"Cronus, it is good to see you," Alen greeted in kind as Cronus placed a heavy hand on his shoulder, the gesture giving Alen a sense of belonging that he desperately needed. "Commander Balka." Alen bowed stiffly, greeting Cors as soon as their eyes met.

"You have news, Alen?" Cors lifted an impatient eye.

"Yes. Commander Nevias summons you for a commanders' call, and Cronus is to report to Master Vantel at dusk."

"Very well. Cronus." Cors bade him farewell before marching off.

"How do you find your new duties?" Cronus inquired as Commander Balka stepped away.

"I'm proud to serve the Torry realm even if my contribution is small," Alen affirmed with deep sincerity.

"A garrison messenger is no small contribution, Alen. It is far more important than you give credit," Cronus said, his praise swelling Alen's heart.

"Thank you, Cronus."

"For what?"

"For everything. Without you, we would have never attained Tro or Corell." He left unsaid that neither Raven nor himself could have navigated a successive course through the wilderness.

"Without you, we might not have escaped Fera at all. We all did our part, Alen. That is the true value of friendship."

"We are still friends?" Alen asked curiously.

"Why would we not?"

"Well, you are of the King's Elite and I—"

"I don't measure my friends by their rank or position, Alen. You should know that, as what we suffered together on our trek across the northern wilds should attest."

"I—thank you." Alen sighed, bereft of words to convey his appreciation. "I must hurry back. Commander Nevias is expecting me."

"Take care," Cronus said as Alen hurried off, disappearing in the mass of soldiers crowding his path.

"An insult to trueborn Torries." Cronus overheard a snide missive cast in Alen's direction, though Alen didn't appear to have heard it. He found the offending voice on the lips of a young soldier manning the outer battlement, a lad of an age and stature to Terin with long brown hair that fell below his polished helm. He stood among a cluster of fellow soldiers, some of whom nodded in agreement.

"An insult?" Cronus calmly asked, stepping in front of the soldier. The young man's eyes drew wide as his friends suddenly backed away, leaving him alone with Cronus.

"I…ugh…"

"You spoke of an insult to trueborn Torries when the palace messenger passed your post."

"I—yes," he confessed.

"What insult were you speaking of?"

The youth stammered, summoning the courage to repeat his comment. "I said…I said that to have a slave of the enemy placed highly in the crown's service is an insult to trueborn Torries."

"A slave of the enemy," Cronus repeated, the words sounding bitter in his mouth. "That slave you speak of has a name. Do you know it?" The soldier answered with shamed silence. "His name is Alen. He is a Menotrist and was born to the bondage that you disparage. What blame can be attainted to the misfortune of our birth? Did he choose such a life? Was it by his hand that fate should consign him such a fate?

"The boy you mock defied the very enemy that surrounds our walls with no army at his back or sword in his hand. His action earned him nothing less than certain death at his masters' hands, and only fate or dumb luck allowed him to aid us in our escape from that foul land.

"He could have continued on to lands safely south with all the riches you could imagine as a crewmate with the Earthers, but he chose to come here instead. He chose to forsake all the comforts that his life had denied him since birth in order to come here to serve in any manner he was able, to fight the very enemy that surrounds us. Such a man is deserving of our respect, not our scorn."

"I…I didn't know," the soldier said ashamedly, his eyes cast down with chagrin.

"Look yonder," Cronus said, not unkindly, stretching his left hand toward the horizon. The boy's eyes followed where he indicated. "The enemy surrounds us with numbers so vast that our realm has no hope to contest by ourselves. Can we truly cast away any who is willing to stand with us?"

"No, we cannot," the boy admitted, suddenly cognizant of the falseness of his words. "I have soiled my honor with my foolish banter, King's Elite. I will not protest whatever punishment you demand of me."

"No punishment is worse than our own shame when we acknowledge it. Just be mindful of easily cast words that disparage a brother-in-arms." Cronus slapped his shoulder, the gesture setting the soldier at ease as Cronus stepped away.

*****

Morac completed his inspection, riding the circumference of Corell, surveying the placement of each legion and any avenues of approach they might have overlooked. He concluded his ride, passing behind the men of the 11th Benotrist Legion, who busied themselves setting camp and hastily erecting palisades to their front. He could see his own pavilion awaiting him up ahead, upon a slow rise north and east, cast in bold hues of crimson and gold.

Drawing near, he could see the standards of the 8th, 11th, 5th, 6th, and 7th Legions positioned before the entrance, indicating his commanders were waiting within. He was delighted to see his own standard raised above the others, bearing his sigil of a glowing golden sword upon a field of black.

A small army of slaves greeted him as he dismounted, bowing deeply before attending to his mount and those of his fellow Elite. Morac removed his helm and passed within. The pavilion was an expansive structure some twenty meters abreast with lavish furnishings, most of which were plundered from Notsu and Bacel. A dozen briefly skirted slave girls hurried to and fro, preparing their master's chamber. Once Morac stepped within, they immediately stopped whatever task they were attending and dropped to their knees, pressing their heads to the ground. Morac strode toward the center of the chamber, leaving the girls in their place of obeisance.

"Lord Morac," General Felinaius, commander of the 11th Benotrist Legion, greeted as the others bowed, receiving their commander.

"Generals," Morac said, stopping at the edge of his table, where a map of Corell and its surrounding lands was already placed upon it.

The others gathered around, each indicating the placement of their legions upon the map. "What strength is your legions?" Morac asked, knowing each was terribly understrength after the battle at Kregmarin and Bacel and their trek to Corell. The 5th and 6th Legions also suffered heavily in their failed assault upon the palace.

"Thirty-eight telnicsss fit for battle," hissed General Concaka, commander of the 5th Gargoyle Legion, his legion suffering casualties throughout the campaign.

"Thirty-six telnics," General Maglakk, commander of the 6th Gargoyle Legion, affirmed.

"Thirty-seven," General Vaginak, commander of the 7th Gargoyle Legion, said.

"Thirty-four," General Vlesnivolk, commander of the 8th Benotrist Legion, said.

"Twenty-two telnics," General Felinaius of the 11th Benotrist Legion concluded.

Morac had detached twenty of his forty-two telnics to secure Notsu and their lines of communication. "Have any of you ascertained the enemy's strength?" he asked, his eye sweeping the faces around the table.

"The garrison, if fully mustered, numbers ten thousand with unknown numbers of auxiliaries and archers," General Vlesnivolk said.

"That is the official number, General, which I could guess myself. What is the actual number?" Morac asked again, curling his lip with the useless answer.

"Fromsss the prisoners we have takensss, we have learned much. The Torriesss have emptied several holdfasts to strengthen the garrison by three telnics, 1,500 to 2,500 archers, and uncounted numbersss of hastily assembled conscriptsss to further bolster their numbers," General Concaka hissed, confident in the information his gargoyles extracted from the flesh of their prisoners.

"Fifteen to twenty telnics," Morac reflected, shifting painfully on his bad leg.

"Their archersss decimated our attack," General Maglakk snarled, painfully recalling his tired gargoyles approaching the palace, Torry arrows riddling his beleaguered ranks before they could place one claw upon the ramparts.

The news soured Morac's mood. Torry infantry could be dealt with, but if they had two thousand archers, he would have to reconsider his immediate plans. His gargoyles were woefully exposed to arrows, and he could not bring his better-armed Benotrist infantry to bear until the main gate was breeched. He was about to ask about that matter when Guyin entered the pavilion, escorting the Naybin emissary Dethine.

"Lord Morac," Dethine hailed, stepping forth to exchange pleasantries as Morac clasped his forearm to formally receive the Naybin champion.

"Dethine, your aid in this campaign is most helpful," Morac greeted, acknowledging the Nayborians' contribution. Their seven telnics were not nearly as significant as the siege engines they brought, especially the large trebuchets that were pounding the main gate. Morac snapped his fingers, signaling his slave girls to rise, and they hurriedly fetched wine and refreshments for their master and his guests. "What progress have you made upon the gate?" Morac asked.

"My people have studied the fortress for many decades, examining it for weakness in the event a large enough army was ever brought to bear upon its walls. The outer walls are several meters thick and even more so at their base. We could hurl stones upon its surface for years to little effect. The only discernable weakness is where the iron gate meets the wall itself. Continuous blows to the same place might crack the wall and expose the iron rods cased within," Dethine explained, going into further detail on the necessity of throwing rocks of equal size to ensure consistency in targeting at this great range.

"And you have cracked the wall?" Morac asked.

"We've opened a meter-wide gash above and to the left of the gate and a vertical gash half as wide above the gate's center. Our rate of fire has waned of late," Dethine lamented.

"Why? We must press our—"

"Our munitions have run thin. Our supply trains ferrying properly weighed ballistae have been ambushed by Torry cavalry," Dethine recalled bitterly.

"Torry cavalry." Morac snorted. His own lines of supply and communication had been equally tormented by the enemy cavalry since Kregmarin.

"We have seized a quarry here," Commander Maglakk hissed, indicating a point some distance north of Corell.

"Yes. I have positioned three hundred men to secure the site. My stone cutters have been working to shape properly sized ballistae. It is a lengthy process, but we should soon see progress. I plan to resume our rate of fire by midday on the morrow," Dethine assured.

"How long until the gate is breached?" Morac asked, his eyes fixed on the north wall of Corell depicted on the map, the image cruelly taunting him like ripened fruit just beyond his reach.

"My lord, even if we break through, the passage through the tunnel is nearly impassable with gates and bulwarks throughout and hundreds of archer slits lining its length. Any attack would suffer tremendous casualties and might never penetrate the palace interior. Our gargoyle soldiers assaulting the upper palace might disrupt the enemy, but they'll fare just as poorly trying to attain the walls. The ancients built these great fortresses to a height that hinders gargoyles from reaching their outer battlements without exhausting themselves," General Felinaius explained.

"I am well aware of our gargoyles' limitations. I shall deal with that problem once I know when the gate can be breached." Morac lifted his eyes to Dethine for the answer.

"I can make no assurances, but give me five good days. If it is not compromised by then, our efforts will have been for naught."

"Five days." Morac nodded his head. "That should be enough time for our engineers to complete their work."

"What work, my lord?" General Vlesnivolk asked curiously.

"Why, nothing short of the Torries' destruction, General," Morac said cryptically, the slightest smile touching his lips.

"And enough time for the 4th Legion to arrivesss," General Concaka hissed.

"Why do they tarry? What task has delayed them?" General Vlesnivolk asked.

"They are tending a very *specific* task, which shall be revealed in all its glory soon enough, once the stage is set." Morac's eyes blazed, alit by the visions of his grandiose plans coming to fruition.

"Then we shall attacksss?" General Maglakk hissed.

"No, we shall attack now, keeping them occupied before we overwhelm them in five days," Morac said.

"Now? But our gargoyles—" General Vlesnivolk protested before Morac cut him off.

"Now, General. We have other means to aid our gargoyles assailing the battlements. I want the palace defenders under constant duress. Perhaps after a few days of carnage, the princess will be more…agreeable to my terms."

"Once she sees your sword illuminating the battlefield in all its glory, she will certainly submit." General Concaka smiled, his lips stretching above his fangs.

"She would if she did not possess a sword nearly my equal," Morac snarled, recalling Terin's sword at Fera. The rumors of a Torry warrior wielding a similar blade was likely Terin, as they chanted his name to counter Dethine's challenge.

"Aye, she may have *one* sword in her service, but we have *two*." Dethine grinned, drawing his sword from its scabbard, hoisting it in the air. A luminous yellow glow danced along its blade.

Morac recognized the nature of the sword immediately, a lesser sister to the one that rode his hip. Though he and the emperor lacked full knowledge of the swords' history, they had pieced together much of their storied lore, enough to know that Dethine's blade was one of the six Swords of the Stars. It was likely gifted to a southern kingdom established by the Tarelian order before falling into the hands of their Nayborian conquerors.

Morac drew his sword, a fiery glow igniting along its length as he stretched the blade across the table, touching the sword to Dethine's, the swords' intensity brightening as they touched. "To the union of our peoples and the bane of our foes!" Morac declared.

The next morn

"KAI-SHORUM!" Gargoyle war cries echoed in the predawn sky. Torry soldiers rushed to the battlements, uncertain of which walls were under attack.

"The east wall!" The cries went out as Torry archers upon the inner battlements released their volleys in the dark. Gargoyle screams indicated that some struck true. Soldiers manning the outer battlements closed ranks as men filed into position, jabbing furiously between interlocked shields at gargoyles clinging to the ramparts. The following gargoyle waves fixed their eyes to the torches lining the inner battlements and watchtowers, using them for direction in the dark. The Torries wisely kept the outer battlements dark to confuse the enemy.

Nearly half of the first wave failed to reach level height to the wall, forcing them to either struggle frantically to gain lift as they clawed desperately at the steep wall or forsake the attack and glide to the surface below. By then, they forfeited the element of surprise with Torry soldiers pouring onto the battlements.

Terin and Cronus hurried into position upon Zar Crest, struggling to make sense of the battle in the cursed darkness. The sound of whizzing arrows and clashing steel echoed along the length of the east wall, indicating the direction of battle. The chaos continued briefly until the eastern horizon was ablaze with a pregnant sunrise alighting the sky. The breaking dawn revealed the crowded heavens with rank upon rank of gargoyles approaching the east wall. A half dozen magantors emerged from their serried ranks, breaking from the gargoyle mass, coursing overhead.

"Shields!" Torry soldiers cried out, lifting their shields overhead as the Benotrist magantor riders soared hundreds of feet above the outer battlements before dropping hundreds of fist-sized stones upon the defenders below. The stones fell like thunderclaps, crushing skulls and smashing flesh wherever they struck true. Even a helm was of little use, exchanging a crushed skull for a death by concussion. Only shields provided the protection needed, but a direct blow along the line where the left hand gripped the shield could break an arm.

Arrow catapults spun into position, releasing their projectiles upon the enemy above, their volleys coming up short. The bold maneuver provided measurable success as a half dozen small breaks in the Torry defense suddenly appeared along the wall. Terin could see several gargoyles strike down Torry soldiers trying to fend them off with their shields raised overhead. Scores of gargoyles drove the Torries back along the wall connecting the two east turrets. Terin hurried off with Cronus close behind.

Once the magantors passed, the Torry soldiers lowered their shields, isolating the gargoyle advance along the wall to a series of small footholds. They struck methodically, thrusting blades between interlocked shields at whatever flesh the gargoyles offered. The rising sun shone directly upon the Torries' eyes whenever they stole a glance at the enemy, forcing them to duck their heads and stab blindly with their swords around the sides of their shields, though they could hardly miss as the following waves of gargoyles funneled into the fissures that fractured the defenses.

The sheer weight of their numbers bulged the festering enclaves, forcing the Torries back. Torry archers directed their fire upon the ramparts wherever the gargoyles took hold, riddling their ranks with thousands of arrows to great effect. One arrow catapult crew upon the inner battlement trained their fire to a cluster of gargoyles pouring over the battlements below, their arrow striking one creature in the chest before passing through two others. The gargoyle footholds began to shrink under such duress until a second wave of magantors appeared overhead, dropping their deadly volley upon the battlements below.

"Keep your aim upon the gargoyles!" commanders ordered the archers. Some tried to target the magantors, only to see their shafts fall hopelessly short. Dozens of Torries dropped along the front with crushed skulls or broken limbs, their fellows struggling to take their place in the shield wall. The gargoyles took advantage of the brief respite, flooding the outer battlements wherever the enemy dropped. The deadly stones struck down scores of gargoyles as well, but Morac was more than willing to sacrifice one for one if need be.

Arrows arced overhead, striking the following gargoyle waves drawing nigh, thinning their ranks before they set down upon the ramparts. Hundreds of gargoyles swarmed the battlements, bulging their small enclaves as the Torries gave ground. Some gargoyles lingering at the battlements recovered enough strength to bound into the air to pass over the Torry fore ranks, landing in the Torry rear. They soared overhead, just above the length of Torry spears thrusting to gut them. They sought out the most vulnerable targets, setting down upon soldiers' heads, the blows knocking unprepared victims from their feet if not snapping their necks altogether.

Their small victories would be short-lived, as the creatures were set upon by Torry blades from each direction. The damage was done, however, one for one. No human would throw his life away, but gargoyle bloodlust trumped self-preservation and reason. Only killing could sate their primal urges. Torry archers again shifted aim to those clinging to the ramparts, killing them before they mustered the strength to fly further ahead.

A significant bulge expanded after the second magantor wave passed with hundreds of gargoyles feeding its expanse, threatening to split the defenders along the east wall. Cronus followed Terin through the shaken Torry ranks, struggling to keep pace, as Terin seemed to glide with ease amid the crowd. Cronus hurried forth the mass of human flesh intermingling with the black-winged forms pressing their front.

A deliberate swing of Terin's blade cut down three gargoyles blocking his path, passing through wings, limbs, and chests in an unbroken arc. His follow-through took more of them with chunks of sundered flesh flying off his blade. Cronus rushed forth, guarding his right flank as he continued on, stepping over the dismembered carcasses littering their path. An errant blade met Terin's sword, breaking where its common steel met the edge of his blade. Cronus drove his sword into the creature's gut as Terin moved on to another, splitting blades at will.

Corry ascended Zar Crest, her gaze catching sight of the melee below. Her eyes, like those of all the others crowding the upper ramparts, were hopelessly drawn to the glowing azure blade dancing amid the gargoyle ranks, cutting a swath to the battlements' edge as the Torries to either flank rushed forth. The gargoyle incursion melted away like snow upon a warm stone. Torry soldiers drove the remnant off the wall, thrusting their swords as they pressed forth with blood splattering their shields.

Cronus struggled to keep pace, hacking desperately at a clawed limb attempting to strike Terin from the side. He felt his sword stop at the bone of the creature's wrist, the blow causing it to drop its sword and retract the stricken limb. Cronus ducked as Terin swung his blade, passing over Cronus and striking a creature behind them, lopping its head.

Within moments, Torry soldiers flooded to either side, driving the remnants of the gargoyles from the palace walls. Cheers rang out along the battlements as the following gargoyle waves broke off, returning whence they came. Torry archers continued firing until the enemy drew out of range, slaying as many as they could.

Cronus lowered his sword and shield, catching his breath as Terin stood at his side, the light of his sword growing dim with the battle's end. Soldiers crowded around them, slapping each of them on the back and arms and shouting their names. "Caleph! Kenti!" the men shouted as Terin lowered his sword, exhaustion taking him as he staggered briefly until gaining his bearing. Cronus sheathed his blade, placing his free hand to Terin's shoulder, acknowledging his fell deed.

*****

Commander Nevias stood beside the princess, surveying the aftermath of the skirmish. Hundreds of bodies littered the outer battlements, including scores of wounded men with a myriad of injuries from missing digits and superficial cuts to severed limbs and mortal wounds. Even those with the slightest abrasions were removed to the Matrons' care, as the enemy was apt to poison their blades.

Overall, they were most fortunate, having suffered 120 dead and an equal number incapacitated. The enemy suffered far worse. He estimated their losses between 2,000 to 3,000 dead and severely wounded. But the enemy thought little of their own wounded, slaying any who could not return to full duty.

"It appears young Caleph is proving most useful, Highness," Nevias said, observing Terin and Cronus pass under a raised portcullis separating the inner and outer battlements below them.

"Yes." Corry sighed, thinking to say something else but unable to put words to thoughts. Terin was fulfilling the purpose of his title as Champion of the Realm, for which her father appointed him, but why was she not pleased? She cringed every time he placed himself in harm's way, waiting for an errant blow or stray arrow to strike him down. The damnable sword instilled a sense of invincibility in those who wielded it, replacing good sense with reckless abandon. But what choice had they? Terin's sword saved many Torry lives this day, and as acting regent, she had the greater responsibility to the realm than to the life of one foolish boy, no matter her fondness of him.

*****

True to his word, Morac continued to harry the Torry garrison. He sent his magantors high above the palace walls several times throughout the day, dropping stones from unassailable heights. The raids were more nuisance than not, but more than a few soldiers were killed or wounded by the simple tactic. The defenders could see their approach from afar during the day and were more than ready to gain cover or raise their shields. The garrison still retained a small number of magantors and sent them aloft after the second wave approached. They managed to slay three Benotrist magantors while suffering one of their own.

By sundown, the enemy renewed their attack, assailing the west wall. The attacks were clumsy and misdirected in the dark of night but were aimed at exhausting the defenders, who were forced to stand to post throughout the night. Torry archers fired blindly into the dark, their errant shafts striking true in the enemy mass. By late evening, the gargoyles shifted tactics, assailing the wall in small groups. Some were able to attain the battlements unseen, clinging to the outermost ramparts until their strength was restored to fly above the inner battlements to wreak havoc wherever they set down. By the break of dawn, the Torries suffered more than a hundred casualties and the gargoyles many times that.

By late morn, Benotrist magantors returned to the sky, depositing their loads upon the palace. Torry magantors contested where they could, managing to bring down two more enemy war birds for their effort while losing one of their own. Weary soldiers slept upon the battlements, their fellows waking them whenever the enemy passed overhead. And so it continued throughout the day, the enemy restricting their attacks to magantor raids until nightfall.

Unlike the previous night, the gargoyles assailed the north wall and in groups of two or three, approaching as quietly as possible, hoping to reach the ramparts unseen. Some stumbled into the wall far below the ramparts, their taxed wings unable to reach the battlements above. They aborted the attempt, gliding to the surface. Others were quickly spotted, skewered by Torry spears before they touched down. Some reached the walls unseen, gathering strength to pass over the Torry fore ranks and attack those gathered where the outer causeway met the wall of the inner battlements.

By the middle of the night, they no longer caught anyone unawares, as everyone upon the palace roof kept constant guard, ever mindful that the gargoyles could drop from the sky at any moment. A third of the garrison remained in their barracks, just below the outer battlements, with soldiers guarding the entryways and stairwells as they slept. Commander Nevias tried to rest as many of his men as possible whilst keeping a strong enough force manning the walls to repulse any full-scale attack. The gargoyle raids were more nuisance than not but further taxed the weary defenders.

*****

The following morn saw the Benotrist magantors renew their assault with the Torries mustering their scant forces to contest them. With most of their magantors departing with Dar Valen, the garrison was left with seven war birds to challenge the Benotrists. With his own magantor still in its stable, Terin begged the princess to allow him to join the others.

"For what gain?" Corry scolded. "We have countered their assaults by making good use of our shields. There is no reason to risk your sword or life for so little," she finished, returning her gaze to the enemy lines in the distance, where they seemed to busy themselves constructing a series of small towers, wondering their purpose.

Terin's eyes were drawn to the magantor skirmish above, where the great avian battled for supremacy. Arrows spewed back and forth as the great war birds twisted in the air. A Benotrist magantor dropped briefly, its right wing struck by a Torry archer upon a passing war bird. The giant bird steadied itself, working its tender wing as it limped from the battle.

The Torry archer rose high in the saddle behind his driver, releasing a second shaft into the wing of another passing magantor. The Benotrist archer returned fire, striking the Torry archer in the shoulder, the blow causing him to drop his bow, which fluttered uselessly away, breaking upon the wall of the Golden Tower.

Another Benotrist magantor swooped overhead of the Torry war bird, plucking the wounded archer from the saddle with its outstretched talons, releasing him just beyond the palace walls. Corry sighed bitterly as the brave warrior flailed his limbs through his descent before impacting the soil just beyond the northeast corner of the palace.

"Shields!" The command echoed through the ranks as the Benotrists released their load upon the garrison with the Torry magantors breaking off their engagement. Terin thrust his shield over Corry's head as two royal guards did the same, protecting the headstrong princess, who refused to leave the command post.

"You should take refuge in the palace, Highness," Terin advised as a fist-sized stone struck near.

"Why?" Corry snarled, stepping clear as the enemy war birds passed to the south, out of range.

"To safeguard your person, Highness. Why risk—" he protested before she cut him short.

"I am acting regent of the realm, Terin. Do *not* advise cowardice when courage is the currency of victory."

"A wise man once said there is a narrow path between foolishness and courage," he retorted, forgetting his place.

"And cowardice and wisdom," she added, impressed by his audacity to address her so freely.

"You can declare standing here under an enemy barrage as courage, yet you claim my actions foolish?" Terin thought aloud.

She lifted an eyebrow, regarding him with annoyed curiosity. "Your acts *were* foolish." Terin thought to reply, but she placed a finger to his lips, hushing him to silence. "I should be safe for now. I am certain Master Vantel has other duties for you to attend." She pinched his cheek, sending him on his way.

*****

The gargoyles renewed their assault just after sundown, this time assailing the south wall. Again, they kept to small groups or individuals, wreaking havoc wherever they could. The defenders were prepared for the unusual tactic but suffered nonetheless. Most of the enemy were dispatched at the battlements' edge, but enough landed behind the fore ranks to slay several dozen Torries.

Alen hurried across the central causeway, passing between the Towers of Celenia and Cot, their massive structures spiraling into the starlit sky. He could make out the shape of the citadels with the torchlight upon the highest floors shining brightly upon the surface of the other. Alen paused, a familiar sensation coursing his flesh, inching along the back of his neck like an insect crawling upon his skin. He craned his neck, noticing a dark blur in his periphery.

There, clinging to the wall of the Tower of Celenia, he spied glowing crimson eyes staring back at him. He swallowed past a lump bulging the narrows of his throat as the gargoyle sprang from the wall, dropping onto the causeway. He jumped back, drawing his knife as the creature hurried forth, its fangs glistening in the dim light, a torch bracketed along the base of the tower illuminating its cruel face.

"Gargoyle!" a soldier shouted from behind the creature, throwing a spear at its back. The gargoyle shifted, dodging the shaft by instinct, the spear grazing its wing. He turned suddenly on his attacker, releasing a guttural obscenity as he stepped forth before stumbling, stricken from behind. The creature's face planted onto the unforgiving stone with Alen on his back, stabbing the gargoyle repeatedly with his dagger. Several Torry soldiers hurried forth, driving their swords into the creature and pulling Alen safely into the clear.

"Splendidly done, messenger," one soldier congratulated him, slapping Alen on the back as they surveyed his handiwork.

"Th-thank you," Alen answered, catching his breath. The uncharacteristic act taxed his lungs. It wasn't his first kill, but the task didn't feel much easier than the last. He was a slave bred for docility. Killing was unnatural to most men, but to him, even more so.

"Perhaps you should wear a helm and armor if you are going to run messages at night," another advised. Alen recognized a single braided cord circling the fellow's shoulders, indicating his rank as a commander of flax.

"I will ask, Commander," he said.

"As well you should. Be on your way. We will clear this carcass," the commander of flax said. "Well done, messenger," he added, and the others chorused his praise. Alen nodded gratefully and hurried on, for the first time feeling as if he truly belonged.

*****

The following morn found Nevias and Corry upon Zar Crest, surveying the enemy in the distance. Along the horizon in each direction, they spotted more of the unusual structures being erected. They were made of lumber drawn from the Zaronan Forest to their west. The sound of axes echoed day and night in the distance, unnerving the Torries with the enemy's industriousness.

The structures were simple platforms that rose some eighty feet into the air. They were too narrow to be siege towers and lacked wheels to ease them into position. From afar, they appeared as observation platforms, but to what purpose? They counted at least a dozen of the makeshift towers circling the castle. Dozens more appeared under construction.

"For what reason?" she asked, her blue eyes fixed on the enemy towers to their north, where Benotrist laborers busied themselves constructing another of the strange towers.

"I do not know, Highness. I suspect they are siege towers of some sort. Perhaps they will add the wheels last, once they are all assembled, in order take us by surprise," Nevias guessed.

"No." She shook her head. "Those platforms are too narrow to support more than a half dozen men at once," she added, pointing her finger toward the nearest structure some one thousand meters in the distance. It wavered unsteady in the light breeze.

"You are right, and none of the completed towers seems of a height to our walls. The Benotrists have no way of using them to attain our battlements, and the gargoyles have no need since they fly," Nevias added.

"Of course," Corry whispered, dread washing over her with revelation.

"Princess?" Nevias asked curiously.

"Summon your commanders. I know their purpose."

*****

By midafternoon, Princess Corry's premonition proved correct as gargoyles scurried up the makeshift platforms. The Torries watched with knowing dread as the gargoyles outstretched their wings, stepping off the edge of the towers, taking to the sky as the towers eased their ascent into the heavens. "To arms!" men shouted, calling Corell's garrison to their posts.

Terin and Cronus joined Master Vantel upon Zar Crest where the princess and Commander Nevias waited. Terin was taken aback upon finding Corry dressed in a short white tunic with polished breast armor and greaves. A shortsword rode her left hip and a helm rested in her right hand. She looked the visage of a warrior queen of old with her golden tresses lifting in the breeze.

Corry ordered every man to arms no matter their station. Even Galen was clad in mismatched armor with outdated bronze breastplate and arm guards with iron greaves and steel helm. A shortsword complemented his belt of knives, which Cronus had witnessed him use proficiently on more than one occasion. They spied Alen hurrying off as they arrived, likely running a message for Commander Nevias.

By the time Terin reached Zar Crest, most of the garrison had emptied out onto the battlements below and the walls of the inner keep. He noticed archers dispersed through the ranks rather than clustered together, wondering the purpose. Neither he nor Cronus attended the commanders' call that Nevias called earlier in the day. Perhaps the dispersing of the archers was a new strategy to combat the change in Morac's tactics.

His eyes shifted further afield, where the gargoyles approaching the castle walls took oddly shaped formations, closing upon the battlements in long lines that stretched to the towers in the distance. What stood out further than the apparent weakness the formations took was that the gargoyles seemed much higher than expected. Realization suddenly dawned that the towers allowed them greater lift, enabling them to soar over the battlements and attain the upper palace without taxing their wings.

Within moments, the first gargoyles passed far above the outer battlements, beyond the range of Torry spears but low enough for Torry archers. Arrows spewed from the outer battlements, riddling the narrow ranks of passing gargoyles. The attacking waves were now some fifty-odd single streams passing far overhead rather than wide and deep ranks struggling to reach the outermost ramparts.

The lead gargoyles in each stream tumbled from the sky, arrows feathering their bodies as Torry archers directed their aim to whichever line was nearest. The following gargoyles broke formation, spreading out as they drew near. Some dove upon the causeway that separated the inner and outer battlements, sweeping down upon the Torries below to little effect, as Torry spears met unprotected flesh. Others drove further before descending upon the upper battlements and turrets but faring little better.

"Ahhh!" Corry looked up as a gargoyle swept down from above, its face contorted with its scimitar outstretched in its right hand. Terin stepped forth, swinging his sword in a high arc, his blade passing through steel and flesh, the blow splitting the scimitar and halving the creature shoulder to crotch. Cronus backed a step as the left half of the creature dropped at his feet while the commanders gathering around them stared dumbstruck at the emphatic blow.

Cronus shifted his gaze across the castle roof, where gargoyles swarmed overhead. An archer atop the Golden Tower struck a gargoyle circling below the citadel, the arrow striking between its wings. The creature smashed into the side of the tower, its body tumbling down its golden wall.

"Remove this carcass before we trip on it!" Commander Nevias ordered his aides, as the slain gargoyle hindered their footing. All across the castle roof, a similar dilemma played out as gargoyle bodies littered the causeways and battlements. Soldiers began tossing the carcasses over the palace walls whenever a break in battle allowed. Despite the chaos, the garrison held their ground, slaughtering the gargoyles wherever they struck, slaying hundreds.

"The east!" the lookouts atop the Tower of Celenia warned. Waves upon waves of gargoyles took to the skies along the eastern siege line. They struggled gaining lift without the aid of the launch towers, which could not facilitate such numbers in so short a time. Their wings would be taxed before attaining the outer walls, but their numbers were not limited like those launching from the towers.

Morac obviously meant to occupy the defenders with those launching from the towers as the greater number approached the palace en masse. They would be most vulnerable at the ramparts' edge and needed their rested comrades to keep the Torries at bay until they were rested enough to advance further upon the battlements.

"I want all archers concentrated on the larger force approaching from the east!" Nevias commanded, knowing their fire was more effective against massed gargoyles than targeting individuals that were difficult to hit.

"We've dispersed them throughout the ranks. It will take time to gather them, Commander," one aide explained.

"There is no time for that. Tell them to stay wherever they are and shoot in that direction!" Nevias growled the obvious, pointing his arm to the east.

"ARGH!" a guard cried out behind them as a gargoyle landed atop him, snapping its fangs, trying to sink them in the soldier's neck as he pinned him to the floor. Cronus marched across the platform, driving his sword in the creature's back as others hacked its wings and legs before pulling its bloody carcass from their comrade. The soldier remained facedown, unmoving with a broken neck.

"KAI-SHORUM!" Gargoyle war cries echoed hauntingly overhead. Cronus turned as three more creatures approached from the north, closing upon the crest in a tight formation. One dipped suddenly, an archer on the wall of the inner keep below, striking its belly. The creature quickly descended, its strength waning with every beat of its wings. The other two continued apace, pushing toward Zar Crest with blood-red eyes.

An archer upon the crest loosed an arrow, the shaft glancing off the helm of one creature, fluttering uselessly astray. His second shaft missed altogether with the third piercing a wing. Both creatures swept over the parapet, dropping onto the platform, swinging their scimitars upon their nearest foes. Soldiers closed around one, swiftly cutting it down whilst Terin finished the other.

Nevias looked despondently as Torry archers felled another gargoyle far above the inner keep, only to have its body crush a soldier below. "Blast!" he cursed. "Tell the fool archers to let them come to us unless they are beyond the palace walls!"

*****

Archers along the east wall directed their fire to the approaching mass, unable to miss the gargoyle horde nearing the outer battlements. Hundreds of creatures slipped from formation, arrows feathering their faces, wings, and shoulders. The dead fell quickly, impacting the ground with their rapid descent. The wounded lingered briefly, forsaking the attack, gliding to the surface as slow as they could manage.

The gargoyle mass met the east wall like the sea breaking upon a jagged shore. Torry soldiers closed ranks before they struck, driving spear tips between interlocked shields, slaying hundreds at the ramparts' edge. The Torries held position, driving the enemy casualties from the wall lest they cluttered the causeway.

The gargoyles from the first wave that launched from the towers shifted to the east wall, falling upon the Torries holding their brethren at bay. Men further back thrust spears into the air, fending off those descending upon them, as the fore ranks focused on the larger threat pressing the walls. The archers had learned their lesson, targeting gargoyles that were not above their comrades lest a falling corpse kill a friend below.

Gargoyle bellies made inviting targets for Torry spears, spilling their innards as they passed. Scores of gargoyles were impaled on outstretched spears, their bodies cluttering the causeway, hindering those holding the battlements. The gargoyles descending from above shifted their attacks to the most forward ranks, crashing down on the wall of shields along the ramparts' edge. They dropped feet first, their impact caving parts of the shield wall, allowing the exhausted gargoyles approaching the wall a place to set down.

Corry nervously observed the happenings along the east wall as small fissures formed along the length of the outer battlements. Gargoyles started to gain greater footholds in several places as Torry swords jabbed desperately to hold their ground. Hundreds of gargoyle corpses littered the battlements, piling up along each bulge in the line, but the Torries could no longer push the dead off the wall.

The following waves used the growing mounds of their own dead to gather upon before garnering the strength to renew their assault after their taxing flight. Torry arrows riddled the festering mountains of corpses, feathering any gargoyle daring to spread its wings or gain its feet. Scores of gargoyle dead were added to each mound, but they only added to the piles, allowing more gargoyles in the following waves to gain a hold.

Catapults along the upper battlements hurled fire ballistae into the piles, igniting the mounting dead ablaze. In several places, the smoke hurt the defenders nearly as much as the enemy. The Torries forsook that tactic, hurling stone and arrows instead. Gargoyles climbed over the fallen, fangs snapping and eyes ablaze, crawling over the dead and wounded to get at the defenders.

"THE WEST WALL!" The cries went out as thousands of gargoyles approached from the west, stretching in endless ranks to the horizon. "THE SOUTH WALL!" others shouted, the enemy approaching from there as well. Confounding their problems, gargoyles continued to launch from their makeshift towers all along the siege lines, allowing hundreds to assail the palace from heights far above the outer walls.

"Concentrate our archers and catapults to the south and west. We must deny them another foothold!" Nevias ordered. Torry ballistae and arrows darkened the sky, cutting large swaths in the approaching ranks. Scores of gargoyles fell upon the foremost ranks guarding the east wall, using their bodies as missiles, dropping upon them from above. Dozens of soldiers collapsed under the weight, breaking bones or suffering trauma of various sorts. Others stepped aside, driving spears into the wretched creatures before they could cause further harm. The defenders quickly learned to combat this unorthodox tactic, but not before the larger formations struck the east wall.

"All reserves to the roof!" Corry ordered. "We must defend every platform and deny them any place to set down!" Nevias acknowledged her command, ordering it so, just as a large hole broke in the center of their shield wall on the eastern battlements. Hundreds of gargoyles poured through as Torry reinforcements swarmed from the inner palace to stem the tide.

"Close the inner battlement gates!" Nevias ordered, though it might already be too late. If the gargoyles secured the outer battlements, they could simply use it to stage their following waves before assailing deeper into the palace. Cronus suddenly realized that Terin was no longer standing beside him.

*****

He raced through the open causeway of the castle roof, passing under the raised portcullis that separated the inner keep from the inner battlements. Soldiers rushed to and fro, hindering his progress as he weaved around and through them where necessary. Many soldiers held their ground, hoisting shields overhead and training their spears on gargoyles circling above.

Terin ignored the threats above, pushing onto the causeway that ran below the inner battlements. He paid little heed to the men lining the battlements above, who faced the threat that waited beyond, or the soldiers passing through the open gate ahead, fleeing the slaughter on the outer battlements. Terin put all else from his mind, driven by a single purpose that called to him beyond the gate.

"Lower the portcullis!" men cried out, relaying Nevias's order, yet men continued to pass under the raised grating, fleeing the carnage without. Soldiers manning the winch wheel released the lock, the portcullis lowering as several gargoyles passed under, chasing a fleeing Torry through the gate, their crimson eyes afire.

Terin stepped between them and their prey, his blade spitting one creature's sword before taking its arm above the elbow and arcing halfway through its chest. He moved on to the second before the first one fell, cutting the gargoyle in half. Split. Thrust. Thrust. He felled two more in rapid succession before slipping under the lowering gate.

"Raise the gate!" Cronus shouted, following close behind, desperate to catch up to his friend, fearing he was too late.

*****

"The east wall is lost!" Nevias growled, cursing their misfortune as the shield wall gave way. Hundreds of soldiers forsook the outer battlements, fleeing to the inner battlements or the north and south walls to regroup. The portcullis along the inner battlements were serried with men passing under them. The men who remained on the outer battlements of the east wall gathered in ever shrinking pockets as gargoyles swarmed over the ramparts.

"Commander!" an aide exclaimed as a brilliant azure light swept onto the outer battlements like a flame dancing freely amid the fray.

"The fool!" Corry gasped, her heart dropping.

*****

Split. The arc of his blade passed through two swords, breaking them on contact, his follow thrust piercing a gargoyle's chest. He removed the blade as quickly as he had thrust, cutting down another to his left. Arrows arced overhead, checking the enemy from swarming over him, though Terin was oblivious of their efforts, the madness of the blade overcoming all sense and reason.

Cronus struggled to reach his friend, nearly tripping several times on the corpse-littered causeway, the bodies of men and gargoyles covering most of the walkway, its white stone surface stained with blood. A creature dropped in front of him, its fangs drenched in human gore as it lifted its glowing red eyes to his, swinging its scimitar with a savage fury. Cronus blocked the hasty swing with his shield, driving his blade in its gut before twisting it free.

The creature stumbled as he chopped its neck and moved on, leaving its twitching carcass in his wake. It was his first kill of the day, as Terin seemed to drive the enemy away, leaving Cronus with little to do but run after him. The enemy either melted away as Terin approached or stood frozen in place as he cut them down, transfixed by his terrible sword.

Terin stepped back as a gargoyle dropped from above, its clawed feet narrowly missing his helm. He chopped its left wing, spinning around it to cut another across the knees as the creature screamed, blood issuing from its stricken appendage before Cronus drove his sword into its chest. Terin continued on as the second gargoyle's knees slid off its severed shins. He moved on as Cronus finished the creature. Most of the gargoyles were now fleeing the madness. Those that remained stood statue still, beguiled by the fell power of his sword.

Gargoyles began to peel away along other parts of the causeway, freeing several pockets of Torry soldiers who were trapped against the walls of the inner battlements. Their weary eyes soon found the source of their deliverance as Terin's blade danced amid the enemy, cutting them down at will. "Forward!" men shouted, surging forth, hindered only by the bodies littering their path.

Terin blocked a scimitar overhead, the blade glancing off his shield as he jabbed his sword into the creature's middle with two quick thrusts. He spun as another creature approached his right, chopping its sword in half and the arm with it at the elbow. He moved on, leaving Cronus to finish his kills. Spill. Jab. Thrust. Spill. Jab. He spun, chopping down three more as his next foe dropped its sword, turning to flee before Terin lopped its head.

He pushed on to the edge of the outer battlements, the enemy fleeing his sword, climbing over the mounds of dead piled upon the ramparts. The gargoyles discarded their weapons, desperate to escape. They spread their wings, jumping off the wall and gliding under the fresh levies approaching the east wall.

The gargoyle reinforcements nearing the east wall were met with archer fire spewing from the upper battlements and their brethren fleeing the battle, springing from the ramparts like frightened douri. The two groups intermingled, the frightened ranks polluting the reinforcements, spreading their madness. Half of the new wave faltered short of the wall, confusion stripping whatever energy they had, weakening their taxed wings and forcing them to the surface. Those that continued on were met by Torries surging across the causeway, meeting them at the ramparts' edge.

As if waking from a dream, Terin found himself standing atop a mountain of dead, catching his breath as the enemy fled, wondering how this came to be. The sound of men cheering echoed in his ears, aligned to either side of him as they pushed the enemy from the walls. Cronus stood to his left, his labored breath heavy with exhaustion.

"It's...not easy...keeping pace with...you." Cronus gasped, struggling with every word as he lowered his sword and shield.

"I..." Terin thought to say something, but the words escaped him. He lowered his sword, its glow dimming as the enemy broke away, forsaking the battle en masse. He could see the distant waves returning whence they came. A gargoyle passed overhead, a straggler who likely launched from a platform. It sped from the battlements, its wings flapping desperately to escape as arrows feathered its back. Terin watched as it faltered beyond the walls, tumbling from the sky.

Craning his neck, Terin could see all the gates separating the inner and outer battlements flung open with reinforcements pouring onto the causeway under their raised portcullis. Torry magantors circled the inner palace, chasing the few gargoyle stragglers that remained. The great avian outstretched their legs, snatching the creatures in their talons before dropping them beyond the castle walls, their grip breaking their wings, leaving them to flail helplessly through their descent.

One figure stood out among the hundreds of soldiers spilling onto the outer battlements, her distinct golden hair trailing her silver helm as she stepped across the dead littering her path, her shield and sword stained with blood.

"Corry?" Terin whispered in disbelief as the princess drew near with Torg upon her right and a dozen Royal Elite fanning out to her flanks, driving their swords into any carcass that might still breathe.

"Highness," Cronus greeted as more men took up position along the ramparts. Terin shifted nervously as her blue eyes met his. He climbed down from the small mountain of corpses piled upon the rampart. He felt suddenly weak as the waning power of the sword exposed his exhaustion.

"You foolish boy." Corry shook her head, wiping the blood from her blade on the hem of her soiled tunic, sliding it into her scabbard.

"Highness." Terin bowed his head as she stepped past them, surveying the enemy fleeing in the distance.

"Foolish but necessary," she added, touching a hand to his shoulder. Terin collapsed, his body surrendering to exhaustion.

*****

Terin awoke, finding himself abed in an unfamiliar room. Torches bracketed along the wall dimly illuminated the spacious chamber. He stared at the domed ceiling above with frescoes painted upon its surface depicting mounted warriors in pitched battle, magantors circling the citadels of Corell, and the fabled waterfalls of Flen in rich detail.

The chamber was filled with sturdy-built furnishings that were more practical than ostentatious, built from solid timber. A wardrobe was affixed to the white stone wall opposite the door, and a long narrow bench rested below a window with closed shutters. His eyes slowly came into focus, adjusting to the light, a familiar voice setting him at ease.

"Lie still, Terin," Leanna soothed, sitting on a chair beside his bed.

"Wh-where am I?"

"Prince Lorn's bedchamber. The princess ordered you brought here when you collapsed," she said, dabbing his head with a cool cloth.

"I…" His mind was a haze, struggling to recall the events of the battle.

"Rest, Terin. There is little for you to do but regain your strength." She placed a hand to his chest, keeping him still.

"The battle? What—"

"We won. For now," she conceded. "Your intervention broke the gargoyle assault on the east wall. The gargoyle attack on the other walls broke soon after. Do you remember any of it?"

"Gargoyles, my sword glowing. It's all jumbled." He shook his head.

"Hmm." Leanna thought pensively before sending a handmaid to inform the princess that Terin had awoken.

"What…what did I do?" Terin asked as she offered him a cup of water.

"What did you do?" She laughed, lifting a curious brow. "You cut a swath through the gargoyle ranks like a child swatting straw men with a play sword. They say you killed a hundred, maybe more. The rest simply fled, all of them."

"All of them?" he wondered aloud. What did that mean?

"All of them. The gargoyles took flight once you ventured onto the battlements. Their cowardice spread among their ranks like a plague. By the time you collapsed, the attacks on the other walls fell apart as well. And you remember none of this?"

He shrugged, only recalling his first steps onto the outer causeway. "Where is Cronus?"

"Helping clear the dead. The battlements are littered with the dead and wounded. We suffered terrible losses on the east wall. Hundreds, maybe thousands, are dead or injured. The Matrons' wards are overflowing. They are gathering the dead in piles to burn in the crematories, but even they are overfull. Many more are piled upon the battlements and set ablaze there. I closed your windows to keep out the stench."

"Thank you, Leanna. I should help the others." Terin began to rise when she again placed a hand to his shoulder, forcing him back down.

"Not until the princess speaks with you."

"Disobedient as always," Corry observed, stepping within, still wearing her blood-stained tunic and armor.

"Highness," Terin greeted as she stopped at his bedside, removing her helm, its shape remaining in her matted hair. Blood stained the skirt of her tunic and smeared across her legs and arms. Her left greave was slightly dented, and her blue eyes were bloodshot from exhaustion and worry.

"Are you well?" she asked, touching her hand to his forehead.

"I, uh, yes. I don't recall what hap—"

"You collapsed. Don't you remember?"

He made a face, uncertain of his answer. "No." He shrugged.

"No?" She lifted a tired brow.

"Well, I remember running beneath the portcullis of the inner battlement and gargoyles surrounding me as I stepped onto the outer causeway. I remember cutting one in half and then…nothing."

"You were probably lacking of water. Battles are very taxing, and men often lose their wits when they lack water," she said, setting his mind at ease, though she believed it not.

"I am well enough to see to my duties, Highness. I should seek Master Vantel. He will—"

"You will rest, Terin. Master Vantel agrees with me on this. The enemy will not launch a major attack this night. We have bloodied them on our walls, slaying many times our number. The only pressing task is seeing to our wounded and clearing the dead," she said, though clearing the dead was nearly as difficult as the battle itself. She feared disease would soon follow before they could dispose of the corpses piled atop the palace and the base of the outer walls.

"I can help with that, Highness."

"To what purpose? We are better served if you save your strength for battle. The enemy will come again. They have no choice now, but not tonight. Using your sword as you did today seems to exhaust your body in ways we do not understand, and it seems it gives you strength as needed but exacts that cost when the need is gone. Now," she said, straightening her back, "will you rest as I have ordered, or must I place a guard to keep you here?"

"I'll obey." He smiled weakly.

"Good boy." She kissed his forehead and stepped without.

*****

"He remembers nothing," Corry said, standing upon Zar Crest, observing the activity below. The stench of burning flesh tortured her senses, the chill night air raising pimples across her bare limbs. Save for two guards standing post at the open stairwell, she and Torg were alone atop the platform.

"Nothing?" Torg asked. "He has never collapsed like that before. Using the sword is draining, as he oft described, but he never spoke of collapsing or remembering nothing."

"What of Telfer?" she asked curiously. "Did Yeltor speak of its effects on him? Did not the Yatin claim Terin having performed similarly, his sword driving the enemy off?"

"He spoke of it taxing him, but not this. Of course, this time, he faced greater numbers. He slew a hundred gargoyles today, maybe more," Torg said, his eyes narrowed in contemplation.

"And drove thousands off, tens of thousands," she corrected herself, that fact weighing far larger than those he slew.

"The legends speak nothing of this power he has unlocked in the sword." Torg scrubbed his chin with his hand, confounded by it all. The swords instilled courage in their wielders and often stripped the nerve of those directly facing them but had *never* sent an entire army in retreat.

"Does Morac and the Nayborian Dethine's swords possess this trait as well?" she asked, fearing the answer.

"We haven't seen them in battle." He left unsaid that her father had, and there were none left to bear witness if Morac's blade could strip away an army's courage. They might not know that answer, as Morac simply waited within his pavilion, throwing his gargoyles upon the walls with little regard to his losses.

"If so, then even General Bode's arrival will count for naught," Corry lamented, envisioning the 3rd Army marching to their relief only to be torn asunder by Morac's blade.

"There is a way to test if Terin is unique."

"How so?" she asked.

"Let another wield his sword," Torg said.

"No. We can ill afford to be wrong, especially now. My fa..." She paused, the word catching in her throat. "My father named Terin Champion of the Realm, believing him a child of prophecy. He died believing so. I shall not dishonor his sacrifice. The sword was intended for Terin, and with him it shall remain.

Just as well, Torg thought, knowing it best not to change what was working. They would have their answer soon enough once Dethine or Morac entered the fray. "King Anthar spoke of Terin with a strange reverence, as if privy to..." Torg's voice trailed.

"Privy to what?" Corry asked.

"There is something we are missing, something about him that—it was the same with his father." Torg couldn't put his finger on it.

"Who is his father, Torg? Truly?" They knew so little of him.

"I wish I knew. I recall his father facing gargoyles in battle *before* he found his fabled sword. The creatures fled from him just as they do Terin," he remembered.

"What?"

"I remember now. How foolish of me to have forgotten, blinded as I was by my hard feelings toward the man. The gargoyles looked at him with abject terror, fleeing the mere sight of him."

"What does it mean?"

"I don't know. Only Jonas Caleph can answer that question." He sighed. They stood there for a time, bereft of words, each lost in their endless thoughts. "You should rest. There is little for you to do this night," Torg advised.

"I shall." She sighed, her heavy eyes struggling to stay open. She stepped away, pausing mid distance to the stair before turning around. "You should tell him, Torg, before it is too late. He deserves to know."

"He does." Torg sighed. It was a conversation he wanted and dreaded, uncertain which he felt greater.

*****

Thump! The ballistae struck its mark above and to the left of the main gate, small stone fragments flaking away. The small hole slowly widened with each blow, as the Naybin catapults pounded the north wall of the palace from dawn to dusk. They renewed their assault at the break of day, the morning sun revealing the carnage of yesterday's battle.

Thousands of gargoyle corpses were piled in small mountains atop the palace and set ablaze. Thousands more littered the grounds below the walls, piled wherever the Torries could gather them and set ablaze, proving the folly of the attack. The stench of burning flesh drifted over the battlefield, curling the noses of the hardiest souls. Hundreds of corpses littered the battlefield between the palace walls and the siege lines, where many gargoyles had dropped dead from their wounds during their retreat.

Thump! The next ballistae hit a meter above its mark, barely denting the powerful wall. The crew quickly reloaded, as the first trebuchet was ready to fire again. They were down to one working trebuchet for three days until the crews worked repairing one of the siege engine's broken cords. They tried various ropes, each breaking under the machine's massive strain. Only moglo sinew was strong enough to hurl the heavy stone without snapping and required great skill in preparing.

Das Doruc stood behind the palisade overlooking the battle-field. The north wall of Corell rose imperiously in the distance, its main gate taunting him as if forged by divine omnipotence, unbreakable and unyielding. Das Doruc removed his helm, raking a hand through his braided dark hair, allowing fresh air to cool his brow.

"We've only sixty ballistae, General Doruc," said Tas Delov, commander of the Naybin catapult contingent.

"Continue firing what you have left, Commander. I want the breach we opened widened!" Das Doruc commanded, pointing his fore digit toward the north wall. General Das Doruc commanded the Nayborian infantry, cavalry, and catapult contingents and coordinated their efforts to breach the north wall. He was second only to Dethine, the Nayborian champion and leader of the Naybin expedition.

"As you command, General Doruc, but we shall expend our ballistae by midmorning," Commander Delov apprised.

"I've already sent outriders to the quarry to hurry their shipment along. I expect them here by midday," Das reassured him, though worried his outriders might not return. His crews were running low on ballistae stones since their resupply caravans were cut by Torry cavalry raiding their lines of communication. Now even their supplies from the stone quarry north of Corell were under attack, forcing Das to reinforce their caravans with most of his cavalry, which seemed to be everywhere in recent days.

Das stepped away from the palisade, its protruding stakes jutting sharply toward the palace, as Dethine's golden mount drew near, galloping through the Naybin encampments that ran behind the siege lines. "King's champion!" he hailed as Dethine rode up beside him with a dozen riders of his personal guard fanning to either flank.

"Commander Doruc, Lord Morac is calling a war council. Attain your mount and follow me hither!" Dethine commanded.

*****

General Doruc followed Dethine within Morac's pavilion. They were greeted by comely slave girls offering refreshment and wine, as befitted their station as their master's guests. Dethine lifted a goblet from the serving tray, regarding the scantily clad girl with a lecherous eye. The girls were clad in diaphanous scarlet cloth wrapped snugly around their chests, lifting their ample bosoms, and narrow strips tucked over a corded belt, draping beneath their waists, one in front and the other behind. Silver collars graced their throats, and iron bands with bells affixed to them were fastened to their ankles. The girls curtsied with practiced smiles before stepping away.

"Dethine, General Doruc, welcome," Morac greeted, waving them forward. He rested comfortably on a cushioned large chair with three other slave girls attending to him. One rubbed his naked feet, another offered refreshment upon a serving platter, and the third was snuggled beneath his left arm. The other girls moved about the tent quietly, save for the soft ringing of their ankle bells.

"Lord Morac." Dethine raised his goblet, honoring their host. "It seems we are alone." His eyes failed to see any of Morac's subordinates.

"They will gather here shortly. I wished to speak with you both before I let them in," Morac explained.

"Concerning?"

"Can you breach the wall?" Morac asked intently.

"We have opened a small hole above the gate, exposing a portion of the gate's support rods," Das explained.

"What of the wall itself?"

"The wall is more than fifteen meters thick at its base, maybe eighteen to twenty-two. It would require hundreds of trebuchets, tens of thousands of ballistae, and several moons to break a hole through it. The weakest part of the wall is the gate itself. If we can further expose the gate's upper workings embedded in the rock, we can weaken its supports and breach the gate with the proper equipment," Das explained.

"How long?" Morac gained his feet, brushing his slave girl aside.

"With enough ballistae"—Das rubbed his chin pensively—"perhaps a fortnight."

"You have *four* days."

"Four?" Das's eyebrows lifted.

"It shall be done!" Dethine assured them. "Plan your assault, my friend. The gate will open to your legions."

"Excellent." Morac smiled. He noticed Dethine's gaze continuously drawn to the girl standing further back, holding a pitcher of wine. "Keya!" Morac snapped his fingers, calling the girl forth.

"Master." She hurried forth, bobbing a curtsy while keeping her eyes trained to his feet.

"She is quite fetching, wouldn't you agree?" Morac said, lifting her chin with his rough hand, gifting Dethine a better view of her comely face. Bright amethyst eyes stared demurely through her thick lashes. Auburn tresses framed her delicate chin and pert nose. A golden collar graced her slender throat, resplendent even in the dim light.

"Exquisite." Dethine regarded her with obvious interest.

"She is the daughter of a wealthy Notsuan merchant. I spotted her standing among the crowd in the city's council forum, a rare flower amid the thorns."

"She is highborn?" Dethine asked bemusedly.

"All my prizes are highborn." Morac swept an open hand across the pavilion, regarding the dozen slave girls of his personal retinue. "What joy is there in collaring peasants and lowborn wenches whose spirits have long been broken? Nay," he said, running a finger along the girl's cheek. "There is such sweet pleasure in fastening a collar to a haughty maid born to privilege, to break them to your will." The girl shuddered as his lips lingered near her ear.

"Breaking her spirit must have brought you great pleasure," Dethine said, imagining her ravishment.

"Ah, she is not broken, not yet. She has submitted in all things but one, the very thing that separates a pure maiden from a plucked flower."

"She is chaste?" Dethine asked.

"Pure." Morac ran a finger along her neck. "The gold collar represents her intact maidenhood. Once I fully claim her, I shall exchange it for silver. I was saving her to celebrate our victory once

Corell strikes its colors. I have only two such maidens in my collection. The rest wear the silver." Das wondered why Morac was explaining to him in such detail the status of his slaves.

"Keya can be yours, Dethine, and Hena"—Morac indicated a similarly striking slave girl standing further back with a gold collar about her throat—"can be yours, General Doruc. Breach the wall in four days and I shall gift them to you."

Slave girls were common and came quite cheap during war, where captives were plentiful, but highborn girls of such beauty were always prized. The gifting of such prizes was considered a high honor among warriors, a sign of esteem and respect.

"Then how shall you celebrate our victory if you gift us your last golden collars?" Dethine inquired.

"I am certain there are other prizes awaiting my collar within Corell." Morac smiled knowingly. "Guyin!" he said, calling for his aide-de-camp.

"Lord Morac," the young Benotrist Elite answered, stepping within the pavilion.

"Send them in!"

A dozen men and gargoyles entered the pavilion. Five were the generals of the legions present, and the rest were a collection of Tyro's Elite. Das was familiar with his counterparts, each general wearing the four braided cords around their left shoulder, indicating their rank as commanders of army. Three of the generals were gargoyles commanding the 5th, 6th, and 7th Legions.

General Concaka commanded the 5th, his wide-set fangs setting him apart from the others. General Maglakk commanded the 6th, his crimson eyes flaring more intensely than the others, as if he was about to explode. General Vaginak commanded the 7th, his extremely narrow build and tall frame standing out among the others. The Benotrist generals Vlesnivolk and Felinaius commanded the 8th and 11th Legions.

The Benotrists had seen little battle since the outset of the siege, a fact that sat poorly with the likes of General Maglakk, who glared distrustfully whenever their eyes met.

"Generals, allies, my fellow Elite," Morac began, addressing each in kind as they formed a semicircle around him. "Casualties?" he asked, cutting to the first matter at hand.

"Four thousand," Concaka said sourly, leaving his legion with thirty-four telnics.

"Two thousand," Vaginak hissed, reducing the 7th Legion to thirty-five telnics.

"Twenty thousand!" snarled Maglakk, the assault on Corell's east wall reducing his once proud legion to sixteen telnics. It would take days to reconstitute his shattered legion into any semblance of a fighting force. Corell was proving far more difficult to crack than Morac once believed.

"Twenty thousand?" Morac questioned, realizing the near destruction of the 6th Legion. "Gather your troops and hold position. The 4th Legion will soon arrive. They shall relieve your troops, and you can reposition to a reserve role."

"Whatsss legion?" Maglakk hissed. "My legion is gone. You"— he extended a digit threateningly to Morac—"have slaughtered themssss!" Morac glared at his legion commander with dangerous dark eyes. "You sendsss us to our death, keeping your fellow humansss safely in their trenches," Maglakk spat, regarding Vlesnivolk and Felinaius.

A violent burst of crimson light illuminated the pavilion as Morac drew his sword, its swift arc striking Maglakk's neck. The others backed a step as the gargoyle's head tumbled in the air before dropping at their feet. Morac's blade shone brilliantly, bathing his face in its fiery aura. "Twenty thousand and one," he said, sliding the sword into its scabbard. "Now let us discuss the next assault."

Three days hence

The stench of burning flesh permeated the air, choking the senses with its noxious fumes. The dead were piled in dozens of mounds atop the palace and below, at the base of the outer walls, where most of the gargoyle corpses were thrown. The mounds were set ablaze days ago with the defenders adding corpses to their piles as they cleared the palace. Whenever the fires died out, they would douse the dead with oil and reset them ablaze.

The largest mound at the base of the east wall rose nearly the height of nine men at its apex, the smoke from its fires drifting into the heavens in billowing clouds of black and gray. Gargoyle carcasses littered the battlefield in each direction, their rotting flesh torturing the noses of friend and foe alike. Morac granted no quarter to allow them to clear the dead, choosing to torture the defenders and his own troops equally. The Torries had worked tirelessly since the battle's end, clearing the castle roof, completing the task by the break of dawn.

Nevias strode across the outer battlements with Sergon Vas, commander of the east wall. Sergon's usually quiet and stoic disposition faltered, if ever slightly, as they walked. His beleaguered telnics suffered the brunt of the gargoyle attacks, nearly 1,500 casualties in all, three-fourths of the Torries' total losses. Several hundred might be fit to return to duty, but most would not.

He had spent his morn in the infirmary, the crowded hall serried with wounded men. Some were beyond saving, lingering until death took them. Those suffering abdominal injuries were certain to perish, often writhing in agony for days before succumbing. Head wounds fell under the extremes of superficial or mortal. Often a puncture to the eye went straight to the brain, though some failed to cut cleanly through. Sergon recalled the Matrons treating one lad with his left eye punctured. It took a dozen men to hold him down in order for the healers to remove the eye, lest infection spread, the boy's screams unnerving the hardiest of souls.

"So many dead." Sergon sighed tiredly as they skirted a small ashen mound, wisps of smoke drifting above the charred remains.

"Such is war. How fares your new commanders of units?" Nevias asked. Seven of the east wall's unit commanders were slain or unfit for duty, decimating Sergon's chain of command.

"They seem competent. The only concern is the sixth unit. It lost its commander, its second and eight of ten commanders of flax. I promoted Lorus Tarv to commander of unit. He is quite young, but the men of his flax speak well of him."

"Very well. What of your rank-and-file replacements?" Nevias inquired, regarding the reserves that filled in the gaps. Most were lesser-trained conscripts or those transferred from abandoned hold-fasts. Once these reserves were spent, the garrison would draw from the civilians who found sanctuary at Corell before the siege. All these reserves currently served in the palace's defense throughout the castle, brandishing whatever weapons were available to them. With so many casualties, there were now more weapons than men to wield them.

"The reinforcements will take time to integrate. The new commanders are drilling them whenever they are not clearing the dead," Sergon said.

"Time we won't have." Nevias sighed as they stopped at the edge of the battlements, overlooking the enemy from afar. Carka birds feasted on the corpses that littered the battlefield while thousands more circled overhead, awaiting their promised carrion.

Further east, the lookouts atop the Tower of Celenia spotted a dark mass along the horizon, gargoyle reinforcements. By midday, they would be well in view of the palace walls, parading behind their banner, a bloody gray ax upon a field of black, the sigil of the 4th Gargoyle Legion.

Why were they so late to the siege? What purpose delayed their arrival? Such questions were foremost in Nevias's thoughts when a lone rider galloped forth from the northeast corner of the siege lines, carrying a solid blue banner, the flag of truce.

*****

The Benotrist herald skirted the north wall, approaching the main gate. The gate raised, allowing him entry, where he was disarmed, blindfolded, and escorted to the throne room. They stopped short of the vast chamber, where his blindfold was lifted before passing through the large open doors. The Benotrist stepped within, his eyes drawn wide in wonder as he crossed the mirrored white stone floor, his image reflecting off its clear surface.

Statues twice the height of a man lined the walls, crafted in lifelike precision. The statues were placed between a series of white stone arches that ran the length of the elongated chamber with spaces between them stained in blue, like a clear summer sky. The marble statues stood in front of the azure walls as if they were giants rising into the sky.

The Benotrist could feel their lifeless eyes upon him as he passed, judging him as a foe trespassing into their sacred hall. He surmised their visage as kings of old, each cast in such lifelike detail that he felt they might come to life and strike him down.

His eyes were drawn to the far end of the chamber, where a large black throne rested upon a raised dais with a lesser throne cast in white to its right. A woman sat on the black throne, her slender form swallowed by the massive chair. She wore a shimmering silver gown, and a thin silver crown with jewels adorning its edge resting atop her golden tresses. He could feel her steel-blue eyes upon him as he approached, her stern countenance tearing away any shred of self-assurance that remained to him. The guards stopped him short of the dais, where he knelt.

"Your name?" Corry asked, appraising the Benotrist kneeling before her.

"I am Guyin," he said, gaining his feet to address her.

"Remain as you were!" a rough-voiced warrior commanded, standing beside the throne clad in dark mail over black trousers and steel guards upon his forearms. He was well-built with silver tainting his dark mane.

Guyin sank back to his knees, less certain of his safety than a moment before. "I am Guyin, two hundred and sixty-second among Emperor Tyro's Elite, steward of Lord Morac and herald of the Benotrist-Gargoyle Empire."

"Lord Morac?" Corry asked darkly.

"Lord of Bacel and Notsu, as right of conquest," Guyin affirmed, lifting his chin as he met her cool blue eyes.

"Lord of Bacel, lord of *ash*. Bandy not such titles before this throne, Guyin, herald of darkness. Speak your master's will, or be gone from my presence."

"Lord Morac seeks parlay with Your Highness." Guyin bowed.

"To what purpose?" she asked icily. "He seeks our destruction, and we his."

"Lord Morac desires to speak with Your Highness on matters of…interest."

"And what matters are these that could draw the princess from the safety of Corell?" Torg asked harshly, standing at her side with arms crossed.

"Lord Morac guarantees your safety, Highness, under the blue flag of truce, mid distance between our lines, just beyond your north gate. Should you agree to treat with him on the morrow, he shall offer a gift as a sign of good faith."

"Gift?" she asked.

"A small boon to demonstrate Lord Morac's magnanimity. We have numerous prisoners attained throughout our march across your lands, women and children mostly, some men. Lord Morac has agreed to release two hundred to your custody upon your agreement to meet."

"Two hundred more for us to feed. Kill them and be done with it, Benotrist!" Torg growled.

"Release the prisoners, and I shall meet your false lord," Corry agreed.

"Your Highness is most wise." Guyin again bowed.

"Spare me your flatteries, Benotrist. You will free the prisoners *before* I meet your master. I expect the prisoners to be in good health."

"As you command, Highness," Guyin agreed.

The following morn

The prisoners were escorted through the main gate after a cursory inspection and questioning, verifying their place of birth. The Torries found them in surprisingly good health considering the rumors of the Benotrists' cruelty. Most were women and children. The few men were of peasant stock. Tradesmen with specific skills were likely kept to apply their trades to the Benotrist cause. Princess Corry received them in the center courtyard, sitting on her snowy mount as they paraded by. They bowed gratefully as they passed, thankful to their regent for their deliverance.

Corry sat on her ocran with bright silver mail over a brief white tunic, her bare legs covered only by the silver greaves running from her ankles to her knees. A steel helm graced her brow, concealing much of her face, save her chin and blue eyes that stared through its narrow slits. A plume of blue feathers ran the middle of her helm from front to neck, arcing backward as if pressed by an unseen gale. A shortsword rode on her left hip and a dagger on her right. Her forearms were girded with armor from wrist to elbow. She looked like a warrior queen of legend, her mere visage instilling hope in her people.

Torg Vantel stood beside her as the people passed, appraising them with far more discernment. He had already vented his displeasure with the arrangement, placing no trust in Morac's assurances. "I'll not sacrifice two hundred of my people to Morac's mercy when I can gain their freedom by merely treating with the cur," the princess had said.

Torg recalled the exchange after Morac's emissary departed. He counseled against it, but the princess stubbornly refused him. She was more headstrong than her father, and he told her so. She merely kissed his cheek and assured him that all would be fine. He loved her as much as his own daughter, having seen her grow up before his eyes.

"I should be your escort," he said to her as another group hurried past.

"You command in my place, Torg. I have chosen my escort well and trust my life to their fell hands." She regarded Terin and Cronus, who waited behind her, each clad similarly to her sans the blue feathers adorning their helms. Torg regarded each of them and shook his head. *Babies guarding babies,* he wanted to say. "See to these people, Torg. I want every one of them armed and ready to stand post, even the women and children," she said.

"Aye, I'll see it done." Every man, woman, and child would fight, as they expected no quarter from the enemy. Everyone knew these prisoners were spared degradation and torture to gain Morac an audience with the princess.

"Come!" Corry commanded, leading Terin and Cronus through the tunnel.

*****

She steeled her heart, riding forth from the main gate, her eyes fixed on the three mounted figures waiting ahead beneath an azure flag. Cronus rode her left and Terin her right, as custom allowed her two escorts. The wind lifted her golden tresses, trailing her helm as she paraded forth. Corry took a deep breath, quelling her pounding heart. If rumors were true, then the man up ahead was her father's killer. Could she guard her tongue in his presence? Or her tears?

Morac awaited her at the agreed upon place—mid distance between his lines and the castle walls. He wore heavy black trousers to conceal his scarred left leg, which he eased from the stirrup, stretching it painfully before she drew near. His healers assured him that it would fully heal in time, but not before this battle was decided. He wore his gold mail over a black tunic with polished greaves and fore guards and a blood-red cape draping his shoulders.

His cruel eyes stared through the empty sockets of the ape skull affixed to his helm, projecting the malice of his caliginous heart. He sat atop a black ocran that stood statue still, its broken spirit obedient to his will. It was one of several that he had ridden throughout the campaign, but not his spirited favorite, which fell at Kregmarin, the one insult inflicted upon him by the Torry king before he took his head. "She comesss!" his companion hissed as the princess drew near.

Cronus recognized the gargoyle sitting on Morac's left even from afar, its unique size and intelligent stare setting the creature apart from its brethren. *Kriton!* he thought sourly as they eased to a trot before stopping before them. Kriton sat on his mount with a pike driven in the ground beside him with a large sack over its top, concealing a bulging object beneath. Looking beyond their host, he could see pikes of similar size driven into the ground, set approximately sixty paces apart in a long line stretching to the enemy siege-works and beyond.

"Kenti!" Kriton hissed, his eyes flickering between dull crimson to fiery red, struggling to contain his rage. Cronus regarded him with a cold stare, stilling his tongue, as protocol required the princess to speak first unless granting that task to her escort.

"Princess," Morac greeted, removing his helm, undressing her with lecherous eyes.

"Morac, I assume," the princess answered dryly.

"Lord Morac, keeper of the golden sword, lord of Bacel and Notsu, prime among Tyro's Elite, anointed to lead these legions in the conquest of your kingdom. He is worthy of far more than the mere utterance of his mighty name, Princess," the golden-haired warrior to his left proclaimed. She recognized the distinct golden braids and Naybin colors as Dethine, the Nayborian champion.

"Lord, slave, peasant, or prince, it matters not what titles you claim. I consign all as friend or foe, Dethine, enemy of the Torry realm," she retorted, keeping her eyes upon Morac.

"As I consign those who oppose me to those conquered and those yet to submit." Morac smiled, though it didn't reach his eyes.

"You asked for parlay, Morac, lord of carrion and bones. Put words to the purpose of our meet!" she challenged, weary of his banter.

"Of course, Highness, though I would be remiss to ignore protocol and fail to properly announce my second and third." He stretched an open hand, regarding his companions. "You have already addressed my third, Dethine, champion of Nayboria and commander of the Naybin contingent." Morac regarded the blond warrior to his left.

"Princess," Dethine greeted her with a mock bow.

"And my second, Kriton, third among the emperor's Elite and keeper of the dungeon of Fera," Morac declared, indicating the gargoyle to his right. Corry stiffened at the mention of Cronus's tormentor, repulsed by the creature's cruel eyes. "And your escort?" Morac asked, though he already knew.

"We can forgo such pleasantries. Speak quickly to your purpose, or I shall end this parlay," she said.

"You wound me, Princess. I expect a lady of such refinement and breeding to adhere to the protocols of state. No matter since I have had the pleasure of meeting your second." Morac regarded Terin, further stretching his false smile.

"The pleasure of your defeat at Terin's hand upon the ramparts of Fera, no doubt," she retorted.

"Lies from the mouth of a coward," Dethine mocked, staring intently at Terin, "a coward who failed to meet my challenge before these very walls."

"A challenge better given in battle, Naybin. You were free to challenge Terin atop the wall during the previous attack. I am sure Morac would have lent you the use of a magantor for you to attain the wall. Or was such an attack beneath you, reserved only for the gargoyles that you throw upon our walls as fodder?" Cronus said.

"Perhaps my challenge was misdirected. You and I before these very walls, Torry. Whenever your fear abates and you gain the courage, I shall meet you in full view of your beleaguered garrison." Dethine shifted his ire to Cronus.

"Lay down your sword and I'll face you now," Cronus challenged.

"You'll face *me*, Kenti, before any othersss. Your blood is mine by rightsss!" Kriton snarled.

"You only hold claim on those chained and helpless, Kriton. I am neither, and when next our swords cross, it shall be your end." Cronus met his feral gaze with equal malice.

"Keep a leash on your pet, Princess, for we stand under the flag of truce," Morac warned.

"Then muzzle your pets if it concerns you so, lord of carrion," Corry rebuked, weary of their banter.

"We need not cast aspersions, Princess. I hope we can agree to end this unfortunate…dispute between our great realms," Morac said.

"Then gather your legions and return whence you came if you truly wish to end this *dispute*," she said icily.

"Ah, but one cannot ask of such from a position of weakness, Princess, and you are *very* weak."

"Am I? It is you that has suffered great loss in your vain attacks. How many troops have you lost, twenty thousand, thirty thousand, more? We suffered far less. We gladly exchange thirty for one."

"Your next exchange will not come so cheap, Princess. My next assault will come almost exclusively from above your walls. My men have doubled the number of launch towers in the past three days." Morac waved an open hand to his left and right, along the length of his siege lines around the palace, regarding the towers that continued to rise along the perimeter. "This alone will greatly lessen my losses. Look to your north wall. How much longer can it endure under the Naybin barrage? Once it is breached, my Benotrist legions will sweep across this field and pour into the palace while my gargoyle legions assail the top. You cannot win."

"A bold claim," she said.

"A promise, Highness, a promise of things to come. Can you not see?" He again outstretched his hands, holding his helm in one hand and the other empty, stretching them to their utmost. "My legions surround you. You are *alone*. Your father challenged my legions with *three* times your strength and failed. What hope have you? If my legions storm the palace, they shall put everyone to the sword, save for you. With you, I shall consummate my victory upon your dead mother's bed with my *trophy* overseeing our physical union." He nodded to Kriton, who removed the sack from atop the pike.

Corry gasped, her voice caught in the narrows of her throat. Her father's head adorned the pike, staring at her with lifeless eyes, his crown resting upon his brow. Patches of tar clung to his flesh and hair, evidence of Morac's means of preserving it from rot. He preserved it for this very moment, freeing the prisoners to draw her forth and present this macabre trophy of his triumph.

"Now you understand what delayed the 4th Gargoyle Legion. Envision the Plain of Kregmarin where the first pole stands, following an unbroken line to Bacel, Notsu, and across the eastern provinces of Torry North to this very place. The heads of the 5th Torry Army and their allies adorn each pike, a tribute to the inevitable fate of your kingdom, Highness, should you resist. Shall I continue from Corell to the gates of Central City, using the heads of your garrison to adorn more pikes, stretching to the west?" Morac sneered, his menacing smile matching the malice of his eyes.

Terin shifted in the saddle, wanting to draw his blade and strike Morac down, but the sword held him in place, suppressing his will.

"You can spare your people such a fate, Highness. They need not die to assuage your pride. Open your gates and surrender your garrison, and I shall spare your men. Your fate would improve as well. I shall claim you as a concubine rather than a bed slave and spare you the indignity of soiling your virtue before your father's eyes." Morac's words were like poisoned arrows, spewing from his lips one after the other. "Think of the others who are sheltered therein. What of Leanna?" Morac said, gauging Cronus's reaction.

"Still your tongue!" Cronus warned, a dangerous fury passing his eyes.

"So she is here." Morac grinned triumphantly. "Kriton spoke of your affection, how you called out her name whilst you slept when you were our guest. Vent your fury upon yourself, Cronus Kenti, for your own tongue betrayed her. Should I storm the palace, be sure that Kriton will visit upon her the suffering you have inflicted upon him tenfold."

"You should have died at the bridge," Cronus spat, burning with anger as he looked into Kriton's soulless eyes.

"Of course, none of this need come to pass. Knowing the Earthers' fondness for Commander Kenti and his fair lady, I can guarantee their safety in exchange for the Earthers' good behavior. They are fond of Caleph as well, though our emperor has other plans for *him*. He desires him alive and whole for some purpose. He has taken a keen interest in the boy since his visit to Fera," he said cryptically. "None of you need die in a vain sacrifice for a kingdom that has already fallen. What say you, Princess?" Morac finished, emptying his quiver into her shattered heart.

Corry lifted her eyes to the heavens, beseeching an omnipotence that seemed to dwell beyond her sight, seeking the strength and words to answer this scion of malevolence. Her father spoke of a deity that spawned creation by mere thought, setting the stars and universe in order, a deity that bestowed strength to those who humbled themselves before its divinity and turned from the dark inclinations of their heart. But if such a being existed, it forsook her father at Kregmarin, and she would have none of it.

She released a breath, calming the trepidation of her heart. The tightness in her throat eased, allowing her to speak without breaking in tears. She lowered her eyes to Morac's, steeling her heart to his aspersions, her gaze stripping away his aura of strength.

"Bring ten more legions and bathe in the blood of thousands, but the towers of Corell shall never bow to your savagery. You ask for parlay to draw me here for little more than childish theatrics and brutish threats, to frighten me in gifting you what it would cost you in the blood of tens of thousands? No." She shook her head. "You called for parlay to take my measure." She removed her helm, her hair lifting in the breeze as he beheld her beauty.

"I will cut open my womb and slash my own throat before falling captive to the likes of you, and not before staining my sword with your minions' blood. Now you know my measure, my worth, my strength. You want Corell? Come and take it!" Corry donned her helm and turned, galloping back to the main gate. Terin waited as Cronus and Kriton exchanged heated glares.

"I'll be up there if you're brave enough to lead your vanguard." Cronus pointed to the palace roof before turning to follow the princess, Terin falling in beside him.

"Soon!" Kriton hissed, his bright-red tongue stroking his fangs.

*****

The land passed into shadow. With the night came a terrible darkness, black clouds shading the sky above, casting doubt in her heart. Perhaps it was an omen of the days to come or a reminder of that fell place where the spirit drowned in the lurid depths of despair. Corry stood upon the terrace that adjoined her bedchamber atop the inner keep. She stared dispirited, overlooking the campfires that stretched to the horizon like stars painting a midnight sky.

The vision of her father's lifeless eyes burned in her memory, haunting her thoughts. She could hear Morac's mocking sneer play in her ears over and over, goading her to act in haste as if she was a simpleminded girl terrified by his cruel theatrics. She would never relent, not to him, not ever. She had given the order that every man, woman, and child would fight to the death.

She would bleed Morac upon these walls, reducing his legions for others to confront. General Bode's 3rd Army could overcome one legion or two and crush Morac if his strength was so reduced. Either way, she was adamant that Corell would be a Benotrist and gargoyle graveyard, not a trophy of their triumph. If Morac was the lord of carrion, she would gift him his own bones.

As hard as she might, she could not suppress her father's memory, his kind heart and gentle eyes. She nearly begged him not to go east, to leave the task to others, but he refused her, speaking of the duty and honor of their house. Oh, how she loved him, his absence leaving a cavernous hole in her heart. If she closed her eyes, she could almost feel his arms around her, feeling the warmth of his embrace.

She tried to direct her thoughts elsewhere, to the mundane details of the palace that any lesser courtesan could attend. She tried to think of the battle to come or other memories to distract her. Only thoughts of Terin sufficed, helping assuage her sorrow. "I need to be strong," she affirmed, though strength was beyond her now as she burst into tears, venting her grief.

*****

Cronus found her atop the inner keep with her arms tucked underneath her, leaning over a rampart, observing the activities below. She could see Galen sitting atop a stone outcropping with hundreds of weary soldiers gathered around him. They were cloistered along the open expanse of the causeway that connected the structures of the inner palace and circumvented the opening that overlooked the courtyard below. The men stood quietly as the minstrel sang one ballad after another, from merry tunes to mournful ballads, lifting and lowering their spirits with each telling. Leanna listened attentively, losing herself in the wondrous tales of loss, war, and love until a warm hand touched her shoulder.

"Leanna," Cronus said softly as she turned, stepping into his arms. She rested her head on his chest, closing her eyes as a gentle breeze played upon her face.

"My love," she whispered, reaching up to kiss him. His lips felt off, cold and distant, his troubled thoughts dampening his passion. She regarded him as they parted, seeing the worry plaguing his green eyes. She had seen him weary, worried, and frightened, but the look in his desperate eyes transcended any emotion she could recollect. "Cronus, what troubles you?"

"I…" He struggled putting words to his raging heart. "Kriton is here."

"Kriton?" She gasped, knowing well the name of his tormentor. Only through much cajoling did she extract the truth from Cronus, trying to glean what transpired at Fera ever since their reunion at Tro. She recalled a night before the siege when he spoke of his harrowing tale and the fate of his men. She knew he omitted much of what he suffered for her sake, but the haunted look in his eyes that night revealed all she needed to know.

"He…he was at the parlay. He overheard me speaking your name in my sleep during my…my time in his keeping." She was trying to piece together what he was trying to say. "I betrayed you," Cronus said, confessing the treason of his tongue, "betrayed you to him in my sleep."

"I don't understand. How did you betray me?" Her heart was aching for the pain she saw in his eyes.

"He knows your name. So does Morac. They…they threaten…" He couldn't say it.

"Oh," she said, finally putting together what he was trying to say. "They have threatened to torture, abuse, or kill me in some unspeakable fashion? Is that what you mean to say?"

"Yes." He sighed.

"And how is this different from their intent with everyone else? What more can they threaten? Have they not demonstrated their savagery time and again?" she reminded him.

"That is different. Those people—"

"Were not me," she answered, finishing his words.

He gripped her shoulders tightly, staring at her with desperate eyes. "I cannot bear to imagine it, to think it!" he said fiercely. "If only I hadn't—"

"Hadn't what, Cronus? Not cried out my name when you suffered so? That is no betrayal, merely a profession of love. Would I not have done the same? Do you know what I thought of to comfort me during your absence?" she asked, touching a hand to his face. "You. I thought of you. I dreamed of you. I…yearned for you."

"I cannot bear him hurting you." He lowered his head.

She hated seeing him so beaten, so low. "Look at me!" she commanded, and he returned his eyes to hers. "They will never hurt me." She lifted the dagger she carried in the belt wrapped around her gown, presenting it before him. "If the palace falls, I'll rip my inner thigh open and be gone in the passing of a breath." His heart ached at the thought of her dying. "Put my suffering from your mind, Cronus. The only obsession I desire from you is killing as many of them as you can."

*****

Torg Vantel stood alone upon Zar Crest, awaiting Terin upon the platform. He ordered everyone else away, needing to speak with his young charge alone. Terin was still off attending errands that Torg asked of him, working feverously to please the commander of the Elite. He shook his head, thinking of how hard the boy sought his approval. Torg was never fond of Terin's father, but Jonas raised him well.

He released a weary sigh, placing the flat of his hand on the rampart in front of him, looking off in the distance. The enemy cookfires dotted the horizon, a grim reminder of their seemingly unlimited strength. He could hear their chants and songs echoing dully in the distant night air. He felt a fool—a lifetime of service to the throne and all his efforts bringing the realm to ruin.

He had known better than to allow Lore to expose himself and the 5th Army to the east. He should have put stronger words to his misgivings. *Bah, he wouldn't have listened,* he reminded himself. Once Lore set his mind to some grand ideal, he couldn't be moved.

He could hear the minstrel's voice echoing from below, where he entertained a number of the men. He didn't look down but listened quietly as he stared off to the distance, the words kindling memories of more festive gatherings in far happier days.

>Kal, Kal, oh ancient king
>That bards write and poets sing

"Master Vantel?" Terin's voice drew him from his melancholy.

"Come, lad." Torg waved him over, keeping a hand on the rampart as Galen's voice faded with the conclusion of his ballad. No cheers followed the final verse as the men stood quietly reflecting on the tale's meaning. A fallen ancient kingdom could easily portend their own demise, or were they to take solace in the legacy of King Kal? The Torry Kingdoms represented the continuance of that ancient realm through their ties to fallen Tarelia.

"Commander Sorus says the main gate is solid, though the catapults have punched a man-size hole above the portcullis, exposing the gate support," Terin reported. Torg sent him throughout the palace on several occasions to gather status reports from different commanders. It was a good way for his charges to learn the lay of the castle and the importance of each post and how it connected to another part of the palace's defense.

"The gate support could be a problem. It shall bear watching," Torg said.

"Commander Sorus agrees. I visited the west wall earlier as you asked, and Commander Balka expressed concern about—"

"The enemy magantors, I know, or at least the absence of them," Torg said, having already spoken to the craggy commander earlier.

"Do you think it means something, Master Vantel?" Terin asked warily.

Torg sighed, thinking on the matter. No enemy magantors had been seen for two days, not even in the distance. Either they were off attending other matters that Morac thought more urgent or were baiting them to send what few war birds they had left to seek aid. Or had Commander Valen drawn them to battle somewhere beyond the horizon?

"It could mean many things, lad—some good, some not so good."

"Which do you think it is?"

"Bah, I always assume the worst and prepare myself accordingly. With all the launch towers Morac has constructed, they don't need magantors to fly above our walls."

They barely held off the last assault. If the enemy came again with more gargoyles able to fly over the battlements, then what hope had they? Terin sighed, his tired mind unable to muster the barest optimism. He wanted nothing more than to retire to his barrack and sleep but waited for Torg to dismiss him. Torg, however, didn't appear in any hurry to do so. There was something that Torg wanted to say but was unsure where to begin.

"Something troubles you, Master Vantel?" Terin asked, scolding himself for being so presumptuous. It was not his place to ask a question that placed him as Torg's equal. Besides, what didn't trouble him considering their situation? Torg surprised him, however, as he answered.

"There is something I meant to tell you long ago, something I've put off for far too long." Torg paused, the words coming harder than he rehearsed in his mind. Terin perked up, his weariness giving way to equal dread and curiosity. He long suspected Torg holding some grudge against his father but could only guess why.

"Does it concern my mother?" Terin asked warily.

"Yes." Torg was annoyed that he was so transparent.

"You loved her," Terin conceded, knowing it true.

"I did, and I do, more than you could ever know." Torg sighed.

Terin felt a sudden apprehension, confirming what he feared to be true. He often wondered the source of Torg's animosity toward his father and could think of nothing other than his mother. "She chose him over you," Terin said.

"Over me?" Torg lifted a brow, confused by Terin's assumption.

"You loved her, yet she chose my father."

"She chose Jonas over her family and honor," he corrected him.

Now it was Terin's turn to be confused. "But you said you loved her?"

Torg stood, rising to his full height, his stern gaze withering Terin under its intense stare. "I loved her since she emerged from her *mother's* womb and was placed in my arms."

Terin backed a step, his eyes wide with disbelief, realizing Torg's true connection to his mother, his father, and himself. He wrongly thought Torg a suitor for his mother's hand. "You…you are—"

"Your grandfather," Torg confessed.

"I don't understand. Why did they not tell me? Why did you say nothing until now? Why the secrecy?"

"It is difficult to answer with few words. If you are willing to listen, I will tell you." Terin was too numb to answer, wondering why his life was a mystery to him but apparently not to everyone else. When he didn't move, Torg took that as his answer and began.

"Your mother was a beautiful child, her beauty only increasing as she matured to womanhood. Beyond her loveliness was her intellect and gentle heart. She caught the eye of every courtesan, commander of rank, patrician, and lord of the realm, but her hand was already promised since her birth."

"To my father?" Terin managed to ask, though fearing the answer.

"No." Torg sighed, revealing the heart of the matter and the source of his ire.

"She broke her betrothal?" Terin asked, wondering to whom she was intended.

"She did not!" Torg refuted, defending her honor.

The more questions Terin seemed to ask, the more confused he became. Betrothals were usually arranged maternally, through the child's mother, maternal grandmother, or paternal grandmother. Once arranged, they were bound by sacred law and could only be revoked by royal decree, especially if the betrothal involved a house as powerful as House Vantel.

House Vantel ruled a vast holdfast in the north central part of the kingdom, guarding the foothills of the Plate Mountains from gargoyle incursions since the founding of the Middle Kingdom. Unbeknownst to Terin, House Vantel served as the guardians of the throne throughout their storied history, their founding patriarch the younger brother, guardian, and confidant of General Zar when the warlord set out from Tarelia to forge the Middle Kingdom.

Torg explained the history of his house as Terin listened, spellbound by a rich heritage he knew nothing about. He asked who ruled House Vantel considering Torg served as commander of the King's Elite. Was Torg the head of his house or merely a second or third son of its patriarch? "My son rules House Vantel, your uncle, Terin, Torgus Vantel, lord of Cropis, regent of the Cropus Region."

Terin suddenly recalled the name of his uncle, remembering it among dozens of other great houses he struggled to learn during his time as a scribe to Minister Antillius. He was surprised to learn that two of his uncle's sons served in General Fonis's 2nd Army, one a commander of unit and the other a commander of telnic. Torg spoke of them with obvious pride, though tried not to reveal it.

Terin felt cheated in a way for not knowing his kin and wondered why it was so. Did his birth bring shame upon his grandfather's house? Was that the reason for his parents to live in obvious exile? To find that answer, he needed to ask the important question.

"To whom was my mother betrothed?"

An eerie silence followed as Torg hesitated. "The king," he relented.

Terin paled, the realization of his father's offense washing over him. "I...I don't..." he stuttered, a thousand questions racing through his mind.

"It's best if I finish the tale before you ask any more questions. The betrothal was arranged by your grandmother and the king's late father, King Lorm III, after Valera's birth." Terin wondered why the king had arranged the betrothal instead of the queen but saved that question for a later time. "My duties at that time were divided between my regency of House Vantel and replacing my father as the commander of the King's Elite. It was my sworn duty as head of House Vantel to sire an heir and replace my father as the commander of the Elite and master of arms of Corell.

"When I replaced my father, he returned to our house to raise my son in my place, just as my grandfather had done in his. It was my grandfather who trained me in all matters of arms and the duties as the head of our house. Upon your mother's birth, I had assumed my place at Corell, bringing Valera and her mother to court, where she was raised alongside Prince Lore. They grew quite fond of each other throughout their upbringing, but as I learned much later, she did not love him." Torg sighed, recalling the memories of those days long ago.

"As commander of the King's Elite, it fell to me to train every recruit to the rigorous standards we require of our king's guardians. That was when I first met your father. Most of the Elite are chosen from the ranks of unit commanders, achieving renown through their proficiency in arms, particularly the sword. A cunning mind is also prized and equally significant to their martial prowess. Your father did not rise from the ranks of the army, his ascension a mystery to nearly all, save a few."

"But my father and Minister Antillius claimed to have served together during the—"

"Oh, they served together throughout the war but never in the army. Jonas was a sworn sword of Lord Teverin while Squid was a scribe and teacher to Prince Lore. Your father came into Lord Teverin's service through his reputation as a swordsman. At the outbreak of the war, Lord Teverin joined Prince Lore and the 5th Army during their campaign along the Plate, where they battled numerous gargoyle incursions.

"It was at this time that Prince Lore and Antillius became fast friends with your father, asking Lord Teverin to release him to his service. This was where I first met him, serving as the prince's protector before joining his father in his campaign in the west. By that time, your father's prowess with the blade was legendary, rivaling the finest swordsmen in the Elite." He left unsaid Jonas's strange ability of sending gargoyles off in tortured fright.

"As good as you?" Terin asked.

"Aye," Torg grudgingly confessed. Terin bit off a smile, not wishing to raise his grandfather's ire. "It was later when Jonas found the sword you now carry somewhere near ancient Pharna. I served at the time with King Lorm, campaigning along the lower Nila. Even there, we heard strange tales of a Torry warrior wielding a mysterious sword at the Battle of Celti.

"At the war's end, Prince Lore returned to Corell with Jonas in his retinue, arranging for his admittance to the King's Elite. It fell to me to train Jonas to the standards of the Royal Elite and hone his martial skills. It was during this time that King Lorm fell ill and passed, forcing Prince Lore to assume his rightful place upon the throne. It was expected that Lore and Valera wed upon his ascension, but unbeknownst to me, she and Jonas had fallen in love."

Terin was dreading this part of the tale, not believing his father capable of betraying the king, nor could he imagine the king forgiving such an affront. "How did the king learn of their indiscretion?"

"Indiscretion?" Torg asked harshly. "Your father and mother were never guilty of such an offense. I dislike your father, Terin, but I never questioned his honor."

"Then what happened?"

"Your father knelt before the king, gifting him his sword, and confessed the treason of his heart, his love for the lady Valera, a love he did not act upon. He claimed his affection for Valera rendered him unworthy of the Elite and feared his action whilst near her. The king called for Valera, asking if she returned Jonas's affection. She confessed the leanings of her heart.

"The king dismissed most of the court before passing judgment, leaving only myself, Squid, and the chief minister at that time, Bal Devorn. Lore told both of them, if he rescinded his betrothal, he would demand of them a price. They agreed, and he placed Valera's hand to Jonas's, joining them in wedlock," Torg recalled, the memory still bitter in his mind.

"What price did he ask of them?" Terin's heart pounded.

"You." Torg sighed.

"Me?" Terin made a face.

"The king told of the prophecy of the one foretold that would find the lost sword of the Middle Kingdom. Jonas was intended to find it, the blade calling to him for a great purpose that had yet to be revealed. King Lore loved your mother deeply with a fond affection, not the burning passion that was alit in Jonas's heart. Valera felt much the same, sharing a deep affection for Lore. They were closer to siblings than lovers, even closer than Lore was with his own sister."

"Sister?" Terin didn't know that Lore had a sister.

Torg winced, cursing the slip of his foolish tongue. "His sister is not to be spoken of. Do you understand?"

"As you command," Terin vowed, wondering the reason for such secrecy. Torg gifted Terin a rare smile, acknowledging the boy's vow before continuing. Jonas and Valera had instilled loyalty and honor in the boy, and for that, he couldn't be prouder.

"The king and Valera were very fond of each other, and she begged his forgiveness for the leanings of her heart, knowing it was beyond the power of her mind to refute. Lore forgave her but demanded a price. He told both of them and each of us that were gathered there that Jonas was meant to find the sword by the very omnipotence that bound his heart to Valera's. The two occurrences were connected and meant that the progeny of their union was intended to wield the sword when the time arose.

"He ordered Jonas and Valera away from court, to dwell in obscurity, free of obligation and influence. He said they would be blessed with a child and that it fell to them to raise that child with honor and loyalty and prepare him for the task that the prophecy foretold. When you came of age, you were sent to Squid to appraise your fitness for your true role. The king did not want you burdened with what was truly expected of you, allowing you to perform as a minister's apprentice for a time before placing you in the King's Elite.

"Your actions before even beginning your apprenticeship rendered his original plan pointless. You captured an ocran thief and befriended Cronus before even attaining Central City. You fought bravely at Costelin and Tuft's Mountain and rescued Corry from

Molten Isle. Then you ventured to the Black Castle." Torg glared at Terin, recalling that reckless act.

"I had to go. Raven needed help, and I couldn't leave Cronus in that foul place." Terin winced under Torg's withering glare, trying to explain himself.

"I'll blame such idiocy on the influence of your sword. The fact that you returned after escaping Fera and fighting at Telfer proves King Lore's faith in the son of Jonas. Needless to say, the king's faith in the prophecies surrounding you have proven true. Now you know the truth," Torg finished, staring off in the distance as the night air pressed his face.

"My mother would have been a queen," Terin said numbly, realizing her sacrifice.

"Aye," Torg said.

"Is that why you dislike my father, for denying her the throne?"

"The throne? The damned chair is a curse to the poor wretch who sits upon it. Nay, I don't begrudge him denying her child a place there," Torg refuted. He never wanted that for Valera in the first place.

"Then why do you hate him?"

"I never hated your father, Terin, nor did I desire a throne for Valera. But my house swore a vow, binding her and Lore in a betrothal. Jonas's meddling ended that, breaking that bond and offending our honor. That was the reason I cursed the day Jonas stepped foot in the palace." Terin sighed, uncertain of his thoughts. Torg regarded him, his countenance softening as he beheld Valera's boy standing at his side. He placed a meaty hand on the side of Terin's face, turning his bright blue eyes to his.

"I cursed Jonas's arrival until the day I learned of your birth. I could not be prouder of you, Terin. You are everything I am not. You are the amalgamation of the finest qualities of each us—myself, Valera, Jonas, and all your kin. I have pushed you hard, boy, harder than any other in my care. Just know I did so to prepare you for the battle to come. All you have done up to this very moment has prepared you for what you were born to do, what you are meant to do. No matter what may come, I know you will conduct yourself as befitting a King's Elite and a champion of Corell and, most of all, my grandson."

*****

He couldn't sleep, his thoughts racing in too many directions. Torg left him upon Zar Crest, where he stood for a time, sorting all that his grandfather had told him. He retired to his barrack before restlessness found him atop the battlements of the inner keep, staring over the ramparts to the north, where the dying embers of the enemy cookfires stretched to the horizon.

"You should be abed," Corry's familiar voice softly admonished.

"Highness." Terin bowed briefly as she stepped to his side. "I can't sleep," he explained.

"Neither can I." She sighed, thankful that her dried tears were unseen in the shadows. Most of the keep was alit, yet Terin found one of the few places where he could lose himself in the dark, a small outcropping on the north face of the inner keep. She ordered her guards away once she saw him, placing her safety in his capable hands.

"Princess, I am sorry about…" He couldn't say it, the visage of her father's desecration playing cruelly in his mind.

She grew disturbingly quiet, steeling her heart lest she crumble before his eyes. She didn't want that, not in front of him. She needed to be strong. Until her brother returned and sat on the throne to claim his kingship, she was acting regent of the realm, and she must hold firm.

"He is gone. Let us speak no more of it," Corry affirmed with as little emotion as she could manage.

"As you wish," Terin said, his soothing voice calming the trepidations of her heart. "You were very brave today," he added, recalling her harsh words for Morac after he presented his macabre gift.

"It was just words, Terin. Deeds are the mortar of victory. Words are merely the colors to adorn them. It is you who are brave."

"My sword has much to do with that." He shrugged.

"No." She shook her head. "You are a child of destiny, born to a great purpose. The sword is merely an instrument of that purpose."

"So Torg has told me," he reflected.

"What did he say?"

"Everything."

"Oh, is that why sleep evades you?" Her tone betrayed her as he looked upon her curiously.

"Did you know?"

"Yes." She sighed. "But it was Torg's place to tell you, not mine, just as I advised him."

"Did everyone know but me?"

"No, only a few, and it should remain a secret as well as we can conceal it. It is best if our enemies learn as little as possible about the champion of Corell."

"I don't feel like a champion," he confessed.

"Your feelings don't shape who you are, Terin. Your actions do. Just follow the leanings of your heart, and your sword will guide you."

"They have magical swords also," he said, nodding his head toward the Benotrist encampments beyond the palace walls.

"Swords they were *not* meant to wield," she corrected him.

"I faced Morac upon the ramparts of Fera." He sighed.

"And defeated him."

"I had help. His sword was too strong. Yeltor aided my cause, and Cronus distracted him, allowing me to knock his blade from his hand and escape."

She knew this tale, believing Terin disparaged his own role as he was wont to do. Her father had placed great stock in the prophecy surrounding Terin. If true, then Terin was born to wield that sword, and she could not fathom it was for naught. If any could defeat Morac, it was him, no matter the nature of their first engagement.

"And Yeltor is dead." Terin's voice trailed.

"He is, but there are others who can fill his absence and guard your side. You do not stand alone, Terin, son of Jonas. You collect friends like a net collects fish, friends that have fought by your side every step of your journey."

"I don't want friends who suffer like Yeltor had only to die on a barren plain. I want friends who live to see the dawn, not die because they followed me to Corell and…" He caught himself too late, knowing where his assumptions would lead.

"And join my father to his foolish end," she completed his thought.

"Princess, I didn't mean to—"

"No. My father acted foolishly, and now he and so many others are dead, their heads adorning pikes, stretching all the way to Kregmarin. I begged him not to go. Did you know that? Then I begged him to take you with him, to guard him as you were born to." Her words struggled through her tightening throat.

"I didn't know." He sighed guiltily.

"He again refused, saying your place was here, beside me," she said past the knot in her throat.

"I should have been there," he lamented.

"No." She shook her head, breaking with emotion. "My father was correct. You would have perished with him, and Tyro would have added your sword to his other, ensuring our doom. My father was right about you, Terin, just as he was right to judge your father and mother with mercy. Had he not and retained his betrothal, neither you nor I would be here. Our very existence rests on that truth and your parents' amorous leanings."

"Perhaps." Terin shrugged. "Or we might have been born to different houses or—"

"No. We are born from specific parents and are an amalgamation of their essence. Remove one parent and we cease to exist. My father understood this, and when your sires confessed their affections, he saw past the betrayal of his heart, to the possibilities that lay with their union: *you*. He chose another wife, one who stirred in him the flame of desire that Valera and Jonas shared.

"Because he did so, I exist, and so do you. We were forged by his mercy and foresight and kindness." She again broke with emotion, overcome by her memories of him. Her strength relented as tears burst from her eyes. Her sorrows betrayed her, tearing the tenuous indifference she placed over her heart.

Terin took her in his arms, forgoing the protocols of her royal position as she stepped into his embrace. His fears of overstepping his place washed away as she clung tightly to his chest. She could hear the beating of his heart, his warmth enveloping her as he held her. She remained in his arms for an eternal moment, losing sense of time as he mended her troubled heart, assuaging the loneliness that had festered since her father's passing.

"Thank you." She wiped her eyes, pulling briefly away, regarding him with watery vision.

"Your father was a great king. He treated me kindly, and if I could exchange my life for his, I—"

"No." She placed a finger to his lips. "He would not choose that, nor would I. Your life is too important. I want you to promise that you will follow this order I give you."

"What order?" He lifted a brow, her tone sounding an alarm in his mind.

"Should Corell fall, you *must* leave. I have ordered the magantor stable attendants to have the magantor that bore you here saddled and ready at the first sign of a gargoyle attack. If we cannot hold the walls, you are to attain your mount and flee. General Bode is somewhere to our west. Find him. If not, find my brother. His armies are near Cagan."

"I will not leave you, not ever!" He gripped her shoulders, his sea-blue eyes regarding her sternly.

"You must. Our realm needs you and your sword if we harbor any hope to—"

"I'll not leave you to *them*, to *him*." Terin couldn't speak his name.

"You'll leave me to no one. I will die before they take me." She lifted her chin in defiance.

"I'll not fight for a world without you. Do not ask me to sacrifice you. I have done all that my father asked, all that Squid asked, all that the king and Torg asked. I have obeyed your commands without question, Corry, up until now. I will not sacrifice you."

"Why?" she asked, realizing that he spoke her name without title or appellation.

"Because..." He looked away, guarding his heart, concealing what he wanted and feared with equal measure.

"Because why?" she pushed, reaching a hand to his cheek, forcing his eyes back to hers.

"Because I love you." Her heart sang, his simple confession sweeping away her loneliness. She regarded him in silence, her eyes examining every contour of his face in the pale light. "And like my father, I want what I can never have." He sighed, turning away, but she caught him by the collar, turning him back to her.

"Say it again!" she commanded, staring at him with terrible intensity.

"I…I love you."

There, upon the battlements atop the inner keep, they kissed. She pressed her lips to his, losing herself in his embrace, the world and its worries falling away like leaves to the wind. She lingered, savoring the softness of his lips. She grew weary of denying the passion that yearned to break free of her restraints, of playing the role expected of her. Her father had failed to arrange her betrothal, freeing her to choose for herself. Terin belonged to the throne. Therefore, he belonged to her, and she would claim him.

CHAPTER 21

Baroom! Baroom! The sound of distant drums echoed throughout the morn as Morac's legions marshalled into position. The 7th Gargoyle Legion waited to the west behind thirty-nine launch towers rising imperiously above their siege lines. General Vaginak's legion was reduced to thirty-five telnics from the previous battles but fared better than his contemporaries. His soldiers chanted their death songs, their guttural hisses echoing their festering rage. The chants would quicken as the time drew near, growing in intensity until the battle cry sounded. Until then, they waited behind their banners, a black whip and gray chain upon a field of green.

The 5th Gargoyle Legion waited to the south, General Concaka's thirty-four telnics aligned behind forty-three launch towers. Concaka's crimson eyes narrowed as he surveyed the length of Corell's south wall and the massive turrets that towered above. He ran his split tongue along his wide-set fangs, gathering the slather dripping from their jagged tips. He would personally place his standard upon the south wall, a black-mailed fist upon a field of white, heralding his triumph.

The 4th Gargoyle Legion waited to the east, their thirty-three telnics aligned behind fifty launch towers. General Tuvukk's legion relieved the 6th Legion, who repositioned to the extreme west, behind the 7th Legion. Tuvukk's gargoyles had yet to assail the palace, having attended the desecration of King Lore and the 5th Torry Army, adorning their heads on pikes for hundreds of leagues. His legion relished a continuance of their grizzly work, hoping to add more heads to pikes from Corell to Central City. Like Concaka, Tuvukk expected to place his banner atop the east wall, a bloody gray ax upon a field of black.

The 11th Benotrist Legion aligned northeast of Corell, its twenty-two telnics holding in reserve, as half its strength remained at Notsu, guaranteeing the dubious loyalty of that city. Morac ordered General Felinaius to guard their supply trains and his personal encampment and respond as needed. The 11th Legion's banners, crossed silver daggers upon a field of black, were driven into the ground as his telnics waited in position behind them.

The 8th Benotrist Legion aligned directly north of the main gate, their banners lifting in the breeze, a gray hammer upon a field of red. General Vlesnivolk's thirty-four telnics were Morac's strongest legion, and to them would fall the task of breaching the main gate. Assembled to their front were two telnics of conscripted Notsu soldiers. They would prove their loyalty to Morac by leading the assault upon the gate. The people of Notsu would fare poorly if they proved less than worthy.

The Naybin contingent waited behind the 8th Legion, their two operational trebuchets lobbing projectiles over the Benotrist cohorts aligned to their front, striking the palace wall above the gate. Dozens of crews, manning smaller siege engines awaited the order to advance, requiring closer range to lob fire projectiles atop the palace walls.

Commander Das Doruc drew his mount up alongside his king's champion, Dethine, overlooking their soldiers in ordered ranks before them. Dethine ordered Das to hold position. The only Naybins joining the immediate assault were those manning the siege engines and the great ram constructed for this very task.

The remnants of the 6th Gargoyle Legion waited far behind the 7th Gargoyle Legion, their might reduced to a mere sixteen telnics. Commander Garsosk was given generalship of the decimated legion, setting his troops along the western approaches of Corell, guarding the east-west road where it disappeared into the Zaronan Forest.

Haroom! Haroom! Horns sounded, signaling gargoyles to ascend the launch towers. Thus began the final assault upon Corell.

*****

Commander Nevias stood upon Zar Crest, observing the gargoyles springing from the wooden towers, their wings fully extended. They stepped off, gliding in brief descent before the flap of their wings gained lift, pushing them ever skyward as they approached the outer walls.

"Archers!" The command rang out with Torry bowmen taking aim. Arrows spewed from the battlements, targeting the gargoyles before they passed overhead, hoping to drop them above empty ground. Few passed through the withering fire, Torry archers winnowing their thin ranks.

"SHAKAH!" the surviving gargoyles screamed, diving upon the upper battlements, their fangs bared through their descent. Most were met with Torry spears, impaling themselves upon their jutting points. Others slipped through, smashing upon the stone walkway or crashing into defenders, breaking bones of men if hit directly.

Nevias observed several launch towers crash under the weight of the gargoyles serried upon their ladders, the product of hasty and poor construction. The damnable inventions allowed the enemy to negate much of Corell's natural defense. Gargoyle waves assailed the castle from the east, west, and south but in small enough numbers to allow his archers to blunt that advantage. He wondered why Morac didn't wait until he had constructed more of the towers. Or why not attack at night, limiting his archers' aim? He eyed the enemy holding back, most of their ranks waiting behind their raised banners, like a great wave waiting to break upon the shore.

"Magantors!" Nevias commanded as a horn sounded, relaying the command. He watched intently as his remaining war birds sprang from their platforms, passing over the ramparts, their paltry contingent reduced to a mere six magantors. Nevias agonized over risking his few remaining mounts but could not abide the enemy towers. There had been no sign of the enemy magantors for days, and he wondered where they might appear. Regardless, he could not keep his own war birds idle whilst the palace might fall.

The Torry magantors swept overhead the approaching gargoyles, pressing on toward the west with balls of flame descending from their talons. Nevias repositioned the archers on the north wall to the east and concentrated his catapults to the north. The larger missiles and fire ballistae would be better served against the heavier armed and concentrated Benotrists should they advance upon the north wall. Hundreds of conscripts drawn from the refugees flooding the castle before the siege ferried bundles of arrows to the archers positioned along the upper battlements.

His eye followed his magantors sweeping over the line of launch towers to the west, dropping their fiery munitions upon the wooden structures before passing on, gargoyle arrows falling short as they sped away. Four of the sorties struck true, three of which erupted into flames. Gargoyles screamed, jumping from the burning towers with fire licking their flesh.

The Torry magantors hurried apace, returning to Corell to reload. Gargoyles springing from other launch towers struggled to overtake them, hissing in vain as the great avian passed over the palace ramparts, Torry archers covering their retreat, dropping the fell creatures as they drew near. Hundreds of gargoyles tumbled from the sky, riddled with arrows as they neared the south, west, and east walls. Others fought to greater heights, where the arrows struggled in the wind, before setting down upon the upper battlements. The few that attained the palace were cut down in quick order. The Torry magantors set down briefly upon the outcroppings of their platforms before returning to the west.

*****

Morac paraded before his serried ranks, his black ocran galloping across their extended front, his red cape trailing in the wind like a bright flame. His dark eyes regarded them through the sockets of the ape skull affixed to his helm, instilling fear and awe in his vast host. Morac drew his sword, the sun playing along its length as he held it aloft. Crimson light burst from its blade, bathing his out-stretched arm with an otherworldly glow. His fellow Elite followed him, Borgan to his right, Guyin to his left, and the others in his wake.

"Kai-Shorum!" Morac shouted, waving his sword before stretching it toward the north gate of Corell.

"Kai-Shorum!" the gathered host shouted, the war cry echoing in the distance, circling the palace in thunderous octaves.

Morac withdrew as the 8th Legion lumbered forth, forming shield walls as they advanced. The bulk of the 7th, 4th, and 5th Gargoyle Legions ran apace, taking flight, struggling to gain lift without the use of the towers. Morac ordered all forces forward, com-plementing the launch towers.

*****

The Torry magantors renewed their sorties, delivering a second attack to the towers to the west. Circling behind the wooden struc-tures, they swept down from above, releasing their ballistae with bet-ter effect. Five more towers were struck, four bursting into flame. *Kagskkk!* Gargoyles hissed in agony, flames caking their flesh as they leapt from the burning wrecks.

With extra archers along the east wall and their magantors clear-ing the towers to the west, the south wall felt the brunt of the gar-goyle assault. Wave after wave passed over the outer ramparts, only half succumbing to Torry arrows before setting down along the upper battlements. The surviving gargoyles converged upon the southwest inner turret and its adjoining walkways.

Torry spears jabbed between interlocked shields as the crea-tures drew near, cutting them down as others followed in their wake. Some were skewered and pushed off the ramparts onto the causeway bellow, but most descended directly overhead, their carcasses falling upon the defenders. Men struggled as the enemy dead piled at their feet. There was no time to clear the bodies, as the enemy fell upon them without respite. The enemy attacks forced many back, crowd-ing the archers behind them and hindering their aim.

"Withdraw!" The order came as the gargoyles started to take hold, swarming over the turret. The Torries backed away, allowing archers atop the inner keep to concentrate their fire upon the surrendered ground. The successive gargoyle waves broke off from the southwest turret for the inner keep itself. Torry archers shifted aim to the new threat as the creatures drew near, their outstretched wings filling the sky to their front. Few reached the inner keep, but the damage was done, as their attack had gifted the gargoyles upon the southwest turret a respite. They branched out, sweeping along the adjoining walkways of the inner battlements.

*****

Terin raced from Zar Crest, Cronus running to keep pace, crossing over the causeways that ran between the inner keep and the towering citadels protruding from the inner palace. They skirted the massive structure of the inner keep, arrows arcing overhead. "Terin, wait!" Cronus shouted as a creature dropped before them, arrows feathering its carcass. Terin dodged the falling corpse, racing across the open area between the inner keep and the inner battlement.

Torry soldiers waited at the periphery as gargoyle dead and wounded littered the empty space in the middle, felled by archers atop the inner keep or tossed from the inner battlements above. Cronus cursed under his breath, swerving between gargoyles, uncertain of which were dead or wounded and avoiding those that were clearly alive. Terin passed between two creatures crawling across the causeway, stabbing at him awkwardly with their curved blades, dragging their useless legs and broken wings. Terin angled to his left, lopping the head of one as he passed, ignoring the other as he continued on.

"Argh!" a gargoyle screamed overhead. Cronus looked up as the creature swept past, its crippled wings flapping with duress, arrows pinioned throughout its carcass. It stumbled behind him, smashing to the unforgiving stone as a Torry soldier stepped from the periphery, driving a spear into its torso. Cronus ignored the scene, rushing to keep pace as Terin sped further ahead, racing up the wide stair that rose to the southwest turret. Terin skipped two steps at a time until meeting a gargoyle halfway up the stair.

"Kai-Sh—" The creature hissed as Terin halved its blade, the swift strike taking the creature's head above the nose, the top of its skull fluttering awry. He spun around the falling corpse as another creature sprang from the battlement above, spreading its wings, gliding through the air with its scimitar raised, its feral eyes fixed upon its prey. Terin lifted his sword, holding it vertically straight as the creature drew near, the blade splitting the gargoyle in half, passing clean through, skull to crotch.

Cronus lifted his left arm, the right half of the creature glancing off his shield as he followed Terin up the stair. Terin bounded up the steps, his feet moving deftly over bodies strewn in his path, splitting blades and limbs as he attained the turret. Split! Thrust! Slash! Split!

He moved apace across the serried platform, effortlessly stepping over the dead piled at his feet. Creatures swarmed over the turret, turning to face him as he drove into their midst. The soldiers who had retreated from the turret held position along the adjoining walkways, staying the gargoyle advance as Terin swept over the turret. Cronus struck down a creature from behind as it approached Terin's back.

Split! Slash! Split! Thrust! Terin dropped two more before spinning around their falling corpses, swinging his sword in a wide arc, cutting parts of three others drawing away. Terin's sword danced in his hand, azure light bursting from its blade, driving gargoyles to madness. In the heat of battle, he felt beset by foes, seeing little beyond the nearest gargoyle. But from afar, he appeared as a lanzar dispersing a herd of douri, the enemy melting away like ice under a summer sun.

Cronus drove his sword into another gargoyle, repeating the thrust three quick times before smashing his shield in the creature's face, knocking it back. Terin was a few paces behind him, slashing another as Cronus spun about, seeking the next foe but finding none. He and Terin stood alone atop the turret, gargoyle corpses piled at their feet or dangling from the trebuchet in the turret's center. Torry soldiers closed from the adjoining walkways, slaughtering what few gargoyles remained. He took a step toward Terin, his foot catching on a dead gargoyle's wing. Cronus face-planted on the pile of dead before gaining his feet, his tunic and armor soaked in blood.

The madness of the sword briefly abated, allowing Terin to catch his breath and clear his vision, taking stock of his surroundings. Gargoyles continued to pass overhead, Torry archers thinning their ranks before they passed over the outer battlements. Hundreds tumbled from the crisp morning air, arrows pinioning their wings, bellies, and faces, as their undersides were fully exposed. Too many passed through, however, setting down on the upper battlements, inner keep, and the observation platforms.

Terin looked to the western outcroppings atop the inner keep, where Torry magantors returned from their third sortie. One magantor swooped past the platform, beset by gargoyles clinging to its back, hacking away at whatever flesh they could manage to strike. One crawled onto the saddle, killing the Torry rider. "Packaww!" the magantor screamed overhead before passing over the battlements, its wings failing as it tumbled from the sky. The gargoyles clinging to it jumped from its back as it crashed just beyond the walls.

Terin saw a gargoyle sweep into the men serried along the upper battlements to the east, the force of the blow knocking two men off the wall, smashing into the stone floor of the causeway below. "Terin, look!" Cronus said, stepping to his side. There, closing upon the south wall like a great caliginous wave came the vast host of the 5th Gargoyle Legion.

They stretched from east to west along the morning sky, two hundred abreast and five rows deep, their leathery wings working laboriously to attain the wall. The Torry archers forsook the hundreds flying over the walls for the thousands approaching the palace en masse. Hundreds of arrows spewed from the upper battlements, disappearing into the dark tide. The first gargoyle wave broke upon the wall, hundreds of Torry spears greeting them at the ramparts' edge.

Hundreds fell from the battlements, blood issuing from their wounds as they tumbled, their bodies bouncing off the wall before impacting below. Others clung to the ramparts, struggling to hold on as Torry swords and spears struck out from between their shields. Archers shifted their aim further afield as the second wave drew near, following the path of the first. Terin looked east and west, catching sight of long waves of gargoyles approaching each of those walls.

"Kai-Shorum!" a gargoyle screamed in its guttural tongue, soaring overhead before an archer atop the Golden Tower drilled a shaft into its neck. It tumbled from the air, just missing a Torry soldier before smashing onto the causeway at the base of the inner keep.

Terin winced as the same archer was struck from behind by another gargoyle, the blow knocking the bowman over the side of the platform that rested halfway up the Golden Tower. His limbs flailed helplessly through his descent before ending with a sickening thud. A Torry soldier cut down the offending gargoyle, driving his sword through its gut and pushing it off the platform.

Scores of gargoyles circled overhead, setting down throughout the upper palace, but the defenders focused on the far greater numbers pressing the outer battlements. Terin held position as the gargoyle second wave was thrown back as quickly as the first, waiting for the enemy to break through before countering their gain. Torry soldiers flooded the southwest turret where he stood, clearing the dead from the floor and trebuchet, tossing the bodies on the causeway behind them. Torry archers followed close behind, taking aim at the gargoyles cresting the battlements below.

*****

The 8th Benotrist Legion lumbered forth, dressing their ranks while maintaining their shield walls. Two telnics of Notsuan conscripts preceded them, rushing toward the north wall in poorly ordered ranks. The vast host swept over the battlefield, their golden tunics and bronze helms contrasting the weathered grass beneath their feet.

"Fire!" Torry trebuchets launched their ballistae from the north wall, smashing the serried ranks with fifty-pound stones and fire ballistae, setting dozens of men ablaze as they struck. Das Doruc ordered his siege engines forward, trailing the Benotrist legion. Once within range, their crews began returning fire, hurling their own fire ballistae atop the north wall. The Torry catapults kept their aim upon the Benotrists below, unable to miss their tightly packed ranks. A Naybin fire ballistae struck true, splashing flame across one of the northern turrets along the outer battlements, caking a dozen men in flames. Some threw themselves from the ramparts, choosing death over the agony of their burning flesh.

"KAI-SHORUM!" the Benotrists shouted, steeling their courage in the face of the murderous fire. The Notsuan conscripts reached the gate first, their fore ranks winnowed by archers firing through arrow slits above. The gate was lowered before the portcullis, a massive block of solid iron that required great winches to lower or raise. The defenders atop the wall over the gate lobbed fire ballistae over the battlements, striking the Notsuans below. Many fled, overcome by fire, smoke, and arrows, while others held close to the wall to either side of the gate, awaiting the Benotrists drawing near.

The Benotrists hoisted their shields overhead, hoping to block fire ballistae from reaching their flesh, but it did little to stop stone ballistae from breaking through, killing those beneath. Men with ladders burst from the formation as they drew near, planting them beside the gate. Fire ballistae struck the first two, flames engulfing the men who were caught climbing up their wooden rungs.

A third ladder avoided that fate long enough for men to reach the hole punched above the gate by the Naybin trebuchets. The hole was nearly as wide as the length of two men with part of the gate supports exposed. The first man to peer into the break in the wall found little room to wiggle through, the way surrounded by solid rock, save for a small gap too small to slip through. "ARGH!" the men trailing him cried out as their ladder erupted in flames, leaving the fellow stranded, sitting on the crevice.

After a moment, he gained his senses, examining the break in the wall and the exposed gate supports. He found a part of the grating from which to wind a cable through. He called out below, and a Benotrist soldier stepped clear of the shield wall, tossing a spear into the crevice with a thin rope attached. The soldier in the crevice caught the spear and snaked the rope through the gate support, pulling enough slack to dangle the rope below, where others took hold. The end of the rope was attached to thicker cables, which wound through the grating, extending to the Benotrist ranks below.

The process took far too long, the soldiers gathered near the wall faring poorly with fire and rock dropping in their midst. Hundreds were crushed from stone ballistae, their bodies littering the grounds before the gate, many with caved skulls with what remained of their faces oozing beneath their broken helms. The fire ballistae were far worse, the gelatinous material clinging to flesh as it burned, seeping around the shields with ease as they splashed in their midst.

The Benotrists continued to draw the cable through the gap in the gate supports under this heavy duress. Once enough slack was passed through, thousands grabbed hold, pulling with all their might. The cable strained under the intense pressure, and the gate support groaned. The soldiers pulling the cables were protected by men to either side, placing their shields over their heads. Torry ballistae rained down upon them, flames splashing upon their shields and passing freely between their seams, burning the men below. Stones strewn from the battlements punched large holes in the formation, as others rushed forth to clear the fallen and take their place.

More Naybin catapults moved within range, losing their volleys atop the battlements to counter the Torries' murderous barrage, though some fell short, striking their comrades gathered at the base of the wall. *Snap!* The gate support gave way, the metal bending outward before breaking, metal shards jutting outward. Hundreds of men stumbled backward as the slack loosened. Benotrist cheers rang out before realizing the gate itself remained untouched. The hole in the wall widened a mere foot, and no path was made to enter the palace through the gap.

*****

Alen ran swiftly along the causeway, passing under the raised portcullis beneath the inner battlement, racing back to Zar Crest from the west wall. He swerved around a dead gargoyle with arrows feathering its carcass. His foot slipped upon the blood oozing beneath its corpse, stumbling briefly before gaining his balance. He continued on, wary of his surroundings, as hundreds of gargoyles now circled above, able to attain such heights by launching from their cursed towers. They might set down anywhere, causing havoc throughout the palace.

Though he was lightly clad to foster his speed, Commander Nevias allowed him a light helm and a shortsword in place of his dagger. He slowed, seeing a gargoyle just ahead exchanging blows with a Torry soldier. Alen drew his sword in stride, hacking the creature's right knee from behind before passing on. He didn't look back to see the soldier finish the creature, the gargoyle's screams confirming the outcome as he hurried on. Speed was essential, and no task took precedence over his return to Zar Crest to relay the next message.

*****

Commander Balka lifted his shield, the gargoyle blade glancing off its edge as he thrust his blade through the creature's middle. Another soldier struck from behind, cutting the gargoyle from wing to neck, driving it to the floor. Cors Balka spat on the flailing creature, delivering several hurried thrusts to make certain of it. "Toss it below!" he commanded, stepping toward a rampart of the inner battlement, overlooking the battle below. His men held the outer battlements along the west wall, though the gargoyles made steady gains with each successive wave.

Even after throwing back six waves, he could see hundreds of gargoyles clinging to the ramparts all along the west wall. Behind him, they tossed the enemy dead upon the causeway that separated the inner battlements and the inner keep. Those slain along the outer battlements were tossed over the palace walls to keep the causeway clear. His men were so tightly packed along the battlements that any corpse caused a compounding hindrance.

"Argh!" a gargoyle screamed above, an arrow piercing its breast before it dropped beyond the palace wall, thank the spirits. Hundreds of the foul creatures circled overhead, able to set down wherever they damn well pleased, Cors cursed. They first targeted the inner battlements and the upper palace but shifted their assaults to the outer walls as their brethren who attained the walls without use of the launch towers approached en masse.

Dozens converged on single points along the wall, occupying defenders who would otherwise strike down their comrades cresting the battlements. Thankfully, those that attained the battlements without use of the towers arrived weakened, spent, and easily slain. Those that attained the skies by the towers needed to occupy the defenders, purchasing time for their weary brothers to recover from their exhausted flight.

Cors Balka scanned the gargoyle siege lines to the west where most of the launch towers were now set ablaze, a tribute to their magantors' fell work. Another of the Torry avian succumbed, beset by gargoyles that slayed its riders and slaughtered the bird just short of the wall.

"Commander!" a soldier cried out in warning as another gargoyle swooped down upon them, stepping in front of Commander Balka. The soldier bladed his shield at an angle to deflect the blow as the creature drew near, its scimitar striking the metal before thrusting its feet into the shield, knocking the soldier back. Cors failed to step clear as the soldier fell into his knee. Soldiers to either side rushed to the gargoyle, cutting it down, its foul blood spraying their faces and limbs.

Cors Balka cursed, unable to rise, his left knee unresponsive. "Hoist me up, lads!" he barked, cursing his stupid injury. Of all the things to knock him from the fight, he never thought someone tripping into him would be the reason.

"All their launch towers are ablaze. Where are these gargoyles coming from?" a commander of unit asked as two soldiers helped Cors to his feet, leaning him against the back wall of the battlement.

"The other walls." Cors groaned, intense pain coursing his left leg. "Our magantors only struck those towers to our west. The other towers are untouched."

"A messenger, Commander," one of the soldiers who helped him exclaimed as Alen rushed along the battlement, stopping short of the west wall commander.

"Commander Balka," Alen greeted, standing rigidly before him with labored breath.

"Report!"

"Commander Nevias asked that you dispatch one hundred of your archers to the south wall," Alen said, relaying Nevias's order. The state of the south wall was far worse than their own. Cors nodded and sent Alen off before dispatching the archers.

*****

"Did they breach the gate?" Nevias asked the nervous messenger who reported the happenings at the north wall.

"Nay, Commander, but they damaged the supports. We will not know the extent until we raise the gate."

Nevais snorted, knowing there was little chance of that anytime soon. He sent the messenger back to the gate to keep him appraised. No sooner had the messenger hurried off than a gargoyle scream drew his eye. Soaring above the inner palace, a gargoyle drove straight toward Zar Crest, its leathery wings outstretched, its feral eyes finding Nevias across that deadly space.

The creature shifted suddenly, an arrow striking its back as an archer atop the Tower of Celenia struck true. The creature dipped just shy of the battlements, twisting in the air as it glided to the causeway below, greeted by Torry swords hacking it to pieces.

Nevias released a breath, acknowledging the archer across from him atop a platform, halfway up the storied tower. He had placed the finest marksmen upon the citadels, for if they missed, their arrows might find a friend upon the crowded battlements. Nevias scanned his defenses, finding the west wall well in hand, though the enemy continued to assail the outer ramparts in endless waves. The Torry magantors finally destroyed the launch towers along the western perimeter and had just flown off to assail the ones to the south. He was down to four magantors and doubted they would last much longer.

The east wall suffered hundreds of gargoyles passing far overhead, but he reinforced their archer complement, and most of the creatures were struck down short of the wall. But this cost them countless arrows for less kills. Eventually, they were forced to shift aim to the larger masses of the 4th Legion cresting the outer battlements, allowing the gargoyles above to pass over the walls unchallenged.

It was the south wall that concerned Nevias the most. It had less archers than the east wall and just as many gargoyles launching from their damnable towers. The only saving grace was Terin, who raced along the south wall, dispatching the enemy wherever they took root, his sword driving the creatures to utter madness. 'Twas the strangest sight as he followed Terin's blade move amid the foe, cutting them down like straw statues and sending the rest in flight, fleeing his presence with all haste.

"Commander, look!" one aide shouted. Nevias followed the direction of his aide's outstretched hand. There, north of Corell, the Naybins brought forth a massive ram. It appeared twice the height of a man with six large wheels and drawn forth by teams of moglo beasts as it lumbered forth. A series of small turrets were erected along its sides, from which large cords were attached and affixed to an immense pike that dangled between them. The pike was the width of a man's height.

From this distance, Nevias could only see the blurred piece of iron affixed to the head of the pike. If he had stolen a closer view, he would have seen the iron head of the massive pike forged in the visage of a gragglogg, its jaws set wide with rows of serrated teeth set in ordered rows and a snout intended to punch through the gate. The machine was built over a great time, long before the war ever began, commissioned by King Lichu for this very purpose.

"Fix all trebuchets to that monstrosity!" Nevias barked.

*****

She stood atop the inner keep as the battle raged all around her. The upper platforms of the inner keep were a myriad of observation posts, most of which looked out in one direction, and larger circular platforms above them that afforded a full view of the palace roof and the surrounding lands. Her blue eyes stared intently through the narrow slits of her helm. Scores of soldiers stood post across the platform with dozens of the finest archers in the realm.

"Kai-Shorum!" a gargoyle hissed, passing just below the inner keep before sweeping down upon the causeway below, swinging its scimitar as it passed mere feet from the floor, striking a messenger across the back. Corry held her breath, hoping the boy would regain his feet, but he simply lay there unmoving as the savage creature continued on. Torry archers brought it down, but not before it felled another with its vicious sword.

The process repeated itself in every corner of the palace roof—gargoyles setting upon defenders from above, their towers affording hundreds of them the strength to attain such heights. They would strike individually or in groups, converging upon specific points.

The larger threat, however, was the tens of thousands of gargoyles approaching the east, south, and west walls. These greater waves were weakened by taking flight from the ground, reaching the outermost ramparts weakened, but their numbers were too great for the garrison to hold back indefinitely. Fortunately, whenever they gained a foothold, Terin seemed to appear out of nowhere to drive them back.

Corry observed him at length as he moved across the southern battlements, slaying scores of gargoyles wherever he went with Cronus guarding his back. The azure glow of his sword shone above the din as her eyes followed him across that deadly space. Gargoyles pressed the southeast turret along the outer battlements, driving the Torries from the ramparts as they swarmed over the massive bulwarks.

Even from afar, she could clearly see Terin pass through the serried Torry ranks with apparent ease, reaching the turret just as the gargoyles began to press their advantage. He met their advance like a hammer striking clay, smiting them in great numbers, their survivors fleeing his presence, beguiled by his wondrous sword. She saw pieces of gargoyles flying off his blade as he cut through their fell ranks.

Torry soldiers followed in his wake, sweeping across the turret, slaying any who lingered, the rest forsaking the battlements as swiftly as they came. The Torries quickly cleared the dead, tossing the corpses over the palace walls while retaking the battlements while Terin moved on.

"Gargoyles!" a soldier cried out behind her. Corry looked skyward as a score of gargoyles circled the Tower of Celenia in a tightly orchestrated formation before sweeping downward upon the inner keep, their feral eyes fixed on the royal standard blowing freely above the battlements, a golden crown upon a field of white. Torry archers across the platform shifted their aim to this new threat, their arrows knocking several from the sky before the rest were upon them. A few were skewered at the battlements' edge, impaled on Torry spears, their terrible screams torturing the defenders' ears. The rest passed over the battlements, setting down in their midst.

"KAI-SHORUM!" they hissed, fanning out across the platform, cutting down an archer who fumbled notching an arrow. Torg stepped forth, blocking a gargoyle sword with his shield, sliding his blade across the creature's knee that was too far forward. He stepped back, allowing the gargoyle to stumble before moving around it, running his sword across its back.

Torg stepped aside as another pressed an attack, glancing the creature's blade off his shield while thrusting his blade into its side. He jabbed two quick thrusts before moving behind the creature, slicing its wing and cutting the back of its knee and passing on.

Galen hurried forth, straddling the wounded gargoyle while grasping its head from behind, slitting its throat as Torg cut down another. The Torry Elite finished the others, following their commander's fluid movements, dispatching the creatures in detail.

"Look!" a soldier cried out as another pack of gargoyles swooped down from the opposite side of the platform, and the archers redirected their aim. Corry's guard moved off to engage the creatures, forgoing Torg's tactic of moving off the line, as they were forced to keep themselves between the princess and their foe, blocking the creatures' strikes and taking what was offered. Arrows whizzed overhead, striking gargoyles further back as more Torry Elite joined the fray.

One gargoyle passed overhead, setting down between her and her protectors, its clawed feet scraping the stone floor as it stood erect, its glowing eyes ablaze. Its gaze fixed upon her with terrible malice. Torg's blade sliced into the gargoyle's left wing, ripping it nearly in half, its leathery flesh dangling to the floor as it screamed. It turned its malice upon Torg, bringing its curved blade across its body toward Torg's head but finding the flat of the old warrior's shield. Torg jabbed several thrusts into its back as it stumbled to its knees, blood issuing from its wounds. Corry stepped forth, driving her sword deep into its side before kicking her foot to its head, freeing her blade.

"Argh!" A gargoyle scream rent her ear, its deafening shriek all too close. She pivoted, finding another creature dying at her feet with a familiar soldier standing over it with his sword pinioned into the creature's back. "Highness." The soldier regarded her. He was small of stature and fair-haired. She suddenly recognized him as Havis Darm, one of the magantor scouts Terin rescued early in the siege. She admonished Terin for risking his life in the endeavor, and now the man he saved had saved her. Terin claimed the sword drove him to do it, and now she wondered if the sword knew the man he saved would save her.

*****

The Naybins brought their massive ram across the battlefield to the main gate, suffering the heavy Torry barrage, leaving hundreds of casualties in their wake. Fires splashed over the siege engine, gaining little hold on its iron-coated timbers. Several moglo teams were set ablaze or crushed by stones, forcing the Nayborians to hasten fresh replacement animals forward to hitch them to the ram. The Nayborians' other siege engines answered in kind, returning fire atop the palace walls.

Gargoyles assailing the palace from the launch towers along the eastern perimeter shifted their attacks to the north wall, occupying and harassing the defenders as the massive ram moved into position before the main gate. The Benotrists worked desperately in clearing the dead from the ram's path, as hundreds of corpses littered the ground before the main gate. No sooner had they cut the moglo teams loose than a dozen fire ballistae struck to either side of the ram, setting hundreds of men ablaze. Soldiers flung themselves to the ground, trying to snuff the flames licking their flesh. Some begged for death, their comrades mercifully obliging.

Morac sat astride his black mount, the beast shifting uneasily as he tightened the reins, keeping it in place. He observed the battle from the northern perimeter of the siege line, his eyes keenly fixed on the Nayborian ram. He winced as fires erupted all around the massive engine, his eyes stinging from the smoke, even from afar. Smoke and ash obscured his vision, lingering in the air for torturous moments until drifting high enough to clear his view. By then, fresh crews replaced the fallen, but flames still lingered across the ram and upon several of the supporting cables.

Moglo teams drew back the great pike to its fullest extent, its cables straining under the severe tension before a Naybin commander released the connecting link, sending the head of the pike smashing into the gate. *Thump!* The sound echoed over the din, metal striking metal with such terrible force to set men's teeth to chatter. The Torries standing post within the tunnel behind the main gate threw their hands to their ears, the sound piercing their skulls. The Nayborians reattached the connecting link as teams of moglo beasts drew the massive pike away from the gate, a small indentation remaining upon the gate where the iron snout of the gragglogg struck.

Thump! The pike struck again, the emphatic blow reverberating with terrible intensity, though the gate wouldn't yield, the indentation expanding with negligible result. Fire and rock rained from above, setting the moglo teams ablaze and pelting the siege engine with one-hundred-pound stones. A rock struck a forward wheel of the ram, snapping it off its axle, causing the pike to tilt off kilter. A second rock struck a middle support tower, its cables dropping uselessly away. Several moglos snapped their yokes, panicked by their burning flesh as they broke free, running north across the battlefield, flames trailing in their wake.

"The fools!" Morac said, cursing the gargoyles assailing the battlements along the north wall. They were tasked with occupying the Torry trebuchets to prevent them from doing what they had just accomplished—raining ruin upon the Naybin ram. More stones dropped from the battlements, striking the great siege engine, breaking two more of its support towers and another wheel. The ram listed severely to its left before snapping its remaining wheels, the disjointed pike rolling to the ground, its final cable attachments snapping. Fire ballistae followed after, arcing further afield, splashing amid the serried troops waiting to storm the tunnel.

The Benotrist legion wavered, men caked in fire throwing themselves to the ground to douse the flames, the macabre sight unnerving their comrades. Many broke and ran, refusing to linger helplessly below those mountainous walls, where the enemy could lob all sorts of fell things upon them. Soon, gargoyle corpses were cast over the palace walls, their bodies killing any they struck below.

Morac snarled, his pounding heart matching the panic that gripped his chest as he beheld the hellish vision. The smell of burning flesh drifted over the battlefield, torturing his nose with its fell odor. It was not lost on his cruel heart that the burnt flesh belonged to his soldiers dying beneath the walls of Corell. The dozens of men fleeing the battle quickly grew to hundreds until Morac ordered them cut down lest he lose the entire 8th Legion. Not even this desperate tactic would hold men to their duty for long unless they had some hope of breaching the gate.

"Kriton!" Morac called out, the large gargoyle drawing his mount up beside him.

"Morac!" Kriton hissed, answering his summons.

"Lead the next foray upon the palace. I want those battlements occupied!" Morac declared, pointing out the battlements above the main gate.

Kriton's eyelids tightened as he studied the jagged bulwarks above through their narrow slits, understanding Morac's intent. "Aye," he acknowledged, galloping off to the east, toward the launch towers.

"Dethine?" Morac called out to his Nayborian counterpart.

"Lord Morac," Dethine answered, ambling his mount forth from his command some paces behind.

"With me?" Morac's dark eyes blazed, challenging his comrade to ride forth at his side.

"Aye." Dethine grinned, drawing his sword, the glow of its ancient blade bathing his countenance in its golden light.

*****

"Packaww!" a magantor's death scream echoed through the air as the Torry war bird tumbled from the sky beyond the southern battlements. Gargoyles clung to its belly, stabbing it repeatedly with their daggers throughout its death spiral, breaking off before it impacted in the field below. Commander Nevias stared despondently as the last Torry magantor met its end. He had expended his last war birds assailing the launch towers along the southern perimeter, setting two dozen ablaze, but the towers along the eastern perimeter stood untouched.

His archers atop the inner battlements of the east wall struggled to drop the gargoyles launching from the towers before they passed over the battlements. Hundreds of the creatures now passed overhead, setting down across the inner and outer battlements. The soldiers manning the outer battlements had thrown back a dozen successive waves, slaughtering thousands at the ramparts' edge, their corpses pilling at the base of the outer wall. His men would often jab and withdraw their spears to use again, but many more were lost, embedded in the creatures they slew. By now, two of every three men in the fore ranks brandished a sword in place of their spear.

"KAI-SHORUM!" the gargoyles chanted, setting down upon the outer battlements, keeping the soldiers there from slaughtering their comrades nearing the wall. Most were quickly slain, their lightly protected bodies easy prey for Torry swords, but even dead, their bodies became a hindrance to the defenders unlike those who were slain at the ramparts' edge and pushed over the wall. Enough gargoyles had set down across the east wall, allowing the successive waves a respite after their taxing flight, clinging to the ramparts before pushing on. With enough rest, many could spring into the air, passing behind the Torry ranks.

Torry archers along the inner battlements fired blindly into the caliginous tide massing along the outer wall, loosing arrows as fast as they were notched. The gargoyles passing overhead now bypassed the east wall entirely, angling for the north wall, setting down across the battlements, their exposed flesh met by fresh Torry spears.

"The enemy ram is broken!" an aide reported as Nevias followed the happenings along the east wall.

"And the gate?"

"It still holds, Commander."

Nevais sighed in relief, taking solace in the victory, freeing him to focus on the greater gargoyle threat overwhelming the battlements. Alas, such solace quickly soured as Morac joined the fray.

*****

Morac rode forth, his blood-red cape billowing in his wake like a rippling flame. His dark eyes stared through the empty sockets of the ape skull affixed to his helm, like soulless embers projecting the malevolence of his twisted heart. Dethine rode beside him, his braided blond locks trailing his helm as they rode apace. A score of Benotrist Elite proceeded them, following their commander into the mouth of hell.

Up ahead, soldiers who held position at the point of a sword greeted Morac with renewed hope, which lifted hearts and stiffened spines. They quickly parted as he rode through their tight formations, his mount running at a full gait, drawing near the north wall as arrow, flame, and rock fell all around, striking down men to either flank. Their screams drowned in a sea of chants as the Benotrists heralded their lord's advent.

"KAI-SHORUM!" Their chants echoed above the din, drifting hauntingly to the ramparts above as Morac drew near. Every ballistae missed him, falling before or behind, to his left or his right, as he skirted the ruined husk of the Nayborian ram that rested in front of the gate. Dethine looked skyward, where hundreds of gargoyles circled above the north wall, falling upon the Torry trebuchets, staying their fire as Morac dismounted, his left leg planting gingerly into the soil.

Though thousands of bodies littered the castle foregrounds, the path before the main gate was cleared to make way for the ram, though the defenders continued cluttering the ground with gargoyle corpses cast from the battlements. Most of Corell's outer walls rose at an eighty-degree angle, blunting the effectiveness of casting bodies on those below. The surface that ran north of the gate was an exception with the wall rising at ninety degrees, making any obstacle thrown over its battlements a deadly projectile.

Morac drew his sword, its golden blade alit a fiery crimson as he stood before the main gate, his fellow Elite surrounding him with shields raised while arrows spewed from archer slits around the main gate. Morac crouched behind his own shield, a massive, long shield with a rounded top and inverted twin arches along its base, keeping his helm below its edge before swinging his sword forcefully across the gate.

Crack! Morac's blade passed through the gate, slicing it like stale bread, iron shards flying off the end of his sword. He swung again, cutting across his first strike, making a large X in the gate as the metal peeled away. A few hasty strikes cut away larger shards of the gate, exposing the light peeking from within. Dethine struck likewise, slicing through the gate beside him. Morac moved aside as a spear struck out from the break he cut in the gate, glancing off his shield. He shifted leftward, expanding the hole further as Benotrist spearmen came to his side, thrusting their spear tips through the hole as those within struck theirs without.

"Argh!" the men waiting farther back cried out, fire ballistae again dropping in their midst. One fellow was struck by a two-pound rock in the center of his helm, the stone cracking his skull. The smaller ballistae did not require a trebuchet or catapult, only a free hand to toss them over the battlements. Another soldier cried out, his sword arm dangling at his side, broken by a falling stone. Another staggered, a hand gripping his opposite shoulder, where a fist-sized rock smashed the joint. Others struggled in evading the stones, as their comrades pressed near to either side, hindering their movement. Some along the periphery broke and ran, though most held their shields overhead, deflecting the rocks. Fire ballistae were another matter, the gelatinous material finding its way around shields and armor, burning wherever it touched.

Morac continued cutting away the gate, its thick metal peeling away like the skin of a tosi fruit. Morac cut east while Dethine cut west, widening the hole and exposing more of the tunnel behind it. Benotrist soldiers filled the breach, driving their spears into the dim light where Torry defenders responded desperately in kind. *Alas*, the main gate of Corell was breached.

*****

He swerved, a Torry arrow missing his wing as he soared over the battlements, arrow and flame spitting in all directions. Kriton snarled as the gargoyle off his left fell away, an arrow finding purchase in its throat, its tortured cries dulled with blood gurgling in its mouth. Another off his right screamed, three arrows piercing its left wing as its right flapped desperately to compensate. He could see others in the rank ahead falling out of formation, felled by Torry archers atop the inner battlements, picking them off in detail. He wanted nothing more than to set down amid their ranks and set things to right, but duty called him elsewhere.

He led his cohorts beyond the east wall, angling right toward the north wall, where the Torry trebuchets lined the upper and outer battlements and turrets, raining ruin upon the Benotrist soldiers below. The crisp air filled his lungs, his untaxed wings coursing the sky as he sped forth, sweeping over the beleaguered defenders below. He quietly thanked whichever Benotrist engineered the launch towers, which enabled him to attain these heights, allowing him to soar above his foes with ease.

Unlike his comrades, Kriton's strength allowed him to bear a larger shield, breastplate, and greaves, further protecting him from the Torries' relentless fire. His distinct armor and red tunic stood out from his brethren, drawing the eyes of foe and friend alike. Torry archers shifted their fire after he passed over the east wall, though to little effect, as he was swiftly beyond them. Only half of the fifty gargoyles in his wave survived their pass over the east wall, and a half more fell before they reached the north wall. Other gargoyles circling the battlements rallied to his call as he angled north, his outstretched wings casting a broad shadow below.

He fixed his eye upon a northern turret on the inner battlements, where Torry soldiers awaited them with shields raised and spears leveled. They surrounded two catapults centered upon its wide stone floor, their crews working furiously, launching fire ballistae over the palace wall. Kriton grimaced, an arrow grazing his right wing. He shifted left before a gargoyle dropped from above, just missing his head as it tumbled from the sky, arrows feathering its chest and skull before splattering on the causeway below. He keenly followed a gargoyle setting down upon the turret, impaled on a spear as it drew near.

Kriton sped forth, closing the gap between them before the Torry holding the spear could dislodge it, the creature sliding further along its slender length, snapping its teeth and stretching to reach its killer as the spear worked its way through its back. Kriton set down upon the creature's back, driving it into the Torry holding the spear, all three tumbling to the turret floor and knocking several others from their feet.

Kriton sprang to his feet as quickly as he landed, cutting down the nearest Torry, who was startled by his tactic. His blade found another across the throat before the soldier lifted his shield. Others collected themselves, closing ranks upon the intruder with leveled spears thrust between their shields.

"Kai-Shorum!" Gargoyle war cries echoed from above, several setting down between Kriton and his foes. The Torries skewered several, driving their spears into them as they set down. Kriton took full advantage of the distraction, throwing himself in the opposite direction, Torry spears glancing off his shield as he severed their tips with his sword, forcing several back as more gargoyles found purchase upon the turret, setting down all around him. Unlike his comrades, who wielded curved scimitars for striking downward as they flew overhead, Kriton carried a straight blade meant for thrusting and melees with a sturdy quillon protecting its hilt.

A Torry blade struck the gargoyle to his left, his sword sliding the length of the creature's blade, cutting its hand. Clawed fingers fell away as the gargoyle dropped its sword. The gargoyle shifted its small circular shield, blocking the Torry's follow thrust before another Torry spear pierced its throat. Another gargoyle set down upon the back of the offending Torry, driving him to the floor of the turret before a Torry soldier lopped that creature's head in turn. Kriton struck down that fellow, moving to his side while striking the back of his knee before striking his back. The blows sent the soldier sprawling atop the other bodies piled before him, and another gargoyle climbed over him, pinning him down while sinking its fangs into his neck. The creature feasted on his prey, blood and gore staining its fangs.

Kriton pressed on, aided by scores of gargoyles setting down in his midst, blunting the Torries' counterattacks as he picked out his targets. Within moments, the chaos spread beyond the turret to the adjoining walkways. Gargoyles commandeered the catapults, hurling fire onto the outer battlements below, striking the serried Torry ranks. The screams of burning men rent the air, their tortured cries solace to Kriton's pointed ears. Men threw themselves over the palace walls, choosing a quick death, their bodies striking the Benotrists below.

More gargoyles followed, expanding their hold on the contested turret, though the rest of the north wall remained firmly in Torry hands. Archers upon the inner keep and its surrounding citadels rained arrows upon them, their dead gathering in great piles, hindering all movement upon the adjoining causeways.

"Stacksss the bodies!" Kriton commanded, ordering the dead to be stacked all around them, forming walls of dead flesh, shielding them from Torry arrows.

*****

Morac stepped aside, his left leg stiff with ill use, as the soldiers of the 8th Legion flooded into the tunnel, the clang of clashing steel echoing off the stone walls within. The defenders slowly gave ground, their disciplined ranks matched by the Benotrist cohorts pressing their front. The two shield walls clashed, spears and swords slashing between their seams. The Benotrist advance quickly eased, their numbers counting for naught in the narrow confines of the tunnel.

The battle was confined to the small group of men in each fore rank, struggling to find flesh to stab in the walls of steel. Few arrows could arc overhead without clanging off the ceiling. Men grunted under the duress, their arms growing heavy hoisting their shields and thrusting their swords. It took an inordinate amount of time for either side to fell an enemy soldier. Those small victories quickly waned, as another easily took their place.

The Benotrists waiting outside the tunnel stood helplessly, unable to advance, as the tunnel was jammed. Balls of flame dropped throughout their tight formations with greater intensity, spreading panic through the ranks. Those nearest the gate pressed their advance, pushing on the backs of those to their front, causing the foremost ranks in the tunnel to stumble forward, their shaky footing exposing them to Torry blades. Dozens fell, stabbed by Torries or crushed underfoot by their fellows. The Torries backed several paces to avoid the corpses littering the tunnel floor. The Benotrists pressed on, struggling to step over the dead without exposing themselves to Torry steel.

The tunnel ran to the central courtyard of the palace, blocked throughout by several gates, each of which was lowered, trapping the men standing guard in between them to fight to the death if the gate to their front was breached. Two Torry units blocked the Benotrists from the second gate—too few to stay their advance but enough to slow them to a painful crawl. To the Benotrists' horror, long metal spears descended from the ceiling through narrow slits built into the stone, striking them at will.

The Torry spearmen stood on the level above, striking downward as the soldiers gathered below, their spears striking necks, helms, and shoulders, impaling men with methodical ease. A spear thrust found purchase between one soldier's neck and shoulder, his cries echoing through the tunnel. A soldier behind him grabbed hold of the offending spear before releasing it, crying out in kind as it burned his hands. The Torries used metal spears with heated ends, hindering the Benotrists from snatching them. Dozens quickly fell, their bodies further hindering their comrades.

Eventually, word spread of the heated spears, and some men dropped their shields, wrapping garments from the dead around their hands to grab hold of the spears. This proved slightly effective, as some succeeded, yanking the long spears free before thrusting them blindly through the slits above. Others called for long spears of their own to be brought forth to return the Torries' favor, but any movement through the tunnel was nigh impossible in the opposite direction with tens of thousands crowding the front to gain entry.

Eventually, the Torries gave way, driven back to the second gate until they were slaughtered to a man, leaving hundreds of Benotrist dead littering the tunnel. The Benotrists were stopped again by the second gate, its massive, thick steel preventing any sort of ram from breaking through.

Only Morac or Dethine could cut through the obstacle, and it would take time to clear the dead from the passageway while contending with the spears before the legion could advance, but Morac and Dethine made their way forward nonetheless.

*****

Split! Slash! Terin's blade cut another in half, shoulder to opposite hip, the creature flailing as its top slid off its torso. Creatures peeled away, fleeing his sword, forsaking their hold upon the turret. Cronus stepped to his side, parrying a hasty blow from the only gargoyle who remained, its scimitar glancing off his blade before smashing his shield in its face, his follow thrust gutting its innards, spilling them to his feet.

Scores of corpses littered the turret, hindering their movement and footing. The scene repeated itself everywhere along the south wall, the enemy advancing with every wave. Whenever they crested the battlements, preparing to pour into the palace, Terin blunted their advance, driving them from the ramparts. Thousands of gargoyle dead piled at the base of the south wall, slaughtered at the walls' edge. Hundreds more littered the causeways of the outer battlements with countless wounded and dying Torries scattered in mounting heaps. With over half the launch towers along the southern perimeter set ablaze, only a trickling of gargoyles soared overhead, often passing over the inner battlements to strike elsewhere.

Cronus yanked his blade free as the creature fell backward, its clawed hands clutching its sundered stomach, its remaining innards squeezing through its fingers. Cronus turned as Terin raced off, running apace through the raised portcullis that separated the inner and outer battlements, forsaking the south wall, as Torry soldiers reclaimed the turret. He could see the defenders' spirits wane with Terin abandoning them, as the sword called him elsewhere.

Cronus hurried after, running as swiftly as his tired legs could bear, navigating the serried causeways cluttered with dead, wounded, and soldiers rushing in every which direction. He passed under the portcullis as archers lining the battlements above fired over the ramparts into the next gargoyle wave approaching the south wall. Cronus was taken aback as he entered the inner palace, gargoyle and Torry corpses littering the causeways in each direction, matching the chaos of the outer battlements. The shouts of wounded and dying men were joined in a deafening chorus of shouts, whimpers, and agonizing screams piercing his ears.

He spotted a soldier with a broken neck lying motionless at the base of the inner keep, screaming as a crippled gargoyle feasted on him. A soldier off his left staggered with a scimitar embedded lengthwise along his skull, somehow still alive with blood oozing down his face. He saw numerous men crawling with broken legs, likely from falling from the battlements above.

A gargoyle carcass dropped at his feet, felled by Torry archers, with several arrows feathering its head and chest. A few paces nearer and the creature would have struck him, an example of the dumb luck that spared some and felled others with no apparent order. Was it fated that some should perish and others live by merest happenstance? Perhaps if he survived the day, he would revisit that question, but now he simply struggled to follow Terin to wherever his sword took him.

They raced between the inner keep and the Golden Tower before turning sharply east, following the causeway through a raised portcullis underneath the inner battlements. The way was blocked by soldiers in tight ranks backing away from the battle without in an ordered retreat. To Cronus's dismay, Terin found a way through the retreating mass, his sword guiding him onto the outer causeway that separated the inner and outer battlements.

Passing through the portcullis, they were struck by a hellish vision. Gargoyles crested the outer battlements along the length of the east wall and its adjoining turrets. The causeway ran red with blood with bodies strewn throughout and piled in towering mounds nearer the ramparts. Arrows and spears spewed from the inner battlements, arcing over the palace wall at the next waves approaching the outer wall. Torry formations were breaking apart as they retreated to the walls of the inner battlements. Gargoyles launched from the mounds of dead, where they could restore their strength after attaining the walls before springing upon the Torries below.

"KAI-SHORUM!" the creatures screamed, crawling over the mountains of dead, their crimson eyes alit. Their curved fangs glistened with insatiable hunger, stripping the fainthearted of what courage the battle left them. They sprang from the mounds of dead, falling upon the Torry defenders, while those launched from the towers dropped from above. Meeting the gargoyles at the battlements' edge, the Torries could easily exchange twenty or thirty to one, slaughtering gargoyles in great numbers, but now that advantage was lost. They traded one for three with every enemy carcass further hindering their movement. The outer battlements were nearly lost as their pockets shrank.

Amid this hopeless slaughter, a great azure light danced along the causeway, stripping the enemy of their courage and wits as Terin cut through their ranks. Split! He split a scimitar striking down from above as a gargoyle passed overhead, the sound of its leathery wings echoing like running water. The blow passed through the metal like thin parchment, taking the creature's left wing with it. The gargoyle tumbled behind him, its left shoulder striking the causeway as Cronus lopped its head. Terin moved along, his nimble feet transitioning from the blood-soaked surface to the uneven contours of bodies strewn along his path.

Slash! He cut a gargoyle across its chest, the blow separating it below its shoulders. He thrust his shield forth, knocking the creature aside, its head and chest slipping off its stump. Split! Thrust! His faintest blow broke a scimitar before he thrust his blade into its master's heart. Withdrawing the blade, he spun around neath an upraised arm. The gargoyle screamed, its sword arm falling away as Terin's follow-through caved its skull, brains and blood staining his blade.

The sword's glow strengthened, burning away the macabre remains, the gargoyle's unclean tissue dissolving into an ethereal mist. He pivoted, planting his foot on the stone surface between two corpses, his blade slashing in a swift arc. His struck cut limbs, blades, and wings, cutting a path through the gargoyles crowding his way, spitting body parts and shards of shattered steel into the air.

*****

The creature hunched over its prey, sinking its fangs into the soldier's flesh, tearing into the meaty part of his thigh, the Torry's screams dying in his blood-drenched throat. Corry strode forth, driving her sword through the creature's back, twisting the blade as the gargoyle lifted its head, gore caking its fangs. She pressed her sandaled boot to its back, forcing the gargoyle down as she yanked her sword free before driving it home again, punching its tip through the creature's back as Galen hurried to her side. He crouched over the creature's neck, running his dagger across its throat.

Retrieving her sword, she backed a step, her eyes searching the platform for other threats. A dozen soldiers lay dead or dying across the white stone floor of the platform, their bodies mingled with the enemy slain, a collage of disjointed limbs and sundered flesh. A few lingered, their tortured moans drowning in the din. Galen dragged the creature off the wounded Torry, stripping its tunic with his dagger to wrap around the Torry's leg as blood pooled beneath his mangled thigh. The soldier's moan faded; his eyes dulled, as too much blood had escaped his wound. Galen gained his feet, his effort gone for naught.

Corry caught sight of Torg off her left, dispatching another creature with effortless precision. He moved across the platform, his deft feet gliding amid the fray, sword and shield shifting in an effortless dance. His blade ran the length of a gargoyle's throat, his shield blocking its flailing sword arm. He moved on as the creature stumbled, finding another from behind, running his blade across its knees. He continued on, allowing others to finish the kill, lopping the sword arm of another, his following strike finding purchase in the creature's heart.

Corry had little respite to marvel at Torg's mastery, her eyes drawn beyond the ramparts of the inner keep, overlooking the east wall. Gargoyles swarmed the outer causeway, cresting the battlements in a massive caliginous wave, driving the Torry defenders back across the breadth of the east wall. Fire ballistae spewed from the inner battlements, splashing amid their masses, setting piles of living and dead ablaze all along the outer ramparts.

Gargoyles attaining the wall now gained sufficient rest to spring forth, assailing the inner battlements, their winged forms passing through the vapors of the smoky air. Torry reserves rushed to the inner battlements, crowding the stairwells that led to the upper causeway, overlooking the outer battlements.

No sooner had she looked upon the sorry state of the east wall than she beheld the glowing azure blade sweeping along the outer causeway, its blinding light driving the enemy from its path. "Terin!" She gasped, her breath catching in the narrows of her throat as he moved north along the causeway. His sword danced in his hand, the gargoyles melting away like snowflakes in a summer sky.

"Highness!" a voice cried out in warning. Corry turned suddenly, sensing danger. A gargoyle loomed behind her, appearing out of nowhere, its blade outstretched as if to strike. She shifted her shield to block the blow that should have already fallen. The creature stood statue still as if frozen in place, its feral eyes drawn wide with surprise. The creature stiffly turned away unnaturally, like a puppet on a stick, until the source of its affliction came into view, another familiar Torry standing behind the creature with his sword driven up through the creature's back and into its throat. The soldier had impaled the gargoyle before it could strike Corry. He twisted the gargoyle away with his blade embedded in its back, easing the carcass to the floor before withdrawing his blade.

Corry blinked, not believing her eyes as she beheld Dalin Vors's familiar face. The lanky, quiet magantor scout was the companion of Havis Darm, who earlier saved her. Both were saved by Terin at the outset of the siege. She had admonished Terin for his foolishness, risking his own life and sword to save these two men. Now each in turn saved her.

*****

Morac moved through the maelstrom, passing between dying and wounded men, their cries echoing pitifully in the dark tunnel. The damnable Torries doused their torches as they withdrew, leaving the Benotrists to advance in the dark. Arrow slits ran the length of the massive thoroughfare, allowing Torry archers to strike them down without respite or retaliation. Upper walkways lined both sides of the tunnel with ramparts running their lengths, overlooking the tunnel floor. It took many men to assail these causeways.

After cutting through the fore gate, his men ran afoul of a second gate and then a third, each time requiring him and Dethine to advance to the front and remove the obstacle, navigating a myriad of arrows and pikes jutting from the tunnel roof. His men covered his head, placing their shields over the top of him.

The tunnel was littered with corpses as he neared the last gate, the twisted mounds of flesh piled hip high in places. His men cleared them away as best they could, allowing him to advance to the gate. His sword issued a mild glow in the sunless chasm, though brighter than Dethine's dull blade. The Naybin warrior stepped to his side as they hacked away at the gate, tearing large shards with each strike.

Within moments the final barrier gave way, light pouring into the tunnel through its sundered remains. Torry spears jabbed through the opening, trying to keep them at bay. His men pressed on, hindered only by their own dead blocking their path. Eventually, the Torries broke, yielding ground as the Benotrists flooded the courtyard.

Morac and Dethine stepped through the breach, their eyes drawn upward, following the walls of the courtyard to the palace roof above, where the clear sky was marred by smoke and arrows passing over the massive opening. Morac stepped to the fore, where his men met a line of Torries holding position across the center of the courtyard.

Split! Slash! His first swing halved a Torry shield, taking the arm with it. The stricken Torry issued a counterstrike, forsaking the pain of his severed limb. Morac blocked the blow with his shield, finishing the Torry as another struck from his left. He cursed their courage as he felled the attacker, cutting the fellow's legs at the knees.

The Benotrists swarmed around him, driving the Torries back but suffering great loss in the exchange. Even with his sword and Dethine's, the Torries contested every step. Archers posted on outcroppings on the levels above rained their fire upon them. More Torries flooded into the courtyard from adjoining tunnels, slowing the Benotrist advance into the castle proper. But Morac had tens of thousands to fill his ranks, and the Torries had but hundreds. Only time stayed his advance, and that time was fleeting.

*****

Split! Slash! He caught a gargoyle across the back as it turned to flee, cutting its spine, its face planting upon the causeway. Terin rushed past, driving further into the gargoyle ranks fleeing before him. Cronus followed close behind, lopping the head of the wounded creature Terin left for him, exerting all his strength to keep pace. At this point, guarding Terin's back was more akin to a handmaid trailing her mistress and cleaning up her mess, as he only trailed Terin to finish his kills. The boy was very greedy, leaving few healthy gargoyles for his friend to slay.

The more Terin surrendered his will to the blade, the brighter it shone, bathing his countenance in its glory. No gargoyle contested his dominion, each forsaking their senses, their courage, and the battle in the face of his terrible weapon. It was a weapon forged for this very purpose: the destruction of the gargoyle curse.

Torry soldiers rushed forth along the east wall, reclaiming the outer battlements in Terin's wake, though hindered by the mounting dead and fires throughout. The gargoyles fleeing Terin's sword collided with those approaching the east wall in the successive waves, slowing their advance and spreading their terror amid their comrades. Cronus followed Terin as he angled toward the north wall, the sword calling him elsewhere. They passed over the adjoining turret that linked the east and north walls, resting at an inverted angle.

Cronus looked up as fires erupted along the upper battlements, flames dancing above the jagged ramparts silhouetted against the clear sky. Terin cut back under a raised portcullis, passing through to the inner palace. They stepped onto the open causeway that connected the base of the inner battlements, the inner keep, the towering citadels, and the vast opening to the courtyard below.

They were greeted by a horrific sight, as scores of gargoyles had overwhelmed a northern turret above, commandeering its catapults and throwing fire ballistae upon the Torries positioned along the inner battlements. Gargoyles passing overhead flocked to their position, further strengthening their hold. Cronus cursed the blasted launch towers that allowed them to soar easily over the battlements and cause such mayhem. His blood ran cold as his eyes found the familiar gargoyle atop the battlement, its distinct armor and large build standing out among its fellows.

"Kriton!" Cronus cursed, the foul creature taunting him, directing his minions as they expanded their hold upon the battlements. Kriton's head peeked above a wall of corpses he piled to shield them from Torry archers atop the inner keep. The tactic worked to great effect with arrows pinioned throughout the makeshift wall.

Terin wasted no time bounding up the nearest stair, attaining the inner battlements and continuing on toward the gargoyle-held turret. Cronus followed, keeping his eye further ahead on Kriton, who didn't seem to notice him as yet. Smoke and chaos greeted them atop the battlement as fire ballistae arced overhead. Men doused in flames writhed upon the causeway, fire lapping their flesh.

Archers lining the causeway fired as rapidly as they could notch arrows, their fire directed at the massive waves approaching the outer battlements from the east, south, and west. A few archers shifted aim to the less numerous gargoyles flying above, though no less dangerous. Cronus could now see further afield, gaining a brief sight of the battle overall. Gargoyles pressed the west wall, driving the defenders back at several points along the outer battlements. The south wall suffered in kind, their defense weakening without Terin driving the enemy off the ramparts.

The east wall had stabilized after Terin swept the gargoyles away, but their successive waves continued without respite and even now started gaining a new hold. Cronus doubted how much longer they could hold back the storm, the enemy too numerous for so few defenders. He could only guess how many thousands or tens of thousands they had slain, but it counted for little against their multitude. Of course, if Terin continued to smite the gargoyles as he had done throughout, perhaps they could endure.

It was at that pivotal moment that Kriton's crimson eyes found Cronus across that deadly space. While every gargoyle eye within their sight followed the path of Terin's sword, only Kriton saw past Terin, his eyes fixed on the one Torry who vexed his waking thoughts. A mere turret and two adjoining causeways separated them with scores of men and gargoyles blocking their path. Their eyes fixed one upon the other as if fate decreed this very moment for them to meet. Cronus tightened his sword grip, steeling himself for this final confrontation with his nemesis.

A panicked cry echoed from the bowels of the palace, faint as a whisper in the wind until growing louder as others relayed its ill tidings, reaching the upper palace in thunderous shouts. "The last gate has fallen! The tunnel is breached!" The Torries along the palace roof faltered, their thoughts briefly consumed by the implication. Nevias ordered half of his reserves to the base of the palace to stem the Benotrist incursion.

Amid the chaos, scores of gargoyles passed over the east wall, bearing fire ballistae that dangled below their outstretched limbs. Men shouted out the coming threat, their voices lost in the sea of panic. The archers shifted fire too late, dropping only a handful before they cleared the wall. Within moments, the length of the east wall was engulfed with massive sheets of flame tearing through the Torries' clustered ranks. Some gargoyles continued on, depositing their wares along the inner battlements of the south and west walls. Torry archers forsook all else as another wave of gargoyles approached the east wall, bearing fire ballistae launched from the damnable towers.

"Kai-Shorum!" the gargoyles hissed in a deafening chorus, pressing their advance on all flanks. The sudden turn of fortune renewed their spirits as they swarmed the battlements. Torry spearmen skewered hundreds at the ramparts' edge, pushing their corpses over the walls, but could not stay the thousands pressing every front. The gargoyles holding parts of the battlements surged forth, springing into the air over the Torry fore ranks. Flames ran the length of the east wall, billowing smoke into the air above the mounds of burning flesh, compromising the Torry defense. Within moments, hundreds of gargoyles emerged through the smoke, their winged forms filling the tortured sky.

Terin shifted to his right, his blade catching a creature passing over the battlement, his sword meeting the gargoyle's helm. Cronus jumped back as half of the creature dropped at his feet, split from head to crotch, its left wing flapping weakly as it expired. He coughed, smoke choking his lungs, the vapors stinging his watered eyes. A guttural hiss echoed off his right. He shifted, his shield blocking a scimitar arcing through the smoke, the blade glancing off his shield as his counter swing cut the offending limb.

"Argh!" the gargoyle hissed, its sword clanging off the stone causeway, its mangled right arm hanging uselessly at its side. The wind cleared away the smoke, revealing the creature standing before him. A Torry spear struck the wounded creature from behind.

"East, withdraw!" The command echoed along the outer battlements, and Torry soldiers again retreated to the inner palace through the raised portcullis that separated the battlements. The outer causeway was a hopeless collage of burning corpses, mounting dead, and mingled ranks of wounded men and gargoyles. Soldiers rushed through the archways, the last men passing under before the gates lowered and doors closed, sealing the inner battlements along the east wall. Nevias ordered additional reserves to the adjoining outer turrets bordering the east wall, hoping to confine the break in his defenses, but the messenger was slain relaying the command, set upon by a gargoyle setting down at the base of the inner keep.

Cronus lost sight of Kriton amid the chaos, forced to guard the inner battlements of the east wall overlooking the outer causeway below as gargoyles swarmed throughout. Torry archers focused their aim on the gargoyles bearing fire ballistae, allowing those below to swarm the outer battlements uncontested. He and Terin joined ranks with others holding the inner battlements, meeting the gargoyles who tested the ramparts.

Torry catapults hurled fire ballistae onto the outer battlements along the breadth of the east wall, igniting the causeway into a hellish inferno. The tactic stayed the gargoyle advance, their guttural screams echoing through the smoke and din.

Terin took advantage of the gargoyle chaos, moving on to the turret the gargoyles occupied along the inner battlements. The causeway was occupied by ranks of men guarding the battlements and trying to advance northward to dislodge the foe. Terin worked his way along the crowded walkway, men moving aside as he drew near, the luminous glow of his blade shining brightly through the chaos. A small pile of dead separated the combatants as Terin pushed to the fore, passing between the Torry shield wall and advancing upon the gargoyles blocking the causeway.

A sudden swing of his blade snapped several gargoyle spear tips, his follow-through finding an outstretched claw, the severed limb flying over the battlement as he stepped over the mound of corpses, driving deeper into their ranks. Cronus rushed to his side as another strike split a gargoyle shield and the arm that held it. Cronus blocked a scimitar, guarding Terin's right, as Terin struck down another. Within moments, the gargoyles melted away, their battle frenzy subdued into frightened retreat. Torry soldiers followed in their wake as they pushed on toward the turret. Bodies were stacked at the turret entrance, forming a wall of flesh. Terin cut away the macabre obstacle, the others following him onto the turret.

Terin moved across the circular platform, dispatching the gargoyles in quick succession as soldiers flooded past either shoulder, clearing the turret. Cronus cursed, not finding Kriton among the foe. He caught his breath, scanning further afield. The outer battlements had fallen to the east, and the defenders pushed back along the south and west. He winced as a fire ballista dropped on the inner causeway below, the heat of its flames warming his face. Two soldiers were caught in the fire, their flesh caked in flames.

Cronus's heart sank as he beheld the rising gargoyle tide cresting the inner battlements, and with Benotrists pouring through the tunnel at the palace base, all hope was lost. Even Terin's blade could not change their fate. Alas, above the smoke-filled sky, he beheld a lone gargoyle soaring over Zar Crest, a fire ballista dangling from its outstretched claw. Torry archers fired with frantic aim, their shafts fluttering awry as the creature passed over the rampart.

Whoosh! Giant talons plucked the gargoyle from the air, pinioning its wings and carrying it off. The gargoyle's fire ballistae fell, striking the edge of Zar Crest, missing its occupants gathered there. Cronus watched in awe as scores of Torry magantors swept over the palace, their gray-and-white feathers glorious in the midday sun, plucking the gargoyles from the sky, like lanzars swatting gnats, before depositing their carcasses beyond the palace walls. Dar Valen had returned from Cropis with all the magantors of the northern realm, his vast host claiming dominion over the palace sky.

"Packaww!" a magantor sounded, snatching a gargoyle circling the Golden Tower, its talons crushing the creature's neck. It soared over the north wall, just above Cronus's head, its rider thrusting his fist into the air, greeting his comrades below. Cronus lost count of the Torry magantors sweeping the sky, simply marveling at the beautiful sight. Torry archers forsook the futility of dropping the gargoyles who soared overhead, leaving them to their magantors. They instead shifted their volleys to the gargoyles crowding the outer battlements.

Cronus suddenly discovered that Terin was gone, losing sight of him while he looked skyward.

"Kai-Shorum!" the gargoyle host cresting the battlements hissed, throwing themselves upon the Torry ranks before the Torry magantors could turn the battle. Cronus's eye found Terin below, on the causeway of the inner palace, racing westward between the inner keep and the Tower of Cot, passing under a raised portcullis leading to the outer battlements. The Torries retreating through the vital artery gave way, moving aside as Terin passed between them, the light of his blade growing brighter with his desperation.

Terin worked his way to the fore, the Torries to either shoulder yielding to the gargoyles pressing their front. Gargoyles sprang from the outer ramparts, crashing into the Torry ranks from above, their weight knocking several over, opening fissures in the line. Terin drove into their dark mass, his blade arcing through the fetid air, cutting limbs, swords, and shields with his first strike. He swung again, the blade's wide arc the most effective means against tightly packed foes. Torg had drilled him ceaselessly to use small strikes to limit his exposure between strikes, but there were too many for that tactic. His second strike cut a wider swath through their formation.

He stepped into the gap, driving further into their midst, azure light bursting from his sword in blinding radiance, stripping the gargoyles of their wits. The creatures' feral eyes quickly dulled before him, transfixed by the ethereal power of the sword and the man who wielded it. The entire gargoyle host along the west wall faltered, fear filtering through their ranks like a poisonous malignancy.

"Forward!" Commander Balka ordered from atop the upper battlements, leaning against a rampart, his damaged knee rendering him immobile. The command was relayed along the breadth of the west wall. The Torries lumbered forth, exploiting the gargoyle pause.

Split! Cut! Slash! Terin stepped over the dead, his nimble feet keeping their footing on the littered causeway. His sword strokes shortened to save motion as he felled two more in his path, and the gargoyles began melting away. He kept his shield tight, though the enemy drew away, ever mindful that an arrow or spear could strike from anywhere or even be cast from a friendly hand that went astray.

Split! Split! A gargoyle hand flew off his blade, his follow cut lopping its head before it uttered a scream for its severed appendage. Terin spun around the falling corpse, his blade running across another's back, rending a gargoyle's wings and spine as it turned to flee.

"Packawww!" a magantor squawked overhead, snatching a gargoyle who sprang from the outer battlements. Terin could hear elated shouts echoing behind him. The madness of the blade dulled his senses to everything but his immediate surroundings, but the faint shouts grew into a deafening chorus, reverberating throughout the Palace. "JENAII! JENAII!"

There, across the southern sky, came the vast host of the Jenaii, their winged forms stretching to the horizon in all their glory. Their pointed ears arced back, their hair trailing their blue helms as they pressed into the wind, coursing the firmament with their multitude dotting the heavens.

"To CORELL!" El Anthar shouted, his command echoing in the wind as the lord of the birdmen outstretched his sword toward Corell, his battle groups relaying his command throughout their ordered ranks. As the Jenaii filled the southern sky, horns sounded in the west. *Haroom! Haroom!*

CHAPTER 22

Haroom! Horns sounded in the west as the banner of the 3rd Torry Army emerged from the Zaronan Forest. Fire ballistae rained from the trees, striking the length of the palisades guarded by the remnants of the 6th Gargoyle Legion. Torry soldiers quickly dressed their lines as they emerged from the tree line, interlocking their shields as they marched forth.

General Bode rode forth, parading before his men, sunlight playing off his steel helm and shield. He needed no flowery words or inspired speech to rouse his men. He merely sat his mount, thrusting his outstretched fist toward the enemy. As one, the 3rd Torry Army marshaled forth.

*****

"Highness!" Galen called out to her as Corry wiped the blood from her blade on a dead gargoyle's tunic, her weary eyes following Galen's gaze to the southern sky. Her breath caught in the narrows of her throat as she beheld the Jenaii host drawing near. The beleaguered defenders began to shout "Jenaii!" heralding their saviors, the chant echoing from the castle walls.

HAROOM! The sound of horns echoed in the west, drawing her gaze to the edge of the Zaronan Forest. "Bode," she said through watery eyes, the 3rd Torry Army emerging from the trees. She could see panic rippling through the gargoyle host, their frenzied bloodlust waning, their swift victory turning to ash.

Within moments, the lead cohorts of the Jenaii swept over the gargoyle waves approaching the south wall, soaring above the exhausted gargoyles with ease, their superior wings working with effortless grace. The Jenaii swept over their foes, their swords slashing the gargoyles' wings as they passed on, the stricken creatures falling out of formation or tumbling to their deaths depending on the severity of their wounds. The Jenaii smashed the gargoyle ranks crowding the southern battlements, sweeping over the ramparts like a cleansing wind.

Amid the Jenaii host, a single blade shone above the rest, its luminous emerald light glowing brilliant amid the fray. Split! Slash! Elos split gargoyle blades like brittle twigs, cutting a swath through their crumbling ranks. The Jenaii continued over the inner battlements, sweeping left and right, half to the west wall and half to the east. El Anthar, king of the Jenaii, circled the command platform atop the inner keep, his gray-white wings closing as he set down, a dozen of his royal retinue setting down around him.

"King El Anthar!" Corry greeted, her heart singing at the glorious sight of two full Jenaii battle groups passing overhead, their ranks stretching endlessly to the horizon. Each battle group numbered twenty telnics, equal in size to a Torry army.

"Princess." El Anthar regarded her, his even voice naturally void of emotion, as a unit of his warriors set down across the platform, slaughtering any gargoyles who remained in their proximity before posting beside their Torry brethren.

"You came," she said gratefully, overcome with emotion.

"Yes, Princess, as our two peoples have done since the Jenaii first stepped foot upon our southern shores. My warriors shall guard you until the battle is decided," El Anthar said, opening his wings as he sprang into the air, disappearing into the serried heavens.

*****

"The Jenaii!" When the defenders first cheered their saviors' name, Cronus found Kriton upon the causeway of the inner palace, cutting down a Torry soldier with dozens of gargoyles gathered around him. Cronus briefly lost sight of him as he passed behind the base of the Tower of Cot before emerging on its opposite side. He hurried to the nearest stair, descending the empty steps, his feet skipping every two as he bounded below.

A magantor plucked a gargoyle standing in his path, carrying it off to its doom as he continued on, swerving around the dead and wounded or men hurrying to and fro. He briefly lost sight of Kriton again as others closed ranks around the creatures, their spears leveled between their shields, herding the gargoyles into an ever-shrinking circle.

Kriton snarled, knocking a Torry spear aside with his blade as another spear found purchase in the gargoyle to his left. Kriton struck the tip of the offender's spear, slamming his shield against the Torry's as his comrade slumped to the floor, its guts skewered.

"Packaww!" a magantor screeched overhead, plucking another of his fellows from his midst, the gale from its powerful wings pressing his face as it flew off. Kriton cursed his misfortune, his gargoyles dying all around him, until his eyes found Cronus working his way toward him through the serried ranks. Anger relit his crimson eyes, their fiery gaze fixed upon his mortal foe.

"Argh!" a gargoyle cried out, a Jenaii sword splitting its skull as the warrior passed overhead. A Torry sword struck down another in Kriton's periphery. Kriton wavered, torn between vengeance, rage, and survival. The Jenaii and Torry magantors now ruled the sky, and Torry soldiers regained dominion of the inner causeway, driving him before their wall of shields. Only one hope remained, and he forsook vengeance and rage for his only chance for life.

"Kai-Shorum!" he hissed, the guttural cry piercing men's ears like nails scratching stone. Kriton retreated to the center of his ever-shrinking perimeter before springing into the air, his powerful wings gaining enough lift to fly above Torry spear thrusts, crossing a short distance before twisting in the air and diving out of sight.

Cronus's eyes followed Kriton's path through the air, his out-stretched wings soaring above the fray, arrows and spears missing his wretched hide until he slipped mysteriously from sight. Cronus's confusion quickly cleared, realizing where his nemesis fled: the *courtyard*.

*****

Torg lowered his sword, coming to stand at Corry's side as her weary eyes surveyed the battle. The magantors and the Jenaii had cleared the gargoyles from the inner battlements and upper palace. The 5th Legion was broken upon the south wall, the surviving gargoyles fleeing southward. The Jenaii battle groups continued east and west over the battlements, falling upon the 7th and 4th Legions. Both legions began to waver, their advances stunted by the Jenaii advent.

The outer battlements of the east wall were awash in flames and carnage, the dead piled along their causeways, rendering much of them impassable. The 1st Jenaii Battle Group passed over the outer ramparts, meeting the following gargoyle waves of the 4th Legion in midair. The two formations clashed in the sky, their collision a maelstrom of leathery black wings and gray-white feathers.

The Jenaii slashed at the gargoyles' wings as they passed over top their clumsy foes. Gargoyles still launching from their towers dove upon the Jenaii from above, their scimitars slashing their wings in kind. Torry magantors swept above their Jenaii allies, plucking the troublesome gargoyles from the sky. Others landed upon the magantor platforms of the upper palace, returning to the fray with fire ballistae, which they deposited upon the gargoyle launch towers along the eastern siege lines.

Corry found Terin's sword amid the chaos engulfing the outer causeway of the west wall, its azure glow illuminating his presence as he cut into the 7th Gargoyle Legion. The Torries manning the battlements could not keep pace, lagging several paces as he cut into the gargoyle mass before sweeping south along the ramparts' edge.

The 2nd Jenaii Battle Group struck the 7th Gargoyle Legion as Terin penetrated their ranks, and the Torries lumbered forth, the combined effect crumbling their resolve. The legion shattered, those upon the battlements forsaking Corell as they sprang from the ramparts, gliding to the surface below, trying to avoid the proceeding waves approaching Corell.

The Jenaii passed over the outer battlements, hacking away at the gargoyles clustered along the ramparts before continuing beyond the walls to strike the approaching gargoyle waves. Corry caught sight of Elos's sword, its blade alit with a luminous emerald glow as he broke from the formation, setting down upon the west wall, just south of Terin.

He landed amid the enemy, his sword clearing his path, Corry following its arc as he cut into the gargoyles crowding near. Granting the creatures little respite to fill their vacuum, he strode forth as they fled before him. With the Torries pressing their front, the Jenaii passing overhead, and Terin's fell blade to their north, none tried to fight back or strike Elos from behind, their red eyes dulled with fright.

The talons protruding from Elos's open boots stepped deftly over the dead littering his path, his penetrating silver eyes further unsettling his foes. The sun shone upon his azure helm like light reflecting off the surface of a tropical sea. His black tunic and light steel mail contrasted with his deep-olive skin and white-gray wings. He was beautiful and terrible to behold, stripping the gargoyles nearest him of their last vestiges of courage, his dark mane lifting behind him as he moved along the ramparts.

He scanned afield, his keen eye finding the azure glow of Terin's blade drawing near. If the Jenaii were prone to smile, he would have happily grinned as they cut through the enemy to reach each other, but his stoic face projected his natural indifference. His blade shifted smoothly in his hands, cutting a gargoyle sword arm at the elbow to his right before slashing a wing to his left, just as the creature sprang from the wall. The gargoyle floundered as it spread its wings, its right unable to compensate. It tumbled from the rampart, bouncing off the wall through its descent. The retreating gargoyles swept around Elos and Terin like water passing around rocks protruding from a riverbed.

Elos closed the final distance between them, cutting down gargoyles with cold efficiency, lopping limbs and heads with minimal movement. Scores of gargoyles fled over the wall between them, hesitating only when those nearest them beheld their fell blades, their eyes transfixed by their luminous glow. Elos and Terin cut into their midst like a sickle cutting dry grass, flesh and gore flying off their swords.

Terin struck one across the back, his blade passing through its spine and wings, its torso slipping from its stump, his sword glowing brighter as it neared its sister blade. He stepped around the gargoyle carcass, his blade passing through another before stopping halfway through the gargoyle's chest. The creature spat blood from its slackened jowls, its eyes dimming as it hung upon his blade. Terin was retrieving his blade, wondering what stopped it from passing through the creature, when Elos's silver blade emerged from the creature's opposite side, his eyes drawn to its distinct emerald glow as it halved the gargoyle.

There, upon the outer battlements of the west wall, the Swords of the Moon met as the last gargoyles of the 7th Legion fled the palace. The madness of the sword abated, though its power intensified as it drew near its sister blade as Terin regarded his friend.

"Elos." Terin smiled, overcome with emotion, while the sound of cheering Torry soldiers echoed all around as they retook the battlements.

"Terin, come!" Elos commanded, leading him back to the palace interior. The battle was not yet decided. The swords could feel Morac's and Dethine's presence at the base of the palace.

*****

Morac stood in the center of the courtyard, directing his men through the adjoining tunnels and stairwells as they poured into the palace. Corell was his, and nothing could stop his legions from completing its conquest. They would fight chamber to chamber, passageway to passageway, and level to level until every last Torry was slain, but an irritating doubt lingered, gnawing its way through his brain.

He looked suddenly skyward, staring through the opening some 160 feet above. Winged shadows passed over its face. He first thought was, his gargoyles had completed their assault upon the castle roof, but the shapes appeared off. His eyes suddenly drew wide with recognition as a gargoyle sprang from the rooftop through the opening above, its wings spread as it glided to the surface with other winged forms chasing after it. "ARCHERS!" Morac shouted, his bowmen adhering his command.

Kriton dove headlong, hurrying his descent, with two Jenaii warriors close behind, slashing at his heels with their swords. His crimson eyes found Morac standing in the center of the courtyard with Benotrists flooding past him as they continued pouring into the palace. Arrows spewed upward from Benotrist archers standing along the sides of the courtyard, their shafts passing over him, one finding purchase in his nearest pursuer's throat.

The Jenaii warrior's wings slackened, his lifeless corpse falling freely, smashing into the courtyard. The second warrior pulled up, circling above the Benotrists crowding below as Kriton set down beside Morac. The Jenaii's wings pounded emphatically, struggling to return whence it came. Arrows grazed his wings and limbs, but eventually, he reached an outcropping halfway up, setting down upon its stone lip.

"Kriton?" Morac asked, his fellow Elite setting down at his side.

"The palace is lost. We must retreat!" Kriton snarled.

"The palace is ours! I have broken the gate!" Morac retorted.

"The Jenaii swarm the battlements, tens of thousands!" Kriton explained, extending his hand toward the opening above.

Morac couldn't forsake the battle now. He had breached the main gate, and his men swarmed the base of the palace. Ultimate glory was his for the taking. His name would reign immortal. Corell had never fallen, never succumbed, until now. Let the Jenaii come. Their wings would count for naught in the confines of the palace. He had more Benotrist soldiers than they had warriors. He was lord of Bacel, lord of Notsu, and by right of conquest, he would be lord of Corell.

"Argh!" a soldier cried out; an arrow embedded in the side of his neck. Morac looked up as arrows rained down upon them. Torry bowmen circled the opening above, losing their volleys into their midst. Men hurried to the sides, ducking within the tunnel openings wherever they could, but the main tunnel was too crowded. Most were hopelessly trapped in the open, suffering the murderous fire.

"Argh!" Kriton hissed painfully, an arrow piercing his left wing. "Stay if you wish," he snarled, wrapping his wounded wing to his side, making his way toward the main tunnel to flee.

"Withdraw!" Morac relented, issuing the command.

*****

The Naybin contingent held position north of Corell with the 11th Benotrist Legion off to their east and the remnant of the 6th Gargoyle Legion to the west. Commandeer Das Doruc stared nervously as the battle soured before his eyes. His siege engines were deployed forward of their lines, hurling fire ballistae over the north wall. He could see several striking true throughout the battle, splashing amid the Torry defenders.

The Torries did not return fire, focusing their munitions on the closely packed Benotrists gathered below their north wall, pouring through the broken gate. They could barely miss, raining fire and stone upon the 8th Legion, killing thousands.

The smell of burning flesh drifted over the battlefield, torturing his senses. Thankfully, the Benotrists had breached the gate and had begun storming the palace, but it would take time to reach the upper battlements and silence the Torry catapults. Perhaps the gargoyles could overwhelm the defenders upon the roof first, but that notion was quashed with the advent of the Jenaii. The birdmen swept the gargoyles from the battlements like an autumn gale stripping dead leaves from a tree.

The sound of horns drew Doruc's eye to the west, where the 3rd Torry Army suddenly emerged from the Zaronan Forest, falling upon what remained of the shattered 6th Gargoyle Legion. He shifted his men westward, closing ranks to receive the Torries if or when they dispatched the 6th Legion.

"Commander, look yonder!" his aide cried out, his hand pointing behind him. Das Doruc turned his mount about, facing northward, his pensive countenance again souring with disbelief. *Haroom!*

Haroom! Horns sounded over the battlefield as a thousand cavalry drew from the north, their hooves pounding the soil like claps of thunder. The Naybins' hearts went to their throats, panic freezing them in place for several crucial moments before gaining their wits.

"About-face! Form to the rear! Pikes!" Das issued the commands, his men shifting, struggling to redirect as the cavalry drew closer. The riders' tan tunics and polished steel breastplates, helms, and greaves marked them as Torry. Das could make out the banners borne by the riders in the center—a charging gold ocran upon a field of gray, the sigil of the 1st Torry Cavalry, and a silver ocran rearing in the air upon a field of green, the sigil of the 2nd Torry Cavalry. Further to his west, he could see a unit of Notsuan cavalry joining their charge.

"PIKES!" he shouted over the din, wondering the delay in their deployment. Only a dozen of the long shafts appeared ready to raise. Without them, they had little hope of slowing the Torry charge. Das Doruc paled further as a beam of azure light streamed across the battlefield from one of the riders, passing through his chest. He slipped from the saddle as more laser blasts swept the Naybin front.

*****

Kato drew his ocran up alongside Commander Connly, pushing the beast to a full gallop as they swept across the open fields, the palace looming behind the Naybin infantry to their south. Laser spat from his pistol while his rifle was slung over his back. The Earther forsook his plans of rejoining his friends in the Ape Empire once he learned of King Lore's fate.

He had spent his time since helping his Torry friends raid Morac's supply routes and slaughtering his foragers and outliers, leaving none to relay the tale of the Earther's threat. It took time until his small contingent rejoined Commander Connly. By then, Connly had joined with Tevlin's 1st Cavalry and Dar Valen's magantors. The Torry commanders happily received Kato's aid, putting his fell weapons to good use.

Zip! Zip! Zip! Kato fired at will, laser fire tearing into the Naybin front wherever they managed to raise pikes. His first target was difficult to place, as his ocran bounced him around as it galloped forth, but he managed to strike a commander of some significance who appeared to be directing his men. He would later learn that his first shot killed General Das Doruc, commander of the Naybin contingent.

The Torry cavalry lowered their lances in unison as they neared the shaken Naybin line. The force of their hooves shook the ground beneath the Naybins' feet as Kato continued his murderous fire. Laser blasts swept the Naybin fore ranks, shattering their line of pikes, melting flesh and steel in a tumultuous maelstrom. The midday sun shone through the clear sky, reflecting off the tips of the Torry lances like a thousand shooting stars drawing across a jade sea.

Kato's pounding heart deafened his ears to the surrounding noise, his eyes fixed on the Naybin line, knowing that one side would have to give. If the Naybins could raise enough pikes and hold their ground, they could bring down the cavalry fore ranks, causing the following mounts to falter amid piles of twisting flesh. The Naybins, however, appeared unready. Only half their line was in proper position, and only half of them wielded pikes. Of those, Kato further thinned their number before shifting his aim to the men to his direct front.

The Torry cavalry struck the Naybin front like hammer striking clay, trampling hundreds underneath. Some stood their ground, holding position. Many broke and ran while others stood dumbstruck and stupid, standing amid their ranks as if their numbers would save them. The Torry cavalry cut through their formation, crushing hundreds more before passing fully through.

Kato saw several ocran off his left go under, impaled on Naybin pikes, their bodies crashing into a pile of twisted flesh and shattered limbs. Others were slowed, unable to cut fully through the Naybin ranks. Men afoot would stab at the stationary beasts, cutting reins or dragging riders from their saddles. Kato watched another ocran off his right crushing a man's skull beneath its hoof, brains squeezing out of its sides like a broken egg. Kato kept tight to Commander Connly, his laser clearing their path through the Naybin line.

"Onward!" Connly shouted, waving his sword toward the Naybin siege engines further south. The 2nd Torry Cavalry continued on, following their commander, as Tevlin's 1st Cavalry regrouped, striking the disordered Naybin infantry a second time from behind. Kato followed Connly, laser spewing from his pistol, riddling the crews manning the catapults just ahead. From here, he could see the Benotrists spilling out of the palace tunnel, forsaking the battle as they fled north and east to rejoin the 11th Benotrist Legion.

The Torry cavalry swept over the Naybin catapults, slaying their crews and setting them ablaze with their own munitions. Kato rode past the flaming wrecks, spitting laser fire at the Benotrists massed before the north wall, keeping them at bay as the Torry cavalry finished their task. Torry fire ballistae rained from atop the north wall, splashing mercilessly into the retreating Benotrists.

"Kato, come!" Connly shouted as the Torry cavalry drew away. Kato fired several more hurried blasts, his laser cutting a swath through the Benotrist infantry before following the 2nd Torry Cavalry westward.

Commander Tevlin led the 1st Torry Cavalry back through the disordered Naybin infantry, striking them from the south side of their formation. Few, if any, pikes were raised, allowing them free passage, crushing hundreds more beneath their hooves. Connly's 2nd Cavalry swept west across the battlefield, enveloping the 6th Gargoyle Legion from behind as the 3rd Torry Army pressed their front. Kato added his laser fire to the battle, firing wherever the creatures were concentrated. He could see their winged forms taking flight, abandoning the battle. Torry infantry poured over the palisades, driving the gargoyles out, as the Torry cavalry cut down those escaping afoot.

General Bode followed his men into the breach, his mount jumping the broken palisade, galloping to the enemy rear as his men fanned out north and south. The gargoyles held a good defensive position but crumbled like stale bread once his men breached the center of their line.

Thousands of civilians and former soldiers had joined their campaign during their march from Central City. Most he left some leagues back, guarding the east-west road, but one particular fellow insisted upon joining the attack and somehow managed to find himself among the first to breach the gargoyle palisade. Any doubts of his swordsmanship ended as he cut down three gargoyles in quick succession before the rest melted away, fleeing his fell hand.

Bode followed the man as he marched northward along the gargoyle line, the creatures mysteriously retreating from his advance as if he was poison. A few stood their ground, only to have the man cut them down, his sword dancing in his hand with deadly efficiency. Bode did not know the fellow's name, guessing his age in his late fifth decade. He was obviously a former soldier, but where or when he served, no one knew.

Bode lost sight of the man when his men swarmed the palisades along the entire front as the Torry cavalry completed the envelopment. When the man emerged from the melee, he remembered Minister Antillius speaking with him during their march, an obvious friend from long ago. Whoever the fellow was, he would be certain to point out his contribution to their victory, as he single-handedly broke the 6th Legion's spirit. The survivors fled south and east, joining the remnants of the 7th Gargoyle Legion fleeing the battle as the Jenaii swept them from the palace walls.

Thus ended the 6th Legion.

*****

Morac and Dethine made their way through the main tunnel, their path hindered by thousands of panicked men crowding the corridor, trying to escape. Arrows spewed from slits overhead, the damnable Torries winnowing their ranks at every turn. It felt an eternity before they passed through the broken main gate, stepping over its twisted frame. Their relief was short-lived, as a fire ballista exploded before the gate, setting a dozen men afire, flames licking their flesh.

The blast heated Morac's face as he lifted his shield, shading his eyes. He kept his feet, following the flow of his retreating men. There was little control or order, only a gaggle of men running to survive. Morac looked for his mount where he left it with a handler. The handler and beast were dead, their bodies lying amid a pile of others at the base of the north wall. He continued on afoot, ignoring the strain upon his tender left leg. Arrows rained from atop the palace as the Torries shifted their archers to the north wall. Up ahead, he caught sight of a rider with two empty mounts in tow, riding toward them while skirting the mob of retreating soldiers.

"Lord Morac!" Guyin hailed, slowing to greet them. "I've brought each of you a fresh mount!" his aide said.

"How goes the battle?" Morac asked as he and Dethine attained their mounts. Guyin's eyes drew wide, his voice gurgling with an arrow feathering his neck, as he slipped from the saddle.

"Hiyah!" Morac yelled, kicking his heels in his mount's flanks, arrows and ballistae dropping all around them. He caught sight of the Naybin catapults burning off his left before scanning further north and west, where the Torry cavalry was decimating the Naybin infantry. Dethine stirred beside him, wanting to intervene but knowing it was folly. They continued on, rejoining the 11th Legion to the northeast, where they could organize a temporary defense and withdraw.

*****

His blade passed through an upraised shield, the metal peeling like torn parchment. The Benotrist soldier screamed, his shield arm falling from its severed stump. Terin took the man's other hand, severing his sword arm at the wrist, his blade moving quicker than the eye, its azure glow illuminating the narrow corridor.

Elos advanced beside him, his sword chopping two Benotrists at the knee, stepping around them to take another across the chest, emerald light bursting from his blade. Terin knocked his opponent aside, the man sinking to the floor, screaming the loss of his hands, his voice echoing off the walls, the pitiful sound haunting Terin's ears. Terin stepped forth as the men blocking his way turned and ran, their eyes driven to madness as they beheld his blade.

Elos regarded him briefly, suspecting the Benotrists' flight was more than cowardice or the breaking of their spirit. Terin's power to strip the courage from his foes extended to *humans* as well as gargoyles. It was a power that transcended the Swords of Light, a power born of his blood, a power beyond their mortal comprehension. The power even extended to his own blade when he was within proximity to Terin, as on the battlements when the enemy fled before him. It was a power he did not possess, nor likely did Morac or Dethine, only Terin.

"Come," Elos said, chasing after their fleeing foe. They continued through the winding stairwells and corridors, following the Benotrists to the base of the castle. The passageways quickly fed into larger thoroughfares, where they picked up others joining the fray. They cut down scores of retreating Benotrists, overtaking them a few at a time.

By now, the Benotrists had ordered a full retreat, horns of friend and foe echoing beyond the palace walls fueling their urgency. They emerged along one of the courtyard's connecting tunnels, their pathway littered with dead and dying men, their bodies piled upon each other in twisted heaps. Men fled back whence they came, stepping over the fallen without regard.

Sunlight shone up ahead through the opening in the palace roof, lighting the courtyard below. The adjoining tunnel was dark, as the Torries had snuffed out the torches when they first withdrew after the gate was breached. Now the dark played against them as they chased the Benotrists back through the palace. The retreating Benotrists tripped over the fallen at several places, struggling to gain their feet before Torry soldiers fell upon them.

A Benotrist soldier stumbled over a leg jutting from a pile of flesh, his face planting upon the stone floor, blood pooling beneath the pile, soaking his bare knees. His hand slipped on a severed ear, dropping his chin back to the unforgiving floor. He failed to rise, Terin's blade taking him across his back before moving on, leaving the soldiers who followed to finish him.

"Wait!" Elos caught Terin's shoulder just before he stepped into the courtyard, stopping at the mouth of the tunnel. The fleeing Benotrists poured into the courtyard from the adjoining tunnels, stopping suddenly as they crowded the main tunnel leading outside the palace, trapping most in the open as arrows rained from above.

The shafts riddled their clustered ranks, finding purchase in necks and limbs, or glancing off helms and armor. Men held their shields overhead, pushing others along or out of their way, trying to hasten their escape while suffering the murderous barrage.

Torry soldiers filled in around Terin and Elos, forming a shield wall, holding position while simply waiting and watching as their archers winnowed their foe. With the battle decided, Terin looked down at his sword, its glow dimming as he felt its power waning. Exhaustion took him suddenly, and the world went dark.

*****

Corry stared out across the lands surrounding Corell, watching in joyous disbelief as their enemy drew away like the tide rolling back from the shore. The 8th Benotrist Legion—or what was left of it—was drawn out in a long, disordered line from the main gate to the northeast. Their weary troops were harried by ballistae and archer fire along the north wall and Torry magantors strafing their columns with fire munitions. The great war birds swept over the retreating Benotrists, dropping the fire ballistae into their midst before returning to the palace platforms to reload.

Commander Nevias coordinated the harassment, granting the enemy no quarter. Elsewhere, the Jenaii drove the remnants of the 4th, 5th, and 7th Legions from the battlefield, scattering them south and east. To the west, the 3rd Torry Army swept over the palisades guarding the western approaches of Corell, destroying the remnants of the 6th Legion before sweeping north and east toward Corell, cutting off the Benotrists still trapped within the palace.

The 1st Torry Cavalry, having twice cut through the Naybin infantry, now circled their disordered ranks, winnowing them further with bows, having broken most of their lances with their previous charges. The 2nd Torry Cavalry followed their envelopment of the 6th Legion by chasing the survivors southward before joining the Jenaii in their pursuit of the 7th Gargoyle Legion.

Corry's eyes followed the trail of laser fire spewing from the lone Earther riding in the 2nd Cavalry, wondering which of Raven's comrades had joined their cause. She lowered her shield and sword, her weary arms relaxing as Torg came to her side, resting his sword hand upon the rampart before them.

"Victory," he stated quietly.

"Oh, Torg." She shook her head, sheathing her sword before embracing him. "VICTORY!" she declared, emphasizing the word with the reverence their triumph was due. The siege was lifted. The battle was won.

CHAPTER 23

Two days hence

Terin awoke on the second morn, sunlight through the open window greeting him as he opened his eyes. He found himself abed in the prince's chamber, suddenly cognizant of the pain coursing through his body as if he had strained every muscle. His first attempt to rise was met with failure before a strong hand forced him back down.

"Rest easy, my boy," a familiar voice advised. Terin turned his head to his left, his eyes struggling to focus as the man's face took shape in the morning light. He made a face, trying to place the man's familiar trimmed beard and mature countenance.

"Squid?" Terin concluded, though his foggy mind was certain of nothing at this point. His voice was barely a whisper, grainy and coarse.

"Aye, it is me, my boy." The Torry minister smiled, offering him a cup of water.

"What...where...how are you here?" he asked, stumbling over his words, his incoherent thoughts jumbling together.

"I rode with Bode's army from Central City. 'Twas quite the adventure, much like our excursion to Molten Isle to rescue the princess. I haven't seen such excitement since the days of my youth, not since you entered my once quiet life." Squid gently laughed.

"The battle?" Terin quickly recalled, wondering the outcome.

"What do you remember?"

"I was standing in the tunnel with...with Elos, I believe. Then...nothing. I don't recall how I reached the tunnel or when Elos appeared. Before then, I remember fighting along the southern battlements at the outset of the battle and then the tunnel." It made little sense.

"Interesting." Squid raked his fingers through his beard, sunlight playing off his gray eyes.

"How long..." Terin coughed, his parched throat constricting his voice. He drank another sip of water.

"You've slept for two days, Terin."

"Two days?"

"Aye."

"Have you been here this whole time?"

"No. I've had other duties to attend. We've taken turns watching over you, wondering when you might stir."

"We?" he asked, his eyebrows knitting together.

"You've many friends, my boy. Cronus, Leanna, the minstrel, and the former Menotrist slave you befriended have all taken shifts waiting for you to arise. Torg and Elos have also taken more than one shift watching over you, but the princess has been here more than any, taking great interest in your recovery."

"Oh." He blushed, embarrassed by all the fussing over him when there were so many others gravely injured. He felt his muscles aflame as he shifted lightly, aching from foot to head, as if he had torn the tissue from every bone.

"Keep still, my boy. Kato said you strained nearly all your primary muscle groups. The sword can mask the pain and grant you strength and endurance to carry you through any danger, but there is always a price to be paid after." Squid needn't explain that the madness of the blade lasted far longer during the battle than any time before, taxing Terin to the extreme. Now his body was paying the price.

"Kato?" he asked, wondering if he heard Squid correctly.

"Yes. The Earther never returned to his ship. He remained with the Torry cavalry to aid our cause. I must say, his help with our wounded has been nearly as fortuitous as his weapon."

"The wounded?"

Squid nodded in affirmation. "He brought with him another of the Earthers' wondrous inventions, a device that can see into a human body to determine what is awry and then correct it. He used it to look inside you and reassured the princess that you merely required rest. His device has healed many of our men, restoring sight to blinded eyes, growing missing digits, and especially mending mortal wounds to vital areas. He claims it can restore missing limbs, but the process is quite slow for such endeavors and will have to wait until the more serious injuries are attended.

"And the battle? How did we...fare?" Terin coughed again, taking another sip of water.

"Victory, my boy, *a glorious* victory." Squid's smile didn't reach his eyes, though. Their triumph was tempered by great loss of life. Thousands were dead or wounded, including 70 percent of the garrison. Commanders Gais Luven and Sergon Vas died defending the north and east walls. Thousands perished in the lower levels of Corell when the Benotrists breached the gate. The 3rd Army suffered nearly 30 percent casualties destroying the 6th Gargoyle Legion and their following engagements with the Benotrist legions.

General Bode slaughtered and captured thousands of Benotrists exiting the north gate of Corell, cutting their only avenue of escape before pressing northeast to engage the remnants of the 8th Legion and the 11th Legion as they withdrew eastward. Many of his wounded might return to full duty once Kato treated their wounds. The Jenaii suffered thousands of casualties but decimated the shattered ranks of the 4th, 5th, and 7th Gargoyle Legions, whose remnants were scattered to the winds. If Squid could hazard a guess, he would surmise that each of those gargoyle legions suffered 50 to 80 percent casualties since the start of the campaign. The 6th Legion was completely destroyed and its marker could be removed from its place on any map.

Squid relayed all this to Terin, glossing over the minor details lest the tale take them into the night in its full telling. He extolled the coordination betwixt General Bode and Commanders Connly, Tevlin, and Valen, along with their Jenaii allies, each playing their part to force Morac's hand before springing their trap. The first decisive blow came days before, when Dar Valen led the vast host of Torry magantors against Morac's war birds, crushing them many leagues north of Corell.

When none returned, Morac hastened his assault, hoping to conquer Corell before the palace was relieved. By that time, the Torry cavalry had nearly severed his supply chains, ensuring starvation if he maintained the siege. Once he committed to the final assault, Torry scouts relayed the news to their forces west and south, converging upon the palace with all haste, striking Morac's legions from behind while their eyes were upon Corell.

"They saved us." Terin smiled as best he could in his weakened state.

"Yes, they did, my boy, but so did you. You held the enemy at bay long enough for others to come to the rescue. Without your sword and unique gift, Morac would've taken Corell long before our forces converged. We each had a part to play in this grand epic."

"The sword was the difference, not any gift on my part," Terin corrected him.

"You believe falsely, Terin. In your hand, the sword strips away a foe's courage. Not so if held by another. Not even Elos or Morac can carry off that bit of magic."

"I saw the enemy flee Elos's blade as well as mine," Terin countered.

"Only when he was near you, another aspect of your *gift*." Squid shook his head.

"Perhaps it is unique to the Sword of the Moon?" he argued.

"Elos wields a Sword of the Moon, the sister blade to your own, and it grants him no such power."

"Perhaps each blade grants a different gift to its master, and mine strips courage from its foes."

"Perhaps, but I think not. There was one other that shared your unique ability, your *father*."

"But he wielded the same sword," Terin pointed out.

Squid shook his head. "Nay. He held this same power *before* he found that blade buried in the ruins of ancient Pharna. The gift is your birthright. It is in your blood. It was the magic King Lore saw in your father all those years ago, convincing the king of Jonas's prophetic significance."

Terin recalled his first encounter with men intent to do him harm in the tavern at Rego when Raven interceded on his behalf. Those men did not seem frightened of him, but he hadn't raised a sword to them at that point either. He then thought of Molten Isle and the pirates he slew there, trying to remember if any fled from him. The fights there were all quite brief, and he didn't remember granting them time to choose between fight or flight before killing them. One question came to thought.

"Why did you not speak of this before?" Terin asked.

"The power was not as obvious then. Often, things are overlooked in the heat of battle, and our first engagements at that time were small in compare to the grand battles you have partaken. To the untrained eye, it seemed that our enemies were merely fearful of Jonas's obvious skill with a blade. Oh, he was a sight to behold, the way his sword danced in his hands. We wrongly ascribed the enemy's irrational fear in his presence to his sword handling, but as I now look back, I remember it differently." Squid's stare narrowed, visions of the past playing again before his eyes.

"Differently?"

"There were times the enemy fled before he could demonstrate his fell hand. 'Twas the strangest thing."

"And he did this without the sword?"

"Yes, but the blade certainly enhanced this ability tenfold or greater, as you repeatedly demonstrated on the battlements of Corell." Terin lay quietly on the bed, bereft of words—or thoughts, for that matter. "Enough of such talk. 'Tis an interesting topic for another time. Now that you're awake, I'll have some food sent up for you." Squid smiled gently, gaining his feet, smoothing the folds of his robe. He cast a mischievous eye toward the outer corridor before regarding Terin one last time. "And I believe my relief has arrived."

With that, Squid Antillius stepped without, hurrying off to meet with Eli Monsh and the council of ministers. The chief minister's sudden appearance was another boon to the realm, having fled Notsu before its submission, riding along with Tevlin's cavalry through much of the campaign.

"You're wake." Corry smiled, passing Squid as she stepped within, asking to be informed the moment he awoke. Squid had sent a servant to fetch her when Terin first stirred.

"Highness." He tried to rise before she ordered him still, sitting upon the bed beside him.

"You gave us quite a fright. It is good to see you awake." She touched a hand to his cheek, brushing his hair behind his ear.

"My apologies for shirking my duties, Highness. I will be ready to resume them as soon as I can dress," he said, suddenly cognizant that he was naked beneath the thick furs, sans his brief undergarment.

"Your duty is to recover before resuming any duties. What good will you be otherwise?" She lifted a brow, admonishing his foolishness. "You have saved us once again, Terin, and it was more than your sword, for that alone wouldn't have turned back the enemy time and again. Only one other could have done what you did," she said cryptically.

He gifted her a smile, happy to see her alive and well. With the flow of battle and the enemy everywhere throughout the palace, he knew no one had been truly safe. His pulse quickened in her presence, her beauty disarming his confidence, and he wondered why a woman so lovely regarded him so fondly. She no longer wore her warrior garb, forsaking the revealing tunic and resplendent armor for a modest emerald gown that draped her womanly form. Even her scent was intoxicating, lingering in his memory long after she left a room.

"There is someone who has been waiting to speak with you. I will leave you in his capable hands, as I have other duties to attend." She pressed a kiss to her fingers and touched them to his lips before gaining her feet and stepping away. She paused at the doorway, speaking quietly with someone in the outer corridor before passing on.

The person she spoke with entered therein, a tall figure in a dark tunic that draped to his knees and a sword sheathed upon his left hip. Terin's curious eyes drew wide as he met the familiar purple eyes of his father with specks of gold tinting their irises. He appeared just as he remembered, his easy smile spreading across his handsome face as he drew near.

"Father?" Terin asked, not believing his eyes. "How..."

"I thought you might need some help," Jonas jested, stopping at his bedside. "I couldn't leave my son here in the palace surrounded by six legions. Your mother would never have forgiven me. I thought to find you under great duress, and here you rest in the crown prince's bed with the princess doting on you." He ruffled Terin's hair. "Of course, the men in our family have oft sought the favors of women far above our station," he added, though Terin noticed a sadness in his father as he uttered the last, as if reminded of a bitter memory.

"When did you arrive?" Terin asked, cursing his blacking out after the battle and missing so much.

"During the battle. I joined the 3rd Army en route from Central City, myself and many other brave fellows, citizens all and armed with whatever we could find. I am still a fair swordsman."

"So I've been told." Terin smiled, proud of his father.

"Is Squid still bragging of my prowess?"

"Yes, but Torg said you were the finest swordsman he ever trained."

"Master Vantel," he said evenly.

"Yes, my grandfather." Terin gave him a look.

"Oh, so he told you."

"Just before the battle, yes. Why didn't you or Mother?"

Jonas sighed, taking a seat by his bedside. There was much he wanted to reveal about his son's rich and tortured lineage. "We wanted you to be your own man, son, to raise you without familial influence other than your mother and I. The king suggested as much, allowing you to grow influenced only by my honor and your mother's love. Names and titles often corrupt and shape our thinking and beliefs and rarely for the good. You were intended to be pure, to choose your own path." He left unsaid that he could not entrust the sword with Terin unless he was certain of his character. It was a mistake he would not repeat with his son, as he had with his *father*.

"Choose my own path? It seems that was decided before my birth, or so I've been told. You are hiding more from me, I know."

Jonas released another sigh, refusing to put words to his son's claim. "One day, you will know everything, son, but ask me not. There is a right time for all things. For now, you need rest and to regain your strength." He patted Terin's leg.

Terin was weary of falsehoods that others claimed were for his benefit. "Are the gargoyles fearful of me or the sword?"

"Of you," Jonas confessed, "just as they are of me."

"I thought the sword—"

"The sword enhances this unique gift. It does not grant it."

"Why? How did we gain this…gift?"

"My mother," Jonas said sadly, a wane smile touching his lips.

Terin made a face. His father had never spoken of his family either, his origin a mystery to everyone except Valera, who fiercely guarded his secret. "My grandmother?"

"A very special woman. As lovely and kind as your mother, as fierce as Torg, and as cunning as General Bode," Jonas fondly recalled, his eyes moistened with her memory.

"Is she gone?"

"A long time ago." He smiled sadly.

"I wish I could have known her." Terin sighed, hungering to know more of his family.

"She would have been very proud of you," he said, recalling the long journey he and his mother endured when he was a child and their many travails, a tale of woe and heartbreak and hope. He thought of how the world would have been a batter place had things happened differently. So much needless death, so much sorrow.

"What of your father? Did you receive any gifts from him?"

Jonas stared numbly for a time, thinking of his sire. "One gift that I recall, the necklace I gifted you before you departed for Rego."

"That was from him?" Terin asked, cursing his carelessness.

"Yes. It was one of my fondest memories of him. He made it of his own hand. It had two images when he gifted it to me, one of your grandmother and one of your great-grandmother. I later added the one of your mother."

"I am sorry, Father, for I lost it," Terin confessed. His mother oft told him to confess guilt, accept the consequences, and be done with it. Withholding bitter truths only delayed the anguish of their telling, torturing your mind until you confessed. He loathed telling his father that he had lost the only token he had of his grandfather.

"How?" Jonas asked curiously.

"When we escaped Fera, it came loose in battle. It is somewhere in the Black Castle, probably a keepsake for whoever found it. I am sorry for my recklessness, Father," he apologized, seeing the concern written upon his father's countenance.

"Things happen in battle that we have little control over, son. Do not trouble yourself over it. You bear enough burdens as it is." He touched a hand gently to Terin's shoulder, though Terin sensed his father was greatly troubled by his admission, and it had nothing to do with the lost necklace.

"Thanks." Terin smiled, the gesture lifting his father's mood.

"I spoke only briefly with Squid, as our time for idle chatter has been quite limited. He spoke briefly of your adventures at Costelin, Tuft's Mountain, and Molten Isle but little of your time at Fera. For what reason did you venture there?"

"For Cronus. He was taken captive at Tuft's Mountain, and I journeyed there with Raven to rescue him, but officially, I journeyed there as an envoy of the realm."

"Envoy? Did you treat with ministers of Tyro's court?" Jonas asked warily, shielding the panic from reaching his voice.

"With Tyro himself. I delivered an offer of peace, but the dark lord mocked the overture," Terin bitterly recalled.

"You spoke with Tyro directly?" Jonas asked, no longer hiding the alarm in his voice.

"Among my other adventures, it seems trivial by compare," he affirmed.

"What did he ask of you?" Jonas asked intently.

"Ask of me?" The question seemed odd. "I don't recall anything specific, just his threats and bluster."

"Hmm," Jonas mused, his gaze drifting, lost in his thoughts.

"Father?" Terin asked, unnerved by his strange behavior.

"You've had quite an adventure, son. We will speak again later. I will remain at the palace for a few days, then must return to your mother."

*****

After his father stepped without, a servant girl brought Terin a platter of food, of which he gladly partook and bestirred from his idleness. 'Twas midday when Kato greeted him outside the throne room, where they were summoned. The joys of victory that permeated Corell still lingered days after the battle, but the grim work of clearing the dead, treating the wounded, and repairing the palace began dampening their spirits.

They passed between the massive open doors of the throne room, a palace steward escorting them to their place in the growing assemblage, standing off the right, below the dais. Terin recognized many of the gathered host from his place along the wall below the throne. Twenty-nine members of the King's Elite stood post behind the throne in their resplendent silver armor and sea-blue tunics. Terin noticed many missing faces among his fellow Elite, casualties of the siege. He wondered how many had fallen at Kregmarin and Corell. Dozens, if not more.

He found Torg standing to the right of the empty thrones, clad in gray mail over black shirt and trousers, his attire a stark contrast to his charges. His grandfather had a natural affinity toward trousers, and Terin couldn't remember seeing him without them.

Terin spotted Alen along the opposing wall, standing amid a handful of his fellow messengers, a number of his comrades having fallen in battle. Standing forward of the messengers were the ministers of the realm, their scribes, and numerous courtesans. Chief Minister Monsh stood forward of his fellow ministers, resuming his duties after his long absence, having spent the siege among the Torry cavalry.

Terin's eye found Squid directly across from him, among his fellow ministers. Squid regarded him with a slight nod, the small gesture reminding Terin of his former master's kindness. He was ever thankful that he was Squid's apprentice rather than serving a strict minister like Lutius Veda, who stood to Squid's left. The ever-serious trade minister maintained his sour disposition as if he had practiced it to perfection. Merith and Aldo stood beside their respective masters dressed in their long golden tunics.

The majority of the assemblage was gathered before the throne, including commanders of rank from the garrison, the 3rd Torry Army, the 1st and 2nd Cavalry, Dar Valen's magantor command, and various commanders representing the Jenaii battle groups. Commanders Tevlin, Connly, and Valen stood among their subordinates, though much of their command was dispatched north and east, harrying Morac's retreating army.

General Bode was noticeably absent, overseeing his troops as they chased Morac eastward. El Anthar and Elos stood prominently to the front of the assemblage, their silver eyes fixed to the throne above with stoic indifference, their regal air masking any emotion they might have otherwise exhibited.

Terin regarded the birdmen with awe as if they were the physical representation of a divine providence sent as emissaries to the mortal realm. He looked for his father amid the sea of faces, unable to find him, Cronus, Leanna, or Galen among the crowd.

"Relax," Kato whispered at his side. It was the first word spoken between them since he disembarked at Tinsay so long ago. Kato had not visited Terin since the battle's end, save for his brief examination, spending every spare moment with the palace Matrons and healing the countless wounded with the wondrous instruments he brought with him from the *Stenox*. But even that device could only work so fast, forcing him to concentrate on those suffering mortal wounds that were not overly large. With tens of thousands wounded or slain, he had to ration care judiciously. In time, he could treat amputations and debilitating injuries; and by the looks of the overflowing Matron wards, the task seemed endless.

He was teaching the Matrons how to use his equipment and how to daily recharge their solar cells, as he was needed elsewhere. Commander Connly asked for his assistance hunting down gargoyles who were dispersed throughout the countryside. If he could pass off his knowledge and device to the Matrons, he needn't have to choose between their needs for his dual skill set of healer and killer. With his services in demand, he became a popular fellow with his Torry friends.

"Am I so obvious?" Terin asked.

"Yes." Kato grinned, regarding Terin's tense posture and nervous left leg that shifted constantly against the hem of his tunic. He shook his head, wondering how Terin could perform in combat with ease, engaging the enemy without respite, and yet act as a nervous school-girl in this formal gathering. Of course, Kato was unaware that Terin was oft berated for his recklessness by the princess as often as he was praised for his daring. He suffered her fury upon his last visit to the throne room after he ventured from the north gate to rescue Jacin Tomac.

"I haven't thanked you for coming to our aid," Terin offered.

"The gargoyles are our enemy as much as yours, Terin. Someday, Raven and the others will realize this and end their false neutrality."

Terin thought that Lorken and Raven had slain too many gargoyles and Benotrists to be considered neutral anyway. How many had they slain at Fera during their escape? Far too many to count as he tried to tabulate the number in his head.

"Her Highness Princess Corry, regent of Torry North and defender of the realm!" a palace steward declared, drawing every eye to the dais as Corry emerged from the passageway behind the throne. She passed between the Torry Elite standing guard behind the thrones, her blue eyes sweeping the chamber as she stepped to the front of the dais.

The assemblage knelt in unison, even El Anthar, as it was customary for visiting royalty to defer to the host regent. Terin was surprised to see Kato take a knee, not expecting such from an Earther, but recalled Kato's respectful deference during their visit at Cagan. He knew Raven and Lorken would never kneel to anyone. Only Torg remained unbent, standing vigilantly at her side as chief guardian of the throne.

"Arise, friends," she greeted the gathered host, her shining blue eyes matching the hue of her sparkling gown. A slender crown nestled atop her golden hair, resplendent in the chamber's light. Terin's throat went suddenly dry as he beheld her beauty. He felt his heart hammering within his chest as he stared at her atop the dais, the tendrils of her silken voice caressing his ears.

"We mourn the loss of many friends and faithful comrades, who gave their lives so that we might endure. Let us take this moment to honor their sacrifice." A silent pall filled the chamber as they honored their fallen before she continued. "So many that perished deserve individual recognition for their great deeds that it would take my lifetime to acknowledge their full sacrifice and accomplishment. I shall name but a few to represent their collective deeds and leave the others' telling to posterity, where scribes shall endlessly labor to chronicle their fell deeds.

"Let us remember Commanders Gais Luven and Sergon Vas, who perished with much of their commands defending the north and east walls. Their stubborn defense slowed the enemy advance upon our walls, without which our Jenaii allies would have attained Corell too late to save the palace. To Commander Kal Sorus, who guarded the main gate of the palace. He and his entire command perished holding the tunnel against Morac and the host of the 8th Legion. They slowed Morac's advance, purchasing vital time with their blood, precious time that we required for the Jenaii and General Bode to come to our rescue.

"To our brave magantor riders, who flew into the teeth of the enemy time and again, setting their foul launch towers ablaze as their number dwindled throughout until none remained. Their sacrifice spared Corell countless gargoyle attacks upon our inner battlements and upper palace, attacks that might have compromised our defense. Let us remember their fell deeds and those of countless others whose names will never be remembered and whose sacrifices were no less significant," Corry acknowledged. Many nodded their heads, their eyes watering with remembrance of their fallen comrades as she continued.

"I have not summoned so many before the throne solely to mourn our dead but to briefly celebrate our victory, a victory unlooked for and, despite our desires, unforeseen. Not all of our heroes were slain in battle. Many are standing amid this vast assemblage, so many that I dare not attempt to name them all. I shall, instead, name a few to represent the whole, a few whose deeds speak well of our people and the soldiers of the realm. Havis Darm and Dalin Vors, come hither!" she declared.

Terin watched as the two men stepped from the crowd, clad in the silver tunics and gray mail of Torry magantor riders. They stopped at the base of the dais and knelt. He remembered them as the magantor scouts he rescued in the early days of the siege, the ones for whom Corry was wroth that he risked his life. He wondered what great deeds they performed to be so recognized before this grand assemblage.

"Havis Darm and Dalin Vors, for saving my life, the crown recognizes your selfless acts, and I so name you to the King's Elite!" She bestowed the tittles as the men humbly accepted, bowing deeply. She bade them to rise and take their place upon the dais beside their future brothers.

Terin was dumbstruck, wondering if his sword knew the destiny of these men and forced him to intercede on their behalf. He caught sight of Havis and Dalin staring back at him after they ascended the dais, standing beside their fellow Elite, their unspoken gratitude evident as they regarded him.

Corry proceeded to name several men whose deeds seemed beyond belief if not for the wonders they all beheld in recent days. One had held a turret along the southern wall after all his comrades were slaughtered, slaying two dozen gargoyles, denying them a hold upon the battlements until relieved. He was also named to the Elite. Another soldier was honored for protecting a dozen archers as his fellow swordsmen were slain, fending off countless gargoyles. He protected them to great effect while suffering multiple wounds, allowing them to slay hundreds with their bows. His brave act, protecting all twelve successfully throughout the battle, saved countless Torry lives. His grievous wounds would have claimed his life if not for Kato's healing device, as the Earther found the poor man dying in the Matrons' ward two days after the battle with several of the bowmen gathered at his bedside. Corry named a few others and could have named hundreds more whose bravery helped carry the day.

"Kato!" Corry said, calling him forth, her eyes briefly regarding Terin standing beside him, her stoic countenance betraying little. Kato slapped Terin lightly on the back before stepping away, a gesture that the Earthers were wont to use to express fondness and friendship. Kato strode across the mirrored stone floor, feeling a thousand eyes upon him. As an Earther, he was accustomed to the curious looks his strange appearance drew. The looks he now received were an odd mixture of awe, revulsion, and gratitude. Their sense of awe would eventually diminish with time and familiarity, as oft happened when strangers met. Their revulsion was quite normal for their primitive culture, and he did not begrudge them that. Their gratitude, however, swelled his heart.

The Torries and their Jenaii allies were good people, just as Tyro's minions were despicable by all objective standards. It was for this reason that he interceded on their behalf. Despite what Raven and the others believed, they had little hope of returning to Earth. Arax was now their home, and Kato could not stand aside and allow Tyro's barbarity free reign. Kato stopped at the base of the dais and knelt, gifting the princess a smile as he stared up at her.

"Kato of Earth!" Corry declared, returning his winsome smile as she beheld his kind brown eyes, wondering how this great man sprang from the same people who spawned Raven. He was everything that Raven was not, extolling kindness, honor, and deference for his host where Raven was often cruel, dishonorable, and rude to extremes. "Kato of Earth, I offer the gratitude of my people for your intervention on our behalf. You killed thousands of our enemies and healed as many of our people with your wondrous magic. I name you friend of the Torry realms!"

Kato bowed deeply to thunderous cheers, a declared friend of the realm carrying the highest honor a non-Torry could receive. The formal appellation granted him sanctuary in every dwelling, holdfast, and city in the Torry realms as an honored guest. Kato gained his feet and stepped away, regarding the princess with a wink, the strange behavior an obvious Earther gesture, which she correctly interpreted as a sign of friendship.

"King El Anthar and Elos, champion of the Jenaii!" She called their most steadfast allies hither. The Jenaii king and his champion stepped forth as she descended the dais to formally greet them. As visiting royalty, King El Anthar would not kneel a second time, as protocol decreed. He stood impassively as she stepped near and pressed her slender hand to his heart, a symbolic union of friendship between their peoples.

"King El Anthar, I offer the gratitude of the Torry realms for our deliverance. Once again, your people have come to aid us in our time of greatest peril. Never has the fate of Torry North been so tested, where the balance of our lives rested precariously upon a precipice!"

"We stand with you always, Princess, against the minions of perdition and the vassals of tyranny!" El Anthar placed his hands to her shoulders, an uncharacteristic mirth gracing his silver eyes.

Corry broke protocol, overcome with emotion, and kissed his cheek. "Thank you." She smiled, her moist blue eyes regarding him with heartfelt joy.

"My pleasure, Corry," he whispered, his stoic countenance softening. With that, he and Elos backed away, returning to their place in the assemblage.

Corry turned, nodding to Torg as she ascended the dais. The craggy master of arms sighed, resigned to her bidding. "Jonas Caleph!" he called out, summoning Terin's sire forth. Jonas emerged from the back corner of the chamber, leaving his preferred place of obscurity, making his way through the crowd as his name drew their collective interest. He took little joy from accolades or attention. Terin had wondered if his father was in attendance until Torg called him forth. He could see what others could not, that his father wished to be elsewhere.

Jonas knelt as he reached the dais before Corry bade him to rise, a beaming smile breaking across her face. "Jonas Caleph!" She repeated his name with great authority, its utterance drawing attention to his kinship with Terin. "Once again, you have rendered great service to the Torry realm, taking up arms in its defense and inflicting great loss to our foe. The men and commanders of the 3rd Army bear witness to your fell deeds in the breaking of the 6th Legion, the enemy fleeing before your presence, sealing their fate.

"But your far greater service to the realm is the role your progeny has taken in his service to the throne, driving the enemy from our walls time and again throughout the siege. Without his brave defiance, our rescuers would have been greeted by Tyro's banners flying above our citadels. Master Vantel speaks highly of your sword arm, and my father spoke equally of your character. Long ago, you forsook your rightful place at court and among the King's High Elite for a life of a simple farmer living in obscurity, remembered only by so few who know your worth. I would not call you again to full service within the Elite without your consent and blessing, Jonas Caleph, but I formally rename you to the King's High Elite to serve as you will."

"I am humbled and honored, Highness." Jonas bowed, shamed by honors he knew he didn't deserve, afflicted by an unspoken guilt he could never confess.

"As you are not a man to treasure flowery titles and appellations, I also bestow upon you a more practical gift that befits your nature," she added, nodding to Torg, who stepped behind the throne to retrieve a sword with a cross-wired silver hilt and quillon sheathed in a black steel scabbard with onyx and sapphires embedded along its length. Corry drew the sword from its scabbard, torchlight dancing along its gleaming steel blade with silver speckles embedded within its folds. 'Twas a magnificent blade handcrafted by Torg himself and gifted long ago to King Lore. "A king's blade for a master swordsman!" Corry declared, descending the dais to present the majestic weapon to Terin's father.

"I am again humbled and honored, Highness." Jonas received the sword in her outstretched hands as Torg presented the scabbard.

"Take your rightful place among your brothers, at least until you take your leave of Corell," she said softly.

Jonas regarded her briefly before looking at Torg, who nodded his approval before ascending the dais to stand among his fellow

Elite. Torg thrust his fist to his heart as Jonas passed, and every member of the Elite did likewise, greeting their lost brother's return.

Corry stole a furtive glance to Terin, whose countenance revealed his gratitude for the honors bestowed upon his sire. She again ascended the dais, her eyes sweeping the assemblage before announcing her final declaration. "Cronus Kenti!" Terin found Cronus on the opposite side of the chamber, where his presence was obscured by the sea of faces between them. Like Terin, he still wore the white tunic and steel breastplate and greaves. They would soon don the blue tunic of a Torry Elite at their formal ceremony, which would happen in the short future.

Cronus's green eyes regarded Terin briefly as he stepped into the clear before stopping at the dais where he knelt. Cronus looked up, greeted coolly by Princess Corry's sudden stern countenance as she fixed her ice-blue eyes to his as if passing judgment upon a condemned man.

"Cronus Kenti!" She scowled, her voice echoing across the chamber with terrible authority. "Your name is uttered across the realm with awed reverence, acknowledging your deeds at Tuft's Mountain and your flight from the Black Castle. My father named you to his High Elite for your skilled blade, high character, and great deeds. Your friends speak well of your person, each risking much to gain your freedom. You have sworn vows to the throne and realm, vows you have upheld with courage and honor," she affirmed.

"Despite your fidelity to the realm, you stand accused"—she paused, letting the declaration hang briefly in the air for all to consider—"accused of breaking the most sacred of vows!" Cronus's green eyes narrowed, confused by Corry's claim. Had he offended someone? Had he broken faith in some way that he was unaware? "We judge men by their deeds and by their words, words they say and mean. A promise was made and yet unfulfilled.

"As princess of the realm, I hold the Royal Elite to the highest tenets of virtue and truth. Vows are to be honored, not left vacant, a mockery of your honor. In this, you are found lacking and wholly unsuited for your place among the Torry Elite!" she declared.

Terin was aghast, not believing the princess would treat his friend so unfairly. He couldn't keep silent anymore, taking a step forward to challenge her judgment, the consequences be damned, but Kato's hand pulled him back. "Relax. This is where it gets good," Kato whispered, a mischievous grin painting his lips.

"Your suitability among the Torry Elite is in question unless," Corry added, enjoying the anguished look passing Cronus's eyes a little too much, "unless you honor your forgotten vow!"

"Highness?" Cronus lifted a confused brow, wondering to what she referred.

"You stand accused, Cronus Kenti. Do you wish to face your accuser?" she asked.

"I do," he said, eager to set things to rights. He craned his neck, following her gaze to the back of the cavernous chamber, where a lone figure passed through the entryway. The assemblage parted, allowing the newcomer to approach the dais. Cronus's eyes widened as he beheld Leanna enter therein, stepping across the mirrored stone floor of the throne room, a shimmering silver gown gracing her feminine form. Her golden hair was styled high upon her head, emphasizing her slender neck. His heart pounded in his chest as her eyes met his across the chamber. He caught her fighting the smile testing her lips.

Cronus suddenly realized what was about to happen, pimples raising across his flesh as he recalled his promise to Leanna so long ago. Her graceful steps seemed to take an eternity as her slipper-clad feet echoed softly off the mirrored stone. She stopped beside him, kneeling carefully with her voluminous skirts before Corry stopped her, bidding her to remain standing.

"Do you acknowledge your guilt, Cronus Kenti?" Corry asked, biting her own smile.

"I admit my guilt, Highness. I swore to wed the lady Leanna upon my return. I have not fulfilled my vow!" Cronus confessed.

"I accept your plea, Cronus Kenti, and shall pass judgment upon your guilty soul. You shall fulfill your vow here and now before this grand assemblage," she said, her eyes sweeping the throne room with her hands outstretched to the gathered host. "Or—" She was beginning to offer the grim alternative when he boldly interrupted.

"I accept, Highness!"

"A wise choice," she said, motioning him to his feet as she descended the dais. Leanna cast a bemused glance toward her betrothed, unable to contain her mirth with his blushing face. "As acting regent of the realm, I declare the wedded union of Cronus Kenti and Leanna Celen by royal decree!" Corry declared, taking Cronus's right hand and placing it in Leanna's left, sealing their matrimony by Torry custom. "Cronus, your bride," Corry said softly, backing a step as they turned to face each other.

There, in the throne room of Corell, he kissed his wife, his lady, his love.

EPIGLOGUE

Moonlight filtered through the window, bathing her bed-chamber in celestial light. She drew a fur cloak about her shoulders before stepping out on the terrace. She breathed the cool autumn air, stepping onto the stone outcropping overlooking the Feran Plain. The open vast expanse surrounded the palace for miles, disappearing in the distance, where it bled into the horizon. It was vast, empty, and lonely, a loneliness that matched the isolation of her heart.

'Twas her last night at Fera, as she would leave on the morrow for her mother's island realm. Her father was wroth with her misadventures in the wilds, chastising her fruitless pursuit of Raven once she knew that she was with child, his grandchild no less. He was equally curious with her sudden interest in acquiring numerous female slaves and arranging their manumission. She had purchased nearly every female slave at Axenville and arranged transport for them to Bansoch, where they would be freed. He wondered if her heart had grown soft or if she had other reasons for her sudden magnanimity.

In truth, Raven's opinion on the barbaric practice had worn on her. She recalled that fateful day upon the auction block at Axenville when she beheld that poor girl subjected to the lecherous eyes of so many men. She vowed no woman would suffer so under her dominion.

Tosha ran her hands over her growing womb, thinking of Raven and his promise to return to her for their child's birth. Could she trust him to keep his word? It was oft at night when such doubts

clouded her thoughts, torturing her mind before bedtime and troubling her sleep. "He will return," she whispered, putting her doubts
aside before returning to her chamber.

"You should dress more warmly." Her father's voice greeted her
as she stepped within. Tyro stood before her grandmother's statue
beside the hearth, the flames alighting his countenance as he turned
from his artistic masterpiece to face her.

"Father." She suppressed the surprise in her voice. She could
not recall his last visit to her chambers, not since she was a child
when he put her to bed, telling her wondrous stories to set her at
ease. Those were difficult times, as she missed her mother dearly.
Despite her parents' schism, Queen Letha allowed her daughter to
visit her father regularly throughout her childhood. Those first visits
were most challenging, as she longed for her home in Bansoch. Tyro
doted on her in those days, a strange contrast to his harsh rule with
the rest of his empire.

He had been studying the statue before she entered, compar-
ing its face to the carvings in the necklace that he held. She noticed
that he never parted with the token, never placing it from his sight.
His councilors feared the necklace was bewitched, beguiling Tyro's
mind, but dared not voice their suspicions. She recalled his interest
in Terin's necklace when it was given to him by Morac after Terin's
escape. His interest had since grown to an all-consuming obsession.

"I am warm enough," she assured him. Most of her clothing no
longer fitted properly, forcing her to wear ever larger tunics that fell
far above her knees. Once he learned of her condition, he became
overly protective. As emperor, he hungered for an heir to his realm,
and her child, if male, became his obsession, though rivaled by his
recent fixation upon Terin's charm.

"You require longer woolen gowns. I have the seamstresses fash-
ioning some for you."

"I am well enough, Father. I leave on the morrow."

"They are already attending to it. You'll have them by morning."

"I shan't break, Father. I *am* the second guardian of the
Sisterhood, not a fair flower to be tended."

"You are my daughter, and I protect what is *mine!*" he said darkly, his golden eyes regarding her intently, his hand gripping the necklace so tightly she thought it might snap.

She found his behavior unsettling, a constant maelstrom of melancholy and simmering rage as he rolled the necklace in his fingers. Others told her that he studied it over and over, day after day, it never leaving his side. He repeatedly asked her of Terin, raking every detail of the boy that she recalled. Most importantly, he asked her how the boy had come to possess the necklace.

"His father gifted it to him," she had said. He thought the claim a blatant lie. The boy was too young to be who he hoped him to be, but then a thought occurred to him, a small morsel of hope in his decades of despair. Perhaps the boy wasn't the one he had long sought, but the boy's *father* was if he still lived. If this was true, he wondered why they sent Terin to his lair to begin with. Who was he really? Did they even know who he was? Did the boy even know?

At first glance, the boy's blue eyes and fair hair were neither remarkable nor familiar, but the shape of his face and the subtle mannerisms that permeated his being were eerily familiar. And he recalled Regula's unease around the boy, a feeling shared by nearly all the gargoyles who encountered him. Only the one he sought had such an effect on the creatures.

"Father," she soothed, touching her hands to his, her caress easing his grip on the necklace. She lifted it as he opened his hand, running her fingers over the carved faces, like she did when she first noticed it gracing Terin's neck. There were three faces cut from bosa stone on the necklace with small pieces of lupec wood carvings between them. Though bosa stone was easily shaped and used for finer carvings, the artist who cut these pieces was exceptionally talented for crafting such detailed images in stones so small.

The faces were female, each striking and diverse in their countenance. She recalled when she first set eyes upon them and thought her father would appreciate the artist's work, who Terin claimed was his father, but she didn't think to bring it up during Terin's brief stay at Fera. There were far too many other matters to attend than the origin of Terin's charm. It was then her eyes were drawn to the center face on the necklace. She recalled noticing it the first time she had seen it but was unable to place it until…

She lifted the necklace to the statue of her grandmother and gasped. "Is it—" she began to utter.

"My mother's visage? Yes," Tyro affirmed.

She stared dumbstruck, wondering how Terin came to possess an heirloom connected to her paternal grandmother. "Whoever carved this must have known her," Tosha said.

"He knew her," he said.

"You know who carved these?"

"I carved two of them before I gifted them to my son."

Thus Ends book two of the *Chronicles of Arax: The Siege of Corell.*

The saga continues with book three: *The Battle of Yatin.*

APPENDIX A

Armies of Arax

Torry Armies

Army	Based	Commander	Size (1 telnic = 1,000)
1st	Cagan	Lewins	twenty telnics
2nd	Rego	Fonis	sixteen telnics (plus four reserve)
3rd	Central City	Bode	fourteen telnics (plus six reserve)
4th	Cagan	Korath	twenty telnics
5th	Corell	Morton	twenty telnics

Large Garrisons

Cropus	Torgus Vantel	five telnics
Corell	Nevias	ten telnics
Central City	Torvin	five telnics
Cagan	Telanus	five telnics

Cavalry

1st	Central City	Tevlin	five hundred mounts
2nd	Central City	Connly	five hundred mounts (1,500 reserves)
3rd	western border	Meborn	five hundred mounts
4th	Cagan	Avliam	five hundred mounts (300 reserves)

Navy

1st	Cagan	Kilan (grand admiral)	sixty galleys
2nd	Cagan	Horikor	fifty galleys
3rd	Cagan	Liman	thirty galleys
4th	Cagan	Nylo	forty galleys
5th	Cagan	Morita	twenty galleys

Benotrist-Gargoyle Armies

Legion	Based	Commander	Size
1st (gargoyle)	Telfer	Yonig	forty telnics
2nd (gargoyle)	Tenin	Torab	forty-three telnics
3rd (gargoyle)	Tinsay	Yatin	fifty telnics
4th (gargoyle)	Fera	Tuvukk	fifty telnics
5th (gargoyle)	Fera	Concaka	fifty telnics
6th (gargoyle)	Fera	Maglakk	fifty telnics
7th (gargoyle)	Fera	Vaginak	fifty telnics
8th (Benotrist)	Nisin	Vlesnivolk	fifty telnics
9th (Benotrist)	Mordicay	Marcinia	fifty telnics
10th (Benotrist)	Pagan	Gavis	fifty telnics
11th (Benotrist)	Nisin	Felinaius	fifty telnics

12th (gargoyle)	eastern border	Krakeni	fifty telnics
13th (Benotrist)	Laycrom	Trinapolis	fifty telnics
14th (gargoyle)	Laycrom	Trimopolak	fifty telnics
15th (gargoyle)	Tuss River	No named general	fifteen telnics
16th (gargoyle)	Destroyed at Tuft's Mountain		
17th (gargoyle)	Destroyed at Tuft's Mountain		
18th (gargoyle)	Destroyed at Tuft's Mountain		

Garrison Forces

Based	Size
Fera	twenty-nine telnics (Benotrist)
Nisin	twenty telnics (Benotrist)
Pagan	ten telnics (Benotrist)
Mordicay	ten telnics (Benotrist)
Tinsay	twenty telnics (Benotrist)
Laycrom	twenty telnics (Benotrist)
Border posts	ten telnics Benotrist) ten telnics (gargoyle)

Benotrist Navy

Fleet	Based	Admiral	Size
1st	Mordicay	Plesnivolk	50 galleys
2nd	Tenin	Kruson	27 galleys
3rd	Pagan	Elto (grand admiral)	80 galleys
4th	Pagan	Pinota	50 galleys
5th	Tenin	Mulsen	97 galleys
6th	Pagan	Silniw	50 galleys
7th	Tinsay	Onab	50 galleys
8th	Tinsay	Zelitov	50 galleys

Yatin Armies

Army	Based	Commander	Size (telnics)
1st	Mosar	Yoria	twenty-five
2nd	eastern border	Yitia	twenty-five
3rd	southern border	Jutol	fifteen
4th	Tenin	Teminas	six

Garrison Forces

Based	Commander	Size
Mosar	Yakue	ten
Telfer	Morue	twelve to sixteen
Tenin	Yanis	twelve (eight never mustered)

Yatin Cavalry

Army	Based	Commander	Size (mounts)
1st	Destroyed at Salamin Valley		
2nd	Mosar	Cornyana	eight hundred

Yatin Navy

Fleet	Based	Admiral	Size
1st	Sunk at the battle of Cull's Arc		
2nd	Sunk at the battle of Cull's Arc		
3rd	Faust	Horician	forty galleys

Jenaii Armies

Battle Group	Based	Commander	Size
1st	El-Orva	El Tuvo	twenty telnics
2nd	El-Orva	Ev Evorn	twenty telnics
3rd	El Tova	En Elon	twenty telnics

Garrison Forces

	Based	Commander	Size
	El-Orva	El Orta	fifteen telnics
	El Tova	En Vor	five telnics

Jenaii Navy

Fleet	Based	Admiral	Size
1st	El Tova	En Atar	twenty galleys
2nd	El Tova	En Ovir	twenty galleys
3rd	El Tova	En Toshin	twenty galleys

Naybin Armies

Army	Based	Commander	Size
1st	northern border	Duloc	ten telnics
2nd	Plou	Rorin	ten telnics
3rd	Non	Corivan	ten telnics
4th	western border	Cuss	ten telnics

Garrison Forces

	Based	Commander	Size
	Plou	Cestes	five telnics
	Non	Rasin	seven telnics
	Naiba	Tesra	three telnics
	border posts		five telnics

Naybin Navy

Fleet	Based	Admiral	Size
1st	Naiba	Gustub	ten galleys
2nd	Naiba	Galton	ten galleys

Macon Empire Armies

Army	Based	Commander	Size
1st	Fleace	Noivi	ten telnics
2nd	northern border	Vecious	fifteen telnics
3rd	western border	Ciyon	ten telnics
4th	Null	Farin	eight telnics

Garrison Forces

	Fleace	Novin	five telnics
	Cesa	Clyvo	five telnics

Macon Navy

Fleet	Based	Admiral	Size
1st	Cesa	Goren	twenty galleys
2nd	Null	Vulet	twenty galleys
3rd	Eastern Coast	Talmet	twenty galleys
4th	Western Coast	Gara	twenty galleys

Ape Empire Armies

Army	Based	Commander	Size
1st	Gregok	Cragok	twenty telnics
2nd	Torn	Mocvoran	twenty telnics
3rd	Talon Pass	Vorklit	ten telnics
4th	Northern Coast	Matuzon	ten telnics
5th	Southern Coast	Vonzin	ten telnics

Garrison Forces

	Gregok	ten telnics
	Torn	ten telnics
	Talon Pass	ten telnics

Ape Navy

Fleet	Based	Admiral	Size
1st	Torn	Zorgon	sixty galleys
2nd	Torn	Vornam	forty galleys

Casian Federation Armies

Army	Based	Commander	Size
1st	Coven	Gidvia	twelve telnics
2nd	Milito	Motchi	twelve telnics
3rd	Teris	Elke	seven telnics

Garrison Forces

Based	Size
Milito	three telnics
Coven	four telnics
Port West	three telnics
Teris	three telnics

Casian Navy

Fleet	Based	Admiral	Size
1st	Coven	Voelin	one hundred
2nd	Milito	Gylan	eighty
3rd	Port West	Gydar	sixty
4th	Teris	Eltar	sixty

Federation of the Sisterhood Armies

Army	Based	Commander	Size
1st	Bansoch	Na	twenty telnics
2nd	Fela	Vola	twenty telnics
3rd	southern border	Mial	twenty telnics

Garrison Forces

Bansoch	ten telnics
Fela	ten telnics

Federation of the Sisterhood Navy

Fleet	Based	Admiral	Size
1st	Bansoch	Nyla	120 galleys
2nd	Bansoch	Carel	80 galleys
3rd	Southern Coast	Daila	50 galleys

Teso Armies

1st Army	southeastern border	Hovel	four telnics
2nd Army	Central Teso	Velen	two telnics

Zulon Armies

1st Army	northern border	Zarento	two telnics
2nd Army	western border	Zubarro	three telnics

City State Armies

Sawyer	five telnics	one hundred cavalry	
Rego	three telnics	one hundred cavalry	
Notsu	seven telnics	two hundred cavalry	
Bacel	eight telnics	one hundred cavalry	
Barbeario	eight telnics		
Bedo	ten telnics	one hundred cavalry	forty galleys
Tro Harbor	ten telnics	fifty cavalry	fifty galleys
Varabis	five telnics		thirty galleys

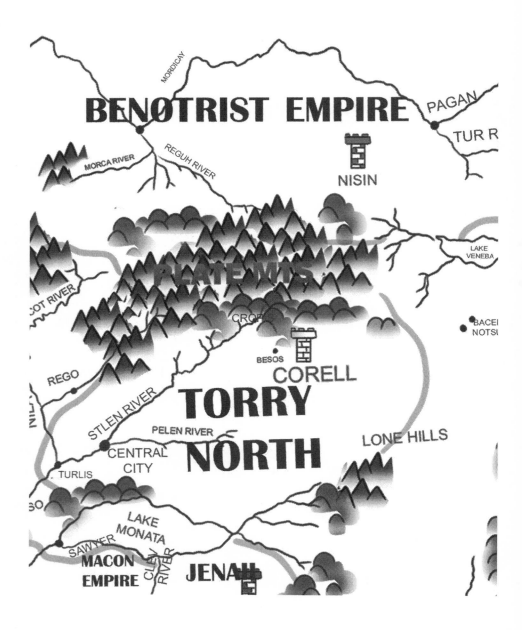

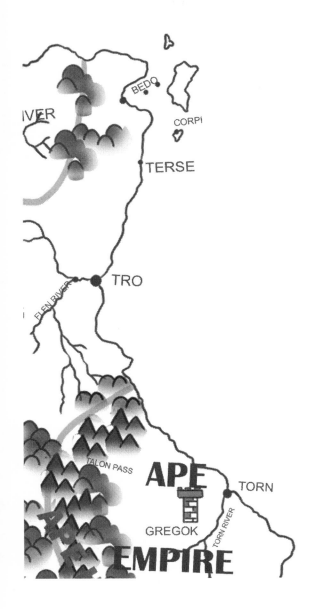

Other Books Available by Author:

Free Born Saga
     Free Born
     Elysia

Chronicles of Arax
     Book one: Of War And Heroes
     Book two: The Siege of Corell
     Book three: The Battle of Yatin
     Book four: The Making of a King

ABOUT THE AUTHOR

Ben Sanford grew up in Western New York. He spent almost twenty years as an air marshal, traveling across the United States and many parts of the world, meeting people from a broad range of cultures and backgrounds. It was from these thousands of interactions that he drew inspiration for the characters in his books. He currently resides in Maryland with his family.

Made in the USA
Middletown, DE
27 October 2023